To Joy

KYMIERA
(Season 1)

by Steve Turnbull

KYMIERA (Season 1) by Steve Turnbull
Copyright © 2017 Steve Turnbull. All rights reserved.

ISBN 978-1-910342-71-8

Published by Tau Press Ltd.

Cover art by Jane Dixon-Smith (www.jdsmith-design.com)

For Joss Whedon.

Episode I: Purity

Chapter 1

Chloe

'Freak!'

The scream came from a voice Chloe recognised, a bully from two years above her. What was his name? She sighed and looked down at her empty lunchbox; she was still hungry. She was always hungry nowadays. Her dad had even made a joke about her having a tapeworm which he thought was hilarious. It really wasn't.

'So you'll do my homework, yeah?'

Chloe was distracted by the shouting behind them but turned her attention to Ashley. If there was Aryan perfection, Ashley was it: blond, blue-eyed, slim and not too tall for the boys. The fact the hair was dyed and the roots needed doing didn't seem to mean much. She hadn't lacked for male attention for years. Until recently.

'My homework, you'll do it, right?'

It was late November; the sky was overcast and the air cold with damp. It was school lunch break. The girls were sitting on a bench at the corner of the wilderness facing the school building. The place had been old fifty years ago. And the vegetation behind them wasn't much of a wilderness—a few trees backed onto a brick wall topped with razor-wire—but then St Gilbert's wasn't much of a school. The roof tiles were broken in a dozen places and rain leaked into the main hall even in a drizzle. Chloe wouldn't have to put up with it too much longer.

'Are you even listening?'

'Why would I do your homework, Ash?'

The cries of 'freak' were getting louder; sounded like the lynch mob was coming their way. Chloe looked off to the left, round Melinda who definitely wasn't listening but just staring into the distance. Beyond her was sad Kavi. She had good reason to feel sad. The misfits and the outcasts.

The mob of school kids, girls and boys, mostly thirteen year olds, some her age, but all following the bigger ones, grew nearer. She couldn't see their victim, who was on the ground.

'You have to do it because I won't have time.'

Chloe dragged her attention back to the conversation.

'Why? What are you talking about?'

'I'm going out.'

'Really?' Chloe ladled as much sarcasm as she could into the word. Ashley had the good taste to look embarrassed. 'And where would you be going?'

Ashley hesitated then the words tumbled out. 'It's about the Purity, and you know Kavi and I aren't good at that stuff.' Her eyes pleaded. She leaned forward and glanced at Kavi as if hoping she'd get some support. It wasn't forthcoming. She focused on Melinda.

'Mel? Chloe could do it for me, yeah?'

Melinda did not even register that she had heard.

'Mel!'

She jumped but still didn't respond; instead she looked at her watch and got up in a rush. 'I have to go.'

'Go where?' said Ashley. Her voice trailed off as Melinda headed away without looking back. 'What crawled up her skirt?'

'Appointment.'

'When?'

'Wouldn't expect you to notice, Ash.'

'Notice what?'

'Exactly.' Chloe glanced at the open lunch box in Ashley's lap. Her friend still had a whole sandwich, made from decent bread and what looked to be some lettuce and tinned meat. Chloe's mouth watered. 'You eating that?'

Ashley looked down then back. 'Homework?'

'No.'

There was another hesitation and then barely above a whisper. 'Please.'

Chloe's hand flashed out like a blur and grabbed the sandwich. 'I'll help.' She took a mouthful and added around it while she chewed. 'But you write it.' Chloe did not expect a thank-you from Ashley, and she was not disappointed.

The sound of someone crying mixed with harsh laughter drifted through the damp air. Chloe leaned back and looked behind Kavi's back. She caught a glimpse of red hair on the ground between shifting feet.

She stood up and took another bite from the sandwich. She twisted her back to remove an ache. Her shoulders and back had a lot of aches and pains lately. Her father said she was training too hard. Her mother said it was just growing pains—which was amusing since she was seventeen and hoped she wasn't growing any more.

Her physio said it was just one of those things and managed to make it tolerable.

The red-haired kid, it was a boy, young so probably new, had managed to get to his feet and the cries of freak had started up again. Now they were getting into their rhythm. They pushed him back and forwards in time to their abuse. The boy had heavy glasses; someone made a grab for them, pulled them from his face and dropped them under the boy's feet. When he tried to get them they pushed him over again.

'I've had enough of this,' said Chloe.

'Oh god, Chloe, don't start anything.'

Kavi came to life. 'She's right; you'll just get in trouble.'

'Again,' added Ashley.

'Trouble's already started,' said Chloe and with sandwich in hand she walked steadily towards the mob.

The victim was on his feet again. His face was streaked with lines of mud and tears. There was blood on his hands. He managed to push his way out through the crowd. They almost let him escape but a foot caught round his ankle and tripped him. He went flying once more and landed at Chloe's feet. She moved forward and stood beside his prone form.

She met the eye of the leader and took a bite out of her sandwich. There was a murmuring. 'Chloe Dark.' Most of them knew her.

She maintained eye contact, chewed the sandwich and swallowed.

'Out the way,' he said. She said nothing. 'Are you deaf or stupid?'

She took another bite from the sandwich.

'You don't look tough,' he said. He broke eye contact and forced a laugh, staring at his cronies so they joined in. It was not convincing.

Some of the younger ones on the periphery were already breaking away and returning the way they had come. The ones closest to Chloe pulled back. She had a reputation. She was not afraid to get into trouble.

But when you try to steal the prey from a pack of hyenas, they're going to fight for it.

She remembered now; his name was Hancock, and with a name like that you either become victim or bully. He'd chosen the latter route. He had the lowest brow and the thickest arms of his gang, though he wasn't the tallest, but he still topped Chloe by several inches. His school uniform strained to hold him in. She could see the reluctance to tackle her in his eyes but he had no choice. There was no way he could withdraw and save face. His position as the leader of the gang was at stake.

'Give me a bit of space,' he said with a smile on his face. The others laughed and took a step back. 'Last chance to back off. I wouldn't want to mess up your face.'

She swallowed and stuffed the remains of the sandwich into her pocket. No point letting it go to waste.

And then he did the stupidest thing he could possibly have done. He grabbed the left lapel of her school blazer with his right hand. She did not think. It was the first thing she had ever learned. The years of training her father had insisted she do just engaged, the way they always did.

It's a dangerous world, Chloe. Freaks round every corner. You have to be confident. You have to be able to look after yourself.'

Her right snaked up. She placed her thumb in the middle of the back of his hand and reached round his palm with her fingers then simply peeled his hand away. She twisted it and applied more pressure. His face held a look of astonishment as he sank to his knees in front of her. Powerless.

'You are such a dick, Hancock,' she said.

'You're not hurting me.'

'You want me to hurt you?' she said and applied more pressure. His face reddened.

'Get off me, you bint! Get her!' His command to his followers was met with silence. They were moving away. There was movement beside her as the victim got to his feet and ran.

'It's people like you make it hard for the Purity to do their job properly, Hancock,' Chloe said in a relaxed tone. 'But let me explain: Having red hair is normal. Wearing glasses is normal. Being a Neanderthal moron like you is also disappointingly normal. You need to find something more constructive to do with your time and more appropriate to your limited intellect. Like making paper doilies.'

'You can't tell me what to do,' he said through gritted teeth.

Chloe applied more pressure. He squeaked with the pain.

'All right, I'll leave him alone.'

'Chloe Dark!'

Chloe dropped Hancock's hand and turned to face the approaching teacher. 'Yes, Miss Kepple.'

Miss Kepple reminded Chloe of diamond: pretty but hard and sharp. She liked Miss Kepple and she thought it was mutual. Miss Kepple taught the Purity class, which also happened to be Chloe's favourite lesson.

'What's going on?'

'She nearly broke my arm, Miss,' whined Hancock. Chloe would have quite happily pummelled his pathetic face into the ground. 'She's a bully.'

Miss Kepple gave him an appraising look. 'Really, Hancock? Is that the best you can come up with? You're in detention for the next week.'

Chloe gasped. Pain like a red-hot poker slammed through Chloe's back slicing across both shoulder blades. It was so intense she went rigid and slipped to her knees.

'Chloe!' Miss Kepple was at her side and holding her hand. 'What's wrong?'

The pain subsided as fast as it had arrived but every muscle in her back ached. She sagged, holding tight to the arm that supported her.

'She's just putting it on,' said Hancock but even he didn't sound convinced. It was as if he was simply mouthing the words.

'Chloe?'

'I'm okay,' she said. She rotated her shoulders and the tension faded to a tolerable level.

'You go see the nurse, right now.'

'I have English.'

'Now.'

Chapter 2

Melinda

Melinda Vogler walked away from her friends and crunched along the gravel path to the small exit at the rear of the school.

She knew they were concerned about her—well, Chloe and Kavi were. Ashley wasn't really a friend; she had only recently been given a reason to join the club of outcasts. Before that she had been one of the bitches who made their lives hell. Though not as much hell as it would have been if Chloe hadn't been there. She always stood up for them. Protected them.

'But she can't do it all the time,' Melinda said to the damp air.

She stopped at the steel gate. Unlike the rest of the school these were hi-tech.

'Melinda Vogler. I have a note,' she said out loud. She did not need to speak. There was no one there to hear her except the machine. And somewhere in Manchester, maybe in the town hall, a wirehead. Melinda shivered; wireheads gave her the creeps.

There was no response as the machine scanned her riffy. Melinda touched the side of her head, self-consciously imagining the signals between the machine and the RFID chip embedded in her skull. You couldn't really feel anything but she always imagined she did. The gate motors ground into action, the barrier slid back and she stepped out into the street. She pulled out her phone and glanced at it. She had to be at the doctor's in forty-five minutes. The Metro stop was a fifteen minute walk.

She set off across the road into the street opposite flanked by the derelict and boarded up terraced houses. No one even bothered sticking up signs here. There weren't enough people around living in the area to make a difference.

One panel of a fence had been plastered with twenty copies of the same circus flyer. There was no year, just the date 'August 20th-25th'. The posters had been there as long as she could remember. There weren't any circuses anymore. Too dangerous. She had never been to one, so she wasn't missing anything and didn't want to risk her life.

A bright orange stain on a window further down caught her eye. That was new. It was on the opposite side of the road and as she came alongside it she read the words daubed on with a brush in bright paint 'SID WILL GET YOU'.

She shivered again, shoved her hands in her pockets and walked on.

The road curved slowly to the right. The junction at the far end of the street came in sight. She relaxed. The houses were sealed tight but you never knew what might be lurking inside. If she had been anyone else, like Ashley used to be, and with friends, they would have joked about the imaginary threat. But the outcasts didn't make jokes about freaks.

There was a dirty white van, veined with rust, parked a few yards into the street from the junction.

It looks hot, she thought and then shook her head as if trying to dislodge the thought. *How can it look hot?* She tried to argue sense into herself but she knew it was pointless. For weeks now every cable, every light, everything with power running through it had looked 'hot'.

She hadn't told anyone—she wasn't stupid. But then she'd had her annual medical scan and now she had to go back. The letter had said it was routine; something had gone wrong with the heart monitor, apparently.

Her dad had insisted it wasn't anything important. Machines went wrong all the time. Of course they did; a lot of the equipment was old and wearing out. But he didn't know she had seen the EEG go very hot and then cold shortly after the nurse had attached the sensors to her head.

It was just a coincidence. The brain monitor hadn't broken because of her. Just coincidence.

The van got really hot as its electric motor spun into life. Melinda froze. It did not race towards her, but pulled gently away from the kerb. It moved sedately down the road and past her. She listened to it retreating into the distance and headed off towards the junction again, cursing herself for being a baby.

That's when she saw the man walking along the other side of the road, looking at her. Perhaps he was just curious to see a schoolgirl out in the middle of the day. He was clean-shaven and quite young, perhaps in his twenties, and not bad looking. She realised she was staring and looked away.

Then someone grabbed her arms and forced them back into a painful double lock. Terror flooded through her. The air cracked and a grunt came from behind. She felt light headed and dizzy. A smell of burning filled the air: clothes and something else. Whoever grabbed her fell back, pulling her as he went. She stumbled backwards, lost her balance and collapsed on him.

The man beneath her swore and she was thrown to the side, out onto the street. She rolled over and hit her head. She lay face to the tarmac. Something hit her hard in the side knocking the wind out of her.

'What the fuck was that?' said a strained and angry voice close to her head. Someone kicked her in the side again.

'No damage!'

'I'll give them no damage,' said the angry one. She was kicked again. She could not breathe and her ribs on that side were in agony. Melinda felt rather than saw the van return. Her ears were filled with the grinding of the side door sliding open.

'Come on, get her inside.'

'I'm not touching her!'

'Not you. Him.'

Something snapped around her upper arm. She cried out with the intense pain. It felt as if it was going to be broken off. The air cracked again with the same dizziness. Ozone and burning wafted by her. Her arm was pulled up, dragging her body with it. Something in her shoulder gave way as she was tossed into the back of the van. Her head smashed into metal.

'No damage?' said the angry voice almost as if he was laughing, but his voice came from a long distance away. The door slammed shut and she felt the motor beneath her glow as the vehicle pulled away.

'Hold her down.'

Something pressed hard in the middle of her back, crushing the breath out of her. A hand gripped her wrist. She felt a surge and the world flashed white behind her eyelids.

'Jake? Jake? Shit,' said one them.

Something stabbed into her leg and her muscles relaxed beyond her control. And the world faded away.

The dirty white van streaked with rust lurched out of the side road and took off towards the centre of the city. Ellen Lomax turned to watch it go. There was a flash of light from inside it and the motor choked for a few moments before recovering.

She shook her head and checked the road carefully before crossing. There wasn't a lot of traffic nowadays. Once upon a time it would have taken ten minutes or more to get across the road and over to Southern Cemetery.

She ambled across the first set of lanes, keeping an eye out for cars, and then the second set. She glanced up at the riffy pylon. Hundreds of graves must have been cleared away to make space for it. The pylons made a grid across the whole city—every city, every town and every village. Even the countryside had them, though not so many.

It took her another five minutes to reach the entrance of the cemetery and the path up to the chapel of remembrance. She glanced back across the road. An electronic billboard switched from showing a woman using a vacuum cleaner to make her house fit for her family to the message she had been seeing all week: The faces of two teenage girls, nearly old enough to be women, with the words 'MISSING. HAVE YOU SEEN THESE GIRLS? CALL THE POLICE HOTLINE NOW'.

Even as she watched it faded out and then came back, but this time there were three girls' faces smiling out at her.

She sighed and headed up to the chapel. It was a relatively modern building, only a single storey and big. When the plague hit there had been so many dead, and such a risk of infection, the corpses had been incinerated as fast as possible. No one knew how many and who they all were. Which had made her deception much easier.

She pushed her way through both sets of double doors; the chapel did not rate automatic doors. The woman behind the desk looked up and smiled as if in recognition. 'Mrs Lomax. Lovely to see you again.'

Ellen had never seen the woman before in her life but that didn't mean anything. The riffy identified her and the pylons tracked her every move. Just as they tracked everybody. The grid had informed the receptionist who she was and the fact she came here every week.

'Please take a seat; there's someone in at the moment.'

It was rare but it happened. As far as Ellen knew she was the only one who had been coming here every week since it opened, seven years after the plague.

'Where's Moira?'

'Moira Fraser? She's moved on.'

Ellen's face must have communicated her sudden horror that the woman must have died—or had something worse happen to her. 'To another department. Town hall.'

'Oh, I see.'

Ellen sat and waited. After a few minutes a man emerged, a few years older than Ellen; he would have known what it was like before. There were no tears in his eyes, just the vacant look that some of them had.

'You can go in now.'

The chamber of remembrance consisted of a circular room with enough stepped bench seating to accommodate fifty people. Ellen had not seen that number of people in all the nine years she had been coming.

She took her usual place one level up from the lowest. The lights dimmed and the images of two bronze panels rose from the ground. On each was embossed an image: one of her dead husband, the other a baby. Inscribed into the holographic panels beneath the man's face were the words: 'ROGER JON LOMAX' and under the other 'JASON LOMAX'.

'I love you, Roger,' she said quietly.

Chapter 3

Dog

The screech of the metal lathe was painful. Dog pressed his fingers into his ears and waited just inside the door of the warehouse. The place smelt of hot lubricating oil, metal, burnt animal skin and pilchards. The fish was still fresh and Dog salivated. Probably the Armourer's lunch.

The screech came to a merciful end and Dog tentatively removed his fingers. There was the sound of metal being moved around, feet shuffling and someone taking a bite out of a sandwich. Good enough. He glanced back at the shadowy bulk of Ralph and signed for him to stay put.

Dog threaded his way through the tables and benches where old machines were covered in filthy sheets of plastic. Most of the lights were smashed but he could see well enough. Ahead, in the middle of the room, throbbed a portable generator powering the lathe and the lights.

The Armourer was short and overweight. He wore a leather apron to protect his clothes from the metal sparks of the lathe—the burnt animal skin—a bench to one side, just out of the main light, had two dozen cheap woven sacks.

'You know I could have been anyone,' said Dog casually.

The Armourer jumped and spun round with a sawn-off shotgun in his hands. Dog cocked his head on one side and stared at it. He raised his hands slowly.

'Am I early for the party?'

'You're late.'

'But fashionably late,' said Dog. He looked pointedly at the sacks. 'And you have party bags.' He reached for one. The Armourer brandished the shotgun. Dog stopped.

'Payment?'

'What about party games?' said Dog. 'I love party games, don't you?'

'Ever been to a party?'

'No, but I've seen them, you know, through windows. They look a lot of fun. I like the one where they all sit in a circle and unwrap a present to music.'

'Pass the parcel.'

'What?'

'It's called pass the parcel.'

Dog smiled, showing a lot of teeth. 'Is it? Fascinating.'

'Where's the payment, Dog?'

Dog patted down his clothes. 'Oops, lost it. Hide and seek. We could play hide and seek. I know that one.'

'Any chance you could be serious?'

'Tried that once, didn't work out. I prefer...' Dog paused and grinned again, '...insouciance.'

'No payment, no shell casings.'

'Are you sure you don't want to play hide and seek?'

The Armourer lifted his gun. Dog sighed and whistled. The sound echoed around the room.

Dog glanced round though he had heard Ralph's shuffling feet as he responded. The big dark shadow detached itself from the dark of the warehouse. Persuading Ralph to come into the building had been difficult and getting him up the stairs had been harder. His coordination was deteriorating; he really wouldn't be much good in the fights. As long as the Armourer didn't realise that.

Ralph was not turning out well. The man he had once been had been replaced by random DNA strands. He lumbered as if his whole body was distorted—Dog had no desire to see what was under the coat he wore. The insect eye that occupied half his face was bad enough. Probably why he had trouble with stairs. But it was the fact his other eye was completely normal that made it so much worse. It was a very sad eye. Even more incongruous was the silver foil protruding from beneath the big hat pulled down hard on his head.

The Armourer looked him over and noted the clawed left hand. He nodded at that and then studied Ralph's face.

'Ugly bastard,' he said. 'What's with the foil? He hasn't still got his riffy?' The Armourer started to look worried and stared around as if the shadows were full of threat.

'Of course not,' said Dog quickly. 'He likes it, won't wear a hat without it.'

'Still making decisions?'

'Oh yes, may look rough but he's still got it up top,' Dog turned to Ralph. 'Say hello to the nice man.'

Ralph shuffled for a moment. 'Ung-ugh.'

'See, he can still talk.'

'And you brought him in daylight?'

'He's got a hat,' said Dog. 'Anyway, Mr Mendelssohn wants five bags.'

The Armourer shook his head. 'For that? No way. He's barely worth two.'

Dog turned to face the Armourer directly. 'You think I'm joking? Yeah, I like jokes but, y'know, Mr Mendelssohn, he doesn't have a sense of humour, not even deep down.' Something tickled Dog's ears; he felt them twist to the sound. 'But you shouldn't insult Ralphie here. He's got a good few months left in him. He's got real talent; he's an excellent fighter...'

'I might see my way to three.'

But Dog wasn't listening any longer. He put his head on one side and turned his ear to a broken window on the other side of the warehouse. He caught the sound of—

'Oh, bollocks.'

Dog slammed his hands over his ears and dived for cover under one of the benches in the shadows away from the Armourer's lathe.

Every window not already broken, on both sides of the warehouse, exploded inward. Shards of glass cascaded through the room covering every surface. Ralph let out a cry of fear drowning out the swearing of the Armourer.

Dog heard the whining of high-speed winches. Shadows appeared at the windows. Moments later double beams of light sliced through the room. One hit the Armourer and his cursing was cut off as he crumpled to the ground. The air filled with the pungent smell of ozone. Another beam hit Ralph but though he reacted with a jerk, it just set him off running. Moving like an unstoppable train into the dark away from the door they had entered by.

Dog muttered under his breath. He'd better come back with either Ralph or the bags otherwise Mendelssohn was not going to be pleased. Half a pilchard sandwich was lying there in front of him. He grabbed it and took a bite.

'THIS IS THE POLICE.' Boomed the heavily amplified voice.

'No shit,' muttered Dog and swallowed.

'REMAIN WHERE YOU ARE AND YOU WILL NOT BE HURT. ATTEMPT TO FLEE AND WE WILL BE FORCED TO USE LETHAL FORCE.'

'Mitchell?' Dog rolled his eyes to the heavens. 'Bloody Mitchell again. How am I supposed to earn a crust with him on my tail all the bloody time?'

There was a crash behind him, in the direction Ralph had gone, and the sound of submachine gun fire. 'Poor Ralph.' Dog jumped up, grabbed a couple of bags from the table and hit the lathe on-button. It ran up to speed in moments filling the air with noise.

It took him less than three seconds to cover the ground to the first door. Armoured police smashed through the window as he reached it. They would be busy following the heat signature of the engine, Ralph and the Armourer. Dog knew he moved so fast his trail would barely show and, to them, that would mean it was old.

There was no time to listen. He pulled the heavy metal-bound door open, slipped through and pulled it shut as gently as possible behind him. There was no lock.

The corridor ahead was empty. There wasn't much light. What there was filtered from the dirty windows in the rooms to the left and right. The place was overlaid with the sweaty scent of the Armourer and his lunches, but underneath that there was only dust and rats. No one had been here for a long time.

The police might have come in by the window but they would have all the exits covered and expected to flush out any prey that escaped the initial attack. He could hear the incoming helicopter. Once it was close enough it would make it impossible to hear anything ahead. Dog had no idea if the place had an exit through the sewers but, if there were any, Mitchell would have them covered.

Dog loped the length of the corridor, retracing the path in the dust he and Ralph had made. He was not concerned about noise; they did not have his hearing, and the floorboards had been well-maintained once upon a time, so did not creak as he sped across them. He bounded through the empty window frame of the far door. The floor of the stairwell was concrete and metal. Dog landed light and came to a halt.

Panels in the ceiling allowed light through there. A couple of panes were missing and the metal banister was slick with damp. The stairs were stained darker with wetness and, in places, green with moss.

Dog froze. There was movement below, just as he expected. He peered into the dimness. There was a figure in the shadows but just a constable from his combat jacket and armed with a shotgun and a Burner. They were dangerous but their ionising beams were less effective in the damp and the voltage just leaked away before it got far.

The constable did not come up the stairs. He was on his own. What was he doing? Taking a leak? He should have been covering the door from outside, instead he'd come in to relieve himself. *Must be a complete rookie.* Dog almost felt pity, but the smell the policeman generated was intense and unpleasant.

Dog knelt and unfastened one of the bags. He pulled out a slim cartridge casing. It gleamed in the half-light. He retied the bag and stood, just as the policeman was adjusting his clothes.

Gunshots went off in the distance. The policeman grabbed his gun probably planning to get back to his position. Dog flicked the cartridge over the rail and stepped back. He heard the sudden movement of boots as the cartridge clinked against the ground.

The boots stopped moving. The man would be looking up.

The helicopter got closer. Dog strained to hear what he needed. A pause and there it was: scraping of one shoe as he knelt down to pick up the shiny thing.

The helicopter's drone turned into a roar as it came lower.

Dog vaulted the banister. The bottom of the stairwell got darker as he did so. The policeman looked up. Just in time to see the bag of cartridges smash onto his helmet.

Dog landed on his feet in a crouch, absorbing the energy of the fall. He used one hand to balance as he swung the heavy bag into the back of the policeman's legs. The man dropped to his knees.

Dropping the bags, Dog pulled at the helmet's velcro chinstrap. It came loose and the helmet tumbled away.

'Sorry,' said Dog and slammed the man's head against the wall. He wasn't unconscious, but dazed. That would be enough.

Dog grabbed the bags, jumped to his feet and dived for the door—coming to a halt just inside.

There were bushes ten feet away, then a drop down to a stream.

More gunfire caught his attention and he heard a roar from the other end of the building. Ralph must be putting up a good fight. Dog felt a little sorry for him, but perhaps getting shot now would save him from the agony to come. Besides—Dog peeked out—no one was looking in his direction.

The helicopter would have infra-red but if he moved fast enough he would be gone before anyone reacted.

He moved.

Chapter 4

Chloe

The school infirmary was sponsored by Utopia Genetics. The money and equipment supplied by the company did not make the school exceptional; every school had an infirmary backed by a genetics company who also paid the staff.

Chloe sat in the hardback chair, leaned back against the pale blue wall and glanced at the door to the examination room. She shivered. It wasn't that she believed she was infected but the idea that a trip into that room could result in a positive diagnosis was scary.

There was compulsory testing by a qualified doctor every year. It was the only way the plague could be kept under control. The stories of what had happened when it struck were unpleasant.

Even her father wouldn't talk about it in detail but he had hammered it home again and again at the FreakWatch meetings that he ran for the local neighbourhood. Most of the older people who attended would nod their heads in agreement. The people who were too young to remember, or had been born since, accepted it.

She turned her attention back to the posters on the wall and read them for what seemed the hundredth time. She had even read the small print.

'Utopia Genetics—Protecting Your DNA'

Chloe looked at the smiling face of Mercedes Smith, the CEO of Utopia Genetics, the largest genetics company in the country. The same friendly image of her smiled out from every poster. There were various messages in the posters: dire warnings about staying alert for anyone exhibiting signs of S.I.D; warnings to stay away from anyone showing strange behaviour; and not to engage in sexual intercourse with any partner who had not been certified clear of the infection.

'Ten Ways to Spot an S.I.D Infectee'

Before an individual had the plague they were a person, but from the moment of infection, they became a freak. She thought about the red-haired kid for a moment. Chloe understood about heredity—not the details but an overview—she'd looked it up on BritNet. The wiki pages had been sponsored by UG.

'Death Cycle of an S.I.D Infectee'

Initially, after infection, there was nothing to see. In fact nothing happened, except S.I.D wormed its way into the stem cells of the body where it lay dormant, waiting for the trigger.

Then live DNA from another source would get into the body. Instead of being destroyed it would be absorbed and replicated. The victim's body would change—the results were uniformly gruesome. They could sprout another arm, or an eye not necessarily human; almost any DNA could be absorbed. And anything encoded into the invading DNA could be reproduced.

It wasn't always visible; it might be internal like a fish's swim bladder.

But once the process started it was unstoppable. There might be multiple infections creating weird monsters. As the physical distortions increased, the pain became greater. Many killed themselves as soon as they realised what had happened. Some later, as the pain increased. Others lost their mental faculties and simply went mad.

Death was a welcome relief for the victims. What the Purity did was a good thing; it helped both society and the infectee.

She jumped as the door beside her opened. Kavi peered in.

'Are you all right?'

'I'm fine, really, just been working out too hard.'

To Chloe's amazement Kavi stepped into the room. She had her hands stuffed into her skirt pockets, probably so Chloe wouldn't see them shaking. Well she might not be able to see her hands, but Kavi's frightened eyes darting to and fro, lingering on the door to the examination room, said everything.

'You didn't have to come,' said Chloe. She really just wanted to tell Kavi to leave. She didn't have to put herself through this.

'No, it's okay, I wanted to make sure you're okay.'

Make sure I hadn't been quarantined as a freak, thought Chloe. She stood up and glanced at the office door. The nurse must have got tied up with something else, maybe even forgotten about her. Chloe pushed her shoulders back. There was still some tension in them. 'Let's go out into the corridor.'

There was a moment's hesitation then Kavi nodded, turned, and left the room as if it was on fire. Chloe sighed. Kavi's father had been diagnosed months before and was gone. He had been collected by the Purity and euthanised. The family had been quarantined. Since their return Kavi had been a wreck and become an outcast, even though she had been declared clean.

She never spoke about the time she had been quarantined along with all the other close members of her family.

Even in the corridor she kept glancing at the door to the infirmary.

'Really, I'm okay,' said Chloe again.

'I was worried.'

'I know. It was brave of you to come.'

'Ashley wouldn't.'

'She's not as strong as you.'

Kavi gave a nervous smile.

'You can go, I'll call you later.'

'If you're sure.'

'Go.' Chloe gave her a gentle shove. Kavi smiled and turned. She had only gone a few paces when Miss Kepple came round the corner, her shoes clipping on the hard surface. Kavi froze.

Miss Kepple breezed past her without even looking; she had her eyes fixed on Chloe. Even in the Purity lessons, Miss Kepple never addressed a question, a look, or perhaps even a thought, at Kavi. It was as if she didn't exist. She had stopped noticing Ashley as well.

Chloe liked Miss Kepple but did not think that was right.

'How is your back, Miss Dark?'

'Much better.'

'Good.' Miss Kepple opened the door to the infirmary, checked the room was empty and ushered Chloe inside. She shut the door firmly.

'I understand you have applied to join the Purity?'

She was so stern Chloe could not decide whether she was angry or not. So she just nodded.

'I would have thought you would want to discuss it with me first.'

'I do, I mean, I would,' said Chloe. 'It was my dad really. He put my name in first.'

'Oh, I see.' Miss Kepple seemed to be adjusting mental gears, and then she smiled. 'Well that's all right. So you would like to talk about it?'

'If you don't mind?'

'After school tomorrow then.'

'Thank you.'

Chapter 5

Mitchell

The warehouse was swarming with police, technicians and forensics. Though mostly for show, since the whole area had been irradiated by the Sanitation squad as the first step. There was little evidence that S.I.D could infect in any way other than direct contact, and more than just a brief encounter.

Detective Inspector Mitchell stepped into the main floor with the plastic-covered machines. It was nearly lunchtime and he was hungry. He had handed over his gun to the forensic scientist responsible for the police side of the shooting and gone through the various administrative procedures. The incident outside had been filmed by drones so there would be no doubt justice was seen to be done as always.

He'd lost count of the kills he'd made.

One of the forensics went past carrying a half-eaten sandwich in an evidence bag. He stopped the man with an abrupt wave of his hand and had him hold up the sandwich. The pattern of large incisors was unmistakable. It was Dog again. That perp was a pain in the backside. When he had first surfaced, Mitchell had assumed Dog was a freak, but he had been around so long he must just be human.

Mitchell walked over to the line of tape outlining the primary area of interest. He glanced around at the lathe and the table of cartridge bags. There were three fully suited forensics combing the area. Mitchell felt rather than saw Yates coming up beside him.

'Any sign of Dog?' he said.

'No, but Kendal's got an aching head.'

'Serves him right. What the hell did he think he was playing at?'

Yates shrugged. He was a good twenty years younger than Mitchell, and a good detective, though he reminded Mitchell of a game show host.

'He was at the low risk end.'

'Computer analyses are crap.'

'You know that, I know that,' said Yates. 'But rules are rules.'

'I want that little bastard.'

'Hey, you got the freak; you know the Super will love you for that.'

Mitchell sighed. 'There's nothing we can do here.' He turned and headed for the door.

As they descended to the first floor there were a dozen moving spotlights flickering and shining into the dark of the building.

Yates went ahead and pushed open the doors. The crowd outside surged in their direction, along with clamouring voices. Journalists with microphones shouting questions. Mitchell hung back, Yates loved this stuff. Let him handle it.

The crowd went quiet as Yates raised his hands. Mitchell squinted into the lights.

'How many freaks have you eliminated now, Mitchell?' A woman's voice pierced the air.

'No comment as yet,' said Yates raising his voice.

'What do you say to the accusation you enjoy killing freaks?'

Yates pushed into the crowd that gave way before him. They may be reporters but they could be arrested if they obstructed an investigation. Mitchell followed. Questions continued to fly.

'Are you following the rules, Mitchell?'

He tried to see who was asking the questions, but Yates moved back and stood directly in front of him.

'Today's intervention has eliminated weapons manufacture that would have put the lives of ordinary citizens at risk,' Yates said smoothly. 'The use of lethal force against an S.I.D infectee can be seen as an act of kindness in light of the degree of abnormality. You'll be receiving images of the infectee in due course.'

Mitchell escaped the crowd and found his car. He slid into the driver's seat. He rummaged around among the empty snack wrappers in the door until he found a half-eaten energy bar. He pulled some hairs off it and took a mouthful.

Yates opened his door and sat down with a cup of coffee.

'Where did you get that?'

'One of the journos.'

'Abuse of power.'

'Want some?' Yates asked. 'Wash that thing down?'

Mitchell took the paper coffee cup. It was barely warm. He took a mouthful and handed it back. The actual coffee content was minimal. 'You do talk a load of crap.'

Yates shrugged. 'They lap it up.'

Mitchell selected Manchester Central Police Station and activated the auto-drive. The car stayed slow over the uneven surface outside the warehouses but accelerated smoothly once out on the sparsely populated main road. Mitchell took another bite of the snack bar.

The screen in the middle of the dashboard flickered into life. A grey background with the androgynous head and shoulders of the police wirehead, Lament. Weird name. The image was completely lifelike if you can call a bald twenty-five-year-old with a voice that was as indistinctly androgynous as the face it theoretically belonged to 'lifelike'. The skin colour was vaguely Mediterranean which meant nothing. The wirehead could be anything it wanted.

'Sorry to disturb you, DI Mitchell.'

'What do you want, Lament?'

'There has been another kidnapping.'

'Not my case. You should be talking to Thomas.'

'He's busy at the scene.' The wirehead's face was capable of expressing emotion. It seldom did. 'You are to proceed to the girl's school and take statements from friends and teachers. The girl's parents have been sent there.'

'Do I get any choice?' said Mitchell. It was a rhetorical question.

The car decelerated abruptly and swung into a u-turn.

'Shit!' shouted Yates, brushing coffee from his trousers.

'Consumption of liquids (hot or cold) in a moving police vehicle is prohibited.'

Mitchell could have sworn Lament was laughing behind the words. The screen went dead.

'Bloody machines,' muttered Yates.

'If he were a machine.'

'God, don't remind me. Those wireheads give me the willies. The idea there's a body in there somewhere.'

'I wonder how he feels about it.'

Chapter 6

Mercedes

Mercedes Smith straightened her dress. The movement was automatic and completely unnecessary. She could afford the very best but she always used the clothes designers on the rise. They struggled hardest to succeed. They worked to satisfy her, because they understood the benefit of having the CEO of Utopia Genetics as a customer.

'You look fine,' said a disembodied voice in the room. She was in her private suite near the top of the UG skyscraper—what passed for a skyscraper here, anyway.

'Spying on me?'

If she could have heard a shrug it would have been there.

'Just doing my job.'

'Giving me moral support is part of your job?'

'The smooth running of your life is my job, Mercedes.'

She allowed Xec to use her first name when they were together in private. She laughed to herself; there she went again, imagining he was really here. The truth was different. Even when he was 'here' she was still completely alone.

'Is there something you want to tell me, Xec?'

'You're ten minutes late for the meeting.'

'I know.'

'That's all right then,' he said. 'As long as you know.'

And he was the only one she allowed such familiarity and, potentially, rudeness. Everyone else was terrified of her, and so they should be.

She sighed and headed for the exit. It was just a couple of floors down to the conference room. There was an elevator but she took the stairs as usual. Her shoes were not quite flats but the heels were no problem. Exercise was important; not that she intended to lose weight. Having generous curves was an important statement nowadays: only the poor were thin.

'Anyone complaining about me being late?' she asked as she came down the final flight.

'You know I'm not supposed to do that,' said the voice of Xec. He preferred to be the faceless entity rather than use a virtual image on a screen. She appreciated that; it made him scarier. She also knew he would do as he was told. She could not imagine what benefits wireheads gained from being paid, but he responded well to a generous income.

'Well?'

'Only McCormack, but then complaining is what he does best.'

Mercedes pushed through into the main corridor. The carpet was well-worn and would need replacing soon. Xec would deal with it as and when it became important.

She was no longer sure about McCormack. As Head of Research he probably thought his position was secure, especially as he knew a lot of secrets—the sort it would take a lot of money to suppress if they got out.

It was not that she wanted yes-men, but she preferred to have people with a more positive attitude. Still, his department was doing good work.

At what point does the balance shift?

The door of the conference room came into view as she turned a corner. She stopped. 'Anyone in his department that could take over and do as good a job?'

'Possibly.'

'That's not helpful.'

Again the silent and invisible shrug. 'I'll have to look into it; the job requirements are difficult to fill.'

'And look into what can be done to remove any possibility of McCormack going to one of our rivals.'

'Apart from the obvious?'

'If it can be avoided.'

'I'll see what I can do.'

Mercedes nodded, knowing that he could see her perfectly clearly.

The upper echelon of executives stood as she entered the room. Almost every one of them was both taller and older: Alistair McCormack with his fake grin, fake hair and Scottish pretensions; Margaret Jenner, shorter than Mercedes and wider, in charge of Administration and Support Services—she also had a very short fuse; Paul Banner, Security and Purity Liaison, quiet but with a sonorous speaking voice, he was hard to read but she had never had a reason to question his loyalty; and Kingsley Upton, marketing, who always seemed to be selling something.

'Sit down, everyone,' she said as the door closed with a gentle click behind her.

'Room secure, Miss Smith,' said Xec.

'Off-the-record protocol, Xec.'

'Yes, Miss Smith.'

The background buzz, so constant no one ever noticed it, went silent. It was a trick Xec had suggested. He broadcast the buzz at all times through every speaker. It was hard to hear even when you listened for it, but you noticed when it vanished.

Anyone with sufficient authority could request the off-the-record protocol. Xec would switch off the buzz and give the impression he was no longer listening. It was a lie.

'Hope we can get through this quick,' said Upton. 'I have seats at the Palace tonight.'

Jenner looked across at him. 'Is that *An Ideal Husband*? We were thinking of getting tickets.'

'Degenerate,' said Banner, his voice rolling across the room. Other people might have muttered the word; Banner did not need to.

'It's just a play,' said Upton quickly. 'Historical.'

'Wilde was a degenerate.'

Mercedes moved in her chair. Their attention focused on her immediately. 'We are more likely to get out of here quickly if we stick to the subject.'

No one spoke. 'Paul, you had something you wanted to communicate to the team?'

All eyes turned to him. 'The sudden availability of new resources and their collection has attracted the attention of the Purity.' He paused for a breath. 'They are sending an investigator to work with the police.'

'Can they do that?' said Upton. He looked at Mercedes as if for confirmation.

'They can do whatever the hell they like,' growled McCormack. 'More importantly, can they trace it to us?'

'I do not think so,' said Banner.

'You don't think so?' cried Upton. 'You know what they would do to us?'

'We all know,' said Mercedes barely raising her voice but it calmed them. 'They won't find out. We have taken precautions. The more important question is what we should do if any more resources become available while this investigator is in the area.'

There was a long silence. It was Jenner who broke it. 'We need to take each case as it comes. If we can ensure the resource is properly suppressed then it should be no problem acquiring it. Otherwise it should be terminated.'

Jenner nodded. Upton continued to look worried.

'I'm loath to lose any resource,' said McCormack.

'What about your life?' said Upton.

Mercedes stood up and leaned forward with her fists pressed against the table top. 'It won't come to that, Kingsley. You know we have protocols in place to deal with bad situations. Margaret is right; we'll just take each one as it comes. Any that risk our exposure will be ignored.'

With that she turned and headed for the door. 'Enjoy the play, Kingsley.'

She noticed the artificial hum as she came out of the room. 'Kingsley may be more of an issue than McCormack,' she said out loud.

'And considerably easier to replace,' said Xec.

'I need to go home,' she said.

'Not the club?'

She said nothing; he knew her very well. Perhaps too well.

'Not tonight.'

Chapter 7

Chloe

Half the lights in the corridor leading to the school atrium were out. There was enough to see by and you got used to it. The passageway was straight and wide. The school had been built to accommodate perhaps two thousand kids before the plague; now there were barely five hundred.

Chloe knew her history: The S.I.D plague had taken a lot of people; no one really knew how many because records had been lost. When enough people died in a business that depended on computers, the passwords were gone and no one could get in.

The riots, panicking and social disorder that followed the worst of the S.I.D plague had been bad but not killed many others. But in a society run on computers that no longer worked, everything had shut down. Civilisation disintegrated in a matter of weeks. Ordinary diseases and malnutrition killed off the weakest of those who were not infected by S.I.D.

It was only the Purity that held off complete collapse.

But still things broke and could not be mended because the industry was not there. Most resources were engaged in ensuring the S.I.D plague did not spread again. It had not been wiped out, just controlled.

The front of the school was all window, which allowed daylight to illuminate the space. Chloe climbed the wooden stairs that curved round to the mezzanine floor. The steps were clean but stained with years of use. Her back still twinged every few moments at the stress of climbing. She was angry at herself. Normally she would have run up them two at a time; now she was like an old woman.

She paused and looked round as a rhythmic whooshing started up in her ears, accompanied by a low throb that sounded like a heartbeat. She turned her head trying to see where the noise was coming from, but the sound moved with her. She pressed a finger in her right ear. The sounds changed in quality but did not diminish. She shook her head trying to clear whatever had blocked up her ears. The sound faded.

She sighed and hoped she was not getting an ear infection as well. That would be too much. She continued to plod up the stairs.

The school lockers were ranged across the walls of the mezzanine floor. Here and there were clumps of other students, mostly older ones who had free periods. She headed for her locker where she could see Ashley and Kavi. A murmur of conversation floated her way. A boy from a nearer group looked her way with a frown on his face.

'...shouldn't be allowed in the school.'

Chloe stopped and touched her ear. He had turned back to his friends but she heard his whispered words distinctly as if she had been standing beside him.

'My dad says all the families should be put in quarantine for years.'

'That would cost too much.'

'Just kill them then, like they used to. Easiest all round.'

Chloe shook her head. Must be a trick of the acoustics; she was a good fifteen metres from them. She strode on.

'I don't get that one,' said the first voice. 'Her dad's in the watch, but she's friends with them.'

Chloe allowed herself a smile and continued towards her locker. People like that couldn't possibly understand. They were the sort that would riot given half the chance, follow the crowd and not think for themselves.

'I still don't get that she likes Kepple.' That was Ashley.

'She wants to get into the Purity.' She heard Kavi say. 'Anyway, *you* used to like Kepple.'

'Well, she used to like me, until … you know.'

'Yeah.'

'But if she wants to get into the Purity, why is Chloe friends with us?'

'Maybe because she's a good person.'

They went quiet as Chloe approached.

'Hey,' said Chloe.

The others nodded.

'Anything wrong?'

'Apart from the usual?' said Ashley. 'Everything's rainbows and teddy bears. Just waiting for the day they find out my teddy bear has three legs and scales instead of fur.'

The school intercom played a jolly tune. They all looked up even though there was no point. The sound of the school secretary's voice pierced the overwhelming quiet that seemed to pervade the place.

'Ashley Crook report to classroom 3B. Chloe Dark to classroom 15A. Kavi Moorthy report to the School Office. Immediately.'

Chloe realised she had blocked out the thumping sound but now she heard two sets of racing heartbeats. Her hands snaked out to grab both Kavi and Ashley by their wrists.

Neither of them spoke but there was panic just beneath the surface.

'No,' breathed Kavi. 'I can't, not again.' She pulled ineffectively at Chloe's grip.

Chloe could hear the voices of the students behind her. She knew they were looking and making judgements.

'It can't be anything to do with your families,' said Chloe. 'It would be one or the other of you, and not me.'

Kavi wasn't listening but Ashley got the point. 'Kepple must have talked. Must be about the fight this morning.'

'She wouldn't,' said Chloe but she was suddenly unsure. 'Look we have to go. I'll take Kavi to the office, it's on my way—'

'Sort of,' said Ashley.

'—yeah, well, I'll be late.'

She was about five minutes late but she had sneaked a peak into the school office, and seen Kavi's mum. Whatever it was, it was not about S.I.D infections. And when she arrived at 15A she was not surprised to see her parents sitting by the wall.

There was a man standing at the main window across the room, looking out. She recognised him immediately as DI Mitchell; he was famous, which meant the other man was DS Yates. She was very confused: What could she have to do with the best freak killers on the Manchester force?

'Mum?'

'It's all right, dear—'

'Please, Mrs Dark,' said Yates. 'We require your presence to interview your daughter, but she is old enough to answer for herself.'

Her mother sat back, her eyes filled with worry. Chloe gave her a smile.

'Miss Dark,' said Yates. 'Please take a seat.'

He indicated a chair in the middle of the room. The rest of the classroom had been cleared with furniture stacked along the walls. If anything looked right for an inquisition, this was it. The room itself was used for the Purity lessons and there were S.I.D information posters on the walls, like the ones in the infirmary.

Chloe sat. The chair was for younger students and a little small.

'We just want to ask you a few questions, Miss Dark— can I call you Chloe?'

She nodded and he smiled. It was the smile of a TV presenter.

'So, Chloe, you know Melinda Vogler?'

'Yes, I know her.'

'And when was the last time you saw her?'

Chloe frowned at the curious question. He must know exactly when she had last seen Melinda. The truth hit her like a brick and she gasped. 'She's disappeared, hasn't she? Like the others.'

There was a movement from the man by the window but he didn't turn. 'What makes you say that?'

'You're DI Mitchell.'

He turned. Chloe could see he was in his fifties at least. He had been a policeman before the plague. Yates stood up. 'No photographs, and no autographs.'

Chloe did not miss the look that flashed from Mitchell to Yates, but she got the strong impression Yates did not care.

'What makes you think she's disappeared, Miss Dark?' repeated Mitchell.

'Because you know the last time I saw Melinda. It's in the riffy records.'

'RFID archive,' said Yates.

'But if you're asking then you don't know where she is right now and the only way that can be true is if she's no longer broadcasting.' Chloe's breath caught in her throat. 'She's not dead is she?'

Her mother gasped and, in the corner of her eye, she saw her father put his arm round her.

Yates glanced at Mitchell, who paused for a moment as if deciding which version of the truth would be right in the circumstances. 'Not as far as we know.'

Chloe breathed out and looked Mitchell in the eye. 'You want to know if she was acting strange or different?'

'I take it she was.'

Chloe hesitated, gathering her thoughts. 'She was sort of withdrawn, I suppose. She said she was going to the doctor. I knew there was something. I should've talked to her.'

'When you say 'withdrawn' can you be a little more precise?'

'She wasn't talking so much. Didn't take part at all, really. Like when you've done something really bad and you're scared you're going to get found out.'

'And what do you think she might have done?'

Chloe sighed and when she replied she was almost talking to herself. 'I don't know. I should have asked her. I should have talked to her. I might have stopped it.' She looked up and stared at Mitchell again. 'You have to find her.'

He shrugged. 'It's not my case.'

'But you're the best.'

Mitchell's stern face cracked into a smile. 'Tell that to my superior.' He turned back to look out the window at the school car park and a distant line of trees.

Yates got up from his chair. 'That's all for now, Mr and Mrs Dark, Chloe.'

He ushered them out into the corridor then turned to Chloe. 'Ever thought of joining the police force, Miss Dark?'

'No, I'm joining the Purity,' she said.

Yates's face fell. 'Seriously?'

Chloe frowned. 'Yes, DS Yates, seriously. Someone has to protect the world.'

Chapter 8

Ellen

Ellen Lomax pushed her trolley around the shop with the
wire shopping basket balanced precariously on the top of it.
A single fragment of red plastic was the only memory of the
handle it had once had. She wandered down the aisles under
the flickering of the fluorescent tubes that remained. Most of
the shelves were empty and had been for so long that the
labels, for what they should have carried, had been removed.

She remembered when supermarkets had been stacked
to overflowing with goods, the small ones cramming it all in
to their limited shelf space. But not anymore.

It was true that nowadays the variety of items available
was increasing slowly. But most of them were forbidden to
her because, as a woman on her own with no job, she did not
qualify. Rationing was still in force and only those with spare
money got to have the limited range of luxuries.

The rations were supposed to be enough for one
person but she was still starving most of the time.

She reached the checkout. It was the boy today, born at
the same time as her son, she supposed, but luckier because
here he sat doing a job that required minimal effort. She
stood in the roughly painted checkout circle and waited while
the boy finished reading something on the screen. Mrs
Lomax remembered smartphones. No one had those, but
there were terminals enough for those who rated them.

The boy—his name tag said he was Carl—ensured she and the basket were inside the circle and pressed a button. Something beeped.

'You got too much,' he squinted at the screen, then looked up. 'Two tins of meat. Should be one.'

Mrs Lomax hesitated. 'I have some cash.'

'I can't take cash.'

She waited and watched the thoughts running through his head.

'I'll get Mr James.'

Mr James took two minutes to arrive, saw who was at the checkout, and sent the boy into the back. He removed the tin of meat from Mrs Lomax's basket and rescanned. There was a gentle and reassuring beep from the machine.

Mrs Lomax fished around in her bag and pulled out an old embroidered purse. She simply handed it to Mr James without a word. He opened it, removed most of the contents, and handed the purse back along with the tin of meat.

Not a word passed between them. Mrs Lomax transferred her purchases to her trolley bag and left, trailing it behind her.

It was dark by the time she reached her street. It was not well-populated, less than one in ten of the houses had people living in them. This was both good and bad. She appreciated having some people around; it made the place a little safer, but there were more eyes to pry. Including the twitching curtain across the street as she made her way up the weed-covered path to her door. She unlocked it and pushed her way into the darkness beyond.

She did not turn the lights on. There was a basic entitlement to power but she preferred to store it up until she really needed it in winter. Her eyes adjusted slowly. She lit the candle on the table. It provided enough light to unpack the shopping and put it away. There was more cupboard space than she would ever need again.

The two tins of meat would have to last the week but, as long as she was careful, it would be enough.

She glanced up. A dark form stood in the doorway. She had not heard him arrive, but then she never did. The threadbare hoodie he owned, that she had repaired countless times, was pulled up over his head, and not even the flickering light from the candle penetrated the shadows beneath it.

'Hello, Jason, had a quiet day?'

She did not expect an answer and did not get one. She got the can-opener from a drawer and attacked the first tin. It opened easily enough. Jason stood and watched.

Using a knife she retrieved from a drawer, she dug out the slab of cooked meat and let it drop onto a plate. Two tins for the two of them for the week. Well, those in power claimed that one tin was sufficient for one person, so two ought to be enough.

She measured off the days on its surface and sliced off two pieces of roughly equal size. They had some carrots left over from the previous week and she put those out on side plates. She could have used dinner plates but it made the meal look even smaller than it was.

Finally she fetched a couple of forks—there was no need for a knife—and placed one plate and fork in front of her chair and the other at the other setting. There had been four chairs for the kitchen table but one was in Jason's room while another had been burnt as firewood last year during the worst of the freeze.

She sat down, looked up at Jason, still standing in the doorway, and waited.

'Jason?' she said after long moments passed. He moved with sudden swiftness, the chair scraped on the stone tiles, and he was sitting there. His face was still in shadow and she realised he had moved the candle. He could be so quick when he wanted.

She picked up her fork and cut off a chunk of meat with the side of it.

'I went to see your dad,' she said. 'I gave him your love.'

She put the meat in her mouth and glanced nervously at him. She caught a glimpse of something moving in the shadow of the hood. She forced her gaze back to her plate. Of course she knew what he looked like; she had given birth to him. She should be used to his strangeness but he had hidden his face even from her for so many years now she could only imagine what he looked like.

'You should eat,' she said. 'It's good.' But he didn't; he just sat there.

'You must eat, Jason. I know it's not much but it's enough.'

And if he ate perhaps he would stop going outside. She did not think he understood the terrors she went through whenever he left, and he had been doing it increasingly in recent months.

She broke the soft, tinned carrot in half and put it in her mouth. In the blink of an eye he was standing again, the food untouched on his plate. His hand moved in a blur and there was a metallic clatter as coins dropped on to the table.

Then he was gone. She heard the tell-tale creaks of the flooring as he went up the stairs and into his room. He did not shut his bedroom door quietly.

Jason

He paused for a moment in the middle of his bedroom. He could not bear to see his mother wasting away. Better she had the food. He knew she would pretend to leave it for him for a while. Then she would convince herself that she had better eat it. Once she had, she would feel guilty about it. But that guilt would not stop her from doing it again.

It wasn't that he wasn't hungry. He was always hungry. It had been years since he had eaten all the bugs in the house. Occasionally a spider would come in from the outside, but it never lasted long.

Likewise all the empty houses nearby. He had eaten bugs when he was a baby—once he had been able to get about on his own—but when he realised how much it upset his mother he had stopped doing it with her around. That had lasted until he was about thirteen but then the hunger had really kicked in. He had to find another source.

Rats were easy to catch—for him—but he was human enough to dislike eating them on principle, and certainly not raw. And, to tell the truth, he hated killing animals. While eating bugs and earthworms came naturally to him, anything bigger was just not on his radar. The local cats and dogs were safe from his depredations. And it wasn't that he didn't like proper food.

So he resorted to stealing food wherever he could find it. He knew what the Purity would do to him if they found him, let alone ordinary people. So he was as careful as he could be, and for Jason Lomax being careful was an easy skill to acquire.

'Don't go, Jason, please!'

He had heard her coming up the stairs, of course, but he had locked the door.

'It's not safe!'

She tried the door handle. They went through this ritual almost every day now.

Jason put one foot on the chair and then the other, tightening the laces on his battered trainers. He would have to see about getting something new soon. If he went to another part of the town he would be able to steal clothes without leading anyone back here.

'Please don't. Your father wouldn't want you to go. If you can't do it for me, do it for him...'

She pulled that argument out once each month, after she had been to the Chapel of Remembrance. Jason had been less than a month old when his father had died. He had never been to the chapel. All he had seen was that one old photograph his mother still had. It didn't mean anything to him.

'I saw a girl being kidnapped today: the one in the news.'

He stopped then shrugged. He picked up the kitchen knife he had honed into a dagger and slipped it into the makeshift plastic sheath that had once held a toy sword.

'They know I was there,' she said. 'They'll interview me. They might search.'

All the more reason not to be here. His mother had a tiffy but he did not because, as far as the rest of the world was concerned, he had died with his father. He glanced around. If they did a DNA check they would know someone lived here but beyond that the room looked much the same as it always had. He had not been part of the real world, and had not decorated his room with anything modern.

He unlocked the door and opened it. There was no light but he could see her perfectly well; it was bright lights he did not like. He did not bother slowing himself down this time; he only did it for his mother's sake normally. He was at the window in a moment, unlatched it and glanced out. It took him moments to satisfy himself no one was there to see him as he climbed out and leapt down to the ground.

He heard his mother closing it behind him.

Chapter 9

Dog

In some ways Dog liked the night. Everyone else in world saw things in colour, he only saw shades of grey, but at night it was the same for everyone—and he had good night vision.

On the other hand he really was a creature of daylight and preferred to spend the nights asleep. As long as he could find somewhere safe; if not it was impossible for him to even close his eyes. Something inside him forced him to stay alert.

That was one reason he stayed with Mendelssohn, although he was seldom allowed to stay the night. The other was the sense of belonging, because being a part of something filled a need. Then there was Delia, another reason he liked to stay, and the reason he wasn't allowed to.

Dog bounded over a fence and into a back garden. This one was well-kept. Into the next—abandoned. His ears pricked as he heard a dog bark but it wasn't nearby. Mr Mendelssohn's rendezvous location coincided with some journey or other that his employer needed to make. Riffy implants didn't work inside metal boxes—and that's what a car was—but when someone got in a car the monitoring system tied them together and the car was tracked instead.

Mr Mendelssohn might run illicit activities but he had a riffy and was on the grid. His route had to have a reason; stopping had to have a reason. No one expected that every person's activities were monitored, but the records could be checked.

Dog leapt up to the top of a high fence and jumped down the other side into a back alley. He had already smelled the cat. 'Boo!' he said as he landed beside it. It scrammed down the passageway as if the hounds of hell were on its tail. Dog laughed quietly. He didn't like cats.

He stood up straight and sauntered along the passage to the end where it gave out on to a road. The lighting was bad and he leaned against an unlit lamppost, half-closed his eyes, and dozed.

The bright lights of a car pulled him back to reality. Even before it had rounded a turn further up, he cocked his head and listened. The sound of the motor was familiar. It was Mendelssohn's limousine. Dog shrugged off his backpack and held it in one hand. He had packed the bullet casings tight to ensure they did not clink as he moved.

The car turned the corner and slowed as it passed him. Dog moved forward, grabbed the handle, and slipped inside as the door opened. He closed it behind him and sat with his back to the driver.

There was a dim light in the car. Mr Mendelssohn was watching a news item on a screen. Dog recognised the warehouse from earlier. There was a lot of commotion, then shouts and some screams as Ralph emerged from the building. He had lost his coat somewhere inside and his full horror was on show for all to see.

But he still had his hat on, Dog noted with a smile. Then he lost the smile as a series of gunshots rang out and Ralph collapsed to the ground. Mendelssohn paused it.

'Mitchell,' he said.

'Yeah.'

'He is annoying.'

'I got the stuff,' said Dog. He plunged his hands into the rucksack and pulled out the two bags of casings.

'All of it?'

'Most of it.'

'Really?'

'The Armourer was being a dick,' said Dog. 'Like he felt he could argue with you.'

Mendelssohn settled back in the chair as the vehicle drove steadily through the dark streets. Not fast enough to attract any attention; not slow enough to look suspicious.

'And you lost Ralph.'

'He ran the wrong way, and besides,' said Dog, 'they had the place locked up tighter than a wirehead's arse. If he'd been with me neither of us would have got out.'

'I dislike losing assets. This will go against your credit.'

'But...' Dog clamped his jaw shut on what he wanted to say. You didn't argue with the top dog unless you knew you could win, and Mendelssohn was not someone you played games with.

'You were going to say?'

'But I have something even better.'

Mendelssohn turned his full attention on Dog. It made him feel even more uncomfortable. 'And what might that be?'

'A freak, down at the fights.'

'There are a lot of freaks at the fights, Dog, they have owners already.'

'No, I mean,' he hesitated. He might appreciate being part of Mr Mendelssohn's pack but it was not a place he wanted to stay. He wanted his own. He thought that this other one might be a way to build a pack of his own. But the devil was driving. 'I mean one like me,' he hesitated again, 'like your Delia.'

Mendelssohn's eyes narrowed and he leaned forward. 'Why haven't you mentioned this one before?'

Dog shrugged and grinned. 'Everyone needs assets.'

The threat passed and Mendelssohn sat back. 'You say no one owns him?'

'No, he's not a fighter. He's a pickpocket.'

'Dime a dozen.'

'Not this one, he's fast. I mean *fast*,' Dog emphasised the last word to make sure his boss fully understood what he was saying. 'And no riffy.'

'Very well. Fetch him.'

Dog did not miss the implied insult. 'I'll need money.'

Mendelssohn looked at his watch. It was a very expensive watch, probably an antique. 'I'm busy for next couple of days so let's meet up at the fights on Saturday evening and you can introduce me.'

'No cash then?'

Mendelssohn did not deign to reply. He pressed a button and the driver slowed. Dog glanced out. They were already out of Manchester with nothing but fields around them. Great. It would take him at least an hour to get back into town. But he wasn't going to complain. He opened the door and threw himself out.

He watched the limousine speed up and disappear into the distance.

Chapter 10

Mitchell

DI Mitchell looked down to check his shoes. They were regulation black and polished to a shine. His reflection in the window showed the neat well-fitting suit with his tie properly tightened.

He raised his eyes slightly and read the reflected clock backwards. A couple of minutes past ten: standard management practice, leave them waiting a couple of minutes after the allotted time just so they would sweat a bit and therefore be easier to manage.

Mitchell was not impressed, nor did he sweat. He had seen enough bosses come and go that another one made no difference. They had lost contact with what it was really like out in the world. Even if they ever had pounded the beat, or even investigated the pathetic crimes of ordinary people, they had forgotten it. They had nothing of value to say.

So Mitchell would go into the meeting, Dix would say things, Mitchell would respond and that would be that. Then Mitchell would carry on doing things his own way because that's the way that worked.

He wondered briefly whether Catherine would have liked what he had become. Probably not.

'The Super is ready for you now, DI Mitchell.'

Mitchell turned and smiled at Siân. She was a few years younger than he was with a warm and friendly voice that perfectly suited her position. He knew she liked him. She had lost her family and he would be a good catch since he too had nobody. But that was not something he considered nowadays. He was not good husband material.

Of course a human assistant was completely unnecessary; Lament could have handled all the Superintendent's appointments easily, just as it handled all the others', but it provided employment in a world that had a limited supply of jobs—or, more accurately, a limited supply of qualified people.

And Superintendent of Police was the sort of job where a real person was expected; it gave the job more gravitas.

Mitchell headed across the deep pile carpet, knocked once on the door, opened it and went inside. Like the antechamber, this room belonged to the old part of the building with high ceilings, thick walls, and oak panelling. It could have come straight out of the Victorian age.

Superintendent Dix was a big man, though most of the largeness was now situated around his middle rather than his shoulders. He was in uniform—it was one of those strange traditions where a detective dressed in civvies while those in the upper echelons wore their almost military costume every day.

He stood up and shook Mitchell's hand. His face had a smile fixed on it.

'Good work yesterday, David,' he said. 'Sit.'

Mitchell folded his long frame into the padded armchair facing the desk. The Super's chair was also well-upholstered but more upright which meant he had the height advantage.

'Excellent press coverage, very pleasing.'

'Thank you, sir.'

'And nabbing the freak too, always good for the headlines.'

Mitchell nodded. He had been in enough of these meetings to know that something bad was coming. But he knew he had not done anything wrong, so it puzzled him.

'The courier got away, sir.'

Dix sat back. 'Unfortunate but can't be helped. The press appreciate the elimination of another S.I.D infectee.'

Mitchell considered that Dix could have been writing the headlines himself, though in truth he was parroting them.

'Just doing my job, sir.'

'Too modest, David; no one is complaining about your clean-up rate and your newsworthy activities.'

'Is there a problem, sir?'

Dix looked as if he were trying to swallow something unpalatable. There was a long pause but finally he managed to spit it out. 'Why are they always dead, David? You'd get a better bonus for living ones.'

Because I don't want them to suffer at the hands of the Purity, sir, because I care that they don't spend the rest of their horrible lives in pain.

'Circumstances, sir. Protection of the public at large. Shooting to wound could easily allow someone else to become infected. We can't have that.' It was an answer that Mitchell practised and repeated. 'But if there's someone who wants me to be less effective?' He let the question hang there.

The *faux* smile returned to Dix's lips. 'Of course, no one wants that. Efficiency is the key note of our operation.'

Wait for it, thought Mitchell. *Here it comes.*

'However we are going to have to reallocate your resources,' said Dix. 'I'm reassigning you to the kidnappings.'

'What? Why?'

Dix lost his smile and for a moment Mitchell thought his abrupt questions had gone too far. The smile was replaced by an introspective frown.

'Things have been taken out of my hands, David,' he said. 'the Purity are sending one of their own investigators from London.'

'Why are they getting involved?'

'Much as I would love to know the answer to that question, David, it is not the sort of thing you ask. Not if you want to have a future.' Dix almost looked scared and Mitchell was surprised at how much he was sharing. 'I need someone with backbone who can handle themselves with diplomacy.'

Mitchell snorted. 'I think you've got the wrong person; diplomacy is more Yates's line. I'd certainly prefer something a little more active than a babysitting job.'

There was a long pause. Dix looked as if he were deciding exactly how much he should say, weighing his words with care. 'I am not asking you to babysit, David. This case needs to be solved and I'll be damned if some upstart Purity agent parachuted in from *London*—' he said the word almost as if he was swearing '—is going to do it before us.'

Mitchell said nothing. Dix looked as if there was still something else he wanted to spit out. Years of experience had taught him one thing, if nothing else; that people wanted to tell you everything, you just had to give them the space to do it.

'None of us like politics, David. We're just policemen trying to keep the peace. But this is important. If the Purity wins this one they'll start sticking their noses into police business everywhere, and at every level. Before you could turn around once we would just be another part of the Purity.'

And that was it. Mitchell could see Dix meant every word of it.

'So, you want me to solve it, while liaising with the Purity?'

'I didn't say that.'

Mitchell got to his feet. 'No sir, you didn't.'

The briefing room was empty except for Mitchell. He had a coffee from the machine and was sitting on a sofa at the side of the room. The lights were off and the blinds drawn, but the room was lit up by the wall screen at the far end.

Lament had given himself a window in the corner of the screen and was currently displaying a map of where Vanessa Cooper had disappeared. There were pictures of the other girls, parents where appropriate, and biographical information scattered ergonomically round the edges.

'Is this it?'

'There is a great deal of information,' said Lament. 'We have three hundred statements and are gathering more related to the new abduction.'

'But nothing useful.'

'No.'

'Little wonder Thomas was having problems.'

'Yes,' said Lament. 'You are showing the same signs of frustration but over a much shorter time period.'

'You can keep the personal comments to yourself.'

'As you wish.'

Mitchell sighed and took a drink of coffee. It was almost all chicory. If there was any actual coffee in it that would be an accident. 'Run me through what you've got, first to last.'

An image captioned VANESSA COOPER appeared in the centre of the screen. She was a redhead and grim-faced. The freckles did not make her seem any less stern or unhappy.

'Vanessa Cooper, age 17.'

'Looks like a rebel.'

'She was found living wild after the plague, aged five. She was brought up in an orphanage, several orphanages.'

'No adoption?' Mitchell found it odd; there were so many families that had lost children, never mind adults, that there had been no shortage of people wanting to adopt.

'There were a lot of fosterings, at least until she was ten, but after that it stops. Seems she was a very difficult child. They kept giving her back.'

Mitchell sighed. 'Poor kid. What have you got on the abduction?'

The map at the back of the screen came forward and overlaid everything else. It was of an area of West Manchester near Trafford Park. The image zoomed in on a few streets. A dot appeared tagged with Vanessa's face.

'Three weeks ago she was walking home from school.' A clock in the corner started to move, faster than normal time, and the dot made its way through the streets. 'The street was deserted as you can see, a couple of people in their homes—' there were tagged dots inside the buildings '—and then this happened.'

The clock slowed to half normal speed. Vanessa stopped, moved backwards, went sideways onto the road itself, paused and then vanished.

'So she was caught and put into a vehicle.'

'A vehicle with no riffy and, unless she went willingly, grabbed by perpetrators who also had no riffy or were blocking them.'

'Any reason to suppose she did not go by choice?'

The image of Lament faded through to the foreground and he shrugged. 'Hard to say. Obviously she had not had the happiest of childhoods and interviews with teachers and orphanage staff revealed that she had no love for society. However there's no behaviour that indicated she was meeting with anyone.'

'What about friends?'

'Yes she had a few; they were attracted by her rebellious nature,' said Lament. 'But again, she had not said anything about leaving. According to reports she had resigned herself to another year and then she was getting out.'

'To where?'

'I really couldn't say.'

'Anything in her things at the orphanage?'

'She had a private room because she was so unpleasant to the others. She really did not like being among other people.'

'With a life like hers...' Mitchell sighed and pulled himself together. 'What about the next one?'

'Lucy Grainger, age 16. Three days after Vanessa.'

The image was of a girl with dark hair that fell round her face. Her nose was rather longer than you might expect and it seemed she wanted to hide it. She had large, round brown eyes.

'Slim build and only four foot six. Only child, unremarkable parents, neither has a job so they're on benefits but having a daughter means they are well looked after.'

'No other children?' The production of children was encouraged, and well rewarded, because the population was still falling. That a family would not have several children was surprising.

'Mrs Grainger has a medical condition that makes it impossible for her to conceive.'

'But they didn't adopt?'

'One moment.' This happened occasionally when Lament was asked a question where the answer was not immediately available in the notes. He had to search the data banks. 'It seems not.'

'Well, not everybody wants to,' and when you might get a child like Vanessa Cooper it's easy to understand why. 'Let's see what happened.'

The map came to the front. This time it was in the north near Heaton Park. The story played out the same way until the moment of the abduction. If Vanessa had been willing, it looked as if little Lucy was not. The movement into the road, where the vehicle was presumably located, was a series of stops and starts. But finally she too disappeared.

'Looks like she dug her heels in.'

'There were scuff marks in the ground at the locations where you see the pauses. Forensics found deposits that corresponded to the shoes she was wearing.'

'But she's tiny.'

'Yes.'

Mitchell sighed. 'All right, bring up Melinda Vogler.'

'Age 17, disappeared yesterday.'

'Yes, I know that. Family?'

'Two younger brothers, father employed, mother not. Nothing special about her.'

'Except she's the third victim,' said Mitchell. 'Let's see it.'

The map came up, south-east Manchester, only a couple of miles from where Vanessa was taken. Once more the map played out the actions. Mitchell noticed the clock.

'Wait,' it stopped, 'this is the middle of the day, a school day.'

'She was on her way to a doctor's appointment.'

'What for?'

'S.I.D check; one of her family members was infected a while back. She was on Protocol 2.'

'Medium risk.' Mitchell's excitement waned. If there had been an infection in the family it meant that the checks had to be done externally and more often. It wasn't unusual.

The playback resumed. It followed similar lines up until she was grabbed. The tag that marked her position disappeared for a moment, reappeared, and then vanished permanently but before she had moved to the road.

'Any evidence the vehicle had come up to her?'

'There's no indication of that,' said Lament. 'However the forensics reports did have something to say about it: there was an electrical burn at the point she disappears.'

'Burner?'

'They say it did not have the same signature as a beam ionising weapon, but definitely an electrical discharge.'

'Enough to kill her?'

'Perhaps but definitely enough to fuse her riffy.'

'If you zapped someone through the head with enough electricity to kill the riffy, I can't think it would do the victim much good.'

'I don't know,' said Lament. 'I'll send a request to find out.'

Mitchell stared at the map. 'So what we're saying is that although there are similarities between the events that show they are all related, every single one of them has unique features which make no sense.'

'The first lacks any confusing aspects.'

'Yes, but that makes it unusual in itself.'

Mitchell drank down the rest of the coffee even though it was now cold. He stared at the map and the one tag for a member of the public who was standing around the corner from the abduction.

'Who's the potential witness?'

'Ellen Lomax, age 56, no family. Both her son and husband died in the plague. Not employed, on minimum benefits. She did not have line of sight.'

'But she might have seen the vehicle. Has she been interviewed?'

'Thomas was going to but he got pulled off the case.'

'So she's been sitting there with possible information for a day and no one's talked to her?'

Lament did not answer. Mitchell got up and stretched. 'That's what I'll be doing.' He headed for the door.

'You're not supposed to do anything until the Purity investigator gets here Sunday.'

'While the trail goes cold?' he headed for the door. 'Have Yates meet me at the car.'

'Yes, sir.'

The sound of Mitchell's shoes echoed along the corridor as he strode towards the elevator. He pressed the button for down.

'Why would someone kidnap teenage girls?'

'Prostitution?' said the image of Lament in the screen beside the elevator.

'Possible.'

'Body parts.'

'Was there anything interesting in their DNA?'

'Nothing in the most recent check-ups. All perfectly normal. Perhaps for deliberate S.I.D infection?'

'What for? They would be useless in the fights.'

'If you deliberately selected the DNA to infiltrate?'

'Okay, I'll give you that one. What else?'

'Sadistic pleasure,' said Lament as the elevator arrived and the doors slid open jerkily.

'Could be, but both those would require someone with considerable resources,' said Mitchell as he stepped inside and hit the button for the car park in the basement. 'Blackmail?'

'None of them have any connection with anything or anyone significant,' said the screen in the elevator car.

'Maybe it's just murder,' said Mitchell. 'Perhaps that's the best we can hope for them.' He lapsed into silence as they headed down.

The doors slid back but Mitchell stood there. 'Any other ideas?'

'Making a cheap wirehead?'

'Would that work with someone unwilling?'

'They didn't ask *me*,' said Lament.

Chapter 11

Chloe

The school day had been weird. Everyone was on edge. That girls had been disappearing was bad, of course, then to have it happen in her own school was worse. But for it to be someone she had known all her life made it the hardest thing she thought she had ever had to bear.

She tried to concentrate but she was distracted by the fact she had missed the clues: All the times Melinda had been down and not talking. All those times she'd failed to help. It was easy to rationalise that it had nothing to do with the abduction; it was easy to think that there was nothing she could have done. But they were just thoughts. It did not make her feel any different.

She had let her friend down.

People kept asking her questions. Students, most of whom she barely even recognised. On more than one occasion she got the idea that even the teachers wanted to ask her about Melinda—but they couldn't, and you could see the look in their eyes.

Chloe was glad that the weird extended hearing effect she'd had the day before was gone. She couldn't imagine what it would be like listening to all those conversations. The bullies had had a field day with their vicious speculations. One idea going around was that Melinda had been killed by a freak; or that she was a freak and had sprouted weird appendages and disappeared into the city. Some bright spark even suggested Melinda had caught S.I.D from Kavi or Ashley, failing to note the obvious flaw in the argument.

The lessons had gone slowly. Her back had ached a bit but no attack like before. She had an appointment with her chiropractor on Saturday but that was still two days away. She hoped she would be okay until then.

She was grateful as the last minutes to five o'clock ticked away and the alarm—an electronic facsimile of an old-style hand bell—sounded through the school to mark the end of lessons.

The rush to the door left her alone. She packed away her books and slung the bag across her shoulder—her back protested a little but not much. She would have gone to her Jujitsu lesson this evening but there was no point with her back in this state. Sensei wouldn't let her train even if she went.

A few stragglers were leaving the lockers by the time she arrived. She unlocked hers and glanced across at Melinda's. There was no personal ornamentation permitted on the outside, or even names. Just the locker number, but she knew Melinda's as well as her own. And she knew the code for the lock.

The police would already have been through it. If there was anything important they would have taken it away.

Chloe unlocked her locker, exchanged books and removed her lunch box, which she stuffed into her bag. She snapped the door shut and turned the code dials a couple of times. They could have had lockers coded to their riffies, but that would have been expensive. Mechanical locks did the trick well enough.

She glanced at Melinda's locker again. It was as if she had decided the moment she first had the idea. There was no question; she was going to look.

The dials turned easily and she pulled the door open. It looked the way hers did. A few school books stacked up, including copies of the ones that Chloe was now taking home to work on. She frowned; there was a book she didn't recognise. She lifted up the text books and slipped out the hardback. It was old, not only pre-plague but well before that.

She read the title: *The First Men in the Moon and Other Stories* by H. G. Wells. She didn't recognise it.

'Chloe Dark!' Miss Kepple's voice echoed around the empty space making Chloe jump. Chloe stared at the open locker that was not hers. Opening other students' lockers was a crime. 'Did you forget?'

Chloe turned with a look of horror on her face. Forget? Forget what? Oh, she was supposed to be meeting Miss Kepple to talk about the Purity.

'I see you did forget.'

'Sorry, Miss, had some things on my mind.'

'Things?'

'Melinda Vogler.'

'Oh yes,' Miss Kepple seemed slightly mollified, 'well, I still need to talk to you.'

'Right away?'

Miss Kepple smiled. 'Oh yes, right now.'

Chloe shoved the storybook into her bag, shut Melinda's locker and spun the dial. Nobody could expect to remember which locker belonged to which student; as far as Miss Kepple was concerned Chloe had been looking in her own. After all, why wouldn't she?

Chloe entered Miss Kepple's office and the teacher closed the door. The room was not large but the fact she had her own, separate from the teachers' staff room, was a reflection of the importance of her job.

'Would you like a drink, Chloe?' she asked. 'Tea, coffee, orange juice?'

'Orange juice?' Chloe could not remember the last time she had had it.

'There are some perks to being in the Purity,' said Miss Kepple. 'We may as well take advantage of them.'

She even had a refrigerator. It was small and floor standing so she had to squat to reach in. She pulled out a glass bottle containing the precious orange liquid.

'Sit down, Chloe,' said Miss Kepple as she walked across to a cabinet on which was a kettle and some crockery.

Chloe looked around. There was Miss Kepple's desk with a hardback chair on this side and a padded one on the other.

'Use the sofa; this is not formal.'

The two-seat sofa, a wooden frame with floral embroidered cushions to sit on and lean back against, was at the end of the room furthest from the window where it just fitted with enough room for the door to open.

Chloe tried to decide which side to sit when Miss Kepple came up beside her. 'Put your bag behind the door and sit there.' With a hand holding a glass containing an inch of orange juice, she indicated the place nearest the exit.

Chloe did as she was told and crammed herself hard against the armrest to give as much space as possible to Miss

Kepple, who sat next to her and held out a glass. She had an identical one in the other hand.

Orange juice was so expensive Chloe could not imagine the value of what she was about to drink. Miss Kepple had a reputation among the girls but Chloe hadn't heard of anyone being offered anything like this before. She wasn't sure if this was a good sign, but she did like the teacher, so it couldn't be all bad.

'Cheers,' said Miss Kepple with a smile and lifted the glass to Chloe.

Chloe felt uncomfortable—despite being slim Miss Kepple seemed to fill the space available. She had very long legs that she stretched diagonally across the room. Chloe felt trapped but she raised her glass as well and took a sip. The taste was heavenly.

'There, good, now we're comfortable.'

Chloe's smile in return was a lie.

'So, what really happened between you and Hancock yesterday?'

Of all the questions she had been expecting, that wasn't one of them.

'I ... he was being a bully.'

Miss Kepple smiled and showed her perfect white teeth. 'It's all right, Chloe. You're not in any trouble, not with me certainly. I'm just interested to know your side of the story now that the fuss has died down.'

But what about Melinda? thought Chloe. *Doesn't she care at all?*

'He and his friends were bullying a red-haired kid—'

'Price.'

Chloe looked confused.

'His name is Price.'

'Oh, yes, well, he shouldn't do that. I mean there's enough things wrong in the world without adding to it by making stuff up.'

'So you stopped him.'

'Yes,' Chloe surprised herself with the amount of emotion in her voice.

Miss Kepple nodded. 'Quite right too. Your father is the chairman of the local community PurityWatch, isn't he?'

We call it FreakWatch. 'How did you know?'

Miss Kepple took a sip of her orange juice. 'It's my job to know everything about everybody.' She must have noticed the worry creeping across Chloe's face. 'The good things as well as the bad.'

But she has no idea that I opened Melinda's locker and have a stolen book in my bag.

'I think, Chloe, that your father has managed to give you a very clear sense of justice. Not only that but you act on it. You know, very few people have the courage to live up to the principles they claim to have. I admire you for that.'

She raised her glass again as if she were toasting Chloe and took another sip.

'Yes…I mean, thank you, Miss.'

'There are too many Hancocks in this world, Chloe,' said Miss Kepple. 'They are ignorant. They have no idea how far things are from what they used to be—how we're trying to rebuild it all. But the Purity understands this and is taking steps to correct it.'

Now that she had started Miss Kepple seemed to be unstoppable and, in some ways, Chloe had the feeling she was no longer talking to her.

'Yes, Miss.' Chloe took a large swig of orange juice, wondering where this was all going.

Miss Kepple drew her legs in and sat up straight. She leaned in towards Chloe. 'The Purity are starting a young people's group called the DN-Cadr-A and we, Purity-appointed teachers, have been tasked with setting it up.' She looked at Chloe as if expecting something but when nothing was forthcoming she added. 'I want you, Chloe, to be my first recruit.'

'Oh.'

Miss Kepple put her fingers gently on Chloe's arm. 'I want you to be the leader.'

Chloe didn't know what to say; all she could think about was Melinda, Kavi and Ashley. What would they think? 'I'm not sure.'

'I am, Chloe.' Miss Kepple ran her hand down Chloe's arm and held her hand. 'I know you are exactly the right person for this job.' The teacher did not remove her hand as she drained her glass. 'You think about it. And just remember that with the power of the Purity behind you, you could do the things you know are right and no one could stop you.'

Chloe drained her glass and wondered how she could extract the hand Miss Kepple was clinging to without appearing rude. She was saved from having to make the decision as Miss Kepple leaned back again, letting her hand drag along and then off Chloe's forearm.

'Some things may have to change, of course.'

'Change?'

'Those girls you hang around with?'

'Kavi and Ashley?'

'Your friendship with them is very noble, of course, admirable. But their family connection with S.I.D infectees has tainted them. They would not be acceptable material for the DN-Cadr-A.'

Chloe's admiration of Miss Kepple took a nosedive. She climbed to her feet. 'I have to be going, Miss. I'm expected.'

Miss Kepple got up and opened the door while Chloe gathered up her bag and put the glass on the armrest.

'I'll see you tomorrow then, Chloe,' she said.

Chapter 12

Melinda

The cold was the first thing Melinda was aware of and she was shivering. She was on her back. Her right arm ached from being stretched above her head. She tried to move it and found her wrist was encased in a metal strap. She shook it and it rattled.

Using her heels she pushed herself up the bed—she wasn't sure, it seemed like it was a bed, but there was no light. She blinked just to be sure that her eyes were open, but the darkness was complete.

She rolled over to her right and felt the edge of the bed with her left hand. Pain lashed through her ribs—she remembered being kicked. She pushed herself up until she was sitting and leaning against the metal of the bed-head. There was no pillow and only a sheet stretched across the mattress, but now that her right arm was no longer stretched above her head she felt a great deal more comfortable.

The place smelled of damp but there was the clinical scent of antiseptic underlying it all. It reminded her of the month in quarantine, but even the Purity cells had not been like this. They may have been no more than a prison but at least they were dry and had light. The amenities were crude but she understood.

Here she had been dressed in a single shift, nylon, and nothing else. In quarantine she had clothes and at least some privacy.

She had imagined that her younger brothers had been terrified; they were too young to truly understand. And afterwards they had been very quiet, even months later they were scared to leave the house and cried when they went to school. In quarantine the whole family was separated and contact with anyone else was forbidden, except for the staff. And they were not friendly.

She understood. Everyone was scared of the S.I.D infection. There was no cure and once infection had set in there was nothing that could be done. It entered your cells just waiting for the foreign DNA so that it could bind it into your genetic make-up and turn you into a monster.

No, the staff were not friendly. She did not blame them; she understood. Every five days they were tested. Under anaesthetic, of course. The pain afterwards, where they had drilled into the bone marrow, was bad but the painkillers were strong.

She rubbed her hip absently. There was a permanent scar where they had repeatedly made a hole.

But this wasn't the Purity. She did not understand this.

She felt the tears welling up but rubbed them away. Crying wasn't going to help.

Who could have done this? The ones who had taken the other two girls, that much was obvious. What did they want?

'Why can't you put the lights on!' she shouted. Her words fell dead around her. She could get off the bed and find out at least on one side. But she was afraid: afraid of the dark; afraid of what might be underfoot; and afraid of monsters in the dark beneath the bed.

She touched her ribs and winced when she found the bruises. She wrapped her left arm around her legs and pressed her right hand into the bed. She rested her face on her knees and let herself cry.

Then there was a light beyond her eyelids, and the slightest feeling of warmth in the air made the hairs on her right arm prickle. She raised her head. The dark was still absolute. There was no light.

What had happened? How long ago? She had been going to the doctor for the check up. The men had attacked her; they had grabbed her.

The silence was broken by a gentle buzzing. She turned her head trying to locate the sound but it seemed to be all around her. Then she saw the glow in the wall.

There was a line of light running from the ceiling down the wall. It branched about halfway down. One line headed off along what she took to be the wall and disappeared further along. The other went down to what must be almost floor level and stopped.

She looked up. There was a line running across to what might be the centre of the ceiling above the end of the bed. In the far corner there was another light, much thinner and less hot, again rising from below. At its top, the same height as the other lights, it spread out into a blob that seemed roughly cuboid.

It was strange. With so many sources of light she could still see nothing. The light seemed to give no illumination at all. She closed her eyes and shook with fear. The lights did not disappear. Worse, they seemed clearer and she perceived all of them simultaneously.

She opened her eyes again and the effect reduced. Even though her eyes did not seem to 'see' the lines of light, having them open focused her attention. She preferred it that way.

But still, she did not understand. What could the lights that were not lights be? Was she just hallucinating? Had they given her drugs? Well, she knew they had done something to knock her out. But something else?

She lifted her hand and put it where it should block out the lights. It made no difference. It must be a hallucination. The EEG had looked hot to her and then it had stopped working.

One of the men had tried to burn her. She had seen the double ionising beams paint across her. She remembered the jolt, as the beams had shone brilliantly white. She had not collapsed; she had not even noticed. Perhaps they missed. And then, in the van, something had happened to Jake, whoever he was.

Then the light came on. She blinked and the images of the lines in the walls vanished. But as she looked around the plastered walls, she could see the size of the room directly corresponded with the impression she had got. Where the line had run down to the floor level there was a power socket. In the further corner there was a wire running up to a camera.

There was movement beyond what she could now see was a plain wooden door and the sound of bolts being drawn.

Chapter 13

Chloe

Chloe wandered along the dark lanes of the park towards home. The clouds were turning black as the sun crawled past the horizon. There had been a brief moment when its rays shone up through a break and illuminated the underside of the clouds in broad red beams, but it hadn't lasted.

She kept her eyes on the path and the surrounding trees. To her right she could just make out the edge of the ornamental lake with a low fence round it. The water reflected the mottled grey above.

The park had been here for nearly two hundred years. The path had been resurfaced with tarmac a long time ago but the weathering of the passing years had caused it to break up. In some places the Victorian cobblestones came through. It was easy to get the edge of a shoe caught and trip.

Most people would have taken the road around the perimeter where there was light and people. Whatever lights the park had once had—there were lampposts—were long gone and no one replaced them. There were more important things to worry about.

Chloe was cautious but not concerned; she had walked this route alone many times in daylight and at night. It gave her a chance to think. And she had a lot to think about.

Miss Kepple was right about one thing; she did have a strong idea of what was right and wrong. That was why she wanted to join the Purity. That was the reason she tried to help her friends. But now she was confronted with what she could only regard as an ultimatum: If she wanted to lead this new young people's group she had to leave Ashley, Kavi and Melinda behind.

That did not seem right.

After all they were not freaks. They just had the misfortune of being connected to people who had been infected. Just like getting the flu. Miss Kepple and the teachers acted the same way as the schoolkids—the only difference was that the adults were hypocritical.

And she was in the middle in more ways than one.

The sound of an approaching bicycle made Chloe stop and move to the side. She looked round but even accepting it was dark there was no sign of it. But she could still hear it bumping over the rough surface of the path. She could even hear its mechanical bell dinging on the big bumps.

She turned her head and stared in the direction of the sound. Long moments passed and then a dim light moved in the trees. It resolved into a bicycle lamp and the rest of it emerged from the shadows. The rider had his head down peering intently at the path and trying to dodge the potholes. She did not think he even saw her as he trundled past.

It did not seem to be making a lot of noise so the fact she had heard it clearly before it became visible was confusing. She thought she remembered that sound travelled over water; perhaps the lake made the difference.

She knew she was trying to convince herself because she really did not believe it even saying it to herself. There was no water between her and where the bicycle had emerged. Even now she could hear it disappearing into the distance but it was out of sight.

She shook her head and walked on. She tried to recall where her train of thought had led her but, as she came out of the park onto the street, she could not.

Spots of rain were starting to fall as she went through the gate of the house and pushed her key into the lock. Even though her father had a job, quite a good one with an engineering company, they could not afford an electronic lock.

A wave of hot air poured out as she opened the door. She had forgotten it was her dad's FreakWatch meeting tonight. She sighed and closed the door as quietly as she could. Voices emerged from the front room.

'What about you, Colin?' she heard her father say.

She recognised the voice of Mr Thackeray from down the road. 'Mrs Wilberforce at 37 insists that there's something odd about her neighbours at 39.'

'Any particulars?'

'Well,' said Mr Thackeray, 'they don't go out much.'

Chloe sighed. These meetings were always the same with petty-minded people whining about anything that did not match their personal expectations.

She did not wait to hear her father's reply but went past the door and through into the kitchen. She was starving again.

Her mother was standing by the screen in the corner, leaning on a chair beside her. The display was filled with the face of a crying woman: Mary Vogler, Melinda's mother.

The table showed signs that dinner had already been eaten. That was usual on FreakWatch evenings. They didn't know how long they would last so her parents ate early, as soon as dad got home from work. Hers would be in the oven. Chloe could smell burnt cheese.

'Of course she's all right, Mary,' said her mother. She was using the earbuds so Chloe couldn't hear the other side of the conversation. She didn't stare because Mary could no doubt see her in the background. Better to act as if she was unaware.

Chloe had to use the oven gloves to get the plate; it was too hot. The heat was getting even too much for the gloves by the time Chloe had managed to grab a mat from a side drawer and get it onto the table before she was forced to drop the plate heavily. Her mother glanced round and frowned at her.

'But you can't, you have to let them go sometime. You know it's not your fault.'

Chloe dug a knife and fork from another drawer and sat down. She could feel the heat of the plate on her face. Dinner was cubed swede and baked fish, all topped with cheese. Where the cheese touched the plate it had burned black.

Carefully, so as not to touch the plate with her hand, Chloe scooped some swede onto her fork and put it down at the side to cool separately. Her stomach growled.

There was an unframed photograph lying on the table. Chloe recognised it immediately. Two smiling couples posing on a road, each woman holding a young baby with the men standing protectively slightly behind.

The two women, seventeen years older, were talking in the corner. One of the men was her father; the other was Melinda's dad, Geoffrey. The street was nondescript; all you could see was a brick wall but there was a road sign saying

Fanshawe Crescent. Chloe brought the fork tentatively to her lips and tried out the food. It was still very hot but she could manage it.

'We have to trust them ... all right, I'll talk to you tomorrow. She'll be fine. Bye.'

Her mother touched the screen at the bottom and it went black for a moment to be replaced by a gentle swirling pattern of interlocking spirals.

'That was Mary.'

Chloe nodded and tried breaking up the food into smaller piles, spreading it out so there was more surface area exposed to the air. It should cool quicker like that.

Her mother came over to the table and plonked herself down heavily opposite. 'I don't know what I'd do if it was you.'

Chloe took a moment to swallow. 'I'm all right. Did she say what the police are doing?'

Her mother sighed. 'They won't tell her anything. Just following lines of enquiry.'

'I should have said something,' said Chloe.

'It's not your fault, sweetheart,' her mother hesitated, 'I just don't know how they can lose children like that. I mean, we let them put these things in our heads so they know where everyone is and can make sure anyone who'd infected can easily be found.'

'It's easy to get round, Mum,' said Chloe. She tried some dinner, it was cooling. 'Get in a car, go underground, wear a tinfoil hat.'

'Don't.' Her mother reached out and grabbed Chloe's hand, thankfully not the one with the fork. 'I don't want to lose you Chloe.'

'I'm not going anywhere,' said Chloe. 'I just wish I could have done something. Why didn't I?'

'Nobody likes to pry.'

'Tell that to Dad's FreakWatch friends.'

'Don't call it that.'

Chloe extricated her hand from her mother's and picked up the knife. She didn't need it; the dinner was soft enough that the fork alone would do. But she suddenly did not want her mother holding her hand.

'They're just a bunch of vicious gossips.' *And no different to everyone else, including the people in the Purity if Miss Kepple is typical.* 'They never actually do anything useful.' The anger and frustration that had been festering inside her suddenly boiled over. 'Nobody does anything. You talk and talk, mouthing words and saying nobody can do anything about anything, it's all too hard, mustn't interfere except when you think someone's harbouring a freak.'

She pushed herself to her feet, the chair almost toppled over but she felt it go and caught it without even thinking.

'I am fed up being told that no one can do anything. We have to do something!'

She grabbed the plate and stormed out of the room and up the stairs. There was silence from the front room. They must have heard her. *So what?*

Chloe did not bother changing out of her school clothes. She dropped the plate on the bed and took up a balanced stance in front of her punchbag. It was an old leather one that had seen better days. Sensei had bought a new one and bequeathed the old one to her.

She slammed a straight punch into it making it quiver. She followed up with a jab from the left. She adjusted her stance slightly—wearing ordinary clothes felt odd; her body was trained to expect her to be barefoot and in her gi.

She ignored what her body expected and slammed punch after punch into the bag. Sequences of one fist then the other, patterns shifting sides. She swapped stance and repeated. As the sweat streamed off her she switched it up and added imaginary blocks.

Her school skirt was pleated with plenty of give. She lashed out with a right side-kick and stretched for a roundhouse with the other leg, striking with her shoe at the top of the bag. Sensei did not think much of roundhouse kicks—they left you open and easily knocked off balance. She put her hands flat on the ground with her back to the bag and kicked up three times. In her mind she was Melinda kicking the people that took her.

Her imagination became her reality. She pushed herself up and spun around. She beat the punchbag with every punch and kick she could muster. She did not even realise she was crying until she collapsed to the floor exhausted and panting. Her back ached but did not seem inclined to inflict pain.

Her stomach told her it was hungry again. The plate of food was almost cold and she ate it all.

Why couldn't she do anything about it? Why did she have to wait?

The police would be investigating, said the side of her that was her mother. *They know what they are doing.*

But they don't know Melinda. She looked up at the picture she had of the two of them making faces at the camera when they were about ten. It made her smile.

She knew she ought to do something, but she had no idea what that could be.

Chapter 14

Jason

The muffled roar from a beast with a hundred throats went up. The two-hundred-year-old warehouse, with its thick, mossy walls and covered windows, was a deeper shadow against the dark of the trees that fought to grow in the cracks between the flagstones. The sky was overcast though there was a patch of silver where the moon hung.

Among the shadows Jason Lomax moved silent as a breath.

The door was shut and guarded. There was no way he would get in that way. Another roar went up. The freaks must be making a good show. Jason did not care. There were other guards set out at the entrances to the industrial estate. They were on the lookout for police or the Purity. They were not interested in shadows.

In the distance Jason heard a car moving along the road. He saw its lights shining out through the mist as it curved around the bends. The collection of warehouses, some converted to empty offices, were on a slope and downhill from the main road. Beyond that road the Pennine Hills stretched away to the small towns in the valleys and the cities on the farther slopes. Jason did not care about those either.

He was here to eat and to steal.

There was a wall that ran alongside the warehouse. He slipped over it in an easy motion and landed with barely a sound on the other side. The silver eyes of a cat stared at him for a moment and then vanished into the dark.

He made his way along the side of the wall until he reached the warehouse proper and then climbed the outside. His bare fingers found easy purchase in the brick and stonework. The years of weathering made some of it unreliable; it crumbled under his fingers, but there were plenty of gaps.

The roof was corrugated plastic, brittle with age. To prevent light from the fights from shining up through it the ceiling crossbeams had been hung with cloths. He could see down through them into the melee of the battle and the chaos among the men who watched it. Mostly men, and a few whores.

The fight organisers were nothing if not thorough. The fights were the big draw and the gambling that went on, but they made their extra cash from the alcohol, drugs and prostitution. They had some of the office space set aside.

There had been a hole in the roof here the last time, just a little higher and towards the middle, but it had been patched. No problem. He climbed along the edge of the roof to ensure his weight only pressed against the solid wall beneath. At the apex the wall was truncated but the roof continued to rise the final few inches. And between them was a triangular gap.

Clinging upside down to the main strut that ran the length of the roof, Jason wriggled through. The sounds from below increased in volume and the moist heat was oppressive. The place stank of men, urine, and alcohol. The shouts and laughter battered at his ears as the scents assaulted him.

He paused to allow himself to adapt to the onslaught. It always took a few moments but his awareness dulled and the volume of the experiences reduced.

He turned his head to check the position and distance and then dropped to a lower metal girder and crouched. His balance was perfect. The girder itself was most likely original and was covered in rust. He needed to take care not to disturb it; while most of it would be caught in the blankets below he could not risk someone looking up.

He did not think he would be caught. He had been seen before and had always got away. Other people were just slow. But better he was not seen at all.

There was the sound of something hard snapping, a moan of pain and an unpleasant squelch. He was deafened by the explosion of sound, the cheers and the complaints, the swearing for pleasure and disgust. He looked down into the cage—sealed to avoid any chance of S.I.D infection—one of the freaks was on the floor. At first glance it did not look too horrific, until you noticed a small second head with extra limbs sprouting from the chest and hips.

The original face was crushed on one side but a very human eye stared up at the thing that was killing it. Something so far gone that it looked like a monstrous combination of a crab and a tree. Its exoskeleton had root-tendrils growing across it. Jason imagined it must be feeding off itself.

As he watched it raised its crab-claw right arm and smashed it into the bigger head. The smaller head set up a childlike wailing before it too was smashed.

Jason shook himself. He did not care.

There would be a break of half an hour while they cleared the cage and brought on the next pair. Barely disturbing the dust and rust, he traversed the length of the warehouse and came to a stop above the rooms used by the women. He could see what went on perfectly clearly. It did not interest him.

There was a small passage between them that led to a toilet. The stench was appalling. Ensuring no one was heading his way, he descended to floor level and, with his hoodie in place over his head, ensuring that his face was in shadow, he stepped out into the maelstrom of people.

Dog

Dog had been careful not to look up. Mendelssohn did not understand the way it was with some of them. This one was used to working alone. If Dog and Mendelssohn turned up the following night without warning and tried to recruit him, they would never see him again. And Dog knew how good the thief was.

He watched as the fellow—he really was very small—slipped out from the shadows that led to the latrine. Dog could barely stand the smell of the place and he was used to it. Ordinary people had no idea what the real world smelled like.

Dog lost sight of his prey was the crowds moved around him. If this sneak was true to form he would make a pass across the room and back, then he would be gone.

He never stuck around long, just enough time to lift a few items. Dog had never actually seen him do it, but he'd seen the results when someone found their wallet was suddenly empty of money. Usually long after this guy had gone. He was so smooth and so fast.

But this time Dog needed to talk to him. The sneak was heading in his direction but would pass him about fifteen feet away. Dog casually stood and headed on a course that would not quite intercept. He was sure the little fellow had senses as good as his, at least.

Dog passed a table and removed a beer bottle. Its owner was busy talking to someone else. He took a swig as he moved and sat on a stool by an unoccupied table. People were still busy sorting out their winnings.

Dog did not look up but watched as the threadbare hoodie moved past. He carefully pulled one of the two packages from his pocket and put it on the table.

'Hey, hoodie.'

There was a blur of motion and he was three yards away. Dog spoke low, certain he'd be able to hear. 'I'm not turning you in. Just want to talk.'

Hoodie did not move.

'Got a couple of pies, thought you might like one.'

The hoodie moved. The pie was gone but he was standing closer.

'Or two. Whatever. Time is money, or pies.'

Dog finally lifted his head and looked into the hood. Nothing but dark.

'My name's Dog.'

The noise and the people flowed around them. Hoodie moved closer but stayed out of reach. Dog could see he was ready to flee in a moment.

'Look,' he said. 'I know you're not the same as everyone else,' the tension in Hoodie's body increased, 'I'm not either. I mean I know you're different. Like me. I'm not going to grass you up. I know you're not S.I.D. You've been like this all your life. Like me.'

Hoodie glanced at the cages; at least, Dog saw a movement that was probably that.

'Yeah, that.'

Hoodie moved a little closer.

'So, anyway. I work for a guy. He knows about us, understands we have special skills. I do things for him and he looks after me. You could work for him too. What do you think?'

This time there was no mistaking the shaking of the head. But in doing it the hoodie over his head moved in the light and Dog saw something in the shadows. In that moment all he could think of was *tentacles*. No wonder he kept his head covered.

'No need to be hasty, my fine young friend. Think about it. You wouldn't have to do this petty stuff,' he gestured around. 'He looks after us; it's like a family. He makes sure we have what we need.'

Hoodie stepped back.

'Look, think about it. We'll be here tomorrow or the next night, okay? You be here, we can talk.'

Hoodie moved and was gone. Dog thought he saw him for a moment in the crowd. He watched above but if the sneak used that exit again he managed to do it without Dog seeing.

Dog sighed and took a swig of the beer he had swiped then reached into his pocket. All he found was an empty pie wrapper.

'Thieving little bastard,' he said without rancour.

Chapter 15

Mitchell

Mitchell stopped off at the cafeteria and paid over the odds for two high-percentage coffees, then returned to the lift and made his way down to the underground car park.

Lament would be watching, of course, or one of his automatic systems.

Mitchell had been a cop before the crash; he had stayed on duty the whole time—almost the whole time. The police had been issued with guns when it became clear how bad things were getting. His official record of freak kills was a fraction of what he'd done before people started counting.

He placed the coffee cups on the roof of his car. The door unlocked as he gripped the handle. He placed the cups inside and then took his seat on the passenger side.

The coffee smelled good.

It was another five minutes before Yates opened the driver's door and climbed in. Once the door was closed Mitchell waved his hand at the second cup in the cavity.

Yates hesitated. 'We're not going anywhere, are we?'

'Not unless Lament decides to give you another lapful.'

Yates picked up his cup and sniffed it. 'Nice.' He sipped it and made an appreciative sound. 'Can't remember the last time you bought me a coffee.'

'I never have.'

Yates took another, bigger, mouthful. 'Very nice.'

For once in his life Mitchell was not sure how to proceed. He was sure he could trust Yates; the man gave the impression he was completely self-centred and he never hesitated in breaking a rule if he felt it would do him some good. The question was: How would he feel about this?

'You know what I'm doing?'

He shouldn't, of course.

'Babysitting the Purity.' Came the instant response. Mitchell shook his head, it was impossible to keep any kind of secret.

The car park was dark, only half the lights worked, and there was no one around. That was suspicious; there was always some activity. Mitchell frowned.

'I imagine you've been reassigned.'

'DI Merchant gets your job. I'm working with him and his DS in an advisory role.'

'He's a good copper.'

'Yeah. Good as in no imagination.'

Mitchell shrugged. 'I may require you to carry out some additional duties.'

'Not entirely above board?'

'Can you do it?'

Yates glanced in the rear-view mirror. 'Sounds like fun.'

They both took drinks from their cups.

'The Purity might be party poopers.'

'Goes without saying.' He turned and flashed his pearly-whites at Mitchell. 'Bigger stakes, double or nothing.'

'You don't have to do this.'

'Who else could you ask?'

Mitchell was silent again. The next thing he said would, at best, get him fired, at worst, who knew?

But Yates spoke before he had a chance. 'Seems to me that the Purity want to solve this important case that the police couldn't. That will give them the justification to get their fingers into a pie they haven't yet been able to touch directly.'

'That's what the Super thinks too.'

'Really?' Yates sounded genuinely surprised. 'Dix figured that out? Can't be as stupid as I thought.'

'He was a good copper too, once.'

'Yeah, bureaucracy's a vampire.'

Mitchell had been keeping an eye out. Still no one had come down into the car park. Not a car coming in or going out. Nobody walking through to or from their vehicle.

'Bit quiet out there, isn't it?' said Yates.

'Let's get this wrapped up. Dix wants the credit for finding the girls before the Purity, but without annoying them.'

Yates made a rude noise. 'He always gives you the easy jobs.'

Mitchell turned in the seat to face Yates. 'He's missing the point. It's our job to find and rescue these girls. With the Purity here we might never see them again even if we find them.'

Yates frowned in noncomprehension.

'Finding them isn't enough. The Purity could spirit them away and accuse us of failure, or anything they like. That would be their best outcome.'

'Are you saying we don't want to find them?'

'Maybe, maybe not, we won't know until the time. But the important thing is that we have to try to rescue them without the Purity getting in the way.'

Mitchell sat back and took a drink. The coffee was getting cold and the taste of chicory was coming through.

Yates drained his cup and opened the door. 'I may have to call you to ask questions on behalf of Merchant,' he said and climbed out. 'Quite often.'

Mitchell nodded. 'We'll work something else out when that's run its course.'

Yates shut the door and Mitchell watched him walk away in the mirrors. *He's a good man*, he thought to himself and drank the rest of his coffee.

Once Yates had gone up in the elevator, Mitchell got out of the car and waited for it to lock itself before heading back into the building. He was halfway to the elevator when there was a squeal of tyres as three cars came into the car park.

Five policemen vacated the elevator as he approached; they were complaining about a delay. Mitchell knew what it meant and wondered whether Dix had given some very specific orders.

Chapter 16

Chloe

Chloe lay face down and stared at the floor a yard below her. She could see Ali's feet as he moved around her. He had given her shoulders a thorough investigation, digging in his thumbs and fingers almost to the point of pain—except she could feel the tension releasing as he did it.

He had tutted. He only tutted when she had really managed to mess up something in her back. Well she knew she had done something bad; she just had no idea what.

'Are you eating properly?' he said as he worked his fingers on her lower spine. Spikes of what seemed like energy ran down her legs and out of her toes.

'More than usual,' she said. 'I seem to be hungry all the time.'

'Maybe you've got a tapeworm.'

'Is this a common dad joke?'

'Well, I could swear you're losing fat.' When he worked his fingers to the sides of her waist it almost tickled but he always managed to avoid that.

'I haven't got any fat, Ali.' When she had first started to visit him, after a bad fall at the dojo had done something aggravating to her left hip joint, she had called him Mr Najjar, and she had been Miss Dark. Over the last ten years they had achieved first name terms. Not that she fancied him; he was in his forties and married with kids. There was a picture of them on his desk.

'No, not a lot of fat,' he said. 'But you have less than you should.' He stopped. 'And you say you're eating more?'

'Yes.'

He grunted an acknowledgement and began to work his way up her spine.

Chloe relaxed and let his fingers take away the strain. He worked on her shoulder-blades.

'What have you done here?'

'You're the chiro, you tell me.'

He dug his fingers in more. She could almost see his frown. 'Did you fall? Did someone put you in a hold badly?'

'Well, I don't remember exactly but I must have done something.'

He felt around some more. 'It's really very solid. Hard to believe you only just did it. You're more flexible than this.'

'Sorry.'

He laughed. 'No worries. Sit up.'

She pushed herself up on the treatment table and into a sitting position while he lowered it until her feet were touching the ground. She was only wearing her bra and shorts but any embarrassment she had felt in the early days was long gone. He was always professional. On the other hand she was aware her bra was a little looser than it had been. But it wasn't something she was going to mention. There were limits.

The way he ran his fingers along the vertebrae of her neck, put his arm round it and the other hand on her head, she knew what was coming. She relaxed as he applied sudden pressure and something in her neck popped.

Chiropractors: the only people licensed to break your neck. She smiled. He checked her neck again and seemed satisfied.

'I want to do a scan of your back,' he said. 'I can't tell what's going on in there. Just get in the booth, will you? Pop your bra off when you get in. Grab the bar and hold still.'

The 3D ultrasound scanning booth was fully enclosed and, he'd said years ago, fully automatic. She had been in it a dozen times and never felt a thing.

She went in and he closed the door behind her. The light inside was subdued but there wasn't much to see. The bar, made of some very light but strong plastic, could be raised and lowered to the person's height and was only there so the patient did not move. The scanner itself was mounted in the ceiling. It descended in spirals so that a 3D image resulted.

'Okay,' he said, his voice muffled by the wall. 'I'm just initialising to scan from your neck down to the bottom of your ribcage. That should show everything we need.'

Moments later the machine whirred quietly. She watched the mechanism descend to neck level.

'It'll take about ten seconds in all,' he said. 'Three...two...one...'

The universe screamed like a banshee.

Chloe gripped the bar convulsively as her body went rigid. Her ears were pummelled by a screech she could not even begin to describe. Like the whine of a dentist's drill but so much louder and pitched so high she should not even be able to hear it.

She was dizzy with the noise; it whirred around her head and descended. The pain of it diminished as it seemed to drop towards the floor. She was panting and her muscles quaked.

Then it shut off and all that remained was the winding down whir of the motor that drove the ultrasound device as it rose up above head height once more.

Her eyes stung as sweat dripped down her forehead. Every inch of her was soaked with perspiration. She sat down on the small bench behind her while she pulled herself together.

Absently, she picked up her bra and put it back on. She pulled herself up with bar and adjusted the straps. Ali tried to keep the place at a neutral temperature but she felt cold as the sweat evaporated from her body. There was an electronic beep from the outside, in the main room.

'You okay, Chloe?' Ali called through.

'Fine, be out in a moment.' Clearly Ali did not know anything strange had happened.

The throbbing in her head was diminishing and her muscles had stopped quaking. She took a deep breath and focused on the door.

Should she tell him? But tell him what? That she'd heard a screaming sound that was so loud it felt as if it was going to make her head explode? She shook her head and regretted it as the throb intensified. No. Any sign of strangeness would bring the Purity down on her and ruin any chance she had of getting in—except as an unwilling guest.

She was not going to let what had happened to her friends happen to her.

She pushed the door open and exited the booth. She smiled at him and then felt embarrassed as he very openly stared at her from head to foot.

'What?' she said.

He did not say anything and found a towel which he tossed across to her. She looked in one of the full length mirrors. Her body was glistening with the slick sheen of sweat.

'Did you run a race in there?' he asked, but pointedly looked away and operated his desk-workstation.

She ran the towel across her arms and legs then rubbed down the rest of her exposed skin. 'Wrong time of the month,' she said.

'Any nausea and fatigue?' he said, not looking up.

She hesitated. 'No, should I?'

He glanced up. 'You can get dressed.' He turned away again before continuing. There was an area for changing near the door. 'Hormone imbalance after ovulation can cause those symptoms. Have you had it before?'

The safest answer was to make everything appear normal. 'Once or twice.'

'Well if you have any serious problem with it you should see your doctor.'

'Okay.'

She finished dressing and emerged from behind the screen.

He smiled. 'You got a ping from your mother—do you want to read it?'

'Probably better, do you mind?'

'Not a problem, I've cued it up,' he said.

He went off to the other side of the room as Chloe sat down at his desk. The machine detected her riffy and her mother's image appeared on the screen.

'Play,' she said.

The image animated and her mother's voice pounded out of the machine. 'HI, SWEETHEART. WE—'

'Pause,' she said quickly.

'My bad,' said Ali. 'I talk to my wife while I'm working here sometimes, need to be able to hear her wherever I am. Try setting three.'

'Volume to three. Play,' said Chloe. The image started up again.

'—got a message that Debenhams has new clothes in. So we're going down there this evening to see what we can pick up. I know you'll be out with your friends but I just wanted to tell you we might not be home when you get in.'

Chloe checked the time on the message: a couple of hours ago while she had been at Ashley's, helping with her homework. She glanced at her watch; they would have left by now to arrive in time to be near the front of the queue. When one of the major shops got a big shipment they would close up while they prepared for the guaranteed rush. It could get nasty. She wouldn't be going as well; she would have to join the back of the queue because people could get very unpleasant about what they perceived as queue jumpers. Mum knew what she needed.

'Thanks, Ali,' she said. As she moved away from the screen it blanked the message and returned to the usual holding screen.

'Not a problem. Make sure you don't strain your back any more than it already is.'

Chloe put on her duffle coat and pulled the hood up over her head. Her black hair was pushed forward to frame her face. 'I won't. Sensei wouldn't let me train anyway.'

'Good. I'll take a look at the scans and let you know when I want to see you again,' he said as he held the door open for her. 'Okay?'

She paused in the doorway. 'Okay, thanks, Ali.' She headed out into the small hallway and opened the front door. It was dark outside.

Ali Najjar

Ali watched as she pulled the door shut. There was a cold, damp draught from the outside and he shut the inner door to keep the examination room warm. The clock on the wall told him he had about twenty minutes before the next patient.

He sat at his desk and brought up the scan of Chloe. It was a little fuzzy in places; she must have moved. Still, if she was hit by that hot flush it was hardly surprising. There might have been cramps as well, but while they knew each other in a semi-familiar way it was only as if they met on a train each morning going to work. It wasn't real friendship. But he liked her.

As the first step, required by the Purity, he fired off a copy of the scan to Chloe's central medical records. Then he launched an image of it on his screen.

He could not afford—and did not rate—a 3D projector but the gesture controls were effective enough with a flat image. He turned the scan and expanded it so it showed the spine between the shoulder blades.

He adjusted the colour controls to make the denser bone structures appear dark blue. The skin stayed white and transparent, while the muscle and connective tissues became shades of translucent green.

There was a whole section where the trapezius muscles, on both sides, looked odd. Normally they ran from the spine up and over the shoulders in wide sheets but here—he adjusted the colours to highlight the tendons as well—they seemed to have new strands running out to thick areas that seemed to have the density of bone.

Could she be developing osteophytes? Bone spurs were usually a symptom of osteoarthritis, and he had never heard of it occurring in symmetric formations, or with associated muscle changes. These were identical on both sides. He went deeper but found the inner musculature and rib structures to be normal.

With a flick of his fingers he restored the image to show the osteophytes, then sat back and stared.

He froze with the sudden realisation of what this meant. It was strange. He spent his life working with muscles and bones while every day he, like everyone else, was bombarded with information about the freaks and S.I.D infections. He glanced up at the poster on his wall with the smiling face of Mercedes Smith.

He had met her once, briefly, at a dinner given for medical practitioners in Manchester. His equipment was part-sponsored by Utopia Genetics.

Chloe was infected. He could feel his extremities going cold with fear—not for himself but for her. He had seen DI Mitchell's latest kill and the shots of the freak he had destroyed. Ali thought about that happening to Chloe.

If he reported her now the Purity would pick her up and she would be disappeared, her family would be put into quarantine—and so would he. He would be signing her death warrant, but no, that had already been signed. She would die one way or another. He would be signing her execution order.

He got up and paced. If he didn't report her the pain would get worse and she, being a good citizen, would go to the doctor and he would report her. Ali liked that option better. All he needed to do was destroy the evidence. He sat again quickly and brought up the details of the scan that he had sent.

Occasionally there were bad images and he would delete them; this was no different. He found the file and issued the delete command. The file was removed.

Ali sat back and felt better. Now it was nothing to do with him.

Chapter 17

Chloe

The Metro train pulled up in St. George's Square. Although her parents were less than half a mile away in the centre of the shopping district, Chloe wasn't going to try to meet with them.

She pressed the button and the doors opened. There were still a few people on the tram heading further in but there was no point joining the queues this late in the evening. There'd be nothing left to buy.

Her destination was just across the way. The huge Victorian monolith that was the Central Reference Library. Her ears were still humming from what had happened in the scanning booth. She made a point of checking in all directions before crossing the tracks; she was not sure whether her hearing was actually working properly at all. First there had been the weird extended hearing in school and then—whatever that had been.

But that wasn't why she was here.

The Central Ref was circular with mock Roman columns at the main entrance with a portico that covered the wide steps that led up to the revolving doors. She pushed through from the cold and damp into the cool and dry. There was something solid and reassuring about the place. The walls were so thick and everything about the construction was massive.

She walked through the riffy scanner. She needed some proper network-connected machines. The one at home had a highly restricted subset of BritNet but as a student she could do more research in here.

The problem was that she felt so helpless. Her best friend had disappeared and the police were clueless—they must be because they hadn't found the other girls and they had been missing for weeks.

She headed upstairs along winding steps that were a yard at their widest and took two paces each. On the next floor she pushed through the fire doors into a corridor that ran around the outside of the building. The windows showed St George's Square and its multiple tram lines.

There was a small area with wooden seating just outside the main terminal suite. She fetched a plastic cup of water from the machine and entered the quiet room.

The fifty seats each had their own terminal and screen. Almost all were empty apart from a few university students scattered about. Chloe had never intended to try for university; the debt level was not worth it. That was another reason to try for the Purity. She had never had any doubt she would be able to get in but now she was beginning to wonder whether it was her best choice.

While history was not a big subject in the curriculum, the most significant events of the previous century were covered. While the militaristic attitudes of the Germans were always decried there was special dispensation given to their desire for a pure bloodline. It was suggested that if they had succeeded in their aims the world would never have suffered from the S.I.D plague.

The purity of the human genome was what it was all about in the end. And S.I.D was the one thing that destroyed it. Nothing was more important, and Chloe could hardly disagree with that—but methods mattered.

She chose a seat out of sight from the other people in the room. Not because she was embarrassed—well, okay, perhaps it was because she was embarrassed. They were older than her and even if it was only by a couple of years she felt naive in their presence. Like a child.

The machine recognised her and the screen came alive. These were not the basic terminals like the ones at home or school; these had full graphics capabilities, another reason to use them.

She watched the graphical display that eventually settled into the search engine for BritNet.

'List of missing schoolgirls in Manchester, unsolved.' she typed.

There was a moment's delay and then 'Authorised. Chloe Dark. 7639572. Title?'

'*School Project.*' Well, it was almost the truth.

A window popped up with School Project in the title and listing names and dates starting with the most recent: Melinda Vogler and the date two days ago. There were eight names in the list. Chloe frowned. 'Eight?' she said under her breath.

At the bottom was another message: 'Related searches: Missing schoolboys; Missing Men; Missing women.'

Chloe clicked the missing boys link and the window expanded to accommodate another twelve names. The dates of disappearance went back ten years and nothing recent. She knew that there may have been disappearances before that but after the systems collapsed it was a while before records became available again.

She had a sudden thought. 'Refine search to abductions.'

The list reduced to a total of seven: four girls and three boys. Somehow that felt better, although it meant that thirteen other children had simply disappeared. Although perhaps people didn't know they were abductions.

'Graph factors.'

A new window popped up containing a graph showing the disappearances over time. There were a couple of older ones but five had occurred in the last year. She wondered why they were only looking for the recent girls, although those were all clustered in the last month, so perhaps it wasn't strange.

Other text tabs were available graphing by gender, date of birth, and other strange things like physical height and weight.

The gender graph showed what she already knew, but the date of birth graph was interesting. Every one of them had been sixteen or seventeen years old when they disappeared. Just like her.

She sat back and stared at the screen. It seemed to mean something, but what? Someone was abducting children of a specific age? Why would they do that? The police must have noticed that too; there was no information that she could find that they did not have and they would have looked at it from every possible angle. Probably angles she could not imagine.

What did she possibly hope to have achieved? There was nothing she could do.

She stood up, picked up the cup of water, and left the room.

Chapter 18

Mercedes

The nightclub smelled of sweat and the sharpness of spirit-based cocktails. If there was a melody to the throbbing music, Mercedes did not hear it, only the drums and the bass. Other people pressed against her. Out in the real world she would have been offended, but not here. This is why she was here. To feel.

She was in her club gear that exposed most of her body. It wasn't the most expensive, just something that anyone who could afford to club might wear. A black filigree masquerade mask hid her features while the reflective purple lipstick made her lips bigger than normal and distracted the eye. Her face was on almost every corporate image; it was likely someone would recognise her and masks were not uncommon.

The club was a rebellion, not just for her but everyone else here. The plague taught everyone to stay clear of everyone else. Simply touching someone could kill you in the most obscene and grotesque way. In this private club everyone touched. Minimum clothing, packed tight, anonymous.

Complete nudity was not permitted—that would just be gross—but people came very close without breaking the rule. The sexual thrill of being crammed against so many other semi-naked bodies was the other part of the appeal.

As she moved to the music she rubbed against the others, arms, legs, hips, backs, chests and breasts, and others touched her. It made her feel more alive than any other time. What she did in the real world was only to make space for this.

The rhythm of the track, if it was a distinct song, gave way to another with a slightly different pattern of beats. It was faster. The lights flashed faster. The air smelled of sweat and sex. There was no gap between bodies to see but she knew there would be many people in the crowd engaged in sexual acts. Standing because there was no room to lie down.

She had drunk a combination of caffeine and alcohol before coming onto the floor, where no drinks were allowed. She briefly wondered what it was like at the beginning of the night when the first people arrived. Did they huddle together in the middle of the dance floor while others arrived and added themselves to the outer edges? Or did they dance apart from one another and the incomers filled in the gaps?

A voice whispered. 'Mercedes.'

She whipped her head round looking for the person who had spoken her name. In the flashing lights the faces of those around her were looking up, or down, or staring blankly ahead. No one was looking at her.

'Mercedes.'

Xec. Her feeling of abandon dissipated like mist. She stopped moving. The dancing crowd was suddenly an irritant.

'Wait,' she said loudly. No one around her gave any indication they had heard, nor was it likely they had as the throbbing track grew in volume infinitesimally and she could feel the bass notes shaking her lungs.

She glanced around and located the entrance a hundred bodies away. She bounced to the music and pressed her way through the flailing limbs.

When she was one with the crowd she moved with it. They were like one raging animal. But now she was separate from it and every movement was an effort as she pushed for the exit. The bodies parted but it was like molasses and now she hated it as hands touched her, trying to hold her back. The animal was selfish and did not like to lose a part of itself to the outside world.

Bodies filled the short passage to the antechamber. The music volume dropped, leaving only a numb ringing in her ears, and she stumbled free. Someone caught her arm but Mercedes shook it free and glared at the woman who had tried to prevent her from falling. Mercedes straightened herself and stalked towards the changing rooms.

The riffy scanner identified her bag to the attendant who passed it over. Mercedes entered one of the booths and shut the door. The door itself was sufficient to maintain someone's modesty while changing but the booths were open top and bottom. There was a stone basin in each with a stream of water running from the lip and down to the plughole.

She was soaked with sweat, mostly not her own, and her hair hung lank about her shoulders. She stripped off the clothes and splashed water from the basin over herself to rinse off the smells. A small tin cup was provided to allow her to drink. She grabbed one of the supplied towels to rub herself down. She detached the mask and put it next to her bag.

'What's the time?' she said. Xec was under strict instructions not to interrupt her when she was clubbing. That meant this was important, but did not mean she had to be pleased about it.

'A little before eight.'

She sighed. She knew she had not been at the club long. She remembered in the old days when clubs did not even get started until well past eleven. Things changed.

'What is it?'

'When will you have access to a screen?'

'When I get back to the car.' She poured water across her back. It ran off into the little ridges in the floor and drained away. There was a red mark on her foot. Someone had trodden on it. She could not remember when that had happened. It was always the same. The driving rhythms and volume drove the adrenaline to the point you didn't feel anything bad. Just the heightened pleasures.

She used the provided towel to rub herself down. A couple of women went past outside. They were laughing. One of them glanced in at her. Mercedes met her eye for a fraction of a second. There was a change in the woman's face: one that said that, even if she had not specifically recognised Mercedes, she knew she was someone famous. Mercedes turned to face away from the door.

'You could just tell me,' said Mercedes as she pulled on her panties. The dress slipped into place neatly and she zipped it up. The sensible shoes went on. She rinsed her club clothes in the basin, used the towel to dry them and put them in the air-tight bag she brought for the purpose. There were a couple of other sets of clubbing outfits as well. One set was never enough for a full night, or even a full evening.

Watch, expensive but not ostentatious, followed by wedding ring though she was not, and never had been, married. It was a defence. Simple necklace which matched the watch, and earrings that matched the necklace.

She gathered up her things, gave the booth a quick glance to ensure she had forgotten nothing, and headed out of the club.

The car drove up to the entrance as she exited. It was raining and cold but it was only a few steps across the cobbles of the back alley to the warmth of the interior.

She pulled the door shut behind her and dropped back into the luxurious leather of the vehicle.

'Drink?' asked Xec. Not that he could have got her one. Mercedes opened the cooler and pulled out a bottle of water. The car pulled away smoothly. Xec was driving since she did not trust any ordinary employee with her dirty little secret. Even the car was not registered to the company, or her, but one out on long term hire from a company in London who asked no questions as long as they got paid.

The screen flickered into life. It showed an ultrasound scan.

'You found another one?'

'I imagine you have not the slightest inkling of the files I have to look through to find these?'

'I'm sure you don't check every file yourself.'

'That would be wasteful.'

'I can't see anything strange about this, are you sure it's another?'

'You think I would waste your time otherwise?'

'Name?'

'Chloe Dark,' said Xec and the image zoomed in on the bony protrusions in her back.

'What am I looking at?' said Mercedes. Her medical training was far in her past and she hadn't practised since the plague.

'Ordinarily I would describe them as osteophytes.'

'But?'

'They are normally associated with arthritis and there is no evidence of that here, plus their development is perfectly symmetric.'

'It could still be a standard S.I.D infection.'

'Playing devil's advocate, Mercedes?' Xec's tone was amused but with an underlying sense of annoyance. 'She's the right age and she's in the right place, the development is atypical to an S.I.D infection. Besides,' he said, 'you haven't checked the name?'

'There were so many.'

'Dark is not a common name.'

'Parents?'

'Amanda and Michael—Mike.'

Mercedes thought hard. It was possible. Theoretically they had been double blind tests—though even the parents had not known anything was happening. All the records had been lost and all they had left was half-remembered names. She had not been party to the details of the tests, just a very junior medically trained administrator.

'Could be,' she said. 'No harm in picking her up.'

'The Purity investigator will be arriving tomorrow.'

'Better get it done tonight then. Where is she?'

'And the therapist that did the scan may be a problem. He clearly realised there was an issue because he deleted the file after he had sent it. I have ordered a clean-up of the spillage.'

'Did I need to know that?'

'I needed approval from your executive level.'

'But you'd already ordered it.'

Xec said nothing.

Mercedes sighed. 'You did the right thing, of course.' She settled back into the seat and took another sip of water.

'Do you want to go back to the club?'

Do I? She wondered. 'No, I've lost the mood.' She paused and looked out at the streets crying in the rain. 'Take me home. And no more calls tonight.'

'As you wish.'

Chapter 19

Ali Najjar

He leaned back in his padded chair and stared at the blank screen—it had long since switched to sleep mode. He was not happy.

He glanced at the picture he kept on his desk of his wife, son and daughter. The current image was three years old, taken shortly after Zalika had been born. She was a crazy three-year-old now, running around and getting herself into everything. She would become very serious about her toys, explaining to her father how they had a bad back and he had to fix them. Which he would, of course.

What would he do if Zalika contracted S.I.D? How would he feel? What would he want the person who discovered it to do?

The idea of some horror distorting his beautiful daughter's features made his hands convulse into fists. It was not something he could imagine easily.

But if it did?

All licensed medical practitioners were required by law to report suspicious symptoms. The penalty was imprisonment. He had already broken that law, but with the deletion of the file he should not be found out.

What would happen to Chloe now? The symptoms would intensify and she would suffer. It might take a while before it became obvious but she would go to her doctor before that and he would certainly report her. They would have her in custody before she left the surgery. There would be questions and tests in an attempt to discover where she caught it. Her family would be quarantined as well.

He looked back at the picture of his daughter. If it happened to her he would want to know first. He would want the chance to prepare to say goodbye properly.

Perhaps he would want the opportunity to run.

He pushed that thought away. There was nowhere to run and no cure. Better let her be euthanised before the suffering became too much. But Chloe still had time.

If he warned her parents they would know what was best for their family. Better they should have a choice than have the decision thrust on them when it was all too late.

It was against the law but he knew it was the right thing to do. He had her address, of course, but he did not have to go to her home, which would have been odd. He could go to the shop and find them.

Making the decision made him feel better. He grabbed his coat and headed out.

John Smith

The man did not think of himself as John Smith; that was just the name he went by. He was just a collection of needs that must be satisfied. When he was hungry, he ate; when he was tired, he slept; when he needed sexual relief, he bought a girl. Those needs required funds and he did what was necessary to provide those funds.

His profession was something he had fallen into easily enough. A client required a person to be removed? He took out the trash. He was a facilitator to an elite clientele. Knowledge was power and, on occasion, the wrong people possessed knowledge that gave them inappropriate power. Unfortunately there was only one practical way of removing knowledge from the world.

Often his clients would try various other methods before they came to him. It was foolish of them to put themselves at risk that way. The cessation of life was the only guarantee.

There was a knock at the door and an envelope slipped under it. He rose from the bed, walked the length of the hotel room with precise steps, he watched his thin fingers pick up the envelope seemingly of their own volition. He had a need and his body satisfied that need.

The outside of the envelope was bare without even the name he used on it. That was as it should be. He used the knife that had come with his evening meal to slice through the crisp envelope.

He extracted the paper from inside it. The code consisted of two hundred and forty-seven letters and numbers in a 16x16 block with the last digit missing. It looked handwritten but very neat and precise. There was no mistaking what each individual character was.

On the desk-cum-dresser stood two small, identical devices, one of which was plugged into the power socket. His riffy. There was a time when he had had a riffy just like everyone else but there had come a time when it became an inconvenience. Everyone knew it was easy to block a riffy: an aluminium-lined hat would do the trick. But that meant you disappeared from the scan. And simply disappearing did not give you an alibi.

A riffy did not, in itself, require power to work. It retransmitted using the energy of the enquiring signal but it could also provide information about the physical state of the person. Replacing that took clever electronics which needed power.

The machines were expensive because they were both illegal and complex. But having one meant he could be in two places at once. Having two meant he could pretend to be someone else.

Creating an identity required the code on the piece of paper. The missing digit was a precaution against interception.

He activated the second device, then keyed in the digit sequence. The batteries were good for a few hours. He put on his coat and headed outside. He took the stairs down to the ground floor. He had chosen this hotel because it had a garden, which meant he could leave without going through reception where his lack of a riffy might be noticed.

The letter Q was freshly chalked next to a modern, though not brand new, car. He walked around the next corner then pulled out his machine. He paused to key in the Q then turned around and headed back.

The car unlocked at the touch of his hand and he climbed into the passenger seat. The car moved off smoothly in self-drive mode. The glove compartment contained information about the potential knowledge leak: sex, age. This car had a link through to the riffy network. He activated it. The target was heading in towards the centre of the city.

John Smith specialised in accidents. It kept him below the radar. If the leaks were plugged in an apparently natural way there was no one to chase. And with contracts usually months apart there was no indication that someone like him even existed.

Michael Dark

His arms were getting tired but he didn't dare put down the bags containing the items Amanda had chosen; someone might try to grab them. There had been a couple of fights but nothing they had been involved in, or even close to.

They had been in here two hours, after queuing for a further two hours. It wasn't just his arms that were tired. His legs ached from the standing, and the claustrophobic stuffiness of the shop, along with the breathlessness of air that had been breathed by too many people, was giving him a headache.

'Mr Dark, isn't it?'

Mike barely registered that someone was actually talking to him.

'Mr Dark?' The voice seemed more uncertain since he hadn't responded. He stopped daydreaming and turned. Black hair, early 40s, Middle Eastern heritage, decent clothes—and no one he recognised. Nervous-looking so not police or the Purity.

'Who's asking?'

The man smiled. 'Ali Najjar, I'm your daughter Chloe's chiropractor.' He did not offer his hand; that was something you only did with someone you trusted.

'Okay, nice to meet you.' This was not a conversation he wanted. He just wanted Amanda to stop rooting through the piles of clothes that remained, so they could go home.

'Can we talk?'

A doubt crossed Mike's mind. The man was not carrying any bags. Could he be freaking? He looked normal enough. His hands and his head were bare. He had walked without any kind of limp. There did not seem to be any suppressed pain behind his eyes. Of course there were more subtle forms of infection. Sometimes they never became visible until the infectee keeled over and died. Occasionally the genetic corruption affected the brain first.

But for now the fellow looked unaffected. 'Are you here shopping?'

'No, Mr Dark, I came here specifically to talk to you. Do you think we can find somewhere a bit more private?'

'What's this about?' he said. 'Chloe?'

'Look, there's a space over by the wall.'

'How did you know where we were?'

'I overheard your wife's message to Chloe this afternoon. She took it in my office.'

Mike frowned. 'It's a big shop and I don't think we've ever met.'

'I asked the store to do a scan for me.'

'And they did it?'

'I told them it was a matter of life and death.'

'You lied.'

'No.'

Mike had not expected him to say that. He should have agreed, or explained it away, or anything except 'no'. There was a sincere look in his eyes. Mike gave in; at least it would be more interesting than just standing here.

There was a rail that now held nothing but empty hangers and behind it a space. They wouldn't be out of sight but it would afford the impression of privacy. Mike adjusted the weight of the bags and headed over to the wall.

'Do you want me to take one of those?'

Mike's natural suspicion kicked in. 'No, it's fine.'

'You're right. You can't be too careful; these things can turn into a riot.'

For a moment Mike thought he was being laughed at, but Najjar's face was perfectly serious and he was making no effort to come any closer.

When they reached the wall, Mike put the bags next to it and stood in front of them defensively. He rubbed his fingers to get some circulation back into them.

'What's this about? If it was Chloe, it would be the police talking to me.'

Najjar looked uncertain again. He glanced around then back at Mike. 'I have a daughter, Mr Dark, not as old as your Chloe. Just three.'

Having to deal with the people who came to the FreakWatch meetings meant that Mike knew that some people had to go round the houses before they got to the point. But in this case he hadn't wanted to talk anyway. 'Perhaps you could just get to the point?'

'Do you love your daughter, Mr Dark?'

'What kind of question is that?'

'How much?'

'What?'

'How much would you sacrifice for your daughter?'

Mike's temper flared. 'Are you threatening me? Where's Chloe? What have you done with her?' He grabbed Najjar's jacket in one fist, but kept him at a safe distance.

A look of terror crossed the man's face. 'Please, Mr Dark, I'm not threatening you or Chloe, I'm trying to help you.'

'Where is she?'

'I don't know where she is,' he said. 'She left my office this evening after I examined and treated her. She didn't tell me where she was going.'

The rational side of Mike's mind made him release Najjar's coat but the anger was still bubbling inside him.

'Mike?' His wife appeared behind him. 'What's going on?'

'I have no idea,' he growled.

'I'm Ali Najjar, Mrs Dark, Chloe's chiropractor.' He took a deep breath and before anyone could say anything else, 'Chloe told you she's had back pain? I found an anomaly in her spine.'

The anger in Mike was barely held in check. 'What exactly are you saying, Mr Najjar? Choose your next words with care.'

Najjar hesitated again.

'What's wrong with my baby?' said Amanda.

'I did a scan of her back,' he said. 'Found something.'

'What sort of thing?'

'Symmetrical osteophytes and extended musculature supporting them.'

'Put that in plain English.'

'Something is growing in her back.'

Mike did not even think. It was fury that propelled his fist into the man's solar plexus. Najjar doubled over and fell to his knees. Mike leaned over him and put his mouth next to the man's ear. 'My daughter is not a freak. Come near us again and I will kill you. Do you know what the penalty is for falsely accusing someone of being a freak?'

Najjar seemed to be fighting to breathe in.

Amanda was on the verge of tears. 'Why would you say this?'

Mike gathered up the bags. 'Come on, Amanda. We're leaving.'

Chapter 20

John Smith

He examined the scanner in the car. The target had been in the shopping centre for an hour but was finally moving out. He had identified his weapon of choice on this occasion and was parked behind it.

The truck was a refrigerated unit for meat. When he found it the last of its contents was being carried into the municipal butchers—The Shambles—for processing and redistribution to shops. There would have been an escort with it when it arrived but that had moved off. The security system for the building had been reactivated just after the driver had returned to the vehicle. He had not moved yet, not that that would have been a problem.

Smith adjusted his hat and got out of the car. In the old days there were cameras everywhere and he would have to have been far more cautious. As it was, riffy-less, the only scanners that now existed could not see him at all.

He walked up to the driver's side. He pulled open the door—unlocked because the driver was already in the vehicle. An ion-beam burner would mark the clothes and killing him now would register in the system as his riffy died with him. Instead the needle carried an efficient neurotoxin that prevented voluntary muscle control. The driver would not be able to guide the vehicle or call for help. It would only last an hour but that was more than enough.

Smith climbed into the cab beside the driver and fastened his seat belt tightly—couldn't have him slipping off the chair while driving. Attached to the dashboard was a picture of a smiling woman and three kids. 'Sorry, pal, collateral damage,' Smith said.

It took a few moments to attach his system service monitor—used by vehicle mechanics—to the truck's computer system, then code the target's riffy into the system, and add a custom command channel. He set the new channel to the default, removed his devices and climbed out again.

There was a faint possibility that his overrides could be found, but he was counting on the destruction of the vehicle hiding that evidence.

As he climbed down from the cab, two people started down the otherwise empty road towards them. He turned smoothly and held the door open for a moment. 'Yeah, okay, see you tomorrow.' And slammed the door.

Instead of going back to his car he headed towards the two people. He still had his hat on to shade his face from any lights. Like a good citizen, when faced with someone he did not know and was not going to talk to, he crossed to the other side of the road. He stuck his hands in his pockets moving positively but not too fast, as if he knew where he was going but was not in a hurry.

The two people passed him without comment. Smith made it to the end of road and paused at the junction with the main road. There were a lot of lights here and a few people moving about. Most were heading away from the centre, going home.

He turned and looked into the window of the shop on the corner. As he did so he watched the two who had interrupted him. They had passed his car and were carrying on at a leisurely pace.

He crossed the small road so the truck was between him and them, then made his way back. Once more he was grateful for the lack of cameras; there was no one to see and no riffy scanner could note his odd behaviour.

He passed the truck on the inside. By the time he emerged the others were gone. He got in his car and checked the target. He was out of the main shops and heading in this direction. He was probably planning on catching the Metro line in Piccadilly Gardens.

Smith activated the truck's motors and put it into auto-drive with the target's riffy as the destination. It pulled away smoothly. Smith followed directly behind. This vehicle also had no active riffy so no system would be able to track it.

Ali Najjar

He could breathe normally again. The shop staff had been kind, especially when he claimed the argument had been over clothes. It was common enough and they had no reason to disbelieve it.

As he came down into the street from the shop he was undecided what to do next. Perhaps he should get his wife, son and daughter, and just get out. People said the countryside had far fewer riffy scanners. It was possible to escape detection if you were careful.

But he would not know how to live and how could he put his wife and kids through that when it was all his fault. Nothing might happen. Perhaps he was wrong about Chloe, but would the Darks risk their daughter just to report him for falsely accusing her? Surely they would be worried it might be true.

He staggered up the gentle hill holding his stomach, which still hurt. He hoped Mike Dark had not ruptured something important.

If they didn't report him then time would pass and if Chloe was a freak—he hoped not—then she and the family would be put into quarantine. He would probably be tested as someone who came into physical contact with her. He might be quarantined for a while.

Better that.

And if she was not a freak then it was an unfortunate false alarm. He knew that was not the case. There was no mistaking what he had seen. And if she was having hot flushes as well? Could be another symptom.

Bright vehicle lights flashed past him as he passed a junction. A car turned out of the side road and illuminated everyone walking up towards Piccadilly Gardens.

He barely heard someone shouting as another set of vehicle lights shone at him from his left. He heard a thump as something heavy mounted the kerb nearby, and the whirring of a powerful electric vehicle motor. Then a wall smashed into him and his entire body screamed in agony for a fraction of a second.

John Smith

He pulled up to the kerb and climbed out. Once upon a time vehicles ran on petroleum products and could be made to burn very easily. There was no longer the industry to support drilling for oil, although coal mines had been reopened.

But his choice of the refrigerated truck was not mere coincidence. What it did have was liquid nitrogen and carbon filament batteries.

When it had run off the road the truck had embedded itself in the wall opposite. There was no question the target was dead. A crowd had gathered around the vehicle and someone was trying to get the driver's door open.

This was the tricky part.

He moved forward through the crowd as if he knew what he was doing. People parted before him. Rather than make his way to the cab he moved just behind it. There was a valve located underneath to bleed off the nitrogen. 'I need to check something, pal,' he said. 'Make sure it's safe.'

Those words alone were enough to get the people close up moving away.

He climbed underneath and pulled the required tool from inside his jacket. He attached a length of rubber tubing to the nitrogen outlet and fed the other end into the battery compartment. He fitted the tool on the valve control and gave it a half turn. The rubber tube went hard as the nitrogen flowed through it. It would shatter when the battery went up.

He stood up. 'Everything's fine,' he said and walked to his car.

As he drove away the vehicle exploded, taking with it everyone who had seen him.

Chapter 21

Chloe

Chloe growled at the rain as she exited the library. She walked to the edge of the steps and faced the wall of water. She had no umbrella and really wasn't dressed for the downpour. But time was getting on and there was no point waiting; the trams were few and far between at this time of night.

She resigned herself to getting wet and stepped out into the rain. She was drenched in moments. People joked about wet rain, the sort that somehow penetrated more than other rain. This was possibly the wettest rain she had ever encountered.

The weather was more extreme than it used to be: the summers hotter and the winters colder. People said it was global warming; it had been a big thing once upon a time, apparently. Too many people running too many machines that burned coal and oil. S.I.D solved that problem.

The Purity taught that S.I.D was the Malthusian solution; there had been only so long that the world population could keep increasing before disease took it—if war and famine didn't get there first. There was nowhere else for the population to go. Of course there were the cults that thought it was a judgement from some higher being. Maybe it was. It didn't really matter.

She supposed that global warming must have been monitored in some way. No one talked about it anymore.

Something had changed in the weather but if it had been a cataclysmic alteration nobody really noticed. Just the older people complained that the summers were hotter and the winters colder.

She crossed the tram tracks and stood under the canopy that stretched across the waiting area. Water dripped from her and the light breeze raised a shiver. Her trip to see Ali had helped and, as long as she stayed straight, her back didn't ache.

She heard the screeching of the metal wheels on the rails before the tram came around the corner. Someone coughed behind her. She jumped in surprise and glanced round but there was no one there. She frowned and turned her attention to the incoming driverless carriages.

She supposed there must be a wirehead somewhere running the trams. Or perhaps they really were completely automatic. Lots of people didn't understand that a computer virus wasn't like a real one; someone had to create it and plant it. Not like S.I.D which was natural. Was a wirehead really better than a computer?

The tram ground to a halt in front of her. The doors opened automatically. No one got off and she climbed aboard the front carriage, glancing around to do the dance of where to sit.

She preferred to have a solid wall behind her. There were a couple of people in the second carriage so she would stay in the front. She also liked looking forward but since she had the choice of every seat in the carriage it was moot. She chose a seat near the rear of the carriage with her back to the patched rubber concertina stretching between the two.

The muscles behind her ears twitched as she heard someone else stepping heavily into the rear carriage. She hoped it wasn't a drunk. It wasn't that she couldn't defend herself—she knew half a dozen ways to kill someone with her bare hands and feet—it was just difficult and embarrassing. Especially if they were friendly.

Just as the doors began to close someone else jumped into the front carriage. She couldn't blame him; no one wanted to wait in that rain. He looked around just as she had, though she thought his eyes lingered on her a little too long, but then he took a seat halfway up the carriage from her.

The tram pulled away, slid across a major junction and into the road opposite that ran between dilapidated buildings. The space opened up and the track climbed above road level. It ran alongside the Central Arena. It was still used for events but much of the ceiling had collapsed. Besides, no one really wanted to spend a lot of time in close proximity to anonymous people. The risk of infection might not be high but why take chances?

The tram curved around the end of the arena and came to a halt at Deansgate railway station. Reflected in the window at the front she watched as the two original occupants got out. The tram moved off again and headed south. They passed through Chorlton and the tram turned more east towards Didsbury. Chloe realised they were near where Melinda had disappeared.

She wondered what the police were doing. Nothing at night probably, she wished that DI Mitchell had been working on the case. She was pleased to have met him in some ways. It wasn't the fact that he had killed so many freaks; it was that he wasn't proud of it. He did it because he had to in order to protect the public, and because in the end they were better off dead.

The rain and the dark obliterated almost everything outside the window. When she was younger she had been scared of being on the tram in the dark and rain just in case she missed her stop.

Familiarity eventually solved that fear. She peered out and recognised the flashing billboard opposite the entrance to Southern Cemetery. The tram stopped. She saw the reflection of the big man in the rear carriage get up and move forwards. Instead of getting off he took a seat closer to the front. Her ear muscles twitched again and she fancied she could hear him breathing over the noise of the rain pelting the roof and the whining of the electric motors.

She shook herself. Why should there be any threat? Even she had adjusted her sitting position on the tram before when she found the place she was sitting had an unpleasant odour or there was something sticky on the plastic seats. It wasn't unusual. Anyway, the next stop was hers.

As long as he didn't get off at the same place.

The tram paused at the red lights, not that there was any traffic going the other way. *Probably just machines*, she thought, *a wirehead would have given them priority*. At least, she imagined that's what they would do, they were people after all.

The light went green and the tram moved off once more. It took about two minutes to get to the tram station. She glanced ahead. With the lights on inside the tram she could see nothing except the distorted reflection of herself and the rest of the carriage. The man seated in front of her was also staring at the window. Lights from outside glinted on his eyes and she could have sworn he was staring at her.

She looked down at her hands and then up again. He was still looking at her.

An involuntary shudder went through her. She had not known the other girls that had disappeared but she knew Melinda, and every one of them was about her age. Was this it? Had they come for her?

Don't be ridiculous, she told herself. Why would they want her?

But the other part of her mind asked: *Why did they want Melinda, or the others, what was it that made them a target?*

She jumped as the brakes squealed and the tram slowed. She got to her feet and went to stand by the left-hand door. The other two passengers did not move. She tried to convince herself she was imagining it but her heart sped up and she could almost feel the adrenaline flowing through her. She just wanted to run. Yes, of course, she had had fights, but they were either in the dojo where everything was controlled, or it was in the playground where she barely needed to exercise the slightest level of technique to dominate.

But this was real—at least in her imagination—and the truth was she was scared.

The tram doors huffed and scraped as they opened. The platform was dimly lit from the lights in the roof of the station. A sheet of rain fell between the door and where the roof started. A wide puddle covered the platform.

Before she stepped down into the rain, a third man emerged from the shadows of the station opposite her. His coat was slick with water reflecting the light and his bald head glistened. She stopped. He stared at her.

'Hello, girlie, want to go for a nice ride?'

Sensei had always said that if a fight was imminent, don't hesitate. Jujitsu was not a clean and pretty martial art; it was about getting the job done with a minimum of fuss and effort. But he was too far away; he would see her coming.

She did not need to look behind her; she could hear the other two—the one with the hat that had sat at the front, the other big and heavy one—as they moved into position behind her.

Baldy took a step forward. One of the men behind her shoved hard. Pain shot through her. All of Ali's work in relieving the tension was undone in a moment. He was strong and caught her off balance. She stumbled out into the rain, caught her foot in the gap and fell forwards smashing into her knees. The agony of it ripped through her.

Behind her, the one with the hat followed her out. 'Easy.'

Chloe caught the movement as he reached out for her. Almost without thinking she twisted and slammed her fist into his groin. He doubled over with a whimper. She improvised a punch up to where she thought his solar plexus ought to be but hit ribs.

Sensei's voice was in her head. You can fight on the ground, but better on your feet.

She grabbed his shoulder and used him to lever herself to her feet. On the way up she slammed her knee into his face and he fell back. At the ferocity of her attack, Baldy had taken a step away but something like a metal vice snapped round her right wrist, serrated edges bit into her forearm as it pulled upwards and lifted her from the ground. She wriggled in attempt to get free.

'We were warned about you and your little tricks,' said Baldy as he came forward. He let fly an untrained kick at her stomach. With her weight suspended from her arm, dragging on her shoulder, she lifted her legs and blocked then snapped a kick at his face. She made contact, and he tumbled back into the dark. Water splashed up where he fell.

Trying to ignore the pain in her right arm, she tried to hit the one that held her in the groin with her fist but couldn't reach. She pummelled his legs with her heels. It made no difference. She couldn't see what she was doing and nothing in her training covered being dangled by her arm. She needed to see her opponent. She relaxed her raised arm and twisted.

Where there should have been skin there were fish scales. The eyes were no longer human but at least one ear was normal. Above her head her arm was gripped in a crab-claw. Freak.

She punched the chest. It was like rock. She shrieked and yanked her hand back. She pulled back the cloth around the arm that gripped her and found a chitinous exoskeleton. But it was just one arm; it wasn't a bear hug. All she needed was leverage.

There was a groan to her left. She released the tension in her arm and twisted back. The one with the hat was pulling a burner from his pocket and, with a pained looked on his face, aimed the twin ionising barrels in her direction. Without even thinking she hooked her dangling legs around the right side of the freak. She strained her stomach muscles and pulled herself round so the big guy's body was between her and the weapon.

Pain lanced through her elbow as it bent unnaturally. Light flashed and the smell of ozone filled the air as her hip went numb. But the freak must have taken most of it. The grip on her arm loosened and she crashed to the ground. The freak collapsed beside her.

She heard the sound of the tram doors closing. Lifting her head she saw she was barely a foot from it. She flung out her right arm, not caring how much it hurt. The doors slid together but stopped on her wrist. After a moment they opened again. The rain poured down.

Get up, she screamed at herself.

'Just stay still, girlie.'

She twisted her head. Over the top of the prone freak she saw Baldy approaching. He had a burner too. She did not move. *How long before the doors close again?* She had no idea, time seemed distorted.

'Get up slowly or I will use this.'

She gathered her aching arms under her and placed her feet against the back of the freak. She heard the click of machinery and something engaged. She twisted her head towards Baldy again. 'Screw you.'

Almost in slow motion, as the door mechanism engaged, she saw and heard his finger tighten on the trigger. She almost thought she could see the twin beams of ionising radiation emerge from the double barrels.

She thrust against the freak and pushed with her arms as the doors closed. She had lost so much weight she soared through the closing gap.

Not fast enough. The beams grazed her again as the ten thousand volts surged through the air. With Chloe moving out of the way the beams struck the ground. The electrical power found the water much more to its liking than ionised air and, as Chloe thudded against the far door of the dry carriage, the station lit up and each man went rigid with the shock. Unable to do anything else, Baldy kept his finger on the trigger until the power in the battery pack was completely exhausted.

The tram motor engaged and its motion, as it pulled away, was the last thing Chloe knew before she lost consciousness.

Episode II: Poison

Chapter 1

Melinda

Melinda now believed she knew what true boredom was. After she had woken up, someone dressed in an all-encompassing rubber suit had come in with some apples, water, bread and cheese.

Melinda thought it might be a woman from the height, but the suit covered everything in loose folds and the visor at the front was fogged to hide the face behind it.

For some reason Melinda had not tried to talk. Her jailer placed the platter at the end of the bed where Melinda had to stretch to reach it. As she ate she realised how hungry she was, having had nothing since breakfast the day before—if it was only the day before.

By the time she had cleared everything she had slowed down and felt satiated. At least they weren't trying to starve her.

Then the person had gestured for the plate to be put back at the end of the bed. She took it and left. The bolt was drawn on the outside of the door again.

And that was it. There was nothing for hours. She just dozed. It was impossible to tell how much time was passing. The light stayed on. She was compelled to use the convenience even though the red light on the camera embarrassed her. But she had put up with it when she had been in the Purity quarantine, she could again.

During what she guessed to be the evening, the person returned with more food. It was hot this time but the utensils were made of wood. The knife barely had any cutting edge at all but that wasn't a problem since the lamb had already been cut up and the rest was mashed potatoes and peas.

But it felt good to have a solid warm meal inside her.

Fattening her for the slaughter?

The trouble with dozing during the day was that, when the lights went out, she was not sleepy at all. And the eerie glowing lines returned.

Now she had physical reference points for them she knew they linked the various electrical devices in the room: the light, the power socket and the surveillance camera. But what did that mean?

The grogginess of the previous night—she had still been suffering from the after effects of the drug they had given her—was gone and with the food she was quite clear-headed.

She closed her eyes.

Sure enough the lines remained in view just as they had before but now she knew she wasn't imagining it. She turned to face the wall behind the bed. The lines remained visible although she knew she was seeing them backwards. It was disorientating and gave her a strange itchy sensation on the back of her scalp.

She turned back and opened her eyes. That definitely felt better even though it made little actual difference.

She experimented. The metal bedstead, when she got her head down to its level, did block the glow but with a curious halo effect on the edges. So did the metal of the chain that attached her to the bed. But she could see the lines through anything non-metal, although by putting one hand in front of the other, lifting and crossing her legs and looking through all those layers of skin and bone the view was a little fuzzier.

By the time she had exhausted all her options she was tired.

She lay down in the bed. It was still cold but she had become accustomed to it. Another thought came to her as she lay there.

How is this possible? She shivered as the truth slid like a needle into her mind. She must be a freak. And she was going to die.

The light woke her. Moments later the bolt slid back and the rubber-suited figure entered carrying the breakfast tray. The person looked the same height but other than that there was no way to know if it was.

But as Melinda ate, the rubber suit kept shifting its weight from one foot to the other, giving off the strong impression of impatience. Over the past day Melinda had managed to relax but new fear spread through her.

She did not finish the food and pushed it away to the end of the bed. It was grabbed up almost before she had let it go and the person left the room, leaving the door wide open.

Melinda stared at it. She saw shadows moving which then resolved into two much taller figures in the same green rubber suits. One of them carried a burner and pointed it at her from beside the door.

She felt her way back across the bed and against the wall as if the extra distance would make a difference. The second figure approached the bed holding a key that was almost swamped by the massive glove.

Melinda stared as this person tried to unlock the cuffs at the bed end. He dropped the key on to the bed more than once as he attempted to manoeuvre it into the lock. Even though she could not see the face, she knew what expression he had when he looked over to the other guard.

They said nothing to one another. The one with the key placed it on the bed out of her reach and unstrapped the glove with a ripping of Velcro. His hand was fleshy and pink while the nails were rough and chewed. He tucked the unused glove into his belt.

Holding the chain with the still-rubberised hand he gingerly placed the key in the lock, behaving almost as if he expected it to bite him. The key turned and the lock snapped open. He quickly pulled his hand back and put it, with the key, into a pocket.

He gave the chain a couple of tugs and Melinda climbed awkwardly from the bed. The one with the burner moved into the room to the other side of the bed, keeping the weapon trained on her.

The floor was cold to the soles of her feet. The first guard walked ahead of her with the chain in his grip. The other followed behind as they headed out into the corridor.

Chapter 2

Mitchell

Night still claimed the world outside the kitchen window. Light from the dim interior bulb gleamed off the spotless surfaces.

It's almost as if no one lives here, thought DI Mitchell as he sipped the tea. It was pricey but not as extortionate as the coffee so was a luxury he allowed himself.

A drop had splashed on the table. He looked at the brown curved surface of it and decided it could stay until he tidied everything away. He wasn't obsessive about cleanliness but when he was at home he had nothing else to do.

The wooden bread bin was half-open. It had a habit of sticking but then it had been handmade. He'd picked it up in a market five years ago. There was almost no metal in its construction. The lid was composed of interlocking wooden slats that ran in grooves in the side pieces. They always stuck.

He had a working fridge, which was more than most. It was the one he and Catherine had bought when they were married. They had been together nearly ten years before things started to go wrong. No children: they had decided to wait. Just as well.

But that wasn't something he liked to think about.

He looked at his watch and then, to double check, glanced at the clock on the wall. Ten to six. The car would be here on the hour and would take twenty minutes to reach

Piccadilly station so he could meet the train from London at about half past.

It had once been a two-hour journey from London. Some of the express trains could still do it, with enough preparation. But the battery electrics took much longer. They had the speed but line maintenance was inefficient; it was too risky. Purity Special Agent Graham had taken the overnight so he could get in a full day's work.

Mitchell carried the plate and cup to the sink. He turned the tap. The water from the boiler on the wall was only lukewarm. He picked up the dishcloth, wrung it out, then wiped down the table, removing the spot of tea.

He went through the motions of cleaning and placed the cup and plate on the drainer before picking up a tea-towel to dry them. The cupboard door squeaked as he opened it to place the items in their correct positions inside.

There was no desire in him to rebel against the tidiness of his home life. Not that he considered it much of a home without Catherine. It was just a place to stay. The same place he had been for the last ten years.

There was a short corridor to his front door. He took his coat from the hook and pulled it on. Lifting the gun from the table, he checked the safety, latched it firmly into his shoulder holster, and buttoned up the front of the coat. He put his keys into his pocket. He picked up the hat and gloves. Of course keys were unnecessary here; the police residence was fully equipped with security and riffy detectors. But he liked keys, they were real, so much in this world was not.

The corridor was carpeted and he walked silently along the passage. None of the apartments, including his own, were numbered or even named. There was no need. Ashburne Hall had once been home to female university students. Now it was used as police accommodation.

He turned right through a fire door into the main corridor. The rooms here were smaller, just single bedrooms with shared facilities while he rated one that was a complete living unit.

This part of the building was nearly two hundred years old and the staircase was original. It flowed down to the ground floor in a wide sweep. Mitchell enjoyed the sensation of the wooden railing, never too cold even on a morning like this.

There was a duty sergeant in the reception. Awake but reading a book. His name was … Andrews. 'Good morning, sir,' he said and got to his feet, putting the book down.

'Car here yet, Andrews?'

'Not yet, sir.'

Mitchell nodded. 'Not to worry. You get back to your reading. I'll wait outside.'

The door slid open and the cold washed across him. He put on his hat, slid his hands into the gloves, and pulled up his collar.

There was an exterior light and he stood under it. It had stopped raining but the air was filled with the frosty earthiness of recent wet. Between him and the main road was open grass that ended in a high wall lined with rhododendron bushes and bare trees.

His breath misted and drifted away slowly.

He heard the car tyres crunching on the gravel and glanced up to see its side lights moving between the trees like a pair of will-o'-the-wisps. The vehicle slid past and made a tight turn in the space provided before returning to stop in front of him. The locks clicked.

Mitchell pulled open the door and slid inside, closing it after him with a solid *thunk*. The powers-that-be had provided the best vehicle available for collecting their important and potentially troublesome guest.

The car moved off the moment his safety belt was fastened. The clock on the dashboard showed the time as six-oh-one.

'Good morning, DI Mitchell.' Lament's pseudo-face appeared on the screen.

'Lament.'

'I hope you slept well.'

'I have nothing to complain about.'

Lament hesitated. 'Can I update you on recent events?'

Mitchell frowned. 'Events?'

'Chloe Dark was found unconscious on a Metrorail tram at three this morning.'

'The girl I interviewed?' Not that he expected a denial—her name was unusual and the reduced population meant name duplication was rarer than it used to be. 'Where?'

'Riffy records showed unusual movement at the stop near her home. No investigation has taken place there as yet due to the lack of light but the area has been cordoned off.' Lament sighed. 'Unfortunately it rained almost continuously for three hours after the event.'

'You think there was an attempt to abduct her?'

'Yes.'

'Does Special Agent Graham know?'

'All information is being transferred to his departmental wirehead; I can only assume he is being kept abreast of the situation.'

'He'll be wanting to interview her as soon as possible.'

The car drove up past the dark shops of Rusholme. The traffic lights changed in their favour as they continued north.

'The doctors have not finished their examination and have sedated her.'

'That's unfortunate,' said Mitchell.

'Yes, she might be unavailable for hours. These things are so unpredictable.'

Mitchell stared at the emotionless face in the screen. The left eye winked.

'Do you have the preliminary reports of the attack?'

'Not officially.'

Mitchell said nothing.

'It seems she had been physically assaulted and burned,' said Lament after a pause. 'She has some defensive wounds. The burns were not serious as if she had not been hit directly. Of course the rain would have reduced the effectiveness. However her right arm was dislocated at the shoulder and there were curious tear marks in her right wrist and forearm.'

'A freak.'

'Most likely.'

'How on earth did she escape?' Mitchell asked.

'According to her records she has martial arts training,' said Lament. 'Jujitsu.'

'Sounds like it almost wasn't enough.'

The car passed through the university and turned right towards the station. The clock said quarter past six.

'I take it our Purity agent will be given the medical report.'

'His department will be sent the official report once it's been completed, verified and filed.'

The car wound through the dark streets. They were empty of vehicular and pedestrian traffic. True it would have been quiet in the old days at this time, but never like this. It was as if the end of the world had come but forgotten to take him.

'Oh, and Chloe Dark's chiropractor died last night.'

Mitchell jerked his head up. 'What?'

'Her chiropractor,' said Lament without a trace of emotion. 'He was hit by a refrigerated truck.'

'And he's dead.'

'Very. The truck subsequently exploded killing nine bystanders.'

'I didn't think electrics could explode.'

'Seems they can.'

'And when will Agent Graham get that information?'

'I can't see that it's related,' said Lament without any change of tone. 'Completely isolated incident. Just an accident.'

'Get Yates on it.'

'Already done.'

Mitchell sat back. There was not the slightest chance this was a coincidence.

The car mounted a series of ramps and came to a standstill at the pick-up point at the rear of the station. The time was six twenty-one.

Special Agent Graham smiled amiably and extended his hand. Mitchell hesitated. You did not shake the hand of a stranger. But this man *was* the Purity; if you could not trust him, who could you trust? And if you implied distrust, what did that say about you?

Mitchell took his hand and gripped it firmly. 'Special Agent.'

He didn't trust the Purity in the slightest, and the feeling was no doubt mutual.

'DI Mitchell, thank you for meeting me.' His tone possessed the relaxed air of someone who knew how much power he could wield. The creases in his suit were knife-straight, and there wasn't a single black hair out of place on his head. He did not look like someone who had arrived on the overnight.

'Is this your first time in Manchester, sir?'

'Yes, it is.' He glanced around at the concourse. A local train had arrived at platform one, and a dozen passengers moved towards the exit. 'It's very quiet.'

'The place will be teeming in an hour,' said Mitchell. 'It's still early.'

'Of course.' He paused. 'I imagine Chloe Dark won't be available for interview for a few hours.'

'I understand she has been sedated.'

'Unfortunate.'

Mitchell shrugged. 'The hospital staff were not to know.'

Graham looked around the station again as if he was assessing a threat.

'Do you want to go to the Purity office first?'

'There's no need.' Graham focused his attention on Mitchell. 'So, they assigned their best killer to nursemaid me?'

'I've been in the job longest, I have seniority.'

Graham smiled. 'The person least likely to screw up.'

Cold was beginning to penetrate Mitchell's coat. 'I couldn't possibly second-guess the Superintendent's intentions.'

'This is not my first assignment of this sort, DI Mitchell.'

'Where would you like to start?'

'Let's try the Chloe Dark crime scene.'

Chapter 3

Yates

'What a fucking mess,' muttered Yates. Dawn was beginning to crawl into the sky beyond the grey clouds but here, at the start of December, it took its time.

The lorry was a tangle of metal. An occasional wisp of smoke floated up from its innards and escaped into the frosty air. The main body of the vehicle had opened like a grotesque flower with the incinerated load at its heart. The bodies of the passers-by had already been removed though chalked outlines showed where they had fallen as the explosion scattered them like seeds.

Market Street had been closed off. Beyond the police barriers to the north, east and south were gawking bystanders with the mist of condensation from their collective breath hanging above them. On the far side Forensics had provided a space for the commuters to shuffle by and rubberneck the accident, a uniform kept them moving.

The cab of the truck was crushed against the wall. The driver was still in his seat, squashed against dashboard and window, while the pulverised remains of the victim had yet to be revealed in full. However, the feet and lower legs were visible if you shone a light under the front axle. Almost no blood though; there had been no circulatory system remaining and nothing to pump with after the impact.

This was a crap job in more ways than one. An abduction attempt was made on Chloe Dark, and the same night her chiro got rubbed out by a truck, along with a bunch of witnesses. A professional job. It had to be murder.

Why would anyone take out a hit on a chiropractor?

The old TV cop shows they ran and re-ran were weird. They had been made before the plague and all their reasons seemed so unnatural. Of course there were burglaries, thefts, prostitution just like always, and sometimes ordinary people broke down and killed someone. But now there was almost always the question of the Purity somewhere in the mix. If you were a detective and you didn't make that number one in your possible motives, you wouldn't solve a lot of crime.

Unfortunately they also had this Purity agent to deal with as well.

Yates saw a well-padded and familiar figure—even more familiar when she was naked and lying in his bed. 'Ria!'

She looked round. The protective goggles she wore acted as an Alice band for her straight black hair. She held up a finger and turned back to what she was doing, digging something from between two paving bricks.

Yates wandered over.

'Hey, Harry,' she said without looking up.

He peered over her shoulder as she prised a piece of metal from the packed earth between the herringbone brickwork. 'What's that?'

She brought the sliver up to her face and stared at it.

'Looks like half of a child's hair clip.'

'Relevant to the case?'

'No.'

'How do you know?'

He stepped back as she stood and stretched. 'There was no child caught in the explosion as far as we know.' She looked across at the truck and then back at her feet. 'It was well-buried and the angle is completely wrong.'

She dropped the metal into an evidence bag and handed it to her assistant. 'You on this case then, Harry?'

'Seems like.'

'Where's your boss?'

'Babysitting the Purity agent.'

Ria nodded. 'Broken up the dream team then.'

'Got anything interesting?'

'It's all interesting, Harry,' she said and pushed up her goggles. 'I like my job.'

There was a stirring in the crowd which parted as a lorry with a crane mounted on the flatbed reversed into the area, spewing methane fumes and smelling of a farm.

'Want to stay for the big reveal?' she asked.

'Sounds delightful,' he said having to raise his voice over the noise. 'But really what have you got? How could a truck blow up?'

Ria gestured to him and he followed her to the imploded window of the shop next door. She pointed to melted metal embedded in the brick work.

'That is probably aluminium,' she said. 'Aluminium can explode under certain conditions.'

'What sort of conditions?'

'It needs to be molten and come into contact with water.'

He raised an eyebrow. 'From a meat truck?'

'Those vehicle batteries hold a lot of power. If the crash twisted the contacts so it all discharged at one time it could

- 175 -

have melted aluminium that came in contact with some rain water collected in the engine.'

Yates thought about it. 'That's a lot of ifs, buts and maybes.'

'Yes it is.'

'Could that be done as deliberate sabotage?'

'Of course, but is that likely?'

Yates hesitated. 'Might be but can you keep it out of the report?'

She frowned. 'I won't be putting the whole thing back together, Harry. That'll be someone else. It's not my area.'

'Who then?'

'Tony Jacobs.'

'Don't know him.'

'Well, don't try asking him for any favours; he's a true believer.'

'Right.'

Yates looked round again. There was nothing here for him. He needed witnesses.

'Can I use your van?'

'Joy ride?'

'I need to talk to the wirehead.'

Ria waved in the general direction of the two Forensics vans pulled up on the corner. 'Be my guest.'

Yates slammed the passenger door and settled back into the chair. The van wasn't warm but it was better than outside. He glanced around. The cab was spotless, not a food wrapper or receipt to be seen. He opened the glove compartment.

Vehicle maintenance manual, a notepad (unused) and a couple of pens. Forensics were weird.

'You wanted me, DS Yates?'

Lament's voice emerged from the speaker before the image materialised on the screen.

'Witnesses?'

'There were quite a lot because of the sale. Uniforms took their statements.'

'And?'

'There was a crash, a delay, and an explosion.'

Yates nodded, public statements tended to lack useful detail.

'How much of a delay?'

'It was exactly forty-seven seconds between the driver and victim's riffy signals stopping, and those of the bystanders.'

Yates stared at the screen picturing how the people must have been crowded round to see if they could help, unaware their lives were about to be cut short. Did you know when you died that fast? Were you aware of the cessation of life?

'Ask me another,' said Lament.

Yates focused on the face. 'What?'

'Here, let me replay it for you.'

The face disappeared to be replaced by a three-dimensional mock-up of the area with figures representing the people involved. The victim crossed the road from Debenhams looking to head up to the tram station.

The lorry crossed the junction and ploughed into him. Some bystanders moved away from the incident, others towards it. One in particular moved straight up to the vehicle, paused for perhaps ten seconds, and then moved away. The other people were edging closer but this one just crossed the street.

The mock-up on the screen zoomed out and switched to a map view. The truck exploded and the nearby dots went red. The other one continued away from the incident.

'So, who is he?'

Lament reappeared on the screen. 'I have no idea.'

For a moment Yates was at a loss for words. 'How can you not know? He has a riffy.'

'Yes, he does. But its code does not match anything in the records.'

'How can that be?'

'There are several possibilities.'

'Like?'

'One: He's been removed from the records. Two: He has a riffy that hasn't been added to the records. Three: He's foreign. Four: He has a device that acts like a riffy but is external.'

'Which one?'

'Well if it was any of one to three then I would have no way of knowing. But it's the fourth.'

'How do you know?'

'Seriously, I seem to be doing all the work. Who did you sleep with to get to be a detective sergeant?'

Yates looked out of the window; it was fogging up and in the increasing light the people outside moved like ghosts.

'Biometrics,' Yates said finally.

'And you win today's prize!'

The screen image dissolved into four lines. The top three were jagged and their peaks increased in size in the same place. The other had a similar underlying pattern but much smoother and without the increase.

'Our surprise guest shows a completely regular and normal heartbeat despite the situation.'

'It's a fake.'

'Yes.'

'Can you track it?'

'It stops about half a mile away.'

Yates sat forward. 'How about where it came from?'

'It will take a while.'

'All right. He won't be there now but send someone to check it out and Forensics when they're available.'

'You want me to send someone else?'

'It's Sunday, I'm not doing any more than I have to.'

'Mitchell won't like that.'

'He's not my dad.'

Lament said nothing.

'I'm coming back to the station.' He looked at his watch. 'Get me a car for about three.'

'Yes, sir.'

Chapter 4

Sapphire

The pair of high heels clicked down the empty hospital corridor. Sapphire Kepple had the confidence of knowing the strength of the Purity was behind her. She paused at the reception. The administrative person behind the desk, not a nurse, continued tapping away at her terminal. Sapphire cleared her throat. 'Chloe Dark.'

'Just a moment,' said the woman. She did not look up but raised a hand. She continued typing for a few more moments, and then hit the return key with a flourish. She smiled at Miss Kepple.

'And you are?'

Sapphire felt the anger beginning to boil within her. She suppressed it as best she could. 'I'm from her school,' she said. 'I'm the Purity officer.'

It was with a certain amount of satisfaction she watched the sunny demeanour of the receptionist dissolve. The woman glanced at the riffy monitor in front of her. The device registered Kepple and her credentials. With her Purity registration, and being a teacher, she was better than next-of-kin.

'Room 313.' The woman was almost trembling. Sapphire gave her a nod and headed for the elevators. She had been here before. There was a lot of security to get

through on the third floor but it wouldn't be a problem for
her.

Chloe

'I'm fine, Mum.'

'You're not fine,' said Mrs Dark. 'You're in an isolation
tent behind sealed doors. You've been attacked. You're
injured.' Her mother looked on the verge of tears again.
Chloe knew the real reason: She had been attacked by a freak;
the possibilities were terrifying. But you didn't talk about that,
so instead her mother talked about the more obvious of
Chloe's injuries: her arm in a sling, with the wrist swathed in
bandages. 'And never mind your arm; have you seen your
face?'

Chloe had seen her face. Against the orders of the
doctor and the nurse, and apparently anyone else who just
happened to be passing, she had climbed out of bed, though
it made her head throb. There was some space between the
bed and the inside of the plastic tent, on one side was a
medical monitoring device set into the wall with its
instrument panel behind a sheet of glass. Chloe's battered
face was mirrored in it.

Outside the tent were a couple of chairs that looked
very uncomfortable even though they were padded. Her
mother was sitting in one, forced to lean back by the shape.
There were no windows. The top of the tent had a noisy fan
that sucked air out constantly so the walls bowed inwards.
Chloe understood why and could imagine the air from hers,
and every other, room being cooked to kill off anything alive
that came from her.

In that time alone, before her mother had arrived, complete with a large badge hung around her neck, she had examined herself in more detail. The arm that was not in a sling was bruised up and down its length where she had parried her attackers' blows. One eye was turning purple and she had a cut across her left cheek which had been stuck together with tape. Her right shoulder ached incessantly, as did all the muscles in that arm and, where the freak had gripped her, it stung. Inside she felt detached although she wasn't sure if that was due to the drugs, or the experience.

Her mother said she had arrived about four in the morning but had not been allowed to see Chloe. So the staff had found her a place to bed down and she had fallen asleep but they hadn't woken her up. Her mother's eyes were red from the crying, and probably the lack of proper sleep. It was now past lunchtime

'We were up all night when you didn't come home, our trace couldn't find you,' said her mother. 'I was going mad. We called the police, but they couldn't find you either. I thought you were gone like Melinda.' Mother started to cry again. 'I was going out of my mind.'

Chloe decided it was best not to say she almost had been gone like Melinda. 'I'm okay, mum. I'm here, aren't I?'

Her mother looked about to burst out crying again. Chloe wondered for a minute whether it might have been better if she had been caught because then she could have found out what had happened to her friend, and maybe they could have escaped together.

There was a knock on the door and, without a moment's delay, in strutted her teacher. 'Chloe, I'm so glad you're all right.'

Miss Kepple approached the wall of the isolation tent and put her delicate hand against it, almost as if she would rather be touching Chloe. 'How are you feeling?'

Chloe shrugged. And then winced at the pain. 'I'm okay.' She wasn't quite sure how to behave with her teacher here; it was strange seeing her out of school.

Miss Kepple turned to Chloe's mother. 'Mrs Dark, you must have been so worried.'

'Oh,' said her mother, 'yes, we both were. My husband. When she didn't come home.'

Miss Kepple acted like Chloe's mother hadn't even spoken. 'Don't worry Chloe,' she said. 'This doesn't change anything.'

Chloe frowned. 'Anything?'

'You can still be in charge of the D-N-Cadr-A. What happened to you doesn't make any difference.'

'Oh,' said Chloe. 'I am ... thank you.' In truth Chloe had hoped it might make a difference; she had decided being part of an organisation that stopped her from seeing her friends was not what she wanted. Even if it meant the displeasure of her teacher.

'I thought I'd leave something for you,' said Miss Kepple. She reached into her handbag and pulled out something metal that glinted under the lights. 'I'll just leave it over here.' She placed it on the personal cabinet that was outside the isolation wall.

'What is it?'

'A badge. It's a badge for your new position.'

The door to the room opened again. A woman in a white coat, a doctor's coat, came in. In her hands she held a portable terminal. She glanced up and took in the two people

- 184 -

in the room, nodded to Chloe's mother, and then looked at her teacher.

'And you are?' Her tone was not friendly.

'I am Chloe's Purity teacher, Sapphire Kepple. I came to see how she is, and to tell her how everyone at the school is thinking about her.'

'Well, I am Chloe's physician, Dr Majeed. Chloe has had a traumatic experience and at this moment, what she needs is peace and quiet. I do not believe you need to remain any longer.' The doctor moved back to the door and opened it. 'You can go back to the school and you can tell them that Chloe thanks you for your regards but, for the foreseeable future, any visits are restricted to immediate family and officials only.'

Chloe had never heard anyone speak to Miss Kepple that way. In school everybody, even the Principal, was terrified of her and what she represented. Chloe wasn't sure but she could see Miss Kepple's left hand was clenched so tight the drawn skin was going white. Then she relaxed and the hand dropped open.

'Of course Dr… Majeed,' said Miss Kepple. 'And thank you, I will pass on the information.' She turned to Chloe, and once again raised her right hand to touch the plastic of the isolation wall tent. 'Bye now Chloe, get well soon, and we'll see you back in school.'

Dr Majeed closed the door on the teacher as her heels clicked out and down the corridor. She turned and smiled at Chloe. 'Well, my dear, you are lucky,' she said and Chloe wasn't sure whether she was referring to the attack, or Miss Kepple's departure.

'Is she going to be all right?' said her mother, escaping the grip of the chair and standing.

'We are still waiting for some results to come back,' said the doctor. Chloe did not need to have that interpreted and, from the look of despair on her mother's face, neither did she. 'However, all the other injuries are superficial. Just bruising, cuts and some stretched ligaments. The worst of those will take no longer than a couple of weeks to heal fully.'

There was an unspoken 'but' hanging at the end of her sentence. Neither Chloe nor her mother said anything.

'However there are a couple of things we should go over.'

'What's wrong?' said Chloe's mother, her fears erupting to the surface again.

The doctor turned a calming smile on her. 'Nothing to be concerned about, Mrs Dark. Just some things I need to ask your daughter and if there's anything you can add I would be interested to know it.'

Chloe's mother sat back down. She gave the impression of trying to relax, but the way she gripped the armrest of the chair was telling. The doctor turned back to Chloe.

'As I said, most of your wounds are superficial, my dear,' she said, 'the blow to the back of your head could easily have been worse than it appears to be, for which we can be grateful, however the reason it's not bad is curious.' She paused.

'What?' said Chloe.

'Yes, what?' said her mother.

'Do you have any problems eating?'

Her mother gave a short sharp laugh. 'The problem is stopping her.'

'Mum!'

'Really?' The doctor looked suspicious. 'You seem like a sensible well-balanced girl, Chloe.'

Chloe hesitated. It was a strange thing to say. 'Thanks?'

The doctor pulled up the hard-backed chair and perched on the edge. 'You know, before the plague, it was not unknown for young women to become convinced they were overweight, even when they weren't, and stop eating.'

'I eat.'

'She does.'

'Yes,' said Dr Majeed. 'But sometimes they would hide it by eating and then forcing themselves to regurgitate. In some cases it was so bad they died.'

'They did that?' said Chloe. The doctor merely nodded, and waited as if she was expecting more of an answer. 'This is about my weight?' Another nod. Chloe thought hard. 'I exercise a lot.'

'Your weight is equivalent to a girl half your age. Exercise is unlikely to account for that. Muscle tissue is denser than fat.'

Chloe just looked at the doctor, not knowing what else she could say.

'But look at her, doctor,' said her mother coming to the rescue. 'Does she look underweight? We've all seen the pictures of people starving, children and adults, does Chloe look like that?'

For a moment Dr Majeed looked as if she were on the back foot. She looked hard at Chloe, waist to chest to face, and finally shook her head. 'No.'

'Your machine must be broken, then.'

Chapter 5

Mercedes

'Let us in, Mercedes!' The voice of Alistair McCormack growled through the intercom system. His face looked abnormally large through the fish-eye lens that focused on him and Margaret Jenner, outside the door to Mercedes' penthouse.

Mercedes Smith ran her hand through her hair—it needed a good wash. She had not had a good night. Xec had woken her at three in the morning to report the failure to snatch Chloe Dark. The following hours had been tedious and filled with stress.

Xec had done his best to cover up and delay the investigation. The rain would have washed away most trace evidence and he had managed to keep Chloe's location uncertain for a while. When she had asked how he managed that, the reply had been an enigmatic: 'I called in a favour.'

After that she couldn't get back to sleep. Possible scenarios kept running through her mind, and none of them had a happy ending. She had expected representatives of the board to turn up a lot earlier. Maybe Xec had kept the information from them as well.

The buzzer on the door rang again. 'Mercedes, we need to talk about this right now.'

'Well?' asked Xec.

She turned away from the screen and looked out on the dismal day. The panoramic windows of her penthouse apartment in Utopia Genetics revealed only the freezing grey mist of a Manchester autumn morning. At least it had stopped raining. 'Yes, all right, let them in. I'm going to get changed.' She turned and headed towards her bedroom suite, unconsciously avoiding the stainless steel glass and leather furniture. She slammed the door behind her.

When she opened it again she had a smile plastered on her face. Her hair was clean and her clothes transmitted a confidence she was not feeling inside. Alistair McCormack and Margaret Jenner were seated opposite one another in the leather sofas with cups of coffee in their hands. Mercedes was awash with the stuff; it had been the only thing that kept her going through the night. The smell of it just reminded her that her stomach was empty.

'Lunch, Xec.'

'Way past that, Miss Smith.'

'Late lunch.'

'Scrambled egg, ham and toast in the kitchen,' said Xec in his most efficient voice.

Mercedes walked past her unwanted guests without acknowledging them. She went around the corner to the breakfast bar where her breakfast waited. She ate quickly, crunching through the buttered toast and washing it down with orange juice. There was also a pill on the plate. She didn't ask Xec what it was but added it to her meal.

When she returned to the lounge she was feeling vaguely human again.

McCormack placed the espresso cup on the glass table where the porcelain clinked as he put it down. The cup looked especially small in his huge hands.

'We're screwed,' he said as his opening gambit.

'No, we're not,' said Mercedes. 'We're a very long way from being screwed.'

Jenner slammed her cup and saucer on to the table so hard Mercedes thought it would crack. 'This is a complete disaster,' she said. 'When this gets out, it'll be all our lives on the line.'

Mercedes settled back into the armchair and crossed her legs comfortably. 'Nobody is going to find out.'

'Don't try that on us,' said Jenner. She was gripping the edge of the leather sofa, digging in her fingernails. 'We have just killed the chiropractor of the girl who failed to be disappeared.'

'It's just a coincidence,' said Mercedes. 'There is nothing to connect the two events.'

'Except,' said McCormack. 'Except he's only her bloody physical therapist.'

'Kindly do not come into my home and threaten me.' Then she smiled. 'The situation is not ideal, I'll give you that. But it is not as bad as it seems. Xec woke me with the news last night, and I have been up for hours. We have been analysing the situation and dealing with the evidence trail.'

Mercedes uncrossed her legs and smoothly climbed to her feet. She turned her back on them and walked over to the window. She stared out into the gloom. 'Xec, what is the state of the evidence of Chloe Dark's abnormality?'

'The records of Chloe's visit to his surgery have been doctored to show no abnormalities. The man's attempt to delete the records has also been obliterated since we control all aspects of the medical data.'

'But he went to speak to her parents,' said McCormack. 'How are you going to deal with that?'

Mercedes turned. 'We don't have to,' she said. 'Since there is nothing in the medical records to suggest there was a problem, anything he said will be the ravings of a deranged mind. In fact, when the police put samples of his tissue through their analysers, they may actually find he was suffering from some sort of infection.'

That stopped them, thought Mercedes, *let them try to make this my fault now.*

'Coincidences do happen in this world,' said Mercedes.

'This is one hell of a coincidence, Mercedes,' said Jenner. 'And don't forget we have a Purity officer looking into the whole thing right now. Do you really think you can pull the wool over his eyes?'

'I don't have to; there is no evidence that connects them. The only conclusion is that this was an unfortunate pair of circumstances.'

The two of them were quiet for a short time, so Mercedes went on the attack. 'But you, Alistair.'

His head jerked up.

'Your men failed to pick her up. Can you explain that?'

'How the hell were we supposed to know she was that good? She's just a kid, like the rest,' he growled. 'We won't be making that mistake again.'

This time Jenner stared at him in horror. 'You're going to try again?'

'What choice have we got?' he said. 'If we leave it too long it'll become obvious. The Purity will get her and then we'll really be in trouble because it will look as if our devices failed to detect her.'

Jenner turned to Mercedes. 'Surely you can't agree to this?'

Mercedes shrugged. 'There's nothing else we can do. Alistair is right; if we don't pick her up she will start to show, and if the Purity get hold of one of our assets, they'll easily make the link with the others and it won't be long before they're here in force.'

'But your goons put her in the hospital and one of them was a freak,' said Jenner, 'they'll test her thoroughly.'

'No,' said Mercedes, 'their tests will find nothing wrong with her DNA. And then they will release her and we will be able to pick her up. This time we won't make any mistakes, will we?' She looked pointedly at McCormack.

'We'll be a lot more careful,' he said. 'We won't make the same mistake again.'

But Jenner would not be stopped. She stood up. 'But they will be keeping track of her. They will assume whoever tried to pick her up will do it again. It will be both the police and the Purity. How are you going to do that?'

'I haven't the slightest idea,' said McCormack. 'We'll have to see how it goes.'

'This really is a disaster,' said Jenner. She picked up her coffee cup, noticed it was empty, and put it back down. 'I need more coffee.'

'Fresh coffee is available in the kitchen area,' said Xec in his precise manner.

Chapter 6

Mitchell

It was around three-thirty, the sky continued grey and overcast but it was too cold to rain. The auto-drive police car wound its way through the Manchester traffic. Although they kept moving, the traffic lights were not always green in their favour, and their progress was much slower than DI Mitchell expected. It seemed Lament was not hurrying them through the late rush hour. The crime scene had been a wash-out.

'How much further to the hospital?' asked Graham. The two of them were sitting in the back. The vehicle was not a limousine so they were side by side. Mitchell could smell Graham's aftershave, not a cheap brand but he hadn't overdone it. Mitchell half-shook his head again as if trying to clear it. This man was not someone to be trifled with, and they would have to be careful.

The car crawled down Oxford Road but, once past the railway station, progress was faster.

'Ten minutes at most,' said Mitchell, 'more likely five.'

The car drove past the old university buildings; there were still a few students but the halls of residence were all empty now. Nobody travelled to go to university anymore. And there were precious few classes of any sort. The government had woken up to the fact that key skills were being lost as people died of old age. Specialised skills were important, but not as much as knowing how to make clothes, or grow food. Or manufacture new riffies for the new population as demanded by the Purity.

That subject was not reported in any detail but advanced chip manufacture was something that drained the resources of the country, and forced them to trade with countries that had the raw materials they needed. But no country had been immune to the plague.

Mitchell was glad he wasn't a politician.

A minute later they were passing the iron railings of the hospital. They turned in through the main entrance and drove through the older buildings and round to the newer ones. Although 'new' still meant sixty years old.

The car came to a halt and the locks popped. Graham didn't wait for the door to be opened for him; he climbed out and hurried to the entrance. Mitchell, older and slower, and probably more willing to tolerate the damp cold, followed. Once he was under cover the car moved away. The two went through into the main reception area. Graham did nothing but walk up to the desk. Something on a screen caught the attention of the receptionist, who then stared at him with barely hidden fear.

Mitchell's riffy identification showed up too, and when she saw it she seemed to relax a little.

'We're looking for the girl brought in this morning,' said Mitchell. The Purity agent had stepped away from the desk and was studying the posters on the wall. 'Name of Chloe Dark, can you tell me where she is?'

She didn't even look it up. 'Yes. Third-floor genetic isolation,' she said, 'room 313...' She pointed along the corridor. 'The lift is that way.'

Mitchell thanked her and turned to where Graham had been, but he was already heading down the corridor. Mitchell refused to run but he did stretch his stride to catch up. The elevator doors were opening just as he arrived.

When they opened on the third floor it became clear that whoever had decorated it had decided that the biohazard symbol was the way to go. The entire length of the passageway, floor and walls, was plastered with the symbol, as well as warnings about S.I.D. He half expected to see it on the ceiling too but it seemed they had managed to restrain themselves.

The first door sealing off the isolation area slid back as Graham approached it. The authority given to him by his riffy was certainly higher than Mitchell's since the door slid back and barred him entrance immediately. Realising that Mitchell wasn't with him, Graham turned and hesitated for a moment as if trying to decide what he should do next. Speaking loudly enough for his voice to penetrate the door, he said. 'You've spoken to this girl before?'

Mitchell didn't bother raising his voice. He simply nodded.

'All right.' There was a manned station a further twenty paces down the corridor. Mitchell watched as Graham headed towards the guard sitting there. He couldn't hear the conversation but after a few moments the guard adjusted some detail on his terminal and the door slid open to Mitchell.

'I've given you temporary access,' said Graham, once Mitchell had caught up. 'As long as you're with me.'

'All right.'

The final door did not open on their approach. Graham touched the button on the wall then turned back to look at the guard. He checked them both over a second time and then let them through.

'Decent security,' said Graham. There was a turn in the corridor and from that point the rooms were numbered from 301 going up on the left-hand side and down from 321 on the right. Room 313 was near the end on the right-hand side.

The Purity agent walked straight in.

Mitchell stepped in after him and took in the scene that was only too familiar to him. The bed, the isolation tent, and the worried relative sitting off to one side. It wasn't only that he had seen this a hundred times before, it was the fact that, once upon a time, he had been the one in the seat.

Mitchell saw the look of recognition on Mrs Dark's face as her eyes flicked from Agent Graham to himself. He nodded at her. 'Good morning, Mrs Dark.'

Chloe was sitting up in bed with her legs over the side. She too recognised him but looked with considerable unease at the man she didn't know. She was wearing a dressing gown which she pulled close around her. Mitchell wondered whether the Purity agent deliberately scared people, or whether he genuinely had no idea of the effect he caused on others.

'Hello, Chloe,' he said. 'This is Special Agent Graham of the Purity. He'd like to talk to you about what happened last night.'

His identification of Graham did not have a calming effect. The worried expression on Mrs Dark's face deepened further. Graham glanced around, his gaze falling on a hardback chair behind the door. He grabbed it and placed it just outside the plastic of the isolation tent. He leaned back and crossed one leg by bringing his ankle up and placing it on the opposite knee. If it had been 40 years ago Mitchell would have expected him to light a cigarette.

'Chloe,' said Graham. 'You don't mind me calling you Chloe, do you?'

She shook her head. If Mitchell was any judge, she would rather the agent were gone completely. She didn't care what he called her.

'If you're feeling up to it, Chloe, perhaps you wouldn't mind telling us exactly what happened last night.'

'I was in the Central Library—' she began.

The agent interrupted. 'We know where you were, Chloe, up until the time the trouble started.'

Mitchell was not impressed with Graham's interview technique. He cleared his throat pointedly.

Graham glanced round at him. 'Interviewing victims is not necessarily my *forte*,' he said. 'Perhaps DI Mitchell would prefer to do this?'

Despite the fact he had been given the opportunity to do what he wanted, Mitchell felt that somehow he had been pushed down into a very small category, that of police interviewer. Nothing so exalted as a Special Agent of the Purity.

'When did you first think there was something wrong?' he asked.

'On the tram,' she said, 'it was when the freak got on, although I couldn't see him properly. But there was a man who'd got on earlier, and I could see him looking at me.'

'You were facing him?'

'No, I could see his reflection in the glass. He was looking at me. Staring.'

Mitchell nodded encouragingly.

'Then everybody else got off and he moved forward closer behind me,' she said. Mrs Dark made a tiny noise. Chloe glanced across at her then back at Mitchell. She didn't look at Graham at all. 'We got to Didsbury and that's when they attacked. I was just getting off.'

'And then you fought them, and you beat them off,' said Special Agent Graham, the tone of his voice indicated how unlikely that sounded.

'My dad wanted me to train in martial arts; he thinks the world is a dangerous place.'

Graham just grunted as if he didn't care what her father thought. He got up from the chair and wandered over to the cabinet by the wall. Mitchell had already noted that there was something small and metallic lying on top. Graham picked it up and examined it. He looked sidelong at Chloe. 'Where did you get this?'

Chloe hesitated as if she didn't want to say. 'My teacher gave it to me, my Purity teacher.'

'Sapphire Kepple.' Graham put the badge back down onto the cabinet. 'I'm done here for now,' he said to Mitchell and, without offering a goodbye, he left the room.

'Thank you for your help, Chloe,' he said, 'and you Mrs Dark.'

Mrs Dark got to her feet. 'Do you know what's going to happen to Chloe?'

Mitchell shook his head. 'I'm sorry, that's for the medics and the Purity to decide.'

Chapter 7

Melinda

She woke in the dark and her head ached.

She did not know what time it was but without even opening her eyes she could see the electrical wires just as she had before. She guessed from their relative positions she was back in her room, in her prison. If it was still the same day she had now been there two days, but the gas they had given her might have knocked her out for longer.

Yes. She now remembered: the gas.

Today—she might as well think of it as the same day— had started just like yesterday. Breakfast offered by somebody impatient, followed by people in rubber suits who forced her to stay as far away from them as possible. They unchained her again and took her for the tests.

She adjusted her position a little and she realised something was different.

Her left arm was still chained to the bed but when she moved it there was no clink of metal on metal. And something was missing from her electrical sense. She had not noticed before but, just as she could see the electricity in the wires, she had known that her chain was metal even in the dark. She reached with her right hand to feel the new binding. It was some sort of plastic cable but tied just as firmly to her wrist.

She was very thirsty and found she had no need to use the facilities regardless of how long she'd been asleep. Were they trying to dehydrate her? They might be. The experiments they were performing on her were varied.

Yesterday it had been mainly samples they were after. She had ended up with her arms like pincushions, and then there were the deeper samples. It seemed they did not care if she were anaesthetised or not. Those had hurt, a lot.

In a room that was as white as every room and corridor here, but resembled a torture chamber as much as a medical facility, they had clamped her to a frame. It provided support but was not solid so they could get at her back. There were straps around each part of her arms and legs as well as across her chest and hips. Her head too was clamped in position. The place was equipped with drills that would have put a dentist to shame. She wouldn't have been surprised if they had started drilling into her head, but yesterday it was just samples.

As they had gone about their tasks, she had closed her eyes and tried not to think about what they were doing to her. Instead she explored the room with her new sense. She saw the power cables. One particularly thick one coming through a wall glowing like a neon bulb and others snaking away like tributaries on a river. And there were machines including computers of different sorts.

So yesterday she had watched the lights glowing, fading, and moving while they had prodded, pulled, poked and sampled her as if she were nothing more than a frog on a dissecting table. She pushed that thought from her mind as soon as it appeared.

And today had started the same way. She had resigned herself to being treated as nothing more than an object. But instead of the dissecting room, she was taken to what looked, for all the world, like a gym. There were all sorts of exercise devices: things like bicycles, machines for weightlifting, and several she didn't recognise at all.

They kept her on the leash, but moved her from machine to machine. The man she had come to think of as her jailer, even though he wasn't the only one, kept hold of the chain while he pointed to a machine and indicated how she was supposed to use it. They did not offer her any better clothing than the hospital smock but she was a long way past embarrassment now.

They did not exercise her very hard but they did attach various measuring devices for her heart rate and blood pressure, and on a couple of occasions she had to breathe into a tube. All of which she found much more exhausting than perhaps it should have been. She wondered whether she was still under the effects of the sedatives she had been given in the first place.

She was allowed a break and some lunch which again was mostly fruit and water. She wasn't sure how much longer she could go on without some solid protein. But it seemed that the morning of exercise was only half of the day—for the rest she went back to the dissecting room. She was strapped in firmly once more and left for a long time.

Since all of the people in the prison apart from her were wearing rubber suits it was hard to tell them apart, but the long wait was broken when a particularly tall person walked through. From his long and confident stride she guessed he must be a man. The others stopped what they were doing and watched him from the moment he entered.

He came over to where Melinda lay in the frame. He gestured with his hand, making a circular motion. An attendant leapt to the frame and turned it until she was hanging by the straps and staring at the ground with her back exposed.

Although she could not move her head she could see his feet as he moved closer. There was the clink of metal on metal, and a scrape as something was picked up from a metal tray.

As she lay there in her cell, recalling the final events before she blacked out—before they gassed her—she tried to focus. The memory was fuzzy and she had to concentrate. She remembered the metal sounds. She recalled his shoes as they shuffled that little bit closer. And then there was the intense pain as something sliced into her skin, along her spine.

She lay in the bed, the sheets becoming damp with her sweat. In the days she had been here, not one of them had spoken to her. The only real flesh she had seen was her jailer's hand. Nor had she spoken to them.

But then, in that moment, as the man cut directly into her skin, all the pent-up fear and anger condensed into a single scream: 'No!'

Her sensitive electrical sense was blinded with white. She did not know exactly what happened next because she could see nothing. People screamed, or cried out in pain. Then everything went quiet, even the constant background hum of the machines was silenced.

The acrid burning smell of plastic filtered through the air to her. A scalpel blade, red with blood, clattered to the floor beside her and the man crumpled to the ground.

It was moments later she smelled the first of the unpleasantness in the air. She tried to hold her breath but, since there was no escape, she had to breathe eventually and that's when she lost consciousness.

Now that she remembered the details she could feel the cut in her back, it stung and stretched when she moved. He could not have been very deep but the mere idea of someone cutting into her back while she was still alive...

No wonder she had responded. Then it came to her— she *had* responded. Though she had been completely tied she had done something, though she had no idea what it was. The idea was outrageous. And yet, it explained everything.

She lifted her hand above her face as she lay there on the bed, the electricity flashing between her nerves and muscles made a rhythmic pattern glowing dimly beneath her skin. Then she focused her mind. She remembered her own panic as the man had cut her open.

And from elbow to fingertip the light in her arm glowed.

Chapter 8

Mitchell

Special Agent Graham was seated at the desk of the hospital office he had commandeered. All he had to do was express the desire for an office to be put at his disposal, and it became so. Mitchell was not impressed. He knew the difference between power given willingly and that extracted by fear. You might say the Purity put the fear of God into everyone, but that wasn't the case: It put the fear of S.I.D into people, even though that was precisely what they were supposed to be against.

'You want a drink?' asked Mitchell into the silence that filled the room. Graham was working on a portable tablet; he appeared to be reviewing files. Mitchell, even though a Detective Inspector in a prestigious force like the Manchester Police, did not rate that level of technology. Instead he had just been waiting, looking out the window at the greyness.

'You think they have any coffee?' said Graham.

'Nothing decent.'

'Just some water.'

Mitchell left the room and closed the door after him. He didn't hurry; he wasn't even sure what they were waiting for. Although it was probably one of the tests to see whether Chloe had been infected with S.I.D.

Mitchell headed along the corridor. He knew that after this short amount of time the S.I.D test would almost certainly come back negative. But that was for the best, for Chloe at least; he had no desire for her to be locked up. But if she was infected it would certainly be a risk letting her go free. Normally she would be sent to Purity quarantine.

He pushed through the swing doors at the far end of the corridor which led to an atrium where he stood at the top balcony looking down. He could take the elevator but there really wasn't any hurry so he headed for the stairs. And then stopped suddenly.

There was a woman pacing backwards and forwards near the reception area. He squinted, wishing that his eyes were not ageing at the same rate as the rest of his body. The woman was dressed immaculately, certainly not like a teacher, but he recognised her: Sapphire Kepple.

She kept walking towards the exit, then stopping and retracing her steps in a slightly uncertain way as if she knew she ought to leave but didn't want to. Certainly curious behaviour. He wondered at the significance of the badge, and the level of interest that one Purity teacher might have in one relatively ordinary girl.

He made up his mind and headed for the stairs. As he descended he became visible to the atrium, and it was when he reached the first level she noticed him. The effect was dramatic. She had just been on her return journey, when she reversed direction headed for the exit and was gone. Mitchell thought that was probably for the best as well. He wasn't sure what Graham might have done if he found her loitering in the hospital.

He found the drinks machine. It did have coffee but there was no question that it would be of the lowest possible strength that could still legally be called 'coffee'. He pressed

the button to make the machine recognise his riffy, ordered
two bottles of water and scooped them out of the basket at
the bottom when they were delivered. Two glass bottles,
plastic ones were rare and expensive nowadays. People reused
the old ones since they never deteriorated, although they did
split eventually and could be crushed. Glass was easier to
make, mould, and recycle.

Mitchell took himself and the bottles up in the elevator,
seeing no reason to climb all those stairs. When he reached
the door of the office he heard raised voices. Then he
corrected himself—there was only one raised voice and it
wasn't Graham.

Putting one of the bottles under his arm, he opened the
door and went in without knocking. The doctor's diatribe
stopped mid-sentence as he broke her flow.

'DI Mitchell,' she hissed. 'I might have expected to see
a murderer like you here.'

'I'm only doing my job, Dr Majeed,' he said, crossing
the room and handing one of the bottles to Graham.

'Well, since you're so familiar with the end results of a
rampant S.I.D infection,' she said. 'Perhaps you'd like to
advise your associate that releasing someone on this evidence
is potential murder.' Mitchell sat down in a chair at the side of
the room and unscrewed his bottle. 'I'm just the tour guide,
Dr Majeed. Special Agent Graham is calling all the shots.'

She stared at him for a moment as if her glare might
drill through him and drop him dead where he sat. Then she
turned back to Graham. 'I can't stop you, can I?'

Graham, who had remained seated the whole time,
slowly climbed to his feet. 'No, Dr Majeed, you cannot.
When her tests come back negative, you will release her.'

Back in the car, Mitchell stared out into the grey. 'You're not releasing her out of the goodness of your heart.'

'Of course not,' said Graham. 'You and I want the same thing here, DI Mitchell. You want to apprehend the people who are kidnapping these girls, and I want to know why they are kidnapping these girls.'

Mitchell sat back and stared straight ahead, not really seeing the back of the passenger seat ahead of him. 'So you want to use her as bait.'

'I think it is the most efficient method, don't you?'

'It might be efficient, but it is not usual police policy to put an innocent at risk.'

Graham laughed. 'Well, lucky for you that I'm here then. Since I don't have those limitations, we'll get to the bottom of this considerably faster than you would with your simple police work.'

Mitchell did not respond.

Chapter 9

Yates

Yates steered the car in towards the kerb, mounted it and came to a halt. He killed the engine and stared down the road at the line of vans already parked.

'You know,' said Lament's disembodied voice, 'if you'd let me drive more, there would be less wear and tear on the vehicle.'

'No, thanks,' said Yates.

Men and women with microphones and cameras stood around open van doors chatting to one another with their coats pulled up around their necks to keep out the cold and damp. Yates wished it would rain heavily but it was one of those days where the dreariness hung in the air like its own cloud. The sky was slate grey and it was already going dark.

'Bloody vultures.'

'Well, the press is certainly on top of this one.' The artificial face of Lament emerged on the screen from its own cloud of grey.

'I wasn't talking to you.'

'Want me to get rid of them?' said Lament. 'I could suggest that there is something really interesting to be filmed elsewhere.'

Yates shook his head. 'That would just get us into trouble.'

'Speaking of which,' said Lament. 'You're going to be interviewing Chloe Dark's parents. Doesn't that conflict with the order to stay clear of that case?'

Yates opened the door, climbed out and grabbed his coat from the back. 'I am merely following a line of investigation related to the death of one Ali Najjar, chiropractor, who died accidentally last night.'

Lament started to say something else but Yates shut the door on him. The locks clicked on automatically. Yates stepped up onto the side of the road and started to walk in the direction of the Dark household. The members of the press jerked their heads in his direction like hyenas, preparing to pounce on their prey. Yates swung his coat behind him and began to shrug his arms into the sleeves. Merely by chance, this action opened his jacket to reveal his shoulder holster and gun. He doubted anyone there didn't recognise him, since he generally spoke for Mitchell, and they certainly recognised a gun when they saw one. They did not try to speak to him but watched hungrily as he walked past.

He used the knocker to announce his presence, firmly rapping it three times before letting it fall back. All the curtains at the front of the house had been closed. A wise precaution considering the powerful cameras owned by the besieging forces.

'Who is it?' It was a man's voice that Yates recognised.

'Detective Sergeant Yates,' he said loudly. 'If you wouldn't mind letting me in, Mr Dark.'

There was the rattling of the security chain and a bolt being drawn back. There were camera flashes from the street, but Mr Dark kept himself behind the door. Yates slipped in when the door was wide enough. It was slammed back behind him and the bolt locked in place.

'Let me take your coat,' said Mr Dark.

Yates shook his head. 'I won't be staying long; I just have a few questions.'

Mr Dark looked expectant, as if Yates was going to question him here in the hall without Mrs Dark.

'Is there somewhere we can sit?' said Yates.

Mr Dark jerked into sudden motion. Pushing past, he led the way back to the kitchen. Yates followed, taking in the dreary furniture and old decorations. The kitchen itself was clean and relatively new. Yates knew from what Lament had told him that Mr Dark ran the local FreakWatch, and had a fairly decent job.

The kitchen was empty.

'I would like Mrs Dark to be present as well,' said Yates.

'She's at the hospital with Chloe.'

Yates examined the room. He noted the photograph of the much younger Darks, with the baby he assumed to be Chloe and another couple whose faces looked familiar—the Voglers. So, the Darks knew the parents of one of the other girls who had been abducted. That was interesting.

'What can I do for you? I mean, I already gave a statement to the police.'

Yates fixed a smile on his face. 'I do understand, Mr Dark, however this is a separate enquiry into a murder.'

Yates did not really consider himself to be a vindictive man, but the wave of horror that went through Chloe's father at the mention of murder was impressive.

'Murder?' He blinked. 'Who's been murdered?'

Yates settled himself into one of the kitchen chairs, which gave Mr Dark permission to do the same.

'I don't know anything about murder. This is nothing to do with Chloe, is it?'

'It's only indirectly to do with your daughter, Mr Dark. I am not part of the abduction investigation. Can you tell me the name of your daughter's chiropractor?'

Unsurprisingly, Mr Dark looked at a complete loss. Yates imagined his wife was the one who kept track of that sort of thing.

'I'm afraid I don't know.'

'Perhaps Ali Najjar?'

'It does sound familiar. That could be it.'

Yates studied him. It didn't take a genius to see that the mention of the murdered man definitely meant something to him. He wondered how far the man would push ignorance considering the evidence available. 'We saw him last night, but then you already know that.'

Yates was almost disappointed, but it did make things run more smoothly. 'Yes, it's in your riffy records. And his.'

A look of horror came over Dark's face. 'He's the one who died? You're saying he was murdered? We didn't have anything to do with that.'

It did not take a lot of effort to make ordinary people say everything. All you had to do was stay silent and they filled in the gaps themselves.

'Was Chloe there?'

Yates leaned back in his chair and rested both hands on the table. 'I'm afraid I can't comment about Chloe; that would be too close to the other case. We have to keep them separate. But I have to ask you why you met with Ali Najjar in the department store last night?'

'We didn't go there to meet him,' said Mr Dark. 'There were thousands of people there. It was just a coincidence.'

Yates stood up, pressed his fists on the table, and leaned towards him. Dark was a large man but Yates had the authority, and he knew it. 'Mr Dark, we have already interviewed some of the other people in your vicinity when you met with Ali Najjar. They unanimously report that what went on between the two of you was more an altercation than a coincidence. Now, perhaps you could enlighten me as to the nature of your disagreement.'

'Clothes,' said Mr Dark. 'We wanted the same clothes. We almost didn't recognise him. You know what it's like when a place like Debenhams gets new stuff in: it's more like a riot. Everybody gets angry if they can't get what they need.'

Yates sat down. 'That doesn't seem too bad; why would you hide it?'

'I was embarrassed,' said Mr Dark. 'Someone in my position—I know it's not much to you but I have a place in the local community—if it was found out I was brawling in a shop sale what would people think?'

'And that's all it was?'

Dark nodded, as if he didn't trust himself with words. He was lying.

Yates got to his feet, smiling. 'Well, that's fine then, thank you very much Mr Dark. I'm so sorry to have trespassed on your time. I'm sure that your daughter will be fine and will be home very soon.'

'Is that all?' said Dark in surprise, also getting to his feet.

'Certainly, that's everything for now,' he said. 'Certainly everything I need to know. If anything else comes up about the problem we will be back in touch.'

And with that he headed to the front door, allowed Mr Dark to unlock it for him, and left in deep thought.

There's something strange about this whole thing.

Chapter 10

Chloe

There was a man in the back of the ambulance with Chloe and her mother as it headed back towards the house. He had a hat, which he cradled in his lap, a heavy overcoat, and was slightly unshaven. Chloe wasn't sure whether he was a policeman or someone attached to the hospital, but either way he was not very encouraging.

'This is not going to be very enjoyable,' he said. 'Your house is overrun with vermin.'

Her mother gasped. 'Vermin?'

'He means the press, mum,' said Chloe.

'Sorry, yes, the members of the press.' He pulled a newspaper from inside his coat and unfolded it. 'This morning's edition of the *Guardian.*'

Covering half of the tabloid sheet was a slightly fuzzy picture of Chloe. It was at least three years old and looked like a school photograph. The headline read THE GIRL WHO ESCAPED.

Chloe stared at it.

'Where did they get that picture from?' said her mother.

'It's like this, Mrs Dark,' he said and re-folded the paper, tucking it back inside his coat. 'Chloe, your daughter here, is now a celebrity.'

'Because I *didn't* get kidnapped?'

'Exactly. It makes you a hero. And that means the press are now encamped outside your house awaiting your return.' He leaned back, put his hands behind his head and stretched his legs. 'And that means it's going to be slightly unpleasant getting from the ambulance into the house.'

'Won't the police be there to help?' said her mother.

The man shook his head. 'Unfortunately she is not *that* much of a celebrity. The police have rather more important things to do, I should imagine, like finding out who the kidnappers are. So there's a few things you need to decide: Do you want to go in with a coat or blanket hiding your head? To prevent them from taking any further photographs.' He ticked off the points on his fingers, that was point number one. 'You could choose to stop and make a statement to the press, though that is not something I would recommend, on the whole. And thirdly we could go somewhere else completely.'

'Like where?' said Mrs Dark.

'Maybe a friend, or a hotel,' he said. 'Although, to be frank, I suspect most places would not make you welcome since there's always the risk of infection.'

'But Chloe was declared free of infection,' said her mother.

The man raised his hands almost as if he were appealing to some god. 'I know, it makes no sense whatsoever, but that's just the way it is. People panic when it comes to S.I.D.'

'So how are we going to get into the house?' said her mother.

Just at that moment the intercom with the driver's cab activated. 'Two minutes to arrival.'

'Well, they are not allowed to obstruct you,' said the man. 'But there might be some jostling. You are not required to speak to them as they have no authority. So my best advice to you is once you're out of the ambulance is just to walk directly to your house. Do not engage with them; do not listen to anything they are saying. If you do get touched, do not respond; just pretend it didn't happen and keep moving. Your husband has been apprised of the situation and I understand he will be in the house ready to unlock the door for you and let you in.'

'You're not coming with us?' said Chloe.

He shook his head with a sad smile. 'Not part of the job.' He turned his coat and rummaged in one of the pockets. 'Here,' he said and handed a bag to Chloe's mother. 'These are her medicines, the instructions are included.'

The ambulance took a right turn at speed and its sirens blasted out. The horn blared as well as if the driver was trying to get people out of the way. The man glanced forward though he couldn't see anything through the barrier. 'The reporters try to get in the way so the passengers will have further to walk,' he said. 'We have to be careful otherwise we'll be taking them back in place of you.' He laughed.

Chloe didn't think it was very funny.

When the ambulance came to a halt, Chloe could hear the noise from outside. There was banging on the ambulance itself, and what seemed like a huge crowd shouting her name.

Chloe grabbed her mother's hand. 'I'm scared.'

'No need to be scared,' said the man. 'I've done this a dozen times.' He headed towards the back of the ambulance.

'But you never get out of the ambulance,' said Chloe.

He frowned. 'Come on, let's be having you.' He gestured for them to follow. Chloe got up still holding her mother's hand. At this point she wasn't entirely sure who was reassuring whom—it was probably mutual.

Through the constant barrage of noise she thought she heard someone say 'who's your boyfriend?'

'The way this works,' said the ambulance man, 'is that I jump out and hold the door while you get down, then you set off to the house. I get back in, shut the door and off I go.'

Easy for you then, thought Chloe. But she had no time to think about anything else. He unlocked the door, and pushed it open. At least one person got slammed in the face and cried out, but that was all that could be heard over the shouting.

There was a semicircle of men and women with cameras calling to her. Chloe realised she had forgotten to get a blanket to cover herself but it was too late. Already lights were flashing, and above the crowd drones floated back and forward. The man jumped out and the crowd backed off a little.

Chloe's mother went first. The distance to the ground was awkward and she stumbled slightly as she landed but the ambulance man caught her arm and supported her. Chloe grabbed the side of the door and stepped down directly behind her mother. The racquet redoubled as she exited the ambulance.

Instinctively she grabbed the belt of her mother's coat and hung on, keeping her head down.

Behind her Chloe made out the ambulance door slamming shut and the engine coming to life. Her mother stepped forward and the crowd parted. The man had been right about one thing, the reporters did seem reluctant to touch them. As the two of them moved it was as if they were in a bubble; the members of the press parted before them, and enclosed ranks after them. It was surreal.

The constant noise was so great she could barely make out a single word and the fact her name was being used so often made it blur and become a meaningless mush of *kl, oh* and *eee*. They reached the gate, its squeak distinct against the wash of sound. The gate seemed to be a barrier they would not cross. They massed against the wall and did not seem shy about going into the garden next door.

Chloe was terrified they might somehow attack and consume the house like locusts. Her mother was reaching up to ring the doorbell when there was a movement in the glass inside. The door opened almost magically before them. They slipped inside and it shut behind them.

The noise cut off, replaced by the sound of locks and bolts being engaged.

'Hi Dad,' she said turning to him.

'I'm so glad you are safe,' he said. But he didn't hug her. He moved awkwardly to the side as if trying to avoid her and that hurt more than anything. She knew what it was: she had been touched by a freak and he was scared.

But whether it was for his health or his reputation she was not sure.

Chapter 11

Yates

DS Yates sat in the passenger seat of the police car and allowed Lament to steer it towards its destination. He didn't like it, he preferred to be in control, but this was probably going to be the most delicate of his interviews and he'd stayed up waiting for Ria. He smiled for a moment and then came back to reality. He was not supposed to be investigating the kidnappings but he needed to talk to Ellen Lomax because Mitchell needed her information and Graham seemed in no hurry.

There were plenty of rundown parts of Manchester nowadays; in fact the majority of it was completely empty. But some were worse than others and this was one of the bad ones. Not bad because there was a great deal of crime, but simply that it oozed hopelessness. As if to reinforce his opinion, it started to rain as the car pulled up by the kerb. The street had probably been quite prosperous in the old days; it was wide and there were trees on each side of the road. Each house had a small garden at the front, and probably a larger one behind. They were terraces, but of decent quality.

But most of the gardens were untended and overgrown. The houses had smashed or boarded-up windows. You could tell which were occupied: They were the ones that still had the majority of the glass intact—probably cannibalised from the other buildings. Nobody had repainted the woodwork on any house in years.

In the old zoning laws, which were still technically valid, this would have been classed as a smoke-free zone. But again the occupied houses tended to have a stream of smoke emerging from the chimneys.

'This it then?' said Yates.

'Obviously,' said Lament. 'Ellen Lomax is inside. In fact, if I am not much mistaken she's peering through the curtains at us right now.'

Yates glanced to his left. There was a momentary movement of what might once have been white net curtains.

'Right, I won't be long.'

'Mitchell and Graham are a long way from here,' said Lament. 'I'll honk the horn twice if they're coming this way.'

'Jesus,' muttered Yates, as he climbed out of the car and slammed the door. 'What a joker.'

He didn't have a hat and hadn't brought an umbrella so pulled his collar up round his neck and looked about. There was nothing important here. There was a button for a bell and, on the off-chance, he pressed it. Unsurprisingly he heard nothing from inside but, through the frosted glass, he made out the darker shadow of someone heading towards the door.

'Who is it?' The voice of Ellen Lomax was thin and lacking in any substance.

'Police, Mrs Lomax. If you wouldn't mind letting me in, I have a few questions.'

The figure behind the door did not move for a full count of five. There was the sound of the chain being unhooked and the turning of the key. Moments later she opened the door, and air barely warmer than outside moved gently across his skin.

He glanced up at the rain then back at the woman in her threadbare dress. 'Mind if I come in?' The question was rhetorical. He stepped forward and she backed away, not scared, just letting him get past.

He stood in the dark hallway as she shut the door, and sniffed. There was a strange odour about the place, a kind of animal smell but nothing he could identify. There had been no dog bounding up to the door or barking. Perhaps she had cats; little old women who lived alone often had cats.

'Please, come through,' she said, and led the way to the front room. If he had been expecting a room unchanged for thirty years he wasn't disappointed. *Strange really, she is only in her forties or fifties at most,* He should have checked that.

'Please, sit down, Mrs Lomax.' Standard procedure was to get them sitting. He would remain standing so he controlled and dominated the room.

She did so.

'Thursday morning, you were at the junction of Barlow Moor Road and Maitland Avenue, opposite Southern Cemetery.'

'Yes?' She looked nervous, but then they always looked nervous. Everyone had secrets and they were usually unimportant.

'Did anything of interest occur when you were on that corner, perhaps just before?' He asked in the least leading way that he could.

'I don't think so,' she said. 'Can I make you a cup of tea?'

He knew she couldn't afford tea, let alone coffee, so he shook his head. 'Perhaps a vehicle?'

'I don't think so,' she said.

He decided to take a different tack. 'What were you doing in the area at that time?'

'Have I done something wrong?'

'If you could just answer the question, Mrs Lomax.'

She shifted slightly in the chair as if she was uncomfortable. 'I was visiting my husband, and my son.'

She must have noticed he was frowning because she added. 'I try to visit them once a week, when I can get the timeslot. They died.'

He nodded. She was someone who had lost her family during the bad times. Just another one of so many. The smell was bothering him. It was very strong and he couldn't make out what it was. 'Would you mind if I use your toilet?' he said. 'I'm afraid I've been on the move all day.'

His question resulted in her rubbing her hands together and hesitating—whatever she was hiding must be upstairs. He could see she desperately wanted to refuse him but it was not something you could deny, especially to a policeman.

'Upstairs,' she said in a rush. 'Keep going round to the left, it's at the front.' He knew he wouldn't have time to do any kind of a search—it wasn't as if she was being kept busy by his partner—so he would have to be quick.

The stairs were carpeted but it was worn like everything else. The same went for the landing. There were three doors in total: one to a small box room at the front which appeared to be the bedroom she used, and one other door that was shut tight. It was locked. The final one was the bathroom.

The smell was definitely stronger up here.

He checked through the bathroom cabinet which contained the barest minimum you might expect. There was an immersion water heater in an airing cupboard. Stone cold. At least she still had running water and the toilet worked. There was nothing here that suggested anything other than a little old lady. So what could she be hiding? Maybe she had the dead bodies of her son and husband in the bedrooms. Maybe that was the smell. He gave a little laugh. No, after all this time they wouldn't smell at all.

He came back downstairs and took a quick glance into the kitchen. It was clean and there was no obvious evidence she was feeding anybody else, and that included the lack of animal bowls on the floor. No pets.

'Well, that's it for now, Mrs Lomax,' he said loudly from the hall. She came bustling out.

'You don't have anything else to ask me?' The look of relief on her face was obvious.

'Not for now,' he said casually. 'Just routine. You didn't notice the van then.'

The hunted look reappeared on her face. 'Van?'

He wandered to the front door.

'Oh yes,' he said. 'The van that was carrying the kidnapped girl, Melinda Vogler.'

A look of horror crossed her face as she absorbed that information. 'But,' he said, 'if you didn't notice anything it doesn't matter.'

By the time Yates had got back into the car and settled himself, the front door was shut and Ellen Lomax was cut off from the world again. Yates glanced at the door of her house as the car pulled away.

'Did she see the van?' asked Lament.

'Oh yes,' said Yates, 'she saw it, and she is hiding something significant. At least it's important to her. So important she's lying to the police.'

Chapter 12

Chloe

She felt numb. Her mother had made her a high-strength coffee, the sort they only kept for special occasions. Chloe had protested.

'This is a very special occasion,' her mother had said. But she didn't make one for herself, or for Chloe's dad. He sat on the other side of the table while her mother sat beside her. The conversation had been stilted. Chloe couldn't understand what he was thinking, or rather she completely understood it, but how could he be like that?

At the earliest opportunity she escaped to her room. She said it was because she was tired and ached. And that wasn't even a lie. In truth she needed to get away from her father and the broken affection that lay on the table between them.

But now she could not even lie down as the events of the previous night ran through her head in a loop. She paced back and forth. The men who tried to take her, the men who had kidnapped Melinda. It was all buzzing away inside.

She forced herself to sit at her desk facing the terminal. The names of her three friends directly in front of her. Normally she would have clicked the button that connected all four of them but one of them was Melinda and she could not bear to think of the pain she would cause Melinda's mother if she rang in like that.

Instead she selected Ashley and Kavi separately, and called them.

The borders around the images of her friends quivered and the sound of the two subdued bell tones rang out. She waited. She did not think it was her imagination that the time they took to answer was longer than usual.

Ashley's face appeared first. She was looking off to the side and Chloe thought she probably had a drink in her hand—she knew that Ashley drank alcohol. Her mum and dad let her. Under the circumstances, who could blame her?

'Hey,' said Chloe.

Ashley flashed her smile, her teeth were perfect. 'Hey,' Ashley looked as if she was studying Chloe's face. 'Wow, you look really rough.'

'Thanks.'

Chloe's face moved to the side and Kavi materialised in the space. 'Oh my god, Chloe, what happened?'

Chloe really didn't feel like talking about it, she just wanted to see them to remind herself what reality was. But she knew her friends deserved some sort of explanation. So she related the details once more, just as she had to the police on more than one occasion, and her mother. It was at that point she realised her dad hadn't even asked.

'And they let you out of quarantine?' said Ashley. Chloe wasn't sure but it almost sounded accusing, as if it was unfair that she should be allowed out immediately after being in contact with a freak.

'Yeah, they did.'

'The Purity must be going soft.' This time there was no question, she was pissed off.

'Look, Ash, I didn't get any say in it. My guess is they want the kidnappers to try again.'

Ashley looked suitably horrified at the idea, but Kavi nodded her head. 'Yes, that's exactly what they would do. You're bait.'

'Shit,' said Ashley.

The three of them sat in silence for a few moments. Kavi looked concerned but then that was a natural state for her face. Chloe felt herself withdrawing into herself again.

'So you totally beat them off,' said Ashley. 'That's awesome.'

Chloe blinked, was it really possible that Ashley was thinking of someone else except herself? It hardly seemed likely.

'We got some extra homework today,' said Ashley. 'I was wondering...'

Chloe burst out laughing, and Kavi was not far behind. Ashley looked surprised, and slightly hurt.

'Why are you laughing?'

It was still early evening but Chloe changed into her pyjamas, wrapped her dressing gown around her, and headed into the bathroom.

Ashley's right, she thought as she stared in the mirror. She really did look terrible. If her skin had been white she would look deathly pale, but the bruise on the side of her face was deep purple. The whole of her right arm ached, and the shoulder on that side looked twice as big as her left where it was inflamed.

She stepped onto the scales. They were an old mechanical set because the battery powered one was so hard to recharge. The numbers spun and finally settled. She stared. It was registering at slightly under three stone. She did the calculations in her head: nineteen kilos. There must be something wrong with them. She stepped off.

Her back was still aching—it had never stopped despite the manipulation, and now the painkillers. She tried to stretch her arms to relieve it but too much movement just made it hurt more.

She wanted to look at her back and there was a way. The small cabinet above the wash basin was mirrored and if she angled it just right, it reflected the image from the full-length mirror. It took a few moments of fiddling and then she tried to twist to make the bathroom light cast shadows to show where there were bumps. It didn't look good; her right shoulder blade looked far smoother and more rounded than it should be. And, if she wasn't much mistaken, there were a couple of small lumps either side of her spine. That must have happened when she landed hard inside the carriage.

There was no point worrying about it; it would take time to heal and she would just have to put up with it until then.

Chapter 13

Jason

After the policeman had left, Jason Lomax climbed back through his window into his room and lay on his bed. He could smell the man. Not just his general scent but every detail of what he'd eaten that day, the car he had been sitting in and hints of the people he had met. Including the woman he had been with, who was so distinct Jason would know her if she was close.

But the man's scent made Jason want to run. He represented everything Jason was afraid of. Policemen were death.

Of course, his mother had fussed over him once she was sure they were safe. She had waited half an hour before she started moving around. She had explained to Jason more times than he could remember about how she had the chip in her head which meant those in power could track her every move. He was not entirely sure how true that was; could they really tell *exactly* where everyone was all of the time?

It was clear enough they couldn't tell where *he* was.

He had planned to go back to the fights tonight. They were busier at the weekends which made it that much easier to pick pockets, and collect physical money. It would take him over three hours to make the trip since he had to do it on foot, while avoiding any person or machine that might notice that he did not have a riffy.

He didn't go downstairs to eat when his mother called him. He listened to her plaintive calls but ignored them. It wasn't that he didn't love his mother, no, it was the reverse. All he had was his guilt for depriving her of food all these years. That was why he went out to find his own, and why he refused to eat the little that was provided for her by the state.

As the light began to fade around four o'clock, he got up and dressed in his outdoor gear. He stood by the window and watched as the sun went down. The sun was his enemy; it was only at night he could risk walking among others without them seeing his face.

He opened the window, slipped out, and closed it tight behind him.

The air was cold and his clothes were thin, but he didn't really feel it. His destination was almost due north from his mother's house in Burnage, up the east side of Manchester through empty estates that stood like lakes of houses with residents living in clumps like islands. He knew intellectually, at one time, the place had been teeming, but it was not something he could really imagine. Besides he wasn't one of them. He didn't weep for the loss of humankind. If any of the few people he passed on the way had even the slightest inkling of his nature their only thought would be to kill him. Or, at best, run.

What was it that guy who smelled like a dog said? Jason was like them, they were like each other? That they were freaks, but not freaks?

Others? More than just the dog?

Jason knew he wasn't one of those S.I.D monsters because, if he had been, he would have died 16 years ago, and probably his mother too. He had been born like this and, in some ways, he couldn't even understand why his mother had not abandoned him. Sometimes he wished she had.

Once past the area known as Hyde, it was uphill all the way. Not that it was particularly steep, and there were a few dips, but this was the way into the hills and the land just kept rising. The quality of the roads changed too; the ones further down at least got some repairs, but up here there were only the farms, and agricultural machines did not need decent roads.

Finally he reached the ancient industrial estate converted for the ancient human pleasure of watching animals fight and kill each other. It disgusted him.

He entered by the same route through the ceiling, as before. There was no action; it was too early. So he waited, resting on the cold girder as the frigid night seeped through his skin.

He might have dozed because when he came back to full awareness the noise level had increased dramatically. A fight was in progress though he was not in the right place to see it. All he could hear were the cheers and jeers of the spectators intermingled with grunts and slobbering mouth movements of something vile.

The floor below was full, the men packed tight.

Jason was stiff from being stuck so long in one position. The air was less cold but it stank of human sweat, and base desire. He paused. Was it too busy? He didn't like crowds. He shrugged off the concern. Denser crowds made it easier; he could reach through a gap and rifle through a pocket. If they felt anything they would just put it down to the crowd. And if they realised what was happening he would already be away before any alarm could be raised.

Just as he had two days earlier, he made his way along the central girder to the far end of the building above the latrines—that smelled even worse—and the rooms for the women.

The toilets were empty and he descended into a cubicle. He pulled his hoodie over his head to ensure his face was in shadow and slipped out into the melee.

He did not push into the densest part of the crowd; there was not enough room to move. He kept just within the edges where the spectators were like particles of matter. They detached from the main group and gravitated to the tables. Or the other way. The density of the crowd's edge was enough to keep him hidden, but not enough to stop him from working.

As far as he could tell, the other one—the one who had spoken to him—was not here. Jason would not risk coming back another day. He would find other fights where he could pillage the pockets of stupid humans. There was no end of them.

Jason squeezed between two men shouting at the cage, their voices hoarse, their bodies sweaty and stinking. He glanced ahead from the shadows of his hood. A man was looking in his direction—no, he realised with a shock, the man was looking directly at him. A yellow armband marked him as security. Jason allowed the two men to squeeze him back the way he had come. Their bodies closing up to hide him.

He needed to leave.

His heart sped up. The world slowed down. He had been moving away from his usual exit. Jason whipped round to head back. The movement of the bodies around him became a slow dance. Without conscious thought he calculated their positions and their motions—at least, as far as he could see.

A gap was opening deeper into the crowd, more or less in the direction he wanted to go. He moved into it, knowing that as far as the normal humans were concerned he was barely more than a blur. If he avoided contact there was no reason for them to notice him.

The trick he had played on the one that smelled like a dog—grabbing the pie from his pocket—was something he had practised when he was young to make his mother laugh. Before he realised how different he truly was.

He jumped as a drone scooted across the room, floating above the milling crowds. It paused close to where he was, and a glance up showed the glint of a camera lens pointed at him.

In the blink of an eye he pulled a coin from his pocket, took careful aim—an action taking less than a second—and launched it, not at the camera, but into one of the rotors.

'Hey!' said the man beside him. Noticing him for the first time.

Jason did not pause. Another gap was developing ahead. That the man would see his unnaturally fast movement could not be helped. He was closer to his goal as the coin struck the rotor. Jason heard the whine change.

The next space opened and he dived forward. The sounds of the battling freaks was close now. His escape route had taken him deep into the densest part of the crowd. He did not dare look behind, because it would reveal his face. He squeezed into a small gap and pushed. He hated coming into contact with people like this. The touch of them made his skin crawl.

Then the person to his left leaned heavily into him. Crushing. Jason smelled the acrid scent of ionised air and burnt skin. They had shot at him but missed. But he could get trapped under the collapsing body.

Jason went down on all fours. The crush of people should prevent the person falling. The floor was sticky and stank of old spilt beer. There was a slippery top layer of fresh booze and sweat. He ignored it and scurried forward. The legs moved slow in comparison to him and he made headway.

Around him the noise level was increasing. Not with shouts for the fight but screams of anger and fear. It was a garbled mess of acrimony and pain. As if some multi-headed, many-legged monster was being attacked.

Someone trod heavily on his ankle and crushed it before slipping off. Weight was piling on top of him. There was nowhere for him to go. Someone's heel ground into his left hand.

Bodies piled up and flattened him. He could barely breathe. Around him there was still swearing intermingled with moans of pain. There was something or someone lying across his back crushing all the breath from his lungs. He couldn't inhale.

For desperate seconds he fought to stay conscious, to keep moving. Then black descended.

Chapter 14

Mitchell

Despite the proximity of the large blank walls of the school, the slamming of the two car doors did not echo. Mitchell and Graham made their way up the steps and into the main entrance hall. There may have been no echo in the outside damp but, once inside, the sound of their shoes reverberated from the clean, polished surfaces. The school reception was off to the right and they headed to it.

'I am here to see Sapphire Kepple,' said Graham. Mitchell noted he had not even checked before he rolled out the name and, in his experience, that meant only one thing: They knew each other.

The woman behind the desk checked the timetables and looked up. 'She's teaching if you'd like to wait.'

'I will see her now,' said Graham. 'I take it she has an office of her own.'

The receptionist simply nodded.

'You will direct me to it and you will send her there immediately.' Before she could respond Graham turned to Mitchell. 'I am afraid you cannot be party to this interview,' he said. 'This is a Purity matter.'

It didn't even occur to Mitchell to argue, since it would only be a waste of time. 'I'll wait in the car.' *Which at the very least,* he thought, *will give me an opportunity to talk to Lament, and perhaps Yates.*

Sapphire

She was trembling as she approached her office. The first she had known of the summons was the arrival of one of the other teachers to take over her class. Her replacement hadn't known what it was about, only that somebody important had come to see her. That alone made her nervous, so she had risked the delay and gone by reception.

She saw DI Mitchell sitting in the car and she knew immediately something was up. When Mrs Henderson told her about the visitor, and how his name had not appeared on the information screen but that his authority was the highest possible, she had asked the receptionist to describe the man.

Sapphire was not entirely sure her legs would be able to stay the distance as she approached her office. *Oh god, it's Chris.*

She paused at her office door and knocked. The command to enter made her feel as if she were a child again, one of the children in the school summoned to the Principal's office. Almost of its own volition her hand grabbed the door handle, turned it and pushed the door open.

He was standing on the other side of her desk, in the place she would normally sit. He was closing one of the drawers. She knew there was nothing incriminating in there but still it made her shiver, and she knew he had done it deliberately. If he had intended her not to see he wouldn't have invited her in so quickly after she knocked. It was just one of his tactics. Yet the fact that she knew made absolutely no difference to its effect.

He looked at her, his face completely impassive. 'Hello, Saffie.'

She stumbled into the room. It was as if, after all this time, she simply lost control of herself again.

'Close the door.'

She shut it then put her hands behind her back and looked down at the ground; she wasn't worthy to look at him.

'Oh, come, come,' he said with a reassuring tone that had the reverse effect. He was like a tiger stalking her. 'We're past that stage in our relationship. In fact, we no longer have that relationship at all.'

She heard the words but they did not carry the meaning he seemed to intend. There was no way she was able to shake him free of her mind.

'Sit down, Saffie.'

She looked to the available seats: the sofa where she had sat with Chloe before, her own chair behind her desk but that was barred to her, and the hardback chair in front of the desk. She moved towards the sofa.

'No, Saffie, here.' He pointed at the chair in front of her desk.

Keeping her head down, she moved to it and sat with her feet and knees slightly apart, hands resting on her knees, head down. The part of her mind that remained rational and independent noted that despite his statement about that part of their relationship being over, he couldn't resist enforcing his will on her.

'So, are you pleased to see me?'

'Of course, master.' She cursed herself, but it had just slipped out. It horrified her to know how easily she could return to that state. She tried again, knowing he was laughing at her. 'I am pleased to see you, Special Agent Graham.' Although she had her head down she could see, with her peripheral vision, when he sat in the chair behind her desk. The chair creaked slightly under his weight.

'There, that's much better,' he said. 'So how has this assignment been?'

'I am doing the best I can,' she said. 'I am teaching them everything they need to know, and everything they should know.'

'But you fail to notice the freaks.'

It wasn't a question and she found that she could not answer. Did he mean Chloe? Was there something he knew that she didn't? Or was it the other girl? Or was he just making it all up to put her under pressure? Not that he had to make anything up to apply leverage.

'The Vogler girl is unquestionably a freak,' he said. 'How is it you did not notice?' The tone in his voice became harder and she felt a tingling in her back at the expectancy of being whipped.

'There was nothing visible to see, sir.'

'And what about this Chloe Dark?'

Somehow the mention of Chloe triggered the strength inside her. She raised her eyes to look at him. He was just looking back at her with his lips in a half-smile that carried no humour, only pain. 'Chloe is not a freak.'

There was a momentary battle of wills as she looked at his face and he stared back commandingly. It was not a battle she could ever win; all she could manage was to look down more slowly than she might have done in the past. 'Chloe is not a freak,' she said again.

'You're not reverting to your old ways?' he said.

She shook her head, scared that if she opened her mouth her words would say nothing but the truth.

'You know,' he said. 'I was opposed to this placement for you, but it was not my decision to make.'

There was no question there that she could answer safely, though he had told her at the time he didn't think being in a school would be good for her. But the Purity administration had disagreed with him. There was a job to be done, she was qualified to do it, and that was all they needed to know.

'Have you been up to your tricks again?'

'No, sir.'

'Are you sure?'

She nodded probably with more force than she needed. 'I'm sure,' she said hoarsely.

She flinched as he stood up suddenly, and cursed herself for reacting. She began to tremble as he walked out from behind the desk and stepped behind her. She knew he had leaned over because she could feel his breath on her left cheek.

'What have you told Chloe Dark about the DN-Cadr-A?'

'I—'

'And don't lie to me, Saffie; I saw the badge you left in her room.'

'She's intelligent, a fighter, a leader,' she said. 'I told her about it because I want her to be the youth leader. I wanted her to think about it.'

He was still there by her ear, still leaning over her. She felt that if he touched her her heart would simply stop.

'So tell me, Saffie, which should I put on your record: the fact that you released information before the embargo was lifted?' He moved to the other side of her head and whispered in her other ear. 'Or that you are trying to seduce female students again? You know what that would mean.'

Her mind was frozen. It was as if he had put a clamp on her thinking processes and tightened it until nothing, not a single thought, could be expressed. It was at that moment she realised her eyes were closed, and she could not even remember when she had shut them. It took all her concentration to force them open again and stare at the desk in front of her.

'I shouldn't have told her about the youth group.'

She felt, rather than saw, his presence move away from her.

'Very well,' he said, 'I'll put that on your record. I released Chloe Dark, and I want you to keep an eye on her. These kidnappers will undoubtedly try again. Their attacks are not random; they want specific girls. As soon as you find out anything, Saffie, be sure to let me know, won't you?'

She said *yes* but it was so quiet he might not even have heard it. But then he didn't have to, he knew she would do anything he said without question. *Anything at all.*

She heard the door behind her open, his footsteps leaving, and the door close behind her.

Her tears were a flood but it was some time before she realised that she could use her hands.

She was not tied to the chair. It just felt that way.

Chapter 15

Dog

As far as Dog was concerned the biggest problem with being off the grid was the lack of easy transport. He had been lying in the dreary room that he regularly used to doss down for the night, in a set of empty terraces in the west of the city.

There were plenty of lowlifes and poor people here, plus those animals that had made a comeback after humanity had lost its fight against the virus. But as far as he was concerned it was empty of anyone in authority, or anyone who might report him to authority. And that's what mattered.

When he first took up residence, he had sealed off the upper floor room. He bricked up the doorway and the window, but cut a large hole in the roof which he covered with a trapdoor. A set of stone slabs in the corner meant he could have a fire, though it wasn't too cold yet. It wasn't even too damp.

Still, the thought of Mr Mendelssohn's home in Knutsford was considerably more attractive, and he had been invited. Just not today.

Before dawn he mounted the ladder up through the ceiling, crossed through several adjoining buildings and then down into a back garden that was so overgrown it was more like a jungle. He could smell cat, and rats, and there was a stream not far away which boasted a whole host of additional wildlife. He had dined on meat he caught and cooked himself more times than he could count. A good burger was better though.

Even though he couldn't take any official transport, that didn't mean he had to walk. He headed through the dark to the nearest main road which carried traffic from the centre of Manchester south through Timperley and Altrincham—both almost completely deserted—and then out to Knutsford: the playground of the rich. As he understood it, it had always been the home of the rich.

There were self-drive trucks on the road, and the mostly redundant drivers never paid much attention to what was going on around them unless they had to. It was easy to wait at traffic lights—he always laughed at that, there was so little traffic at this time of day the lights were completely pointless. A truck would pull up and, once he was sure it was going where he wanted, all he had to do was climb on the back.

And half an hour later he was close to his destination. Unfortunately the lights at the junction where he wanted to get off were green and his vehicle barrelled through them, though still keeping to the speed limit. Choosing his moment he leapt off backwards and came to a running halt, watching the red lights of the vehicle disappear into the distance. It had been one of the long-distance trucks and was heading for the motorway.

It was always risky in Knutsford. Unlike the city you couldn't take the chance of running through backyards because security was everywhere. The richer they were, the more worried they were about losing what they had.

The rain had started as he was coming out of the city proper and he was already soaked through. Dawn turned the blacks into greys but everything was glistening wet. Mr

Mendelssohn's house was a quarter mile away, hidden down a back road in its own grounds among half a dozen other similar buildings.

It took him fifteen minutes to negotiate the back alleys and track, to come out a short distance from the main gate to Mr Mendelssohn's estate. One advantage of the paranoia-driven security was that every driveway entrance was hidden from the other houses. He reached the gate. If he'd had a riffy they would have known he was there already. So instead he knocked.

He took a few steps back and glanced up at where the security camera turned and twisted to point at him. He grinned and gave the guard a wave. There was a grinding of an electric motor, the sound of bolts being drawn back, and one of the two massive wooden gates moved back slightly. He slipped in and it slammed back almost instantly.

A pale round face peered out from the guardhouse.

'Jeez, Brian,' said Dog. 'Watch it with those gates, you could have had my tail off.'

The guardhouse was a small wooden shed with a door and window. The door was yanked open and Brian Ekings, in his grey security uniform always tight around the middle, stared out through misting glasses.

'You've not got a tail. Anyway, how'd you know it was me?'

Dog grinned. 'Aftershave, mate.'

Brian frowned, and rubbed his beard. 'I can't afford aftershave.'

'Must be something else then,' Dog said with a shrug and closed the gap to the door with the rain still beating on

- 247 -

his head. 'You going to let me in?' Brian retreated further into the shed, Dog followed.

'Stay by the door, you'll get water everywhere.'

Pushing the door shut, Dog leaned against it and dripped onto the wooden floor. The end of the shed where he stood had a couple of small cupboards and a shelf with a toaster and microwave both looking the worse for their age. The end that Brian had retreated to was filled with monitors and other surveillance equipment but rather than looking at a screen, the security guard was studying a sheet of paper on a clipboard. He looked up.

'You're not on the list for this morning,' he said slightly shaking his head. 'Can't let you in if you're not on the list.'

'Yeah, but you're not gonna make me go back out in that, are you?' Dog jerked his thumb at the door and then pointed at the ceiling where the rain continued to thrum down.

Brian shook his head more firmly. 'Mr Mendelssohn's rules, Dog. He'll have my guts for garters if I let you in before your time.'

'I don't think your guts would make very good garters,' said Dog seriously.

'Oh, very funny. It don't change nothing, can't let you go up to the house.'

'You mean you'll let me stay here,' said Dog, 'that's really kind of you, Brian, thanks very much, appreciate it.'

Brian looked for a moment as if he was going to object, Dog jumped in. 'Shall I make us a cuppa?'

Mr Mendelssohn went out about half an hour later. Dog stayed behind the door as the black limousine crunched up the driveway. Brian operated the gates and noted the details in his logbook using real ink in real pen on real paper.

'Mr Mendelssohn really doesn't like computers, does he?' said Dog.

Brian set the doors to close. They wound shut and the mechanical locks clicked into place. Brian glanced up at his guest. 'Computers get hacked,' he said. 'Or viruses.'

It took another two hours before Brian became so annoyed at Dog he allowed him to head up to the house, alerting the other guards to his presence. He even lent Dog his umbrella.

Dog followed the gravel drive past manicured lawns and carefully organised flowerbeds. The cleverly placed trees hid the house from the driveway. Dog took deep breaths through his nose, tasting the scents. Out here in the country, you could barely smell the decay of civilisation. Of course Mr Mendelssohn had his own sort of decay, thought Dog, as he avoided staring at the armed men placed at strategic locations on his approach. These men weren't armed with Burners. Their guns, like Brian's, were designed to kill and their owners knew how to use them.

The house itself was nearly seventy years old and sprawled across the valley, bridging the stream that ran there. There was one wall which was much older than the rest, maybe 400 years, and the way the stream split into two channels made him think it had been a mill once upon a time. The fact the house was called Lower Mill tended to confirm it.

He was searched before he was allowed in but that wasn't unusual and he didn't carry any weapons anyway. The one thing he didn't do either at the door or back with Brian was mention Mendelssohn's daughter, Delia. But she was the real reason he was here early—he wasn't fooling himself.

The first stage of his plan had been partially fulfilled in Brian's shed where he had managed to get a few things to eat, even if only dry sandwiches and a bit of toast. Once in the house he headed directly for the kitchen. The cook was there and she would only allow him a cheese sandwich. But that was fine because the cheese was a big slab of Cheddar and the bread thick enough to make a good door wedge. He ate it voraciously.

Feeling a bit more human, or at least what passed for human with him, he headed for the swimming pool. It was the middle of the day, Delia was home (as always) and that was the only place she would be. He stepped through the doorway and leaned against the wall. The surface of the pool was barely moving, almost like glass.

A dark form moved beneath the surface as if it were a wave, undulating through the water. The pool wasn't big, perhaps only 30 feet, and she covered the length in just a few seconds. When she reached the far end, she tumbled over and thrust away from the wall, once more sliding swiftly through the liquid.

And so it went on, backwards and forwards, backwards and forwards, one end to the other, barely making the surface ripple.

Dog glanced at the clock; if he was not much mistaken he'd been watching for perhaps fifteen minutes before the undulations changed. The dark shape twisted in the water, and thrust upwards. She burst like an explosion from the water, showering the poolside with glittering droplets.

Delia Mendelssohn landed on her feet. The flood of water she had brought with her cascaded back into the pool. Within moments her skin looked dry, though a little shiny. The flattering, deep blue swimsuit glistened. Delia was well muscled but not excessively so. She reached back and twisted her hair, pulling it over her shoulder. The light caught her, emphasising her curves—Dog knew it was no accident.

Delia glanced at him. 'If my dad knew you were watching me like that, he'd bloody kill you.'

Dog grinned.

Chapter 16

Yates

DS Yates cradled his coffee in both hands as he walked the long straight corridor to the office where he and half a dozen other detectives had their desks. The door at the far end opened with a slight squeak and allowed him through. In the last set of desk reassignments he'd managed to bag one by the window, even if it did look out onto the car park. Between that concrete monstrosity and his building the street below ran straight to the law courts. The sky had been clear overnight. It was cold and the coffee mug was not thawing out his fingers.

He didn't switch on his terminal, but instead stared at the blank screen without even seeing it. How was he supposed to be finding the girls without the Purity's knowledge? The only lead he had was a dead chiropractor.

Why had they gone after the chiropractor? Obviously because he knew something and they were afraid he would tell. And he had told somebody; he had told the Darks. But they weren't talking. And he really couldn't pursue that line too; the connection with the kidnappings was just too close. He'd been pushing it by interviewing Ellen Lomax.

All right, so the only way he could proceed was on the murder of the chiropractor. A fake riffy, electrical lorries exploding: there was a lot of science here, none of which he understood.

'Penny for your thoughts.'

Yates barely jumped. 'Morning, sir. The Purity let you off your leash then?' Yates turned in his chair but didn't bother to get up. Mitchell loomed over him.

'You might say we are in a holding pattern.'

'A holding pattern?'

Mitchell glanced around, found an unoccupied chair and dragged it over to Yates's desk. He sat in it and leaned back. 'Agent Graham is waiting for something to happen to Chloe Dark.'

Yates pushed himself back slightly and turned to face his boss. 'He's not concerned he's putting her at risk?'

Mitchell gave a noncommittal grunt. 'How are you doing on your investigation?'

'Well, the dead therapist spoke to the Darks. Mr Dark claimed it was an argument over clothes. The woman, Ellen Lomax, who was on the corner when Melinda Vogler got nabbed, she's hiding something too. The assassin who killed the therapist doesn't have a riffy, but used a fake one and knew how to blow up something that shouldn't be able to explode. So, on the whole, I've got a lot of pieces and none of them join together.'

'Yes,' said Mitchell looking away and out of the window to where the sun was reflecting off the Utopia Genetics building that stood high above the rest of the city. 'What's your next move?'

'Get some more information and see if I can't get some new ideas.'

Mitchell climbed to his feet and slid the chair back to where he found it. He scanned the office, less than half the desks were occupied. 'Well, seems fair enough, what sort of information were you thinking of getting?'

'I thought I'd start with science.'

The woman at reception had directed him to the third floor of the University Department of Cybernetic Interfaces. According to Lament, Professor Hudd was his best option for information.

He pushed his way through the door into room 2.10. It was a small lecture theatre that could seat a hundred people. There were just three students sitting at the front with their lecturer standing directly in front of them. Yates glanced at his watch; it was coming up to 12:30.

He couldn't hear what the lecturer was saying but after a few moments the students got up and filed out in his direction. Each one of them gave him a look of confusion and a lack of recognition. In this place his coat and suit were definitely not *de rigueur*.

'Can I help you?' The woman at the front was looking at him. She looked to be in her fifties and wearing a dress with a cardigan over the top of it. The room was not heated.

'Yes, if you're Professor Hudd.' He took the opportunity to move down.

'You're a policeman,' she said.

'You have some sort of special detector for police?'

'Oh no,' she said, 'I can tell from the smell.'

Yates was surprised. He certainly wasn't expecting such a casual insult. 'I have to say, honesty makes a refreshing change in my line of work.'

'I imagine it does, maybe you should try it?'

Yates grinned and held out his hand to shake. 'Detective Sergeant Yates.'

She glanced down at it as if she wasn't sure whether she wanted to touch him. Then she reached out her hand and took his. Her skin felt normal enough but after a few moments she began to crush his fingers. She went just far enough that he felt one of the joints crack, and then she released him. 'Quite a grip you've got there, Professor.' He gave his hand a shake and rubbed his fingers with his other hand.

She gathered up her books and papers. 'I'm a walking example of the subject I teach,' she said. 'But it was your lot that made me like this, so don't expect any kindness from me.'

She brushed past him and headed towards the door. Yates turned. 'I'm really not after kindness, but I am after someone who could explain some things to me. Like a riffy that is not actually in a person.'

She hesitated, came to a halt, and looked back. 'You'd better come along to my office, then,' she said.

Professor Hudd's office was not small. It would have done as her lecture room since it was big enough for all the students in her last lecture, with room for a few more. It was on a corner looking out across Oxford Road to the old university building.

'A riffy outside of the person?' she said.

Yates was disappointed. It looked like she had a nice collection of alcohol in a cabinet in the corner and she hadn't offered him any of it.

She must have seen him glance in that direction. 'And I don't give drinks to policemen.'

He thought the level of animosity was getting a bit much. 'We have reason to believe a crime was committed by someone who did not have a riffy, but was carrying a fake riffy unit. Is that possible?'

Infuriatingly she went to the drinks cabinet and poured herself something that looked suspiciously like a whisky. Clearly being head of the department had benefits. 'There's no reason why it's not possible,' she said. 'And I can see that in committing a crime it could be useful. But there are issues that whoever built it would have to deal with.'

'Such as?'

'It would have to mimic the biodata a riffy reports when queried.'

'When queried?'

'Our systems don't have the bandwidth to be able to continuously track everybody, all the time. It uses heuristics to locate or trigger an alarm when someone is perhaps undergoing a stressful situation. At which point it would increase the frequency with which monitoring occurs.'

Yates looked around. 'You mind if I sit down?'

'Why, is it too hard thinking and standing at the same time?'

'Frankly, yes,' he said. 'This is your subject, not mine, I need to understand it in order to catch someone who committed murder, and I really would appreciate it if you would knock off the attitude.' He really hadn't meant to say that last bit but it just slipped out, because her needling really was getting to him.

'I appreciate honesty as well, Detective Sergeant Yates, so you sit down there and I will explain it to you.' She paused then added: 'Using simple words.'

Chapter 17

Chloe

Chloe woke to the smell of frying bacon, which made her stomach rumble. The thought of how much money it must have cost her parents barely crossed her mind. She pulled on her clothes, washed and headed downstairs.

The events of the past couple of days were already like a dream, but she caught a glimpse of the vans still parked outside with the milling reporters moving backwards and forwards. Almost as if they were interviewing each other.

She headed into the back. In the kitchen it was darker than she expected, then she realised her mother had kept the blinds drawn over the window. She pursed her lips. It was very far from being a dream.

There was a plate of bacon and eggs and buttered toast along with another mug of what smelled like full coffee. Her mother must have noticed her staring at the window.

'Some of them got into the alley round the back and were climbing on the walls,' she said. 'They were taking pictures into the house.' Although her mother was smiling, Chloe could detect the underlying tension.

'They'll go away when it all blows over,' she said. 'Something more important will come along.' She sat down at the table, picked up the knife and fork then glanced up at her mother. 'This is for me, right?'

Mother nodded. 'Hospital food is really bad, and you hardly ate a thing yesterday.'

But Chloe was already tucking into the food, relishing it going down. She had considered bringing up the question of her weight with her mother, especially after the doctor's comments. But with the concern over her contact with the freak she thought it would only worry her more. And then there was the reaction of her father yesterday. She glanced at the clock. It was half past nine and he would have left for work two hours ago. It wasn't that he was trying to avoid her.

'I thought I might visit Aunt Mary today,' Chloe said. 'Do you think she'd mind?'

Her mother was busy putting crockery into the sink but she turned. 'Why would she mind, love?'

Chloe hesitated, remembering her friends' attitude with her not being quarantined. 'Because, you know, Melinda didn't get away from those people.' *And she might blame me.*

'No, of course not, I'm sure she'd really appreciate you visiting.' Her mum glanced up and stared through the wall as if she was looking at the reporters. 'Might be a bit difficult getting out though.'

Chloe munched a piece of bacon then washed it down with a mouthful of coffee. 'Well, they're not actually allowed to do anything to me, are they? The man in the ambulance said they couldn't touch me and if I don't want to talk to them, I don't have to.'

Her mother glanced up again at the line of reporters she couldn't see. 'But still, love, they'll be crowding you, and shouting questions. Are you sure you want to put up with that? Would you be all right?' She glanced at the screen in the corner. 'You could just call her.'

Chloe had just bitten into the toast and was chewing a mouthful of it. She opened her mouth to speak when her mother said. 'Don't speak with your mouth full.'

Chloe dutifully chewed and swallowed the toast. 'It's not the same, is it?' *And besides, there are some questions I want to ask her that I don't want recorded or monitored.*

Next to the terminal screen was the photo of Chloe's mum and dad with Melinda's mum and dad holding them as newborns. Chloe knew their parents had been friends, for at least as long as she'd been alive, and that she and Melinda had birthdays very close together.

Her mother was washing up with her back to her. If Chloe talked to her about it, it would be too obvious what she was driving at. But the fact remained both she and Melinda had been attacked. And the only thing they had in common was that their parents knew each other, and they were almost exactly the same age. All she had was that picture of her parents, and Melinda's, on a street somewhere in Manchester.

She knew there had to be something. It could not be a coincidence.

Chloe's mum hated having the curtains closed in the middle of the day but, in order to help Chloe escape without drawing too much attention, she had pulled the ones in the front. She had even found a blanket to put over the glass of the front door.

In the dim light from the grey day seeping through the gaps, Chloe wrapped herself up, put on a scarf and tucked her hair into a woolly cap. She could feel her pulse racing. Her mother went to the door and as quietly as possible pulled back the bolt. Having the bolt on during the day was another thing that was completely unheard of—her mother had rules.

'Are you ready, dear?'

Chloe grinned. 'It's just like being in a competition, I'm always nervous before it starts. Once I get going it will be fine.'

Her mother gave her a hug. 'You be careful, dear, it's not just the reporters.'

Chloe looked her in the eye. 'It's all right, Mum,' she said. 'Those people won't try that again in a hurry. And certainly not in broad daylight. Besides, I'll have all these reporters following me.'

Mother sighed and nodded. 'All right then.' She made it obvious she was getting ready to open the door. Chloe took a deep breath. Her mother turned the lock and pulled the door open a little. Chloe slipped through the gap and heard it closing behind her.

It seemed most of the reporters were not expecting her to leave. Only those directly in front of the house noticed the movement of the door and glanced her way. Some of them were quicker than others. They grabbed their microphones; cameramen swung their cameras into position on their shoulders.

When Chloe stepped out from the alcove by the front door, she noticed for the first time how light she was on her feet. As the camera lenses came to bear on her and the first of the drones whirred into life, she got a crazy idea. If she really was as light as people kept saying—

She barely completed the thought before she leapt sideways towards the house next door. The strength of her muscles had not diminished at all. Pushing off, she almost flew halfway across the next-door garden.

She took several long strides and jumped the next fence. This house didn't have a gate so she slipped out onto the road. She glanced back and noticed the number of vans outside the house was less than the previous day. Some of the reporters must have already left for other stories. And that meant she was already past the majority of them. She accelerated into a run. It was strange at first as each step pushed her higher off the ground than she expected, but she adjusted by leaning forward to push more forwards than up.

That was about the time she realised the shouting had started up behind her, with the whirring of drones filling the air. Although all the sounds were mashed together, she could hear each of them individually. And they were getting quieter. Within moments she was at the end of the street. She turned right and sped off up the road. While she had no idea how fast she was going, it was certainly the best speed she had ever managed.

And then she heard a drone closing in on her. Someone had been quick and clever enough to make it cut the corner over the top of the roofs. She had no idea what their top speed was but she suspected it was more than she could manage.

She felt invigorated by the run, right up until the moment the pain in her back kicked in. Excruciating lances of agony drove through her shoulders. Her shoulder had still been sore from the attack, but this was something different. Waves of pain throbbed through her and she stumbled to a halt against a tree.

The drone still buzzed above her and now she could hear cars and vans approaching. She needed to move. The onslaught of pain subsided to the level of a bad period, so she shoved her hands into her pockets and, with her head down, stumbled the last few hundred yards toward the Voglers' house.

The reporters were shouting out of their vans and cars, trying to get her to say something as she took the last few strides to the house. There was actually one stalwart reporter still parked outside the Voglers' and he was out of his van waiting for her.

The pain in her back was still taking most of her attention. She tried to go round him but he stepped directly in front of her. Without thinking she sidestepped him, hooked a leg round his, nudged him with her elbow and he fell flat on his back too surprised to cry out. She stepped over him and pushed through the gate into the Voglers' garden.

'Oy! You can't do that, that's assault!'

He was right, it was assault. And it was probably recorded on a half-dozen cameras. She felt terrible—she wished she hadn't done it but it had been pure reflex. She grabbed at the knocker but the door opened before she had even struck once.

'Come in, dear,' said Melinda's mother, grabbing her by the arm and pulling her inside.

Chapter 18

Jason

'Ugly little shit. That face.'

'Got black fur all over his body. Jeez.'

Jason could feel cold air across his body. Everywhere. He was naked. He tried to cover himself but his hands were tied behind his back, and his ankles together so tight it hurt. He opened his eyes. All he could see was an old stone wall, mouldy with damp and crawling with insects. He was hungry but he restrained himself.

'It's awake then.'

A hand grabbed him roughly by the shoulder. The fingers dug into his skin and turned him over.

The iron-strutted ceiling told him he was still in the old warehouse, or at least something like it. The air smelled similar but there were far fewer people here. Daylight filtered through gaps in the blacked-out windows.

'We should just kill it and burn the body,' said the man who had turned him over, the second one to have spoken. He was bald and there was some sort of tattoo across his head, might have been a bird.

'After the damage he did last night? He needs to make money for me.'

Jason still couldn't see this one but he sounded older. And he was the one who was running the fights maybe? But what damage had Jason done? All he did was try to escape. If they hadn't tried to stop him nothing would have happened. They probably didn't see it that way.

'He'll be useless in a fight. One of the big freaks will crush his skull in no time. He's got no muscle.'

'But he's fast. You saw the drone footage. Too fast to see. He'll be able to stay clear of the hulking ones, get round behind them and ... do something.'

The one Jason thought of as Baldy propped him up against the wall in a sitting position. Now that he had a view of the rest of the place he could see it was mostly empty. The one who seemed to be the boss was sitting in one of the chairs, leaning on the table beside him with what looked like a glass of milk beside him, half-drunk. Jason tasted the air. It was milk, and something else. The man looked as old as his mother.

Jason realised his mother would be frantic. It was true he stayed out all night most of the time, but he always came back before the world woke up. Only a couple of times he'd made a mistake and got trapped somewhere, or been so far away it took longer to get back than he expected.

When he had arrived home those times his mother was in pieces.

There was nothing he could do.

'What shall we call him then?' asked Baldy. 'Tentacle boy?'

'Hah, yeah, I like that. Those things look like they come out of his nose—if he had a nose.'

'No-Nose Boy.'

They both laughed. 'He's not gone crazy yet though. You think he'll fight?'

The old man grinned and looked straight into Jason's eyes. 'He'll fight. When the Russian Crusher is trying to tear his face off, or the Disley Demolisher grabs him by the balls…' The old man got up and crouched down in front of the gently waving tentacles protruding from Jason's face. 'Yeah, when he's face to face with something that just wants to kill him, he'll fight. Because his fucking life depends on it.'

Jason listened to the words. He could smell the death in this man, not the death he brought to others, but the illness deep inside him, the one that was eating him up. Jason had been close to enough people to know when they were ill, and he had come to know that smell. This man had his very own monster eating him from the inside. That's why he drank milk, to appease the cancer.

Even though he might not live through the day, Jason was pleased to know that this man would die in agony. There was a justice in that.

Chapter 19

Dog

One thing Dog enjoyed, more than just about anything else, was when he managed to get a good workout with Delia. It was a pity her father didn't see it quite the same way.

'What have I told you about playing with my daughter?' shouted Mendelssohn slamming open the door of the gym. The sound of it reverberated around the room, bouncing off the stone walls. To both Dog and Delia it was deafening.

It would have been an easy return, but now the shuttlecock landed with a gentle bump at Dog's feet. He stood there, racquet in hand and glanced across at Delia the other side of the net.

He opened his mouth to say something —

'Just don't,' shouted Mendelssohn striding across the floor towards them. He pointed at his daughter who was quite modestly dressed with a fairly thick top over her sports bra, and shorts neither tight nor revealing.

'You get changed into something more decent!'

Her long hair was tied back and her eyes, unnaturally large and dark blue, gave back the same attitude that her father was giving to her.

'We were just playing badminton, Dad.'

'You do not play with the hired help.'

If Delia had anything further to say she managed to keep it inside as she stalked to the door, dropped her racquet and slammed the door after her.

'If I catch you just one more time with my daughter,' he said like an explosion waiting to happen. 'Your contract will be terminated.'

Dog was not entirely sure what he should say at this point. He had a feeling anything that came out of his mouth might be a flippant remark that would get him shot. He felt, just at this moment, it might be best if he said nothing at all.

Unfortunately it seemed Mr Mendelssohn was expecting a response. 'Well?'

'I—her —'

'Why do you persist in contravening my instructions?'

Dog was quite sensitive to heat and right now the hottest thing in the room was his boss. 'It's just in my nature.'

'It's in your nature to disobey me?'

'In my nature to want to play.'

Mendelssohn closed his eyes. 'I have spent a lifetime protecting my daughter. I will not have her tainted or threatened or corrupted by some stray off the streets.'

'I think of you as my family, sir,' said Dog.

Mendelssohn roared, 'We are not your family, you stupid animal; I am your employer. We are not family; we are not related; you will have nothing to do with my daughter. Do you understand?'

Dog took a step backwards, looked down at the floor, and felt as if he were shrinking. 'I'm sorry.'

Mr Mendelssohn headed for the door. 'Get yourself cleaned up. Be ready to leave in an hour. I'm going to have

dinner then we will get out to the fights.' His final words were
punctuated by the closing door.

Dog retreated to the front of the house. There was a small
room there, lined with books. Real ones. It was the one room
Mendelssohn did not seem to mind him using, as if no one
else did.

He closed the door to shut out the rest of the house
and the constant noise. In here the scent of Mendelssohn was
almost missing. He never sat in the big red armchair with its
worn upholstery. No book carried his smell.

But every now and then he would come across one that
had the peculiar scent of Delia. Dog edged round the room; it
was a game for him to find the most recent book she had
touched.

He found it. *Treasure Island*. He brought it to his nose
and breathed in. She did smell strange. Like her father, of
course, and her mother too—though she was seldom
around—but Delia had her own special scent. Like nothing
Dog had ever found anywhere else, and he had sniffed a lot
of people.

It was about ten minutes later he perked up his ears.
Delia and her father were arguing again. A few words came
through clearly: 'boy', 'no friends', 'lonely' but the one from
Delia that carried the most emotion was *bored*.

It went very quiet after that. Dog buried himself in the
book and Delia's scent.

Chapter 20

Chloe

Chloe wasn't even out of breath. She shucked off her coat and hung it on the hook behind the door as she had done so many times before. She felt the urge to run upstairs to Melinda's bedroom, because that's what she always did. But Melinda wouldn't be there.

So instead she stood in the hall with the woman she called Auntie who, without warning, threw her arms around her and hugged her as if her life depended on it. Chloe didn't know what to do with her arms—whether to hug back or not. In the end she put her arms around her Aunt Mary's waist. And they stayed like that while her aunt cried very quietly.

'Sorry,' said Aunt Mary, as she finally pulled away and sniffed, wiping her eyes with the back of her hand. 'Why don't you come through and have a cup of tea? I've got some nettles fresh from the garden. Probably the last of the year; it's going to snow soon.'

Chloe hated nettle tea, but she wasn't going to say that. Not now. So instead she said, 'Thank you, that will be lovely.' And she followed her Aunt Mary into the kitchen.

Melinda's house always smelled strange. Her parents were very keen on making stuff for themselves, growing their own food where possible, but then Mr Vogler earned far less than Chloe's father and in order to maintain any decent lifestyle they had to save where they could.

And that meant drinking nettle tea.

'Who were you running from, dear?'

'Reporters and their drones.'

Her aunt filled the kettle and put it on the stove. She pressed the automatic lighter and it clicked three times before the hissing gas erupted into flame.

There were similarities between the two houses, of course: there was the terminal in the corner and beside it another copy of that picture.

'I'm really sorry, Aunt Mary,' began Chloe.

Mrs Vogler pulled up a chair and sat. 'You don't have anything to be sorry about, dear.'

She leant across the table, her arm stretched out with the palm face up. Chloe took it. 'I mean...' She hesitated, how could she say she was sorry she hadn't been kidnapped too?

'It's not your fault, Chloe. You were lucky, you managed to escape.'

'But—what I mean—I wish it had been me and not her.' It all came out in a rush and for the first time Chloe felt like crying. More than just a feeling—tears slipped down her cheeks.

Her aunt came round the table and, still holding onto Chloe's hand, put the other arm round her shoulders and squeezed. 'Don't be silly, dear. I understand what you're saying, but that wouldn't make it any better. You know you're like a daughter to me too. Just as Melinda is like a daughter to Amanda. You might as well be sisters.'

'Pretty funny if we were,' said Chloe and sniffed. 'Our skin doesn't match.'

Aunt Mary gave her another squeeze and went back to her chair. 'Well, it does happen, Chloe dear. Genetics is a funny thing.'

Chloe noticed, when she said that, that her eyes flicked in the direction of the photograph.

They sat in silence for a few minutes more while the sound of the kettle grew until it was bubbling away. Aunt Mary added her crushed nettle leaves to the pot and poured in the hot water. The sound of the porcelain lid going onto the teapot rattled loudly in the quiet room.

Aunt Mary brought the teapot to the table with a couple of chipped brown mugs. The same ones that she had had for years.

'How did you meet Mum and Dad?' said Chloe, finally deciding that the best approach was just to ask.

'At a clinic.' Once again the glance at the picture, almost as if she was holding back. This was something new; mother never mentioned a clinic but perhaps it was just a doctor's surgery.

'The antenatal clinic?'

Aunt Mary placed the tea strainer on Chloe's mug and poured in the slightly green liquid. She repeated the action with the other mug and then handed it to Chloe. It was little better than slightly flavoured hot water.

'Not the antenatal clinic, no. Before that. Neither of us went to an antenatal clinic. That was when the troubles started, well, when it became serious and things started going wrong.'

'So what clinic was it?' Chloe tried to keep her tone light as if she was making polite conversation, when in truth she was desperate to know. Her mother had never said anything like this. What sort of a clinic did you go to *before* antenatal?'

'It was the IVF clinic.'

'What is —' She was cut-off as Aunt Mary jumped to her feet.

'I don't think I should be talking about this to you, dear. If you want to talk to anybody, it should be your mother.'

Chloe didn't push the point. The reaction was not what she was aiming for, and she felt guilty for upsetting her aunt.

She spent the rest of the afternoon helping with housework by doing some cleaning. Aunt Mary asked her if she would mind cleaning Melinda's room. She did but it was possibly the strangest thing she had ever done. She tidied up the desk, brushed the floor and remade the bed. It was weird. She kept turning around and expecting her friend to be there, but she never was. Chloe understood why her aunt couldn't bring herself to clean the room; it was bad enough for Chloe herself.

Then she heard Aunt Mary putting a call in to someone. Her mother answered. They exchanged pleasantries after confirming that Chloe was there.

'She's upstairs cleaning.'

'That's sly,' said her mother with a little laugh. 'You need to let me know how you persuaded her.'

'She asked about how we met, Amanda.'

There was a long pause. 'What did you say?'

'I wasn't thinking, I mentioned the IVF clinic. I'm sorry.'

'Did she know what it means?'

'I don't think so,' said her aunt.

'I suppose we should have told her but it never came up.'

'It wasn't a wrong thing. There's no reason to be embarrassed about it.'

'Maybe not wrong then, but it's not the same now.'

'I'm sure she'd be fine about it. She's a sensible girl.'

'Did you ever tell Melinda?'

Her aunt sighed. 'No. Like you said, it never came up.'

It had been a sunny day but the light was fading. Chloe tuned out of the conversation and stared through the window at the darkening world. What was IVF and why did it matter? Something that was bad in the world today but hadn't been before? There were a lot of those.

After Aunt Mary had hung up, Chloe went downstairs and said she had to go. Her aunt gave her a hug although, when she squeezed, Chloe's back hurt again. This time it almost felt as if there was something there, digging in.

'Those reporters are still outside.'

'Maybe if I went out the back?' said Chloe. 'Most of them seem to be out front.'

She got her coat on, and her aunt gave her an extra scarf because the temperature was dropping fast. She opened the back door just a fraction, and the sound of a couple of whining drones filtered down from above.

'Will you be able to see all right?'

Chloe looked out the window. It was that strange twilight moment between light and dark. 'I'll be fine.'

She turned to face her aunt. 'They will find her,' she said. 'But if they don't, I will.'

And with that she made a run for it.

Chapter 21

Dog

A little over an hour later, as the light was beginning to fade from the grey sky turning everything into black, Mr Mendelssohn's car ground along the gravel drive and came to a halt at the front of the house.

Dog emerged from the snug adjoining the entrance hall as Mr Mendelssohn put on his coat, hat and gloves. Although Dog had been mulling over the situation, he was not really sure he had done anything wrong, but he would try his best to keep to Mr Mendelssohn's rules. It had just become harder over the last few months, as Delia seemed to be paying him more attention and, to be truthful, he liked it.

Mr Mendelssohn opened the front door and headed out into the dark. Reflected distortions of the house lights shone on the black paintwork, mirrors and windows of the car. Dog headed after his master but glanced back into the house. Delia was wearing that clingy long dress again, the one that emphasised her torso and hips, and came down into what almost looked like a mermaid's tail. She grinned at him and gave him a little wave. He perked up slightly but the gruff 'hurry up' from Mr Mendelssohn squashed that feeling as soon as it appeared.

The car was speeding smoothly towards the city centre.

'Where are we heading?' said Mr Mendelssohn after a long period of silence.

'Vale Mill.'

'Did you get that, George?'

'That the place past Ashton?' said the driver.

Still trying to be quiet in front of Mr Mendelssohn, Dog nodded. Then he realised the driver couldn't see him. 'Yeah, that's the one, off the Huddersfield Road.'

George grunted. Dog wasn't sure whether it was George or Mr Mendelssohn who activated it but the privacy glass rose up between the back and the front of the car. For some reason, it made Dog feel a little uncomfortable.

'I may have been slightly hasty in my remarks.' Mr Mendelssohn's words were curiously detached, as if someone were holding a gun to his head as he said something he did not want to. 'If my daughter wishes to——' he hesitated as if searching for the right word '——play badminton with you, or something of a similar nature, and I mean similar as in a court game.' He took a breath. 'Then that will be acceptable.'

'Oh.'

'Oh? Is that all you can say?'

'If those are your orders, Mr Mendelssohn, sir, then of course I will carry them out.' Dog could barely keep in his enthusiasm; if he'd had a tail it would have been wagging.

'Yes, my orders.'

And that was the last thing he said for the rest of the journey.

Mr Mendelssohn's car crawled along the ill-kept side road with its lights off, but the sky had cleared and there was moon enough to see by. Even so the wheels kept dipping into deep ruts and potholes making the ride less than comfortable despite the suspension. George turned in through a gate and crawled through the ancient industrial estate with three- and four-storey buildings on each side.

The slope was considerable as the car inched its way through the darkness. Once out of sight of the road George turned on the sidelights, highlighting the moss-covered walls and the grass growing up through the cracks. It was hard to see where the fights were taking place; the blackout on the windows was thorough. There were a few more cars parked, but the limousine pulled up as close as possible to the main building and then turned in until it was facing the wall. George killed the engine and lowered the window between them.

'You want me to stop here, sir?'

'This will do fine.'

The air was freezing and the dew on the grass was turning to ice with the cold. George got out of the car, helped Mr Mendelssohn on with his big coat and handed him his hat. Dog didn't have any additional clothing available but he didn't feel the cold that much. At least not if he kept moving.

Mr Mendelssohn headed further up the slope with Dog in tow.

'Are you aware,' said Mr Mendelssohn, 'there was trouble at the fights here last night?'

This was the first Dog had heard of it, but then he didn't have the information sources his boss had. 'I didn't know. What happened?'

'While reports are not entirely clear, it seems that there was a thief running around.'

'A thief?' Dog was a little bit worried.

'Yes, apparently it was a freak itself in the early stages.'

Oh shit. 'Oh, really?'

They were approaching the entrance. Mr Mendelssohn knocked on the door. 'Yes, Dog. And if it's the one you were going to show me we'll get to see him in a fight.'

'Couldn't possibly be the same one.'

Dog followed his master inside.

Mr Mendelssohn did own some fighting freaks, but as they sat there, on a slightly raised platform away from the unkempt masses, his boss chose not bet on any of the fights.

Perhaps it was a professional courtesy. Or perhaps the promoter of these fights might not appreciate if someone else was muscling in on his position with privileged information.

Whatever the reason, they simply sat there at the table. They were served drinks—Mr Mendelssohn refused any of the food—and watched the crowds.

It was about 9 o'clock in the evening, after a monster with what looked like insect parts had been crushed and pummelled by a freak that was so far gone it took trank guns to slow him down in order to get him back in his cage.

Dog had been scanning the area, and the scents in the air, for his little thief, though he still had hopes that maybe it was somebody different. This could end up being very awkward. He still owed Mr Mendelssohn the money for the incident with the Armourer, and if this replacement didn't work out, he had no idea how he would be able to get the money.

The remains of the insect freak had been cleaned out of the fight cage and washed down the drain, when the ringmaster entered, and announced the next fight. He introduced it as being a special something. Dog groaned as he caught a whiff of his little thief, plus the scent of fear. The guy was so small there was no way he could stand up to one of those big maulers.

The gate at the back was opened and the thief was pushed inside. Dog found it curious the way the crowd reacted. The thief was covered in black fur—very short but thick—and he was wearing shorts of some sort but nothing much else. He looked perfectly normal, not counting the fur, as long as you didn't look at his face and the four tentacle-like protrusions where his nose ought to be, but with a perfect mouth and perfect eyes and normal black hair.

Yes, it was the crowd that was weird. They reacted in a shocked way, horrified, and yet these were people that watched monsters with outrageous and grotesque body parts, things that were insane, trying to tear each other to pieces and yet they were disgusted by this simple creature.

'So, this is your thief, is it?' said Mr Mendelssohn.

'Yeah, that looks like him.'

'It's because he looks so normal.'

For a second Dog wondered whether Mr Mendelssohn could actually read his mind. Silly idea. 'Yeah, funny that.'

A roar went up from the crowd.

Dog saw what was coming and groaned; it was the Friesian. He didn't like to frequent the fights too much; it reminded him of how precarious his own position was. But he'd seen the Friesian. She'd been caught early before she came to the attention of the Purity and before she'd gone completely off her head.

So he'd seen her degenerate over the past few months. Her skin had become mottled black and white and her left arm had become a strange combination of a bovine leg and hoof that bent like an arm. It gave her one hell of a punch.

The rest of her face had become distorted as well; she'd lost all her teeth and her hair was gone. And now, he guessed, she was in constant agony. She was barely controllable. The keepers were using cattle-prods to manoeuvre her along the tunnel into the holding bay. Rather than run before them, she lashed out instead. This was why he hated the fights so much.

The smell from the little freak was getting worse. Dog knew he didn't have the killer instinct. This really wasn't going to last very long.

'So this was what you wanted to trade?' said Mr Mendelssohn.

'That was the idea, sir,' said Dog.

'She's going to make mincemeat out of him.'

Dog could only agree.

The final announcements in the betting were made, the odds were announced and only an idiot would have bet on this fight at all. The Friesian was going to win; the odds on the little guy were a hundred to one. Dog jumped up and waved to one of the betting runners.

'Put this on the little hairy freak,' he said and flicked one of his few coins at the runner. The runner caught it dexterously and nodded, and then disappeared into the back.

'Got to show willing and support,' said Dog in response to the strange look that Mr Mendelssohn was giving him.

'That's my money you're spending.'

Dog shrank back into his chair to watch.

The Friesian had stopped smashing at the walls of the isolation cage; she just stood there looking down at her next victim. At this point, as far as Dog could remember, she had about five kills to her name and that was impressive. The cage door went up. The Friesian stepped out. What Dog had taken to be boots turned out to be another set of hooves on her feet, the change had been pretty smooth. She was lucky.

The thief backed his way up to the cage bars behind him as the Friesian clopped steadily forwards. She loomed over him. With a cry that was somewhere between a scream and mooing, she lashed out with her left. Dog could see it was on target.

The hoof crashed resoundingly into the bars of the wall cage. The thief wasn't there anymore. Dog could barely believe it—though, when he thought back, he did remember seeing a blur. God but that kid could move.

The outcome was obvious. The Friesian, confused by her first miss, focused once more. She pounded towards the thief and slammed her hoof again into thin air; this time she struck nothing and fell forward onto her knees when her momentum met no resistance. The crowd laughed, but as it happened again and again, with the Friesian attempting to pummel the thief into the ground and the thief never being there when the blow arrived, the crowd started to boo.

'This kid is trouble,' said Mr Mendelssohn. 'He needs to do something.'

'Only for fighting, sir,' said Dog, 'just look at his speed, just think how useful he'd be to you.'

Mr Mendelssohn sat there and watched the travesty of a fight go on for another minute, with the crowds becoming more and more restive. It could turn nasty.

'Right, I have seen enough,' said Mr Mendelssohn with a certain amount of finality. Dog was concerned about what exactly that meant.

'What are you going to do?'

Mr Mendelssohn stood up, put a couple of fingers in his mouth and whistled so loud the entire room came to a halt. Even the Friesian stopped moving. Dog slammed his hands over his ears, obviously Mr Mendelssohn was not aware of the ultrasonic components in his whistle; it was very piercing.

Having got their attention, Mr Mendelssohn called out across the room. 'Separate them, I'll take him.' And then sat down again.

Dog looked at his master. 'You already knew this was going to happen and you already fixed it.'

Mr Mendelssohn didn't reply; he just took a drink from his cup and smiled. 'Don't think for a second, Dog, that this lets you off the hook. I've had to pay good money for this piece of flesh; he better be worth it.'

'He will be. Just look at him; he's the perfect thief.'

'We'll see, but right now my main concern is thinking of some way of persuading him to stay. Because I don't think there's any way we would be able to hold him if he chose to escape.'

Which added to Dog's worries. If this new guy ran away the price that had been paid for him as well as the money owed from the Armourer would all be on Dog's head. And that wasn't a price he was willing to pay. He'd better get thinking.

Then he brightened up. *On the other hand, it's someone else to play with...*

Chapter 22

Chloe

Mum had ordered an auto-taxi to take her to school. There were still a few reporters and their vans on the doorstep though their numbers were dwindling as nothing continued to happen.

Dad had been muttering about his position in the FreakWatch. After what had happened to Chloe, chances were Dad would get voted off the committee at the next AGM. Maybe even kicked out completely. Chloe was glad about that; she knew exactly what some of those do-gooders would be thinking.

Was that why he wasn't talking to her? He'd barely said a word since she had arrived back home. Whatever room she went in, if he was there he'd find a reason to leave. It hurt.

The taxi pulled up outside the front of the school at a little before half-past eight, just as the main body of students were heading inside. A few of them glanced in the direction of the taxi as it arrived, then went back to whatever they had been doing. It wasn't unusual.

When she climbed out, things changed.

There were two reactions. The majority took one look at her and hurried into school. The others stared. She looked back towards the entrance. The reporters were there, filming from the edge of the school grounds. Two buzzing drones floated high up, they did not trespass either, but their lenses were almost as long as the ones on the ground.

The shots of her bounding across the gardens and running like a wild thing to her aunt's house had been plastered across the newsfeeds. There were mutterings about the Purity letting a freak walk free. On the official news there were experts who pointed out it took months for S.I.D to take hold and, even if Chloe had been exposed, she wouldn't have been showing any signs yet.

Then there were the ones who said that the reason she escaped being kidnapped was because she was already one of them. Part of some secret cabal of freak-lovers. Chloe had managed to put up with half an hour of that before she turned it off and cried into her pillow for a long time.

Chloe lifted her bag on to her shoulder—carefully because her back was feeling particularly tender—and walked up the broad steps.

'Freak!'

She kept her eyes fixed on the door.

'Freak!'

She knew the voice. Hancock. And now there was nothing she could do. It was okay to defend the weak from persecution but she could not save herself from the same thing, especially not with the cameras on her. Anything she did would just reinforce the problem.

She wished she had stayed at home.

The day went slowly. She tried to concentrate on the subjects and the work she had missed. But what had happened to her, and what people wanted to believe, got in the way of everything.

It wasn't just the other students; it was the teachers. Not all but most.

Ashley and Kavi were fine, of course, but that just meant they got caught up in the abuse hurled at her. After all, both of them had also had family members who had freaked out. They had both been quarantined, so they were the 'other' as well.

The Purity class was the final lesson of the day. Chloe hung back with Ashley and Kavi, wanting to be sure that Miss Kepple was already in the room before she entered. She was.

The teacher smiled as Chloe came in. Chloe found it almost as unnerving as the animosity of the others. The smile faded as Ashley followed her with Kavi behind. Their usual seats were not occupied. The posters on the wall seemed to be screaming at her. The ache between her shoulder blades was intensifying. Chloe wondered whether the doctors had missed a spinal injury. It didn't seem likely. She rotated her shoulders a couple of times and the pain lessened a little.

Miss Kepple rose from her chair behind the desk. The murmuring among the students dropped away.

'I think,' she began, 'that today we should take a break from the curriculum.'

Some of the students took this to mean she was cancelling the lesson and started to pack their books back into their bags.

'By which I mean,' said Miss Kepple looking directly at Chloe, 'we have something of a unique situation.'

The eyes of the students followed her gaze and also stared. Chloe might have had good hearing but, looking back at the faces around her, she was glad she was not a mind-reader. What was Miss Kepple playing at?

'Chloe Dark was attacked by an S.I.D infectee.' There were murmurs. Chloe felt as if she was a rodent on a dissecting board. 'I'm sure some of you must have questions. Now is the time to ask them.'

The silence was suddenly intense. No one seemed willing to be the first. Or was too embarrassed to put any question they had out into the world.

Miss Kepple walked the length of the room between the desks until she was standing at the back. No one dared turn their head. 'Nobody has any questions? Perhaps I should be flattered that my lessons have clearly been so complete that you all understand everything.'

There was a long pause. 'O'Donnell!'

The boy directly in front of Chloe jumped. 'Miss?'

'Don't you have a question for Chloe?'

James O'Donnell was not one of the people who had shouted at her; he was always pretty quiet. He wasn't very bright and wore cheap glasses with heavy lenses. Despite that he was seldom bullied because he had a strong right fist which he was happy to use as the need arose. Chloe quite liked him even though they moved in different circles.

'Well—'

'Stand up, O'Donnell, face the rest of the class and if you're going to ask Chloe a question at least look her in the face when you do it.'

His chair scraped as he stood. He had to turn to face her, and she had to lean back because he was standing.

'You had a fight with a freak?' There was a hint of admiration in his tone.

'Yes—'

'Go and stand at the front, Chloe, so everyone can hear your answer.'

Chloe felt her face flush and in that moment she hated Miss Kepple. But she wouldn't let anyone know how much she loathed being in front of the class. It was bad enough when just doing an ordinary presentation, but this?

Maybe if she just pretended it was a demonstration in front of the Jujitsu class. She had done those so often it didn't even cross her mind to feel awkward about it. Even though sensai might be about to throw her across the mat, or twist an arm or leg into a painful position.

She lifted her head and strode to the front. She turned and saw Miss Kepple lounging against the wall at the back. Then Miss Kepple winked. Chloe stared, what was the teacher playing at?

'Ask your question again, O'Donnell.'

O'Donnell cleared his throat. 'Did you really fight a freak?'

'Yes, sort of.' She undid the button of her cuff and pulled up the sleeve to reveal the bandage and the visible bruising, which by now had become a livid purple stretching to her elbow. There were appreciative noises, and some of disgust. 'It had a claw like a crab. It grabbed my wrist so I was hanging.'

'But it wasn't just the freak, was it, Chloe?' said Miss Kepple.

'No, Miss, there were two others.'

'And were they freaks?'

'No, Miss, well, they looked normal.'

Miss Kepple nodded at her arm and Chloe sorted out her sleeve. 'You see, the criminal element are not averse to using freaks in their crimes. They don't care about the importance of the Purity.

'Sit down, O'Donnell. Who else has a question?'

And so it went for the rest of the lesson. Chloe relaxed a bit until Kavi stood up. Chloe stared at her, terrified of what she might ask.

'Why aren't you in quarantine?' Kavi's voice cracked as she asked the question, as if she were about to cry. And Chloe did not blame her. Why should she get away with being released, when Kavi and the rest of her family had been locked up for months? 'How is that fair?'

Chloe glanced at Ashley, and found accusation in her eyes too. 'It's not.'

'The doctors declared that Chloe is not infected, therefore she has been released,' said Miss Kepple. She strode to the front of the class and glanced at her watch. 'Well, this has been a very enlightening lesson for us all, I think. It's a bit early but I think we should finish there.'

The words of release had the required effect and the room was filled with the sound of the students packing up and leaving. Chloe made to go back to her seat, although Ashley and Kavi had yet to move.

'Stay here please, Chloe, I want to talk to you.'

So she stayed at the front, feeling awkward as the other students left the room. None of them came near her, sliding between the desks in order to exit away from where she stood.

Realising she wasn't returning to her desk, Ashley and Kavi followed the others out. Not even looking behind.

'Sadly, that is the kind of reaction you can expect even from people you think of as friends,' said Miss Kepple. 'Collect your books and come to my office.'

Chapter 23

Sapphire

Sapphire was scared.

She stood in the centre of her office in indecision.

The knock came on the door again. Chris would be so angry if he knew she had invited Chloe back again.

But it wasn't for bad reasons. It was for good reasons.

The Purity had always been good to her. She had qualified and received the training. She helped to keep the perfection of the human genome intact.

She had never killed a freak, of course. She had seen them. Disgusting monstrosities in the holding cells of the Purity. They made nightmares pale into daydreams—because they were real.

'Miss Kepple?'

Chloe's voice penetrated the door, and penetrated Sapphire's concerns.

She never thought of herself as Saffie, or even Miss Kepple. Those two people were merely constructs she used sometimes. Miss Kepple was a stern teacher, while Saffie did not come out much. She existed only for Chris. She was obedient and did nothing without her master's permission.

But the real Sapphire was a hard blue crystal. Beautiful and strong.

'Come in, Chloe.'

The door opened and Chloe looked in. 'I'm sorry, am I interrupting?'

Sapphire smiled her icy smile. 'Of course not, my dear. Come right in, and shut the door. Orange juice?'

Chloe did as she was told while Sapphire went to the cooler and poured two glasses from the bottle. It was the last of her supplies but it was worth it. Chloe deserved it.

The girl was standing in the middle of the room, just where Sapphire had been standing and with the same look of indecision on her face. 'Put your bag down, and you can take your coat off. We have things to talk about. We'll use the sofa.'

Once more Chloe did exactly as she had been asked. It was so lovely to have a girl that could follow orders so precisely. It was almost as if Chloe had become Saffie, and Sapphire was Chris—though she would never hurt Chloe. Never. Only the best things for her.

In a few moments they were seated as before, each with their orange juice in their hands. Sapphire's knee pressed against Chloe's. The girl looked pensive, of course; she did not know what was going to happen but she would do as she was told.

The genuine look of pleasure that passed across her face when she sipped her juice transformed the worry into beauty. Chloe was a delight, and her strength would be such a benefit to the Purity—once Sapphire had honed it into a tool.

'Miss Kepple?'

The serious face had returned and Sapphire was concerned. She did not want her protégée to be sad or concerned, everything must be perfect.

'What is it?'

'Can I ask you something?'

'Of course, you can ask me anything.'

'There's an abbreviation I came across, and I don't know what it means.'

'Did you ask BritNet?'

'I didn't want to, just in case it was something bad.'

'What is it?'

'IVF,' said Chloe. 'I think it has something to do with babies or pregnancy.'

Sapphire stood up and took a couple of steps towards the window, though the loss of the touch of Chloe's knee was like the rending of her heart. She must have said nothing for too long.

'Do you know what it is?'

'It's a medical term,' said Sapphire. 'A complex process. We don't do it anymore.'

She heard Chloe getting to her feet behind her.

'So it's not a bad thing?'

'It was common enough before,' said Sapphire. 'How did you hear about it?'

'Melinda Vogler's mother mentioned it,' said Chloe. 'What is it?'

Sapphire could feel Chloe behind her. All she wanted to do was put her arms around the girl and kiss her, but she had to go slow. If Chloe was unprepared she might lash out—and while Sapphire had known about Chloe's hobby she had not realised how potent a skill it was until she had fought off her would-be kidnappers. She did not wish to be on the receiving end of such a defence.

'It was a process used to help a couple conceive a child.'

'Oh.'

'The woman's ova and the man's semen were collected and then combined outside of the body. When a successful impregnation occured the viable embryo was returned to the mother's body. I understand it was a very long and uncertain process, and quite stressful for the mother.'

'I see.'

'Does that answer your question?'

'Yes.'

Sapphire sighed to herself. The moment had passed. In all these things there was always the ideal time when she could touch without her partner becoming upset. Especially if there was a moment of vulnerability, but that time had gone and they had moved on. Where had this IVF nonsense come from?

She turned to face Chloe, only to discover there were tears falling from her eyes. Chloe turned her head away to hide her face and tried to wipe away the tears with her bandaged wrist.

'Oh my child, whatever is the matter?' She was concerned, of course, but the vulnerability she hoped for had arrived so unexpectedly. 'Are you crying for your friend?'

Chloe sniffed. Sapphire relieved her of the glass and fetched a handkerchief from her desk. 'Here,' she said and reached out gently to touch Chloe's cheek. She felt her warm smooth skin and gently pressed to make her turn her face towards her. With her other hand she dabbed the tears from Chloe's eyes.

The perfect opportunity had arrived. It was now or never.

Sapphire took a step forward so that there was barely an inch between them. Before Chloe could react Sapphire wrapped her arms around the girl. She felt her body tense up. 'Just cry on my shoulder, Chloe.'

Perfect.

The girl relaxed immediately and allowed herself to be drawn in close. Sapphire closed her eyes. She breathed in deep through her nose bringing the wonderful scent of the girl to her. It had been so long.

And Chloe really was crying. It was beautiful how she cared so much for her friend. 'Let it all out, Chloe.' The girl's body sobbed within Sapphire's arms as she placed her hands flat on the girl's body. She could feel the roughness of the jumper on the outside. The rigid bump of her bra strap.

Sapphire reached further. Pressed a little harder. Ribs, the curving shape of her back, her spine. Moving boldly so as not to give the impression she was simply feeling the girl's body but truly offering consolation, Sapphire moved her hand up the girl's spine.

And found two bumps. She frowned. Had she stretched too far? Was she touching the shoulder blades? No.

Two hard bumps a couple of inches apart. A kink in the girl's underwear?

Sapphire squeezed.

Chloe jerked away with a squeal of pain through the tears. 'What are you doing?'

Sapphire stared at her without seeing. Two lumps, hard but covered in skin. The thought tried to beat its way into Sapphire's consciousness. Lumps where there should be perfection.

Something curdled in Sapphire's stomach. She did not even try to hold it back. Her dinner mixed with a little orange juice returned to the outside world.

'Miss Kepple!' Chloe sounded terrified. 'Are you all right?'

Another spasm dumped more of her insides on to the carpet. Through an acid-raw throat she managed to speak. 'Get out!'

Although unable to concentrate on it, Sapphire was half-aware of Chloe gathering up her coat and bag, fumbling with the door handle and flying from the room.

The stench of the vomit filled the room. She retched again, but her body was just going through the motions as there was nothing left to come up. She retched again one final time.

Exhausted she sat back in the hard chair and stared at the wall. With the handkerchief she had used to wipe Chloe's tears she cleaned round her mouth, wiping away the lipstick in a bloody red smear.

Lumps.

Lumps in Chloe's back.

Chloe was a freak. Sapphire felt as if her heart was breaking. She almost reached for her phone. She needed to tell her seniors; she needed to call Chris. He would thank her and maybe love her again.

But she didn't want Chris. She wanted Chloe.

Don't be silly, she told herself, *Chloe is just your perversion. There is nothing there that is true.*

But she did not find herself very convincing.

She needed to think. She needed to understand. She did not need to tell anybody anything. This fact alone would put Chloe truly in her power; Sapphire could protect her. She would keep the Purity from her and everything would be all right.

She had probably just imagined it anyway. There was nothing that needed to be done.

Except clean up the mess, and get herself home.

Tomorrow she would know what to do.

Chapter 24

Chloe

Chloe had not slept well. She had spent the whole of the previous evening in her room, and for part of it she had simply cried. Her encounter with Miss Kepple had left her confused.

The teacher making a pass at her was not the upsetting part. The fact Miss Kepple was into girls was talked about in hushed tones in corners, or laughed about at parties. It was also considered to be odd because lesbianism—everybody knew what it was called—was not considered acceptable to the Purity.

As far as anybody knew, despite all the talk, she had never gone beyond looking, and perhaps a touch that went on a little too long. What had happened with Chloe was unheard of. It suggested the teacher really liked her, in *that* way. Which if viewed from a certain light was almost flattering but, on the other hand, a bit difficult since Chloe didn't feel the same.

And, Chloe had to admit, she really hadn't minded when her teacher gave her a hug because she really needed it at that point. Even if Miss Kepple did have wandering hands. But it was the wandering of those hands that had really bothered her. Because Chloe had felt what her teacher had felt: the lumps on her back.

And then Miss Kepple had thrown up. Now that was a harsh judgement. She had thrown up and screamed at Chloe to get out. Which was why Chloe spent the first two hours in her room lying on her bed and sobbing into her pillow. Then Ashley and Kavi had buzzed her.

Chloe had cleaned herself up as best she could and taken the call. Of course they wanted to know why she had taken so long in answering, and then they wanted to know why she had been crying because there was no point in denying it; she looked terrible.

Chloe wasn't sure why but she didn't usually like to share her personal pain with her friends, although she was always willing to listen to theirs, but this time she told them what her teacher had done, how she had behaved. Ashley had laughed of course, while Kavi had been sympathetic and horrified.

It finally dawned on Ashley that Chloe was genuinely upset—a difficult concept for someone who was always lying about the way she felt.

And, of course, they had asked her how she had escaped from the teacher's evil clutches. So having got that far, Chloe told them the rest, except she didn't mention the lumps. It would scare them. It scared her.

Ashley asked if she wanted to come round and spend the night. How it would be good for them all to have a sleepover again. Chloe managed to stop her by using the reporters still camped out on her doorstep as an excuse. There were even fewer now, but still some waiting for a story they could actually use, preferably an exclusive. Like a teacher lusting after a student, or a student with lumps in her back.

Her friends had been online for about an hour when Chloe told them she wanted to grab something to eat and then get some sleep. Ashley made some smart-arse comment about Chloe being hungry all the time, and that cut even deeper into Chloe's confidence.

She was glad they had called but relieved when it was over.

She dozed fitfully. The lumps between her shoulder blades terrified her. And lying face down or on her side, she found her mind filled with random thoughts. She woke with the suddenness of a thunderclap.

Her mum and dad were talking downstairs, the words were indistinct noises until she tuned in and then she could hear them as if she were standing with them. But there was nothing of consequence: Dad's day at work; Mum's day in the home; and the price of food.

Chloe wanted to scream at them. She wanted to demand to know why they weren't talking about *her*. Wasn't she the most important thing in the family right now? Wasn't she the one suffering? She had been attacked!

Couldn't they see why she had been released? Didn't they know that Special Agent Graham was just waiting for the kidnappers to strike again? Why weren't they talking about that? Why didn't they care?

And when she finally did get to sleep properly she dreamt she was falling endlessly—falling but never hitting the ground.

When she woke again, Chloe was starving. She had been hungry the night before, but hadn't eaten. Now she was ravenous.

She headed downstairs and dug out everything she could find in the fridge that she could cook and eat. While two slices of bread were toasting she ate a third with a spoonful of cold baked beans—then poured the rest of them in the saucepan to heat up. She looked at the carton of eggs and, barely giving it a thought, broke two raw eggs into a glass and gulped them down. Then crunched through the shells.

In the back of her mind she had the idea that perhaps she was behaving strangely, but she needed to eat and that thought overwhelmed everything. By the time she had finished off most of the loaf, the other four eggs from the carton, the baked beans and bacon, and eating it between two more slices, her mother came in.

'Aw, sweetheart, you didn't have to make breakfast.'

Chloe stood up and washed down the final part of the bacon sandwich with the last of the milk. 'Sorry, didn't. Very hungry. Got to do homework.'

And with that she pushed past her mother and bounced up the stairs four steps at a time. A moment later she shut the door and locked it.

Chloe couldn't remember ever hearing her mother swear in her presence. But with her every sense sharp, she heard her mother in the kitchen moving around opening the fridge, looking at the mess that Chloe had made. Accompanied by a string of profanities, some of which Chloe didn't even know. But she didn't call Chloe down, instead talking to herself she said that Chloe was still recovering from the attack, and justified every action as the product of stress.

Chloe threw herself on the bed and dozed for a while longer, not exactly sleeping but digesting. New energy infused her muscles. She hadn't realised quite how exhausted she had become.

It was a knock at the front door that brought her back to full consciousness. She glanced at the clock. It was only nine-thirty. She heard her mother going to the door, and her father in the kitchen saying something about the rudeness of people calling so early. Outside, Chloe heard the drones come to life and the slight increase in chatter from the reporters, although she couldn't quite make out what they were saying.

'Good morning, Mrs Dark.'

Chloe sat up on the edge of the bed rigid. It was Miss Kepple. What the hell was she doing here? Oh God, was she going to blame Chloe for what had happened yesterday?

'Oh, Miss Kepple, isn't it?' said her mother.

'Do you mind if I come in? The reporters…'

Chloe heard the clicking of her heels as she stepped inside, before Chloe's mother had even given her permission. How like her.

'Yes, of course. Can I take your coat?'

'That won't be necessary, Mrs Dark. Is your husband here?'

'Who is it, Amanda?' Her father called from the kitchen.

'It's Chloe's Purity teacher, Miss Kepple.'

Even though it was certain that her mum and teacher couldn't hear it, Chloe was well aware of what her father said under his breath.

'And Chloe?' said Miss Kepple.

'She's upstairs, in her room. Do you want me to fetch her?'

'No,' Miss Kepple's denial was quick and urgent, as if whatever it was she wanted to say was most certainly not for Chloe's ears.

'Well, I couldn't stop listening even if I wanted to,' said Chloe to herself.

Once they were all in the kitchen and had exchanged pleasantries, her mother asked. 'This is about Chloe?'

'Yes, yes, of course it is,' said Miss Kepple, she seemed hesitant. Chloe wrapped her arms around herself; Kepple was going to tell them what happened yesterday. Why would she do that?

'Yes,' said Miss Kepple again. 'I'm sorry, I'm not entirely sure how to tell you this.'

'What?' said her father, the tone of his voice was a dangerous growl. Chloe had never heard him like this before. 'You want to tell us something about Chloe, and you don't quite know how to say it?'

'That's correct,' said Miss Kepple. She had spoken very carefully as if she were now uncertain as to whether he already knew.

But knew what?

She heard the chair in the kitchen scraped back. 'You're here to tell us that Chloe is a freak as well?' said her father.

There was a long pause. Chloe frowned. Why would he say such a thing? *As well?*

Ali? She had heard what had happened but so much else was going on she really hadn't had time to process it. She frowned. No, the truth was she had forgotten about him.

He must have seen the lumps in her back during the ultrasound, and not turned her in to the Purity, and he didn't tell her either, but he went to her parents—he died near Debenhams on the night she was attacked. Chloe got to her feet. She wanted to run but she couldn't move. Where could she go?

'Yes,' said Miss Kepple. 'Yes, that's what I was going to tell you. But you already know.'

And then her father exploded. His anger was like an elemental force. He was deafening as he roared at Miss Kepple to get out and to shut up; and how dare she come into his house to accuse his daughter of being a freak.

There was a lot of noise with chairs falling over; doors opening and closing; somebody bumping into something else, maybe the table; crockery falling and smashing; high-heels retreating down the hall; scrabbling at door locks; and her father screaming 'how dare you' before slamming the door on her.

The drones whined in the background. Chloe sat down again.

Her father was wrong, of course. Despite his treatment of her during the week, he was wrong. He might be convinced she wasn't a freak, but even Miss Kepple had felt the lumps on her back. And Chloe could see them in the mirror now. She was a fraction of her expected weight. Then she laughed at herself bitterly: not forgetting the fact she could hear things no normal person could possibly hear. The screaming in the ultrasound machine had been because she could hear sounds beyond the normal range of human hearing.

And all that meant only one thing:

I'm a freak, and I'm going to die.

Episode III: Flight

Chapter 1

Mercedes

She did not think even Xec really understood how much she preferred the Utopia Genetics office tower when it was deserted over the weekend. She could relax and feel genuinely alone without the staff working in the offices below her. Even on a weekday, like today, not all the floors were occupied; there just weren't enough people. The rest of the building was sealed off or used for undocumented purposes. There had been an argument, at one time, that they should keep all their assets and acquisitions in the building on one of the higher but unused floors. Her personal reasons for not wanting freaks close to her was not something covered in the meetings; however she was very glad when it was agreed that older buildings out of town would be used instead.

Unfortunately this was not a typical Monday. And the other members of the board had decided they wanted an extraordinary meeting to discuss the latest problem. Mercedes shook her head as she walked the length of the corridor towards the meeting room.

'They're well within their rights, Mercedes,' said Xec.

'When I want your opinion, I'll tell you what to say,' she said. 'And before you say anything else, yes I know that's not opinion.'

'Sorry for breathing.'

Mercedes scowled, which she knew was not a good look for her, but there were times she hated that smart-arse machine. *And yes, Xec, I know you're not actually a machine and some part of you somewhere is breathing.*

She paused at the door to the meeting room and closed her eyes. Was this really worth the stress? She could just resign. But if she did, her successor would probably do everything in his power to terminate her. It was not safe to have someone with her knowledge floating around society.

She had never hesitated before entering the boardroom before.

She grabbed the handle and went in.

She had barely sat down, ordered Xec to switch off his monitoring, and brought the meeting to order when Kingsley Upton let loose.

'Did you know this freak was so powerful?'

Upton had been addressing her, which technically was the correct thing to do since she was the chair; however, it annoyed her. 'I think you're asking the wrong person, Kingsley. What do you have to say, Alistair?'

'Yes, well, no,' said McCormack.

Upton leapt to his feet. 'What the hell is that supposed to mean? One of your senior researchers has been fried by a fucking freak, *while she was completely immobilised.* And she destroyed all the electrical equipment in the room. Expensive equipment.'

McCormack lounged back in his chair. 'What do you expect me to say Kingsley? This is how things go. This kind of research is dangerous. Sometimes people get hurt. And sometimes they die.'

Upton was still on his feet. 'And that's all you've got to say? It happens?'

'Yes. It happens.'

'All right Kingsley, that's enough,' said Mercedes. 'It wasn't McCormack's fault. If anything it was the researcher. What can you tell us about it, Alistair? What additional protocols should we now be putting in place?'

McCormack got slowly to his feet and stared at Upton until the latter finally sat down in a huff. 'Yes, well, it seems the researcher in question was a little hasty. They had not completed their anatomical analysis of this particular asset. Although clearly we now have a much better idea of what she can do.

'In terms of new protocols, existing ones are satisfactory. If the researcher in question had not broken the rules, he would most likely still be alive today.'

'Most likely?' Upton growled from his chair. 'So, you're saying it was his own fault he died and all that expensive equipment was ruined? And you're not going to do anything about it?'

McCormack looked Upton in the eye. 'Yes, that *is* what I am saying. On a more positive note, it does mean other researchers are going to be much more careful. What we can say is that thus far we have been unable to recognise any commonalities between the modified DNA structures of those we have collected so far.'

Mercedes was looking at Paul Banner; if anyone was likely to betray them it was him. Although after all this time there would be difficult questions asked as to why he hadn't reported Utopia Genetics before. 'How do you see the situation, Paul?'

'I can't see any particular security impact here,' he said. 'It was an accidental death, as McCormack said. The researcher failed to follow established protocols and was electrocuted.'

'The next-of-kin has already been informed,' said Margaret Jenner. 'They will receive the usual pension. I don't see there being any particular issue here either.'

Mercedes turned her attention back to Kingsley. 'So, does that answer your concerns?'

'Yes .' His eyes said something completely different. 'While we're at it, what's the latest on re-acquiring the asset we lost?'

Mercedes smiled. 'We just have to play the waiting game with that one. Alistair?'

'Well, I have the team in place, this time with additional backup. We have her under constant surveillance, not only monitoring her riffy, but we have a plant in the reporters outside her door and people to keep her in view whenever she goes walkabout.'

Jenner caught Mercedes' eye, and she nodded to her.

'Did you watch the news reports about the girl?'

McCormack sat up straight. 'Anything in particular?'

Jenner looked at him across the table. She didn't look very happy. 'I understand from our records that apart from the changes of her upper spine she's also lost a lot of weight.'

McCormack nodded. 'Aye, that's the information we've been getting.'

'She's on film leaping a ridiculous distance for someone of her size, and running very fast. I've seen the footage myself.'

Upton had a self-satisfied smile on his face, as if he was happy that there was a problem.

'I hadn't seen that,' said Mercedes, 'but I'll have Xec see if we can do something about it.'

'Aye,' said McCormack, 'can't have that kind of evidence floating around.'

The meeting dragged on for another few minutes but they had covered all the ground they wanted to. And Mercedes was glad that she had managed to direct most of Upton's anger towards McCormack, who didn't give a damn about it. Still the footage that Jenner described certainly could be an issue; it wouldn't be possible to suppress it now, but they might be able to discredit it.

What bothered her more was that Xec apparently had not known about it either. Otherwise he would have told her.

Wouldn't he?

Chapter 2

Dog

Mr Mendelssohn's limousine crunched away from the old warehouses and out on to the main road. In the rear passenger section Dog stared at their new guest. Mr Mendelssohn had chosen to ride in the front, with the privacy window rolled up.

It was dark in the compartment with only a small light in the ceiling providing limited illumination. It made the shadows even deeper than they already were and emphasised the horrific look of the thief's face. Dog wasn't sure he would ever get used to it. Everything else about him was so normal, if you didn't count the fur. The smell coming off him was interesting though. If you subtracted the stench of the fights, and the kind of dirt anybody picks up from hoofing long distances, the boy was really clean. In fact, Dog was pretty sure he could smell soap. His fingernails were dirty, but cut neatly short, as were his toenails. No one who lived on the streets took that much care of themselves. He must have somewhere to stay.

The journey continued in silence. More than once, when the car slowed, their guest tried the door. Normally Dog would be able to see it coming and do something to stop him, but this kid was so fast he'd tried to open the door and failed almost before it registered.

'You're not getting out,' said Dog after the fourth attempt. 'Look, just go with it for the moment, okay?'

The kid's face was unreadable because of the four tentacle things where his nose ought to be. His mouth was there underneath in the proper place, more or less.

'What you going to do anyway?' said Dog and nodded at the plastic ties round his wrists and ankles.

The kid sat back.

'Don't say much, do you?'

Nothing.

'Can't say I like having him here,' said Mr Mendelssohn the following morning.

'Yes, sir,' said Dog. He wasn't really sure what the problem was, since Mr Mendelssohn kept the place tight, and it was his decision to bring him to his home anyway. After all, he didn't want anybody discovering Delia, but maybe that was the point. They were all the same.

'This boy cost me money, Dog. And that debt is yours, until he gets to pay it off.'

'I'm still not quite getting what it is you want me to do.' Dog looked across the garden to the small building a couple of hundred yards away. It was Mendelssohn's wife's studio when she was here, which was almost never. It wasn't something that was talked about.

'I can't have him running away. He needs to work. I need you to convince him his best interests lie here with me. Right now he's tied up, but he's no use to me like that. I don't care how you get his cooperation, Dog; you can bribe him, threaten his family, assuming he has one, whatever you need to do. But he stays with us. Is it clear now?'

Dog glanced out at the building. It was a squat brick-built thing like a wart on the rolling meadows of Cheshire. He nodded. 'Yes, sir.'

Mr Mendelssohn leaned over him. 'You just make sure you do.'

Dog collected some food from the cook. He wasn't sure what the little freak would want to eat, but except for those weird nose tentacles and the fur he looked to be pretty normal. Yeah, apart from those.

Delia stopped him at the back door.

'We going out?' she asked. He didn't turn round for a moment but instead took a deep breath in through his nose and across his tongue so that he could taste her scent. He really did like it a lot, even though she was wearing the moisturiser. He turned round, her skin shone with the cream she put on it. Every square inch, as far as he knew, or could imagine. And her hair was wet, as usual.

'I am. We've got a prisoner out in the studio,' he said.

'That kid you and Dad brought in last night?'

Right, of course, she never really slept.

'Yes, the kid we brought in last night who is now our prisoner in the studio. But I'm not sure how much your dad wants you to know about it.'

Delia smiled the smile that tended to get him into trouble. 'You know I can wrap him around my little finger.'

'Yes, but if you got hurt your dad would kill me, and if you were dead you wouldn't be there to do the protective wrapping.'

'He'd kill you for a lot less than that.'

Dog might pride himself on being a bit of a rogue and a joker, but he would certainly never touch the daughter of Mr Mendelssohn, no matter how much she wanted it. 'Well look, I need to check him and make sure he hasn't broken loose and wrecked the place, or escaped, or turned into some sort of raving monster that would tear you to pieces.'

She giggled.

'But if he's still tied up, I imagine you could probably get to know him a bit better.'

'I could just follow you.'

Dog sighed. 'Yes, you could do that, but you want somebody to play with right? And if something bad happened then I'd be gone and you'd have nobody.'

He thought perhaps his logic was working, because she didn't argue this time. Instead she went to the door, opened it and held it for him.

'Thanks. I'll come back and tell you all about it, okay?'

With the bag of food in one hand, Dog unlocked the studio door. The main workroom smelled of old clay and oil paints. There was a workbench along the back wall facing the floor-to-ceiling windows that made up the opposite north-facing wall. There were several tables, and a pottery wheel, with stools and chairs scattered about. They hadn't cleared out the tools last night, and in daylight he looked at the ranks of chisels, gouges, hammers and all the other things he had no name for that could be used as nice stabbing or cutting weapons. What a great place to put a prisoner, he thought.

Their new acquisition, however, was upstairs. Dog went through the opposite door which led into a small hall with two other doors leading off and a spiral staircase to the living area.

Dog wasn't quite sure of the whole relationship between Mr Mendelssohn and his wife. What it amounted to was that sometimes she was here but most of the time she wasn't. The studio was covered in dust and the remaining scents were so old he didn't think she'd been in here for years.

The freak-boy was where they had left him: handcuffed to the radiator pipe. He straightened up as Dog came through. He had tried to pull off the cuff. There were scrape marks on his wrists and the pipe, and the smell of blood. Dog felt sorry for him.

Apart from the radiator, this room contained a couple of sofas, an armchair and a table for eating with four hard-back chairs round it. A door on one side went through to a kitchen, and on the other, to the bedroom. Dog put the bag of food down on the table, pulled one of the hard-back chairs round so he was facing the prisoner and sat down.

'Look, I don't like to see you chained up like this. It was just a precaution until we could talk properly.'

The weird nose with its five prehensile-looking tentacle things that stuck out a few inches was quite distracting. Although Dog relied a great deal on his sense of smell and people's overall body language when he was talking to them, he still liked to see their faces. But this fellow was just too weird.

'I know you can move pretty fast, so I am going to take precautions. Like I said, what we really want to do is talk to you, so if you could refrain from trying to escape at least until we've had a proper conversation, I would really appreciate it.'

He looked expectantly at the prisoner, hoping for some sort of response, but he was disappointed. The kid didn't move and there was nothing in his face Dog could interpret as being agreement, disagreement, or even hate.

Dog pulled another set of handcuffs from the bag of food. On the one hand he was relaxed in his attitude towards life and had no desire to imprison people, but on the other was Mr Mendelssohn and the debt. He wanted to be able to pay off all his debts so that he would be free at some point. Not that he was entirely sure what one was supposed to do when one was free. Having a family and a place to call home was what really appealed.

Staying alert he crossed to a few feet away from the prisoner. 'If you wouldn't mind giving me your free wrist, I'll attach you to me and then we'll go and get some food. How's that?'

He stared into the eyes of the prisoner, trying not to be distracted by the nose tentacles. He looked for some sort of agreement, maybe if he just said okay that would help. But nothing. Dog attached the cuff to his own wrist and then held out the open part of the other cuff to the boy. The boy's eyes flicked towards the cuff and its open jaw. Then he looked back into Dog's eyes. It was a long moment. Dog could not imagine what might be going through the kid's head. Then slowly, and that in itself seemed strange for this freak, he let his free hand stretch out and into the cuff.

When Dog reached to close it, there was a blur. He got pulled forward off-balance. Another blur. A chink-chink of metal. A movement of air across his cheek as he continued to fall forward. Dog caught himself on his hands only to see his wrists were handcuffed together. The freak-boy was no longer in front of him and the other pair of cuffs was dangling loosely from the radiator. The key that had been in Dog's pocket was now in its lock.

'Shit. Shit. Shit.' Dog glanced towards the exit. Nothing. The boy had already gone. 'Shit!'

Sudden noise behind Dog nearly made him jump out of his skin. He whipped his head round. The prisoner was sitting at the table investigating the bag of food.

Forcing his breathing to some level of regularity, Dog plucked the key from the other handcuffs and unlocked the ones around his wrists. Behind him, the sound of munching as the thief chewed his way through a cucumber and cheese sandwich.

Chapter 3

Mitchell

The door opened cautiously. Mitchell saw a tired and thin woman. He knew from the records she was no older than him, but she looked it. Much older, and poorly nourished from the minimum food rations everyone without an alternative income suffered.

Protected professions got additional rations, apart from also having the money to pay for extras. Police got plenty, and Graham, standing slightly in front of him, did not have any nutritional deficiencies—the Purity was the most protected profession of them all.

Mitchell wondered whether Graham had any clue what these people had to live on. Well, he might have been told, but he had probably not experienced it. He was in his thirties, he would have been aware of the fall, but his accent betrayed a protected lifestyle. His parents would have been able to ride out the privations for as long as money continued to have value.

They might not even have been in the country. There were places where S.I.D had less impact—those places that had less reliance on computers.

Mitchell had not bothered listening to Graham introducing them. Ellen Lomax betrayed more fear than most, but it didn't mean anything. Nobody truly liked the

Purity, he wasn't even sure Purity agents even liked each other.

He followed Graham inside and removed his hat as he did so. Proper hats were old-fashioned and, apart from a few hobbyists, no one really knew how to make them. Cloth caps were the mainstay, but Mitchell kept the old fedora Catherine had given him. He had hated it when she bought it. Now he treasured it.

'Good morning, Mrs Lomax,' he said as he passed her. She shut the door and followed them. Graham had gone into the front room. The furniture was old and threadbare, but the wooden surfaces were free of dust. They didn't sit.

'How do you feel about the Purity, Mrs Lomax?' said Graham.

Mitchell suppressed a laugh. What kind of question was that? Almost as if he was doing a survey for a manufacturer of cleaning products, or selling a cult.

The woman hesitated. 'We need it.'

Graham nodded. 'You understand that we are the only thing that stands between you and chaos?'

She said nothing. Her arms were wrapped around herself as if she were holding in her grief and anger. Mitchell could see it even if Graham couldn't. Ellen Lomax's record covered the death of her husband and son, in a fire set by a mob. She was still angry.

'Mind if I use your toilet?' said Mitchell. It earned him a hard look from Graham, as if he didn't understand it was simply an excuse to look round.

'Upstairs on the left at the front.'

Mitchell left the room as Graham started questioning Mrs Lomax about the van that had stolen away Melinda

Vogler. There was no chance he would come up with anything new from her, she hadn't seen anything—or, if she had, she wasn't telling.

He climbed the stairs slowly. The place was spotless, not a hint of dust anywhere. She must fill her time cleaning. Not that there would be much else for her to do. She didn't even rate a terminal. A technological have-not on the edge of society with nowhere to fall.

At the top of the stairs he looked around. There were three doors. The one to the front of the house was the bathroom. Yates had already checked it, and Mitchell wanted time to look at the other rooms.

The door next to the bathroom opened on to a room with a double bed and windows that looked out on the street. Two cupboards, one empty and one with Ellen's clothes, such as they were, and mostly old. The dressing table had glass containers that might once have held beauty products. Now gone dry. Drawers with underwear, some bulkier items like jumpers. Nothing of interest hidden beneath them.

That left the final door Yates had mentioned.

Mitchell had come prepared. It wasn't a complex lock and the picks made short work of it.

The smell was the first thing he noticed. Definitely a different smell, and not musty with age. A bed, properly made, cupboard with clothes all relatively modern and in a better state of repair than Ellen's. Young person clothes. Shoes. He reached down and checked the size. Someone small, or not yet fully grown.

He knew he was eating into 'taking too long in the toilet' territory, and he did not want Graham getting curious. He glanced round. There were no dirty clothes on the floor, so he dug into the back of the wardrobe and pulled out a shoe that looked like it had seen a lot of wear. He shoved it in his pocket.

Relocking the door took only a moment. He went back into the bathroom and flushed the toilet. He opened the window a fraction, as if he'd left an unpleasant smell, and made a big show of coming down stairs.

He walked through into the front room to find Ellen Lomax sitting in one of the armchairs curled up and in tears. Graham was leaning over her. 'We can take everything away from you. What else did you see?'

She shook her head. 'There was nothing, I didn't see anything. It just came round the corner fast and drove away.' Her voice was strained but still strong. Mitchell felt a certain pride in the woman. Bloody southerners coming up north and thinking they knew what the people were like.

She was not as completely broken as she appeared. There was someone in her life she needed to protect and she was willing to protect them with her life if need be.

Mitchell understood that. Had she taken in a stray kid to replace her son? Not properly adopted and then hidden from the Purity so they didn't have a riffy? Possible.

'There's nothing upstairs,' said Mitchell. As if he had not noticed Graham's unacceptable behaviour—well, unacceptable for the police, the Purity could do as they pleased. And usually did. But Mitchell's comment had been designed to interrupt Graham's flow.

Graham glanced up at him.

Mitchell continued. 'She obviously knows nothing, what would you expect from someone like this?'

Graham looked at the crushed woman in front of him. And stood up and away from her. Mitchell noticed gloves on his hands that had not been there before. Would he really have resorted to violence? Easier to imply that she was too inferior to be of value. That was a concept Graham could understand.

'What did you find?'

'Toilet.'

Graham's eyes were piercing, as if he was trying to see through Mitchell.

'Her bedroom and another one that no one is using.' Not even technically untrue, nobody was using it *right now*. And he didn't mention the fact it had been locked, that would have made it far too interesting.

'All right, let's go.' Graham stalked out of the room.

'If you think of anything, or you need to talk to anyone,' said Mitchell—he rummaged in his pocket and pulled out an old business card with his details. 'You can reach me on this number.'

Ellen Lomax took it out of his hand almost on automatic. Mitchell knew what was going through her head. Mitchell had just lied to the Purity, to protect her, and that put him on her side. If she really hadn't been hiding anyone she could have got the Purity off her back by revealing his lie.

But she didn't, which only confirmed Mitchell's ideas.

He took his leave and followed Graham out into the street. Graham was standing just outside the gate and staring around. 'Most people try to live in groups,' he said. 'For safety, and for the comfort of having others around them.'

'But?'

'Lomax lives in a house on her own.' He gestured briefly with one hand. 'People do that when they have secrets.'

'Sometimes the secret is only a hate and loathing for everyone whose family survived when your own did not.'

Graham turned to face him. 'Like you, Detective Inspector Mitchell.'

'I have had to come to terms with it.'

'Have you?' said Graham. 'The most effective killer of freaks in the country? Are you sure you aren't deluding yourself?'

'I don't let my personal feelings get in the way of my work, if that's what you mean.'

Graham said nothing more and they got into the car.

Chapter 4

Dog

Dog hated watching other people eat, especially when he didn't have any food of his own. And the way that freak-boy ate was even worse. His nose tentacles floated above the food as the kid held the sandwich, or whatever he was eating, underneath them. For a moment they would waft backwards and forwards as if he was sniffing it, then he would put it in his mouth and eat it normally. He had teeth and a tongue. Unfortunately what he didn't seem to have was a voice.

Dog thought he was being extremely tolerant. He didn't talk; just waited. Salivating.

Finally the eating was done. The freak-boy sat back in his chair.

'Thanks for not running away,' said Dog. 'You see, Mr Mendelssohn, my boss, well, he's not so understanding of people who fail him. Not that he's unfair, but still, if you'd run away he wouldn't have been very understanding of me.'

Dog waited expectantly for his ex-prisoner to say at least something. A thank you would have been nice. Nothing. The boy glanced over Dog's shoulder as if he hadn't even spoken.

'Look, I don't want to be rude or anything but—'

The scream that broke through the room had qualities that Dog was sure would break glass. That was one of the things about Delia, she could move silently when she wanted to. Still, Dog was pleased to see he wasn't the only one to slam his hands over his ears. Freak-boy hadn't much liked her scream either.

'For pity's sake, Delia,' said Dog. 'Anybody would think you hadn't seen a bloody freak before.'

He turned and saw her standing in the doorway. She had an odd taste in clothes, when she wore them, not that she ever went naked, but she spent a lot of time in the pool. On this occasion she was wearing one of those tight dresses that emphasised every curve down to her hips, then spread out. The pattern on this one gave the impression of some sort of fishtail. Dog didn't think it was very subtle, but she was a bit weird. Nice, but weird. Over the top she wore a pink cardigan for warmth. She liked pink.

'Sorry,' she said, 'I just wasn't really expecting...' Her voice tailed off and she waved her hand in the direction of the kid and his tentacle face.

'No need to apologise to me,' said Dog. 'You could try apologising to freak-boy here, but he's not very talkative.'

Jason

The girl had screamed so loud it hurt. Slamming his hands over his ears had been his reaction, but the time taken even for him to get his hands to his ears was plenty enough for her to do damage.

He'd never heard anyone scream like that. And on his nights out, when he had not been careful enough and had been seen, he had heard plenty of screams.

She was calm now. She and the Dog were talking to each other. He thought he should probably be listening, but

- 334 -

he was lethargic after the amount of food he had eaten. He
hadn't eaten that much in years; in fact he couldn't remember
the last time. She wasn't wearing perfume, like the Dog, but
there was something else artificial about her. And rotten fish.
She must eat a lot of it. The scent of artificiality pervaded the
human world. Both the women and the men poured stuff on
their skin to change the way they smelled. This Mr
Mendelssohn had it last night, although it wasn't
overpowering. Unlike the driver, who wore a scent that was
like having your nose dragged across sandpaper.

But it was odd, he thought to himself; this Dog had said
something about them being the same, about them smelling
the same. As far as Jason knew, his sense of smell was so far
beyond humans they were like the blind where he saw
everything in vivid colour. Except it was scents. He knew
what Dog meant. There was something they all shared and it
was distinct now he was looking for it.

But apart from that, Dog did smell a bit like a canine.
There were overtones, though he was clearly human too, as
much as Jason was human at least.

And this new one, she had an overtone as well,
something Jason had never experienced before—and it
wasn't the rotten fish. He took a deep breath in through his
nose. It folded out to expose the extra-sensitive surface on
the inside. Yes, there was something similar about the three
of them. He homed in on the specific scent, sifting it from all
the others. They were freaks but not freaks, and they shared
this smell.

'Why is he staring at me?' said the girl.

Dog had said her name was Delia.

'What do you mean, staring at you?'

Jason put his attention back on the world through his eyes, rather than simply through his nose. She was staring at him.

'See?' she said. 'He's still looking at me.'

Jason was aware of a slight change in the way the Dog smelled. He wasn't sure what it meant, but it seemed aggressive.

'Hey, freak-boy, it's rude to stare at people.' Dog turned his attention back to the girl. 'I don't think he's been around people very much. He doesn't know how to behave.'

Jason turned his attention to Dog; he was definitely more aggressive now.

'What's his name?' said Delia.

Dog shrugged. 'No idea. He won't talk.'

'Perhaps he can't talk,' said Delia. 'I mean, look at his face, maybe he doesn't have any... voice.' She had hesitated as if she was searching for the right word but failed to come up with it.

'You mean larynx,' said Dog loudly and clearly. 'Well, freak-boy, can you talk?'

Delia laughed at him. 'He's not deaf.'

'Anybody would be deaf after that scream.'

Delia moved up close, no longer scared apparently. She hunkered down so her head was at the same height as Jason's. 'Are you a mute?'

Jason found her scent to be... now even he couldn't quite figure the word he wanted. He finally settled on attractive. He nodded.

'You poor thing. That's terrible.' She reached out to take his hand, but he moved it and her fingers came down on his leg.

She jerked her hand away. 'So sorry.' She turned to Dog. 'His fur is so soft.'

Dog pushed back his chair with a scrape. 'I think you better be going now, Delia. Your dad would throw a fit if he knew you were in here. How do we know he isn't dangerous?'

Delia stood up. She was taller than Dog. 'Well, you weren't getting very far with him, were you? You hadn't even found out that he couldn't talk and you've been trying to have a conversation for hours. You need me.'

'All right, I'm grateful you discovered he's dumb,' said Dog. 'But your dad would explode if he was here and saw you with him—not tied up.'

'He's not going to find out, is he?' she said. 'Not unless you tell him.'

'You need to leave,' said Dog.

'I'm staying here,' said Delia.

'I'll chuck you out.'

'I'd like to see you try.'

Delia crossed her arms and set her feet as if ready for his attempt. Dog just stared at her, and then sat down. 'Fine, whatever, the important thing is that freak-boy—'

'Why don't you find out what his name is?'

'Because he can't talk, as you so cleverly discovered.'

'Well, maybe he can write.'

All the time the two of them had been arguing Jason had the feeling they wouldn't even have noticed if he left.

'Well, as long as you're here,' said Dog, 'you might as well help. Let's see what else we can get out of freak-boy.'

Jason looked up at Delia; at this particular moment she seemed very tall indeed. And she put her fists on her hips, like his mother used to when she got angry with him.

'Listen, why don't you start treating him with some respect. You might get what you want a bit faster.'

'What would you suggest?'

'Well, stop calling him freak-boy for a start. I mean, seriously, pot-kettle-black' said Delia, then she turned her attention to Jason and came down to his level again. 'Can you write?'

Jason was confused. He spent all his life running away from everyone except his mother, and now in the space of just two days everything had changed. He had a full stomach, and people were talking to him. It didn't even matter that Dog was rude. It was just someone was talking to him as if he was really there, and not some sort of ghost. Not some sort of night demon that scared people as he flitted through the shadows.

There were no shadows here, and he couldn't hide even if he wanted to. And just at this moment, hiding was the last thing he wanted to do.

Chapter 5

Dog

'Well?'

Mr Mendelssohn had summoned him at around seven in the evening. He had entered his boss's inner sanctum: an office with no windows in the middle of the house. To Dog's eye it was part of the big lounge area that had been partitioned.

But the partition was steel and stone. The door was heavy and moved like thick oil on its hinges. The office itself, as much as Dog understood these things, was just an office. Papers, folders, filing cabinets and that ancient typewriter. Nothing electronic, just the electric lights.

Mr Mendelssohn stood behind his desk drinking his pure coffee. Its scent made Dog salivate.

'His name's Jason Lomax, and he can't talk.'

'And?'

'He can see the benefits of being part of the team, but he's worried about his mother.'

'That doesn't sound good.'

'She's kept him secret all these years, she's not about to start telling anyone now. Harbouring a freak is—'

He stopped. He didn't need to tell his boss the penalty. He was fully aware that, of all his crimes, that would be considered the worst. And the punishment was execution—

after all, you couldn't trust anyone who put their own interests above those of the whole human race.

'So?'

'I thought I might pop over and have a chat with his mum. Apparently she'll be worried sick because he's never been away for so long.'

'But he'll work for me?'

'Yeah, he will.'

Mr Mendelssohn smiled. 'Excellent. I have just the job to try him out.' He sat down and started looking through the papers in a folder. Dog stayed where he was. Mr Mendelssohn looked up.

'Why are *you* going to talk to his mother?'

'He doesn't like going out in daylight—who can blame him, you've seen his face—and...'

'And?'

'He wants to stay here,' Dog said. 'I know that's totally out of the question and I told him so. Ridiculous, after all you don't like me staying here, and there's your daughter, of course. Too much temptation.' It came out in a rush, and somewhere along the line he lost control of his mouth.

Mr Mendelssohn stared at him for a short while, holding his coffee cup halfway to his mouth.

'He can stay here.'

'What?' said Dog. 'I don't think that's a good course of action, sir.'

Mr Mendelssohn put his head on one side, in a way that made Dog think he was being made fun of. He never did that cute head thing that real dogs did. Did he?

'Are you arguing with me?'

'Of course not, sir.'

'He can stay.'

'Yes, sir,' said Dog, 'so, can I—'

'No.'

Knutsford to East Manchester was a bit of a distance, ten miles or so, and even though Dog had settled into an easy trot that ate up the distance it still took over two hours.

There had been a gang on the main street in Altrincham. He'd been moving so comfortably—and the wind was in the wrong direction—that they saw him at the same time as he saw them.

They didn't have his skills, but dodging them had delayed him by another half hour.

When Dog arrived in the street that Ellen Lomax lived in, he saw a car driving away. Not just any car, he recognised a plainclothes police car when he saw one. They smelled.

Worse still: when he reached the gate he caught the unmistakable whiff of DI Mitchell. Just as well he hadn't turned up much earlier, they might have caught him here. He'd never live it down if he was caught on a mercy mission, as opposed to working some heist.

He was surprised how difficult he found it making his way up the path accompanied by Mitchell's smell when every part of him just wanted to run.

It was also pretty weird knocking on a door, like a normal person. And in daylight too.

He waited; he could hear someone moving around inside the house but no one came to the door. He knocked again a bit harder. He looked around. This was not much of a place to live, nobody to help you, nobody to be friends with, and of course no one to spy on you. And no one to report you to the Purity, or the police, for harbouring a criminal.

From what he could tell the person inside the house had stopped moving. He turned back to face the door. He didn't want to make a fuss and he certainly didn't want to scare her. But he really did need to speak with her.

'Mrs Lomax, I need to talk to you.'

As far as he could tell there was nobody else in the area, but you never knew what tech they might be pointing in your direction; mind you, if they were doing that they already knew that someone who didn't have a riffy was standing outside her door. Oh well, in for a penny, in for a pound, whatever that meant.

'Look, Mrs Lomax, I need to talk to you because I got a message from your son.' There was a sudden movement inside the house. Dog wondered whether he'd said the wrong thing. 'I've met him. He sent me to give you a message. He's alive, he's fine and with friends.'

Dog slumped down in the doorway. He preferred that because he was not quite so visible. Maybe he should have gone to the back door. He sniffed.

There had been someone else with Mitchell. Not Yates but someone he didn't recognise at all. He wore perfume and, if Dog was any judge, it was a proper one and that meant expensive.

There was movement inside the house again, someone getting closer to the door. She wasn't moving fast, just cautiously. Of course he wasn't visible in the glass anymore. She might have thought he'd gone, and he really didn't want to surprise her.

'Hello, Mrs Lomax,' he said being careful not to raise his voice. The movement inside the house came to an abrupt halt. 'I know you can hear me. And I know you're just the other side of the door because I can hear you. I can hear the way Jason can smell.'

There was no movement from behind the door, and he just sat there for a while. He could hear her breathing; there was something wrong with her.

'Who are you?'

'Well now, that's actually a really interesting question,' said Dog. 'Jason told me you've been hiding him ever since he was born because he's different. I'm different too.'

There was another pause. 'You've seen him? He didn't come home last night or the night before.'

'Yeah, he's all right. Look, do we have to do this through the door? Somebody might go past and wonder why I'm sitting here, and I don't like being out in the open in the same way that he doesn't.'

Eventually she unlocked the door and let him in.

Chapter 6

Chloe

Chloe lay face down in her bed. She had pummelled her punch bag until she was completely exhausted, and the hunger gnawed at her. She had tried to block out the sounds from the rest of the house using chewed up bits of paper shoved in her ears. It made no difference. She could hear everything.

And not only in this house, in the houses either side she could hear the people moving around and talking—although thankfully their words were sufficiently indistinct that she couldn't follow them. But it wasn't just the hearing: she knew where they were in relation to herself, and she felt like she was going crazy. And then she wondered if that's what it was like for a freak, a freak like her. Did their senses become so twisted and confused they simply couldn't take it anymore?

She shook her head, rubbing her nose in the wet patch on her pillow, made damp from tears. She knew that wasn't what happened. Freaks went insane because the virus got into their brain, that's why some of them lasted longer than others. Sometimes they died quickly because the modification to their body was simply fatal. Sometimes they simply went mad without any other physical sign. And sometimes they just went mad because something grew inside their head.

It just didn't make any sense. When had she become infected? When would they be coming for her?

Mum and Dad didn't believe it. If they had, they would have reported her—wouldn't they? That confused her as well. Dad was in the FreakWatch and he wasn't talking to her as if he thought she was a freak, but they hadn't said anything. What did that mean?

And she'd had a check-up in the hospital. Nobody had suggested any problem, and there was no indication she was infected. If she was having physical changes she must have been infected ages ago and it would have shown up in the tests. It must be something else, it *had* to be. But what?

She could hear everything. And her body weight was a fraction of what it ought to be. And she was always hungry. And there were two lumps in her back.

So she was back at square one. She had all the symptoms of being infected with S.I.D, and nobody thought she was. She had no idea whether she was supposed to feel happy or sad about that. All she felt was confusion.

Chloe woke from her doze at the sound of someone approaching the front door. Two people, a man and a woman from the footsteps. They knocked.

'Oh, who's at the door at this time?' said her mother.

Chloe was a little surprised that her mother hadn't realised there was somebody at the door until the knock. She had to remind herself she was the weird one here.

Her father made a noncommittal grunting noise and then said, 'Better not be one of those news reporters, or that bloody teacher.'

She heard him stomping out of the kitchen along the hall. It wasn't so much that she heard him moving, more that she could visualise his exact position as he got up from his chair, pushing it back, moving around the table, going through the door and then along the passage.

'Who is it?'

'It's me, Colin, and Chardonnay,' came the voice from the other side of the door.

If Chloe hadn't already had her eyes shut she would have closed them in disgust. The stalwarts of FreakWatch.

Colin Thackery, the man who thought that Mrs Wilberforce down the road was harbouring a freak, or might possibly be one herself, just because she spied on his little trips to number 15. He thinks nobody notices, but everybody knows.

And Ms Chardonnay Jones-Willis, who liked to be the centre of attention for the sake of it. Chloe wondered if she possessed a single brain cell inside her bleach-blonde head.

Except, of course, Chloe was well aware that Ms Jones-Willis (never married) did actually have an opinion on one thing: a poorly disguised dislike of people possessing a dark skin tone, or people with a slightly tinted skin tone, or people with eyes of a slightly different shape to your typical Anglo-Saxon; in fact a dislike of anybody who didn't conform to her personal ideal of genetic purity. That list of intolerance included Chloe and her parents, but freaks were the worst offenders, and she was allowed to express her hatred of those without let or hindrance.

Her father let them in, of course, and escorted the two of them through into the sitting room. He had taken their coats, hung them up in the hall, and asked his wife to make everybody a nice cuppa. It was all so very British. *It was all,* Chloe thought, *so very false.*

Finally, everybody was settled in their chair with the finest crockery and tea so pale it would suit even Chardonnay's standards, and all the pleasantries had been done with while Chloe became very bored.

'So, to what do we owe the pleasure?' said her father, though Chloe somehow doubted there was any pleasure to be had. Her father did not like people visiting unannounced.

Chloe could imagine Ms Jones-Willis looking pointedly at her companion, willing him to do all the talking.

'You must be feeling a bit of strain,' said Colin as his opening gambit. 'I mean to say, this whole thing with Chloe being attacked, the police and the reporters, you must have an awful lot on your plate.'

'An awful lot,' said Chardonnay.

Chloe muttered to herself, 'Is there an echo in here?'

'It's not been easy,' said her father. 'But we manage, keep our chin up.'

'Of course, of course, and you're doing a splendid job, Mike.'

'Splendid.'

Chloe thought it was lucky for Chardonnay that Chloe herself was not in the room at this moment, because she had a strong desire to slap the woman. Mind you, she'd had exactly the same desire every single time she met her. Chardonnay was one of those people that insisted on treating children, regardless of age, as some sort of unintelligent two-year-old. She spoke in a baby, sing-song way and attempted bribery with the promise of sweets—that never materialised.

'Yes, we're doing okay,' said her father. 'And I appreciate your concern. I still don't quite understand why you're here?'

'We just wanted you to understand that if you need any help at all, we are here for you.'

'Here for you.'

Chloe was incredulous; could the woman not actually hear herself?

'Well, thank you again. I appreciate it. Thank you for dropping by.' Her father seemed to be completely nonplussed; Chloe could tell that they didn't look like they were going to move any time soon, sitting back as they were holding their cups and saucers. She pushed herself up on the bed and shook her head a little. How could she possibly know that they were sitting back in their chairs holding their cups and saucers?

'Overactive imagination,' she muttered to herself.

She said it, but she knew she was right.

'So,' said Colin, 'if you would like somebody else to take over the meeting, perhaps hold it in somebody else's house, then obviously we'd be happy to do that.'

Chloe waited for the echo, but in this case it didn't come. She was quite disappointed; it was like waiting for the other shoe to drop.

'I am quite happy to continue to host the meeting, after all I am the chairman and I have some responsibilities,' said her father.

'But of course, I was only saying.'

'Only saying.'

Her father got to his feet in a rush, she heard him plonk his cup and saucer down on the table. 'Well, like I said, I'm very grateful for your concern and really appreciate your offer of assistance, but, as I say, at the present time I do feel able to continue to host the meeting. So that's what we'll do.'

'Of course, your daughter—'

If Chardonnay had been about to echo Colin's words she was interrupted and drowned out. 'Don't you dare bring my daughter into this,' said her father, with barely restrained fury. 'If you think you can force me to resign my position with your innuendo and petty schemes, you've got another thing coming.' Chloe heard him storm out the front room to the coat hooks and then return to the door. 'Well, I am afraid I'm a little bit busy right now so we'll have to cut this meeting short. It's been *lovely* to see you, but I'm sure you want to be on your way. Right now!'

Chloe grinned and silently applauded her dad. Perhaps he wasn't taken in by these puffed-up whatevers. And she was very happy with the way he had defended her, even though he was probably wrong.

Chapter 7

Chloe

She had not left her room the entire day, except to visit the bathroom, and she made sure that no one heard. Her mother had come to the door twice asking her if she wanted something to eat, or a drink.

She hadn't, well not the first time. Second time she had, but was not going to let her mother dictate her actions. She was sulking and she was an adult, almost. Damned if she wouldn't manage a full-grown adult sulk.

The world outside got dark about five, and the pressure from her stomach finally persuaded her to act. She still refused to go downstairs; if she did that her parents would have won.

But she could go out of the window.

Her bedroom, the smallest one in the house, had its window at the back. There weren't any drones now. If the remaining reporters had them they weren't running them constantly. Besides, with her new improved hearing, she could easily tell if one was near.

She added a big jumper and a jacket, then changed into her boots. Shoes were particularly expensive nowadays and in short supply. But there was a cobbler nearby in Didsbury who tanned his own leather. He had a couple of apprentices because, when all was said and done, people would always need shoes. It was a safe profession.

There were moves by the government to get rid of the old child labour laws and make school compulsory only up to age thirteen. Pure sciences were being discouraged and practical skills given priority.

Chloe didn't care about that since she had her own path mapped out.

She stopped with her left boot only half-tied.

She *used* to have her path mapped out. Only a week ago, the Purity was the way she wanted to go. But things had changed. Despite Miss Kepple, Chloe was not sure whether the Purity would even want her now. Even if her physical problems were entirely normal and treatable. Even if the hospital had declared her free of the virus.

She focused her attention back on her bootlace. She could feel the lightness in herself now. She had not tried to weigh herself again, she was almost scared of what she would find, and yet as far as she could see she looked normal enough. She had never developed much up top and her training had always kept her trim.

Her stomach reminded her it needed feeding.

The window opened on a catch that hinged on the right. Cold air poured in. The grass looked a long way away, but she was used to falling and absorbing the energy by rolling. And she was so much lighter. Still, she had a lifetime of knowing that big falls would hurt; it was a hard instinct to overcome.

She didn't want to let all the warmth out—her parents might investigate the draught—so she planned to close the window behind her, but if the latch wasn't on she could probably get it open again. Assuming she could climb back up.

She retrieved a small torch she kept in her desk drawer and shone it on the wall outside her window. There was a ledge. Pocketing the torch, she swung one leg out and then squirmed her way over until her foot found the support. Holding tight to the window frame she put her weight on it and lifted her other leg out. Her flexibility was another benefit of training.

Taking care not to make a noise, she moved sideways and pushed the window shut. Now she was clinging precariously to the outside of the house. Fingers clamped on the tiles that stuck out from the frame and overhung the wall slightly. She bent her legs and jumped backwards.

The sense of weightlessness overtook her and, without any volition, she gave a little squeal. The ground was coming up fast, but even closer was the washing line. She had forgotten and not seen it in the black.

She tucked into a ball and felt her body turn. She straightened and plummeted to the ground, feeling the washing line tug across her coat and flick her chin. Her feet met the ground. She bent her legs automatically.

And came to a stop crouching in the garden. She put her hands down on to the wet grass and dirt. She didn't need to roll, but she was aware she had done a three-hundred-and-sixty degree turn in the air. As if she were diving into the public swimming pool from a high board. Not that she ever had; she didn't do that sort of thing. To be honest, she had always been a bit afraid of heights.

Chloe of a week ago could not have done what she just did.

The light was on in the kitchen and she could see the shadow of her mother moving around behind the blind. She realised they would know she had left the house if they checked her riffy—parents had the right to track their children. But if they did not think she had left the house, they wouldn't check.

She ran to the end of the garden and in an easy jump scaled the fence to land in the alley at the back. She set off at a run. She was surprised at how easy it was. Her eyes were adjusting to the dark and she managed to avoid the worst of the bumps and ruts. She was able to dodge the dustbins.

A dog barked as she passed one house, but it was just a warning not an attack. She surprised more than one cat as she ran.

She got to the end of the alley, which ran parallel to her street, and came out on to a main road. There were some lights here but she kept to the shadows, still running. She felt as if she could run forever, even in these boots, because she was so full of energy.

And it was so good to be out, away from all the pressures. Away from her parents, away from the reporters, and away from the Purity and the strange Miss Kepple. As she moved she found it comfortable to let out a little noise on each breath. Somehow the running made the pain in her back ease as well.

This was what she needed; this was what she had always needed.

She had no idea where she was going, her body still demanded food, and every now and again she noticed a rat or a mouse lurking in a corner. And every time she got the idea that she might eat them—before her mind took over and rejected it. She chose not to ask herself how she could even see them.

Clearly she really was too hungry right now, if she was thinking about eating vermin.

Then she smelled it. It was beautiful. She realised she had covered at least a mile and a half because she was in the north part of what used to be Burnage. And there was a traditional chip shop. The owners claimed it was the only real chip shop left in Manchester—which was a convenient way of negating the others. But whatever the truth, the place had a reputation.

Ashley had been to their restaurant, of course, and said she had had a piece of cod with chips and vinegar. She had claimed it was the best thing she had ever tasted. It cost, though.

Well, Chloe had money on her personal account, and the smell was heavenly.

She followed her nose. The smell led her up a side road, and across three gardens. She didn't care. She could see well enough and leapt each hedge and fence as if she were a deer. She landed finally in front of a line of shops. The smell was overpowering and light poured from the single open frontage.

She stopped running. There were people around— couples, people alone, others in groups—but they barely gave her a glance. This was freedom, she realised, to be in a place with no one to know who you are. Nobody telling you what to think or do.

On the other hand, she had never been in a place like this, at least not alone, and not at night. She stuck her hands in her pockets and tried to think herself into confidence. After all, no one could touch her. And if they tried, well, she knew how to look after herself.

Stepping into the shop was like walking into an oven. A very noisy oven.

Chips and fish were hissing and bubbling in the hot oil. From the restaurant section in the back came the noise of people talking and the occasional piercing screech of a table or chair leg shifting. A big serving counter stood between her and the cooking area. Well-to-do people lounged in the take-away zone. Half a dozen staff worked behind the counter, and above them was the menu.

Chloe stepped out of the way and read the prices. A lot of items had *subject to availability* next to them. There was a chalk board on a side wall which listed just what fish and other meats were available. Almost everything was crossed off, except scampi. She had no idea what that was, but the price, with chips, was within what she thought she could afford.

'What would you like, love?' asked a middle-aged woman with a sweaty red face. She seemed impatient, though Chloe knew no one had come in behind her.

'Scampi and chips?'

'Right.' The woman turned away, gathered up a portion of small round balls and tossed them in a fryer. They sizzled noisily, which went some way to hiding the sound of Chloe's stomach. It also hid, for everyone else except Chloe, the sound of a gun being cocked.

Chloe had never heard a real one before, but the sound itself seemed to be in the shape of a gun. And it was located just to the right of Chloe's spine, at stomach level. She could also picture the man, taller than her, lots of mass.

At that moment the woman behind the counter turned back.

'Yes, dear, what about you?' she said to the man behind Chloe.

Chloe had received a lot of training in disarming a person with a gun, but it had never involved having someone else in the line of fire. If Chloe moved now, and he fired, he might hit any one of the others here. And if she didn't move, and he fired, he could still hurt other people as well as her.

But she knew exactly where the gun was.

Rather than letting her muscle memory respond, she snaked her hand behind her back and slipped two fingers behind the trigger. He reacted to her movement and tried to fire, succeeding only in squashing her fingers, which hurt. Without any further hesitation her training kicked in. She spun on the spot and lifted her arm so he was pointing the gun at the ceiling. Her knee impacted with his groin. He groaned and bent over. Her knee lifted again and smashed into his face, breaking his nose with a satisfying crack. The gun came loose in Chloe's hand; she got her fingers out and tossed it under a table.

She stepped back into the ready pose: hands raised, knees bent. All he did was fall to his knees. She stepped in, grabbed his wrist, twisted it back and round. Using her limited weight she forced him to the ground. Holding the wrist in one hand, she reached for the other and brought that up into a double arm-lock.

She pushed his wrists up hard behind his back to make sure he was fully immobilised. He groaned in pain. Chloe knelt on his hands. Her fingers really hurt; she hoped he hadn't broken them. She flapped her hands and made fists. Well, if they were broken she wouldn't have been able to do that. Just bruised then.

Applause broke out around her. She looked up in confusion. The other people waiting for their food were staring at her, some smiling, some clapping their hands.

'That was amazing,' breathed one.

Chloe looked back at her prisoner. His hat had slid to the floor, it was woollen on the outside but inside it looked like chain mail; just as well she hadn't tried to hit him on the head.

She picked it up. She knew what it was.

'Need any help?' It was a man in his forties, wrapped in a heavy coat.

Chloe got up carefully, making sure she maintained pressure on his wrists. It didn't take skill, as long as his arms were held there he could do nothing.

'You could put your foot there,' she said, pointing at where his wrists crossed. She held the attacker's elbows while the man placed his foot.

'Ow.'

'You don't have to press hard,' said Chloe.

'But it's okay if I do?' he asked with a grin.

Chloe gave a half-smile. 'Yeah.'

'You know the old actress, Michelle Yeoh?' the man said.

Chloe's smile got wider. 'She's my hero.'

The man gave her a conspiratorial nod. 'You do her proud, Chloe.'

Chloe's smile vanished.

'Don't be surprised. You've been all over the news,' he said.

Chloe took the attacker's hat and crammed it on her head. It was a bit big and she had to adjust it so it didn't cover her eyes. The metal inside made it heavy.

'Here you go, love,' said the woman behind the counter, and passed a paper bag heavy with food.

'This isn't mine,' said Chloe.

'Yes it is, love, and no charge.'

Chloe could barely believe it. She managed to cough out a 'Thank you.' And headed for the door.

She ran.

Chapter 8

Yates

The car pulled up outside the chip shop in Burnage. Yates noted they weren't far from DI Mitchell's police residence. The posh one. Yates himself didn't rate anything so plush, he got a single room that was paid for out of his wages.

'So what's this little prick called?'

'Lemon Grainger,' said Lament from the dashboard.

'Lemon? Seriously?'

'Don't ask me. I just hand out what's in the records.'

Yates got out of the car, and the delicious smell of fried fish and chips hit him. It almost made getting pulled out of a quiet evening worth it. Especially if he could cadge a freebie. He adjusted his suit—he hadn't picked up his coat, having come out in a rush—and he was already regretting it. He wasn't entirely sure why he was the one to be sent, a uniform could have handled this.

He followed the streaming light and pushed his way through the steamed-up glass door, and almost stumbled into the man on the floor. There was a woman digging a nasty looking heel into his back.

Yates pulled out his warrant badge and flashed it. They needed physical identification for this sort of situation. Not everybody had a riffy detector linked to the net. Very few, in fact. 'I'm Detective Sergeant Yates, and I'd like to know what the buggery is going on here.'

A bunch of people spoke up immediately. Yates got the gist of it but perked up the moment someone said 'Chloe— the girl who escaped'. He feigned disinterest, though clearly *this* was the reason he was here.

Yates held up his hand to stop the chatter and explanations. Over in the restaurant section people glanced in his direction but did not crowd. He got the impression they were looking for Mitchell. Being a side-kick had its disadvantages.

He walked over to the counter and leaned against it. Then stood up straight—it was very hot. He smiled at the woman. 'You were here the whole time?'

'I work here.'

'Who came in first? The girl or the—' he looked back and down at Lemon Grainger's face, one cheek flat to the greasy floor, '—him?'

'Chloe first, him almost immediately after.'

'Did you notice a vehicle outside?'

'I was just serving.'

'Anyone else?'

The remainder of the patrons shook their heads. Yates looked at the condensation on the windows, it would be impossible to see more than lights anyway.

'Get her off me!' said Lemon from the floor. 'Ow! Oi, Yates, she's assaulting me.'

Yates allowed his gaze to wander from the dagger-like heel digging into Lemon's back, up a leg to where a knee-length dress started. She had hips but the rest of her body was bulked out with a padded coat. Black hair, nicely done make-up and brown eyes looking at him.

'You going to arrest me for assault, DI Yates?' she said through pale peach lips. It was almost a smile but there was an underlying concern. The Mitchell and Yates team were not known for mercy—but then they were usually dealing with freaks.

'There was mention of a gun?' said Yates. The woman behind the counter handed him a paper bag with handles. Unfortunately it contained the gun rather than some fried cod. Yates pulled the cuffs from his pocket and went down on one knee beside Lemon. The ankle was really quite attractive, and he thought he might like to get to know it better if he was off duty. He attached the cuffs and looked up the legs. 'You can remove your foot, Miss ...?'

'Simpson, Elaine Simpson.'

Yates got to his feet, dragging Lemon Grainger with him. 'Thank you for your diligence in keeping this villain under control.'

'We took turns,' she said.

'You should remain in the area for interview, Miss Simpson.'

'I thought it was called debriefing,' she said.

Yates smiled. 'We can do that too.'

'Seriously?' said Lemon Grainger.

Yates accidentally hit the perp's head against the door frame.

'Ouch. It was a fucking nightmare,' said Lemon. 'You took your bloody time getting here.'

Yates cuffed his ear, 'Language', then looked hopefully at the woman behind the counter. Unfortunately there was no sign she was preparing any food for him. And he was not the sort of person that would ask. That would be against regulations. Not that he had a lot of time for regulations—with that thought he cuffed Lemon a second time.

'What was that for?' said Lemon, reminding Yates of whining child.

'Regulations.'

Yates thanked everyone for their help and pushed his prisoner into the cold, and very helpful, darkness. He took Lemon around to the far side of the car, and punched him in the gut. Lemon doubled over and struggled to breathe for a few moments.

'What was that for?' he said when he could finally speak.

'Lack of information.'

'But you didn't ask me anything.'

'You know what I want, Grainger.' Yates hesitated. 'Why have you got such a stupid name?'

'My mum liked citrus fruits; got a sister called Clementine.'

'Your mum must have really hated you.'

'You leave my mum alone.'

Yates punched him again but barely had time to dodge as Lemon threw up. It took him longer to recover this time.

'Will you fucking stop that? That's police brutality, that is.'

Someone came out of the chip shop carrying a bag. Yates looked at it greedily. He was getting cold.

'Where did you get the gun, Lemon?'

'I don't know about no gun.'

Yates slammed his head against the car. 'Where did you get the gun?'

'Armourer sold it to me.'

'And where'd someone like you get the money for that?'

Lemon hesitated. Yates went to hit his head again. 'They'll kill me.'

'If you don't tell me, I'll kill you.' Yates unclipped his gun and took it out. 'Just a bit of paper work, I mistook you for a freak. With a lemon for a head.'

He pressed the gun against Lemon's chest.

'I can't—'

Yates moved the gun to between Lemon's legs. 'Won't kill you, Lemon, but the ladies won't be interested.'

A shot rang out.

Something warm splashed on Yates's cheek.

Lemon became a dead weight.

Yates threw himself to the side as another bullet went through Lemon's chest and shattered the car window. The shooter was behind him. Yates rolled over twice then came to a stop, his gun held steady in both hands, trying to see where the shot had come from.

Nothing.

There was the sound of a car starting up and driving off in the distance, but it might not have even been connected.

A couple of faces looked out tentatively from the chip shop.

'Stay inside!' shouted Yates. They disappeared back and shut the door.

This is a stupid fuck storm, thought Yates. He stood up warily, keeping his gun ready, watching for a flash—not that anybody could dodge a bullet. If he saw a flash he was a dead man. The sniper was good, professional too. He'd taken out Lemon with a headshot from a couple of hundred yards at least.

The sirens tickled his ears, then got louder and more distinct. The ambulance arrived first, followed closely by a couple of police vehicles. Heavy duty armed response, of course. Lament probably should have called them as soon as the first shot went off. Yates was grateful he hadn't fired when Lemon was hit, they might have tried to shoot him too.

A couple of the streetlights flickered on, bathing the area in sickly yellow.

It took twenty minutes for support to arrive and relieve him as the most senior person at the scene. Lament provided a second car since the first would have to be processed—and repaired. The paramedics checked him over and, apart from a tear in his suit and a couple of bruises, they declared him fit.

Yates sat in the passenger seat while Lament replayed the event. There were no riffies registered in the area the shots came from, which was no surprise to anyone, and no vehicle riffy driving away after the incident.

Also, Lemon Grainger had not registered a riffy until he attacked Chloe in the shop. Then he had just appeared.

'Wearing a hat,' said Yates.

'Obviously.'

'Is there a hat among the evidence? I didn't see one.'

'You've got a call coming in,' said Lament and his face disappeared to be replaced by a tired-looking Mitchell.

'Looks like you screwed up royally, Yates.'

'I did nothing wrong, sir,' said Yates. He did not appreciate it when blame was sent in his direction. Even less when he didn't deserve it.

'You saying you didn't screw up?'

'I'm saying someone was very keen to make sure Lemon Grainger couldn't tell us anything.'

- 366 -

Mitchell absorbed that. 'You should have brought him in first, then questioned him.'

'If I had, my powers of persuasion would have been curtailed.'

'And you got nothing.'

'Sir.'

Mitchell changed the subject. Something Yates appreciated in his boss was that he didn't dwell on mistakes, he'd point them out then move on. 'So what the hell was Chloe Dark doing there anyway?'

'Getting a takeaway apparently,' said Yates. 'No one saw fit to point out to her that if she goes wandering around on her own she's setting herself up for an attack. Speaking of which, how's the baby?'

Mitchell frowned. 'Slow, vicious, and he's got some history with the school teacher.'

'Want me to talk to her?'

Mitchell shook his head. 'Best not, until I can find out which side she's on.'

'Are we on different sides now?'

'We always were.'

Yates let it drop. He was aware that Mitchell's drive to kill freaks came from something very personal and nothing to do with the Purity. His wife had been infected and died. But it was not something they discussed.

'What do you want me to do?'

Mitchell spent a few moments thinking. 'Let it go. Write it up as normal. Carry on with your usual investigation. I don't think Graham will be too pleased to find out you're involved with this side of the action.'

'Paperwork's going to be a pain.'

'It always is.'

Mitchell signed off and it did not seem as if Lament had anything additional to say. The paperwork could wait until the morning. Luckily, there was no need now for him to provide a complex explanation of how his gun came to be drawn.

He glanced up and noticed the Simpson woman step out of the chippy. She paused in the light and peered round at all the police activity. She seemed to be searching for something, and then she found him.

Yates grinned, got out of the car and gave a casual wave. He leaned back into the car.

'Won't be needing the car for the rest of the night, Lament.'

He slammed the door and headed in the direction of the chippy.

Chapter 9

Mitchell

There was a bar in the old hall of residence where Mitchell lived. He seldom used it. It wasn't that he didn't drink, and it wasn't that he couldn't afford the drink. The truth was he didn't like socialising, and the rest of the police who lived here, or visited, were bachelors.

However on this Wednesday night, when Special Agent Graham had given him the evening off, Mitchell made his way down to the bar. There were only five or six other men there. He knew them all by name, but he got himself a whisky and a booth, and made it clear he was not interested in talking.

It was still early and none of the others were drunk enough to penetrate the unseen wall of his unfriendliness.

It was about half an hour later that Yates walked in. He greeted everyone, he chatted and joked, he talked about sport and women with that look on his face that told Mitchell he had recently—as Yates preferred to call it—*engaged with the public.*

Casually, as if it were the natural thing to do, Yates moved away from the main group and drifted over to where Mitchell was sitting, nursing his barely touched drink. Yates dropped himself onto the bench of the booth opposite and put down his half glass of beer.

'Evening, sir,' said Yates. 'Living it up as usual I see.'

'Shut up.'

Yates gave a quiet smile and drank from his glass. 'So there was another attempt on Miss Dark's freedom tonight?'

Mitchell nodded.

'But no particular investigation?'

'Our extra Special Agent decided that further investigation was not in order.'

'Have you read the reports? My report?'

Three of the other policeman in the room had gone over to the billiard table. Mitchell watched them as they set up the balls and chalked their cues. They had no interest in Yates and himself.

'I've read them,' said Mitchell. 'What did you leave out?'

'Our young lady is now in possession of a good quality hat.'

Mitchell tasted his whisky. The liquid slid across his tongue and down his throat. He savoured the flavour. 'Is she now? That complicates things, if she knows how to use it.'

Yates laughed. 'Well, I think she knows you put a hat on your head. And she's not stupid, kids today know how to bypass their riffies. And that means she can disappear if she doesn't want us to track her.'

Mitchell looked him in the eye. 'Any reason to think that she might do that?'

Yates shrugged and drank down the rest of his beer. He wiped the back of his hand across his lips. 'No, no particular reason. Though I do notice that, despite the safety element, there is an underlying resentment in the general populace towards twenty-four-hour personal monitoring.'

Mitchell reached into his pocket and, without lifting his hand above the level of the table, put something on the seat within reach of Yates. His DS didn't even glance at it.

'Is that for me?'

'You went to see Mrs Lomax, right?'

'You know I did.'

'I got into that room, the locked one.'

'And you decided to bring a shoe. That's very innovative of you.'

'Just get it checked out. How long since it was last used and whose DNA is on it.'

'All right, just going to get a refill.'

Yates went to the bar and he got himself another beer. He watched the billiards game for a short time. Mitchell finished off his whisky. His watch said it was only nine-thirty, but there were always more books to read and it was the best way to fill the time. Yates eventually wandered back and sat down again. This time he moved further in on the bench and pulled the shoe closer. Mitchell got up. 'I'll talk to you tomorrow.'

'Roger that, sir.'

Yates

Yates sat in the booth for a few more minutes and then squeezed the shoe into his coat pocket. He left his half-drunk beer on the table and headed into the foyer. There was a small door into the cupboard under the stairs, and there he sat down in front of the terminal screen. He punched in the code for Ria MacDonald.

There was a pause before it rang at the other end and another twenty seconds passed before the screen cleared. Her hair was slightly dishevelled and she was in her dressing gown. In the background he could see her bed. She only had the one room.

'Harry.'

'Ria. You settled in for the night, or do you fancy a drink?'

She put her head on one side and looked at him suspiciously. 'What do you want, Harry?'

'I just want a drink with my favourite forensics officer.'

'Yeah, like I really believe that.' She pursed her lips for a moment. 'You know forensics people do talk to each other. We even gossip occasionally.'

'I have no idea what you're talking about.'

'You and one of the witnesses, last night?'

Yates smiled. 'I just thought there might be more information that I could get out of her, with a more thorough interview.'

Ria laughed. 'You are a bloody terrible liar,' she said. 'Where are you?'

'Ashburne Hall.'

'Is your lord and master going to be with us too?'

Yates did not fail to notice that she had agreed to come tacitly. 'Just you and me. I'm paying.'

'You certainly are,' she said, and reached for the off switch.

'Oh and Ria—' she paused '—bring a large handbag.'

Chapter 10

Chloe

Chloe's back had been really hurting that morning. She couldn't lie on it anymore. The lumps continued to grow. It wouldn't be long before it would be impossible to hide them underneath her clothes. At this rate it might only be a couple of days.

She understood now why she was so hungry all the time.

For a time, she wasn't even sure how long, she just stared at the clock. Not seeing it. It was all so unreal. The thoughts kept circling in her mind. The way she was changing meant she was a freak, but if she was a freak why had the hospital let her out?

If she had been infected by the freak when they tried to abduct her, then perhaps it wouldn't have shown up—the infection took time to get established. It had been less than 24 hours and she knew it took weeks or months.

But her changes had been going on much longer. The first time she had noticed herself being particularly hungry had been weeks ago. And in that case an S.I.D infection should have shown up easily and they would not have let her out. But that also meant she would have had to have been exposed a long time ago and she couldn't think of any situation where it might have happened.

But they might have let her go if the Purity told them to. Somebody had tried to grab her twice, the way they had taken Melinda. It wasn't random. So the Purity, and the police, wanted to catch the kidnappers and had let her go so she could be bait. But that meant they were risking everyone else with her infection.

Would they do that?

And that brought her back to the fact that she had been declared free of infection in every recent test. Despite the obvious.

Eventually she had come to her senses and got herself moving again, but it was hard. She had eaten breakfast in silence with just her mother there, and she was still starving when she'd finished.

Her parents hadn't commented on what had happened last night. Chloe wasn't even sure they knew she had been involved in the events at the chip shop. Nobody had come to interview her, but they must have known because of her riffy. Bait. That's all she was, just bait. What was in the news was that a man had threatened customers in the chip shop, and that he had been shot dead. Chloe could read between the lines: he had come for her but screwed up. He got himself arrested and perhaps someone had shut him up before he revealed anything. She shook her head. It was just like being in some kind of TV show.

'Seriously, I just can't believe it,' said Ashley, as they passed through the gates and headed up towards the school between the trees that flanked the road.

'Can't believe what?' said Chloe.

Only the most stubborn leaves still clung to the trees. The ground was carpeted in brown mush.

'I can't believe they're letting you walk to school.' Chloe was amused by Ashley's outrage. She was probably more concerned about herself. 'I mean, it's like they don't care if the kidnappers try again.'

Kavi, on Chloe's right, leaned forward to look at Ashley on the other side. 'Don't you get it?'

'Get what? The fact that they don't care?'

Kavi glanced up at Chloe; she shrugged.

'Chloe's bait.'

It took Ashley a noticeable amount of time to get it, and then she came to a stop. 'You're not serious?'

There was less catcalling and name-calling from the other students this time. Perhaps they were remembering how dangerous Chloe could be after the discussions in the Purity lesson. Or maybe she just wasn't interesting enough anymore.

'It makes sense, Ash,' said Chloe. 'They want to find the other girls, now maybe these people are after me and maybe they're not—' *as if* '—but if they are, the police want to be able to catch them. Maybe catch them in the act.'

'Yeah, but you could get hurt.'

'That's already happened,' said Chloe with a laugh. 'They're keeping an eye on me. When the other girls disappeared it took a while to notice. But they'll be tracking me all the time, so they'll be on the scene with drones and all sorts. Their priority is to find the other girls. I'm okay with that.' Chloe headed up the steps into the school. Ashley and Kavi started after her, hurrying to catch up.

'You're okay with it?' said Ashley.

'Oh yes. I'm sort of hoping they succeed, because if they take me to where Mel is, I'll pull that place apart.' She knew her words were just bravado, but it shut Ashley up. At least for a while.

The morning lessons dragged. Finally the lunch bell went and the three of them slipped out to their bench beside the forlorn-looking trees. There were a couple of evergreens among them but their dark foliage didn't make the area any more cheerful.

Chloe sat down gingerly. The back of the bench didn't reach up high enough to touch the lumps in her back, but the whole area was tender. Chloe got her lunch out of her bag and looked at the meagre sandwiches plus an apple from the garden; unfortunately it hadn't been a very good crop this year and the apples were tasteless.

Chloe could hear small animals moving beneath the leaves behind them: a hedgehog, a squirrel, and a couple of birds. Her stomach rumbled just thinking about eating them. She shook her head and focused on the sandwiches. As long as she didn't start eating people. She was happy to note that, despite her hunger, her friends didn't register as food. Although Ash's lunch did.

'Still hurting, Chloe?' said Kavi.

'It's just backache.'

Chloe noticed a movement and turned. Ashley was sitting there holding out her lunch. Chloe had to resist the temptation to simply grab it all. 'What?' She made a point of starting in on her own sandwiches.

'Just take it, Chloe,' said Ashley. On her other side, Kavi had her lunchbox open and was offering the contents to Chloe.

'You need this more than we do.'

Chloe opened her mouth to argue, then changed her mind and stuffed the sandwich into it. She swallowed it hard and fast. She grabbed the boxes from her friends. She didn't mean to snatch but that's what she did and they didn't complain. Chloe emptied the contents into her own box and handed the empties back. She gulped it down as fast as she could.

Her friends didn't watch her eating. Ashley stood up and took a step away. She kept her eye on the path towards the school. Kavi watched the other direction, towards the back exit. Almost as if she was expecting Mel to come walking back.

For five minutes Chloe focused only on the food. She had a bottle of water and used it to wash the food down faster. Mouthful after mouthful.

She finally settled back and realised what she had done. 'Oh God, I'm really sorry.'

'Was it nice?' said Ashley, holding her empty lunchbox almost accusatively.

'Look, Chloe, we figured it out you know,' said Kavi. 'You've been like this for weeks, and you're getting worse. We think the kidnappers are trying to get you because of what's happening...' Kavi's voice trailed off. Her hands were shaking. And Chloe realised she was going through the same thing she had for her family. 'You should have told us, Chloe.'

'I didn't know.' They deserved more. 'I only realised myself this week.'

The three of them were silent for a while. When Ashley finally sat down again, Chloe did not fail to notice she sat so close their knees were touching. It almost brought tears to her eyes.

'I wouldn't mind if you didn't want to be around me,' she said.

'You really are stupid,' said Ashley. 'We've been through this before. You haven't. We know what's going to happen to us when they decide to admit—I mean, you were willing to be our friend despite everything. We owe you.'

'What about you?' said Chloe turning to Kavi. 'You okay with this?' Kavi reached out and took Chloe's hand in hers. Touching bare skin to bare skin. Ashley noticed and grabbed Chloe's other hand. Chloe felt like she was going to cry.

'Don't you dare start,' said Ashley. 'If you start we'll all end up doing it. And that would just be stupid.'

Kavi shifted a little. 'Does anybody else know?'

'Miss Kepple knows.'

'Fucking hell,' said Ashley. 'And she hasn't reported you?'

'Not really a surprise,' said Kavi. 'Considering.'

Chloe sighed. 'You noticed that as well? Is it that obvious? Is there anything else I should know about me?'

Ashley laughed. 'Honestly, Chloe, everybody knows. Couldn't you tell the way she looked at you?'

'I didn't realise.'

'God, sometimes you're stupid.'

Then Ashley started laughing, and Chloe couldn't help herself hearing Ashley, and even Kavi giggled.

Chapter 11

Yates

The unmarked police car pulled up in an alley. In the side mirror Yates could see the people and cars moving backwards and forwards on the main street behind him. He glanced at the screen showing a map rather than Lament's fake face. He was grateful for small mercies.

'He calls himself Greedo,' said Lament's bland voice.

'Are you serious?' said Yates. 'Doesn't anybody have a sensible name?'

'His real name is Bob Randall, but I suppose he just wanted to sound a little more exciting.'

'Whatever. How do I recognise him?'

'He favours a hoodie rather than a hat, but is not wearing it right now,' said Lament. 'If you look at the map, I've highlighted him a couple of streets over.'

'Is he on his own?'

'If you mean does he have customers, you can see there are others near him.' As Lament spoke one of the riffy dots vanished then reappeared. 'I don't think they'll give you any trouble.'

Yates got out of the car and slammed the door behind him. Facing away from the main street, he unclipped his gun and checked it. He reviewed his options. He could go out onto the market. There would be more people to give him cover, but if this Greedo had any lookouts that would make him easy to spot. Or he could take a back route, but again, they'd see him even sooner. Yates glanced up. All the buildings in this area were only about three storeys high and they either had flat roofs or at least a ridge you could walk round.

He turned back to the car, opened the door and leaned in as if he was talking to an occupant. 'What if I went over the top?'

There was a pause. 'You could do that, but there is no easy way down on the other side, and it's not like you're some superhero.'

'Lot of help you are.' What he really needed was backup, but they were always stretched so thin he'd be lucky if he got anybody in the next few hours.

'Can I make a suggestion?' said Lament.

'What?'

'I could be your partner.'

Yates laughed. 'Oh yeah? What can you do? Change traffic signals on them?'

'Better than that,' said Lament. 'I may not have legs.' The car engine started up and Lament rolled forwards, Yates jerked away and the door slammed shut. The side window rolled down. 'But I do have a car.'

Yates thought about it. 'All right. I'll go round by the main road, when I'm getting near them you come at them from the other direction. Distract them.'

'Yeah, that's the plan.'

The window rolled up and Yates headed out towards the main road.

The street was busy but not so much that he had to dodge people as Yates made his way past the storefronts.

There was a cafe, with a few patrons, but this wasn't one of the better areas. The people here didn't have a lot of money, the place just happened to be in the centre of some population groups. This was an area where the criminal classes thrived.

Yates glanced down the first side road. As he crossed it he saw the car slide across the next junction down. This might just work, he thought. He kept his head down not just to hide his features, but the wind had a biting edge to it, a precursor to the vicious cold of winter to come.

The place had a butcher and a baker, both empty of stock, closing up for the day. If they had had anything to sell that morning, it was all gone now.

Yates glanced ahead and then cursed as he locked eyes with a giant of a man. He recognised Big Jim Cotton at exactly the same moment that Big Jim Cotton saw him.

Big Jim wasn't the brightest star in the firmament, but he possessed the natural talent of perps to recognise trouble when it was heading his way. He turned and ran.

Yates accelerated after him. He could only hope the wirehead would notice and act accordingly. Big Jim had already disappeared into the next side street before Yates had managed to close the gap by any significant amount.

He pounded round the corner and ran straight into what felt like an iron bar as Big Jim elbowed him in the chest. He stumbled back as waves of pain rippled out from his ribs. He drew in a painful breath. As he pulled himself together, Big Jim was off again, shouting a warning down the alley.

Yates forced himself into a run again. Each step sent a spike of pain through his chest. At the very least the bastard had bruised a couple of ribs. Maybe even cracked one.

He looked up at a blast of noise at the other end of the street, as the police car pulled round the corner with its horn letting rip. Big Jim was still running and closing in on a small group. They were exploding away from a man pulling his hoodie over his head and throwing his knapsack across his back.

Big Jim was just coming up to Greedo as he took in Yates pounding towards him, and then the car still blaring its horn in the other direction. Yates wasn't sure there was much Lament could do; the anti-collision system in the self-drive would stop him from deliberately running down a pedestrian. But he could probably scare the bastard.

Apparently Greedo decided the car was full of police and it would be better to take on the one alone. As the perp started towards him, and Big Jim realised he had to slow down and turn back, Yates came to a stop. He reached inside his coat, pulled out his gun and aimed it at the oncoming man.

'Armed police!' shouted Yates, and thought, not for the first time, it was ridiculous they still had to use the pre-plague weapon protocols. So he improvised. 'And if you don't stop right now, you fucking lowlife, I'm going to blow your bloody head off.' Better.

Greedo came to a stop and raised his hands. Big Jim came puffing up beside him.

'And you, Big Jim, just lie down on the floor. You know the drill.' The car rolled up behind them. Lament cut the horn and, after a moment's echo, the street became silent.

Yates walked up to them. 'Afternoon, gents. I'm after some information and I won't even arrest you if I hear what I want to hear.'

Yates left Big Jim lying in the road with his hands and ankles cuffed. You couldn't be too careful with someone that size and no backup. He bundled Greedo into the back of the car for a little more privacy. He unholstered his gun once more and laid it on his knee with the safety on, just for effect.

Greedo sold hats. A convenient tool for your average ne'er-do-well. A good hat could block a riffy signal completely, while a cheaper one would blur it a bit and had to be pretty close to a pylon to register. Greedo made a wide range of them suitable for all pockets—though anyone buying a cheap one was a fool to himself. There was no doubt that Greedo's own hat, sewn into his hoodie, would be the best he could make.

Yates opened the backpack. There was a good selection with styles for both men and women. On the outside they looked perfectly normal, but turning any one of them inside out showed different layers of metal. There was one cloth hat with a lining of silver foil. Yates laughed. 'What's this one sell for?'

'Whatever I can get for it. You interested?'

Yates didn't bother to answer. He threw it back into the bag then rummaged deeper and pulled out a very heavy woolly hat. The interior was crisscrossed with wires making an intricate mesh; there was a component board and a battery pack. 'Sophisticated.'

'For your more discerning hat wearer,' said Greedo. 'You said you weren't going to arrest me.'

'I did say that, but I can change my mind. I'm fickle like that. Just owning one of these is worth a month in the clink.

And selling them?' said Yates. 'They'll throw away the key. This sort of thing is putting the population at risk. It's not something we can take lightly.'

'It's all a bloody lie, you know?' said Greedo with sudden passion. 'The Purity is a fascist organisation. They just use S.I.D to scare people so they can keep them under their thumb, keep them controlled. You should be helping me not interfering with me.'

'So you're doing this for the people?'

'That's right. It's like a public service.'

'Which you charge for.'

'We've all got to make a living.'

Yates threw the hat back in the pack, tied up the fasteners and tossed it into Greedo's lap.

'This is all very interesting, but I'm looking for something a bit more hi-tech.'

'I don't do hi-tech; I just do hats.'

Yates picked up his gun casually and checked it. Greedo gave it all his attention.

'What I'm looking for,' said Yates, 'is a device that can act like a riffy.'

Greedo clutched his bag closer around him and tried to squeeze further into the bench corner. If he could have squeezed through the metal body of the car he would have.

'I don't know anything about that stuff. I mean, is that possible?' he said in a sudden display of feigned innocence.

'You know it is. And I want to know who I would talk to if I wanted to get hold of one.'

'Honestly, I have no idea where you would get such a thing, if such a thing could possibly exist.'

'Oh, I think you do know,' said Yates, 'and if I need to jog your memory, I will.'

He slid off the safety catch of his gun with a very distinct click.

Chapter 12

Melinda

The room was dark again, save for the eerie glow of the electrical wires. Melinda turned over, wondering whether she would ever get used to the weird sense she now seemed to possess. She suspected she had killed the man who dug the knife into her back. There was some faint feeling of remorse in her, after all she had been brought up to believe that, on the whole, killing people was wrong.

Unless they were freaks, in which case you were doing them a favour.

But it seemed she had now gone down that road and somehow she did not feel that dying was an option she would choose. Who were these people who had her? Were they the Purity?

She didn't think so.

Did it mean the other girls that had been taken were like her? That they were freaks too? Probably. But how had they known? And how come they discovered and picked them up before the Purity?

Melinda twisted slightly on the bed and pain shot through her back. The bastard. She was glad he was dead. Vivisection without an anaesthetic? What kind of monster did that? But she had zapped him, she had felt it. She remembered what had happened in the van when she was picked up. It had been confusing at the time, but she had used the zap twice, knocking one person out and stopping the freak.

It wasn't until they'd got the drug into her that she had stopped resisting. And the burner? She had seen it hit her. Smelled the burning clothes and skin, but it hadn't even slowed her down.

A burner worked by hitting the victim with a very high voltage transferred along the twin ionising beams.

She sat up in the dark. It was obvious she was generating electricity as well as being able to perceive it. That's why her captors wore rubber suits, so she couldn't zap them too. But nerves ran on electricity, so if she was generating it she must also be blocking it from her own nerve tissue. And the burner had no effect because it works by hitting the nerves. Either that or her nerves were built to carry the current.

For the first time in several days, she smiled. They were scared of *her*. She had the power. Literally.

She had never really understood all the physics lessons she'd had about electricity, but she had made circuits with bulbs and motors, as well as seen static electricity experiments and spark machines. She reached her free hand across to her bound wrist—with a little concentration she could effectively see in the dark. At least she could see where her own body was. The all-round electrical sense showed the faint glow of her body in relation to the wires in the walls.

Melinda liked horror films, even the less effective TV ones from before. She had seen the special effects where people's bodies had been stripped of their flesh, showing muscles, or blood vessels. When she focused her sense on her own body that was just what it was like, except it was the nerves she could see. Most nerves were in the outer layers of the body, so that helped with the illusion, but there were also major nerve channels that ran deeper. And then there were those great blocks of light located above where her lungs should be. If she had been using her eyes they would have been hard to see, but her perception worked through her own muscle and bone.

She stared at the glowing tissues inside her. She knew they were her batteries, generating electricity biologically and storing it. They would have some maximum capacity, and would run out if she used the power faster than it could be recharged.

Thinking about herself in this way was odd.

On the previous occasions she had used the power it had been as a reaction. She had not initiated it, but simply reacted to a threat. The big question was whether she could do it at will, and whether she could control it.

She focused her attention on the batteries and held up her finger. She tried to imagine the electricity flowing from the battery to her finger. Nothing happened.

She remembered her physics teacher, Mr O'Neill: 'Electricity has to flow from a high potential to a low potential.' The whole flow thing was important, but there was also 'ground' which was ...? Nope, she couldn't recall the thing about ground.

So did she have to complete the circuit? She brought the tips of her index fingers together and concentrated. And jumped as the upper part of her body flashed with inner light, as did her fingers. She pulled them apart and rubbed with her thumbs. Her skin was hot. It was almost painful.

She laughed out loud. It could be controlled, maybe not a lot of control, but she could make it happen when she wanted to. Those people in their rubber suits, they didn't need them, she couldn't just zap anyone, she had to get both ... she searched for the word ... poles in contact. She had done it with the people who had attacked her, but the man yesterday?

How had she done that? There must be more to this trick.

Her happiness was cut short as the truth hit her. She must have been infected with S.I.D, maybe not from her uncle, but from somewhere, and she had been given, what? Electric eel genes? There was all sorts of speculation about freaks in school. Despite the lessons, they all knew there were things they weren't told. Whether there was a limit to the DNA that could be inserted, and what would cause a real mutation.

But it didn't really matter. She was here and she was going to die, but there was one thought in her mind: she was not going to let them experiment on her. She might be a freak, but she was still a person. At least for now.

If she was here, where were the other girls that had been kidnapped?

Were they here as well? Or were they elsewhere? Or were they already dead? If they liked to cut people up alive, she supposed they might be.

But now the thought was in her head she needed to know.

She needed to escape this room.

Chapter 13

Sapphire

Sapphire Kepple settled down into a large armchair with a large cup of coffee, and relaxed. She was glad to be home, and, as a Purity officer, she was able to demand and get reasonable lodgings. The lounge-kitchen with the table and the big chairs also had her terminal, which was currently playing some old movie. She had a separate bedroom with good-size wardrobe for all her clothes, and she did like her clothes. The bathroom was small, but it had a bath and the building had hot running water in the evenings.

She jumped when somebody banged on the door. Hot coffee splashed over her thin dressing gown and soaked through to her skin. She swore, and then stared in fear at the door. Who could it be? There were guards at the entrance, people couldn't just walk in. That meant it was somebody from the building, but she didn't talk to anybody from the building. Except the daughter of Mrs James at number 33. Not that Sapphire fancied her or anything, she wasn't very bright.

The hand thumped on the door again. 'Saffie, let me in. Or I'll huff, and I'll puff, and I'll blow your door down.'

Sapphire's thoughts ground to a halt. He was here. 'Oh God,' she said under her breath.

'I know you're in there, Saffie. I'm going to count to three and if the door is not open by that time, you may regret it. But you'll enjoy it too, of course.'

The thought he might touch her galvanised her. Still clutching the mug of coffee, she pulled herself out of the armchair and across the room just as he reached two.

'I'm here, I'm here! I'm opening it.'

She fumbled at the lock and managed to get the bolt back and the door open as he reached the final number. 'What do you want?'

He glanced down at the mug in her hand and the wet patch across her breast, and then back up to look her in the eye. 'Cup of coffee and a chat. That would be lovely.'

He took a seat at the table with the wall behind him, so that he could see the whole room and across into her bedroom. She busied herself in the kitchen area making another cup of coffee.

'This is a nice place.'

'Yes. I'm glad you like it.'

'What's important is whether you like it.'

The hot water boiled and she gave it a few moments to cool slightly. 'I do like it. But I think it needs a coat of paint.'

'Yes, the white walls are a bit sterile.'

With her arms wrapped tightly around herself she turned and faced him but couldn't bring herself to look him in the eyes. 'What is it you want, Chris?'

'We need to talk about Chloe Dark again,' he said.

She panicked; her heart pounded, how could he know what she had decided? How could he have found out that she wanted Chloe and to hell with the rules of the Purity? Even thinking such a sacrilege tore at her.

He smiled that irritating, perfect smile. 'Is that coffee ready?'

'I don't have any milk.'

'Milk spoils it. I'm fine without. Why don't you bring it over, sit down and we'll talk.' Sapphire did as she was told. She could feel herself going cold as she sat there, so close to him, her body reacting with the fear. But he made no effort to touch her. He didn't need to, his presence was enough and his voice too much.

'This Chloe thing has been going on a bit too long for my liking,' he said. 'It's been, what, five days? And apart from that ridiculous attack last night, they haven't tried to take her again.'

Sapphire frowned. 'What attack? The chippy? Chloe was there?'

'Yes, yes, that was someone overstepping their mark. Unfortunately they shot him before we could get any further information. Quite honestly, after the first attack and now this, one wonders whether they have any competence at all. It's a miracle they managed to abduct anybody.'

'But is she all right?' She realised the stupidity of the question: Chloe had been at school today, she had seemed fine. She wrenched herself back to the present. He had said something about things taking too long. 'What are you planning to do?'

He gave her that smile again. 'It's less what I'm going to do, Saffie, it's what you're going to do. You are going to arrange to meet her, tomorrow evening at this restaurant in the middle of town.' With careful deliberation he took out his wallet, pulled a card from it, placed it on the table and slid it across to her. 'It's in a position that makes it relatively easy for someone to set an ambush. You get her there, the abductors will try to take her and then we will get them.'

'But she might get hurt.'

'I know, Saffie. She might even be killed. But if you don't do this, that could happen anyway. And, after all, it's not as if you're personally attached to her. *Is it?*'

She finally looked up into his face. His eyes ground through her defences and she knew he knew everything. And his unspoken threat was a chain round her neck.

Chapter 14

Chloe

It was lunchtime, but the light outside, under the cloudy sky, was so dull it might as well have been evening. Chloe found herself once more summoned to Miss Kepple's office. She shook her head as she wandered down the empty corridors. Seriously, if everybody knew that Miss Kepple fancied her they were going to be completely convinced that they would be doing something they shouldn't in the woman's office. It was really embarrassing.

There was a weird contradiction on the subject of homosexuality under the Purity. There were plenty of people old enough to remember the acceptance of other sorts of relationships than just man and woman. Of course, there were those who still claimed the reason for the plague was that it was vengeance on immoral behaviour. But the Purity also seemed to frown on such things. The definition of purity seemed to extend beyond just genetics, it was something that affected all behaviour since, they said, all behaviour was derived from your DNA.

It made Chloe's dad a bit difficult to be with, to be honest. He was proud of having the name Dark to go with his skin, and would repeat to anyone how some people thought that their 'kind' was somehow less intelligent. Something that was patently untrue; the fact was human DNA was basically the same regardless of who you were.

So it seemed to Chloe it was a bit unfair to say that people who liked people of the same gender were somehow deviants, like S.I.D freaks. But they didn't come right out and say it, it was just implied.

But then, she was less than human now, with whatever it was infecting her. The foreign DNA that the S.I.D virus had somehow managed to slip into her. She couldn't imagine when it had happened but now she was going to die.

She found she had come to a halt outside Miss Kepple's office. She stared at the door.

Well, if she was going to die because she was a freak, she would make sure she helped all the kidnapped girls first, before she lost her mind.

She knocked on the door and heard Miss Kepple's voice inviting her in.

Sapphire

Sapphire sat at her desk and watched the door open. Poor Chloe. She was bearing it well, but that was why Sapphire loved her: she was so strong. She wanted to deny Chris and be able to say *no* to his face. But she wasn't like Chloe, she just wasn't that strong. But there were things she could do behind his back.

Chloe stood at the door, still holding the handle and looking uncertain. Sapphire realised she was daydreaming. 'Come in, Chloe. Shut the door, sit down.'

The girl came in but again hesitated, as if she was not sure whether she was supposed to sit on the sofa or the hard-back chair on the other side of the table.

Sapphire waved her hand at the chair in the middle of the room. 'Just there, sweetie, we don't really have time for a cosy chat at the moment.' She studied Chloe's movements as she came to the chair, dropped her shoulder bag and sat. It was amazing how graceful she was. It was her training, of course.

Once Chloe was settled, Sapphire thought over the things she had been planning to say, and what Chris wanted.

'Chloe, thank you for coming.'

She paused for Chloe to speak. But she didn't. Her eyes were dead.

'Well, the first thing was I wanted to apologise for what I—I mean, what happened before. You see I wasn't feeling very well, and my reaction, what I did, had nothing to do with you personally.'

Sapphire looked into Chloe's eyes. They were dark brown, almost black. Eyes you could fall into. She shook herself mentally. 'And what I said, I was just embarrassed. Really I'm very sorry for what I said and what I did.'

Still Chloe said nothing, just looked across the space between them. Sapphire was the first to break their gaze. She looked down at her desk and leant forward with both elbows pressed against the wood laminate. She held her hands together as if she was praying, but Sapphire Kepple did not know how to pray. She glanced back up at Chloe's immobile face.

She knows, Sapphire thought to herself. Of course she does, she's not a fool.

With her head still down, Sapphire spoke again.

'I'm sorry, that was a lie. I felt your back.' She spoke each word slowly and separately, as if that would make them easier to say. 'I was surprised. I mean, I was shocked. I don't know what else to say, I'm sorry.'

She looked up again, as if she was a supplicant hoping for forgiveness, or absolution. But Chloe was distant and did not give it.

'I want to help you, Chloe.'

'Nobody can help me.'

She was right, of course, there really was nothing Sapphire could do. She could not change Chloe's fatal destiny.

'But we could talk,' she said. 'Your parents, they don't know yet, do they?'

Chloe was silent again.

'Look, perhaps we could meet, in the evening, tonight.'

Chloe crossed one leg over the other and placed her hands protectively in her lap. 'I don't want to go to bed with you. And even if I did, you might get infected.'

She knows everything.

'No, I don't...I—I didn't mean that,' said Sapphire. 'I meant a public place, a restaurant. I could tell you what you could do. I know how the Purity does things. I might be able to help you, at least a little.'

The harshness of Chloe's gaze softened a little. 'All right,' she said, 'I will meet you.'

Sapphire smiled and opened a drawer. She extracted the card that Chris had given her. She placed it on the table, and slid it across towards Chloe.

The girl looked at it. 'Expensive.'

'Nobody will know us.'

Chloe got up, picked up her bag and slipped it over her shoulder. She went to the door, opened it, and then turned back. 'What time?'

'Nine o'clock?'

'I'll be there,' said Chloe.

Chapter 15

Melinda

Another day of inactivity followed. They continued to feed her, but she was not taken for any tests. Evening came and the lights blinked off.

Her patience was running out.

The energy she could see flowing through the wires did not change. She had assumed she was under constant surveillance, but perhaps that wasn't the case. Just because there was a camera did not mean they were watching her every minute of every day. As far as any watchers might be concerned, she did nothing much except eat and excrete. They couldn't read her thoughts and that was where the danger lay.

There was only one way to find out whether she was being watched, but it was probably going to hurt.

She worked her tied wrist so she could get the index fingers of each hand on either side of the plastic tie that held her. Attempting to keep the power level low, although she had no idea how it might work, she imagined the electricity flowing through her fingers.

There was a crack as a spark flashed from one finger to the next around the plastic. She grimaced and held the pain inside. They might be listening too. The fact the electricity generated light couldn't be helped.

She rubbed her fingers along the tie itself and detected a slight indentation where there hadn't been one before. It was working. She got in position again and zapped the plastic. She found she could maintain the spark for a few moments, although it was like having needles jabbed into the tips of her fingers.

The smell of burning plastic filled her nostrils and she could see, by the light of her work, globs of plastic forming and dripping away. The heat increased and she had to stop. She jammed her burned fingers into her mouth. The skin was hardened and numbed. She wondered if she'd destroyed all the nerves in the tips.

Holding the plastic tie in her free hand and using the strength from both she jerked it taut. It snapped and she fell back on to the bed. She gave a little grunt of satisfaction.

Got you, you bastards.

She stood up and stretched. The cut in her back seemed to have healed fairly well and only pulled a little. She wished there were proper clothes she could change into, but she was stuck in the unflattering and revealing hospital gown.

She lay down on the bed and waited for the alarm.

Time passed and nothing happened.

The next problem was going to be the door. She went over to examine it. She had never heard any bolts, just the sound of the key which was always withdrawn after locking.

She tried something new. The lock was metal, steel probably, so it would carry a current. She touched one index finger to the top of it, the other at the bottom and gave it a little burst of power. Her electricity sense saw it light up as the power went through it. She already knew she could see through a solid object if there was an electrical field behind it, but up to now it had either been the wires in the walls, or the confused glow of electrical circuits. Now, as her power ran through the metal of the lock, she could see it in three dimensions.

Taking her time—she had hours before breakfast—she examined the mechanism, using occasional flashes of power to check it again. Her initial excitement wore off; there was nothing she could do with it. She might be able to see it but she couldn't make it open.

Eventually she sat down on the cold stone floor with her back to the door. If she could have generated magnetism it might have been a different matter. She would have to wait until someone opened the door for her, and that would mean tackling two men.

Perhaps she should have taken up Chloe's invitation to join that jujitsu class.

She went back to the bed and curled up beneath the single blanket in the cold.

The sound of the key in the lock brought her awake. It was only when she realised her wrist was not attached to the bed that she remembered she had freed herself the night before and was planning an escape. She slammed her wrist up to where the other end of the plastic was attached to the bedstead by way of pretence.

The *iron* bedstead.

They were coming through the door. Melinda sat up slowly, rubbing her eyes as if she were tired. She sat on the edge of the bed as the first guard came in, with the usual burner trained on her. It suddenly occurred to her how surprising that was. *They didn't know.*

If there was any time the cameras would be on it would be now, while they were in her room, so she could be monitored. The second guard entered with her breakfast, and moved to the bed. Melinda slid her free hand down to the metal of the bedstead under the thin mattress, and with the one that was supposedly tied up she grabbed the top of the bed to make a circuit.

As the second guard placed the tray on the bed, Melinda blasted power through the metal. Melinda watched as the room lit up with power. All the guards carried electrical equipment. She saw their circuitry glow for a moment. The wires in the walls lit up in sympathy. The camera made an audible pop as its little red light went out. The room went dark as the bulb overloaded. Moments later the power she'd generated was eclipsed by the burner. It shone like a supernova and Melinda felt herself twisting up, as if her insides wanted to turn somersaults. The guard holding the weapon cried out in pain.

The light went out and Melinda recovered. She threw herself at the second guard. Their rubber helmets were not sealed, and she slid her hands up inside. She felt skin with both hands and zapped—trying not to kill him. The effect was instant. He crumpled to the ground, dragging her with him.

The burner hit the ground with a clatter. The first guard was grasping for the door in the dark. Melinda could see his shape in the electricity of his nerve endings. His heart pumped furiously.

He was facing away from her. She got behind him and put her foot against the door to stop it opening any further. He tried to turn. She couldn't get her hands inside his helmet.

He grabbed her arm with his gloved hand; she yanked it away and his glove flew off with it. He grabbed her wrist more firmly with his bare hand. This time she managed to get her hand inside his helmet. And it was over. He dropped like a felled tree, and the light went out of him.

Her extra sense told her that the other was still alive, but this one wasn't.

She found she didn't care.

The hall was dark, but she had been along it enough times to know where she should go. She knew there were cameras at strategic positions, but they weren't functioning either.

She hadn't blown the whole place, and a distant light revealed the end of the short corridor. She peeked round the corner. Nobody yet. The nearest working light was at the far end, shining through the double doors.

They would be coming soon. She checked her battery by looking inward. It looked dimmer, but she still had plenty of juice.

The next corridor was similar to the one that led to hers, and through the door she could see the form of someone else. She scooted down to the end. Her door had a board outside it which gave her name. Bringing her index fingers close together she made a light. *Cooper, Vanessa. Asset 25.*

Melinda was room 26. Were they really holding that many?

'Vanessa?'

'Fuck off.'

Melinda blinked in astonishment.

In the distance there was a crash of something heavy impacting with something yielding. Were they coming already? If they were, why would they be smashing stuff? They have keys.

'I'm a prisoner too.'

'Just piss off.'

'But—'

'Here to rescue me?'

'Well, yes.'

'Got a key?'

'No.'

'Good luck.'

Melinda backed away. She knew Vanessa Cooper was one of the abductees. So why was she being so weird?

Another crash followed by splintering.

'I'll be back,' said Melinda and ran back to the main corridor before Vanessa had a chance to deliver some caustic reply. As she reached the end, Melinda heard something heavy stomping in her direction. *Freak.*

She was expecting a massive monster out of a nightmare, but from the next corridor came something surprisingly short. And not at all nightmarish. In the dim light the silhouette resembled a turtle walking on two legs. No taller than Melinda herself.

They stared at one another for a second. As her eyes adjusted, Melinda realised there was a girl's face in the middle of a hairless head with some sort of bump in the forehead. Her attention was caught by shadows moving behind the double doors at the end.

'Who are you?' said the turtle. The voice was a girl's.

'Melinda.'

The double glow of a burner snaked down the corridor and hit the turtle. She didn't even flinch.

'I'm Lucy,' said the girl. 'You killed the lights?'

The burner fired again. This time the beams swept across Lucy's back and hit Melinda. It tingled and she smelled smoldering cloth. Melinda side-stepped to put Lucy between her and the gun.

'We can't get out,' said Lucy.

'But we're free.'

'No, they have gas and real guns. I've tried.'

'What do we do?'

There was shouting.

'You do electrical things?'

Melinda nodded.

'Then you have to get a message out.'

'They tried to cut me open!'

'Better act fast then.' With that Lucy ran at her and jumped on her, carrying her to the ground. It felt like the time her dad accidentally fell on her.

'Fight me,' said Lucy.

Melinda struggled. Lucy's skin was solid but jointed, as if she was wearing armour. Melinda tried to zap her but it had no effect.

Men rushed up around them.

'I got her!' shouted Lucy.

Melinda felt the prickle of a spray injection and then everything went fuzzy.

Chapter 16

Yates

Yates stared at the neutral image of Lament on the screen.

Lament spoke. 'I don't need gratitude, DS Yates.'

'Of course not, you're a machine.'

'I am not a machine.'

'A lot of you is.'

'I am connected to a lot of machines, yes, but I am not one.'

Yates looked out at the buildings flicking past as they shot through a residential district. The wind was up and blowing ice crystals across the roofs in gusts of white. He shivered even though it wasn't cold in the car.

'How many things are you doing right now?'

'A few.'

'You're evading the question,' said Yates.

'I didn't know this was a cross-examination.'

'And you're still evading it.'

'Would a machine evade the question?' said Lament.

'This is pointless.'

'On that we agree.'

'Are we there yet?' said Yates.

The car drew up outside the closed ironwork gates to a facility based in the south of the city. Yates waited while the wirehead negotiated with whatever security system the company employed. Old-style cameras were mounted on the stone pillars.

After a couple of minutes the gates swung inward.

The roadway was crumbling tarmac with weeds growing in the gaps. Clearly they didn't feel gardening to be as important as security. Which was fair.

'Briefing?' said Yates.

'Biotech Control Systems, a wholly owned subsidiary of Utopia Genetics, is run by James Cochran. There are twenty employees of which ten are key research staff. The person we want is Kieran Mortimer, research assistant. Age 56.'

'I'll talk to Cochran.'

'Not much choice there, they aren't going to let you talk to anyone else.'

The dilapidated building was built in the 1950s by the look of it. Perhaps it was one of the old university buildings scattered across Manchester and its suburbs. No doubt Lament could have told him. The central section and the right wing, as you looked at it, were burnt out completely. You could even see daylight through the downstairs windows.

Only the left wing was in use. The windows were all covered but light bled out around the edges of the blinds. The car drove off the tarmac and on to a rough roadway of brick and stone. It was far from level and water splashed up as the wheels dipped into muddy holes.

They drew up by an entrance that looked as if it had been hacked from the original wall. Yates got out and wished he'd brought his coat. It was bloody cold, and the wind cut through his clothes.

Inside the building it was still cold, but at least there was no wind. The receptionist looked up as he came in.

Beside her desk stood a man in casual clothes, including a thick polo-neck jumper. He was over fifty and strode forward as Yates entered. He didn't offer his hand to shake.

'Detective Sergeant Yates, a pleasure to meet you in person.'

'Is it?'

'Well, my wife is something of a fan of DI Mitchell, and yourself, of course.'

'I bask in his reflected glory.'

Cochran had an easy smile that came readily to his lips. Yates found it immediately suspect.

'And you are?'

'James Cochran, and this is my facility. How can I help you?'

Cochran stopped and waited for Yates to take the lead.

'What do you do here?'

'That's confidential, naturally. Much of our work is done on behalf of the Purity, as well as Utopia Genetics.' He beamed at Yates. 'We're working to make life better for everyone.'

If I wanted the brochure text, I could just read it.

'Mind if I look around?'

'I can give you a tour, but the work is commercially sensitive, and I imagine most of it will be over your head anyway.'

Yates knew how to handle this level of condescension. 'This is just routine, Mr Cochran. A crime has been committed and we have to investigate all possible avenues.'

'But here?' said Cochran. 'What crime?'

'Unfortunately, that's confidential.'

The smile on Cochran's lips became wooden.

Score one for the away team, thought Yates.

The tour was as boring and uninformative as Yates expected it to be. Each research lab was behind a wall of glass and everything that looked potentially interesting was hidden behind something else, or, in some cases, covered by a sheet. But ultimately it wasn't why he was here. Although he did notice the machine for 3D printing of different types of embeddable chips—and when Cochran said 'embeddable' he was talking about insertion into 'biologics', as he liked to call them.

Yates's name for them was *people*. For some reason he felt as if his own riffy was itching, which was ridiculous because it was too deep to have a surface effect.

In the same room as the 3D printer was the 56-year-old research assistant, Kieran Mortimer. Yates hadn't seen a picture, but his name was on his badge. He glanced up and, if Yates wasn't mistaken, blanched.

Yates knew there was a particular look to the police. They had a presence, and in some cases it was an advantage to be known as the sidekick of the most effective killer on the force. So Yates grinned at him and winked.

'The fact is,' said Cochran, though Yates had been barely listening, 'the work we do also benefits the police.'

Yates turned to him. 'How's that?'

'With improved riffies you can track people more accurately, and get better bio-scan data.'

'I'm not sure you understand the nature of the police, Mr Cochran,' said Yates. 'We're here to remove criminal elements from society so that everybody has a better chance to live a decent life.'

Cochran laughed. 'And I thought it was all about control.'

'You would be confusing us with the Purity, sir. An easy mistake to make, but when your house has been broken into and your wife attacked, I think the *biologics* you'll be wanting are the ones that solve crime.'

It was almost dark when Yates got back in the car. The heating was on full, but it took a while for him to thaw out just from the walk from the building.

'Did you get what you wanted?' said Lament.

The car moved out on to the tarmac and picked up speed.

'Oh yes, the cat is very definitely among the pigeons. If you would be so good as to track Mr Mortimer, I'm sure it will turn up some leads.'

Chapter 17

Mitchell

'I want an armed team available this evening from seven,' said Graham as he walked into the detectives' open-plan office. His voice was loud and although he was looking at Mitchell as he said it, it had clearly been intended for everyone.

'What's this about?' said Mitchell turning in his chair.

Graham's entrance had made sure that everyone in the room was listening.

'Chloe Dark will be heading into Manchester town centre this evening. She will arrive at a restaurant for nine and somewhere along the way, before, during, or after, another attempt will be made to abduct her.'

'And what makes you think that?' said Mitchell, although there was no doubt in his mind that Graham had somehow managed to engineer this.

'It really doesn't matter how I know,' said Graham. 'Let's just say that it's an absolute certainty.'

Mitchell climbed to his feet slowly and crossed the room to where Graham was standing. 'Would you mind,' he said quietly, 'if we have a private conversation about this?'

The special agent smiled. He glanced at the meeting areas that lined one side of the room; none of them were occupied, so he took the nearest. Mitchell dropped the blinds.

'What was the meaning of that display?'

'Are you questioning my methods, Detective Inspector Mitchell?'

'I am not questioning your methods, because I don't understand what you're doing.'

'Don't you? I don't underestimate you, so I think you know exactly what I'm doing.'

Mitchell took a deep breath, grabbed one of the chairs, and sat down. 'You think there's a mole in the police department?'

Graham took the chair on the other side. He sat down casually, as if he really didn't care about anything. 'There may or may not be a mole,' he said, 'but I'm making sure the kidnappers have every opportunity to find out.'

'And you think that obvious display will be taken seriously?'

'They can't afford to ignore it.'

'Since I don't agree with your methods, I'm certainly not going to agree this is a good idea. How did you engineer it anyway?'

Graham smiled. 'Chloe's Purity teacher invited her to dinner.'

That did surprise Mitchell. The girl had already been attacked once, why would she take the risk?

'You realise she's managed to pick up a hat? A good one?'

'Yes, I'm just as capable of reading a riffy record and police reports as you are. She got it from her attacker at the chippy. Quite resourceful, wouldn't you say?'

'So how are you going to track her?'

Graham gave that infuriating grin again. He reached into his jacket, pulled out a card and skimmed it across the desk. Mitchell slammed his hand down on it before it flew off. He examined both sides. It was like a business card but blank. Then he noticed it was thicker at one end. He rubbed his thumb and finger across it. 'A riffy?'

'Of course, the original RFID chips were developed to track objects. It doesn't require any power, so we put one in a card. We give the card to someone and they think nothing of it. Even if they wear a hat, it makes no difference.'

Mitchell frowned. He hadn't even been aware the pylons could track nonhuman riffies.

'She might not take it with her.'

'Well that's true, of course, but then nothing is certain in this life, is it?'

The team was ready by six-thirty. Fully equipped with weapons and armour and riot gear, 30 men waiting in the car park for their transport. Mitchell came down in the lift.

The doors slid open and Yates was waiting for him.

'Well, this looks like fun.'

'Special Agent Graham thinks he's got it all worked out.'

'And you don't?'

Mitchell shook his head. 'No plan survives first contact with the enemy.'

'So what's your alternative?'

'I haven't got one,' said Mitchell with a shake of his head. 'We'll just go along with it, and as soon as things go sideways we'll improvise.'

'Just like always,' said Yates.

Mitchell headed out into the car park. He nodded occasionally to the officers he recognised, greeting the ones he knew better. Yates followed him and checked his gun.

'You're not overly curious about what we're going to be doing,' said Mitchell.

Four armoured police riot vans squealed into the car park and headed in their direction.

Yates grinned. 'Chloe Dark is going to travel into the city centre from Didsbury. She will probably take the tram so we'll need to shadow it so, if the kidnappers try anything en route, we can be there fast. Once in the centre we follow her to the restaurant. The riot squad will be deployed ready to move while we keep an eye on the area. When they try to grab her, we grab them instead.'

'You don't need a briefing then.'

'Everyone and their mother knows the plan.'

Mitchell frowned. 'Looks like that part of the plan worked too. He wanted to make sure they try for her.'

'Do you think they're so desperate they'll risk open confrontation?'

'I don't know,' said Mitchell. 'But the abductions of these girls are not random. If they were, they would go after somebody else. But they've tried to take the Dark girl twice. They want her specifically. And for that reason this plan might just work.'

'Do we want it to?'

Mitchell gave Yates a long look.

'If this works then the Purity wins.'

'If it doesn't we lose Chloe Dark as well.'

The four vans slowed and stopped as if they were all connected like a train.

'But if they really do want her,' said Yates, 'and they know how well-equipped this operation is going to be, then it's going to be a bloody war.'

Mitchell sighed and climbed into the front of the first van with Yates at his side.

'I know, and that's what's bothering me. How the hell are we going to find the other girls if the only result of this is a massacre of our men and theirs. Whoever they are.'

Chapter 18

Mercedes

'Mercedes, there appears to be something happening.'

Xec's voice crept quietly into her consciousness. She was meditating on her yoga mat. She had only taken it up recently as a way of dispelling some of the stress. Some people said that as you got older, the stress of life became less important. It was not something she had noticed.

She opened her eyes, and stared at the grey window. Outside shreds of clouds streaked across the sky, driven by the high winds.

'What are you talking about?'

'I have noticed some orders from Paul Banner. He is mobilising forces.'

Mercedes unwound herself and stood up on the mat. She glanced at the clock. It was still early in the morning.

'When you say mobilising forces, what exactly do you mean?'

'It would appear he has received some intelligence, and is spreading the word among the criminal classes that our currently targeted asset will be at a certain restaurant this evening.'

Mercedes did an abrupt turn and headed towards the bedroom. 'Tell him I want to see him and Alistair McCormack in my office in an hour.'

'Already done.'

Mercedes Smith was not one to play executive power games, at least not with her staff. She was sitting waiting for them when Banner and McCormack were shown into her room. They sat in the two chairs provided without being asked. From behind her large, impressive oak desk Mercedes steepled her fingers and looked at Paul Banner.

'We know where she is going to be,' he said. 'We also know the police will be there in force, to protect her, and to apprehend us.'

Mercedes let her gaze slide from him across to McCormack. She waited.

'We can't let her get away, Mercedes,' he said. 'We know from the others that they develop very fast once they start. It wouldn't surprise me if the people around her have already noticed.'

Mercedes sat back. 'And this is the best idea that you could come up with? All-out war?'

Banner leaned forward. 'We don't have any choice. You said yourself, we have to pick her up before she becomes the object of interest. If the Purity get their hands on her, and they realise just what they've got...'

'Have you considered the consequences?'

Banner nodded. 'Of course I have. You don't think I like this, do you? We are going to have to get in there and get her out while our shock troops distract the police.'

'Yes, but it's not just the police is it? It's the Purity as well.'

'May be true, but the Special Agent can only operate through the police. He's from London, he has no connections here.'

Mercedes raised an eyebrow. 'You're saying that? You, a trusted member of the Purity?'

'You know where my loyalties lie, Mercedes.'

She turned back to McCormack. 'How important is this asset? No bullshit, Alistair.'

'You worked with the doctor back at the clinic, Mercedes. He was a genius; it wasn't just that he could get foreign DNA to merge perfectly with the existing DNA. It was the fact that he could trigger it at certain times and some of his experiments using multiple DNA sources—'

'Yes, I know, he was an artist.' He was also a lech and a misogynist with a very nasty sense of humour. He played games with the cells; each time he worked on a new one he was trying to outdo his previous work. If there was ever a real evil genius in the world, he was it. 'But if we were, instead, to just blow that restaurant up with her inside it? What if we were to wipe out all traces of her?'

'Well, that would work, of course, but each asset helps us understand what needs to be done to reproduce it. This might be the one that holds the key.'

Mercedes sighed. 'Yes, all right. Fix us a drink, will you, Alistair?'

McCormack got up and went to the drinks cabinet alongside wall. Mercedes turned her attention back to the security chief. 'So how exactly is this plan going to work?'

'Xec,' said Mercedes. She studied the window, staring out across the Manchester landscape, windswept and grey with cold and frost. The cold seemed to radiate from the glass she stood so close to it.

'Yes, Mercedes?'

'This plan of Paul's. It could go wrong so many different ways.'

'That's true of any plan.'

'You heard what I said to Alistair?'

'About blowing the place up?'

'Do you think we could arrange that?'

Xec hesitated. Mercedes glanced up; Xec *never* hesitated. 'There would be a considerable amount of collateral damage. Could be a lot of important people, with important friends.'

'And if it can't be traced back to us then it's not an issue.'

'If you say so.'

Mercedes glanced at the nearest screen, even though Xec never showed himself. Cold feet? From a wirehead? 'You have a problem with that?'

'My primary concern is your protection, Mercedes. This alternative would put you at risk.'

'Let's have it as a backup, because I really don't like Paul's plan. Too many moving parts.'

'Under the circumstances it's the best option—if you want the asset alive.'

'I know. And Alistair is completely right, we have to get this girl off the streets as soon as we can.' She turned round and looked at her office. She didn't belong here. When she had been a trainee nurse before the fall, all she wanted to do was help people. But she hadn't been able to qualify, there was something about exams. She just couldn't do them. So her grades were insufficient and she got booted from the course. The best she could do with her limited medical training was to be an assistant at a facility. Someone who could understand the words, even if they couldn't do anything useful.

So she had worked in the clinic, and she knew enough to be aware that what was going on there was neither legal nor ethically sanctionable. Unfortunately, she had not been able to apply the blackmail which she had so carefully planned before everything went crazy. But again, because of her medical training, she had been one of the ones to establish help for people, advice on how not to get infected. She may not have been able to handle the medical exams, but she knew how to manipulate people. And she had built this. But, on the inside, she still felt like that girl who been told she had failed the nurse's training.

'Paul is a weak link. I think we need someone stronger in that position.'

'I thought your primary concern was Mr Upton,' said Xec.

Mercedes nodded. 'Yes, he is a concern too. But Paul knows too much, and no matter how many barriers he puts between himself and this plan, a dedicated policeman will be able to track it back to him.'

'So you wish to remove the link from the chain?' said Xec.

'Yes, I think that would be best, after tonight, of course.' It was a shame. She really quite liked Paul. However, his removal would also put the fear of god into Kingsley, and hopefully that would reduce his outbursts and keep him in line. Yes, all in all this was the best option.

'Of course, Mercedes.'

Mercedes turned to look out of the window again. She had a gut feeling that this evening was not going to turn out very well for a lot of people. However, as long as it turned out all right for her and the project, that would be fine.

Chapter 19

Chloe

Chloe examined the hat in greater detail. The inner woollen surface was interwoven with an intricate network of metal strands connected to a circuit with a battery. Chloe knew, just like everybody else, the riffy signal was blocked by metal. It hadn't occurred to her before that there might be levels of blockage, but it was obvious when you thought about it.

The further you were from a riffy pylon, the less likely it was to be able to pick you up, and now that she thought about it, it was clear the protection you got from a layer of metal would vary with all sorts of factors. By the look of this, running some sort of signal through the wires added to its effectiveness.

Chloe's mother had not even commented when she ate everything she could lay her hands on that evening. Whatever the changes going on in her body, they demanded a lot of nutrition. Chloe could not believe her parents did not now realise she was infected, but they continued to say nothing. She didn't understand. Why didn't her father turn her in? After all, he was the head of FreakWatch. If one of them became infected, would she have turned them in? No; not even her father.

She spent half an hour on the phone to her friends. They didn't say much. Chloe didn't tell them what she was going to do, but she must have communicated it somehow.

When Chloe finally said goodbye, Ashley didn't joke, she gave her own 'bye' and cut off immediately. Kavi said 'be careful' before she too cut the line.

Chloe laughed, just like her to say that, and then she cried. She would probably never get to speak to them again.

She desperately wanted to say goodbye to her parents, but if she did they would realise she was planning something and try to stop her. She didn't want to leave them with that kind of fight unresolved, because there was nothing they could say or do that would stop her.

She got dressed, putting on double layers of clothing, it was going to be cold tonight and the chances were she would be spending most of it awake. There was little chance she would end up back home in her own warm bed any time soon, if ever. She located the card with the restaurant details and slipped it into her jeans.

Even through the window she could hear the distant sound of a drone. They were watching her this time. Whether it was the good guys or the bad guys she had no idea. Were there any good guys in this? Once word got out she was a freak, the good guys became the bad guys—to her anyway.

She laced on her boots, locked her door, opened the window and listened. Turning her head, she located the drone at the front. With deliberate movements, she activated the power in the hat, but didn't put it on.

After she had closed the window behind her, she threw herself out into the freezing night and pulled on the hat mid-fall. She leapt the fence at the end of the garden and ran as fast as she could up the alley. Once again, she found it natural to make a noise each time she breathed out, and when she did her surroundings seemed to become clearer.

Following the same route as before she headed north on foot. She had considered taking the tram, but after her previous experience she decided against it. It was not that she was scared, it was just too limiting.

So she ran.

She had not weighed herself since getting back from the hospital, so she had no idea how much more weight she had lost in the last week. All she knew was that in the mirror she appeared exactly the same as before, well, not *exactly*. Her muscles were better delineated, as if the skin was drawing back around them. Getting tighter. Was she just going to waste away to nothing?

On the positive side, it meant that her strength remained the same as it always had been, so the amount of effective power she could generate increased. With the hat on her head and a cold dry night with the first frost ahead of her, she took to a main road and ran. As her speed increased, she found every pace was so much longer than it ever had been before. It was like bouncing on the moon. Just as she had before, she leaned further forward so her legs thrust her forward rather than up.

The route into Manchester was easy enough; the main roads took her straight to the centre with only the occasional major crossing and junction. It was still early evening so there was a fair amount of traffic, and at the first junction she almost didn't brake soon enough. One self-drive car swerved off to the side to avoid her and she caught a glimpse of the passenger staring at her in astonishment as she finished crossing the road at high speed.

From then on she took it slightly easier. Still moving fast, but at a more leisurely pace, she realised she wasn't becoming exhausted. She could feel her heart rate had increased. It held steady while her breathing was only a little faster than usual, but her breaths were deeper. It seemed that whatever creature it was she had been infected with was built for running.

The buildings got higher. The architecture became more modern and the road she was on was carrying her directly to where she wanted to be. As she approached the city centre, she had to slow down until she was doing what appeared to be an ordinary trot. The length of her paces was not much greater than it might otherwise have been. People did not stare. She was just somebody else in the evening bustle.

She went past the old university buildings, across the canal, and into Piccadilly Gardens. The restaurant she wanted was in one of the side roads going off to the north.

On the west side of the square was the Metro station, the main interchange between trams heading south to north and west to east. To the north, the road she had been following continued into the main shopping area, though the majority of shops were empty nowadays. Diagonally across from her, a short distance along Market Street, was Debenhams. The place where Ali had died. She set off in that direction and pulled off the hat as she did so.

It was all part of the plan. Her plan. Not the police's, not the Purity's, not the kidnappers', hers. She had not wanted to be picked up on her way into town because she still wanted to talk to Miss Kepple. But now she was here, the bad guys needed to know where she was, as did the police, assuming they hadn't been following her with a drone all evening. She had no idea how it was going to turn out, but when they tried to take her she would be ready. And somehow she would get the information she wanted from them.

It took Chloe a couple of minutes to cross the square walking at a normal pace. She looked at the memorials for the dead. She supposed Piccadilly Gardens had once been green with grass and flowers, but now it was mostly stained concrete with giant pots for flowers that were overgrown with weeds.

She walked along Market Street, parallel to Debenhams. There were no police, no blue and white tape, but there were barriers where the lorry had struck. Apart from the shops casting their treacherous lights, the place was in shadow. She stared at the wall. A man had died here. Someone she knew. A person she considered a friend, who had discovered something about her, and had been killed. The police had reported it as an accident; how could it be anything else since there could be no motive? But the motive was standing at the scene of the crime, staring at one half of the murder weapon.

'I'm sorry, Ali,' she said in a whisper brushing a tear from her eye. Another reason to find the girls, to find her friend, and do something useful before she ceased to think and became a monster.

She turned on her heel, checked the traffic before crossing towards Debenhams and turned right. Three streets further down she took a left, walked past a square and found the entrance to the restaurant down some steps.

Chapter 20

Chloe

Chloe took a deep breath and steeled herself. She had never been in a place like this, a restaurant in the middle of town. The closest she had ever come was the chippy, and that hadn't turned out well. This wasn't going to turn out well either. She checked her watch, it was nine-oh-five. Hopefully Miss Kepple would already be here, otherwise it could be embarrassing.

She walked from the freezing cold through the double doors into a maelstrom of heat and noise. She was astonished; the place was packed. Everyone was sitting so close to each other it seemed almost obscene. The place was a confusion of movement and lights. From another room music was playing loudly and there was a wall of talking that flooded her ears. She had managed to gain some skill at tuning out the noise but this was just so much. All her senses were being overwhelmed. And the smell: there were the delicious food smells, but also all the people, so many people, sweating, perfumed and a smell that seemed to be like their emotions bubbling up through their skin. She felt like she could smell anger and lust, hate and love.

She realised there was somebody in front of her, talking to her. Chloe focused. A woman in a uniform asking her whether she wanted a table for one. Chloe shook her head.

'No, I am meeting someone. Kepple? A woman.'

The waitress's smile was all lipstick and brilliant white teeth. She led the way through the throng unconcerned at the way she brushed against people in chairs. Chloe tried to avoid everybody although it was not entirely possible. It was easy to see from the quality of their clothes that these people didn't suffer the way her family did. She hadn't realised there were so many rich people in the world. Everyone she knew struggled to make ends meet.

The waitress moved to one side and suddenly Chloe could see Miss Kepple. She stood as Chloe approached, and smiled. Chloe was surprised at how genuine her smile seemed to be. Miss Kepple actually reached out her hand to shake. Chloe steeled herself. Her teacher knew she was infected and yet she was still willing to shake her hand; why? Chloe took it and Miss Kepple squeezed hers a little, not so much a shake as just a touch.

'Take your coat off Chloe, sit down.' Chloe was reluctant, she might have to leave in a hurry and she didn't want to leave it behind. The waitress offered to take it from her but Chloe shook her head. She laid the coat over her knees when she sat, and put her backpack at her feet. She might be parochial, but she wasn't stupid.

The waitress handed a menu to Miss Kepple, then held one out for Chloe. Chloe took it, and stared at it without really seeing anything. How could she focus on this when there was so much going on? She put the menu down in front of her and looked at her teacher sitting opposite. Miss Kepple was wearing a black dress that left her arms uncovered, exposed the curve of her neck and was slit at least as far as her waist. She wasn't looking at Chloe, but studying the menu. Her hair is brown, thought Chloe. She'd never really noticed before, you just didn't look at teachers that way. Her hair had been done in ringlets, pulled up, and seemed to cascade out back. It was pretty. But her skin was so pale, almost like ice. Miss Kepple looked up and smiled at her.

'Chosen already, Chloe?'

'I—' Chloe was about to say that she wasn't hungry, almost as an automatic thing, but she was very hungry. The run had taken it out of her. '—I don't know what to order.'

'I'll do it for you.'

Chloe looked around at the people, so many of them packed in so tight. S.I.D would run rampant here, she thought. Am I infecting them just by being here?

'Don't worry,' said Miss Kepple. She reached out her hand and placed it on top of Chloe's. So much touching. 'You can't infect them.'

'How did you know I was thinking that?'

'Because you're a good person, Chloe, you always think about other people. That's quite an unusual trait, especially nowadays.'

At a signal Chloe didn't notice, the waitress returned and Miss Kepple ordered food. Chloe's ears buzzed with the noise of cutlery and the incessant chatter. She would tune in for a moment to something someone was saying, and then it would be gone again. But she felt hyper-aware of her surroundings; it was as if she knew the position of every person every chair, every table, even down to the light fittings. Even, to some extent, she felt she knew the shape and size of the other rooms: there was the kitchen, the office where two men sat talking, the space behind the bar, the room where people packed together dancing, and another space somewhere deeper in, identified only by its emptiness.

Drinks arrived. Miss Kepple had red wine. She had ordered lemonade for Chloe. The teacher picked up her glass and held it halfway across the table.

'To you,' she said.

Chloe realised she was proposing a toast; she lifted her own glass and Miss Kepple tapped it with hers. Chloe brought her glass to her lips, she only meant to take a sip, but as the tangy liquid touched her mouth she couldn't resist drinking it all down.

Miss Kepple smiled indulgently and took another drink from her glass. 'You are thirsty.'

Chloe glanced around again, there was nobody looking at them but she felt self-conscious, as if she did not belong. She placed the empty glass back down on the table.

'Why am I here?'

'I could ask you that.'

'You said I should come because you wanted to talk to me.'

'And you came, despite the danger. What do you think I could possibly say that could be that important?'

Chloe did not have to turn her head to hear the sound of the door to the outside opening and four people come tumbling in, clattering down the stairs. She knew, and did not know how she knew, they were not talking to one another. In this place everyone talked, incessantly, especially when they had nothing to say.

'Why am I going to die?' said Chloe.

For some reason that statement seemed to rub any bonhomie from Miss Kepple's face. She shook her head. 'Everybody dies, Chloe.'

'I'm not ready to, it's not fair.'

'Quite frankly, Chloe,' said Miss Kepple. 'I had imagined you were more mature than that.'

Chloe felt her heart beating faster. 'I can be whatever I want to be.'

'Utter nonsense. Don't be a stupid child.'

This seemed to be a different Miss Kepple to the one that Chloe knew at school. 'So what did you want to talk to me about?'

It was at that moment the waitress came over. She placed a bowl of soup in front of Miss Kepple, and a large plate with a fish *hors d'oeuvre* in front of Chloe. Chloe's hunger took over. She forgot the conversation and dived into the food, barely remembering in time to at least use a fork.

They spent the next couple of minutes in silence while they ate, or, more accurately, Miss Kepple delicately spooned her soup and dunked her bread. Chloe excavated the plate in front of her and left only smears of grease as any sign there had been any food there.

'I see it hasn't dulled your appetite.'

Chloe wondered if she was making fun of her. 'I'm hungry all the time.'

'You know Chloe, there are such things as clean transitions.' Miss Kepple finished her soup and laid her spoon down. She sat back in her chair with her hands in her lap.

'I've never heard of that.'

'No, it's not on the Purity school syllabus because people misunderstand it.'

'Is that what you think I have?'

Chloe saw the waitress come up to them without turning her head. She began clearing away the plates. By the entrance, one of the four people who had entered seemed to be arguing with the person at the door. They wanted a table but they hadn't booked. Apparently there were no tables available.

'A clean transition is when the acquired DNA seems to merge smoothly with the infectee's own DNA.'

Chloe felt a surge of hope, but Miss Kepple did not seem happy. 'It doesn't end well, Chloe. An S.I.D infection never ends well.'

Chloe's moment of hope was ground into the dirt.

'Is that it?' said Chloe.

Miss Kepple looked awkward; she examined her hands and seemed to shrink. 'I was ordered to lure you here.'

'It's that agent, isn't it?' said Chloe. 'He's trying to flush out the kidnappers.'

Miss Kepple nodded and Chloe gave a humourless laugh.

'Well, that's fine by me.'

'You want this?'

'Three girls, maybe more, and one of them my best friend, have been taken by these people. I need to help them, while I still can.'

Miss Kepple laughed. 'You really are amazing,' she said. 'Such selflessness, and all it's going to do is get you killed.'

'What's wrong with that?'

'You're being used. Chris doesn't care about you. He doesn't care about the other girls.' She waved her hand around indicating the people around the room. 'He doesn't care about these people here. He was the one that said I should come here to this restaurant. He must have known it would be crowded. If the kidnappers come in force to get you Chloe, it could be a bloodbath. It'll be a war, with the police on one side, the kidnappers on the other, and everybody else in the middle.'

Chloe felt a rising panic. She had been so sure she knew what she was doing. She didn't want anybody else to get hurt on her account. Especially if they weren't even aware of what was happening.

'I need to get out.' She pushed back her chair. It screeched across the stone floor, sending shivers through her. Miss Kepple stood up.

'What are you doing?'

'I'm leaving.'

'You can't. You mustn't.'

'What are you talking about?' said Chloe. She pulled on her coat and started to do it up. 'I can't stay here. I can't let these people get hurt,' she said in an intense but quiet voice. Carefully she pulled on her backpack and settled it between the lumps on her back; as far as she could tell they were a couple of inches long now.

'But Chris hasn't arrived yet.'

'Who the hell is this Chris?' said Chloe. She saw in Miss Kepple's eyes the diminishing of power as she shrank into herself at the man's name. 'He's your lover?' She gave a bark of laughter. 'And I thought you liked girls.'

Miss Kepple reached out her hand. 'It's not like that; it's you I want.'

Chloe looked incredulous and shook her head. 'No, no, I am sorry. I like you, as a teacher, or I used to. But I can't have a relationship with you.'

Chloe had never seen someone get turned down before. Let alone been the person doing it. Less than a minute ago she hadn't really understood she was in that position at all. The way Miss Kepple seemed to deflate, the broken look on her face as she sat back down in her chair. Chloe felt terrible, but the truth was the truth.

'Then you'd better run,' said her teacher. 'Get away from the kidnappers, the police, and especially the Purity.'

A couple of people sitting nearby were looking in her direction. One of them, a woman, peered intently at Chloe's face then turned and whispered something to her companion, who also stared.

Definitely time to go, thought Chloe to herself. She glanced one more time at her teacher who was wiping her eyes. *Oh, for God's sake.*

She took a deep breath, turned, and headed for the door.

Chapter 21

Chloe

Chloe squeezed her way through the gaps between the tables and chairs. She noticed their waitress carrying two plates of food. She almost wished she'd waited. But there was no time for that. The four who had come in late and didn't have a table were lounging near the bottom of the stairs, drinks in hand, probably hoping for one to come free. They won't have long to wait, thought Chloe, unless Miss Kepple decides to stay for the main course.

Chloe needed to get outside before any trouble started. She thought perhaps the police had been watching her, even tracked her while she was coming into town. But she didn't think the kidnappers could know where she was until she removed the hat.

She headed for the stairs. As she passed the bar area, one of the four laughed, though it was more of a cackle. He seemed to slip and stumbled in Chloe's direction. She dodged to the side only to come up against one of the others.

'Careful there, love,' he said.

Chloe heard and felt it at the same moment: a quiet hiss and a prickling sting in her side. She reacted without the slightest thought. She swung her left arm backwards as she turned away from the sound and pressure. Her arm struck his, knocking it away. She kept lifting, his arm caught in hers.

Within moments his wrist was on her shoulder. She drove her elbow down onto his forearm and something snapped.

He screamed with the pain and she shoved him away.

In her mind's eye she saw the other two coming up behind her. The one who started it was in front of her. She jumped. High and forward.

There was the double hiss of aerosol injectors behind her as she soared upward, but they were too far away to penetrate. She was halfway through the flight up to the first half level of the stairs, when she reached out and grabbed the vertical support. It was iron, painted green, and slick with condensation. Her momentum carried her through one hundred and eighty degrees, until she was heading back towards her assailants. She planted her feet in their faces, using the push to launch her back up the stairs.

She hit the opposite wall hard, halfway up, but used her arms to absorb the energy. She dropped back onto the upper flight of stairs and ran upwards. Behind her they were pulling out guns; she heard them click as the safeties came off. She reached the door, grabbed the handle and yanked at it, jamming her feet into the lower step and pulling hard to make it open faster. A deafening shot thundered in her ears. The wood of the door beside her splintered. *I thought they wanted me alive.*

The door was open enough. She slipped through. Her backpack caught for a moment but it barely slowed her down.

Outside, under neon lights, the freezing wind tore at her exposed skin. There was no time to deal with it. She focused. Rather than run she paused and looked around deliberately, peering into the shadows. Her ears were still ringing from the gunshot.

This area of Manchester was arranged in blocks with the roads criss-crossing at right angles. Most of the buildings were a couple of hundred years old. Warehouses from the heyday of Manchester's industrial past. They were modernised inside, but grim and dirty outside. And in the dark, they were just black. What she did see were men in uniform, lurking in the shadows of the streets across from her, and to the south in the direction of Piccadilly Gardens. Police.

In the other direction there was more movement. Darker figures, moving surreptitiously. The kidnappers. Should she call them that? They had resources and people. They had access to the riffy grid. And they just wanted her.

The door behind her opened. She felt the rush of warmth accompanied by shouts and screams. She spun on the spot. She could not make out the face of the man silhouetted against the lights of the restaurant. She jumped. Straight up with as much power as she could muster. In school games she managed a creditable high jump, but that was before. This time she soared two floors in a moment.

'Fuck!' echoed up from below her.

She had tried to jump in towards the wall, but at the highest point she was still too far to grab anything. She had no way to gain any purchase, nothing to push against. The problem lasted for only a moment. Gravity took charge and she began to fall.

But she was still moving in. She hit. Desperately she tried to find something to grab on to. Rough stone tore her nails as her body dragged down the side of the building. Her foot caught on a ledge but for only a moment before it slipped off again. There was a window to the right. Her arm lashed out and she hooked her fingers round the edge. Her weight still dragged her down but she hit a gap between two stones and her fingers anchored her. She swung lightly in towards the window just as another shot ricocheted off the stone where she had been.

The air filled with a short burst of machine-gun fire. Glass smashed, wood splintered, flesh erupted. The man below her made a disappointed sound and collapsed. She heard his gun rattle onto the stones.

The police didn't use machine guns. As far as she knew.

She pulled herself lightly up to the window. Being an old building, the ledge was almost as deep as her foot. She glanced north. The kidnappers—the name would have to do—were moving forward. She knew now they definitely wanted her alive; that was why they had shot the man below her.

She adjusted her grip and found she could hold on to the window frame quite well. She felt a little more stable, but the wind was getting up and whipped her hair.

She wasn't so sure about the police. Somewhere out there was DI Mitchell, the man she admired for his ruthless termination of freaks. Not something she wanted to happen to her. And that Purity agent, the one who had been happy to put her in this position—but for what, she was not sure. Did he really just want to help the police catch the kidnappers?

She shook her head. This was not the time.

She shrugged off her backpack, then, balancing precariously, opened it and pulled out the hat. She pulled it down over her ears and then pulled up her hood. She tied off the laces so it wouldn't slip off. Her ears appreciated being out of the wind.

There was a sudden fusillade from the ground. Muzzle flashes from the police lit up the scene like a stroboscopic nightmare. She could see the kidnappers had moved up a long way. They were now at the first junction. There were a lot of them, maybe twenty. The police were not firing wildly but controlled. They were making every shot count and keeping the kidnappers pinned down.

Chloe snatched her leather gloves from the backpack, pulled them on and returned her backpack to its proper position. She needed to move but she had no plan. Things hadn't gone quite the way she expected.

While the police and the kidnappers were busy, she swung out on to the wall and climbed. Someone had seen her. Shots from the kidnappers' side peppered the wall near her, but they were only trying to scare her.

Well, they had succeeded, she *was* scared, but she was not going to stop.

The climb was not hard. The wall had plenty of ridges and holes, some made by the gun shots. And her lightness meant her arms were not under stress. At least not at first.

Whoever had been shooting at her stopped. Beneath her they seemed to have reached an impasse. There was the occasional shot but nothing more.

Her hand slipped. She woke up. She was still clinging to the side of the building but for a moment she had lost touch with reality. The drug from the aerosol was taking effect. She shook her head and concentrated on climbing again. Craning her neck, she looked up: almost there.

There was the sudden sound of vehicles to the north. She stared beyond the knot of kidnappers, at vans turning into the road heading their way. The police had outflanked them. The police had been expecting the kidnappers, but apparently not the other way around. She was just the bait dangling for the kidnappers to take, and be hooked from the water.

Chloe giggled.

And caught herself. She had stopped climbing again. Despite the wind cutting through her clothes she was definitely feeling drowsy.

She rubbed the back of her gloved hand across her forehead and then rubbed her eyes. She reached and got her hand over the top of the building wall. She yanked herself up and tumbled onto the roof, landing awkwardly on her backpack.

Maybe she could just stop here. No one could see her. She could rest.

No!

She rolled over again and pushed herself onto her knees. She tried to pinch her own cheek with her gloved fingers. It didn't work. Something inside her found that very funny.

Chloe got on her feet. She needed to get out of here. Miss Kepple was right. The worst that could happen to her parents would be that they were put into quarantine for a while. And her friends. No one could deny she was a freak anymore. But if she went home she would get locked up, and the kidnappers might still come after her.

With her drugged, the kidnappers would have the upper hand. She needed to disappear.

It was then she saw the figure. Outlined against the skyline of semi-lit buildings, against a darker sky.

'I will shoot you, Chloe Dark.' The voice was not one she knew. A man with a northern accent.

She looked around. The top of the building was flat. There were ventilation pipes and a brick structure that was probably where stairs came out. He was close to it, most likely had just come up the stairs.

She giggled out loud but suppressed it immediately.

'So, one of our operatives did manage to inject you,' he said. 'You may as well give up now. If you come with me I'll get you away and no one will be hurt.'

The streets below erupted in gunfire. The police barrage had started. There were screams as men died. Then there was another sound, a repetitive, deep-throated drone from somewhere nearby.

'There's not much time, Chloe.'

Chloe glanced to her left. It was about fifty feet to the edge of the building and then the blank gap to the next one. Similar to this building and running parallel to Market Street. Then another street, with a low building, and then Debenhams rising like a cliff.

'There's nowhere to go.'

He took a step towards her. She ran.

The fifty feet seemed to disappear beneath her feet in no time as she accelerated. The ground beneath her feet was lit by the glow of a burner. She could feel the electricity crackling, but nothing touched her.

The gap rushed at her. She threw herself up on to the parapet wall and with a huge thrust of her legs launched herself into the void. She kept her arms out slightly for balance as she flew. The freezing air forced her eyes shut, but she had the distance.

She was past the highest point and descending. She opened her eyes, bent her legs, and landed. She let her legs absorb the energy of the landing and rolled. The backpack jammed into her back and the two lumps shot with pain. She grunted as she ended up in a sitting position. The twin beams of the burner flicked above her. She ducked and lay flat, praying the parapet would hide her.

The thumping noise grew louder and the scream of a powerful electric engine filled the air. A white spotlight shone down. The helicopter crouched on the other building.

She leapt to her feet.

'Who the hell are these people?' she shouted. Her words were lost in the roar of the rotors. She jumped up again and cleared the wall by at least ten feet.

She set off again. The next jump would be bigger, but she had a confidence now. She could do it.

She almost didn't.

Her stomach slammed into the parapet wall opposite with her legs dangling. Her breath was forced from her and she hung there gasping for breath. The rotor frequency of the chopper increased. It was taking off and would catch her in moments.

But people in a helicopter couldn't do anything to her.

The burner's beam wavered near her and then sliced in her direction. She jumped out of the way and smelled ozone.

The roof this side of Debenhams had radio pylons reaching up a good distance, which would stop the chopper getting in close. She ran at the brick cliff-face. There was a maintenance ladder going up.

She wondered whether she ought to go down, or in, but she felt driven to climb, to get more height. She trusted her own instincts. Inside a building she could be cornered and trapped—and it didn't matter which side did it, it was not something she wanted.

So she climbed. When she had been training with Sensei the one thing she had always lacked was upper body strength. Any attempt to support her own weight, let alone move, was doomed to failure. She couldn't hold on.

Losing perhaps three-quarters of her weight had changed that. The ladder was inside a cage. She started using feet and hands, but it was awkward and slow. Then one of her feet slipped and she almost fell, except that she was hanging by her arms without any noticeable effort.

She reached for the next rung. Easy. And the next; and again. Moments later she was climbing fast, hand over hand, her feet dangling.

The helicopter's spotlight caught her again. Blinding her for a moment. The burner lashed out but did not make contact.

She got to the top of the Debenhams building. It was higher than the surroundings and she couldn't see where to go. But she felt the urge to keep heading east.

She ran to the far side. There was a long drop to the other side—Market Street—she could make it easily enough. If she could survive the landing.

The helicopter appeared, dogging her every step. She ran back to the ladder, took a deep breath and gave it everything she had. The helicopter moved fast, it side-slipped in the direction she was running and disappeared below the level of the building.

They wanted to force her to stop. But they wanted her alive, they wouldn't let her get chopped to pieces by the rotor—which would probably kill them too. Without looking she jumped, and flattened herself as if skydiving to reduce her terminal velocity and give herself more range.

The helicopter was directly in her line of flight. She could not steer. She could not avoid it.

She saw with interest the look of panic on the face of the pilot. Reacting fast, he increased the rotor speed. Chloe flew at him. The chopper rose with painful slowness. Chloe felt the wind from the edge of the rotor and the down draught as it altered her trajectory. Instantly she knew she wouldn't make the opposite roof.

She passed within a couple of feet of the passenger and pilot. She felt strangely detached. The undercarriage was coming at her; she reached out an arm and hooked it round the skid.

Even with her reduced weight, the force of her deceleration felt as if it were ripping her arm from its socket. She swung up and hooked both legs round the skid and switched arms.

She hung there, dazed. She had not even thought about her actions, it had all been so fast it was automatic.

From the behaviour of the chopper it seemed they did not initially realise what had happened. The front tilted down and the whole machine did a three-sixty as they searched for her body.

She felt faint again. The adrenalin had kept the drug at bay but there was enough of it in her system still. She deliberately bit her tongue so the pain kept her awake.

The helicopter accelerated. They knew they had her. But they knew she was drugged so were concerned she might drop off at any time.

The chopper kept low, and Chloe felt it change direction as it flew out over the Irwell River. By staying close to the surface it used the surrounding buildings as cover.

Chloe's mind was shutting down. The river. She needed to float. She let go with her hands and, hanging upside down, got rid of the backpack. It fell away.

Letting go herself seemed harder; her legs gripped the skid solidly. She focused. And then threw her arms and legs outward.

Moments later the water hit her like concrete.

Chapter 22

Mitchell

Mitchell pulled his collar even tighter around his neck and tugged his hat down. What a mess.

The streets were illuminated with the flashing blue and red lights of police vehicles and ambulances. At the far end of the street the paramedics were checking the bodies of the kidnappers' forces.

Kidnappers? Whoever they were they had a lot of resources. Nobody went to this much trouble to grab one specific girl. She was special.

The wind abated for a moment, allowing the sound of pathetically moaning criminals to drift down to him. He wandered up to the doorway of the restaurant.

Heat was pouring out of the open door. Inside he could hear the constant hubbub of the diners. Uniforms were busy taking statements. The guests were coming out in dribs and drabs, but being sent out the back way so as not to contaminate any of the crime scene.

Special? If he hadn't seen it with his own eyes he wouldn't have believed it. She had leapt straight up about thirty feet. He was old enough to remember the line *able to leap tall buildings.*

After she had gained the roof things got sketchy. One of the police snipers had seen her on the roof, and the double beams of the burner. It seemed the big attack was just a diversion. It was very unlikely any of the foot soldiers had any idea who had employed them or why. He had already heard they had been told there would be a reward for every cop they brought down.

But someone had supplied their weaponry. There might be a lead there.

The police sniper couldn't see where they had gone, but he had seen the helicopter. They had all seen it, and it had gone chasing across the rooftops.

He had asked for data but he already knew: a helicopter without a riffy.

It had paused at Debenhams, gone around the other side, and then made off along the Irwell. And that was that.

Had they caught her? It seemed likely, but there was no way to be absolutely sure.

Mitchell glanced back down the street. He saw Special Agent Graham talking to someone he didn't recognise. Probably one of his buddies. If they had friends in the Purity.

With a shake of his head, Mitchell headed back in Graham's direction. There were a lot of things Graham wasn't telling him, and he thought maybe now he could get some answers.

Episode IV: Abyss

Chapter 1

Chloe

She dreamt she was falling. There was nothing below her, nothing above. She fell through velvet black. And then, as in all falling dreams, she woke with a jolt. Her face was glued to something that clawed at her skin while her arms and legs were numb.

There was light beyond her eyelids but she didn't want to open them. She was tired. Every part of her wanted to go back to the velvet black. Ice snapped and cracked, and the empty wind whistled through the eyeless windows of broken buildings.

How did she know that? Though her eyes were closed, she could see. Buildings, their windows either boarded or broken open. A roadway that ended in an abrupt drop to where she lay. And all about her cold, frozen mud. Behind, away from the buildings, lay a river, some parts of the surface moved, bubbling and gurgling, the rest frozen solid. The wind shifted and the wailing of the ancient and broken walls faded. And with it went the image in her mind.

I am lying in freezing water.

She was not flat, face down, but slightly on her side with her right arm higher than the rest of her. Though she could barely feel the position of her bones, she bent her arm and opened her eyes. Her hand was caked in black mud. She curled her frozen fingers into a fist; lumps of mud fell on to the dirty ice but the rest clung to her. More mud fell away when she spread them again.

She placed her palm flat on frozen mud and pressed down. The ice gave way and her hand sank into it. The mud sucked at her hand, but she kept pushing and turned herself over. The mud tried to hold her and ice cracked under her back. Her heels broke through the thin ice and sank into icy water.

She stared up at the greyness of the sky. Darker grey clouds scudding across it. Down here at ground level, so close to the ground she was part of it, she barely felt the wind, but she stretched her hand up and could feel the moving air.

I am cold, and lying in a river. If I don't get out of the wind, if I don't get out of this water, I will die from hypothermia.

The two betraying lumps of flesh and bone in her back pressed against the ground. Unlike the rest of her extremities, those two growths that were not her were warm enough that they were not numb.

Why not just die here? After all, I have no future.

The wind shifted again and the blank stone faces of the walls wailed at her; once more she could see without seeing. But she did not care.

I am going to die. And so is Melinda. And the other two.

She remembered, from her research, there were more than two. Other girls, and the boys, and yet no one was looking for them, at least so it seemed. But perhaps everything was a lie.

She heard someone cough. It was not a pleasant cough, but the kind that tore your lungs out and left you in excruciating pain while dreading the next one. So you tried to suppress it, tried to make sure it didn't happen again. But nothing you did was ever enough; it was the kind of cough that always beat you.

But it was far away and no threat to her. She corrected herself: the owner of the cough was not a threat.

She realised she was not shivering, and that was a bad sign. If she did not move now, she would never move again. The carrion crows and the fish would feast on her.

She laughed at herself, at the sheer pretension of being eaten by crows. The sound of her own laughter gave her strength. Using her elbows she levered herself up and then pushed herself until she was sitting in the water, facing across the river. She felt the wind on her face but her hoodie still clung around her head and held the drowned hat over her skull.

The electrics are probably ruined, she thought, but the metal should provide sufficient protection. For a moment she couldn't remember why that was important, then her eyes focused on the riffy tower on the far bank. The half-frozen river matched the image she had seen in the wind. To her right, perhaps a couple of hundred yards away upriver, was an old bridge, but then all the bridges were old. There was no reason to build new ones. In the other direction, the river broadened into trees and perhaps fields, but she couldn't see as it curved away to the right. There were a few residential houses strung out along its length, but not much sign of life. Just the man who had coughed.

Perhaps she could just sit for a while. She wanted to go back to sleep.

But I've got this far, perhaps I can get to my feet.

Slowly, because all her joints were stiff, she turned over again until she was on all fours. The grasping river mud sucked at her legs as she moved forward. The surface was covered in ice but it was barely the thickness of a pie crust, and so fragile it cracked easily. Her hands and knees sank into the water with every movement.

The change in orientation made her dizzy and she did not think she would be able to stand. Instead she crawled up the muddy bank until it turned into ice-caked sand. And she sat down again under the lee of the three-foot walls that led up to the wharf.

Looking back she could see her trail in the mud and sand, barely six feet long. Just crawling that distance had exhausted her. She closed her eyes again.

The memories of what had happened the previous night came to her. It had to be last night, otherwise she would be dead. She remembered jumping from building to building like some sort of crazed superhero. And throwing herself at a helicopter.

Lying there, with the water lapping across the ice, she could not believe what could possibly have come over her to do such a thing. Perhaps it was the drug they gave her. She laughed again, as it came to her that she thought she could fly. But it had happened, it was in her dream, she had fallen until she hit something.

She heard the coughing again. And, coming and going with the vagaries of the wind, she smelled burning wood. Burning wood meant fire. Fire meant warmth.

Her body did not want to move.

'I can't do this.' Her voice croaked as she formed the words so her ears would hear it.

She thought of Melinda again, and the others.

'I can't do this.'

Who was she trying to convince? Of course she couldn't do it, but that didn't mean she shouldn't try. And then she swore at herself. She hated the logical side. She was not dead yet, said the part of her that always made so much sense. *While there's life there's hope*, said that trite and irritating voice.

'Will you shut the fuck up?'

It was almost as if the sound of her own voice woke her. As if, up to that moment, she had still been in the falling dream. But now she had hit the bottom, and come awake.

'I have to move,' she told herself in a voice that was barely her own.

Using the wall behind her, she pulled herself to her feet, her muscles stretching painfully, joints cracking as they straightened.

Looking each way along the wharf she couldn't see a way up, but it wasn't high, barely above her waist. There was no sign of movement except for smoke drifting up from one of the buildings and then getting ripped away by the wind.

It was just as well she had become so light. The cold had drained strength from all her muscles but she was still able to pull herself up and roll onto the surface of the wharf. Here she was fully exposed to the biting of the wind. But she got to her feet once more and plodded steadily, if a little uncertainly, in the direction of smoke and fire.

She staggered round the building once. The lower windows were boarded-up, every doorway filled in. It took a second, stumbling pass for Chloe to locate the entrance. A hole in the brickwork which, at first glance, looked as if it was filled with bits of broken wood and stone fallen from above, but it was betrayed by the sound of the wind gusting through it. Behind the disguised entrance she could see, in her head, a crawlspace clear of debris and easy to navigate. Chloe lowered herself to her hands and knees, and crawled inside.

The wind must have changed direction again because it suddenly screamed through the buildings, providing her with a vivid mental image. The tunnel led a short way and turned sharp right. A man stood at the exit holding a stick raised above his head. He was clever, she thought. The semi-hidden entrance meant he could protect himself against marauders. But she was not a marauder; she just wanted to be warm. The threat focused her wandering mind.

She crawled forward, not hiding the sound of her movement, giving no clue that she knew what was waiting for her. She reached the exit and, for the briefest moment, put her head out, then immediately pulled it back. The descending club glanced across her scalp. Without hesitation she grabbed it and, bracing her knees against the sides, pulled for all she was worth—which was not much.

But the attempted blow had him off balance and her pull finished the job. He fell forward with a cry and landed across the entrance. Chloe pushed herself out, grabbed his nearest arm, and twisted it behind his back until he cried out in pain.

'I don't want to fight you,' she said. 'I don't want to hurt you, but I won't let you hurt me. All I need is to get warm. I fell in the river. I need to be near your fire. Okay?'

'Okay,' he said.

The effort had drained her of all her remaining strength. She staggered away from him and dropped heavily into a sitting position.

Chapter 2

Mendelssohn

Mendelssohn heard the car crunch on the gravel outside the house, so he was not surprised when his wife put her head round the door. He glanced up. She looked like hell, with her hair tangled and make-up smudged.

'Hi honey, I'm home.'

'Kind of you to drop by, Lily.'

'I'm going to freshen up,' she said, and stepped further into the room. It was gone ten in the morning but she was still wearing her clubbing gear. Which meant not very much at all.

He put down his pen, leaned back in his chair, and stared at her. 'Your studio is currently occupied. You have to stay in the house.'

'Why, who's here?' she said. 'Finally decided to move one of your bits on the side in?'

'My dear Lily, you know as well as I do that I have never been unfaithful to you. It is a continual disappointment that you do not return the favour.' He picked up his pen and made to go back to work.

'So who is it?'

'Business,' he said without looking up.

For a moment, she was silent, as if she was going to argue with him, but her sense got the better of her. He had made it quite clear that if it was business, then it was law. She left the room and he could hear her shoes on the parquet flooring all the way to the stairs and then up to the next floor.

He sat back again. He had lost the flow. He dropped the pen and spun his chair around so he could look out of the window. The remnants of autumn's fallen leaves were racing across the lawn. Despite the warmth of the room, and the triple glazing, the corners of the window showed frost inside the first layer of glass.

He sighed; even walking across to the studio would be like mounting a polar expedition, but there was little choice. He headed out of the hall and equipped himself with quilted coat and hat. As an afterthought, he called for his car to drive him the couple of hundred yards.

'So, can you play table tennis with yourself?' It was Dog speaking. Mendelssohn mounted the stairs to the kitchen area and heard the question echoing back. 'You know what I think, I think you should learn how to do sign language, and then we could all talk to each other.'

Mendelssohn frowned. When Dog said 'we all', who exactly did he mean? He wasn't just referring to himself, he must be talking about Delia as well. Mendelssohn suppressed the wave of anger. He knew, on a rational level, he shouldn't be so protective, but when it came to his daughter he was not rational.

He stepped into the kitchen diner and was glad to see his daughter wasn't there. 'You'll learn sign language on your own time,' he said.

Mendelssohn looked at the new freak, Jason, and flinched. It was crazy. He'd seen, even owned, so many freaks that the reaction was nonsensical. But this kid, with that face. Mendelssohn shook his head. Maybe it was because everything else about him was so normal. Still, that was irrelevant. If the kid could do the job, that's all he cared about.

Dog jumped up from his chair and came over to him. That was another thing Mendelssohn didn't like. Dog really didn't have a very good idea of personal space. When he was being friendly, Dog liked to get up close and even touch. Mendelssohn knew he couldn't catch S.I.D but, with his years of discipline in not touching anyone, he flinched.

'You've got the plan sorted out?' said Dog cheerfully.

And that was another thing. Dog had a knack for knowing what he was thinking, and as someone who liked to keep his thoughts and feelings hidden, it was a talent he did not appreciate.

Mendelssohn went to the window; this place was not as well insulated as the main house, and he chose not to remove his coat. Instead he pulled out one of the kitchen chairs, sat down and crossed his legs. He looked the tentacle freak in the face, and saw that his eyes were blue. Such normal-looking eyes.

'You owe me a lot of money,' said Mendelssohn to the boy. 'Buying you out of the cages cost more money than I would expect you to make for me in five years.'

The boy did not react. Or if he did it was so fast it wasn't noticeable. Mendelssohn almost had an impulse to check his wallet.

'But if you're as good as you seem to be, and you do a few jobs, then you should be able to make that money for me in no time. Do you understand?'

Mendelssohn caught a movement in the corner of his eye. It was Dog nodding his head enthusiastically in an effort to make the new boy respond. Jason's eyes flicked at Dog, and then back to Mendelssohn. He nodded once.

'I'm glad we understand each other. I see that Dog has gone through your induction thoroughly.'

He took off his mittens, undid the top of his coat, and pulled out a large envelope from an inner pocket. He opened the envelope and unfolded a map. It showed the west of Manchester with the River Irwell winding through it. There was a hospital marked.

'We're going to start with a nice easy job. All I want you to do is to go to the hospital and acquire some equipment.'

There was a blur of motion and Jason was halfway across the room towards the exit.

'Dog, will you reassure our new friend this will not be a difficult thing.'

'He's right, Jason. He wouldn't ask us to do something we couldn't do because you know that would be silly. But, honestly, Mr Mendelssohn, a hospital? Apart from the public areas that'll be like Fort Knox.'

'You even know what Fort Knox is?'

Dog stood up straight. 'Yes sir. I've seen all of the James Bond movies. That's from *Goldfinger*, Fort Knox is the place that has all the gold in it.'

Mendelssohn closed his eyes, counted to five, and opened them again. 'That's not relevant. The hospital will be receiving a delivery of equipment this evening, at around six. Depends on the traffic. I want you to acquire the truck carrying the equipment. Best to do that before it gets inside the hospital.'

Dog leaned over and looked at the map. He reached up and flipped through the other sheets of paper underneath. There were more detailed maps, information about the truck, the shifts, and personnel. 'We might need some minor equipment as well, sir.'

'You can have what you need, within reason.'

Dog looked over to where Jason still stood in the middle of the room, and then back at Mr Mendelssohn. 'Jason was wondering what could be done to assist his mother?'

'Do this job for me properly, Jason, and I will ensure your mother gets a better meal than she's had in years. Keep doing the work for me and she'll be very well looked after. I'm a businessman, I reward good work.'

Chapter 3

Chloe

'You should take your clothes off.'

The old man had built up the fire. It looked like he had quite a stock of wood, all piled up in neat rows. Sensible when preparing for the winter. She thought of him as an old man, but when she looked into his face she realised he was only in his forties. But his face was lined with deep wrinkles, and his hands were grey with ingrained dirt. His fingernails were black and broken. One of the reasons he'd missed her with the stick was the number of layers of clothes he wore. She wasn't sure but there were at least three coats and three pairs of trousers as well as hefty boots and other layers underneath.

And he smelled bad, of course.

Despite the fire, she was cold and shivering, though, under the circumstances, that was probably an improvement.

'You should take your clothes off,' he repeated.

'I'm not taking my clothes off,' was what she tried to say, but her teeth chattered so much the words came out garbled.

He looked at her across the fire. 'If you don't get dry, you'll catch pneumonia and die. It's no skin off my nose, but I thought I'd offer the advice.'

It was strange how the refined quality of his voice was completely at odds with the state of him. She also knew he was right. But that really didn't make it any easier. There was no point in being coy about it.

'I am not taking my clothes off so you can look at me,' she said controlling her trembling jaw muscles as much as she could. 'I'm not going to be naked in front of you.'

'Well, it was worth a try,' he said. She frowned.

He got up from the fire and shuffled across to a wooden box by the wall. It was raised off the ground on lumps of rock and brick. The box itself looked quite old and had a decent lock on it. He opened it, pulled out a blanket, and tossed it across to her.

'I'll not move from the heat,' he said coming back to the warmth, 'but I'll face in the other direction while you get changed. Lay out your clothes facing the fire so they dry faster.' And with that he turned his chair around so his back was to her.

She had seen those tricks in the movies where people said they wouldn't look and then used a mirror, but he didn't have one. She shivered again. She really did need to get out of the wet clothes. Keeping her eyes on him as much as she could, she stripped down. Although when it came to her underwear, she hesitated.

'Finished yet?'

'No,' she said quickly.

'Hurry up. My toes are getting cold.'

Chloe took a deep breath and peeled off the rest. The temperature must have been below zero but the radiant heat from the burning logs warmed her skin, and she was certainly grateful for it. She picked up the blanket, wrapped it around herself—it caught awkwardly on the lumps on her back—and sat down. The cold from the stone she was on sapped the meagre warmth from her behind immediately. She began to pick at the laces of her shoes which, being wet, were virtually impossible to undo.

'I've finished,' she said quietly, almost hoping he wouldn't hear.

Without another word he turned his chair back. He glanced at her face, raked the shapeless blanket that covered her with his eyes, and then looked back down into the fire.

And there they sat for a long time. Chloe continued to pick at the shoe laces and eventually managed to untie them. They and her socks were added to the steaming clothes.

Perversely, despite the temperature—and lack of clothes—she warmed up and the shivering got worse. She couldn't stop her teeth from chattering. She wondered how long it would take for them to come loose.

The man glanced up at her again. 'Walk around.'

'Are you a doctor?'

'You don't need a doctor, girl, you need a survivor.'

'And that's you?'

'You seem ungrateful for someone who would be dying of hypothermia,' he said. 'Do you know how to build a fire?'

She didn't. Chloe tried to swallow but her throat was dry. 'Sorry.' She was acutely aware that if she got up and walked about, at some point she would have her back to him. And when that happened he would be able to see her deformity.

'Well?' he said. 'Are you going to walk?'

'I'm a freak.' The words came out in a rush. She'd been planning to wrap it up in some fancy talk, and be apologetic, slowly revealing the truth. But when it came to it, the words fell out of her mouth.

He lifted his gaze from the fire and looked at her with cold blue eyes. 'It was either that, or you were a runaway. And, to be honest, I don't think kids run away from home the way they used to. The world is too empty and too dangerous.'

'Aren't you scared?'

'I've seen freaks.'

'Of being infected?'

'What's your name?'

She hesitated, but there was something persuasive about him. Or was it just that he seemed to engender trust. Why was he here?

'Chloe.'

He nodded. 'Good. Only ever give the first name, unless you really trust someone. Names are valuable.'

He had avoided her question and come out with some complete nonsense. Maybe he just gave the impression of being rational, perhaps he was crazy. What sane person would choose to live out here?

'Why aren't you scared?' Her whole body shivered so strongly it almost knocked her off her seat.

'I'm sure you can talk while you're walking.'

She stared at his face. There was so much hair from his head and beard it was hard to see to the skin underneath. It probably helped to keep him warm. It wasn't even past midday, but the heavy clouds made it half-light outside, and even darker in here. The light from the fire's flames flickered, casting thick shadows that moved.

She was barefoot and her main concern was cutting her feet on glass or sharp stones, but the area round the fire looked safe enough. Making sure she had a firm hold on the blanket she got to her feet. The concrete floor around the flames was warm. For the first time she noticed the man's fire was built up on bricks and rested on a curved sheet of metal. She wondered why. Although the radiant heat from the metal certainly helped to warm the air.

'I'll just stand here,' she said. Her feet were warm and it felt as if it was moving up her body in waves.

'You need to get your blood circulating faster. Walk.'

She glared at him and then shrugged. She turned to walk off at a tangent, then hesitated again as she imagined how he would see her back. Oh well.

She walked away from him, less concerned about him looking at the thin material covering her body than the two places on her back where she could feel the blanket pushed away from her skin. Now she came to put her attention on it, it was an unusual sensation—but seemed expected in some way. As if her new body shape was entirely natural.

Carefully testing the ground as she stepped, she moved away. It was dusty and dirty but there seemed to be no large pieces of stone, or glass. She kept going until she could no longer feel the heat of the fire and turned round.

A wave of embarrassment went through her. He was staring after her.

From this new position she could take in the whole space. She guessed it had originally been a warehouse for goods coming in along the river. She did not know a lot about architecture but the place looked very old.

Rusted iron girders crossed above her about fifteen feet from the ground. It looked as if there had once been another floor. Here and there were rotting planks but most of it was gone. The upper floor had the empty windows where the wind blew in. At this end the roof was intact, but it had collapsed at the far end. The state of the place was such that she guessed most people wouldn't give it a second glance.

A good place to hide.

She walked back. He was right; getting her circulation moving did help. She was still shivering but not so much, and only occasionally. He watched her walk back.

'You move like a dancer,' he said as she returned. 'Poise.'

This time she did blush, but his words didn't carry any crude overtones. It was simply an observation.

'Jujitsu,' she said by way of correction. He made a noise that sounded like assent. She turned round before she got too close to the fire and walked away again, more confidently this time and quicker.

He was watching her again when she turned round. She accepted it this time.

On the return from her third trip the cold was crawling back though her skin again. She had gained enough confidence to check her clothes while he watched. They were warm and wet still, although some parts had reached the level of damp that could be worn. Better they were drier though.

Chapter 4

Mitchell

Mitchell had woken up at nine still seething. He managed to burn the toast, and even make himself a bad cup of coffee. He knew he was not helping, but his anger at the events the previous night had been building up inside him. He wanted to tackle Graham immediately after the disastrous battle with the kidnappers, but there was too much to do, too much organising of roadblocks and starting Forensics on their tasks. Not to mention all the interviewing, and making sure nobody disturbed the various parts of the crime scene which now covered several hundred square yards, the tops of buildings, and, as far as he could determine, the river.

Lament sent a car. And, if Mitchell was not much mistaken, all the traffic lights in his direction were green. He arrived at the police headquarters in a fraction of the usual time. What Lament could not do was make the lift travel any faster, even though there was one empty and waiting for him when he arrived.

Mitchell stood outside the room assigned to Special Agent Graham. He forced his anger down until it was a tightly-wound spring. He knocked firmly but not aggressively.

'What?' said Graham's voice.

Mitchell went inside. The room was pretty basic: desk, chairs, small table for friendlier meetings, unused. The view from the window was directly onto the car park, although the skyscraper of Utopia Genetics could be seen behind it. Graham was sitting at the desk, staring at his terminal. He was still the perfectly presented Purity officer, but now there was an underlying uncertainty. He didn't look up.

Mitchell shut the door and sat without being asked. He had a feeling it would get the agent's attention, and he was right. Graham turned to look at him. Perhaps he wasn't the perfectly presented agent anymore; he had shaved this morning, but his eyes told the tale of how little sleep he had managed.

'I've just ordered Chloe Dark's parents into quarantine. And I'm wondering about everybody else she's been in close contact with. What do you think?'

'Where would you stop? The whole school? Everyone on the trams she's been on? Me and Yates?'

'We don't have the facilities for that many.'

Mitchell leaned back in the chair. It creaked. He laid his hands in a relaxed position across his stomach. 'I'd be curious to know how often, when family or friends of freaks are put into quarantine, they exhibit symptoms of infection?'

Graham stared at him blankly. 'That's not my department. The Purity protects society.'

'I must admit, Special Agent Graham, I have been wondering where exactly in the hierarchy of the Purity you sit.'

'High enough,' he said, 'that it's no concern of yours, DI Mitchell.'

Mitchell twisted his body slightly in the chair and crossed his legs. 'And how do your seniors feel about the debacle last night?' The death toll had now reached twenty-one, of which three were police officers, one of whom he had known personally.

'Last night was unfortunate,' said Graham.

Mitchell uncrossed his legs, slid forward in the chair and leaned toward Graham, who flinched when he raised his hand.

'Unfortunate?' Mitchell counted off on his fingers: 'We failed to catch the kidnappers, Chloe Dark is gone, three police officers are dead, a further eight are injured, and eighteen criminals are also now dead. And while the latter may not be seen as a great loss, we can't interview them.' He paused for a breath. 'Let me count the good things that came about last night.' He paused. 'Oh yes. None.'

'We can still find Chloe Dark,' said Graham.

'Your card is still functioning?' Mitchell got to his feet. 'Why are we sitting here talking?'

'I told your wirehead to send someone to the area for a scout around.'

'You fucking idiot!'

Mitchell was out of the chair and across to the door almost before his final word stopped echoing around the room. He flung himself through the doorway and down the corridor. 'Lament, pull back whatever officer you sent to track the Chloe Dark riffy. Get a squad together, fully armed and ready to move. And I need a car right now.'

The screen at the lift door lit up. 'Orders received and understood, DI Mitchell. However, I cannot recall the officer sent to investigate. Special Agent Graham has seniority.' The lift doors slid open as Mitchell arrived. He spun on the spot to see Graham almost running down the corridor after him.

'Hold the doors, Lament.' As Graham came through they slid shut and the lift began to descend instantly.

Graham was panting. 'Your insubordination aside, Mitchell, why was that wrong?'

'Because whoever these kidnappers are, they are ruthless, organised and well-armed. And you're sending one officer into the area. Given what you managed to achieve last night, I would have thought you might have been more circumspect in your orders.'

'I only sent one man.'

'You shouldn't have sent any. We need data before we do anything.'

They arrived on the ground floor. Mitchell did not run, but he covered ground fast. People dodged out of his way. The car was pulling up as he exited the doors with Graham in tow.

'Lament,' said Mitchell as he jumped into the car. 'Special Agent Graham here is going to rescind his order.' Graham landed on the bench seat in the back of the car and slammed the door. 'Aren't you?'

Graham looked daggers at him. 'Yes, call him back if he can do that without it being obvious.'

Mitchell half-turned in his seat to face Graham as the car sped away. 'The police officers of the Manchester division are not soldiers, Special Agent Graham. It is their job to protect the populace from criminals. We are not your private army.'

He turned back to face the front and watched the cold streets of Manchester flowing past. He wasn't sure what Lament was doing with the traffic, but there wasn't any. As far as he knew Lament was not in charge of traffic control. One of the council wireheads did that.

'Special Agent,' said Mitchell, 'if you would be so kind as to inform Lament of the riffy code you have been following, that would probably be useful.'

Graham put his hand into an inside pocket and pulled out a sheet of paper. He unfolded it and held it up for Lament's camera. There were no letters or numbers written on the sheet, but Mitchell saw a circular pattern of blobs which represented a visually encoded version of a riffy number.

'It will take me a few minutes to coordinate this with the riffy grid,' said Lament.

'In London, the Purity are in charge of the riffy grid,' said Graham.

'In Manchester,' said Mitchell, 'we keep the riffy grid under separate control. It avoids putting too much power into the hands of one organisation.'

The car zipped through the centre of Manchester and out the other side to where the river Irwell split Manchester from Salford.

'Giving up things like radar and video in favour of the riffy grid was a mistake,' said Mitchell. 'It's far too easy to bypass it. If we still had proper radar coverage we'd know where that helicopter went.'

'The price of progress,' said Graham.

'You call this progress?'

The car came to a halt at the side of the road. 'I've cordoned off the area,' said Lament. 'The armed squad will be here in five minutes.'

Mitchell climbed out of the car. He hadn't picked up his coat on the way out, and the wind leached all the heat from his body in moments. Graham got out the other side; he was also inappropriately dressed. He shoved his hands in his pockets.

The front window wound down automatically on Mitchell's side.

'DI Mitchell?'

He leaned down and put his head inside the car. Lament's image looked out expressionlessly from the screen. 'There's nothing here, sir.'

'What do you mean?'

'The signal is here, but there's nothing else. It's underneath the bridge. It's not coming from inside anywhere.'

'Dead and drowned?'

'I couldn't say.'

Mitchell straightened up and looked in the direction of the bridge for a few moments. He looked at the buildings around it, they were all modern, relatively speaking, and for the most part they were in use. It was highly unlikely some powerful criminal organisation was based here.

He started to walk in the direction of the bridge.

Graham called after him. 'Where are you going?'

Mitchell took no notice. He lengthened his pace and sped up. This had two desirable effects: it helped to keep him warm, and put distance between him and the Special Agent. Unfortunately not for very long. He heard the panting breath and the slapping footsteps of Graham once again running to catch up.

'What are you doing? I thought we were waiting for the squad.'

'Just look around you,' said Mitchell, still striding ahead, 'there's nobody to fight here. Lament says the signal is coming from under the bridge.'

There was a rusted iron stairway heading down. Mitchell took it slowly and ended up at the edge of the water, frozen around the banks but still flowing in the middle. He could see something dark lying on the ice. He took out his flashlight and shone it.

A backpack, and no Chloe Dark.

Chapter 5

Chloe

'Let me see your back,' he said. A wave of fear went through her.

'No.' She stepped away from the fire and faced him. 'If you try anything, well, I know how to kill you.'

She thought she saw a smile hiding in the facial hair. 'I don't doubt it. I can see your muscle, and your control, though you look a bit thin.' There was definitely a hint of humour in his voice; he was laughing at her.

'I don't need you to look.'

'Have you seen it?'

She shook her head. 'Not properly.'

'Don't you want to know?'

'That doesn't matter; I'm not having a complete stranger examining me when I'm naked.'

He moved a little, resettling himself in the chair. 'Why don't you sit down?' He waved his hand at the place she had been sitting in before, across the fire from him. 'I'm not going to throw myself through the fire at you.'

To be honest, she was grateful. The cold was getting to her now that she had warmed up. At least her extremities had ceased hurting.

'You asked me who I am,' he said. 'I am Julian Delacroix.'

He said his name with a flourish, as if he expected her to recognise it. She didn't.

'The Delacroix Ballet?'

His voice was so hopeful she laughed and then slammed her mouth shut because she sounded hysterical.

'Sorry.'

This time she knew she saw a smile under the beard. 'Not to worry, it would be too much to think that a second rank ballet company would be remembered after all these years. It's not as if they put us on the television. Not like Rambert.' The jealousy was evident in his tone.

'I haven't heard of him either,' she said in an effort to make him feel better.

'I was the choreographer of the Delacroix, and I got some very good notices for my productions.' He must have seen the confusion in her face. 'Reviews.'

'Sorry.'

'Never mind, that's not the point, Chloe.' He took a breath. 'The point is that in a ballet company, especially one further down the rankings, one loses all embarrassment. I worked with a hundred dancers, and saw many of them *déshabillé*.' He glanced up and recognised the non-comprehension. 'Naked, darling. In fact some productions required nudity on stage.'

Chloe wasn't entirely sure how she felt about this. She did not doubt he was telling the truth. It explained the way he spoke, for a start.

'So you're saying you're not interested in my body?'

'I am curious to see what S.I.D is doing to you.'

'Why aren't you scared?'

His words seemed to dry up. It was almost as if a black curtain had dropped over him. 'I watched half my girls and boys die.' He lifted his arm and moved it in a graceful arc, as if taking in the room they were in. 'And this is my punishment.'

'Punishment for what?'

'Not being able to stop their suffering. Not dying with them.'

Chloe Dark and Julian Delacroix stared at one another across the fire that was turning to hot embers, glowing red, while the grey sky's light filled the space.

Chloe stood up and turned her back to the heat. She loosened the blanket around her shoulders but it caught on her lumps. She heard him move. The ghost image of him standing and making his way around to her filled her mind's eye. Not as complete as it sometimes was, but if she had wanted to she could have floored him with a single blow without even having to look.

'The blanket's caught,' she said.

'Shall I move it?'

She could not bring herself to say anything and just nodded. Something in the fire snapped noisily. She got the instant picture of him raising both hands to take hold of the blanket.

It pulled against her grip at the front as he lifted the coarse fabric away from her back and brought it down.

He stepped to the side so his shadow no longer hid her back. He let go of the blanket and it dropped until it hung in a loop to her waist. She pulled it tighter.

Something touched her in a place she had never felt before. A muscle she did not know she had twitched, and something in her back moved.

She jerked away. 'Don't!'

He backed off.

'Don't touch me!' She was breathing heavily, and shivered again but this time it was not from the cold. 'Don't touch me,' she repeated more quietly.

'I needed to know.'

'Know what?'

'What is growing in your back.'

Chloe struggled. Did she want to know? 'What is it?'

'Well, in the first instance it is perfectly symmetrical. They are growing together and they are the same thing.'

'But what?'

'I'm not an expert.'

'What!'

'I'm not sure.'

'Either you know or you don't!'

'You're getting upset.'

'I'm not!' She stopped and forced her voice to some semblance of normality. 'What do you want to do?'

'Touch you.'

'What exactly?'

'Feel them. I may press a little hard, as if I was squeezing your hand to count the bones.'

'Why?'

'I want to count the bones.'

'You're a complete bastard, did you know that?'

She got the very strong impression he was grinning. 'It has been a very long time since I've had that opportunity,

Chloe, and believe me when I say I am relishing every damn moment of it.'

Chloe laughed. She could hardly believe any of it. It was like some nightmare that she would no doubt wake up from—hopefully soon.

She stepped back closer to the fire and he moved up to her. 'I'm sorry I haven't washed my hands.'

'Just get on with it,' she growled but not very seriously. And then she held her breath, anticipating his touch.

She could feel his individual fingers as they came into contact with her skin, and his thumb on the other side. The pressure between them increased. She felt tender, as if she were bruised, but put up with the pain. He moved around, squeezed more and then transferred to the other side, going through the same actions.

'Well?' she said when he finally released her. She stepped away and turned to face him. He wasn't that much taller than her.

'Hands.'

'What?'

'Feels like hands.'

A wave of revulsion went through her as she imagined someone with hands sticking out of her back.

'Just hands?'

'Arms too, seems like there's an elbow joint and a wrist.'

'Oh, god.' She turned away and stared into the embers. 'Oh, god.'

'It could be worse.'

She looked up at him. 'Worse?'

She was getting used to the excessive facial hair and saw the look of pain on his face.

'Much worse,' he said in haunted and distant way.

He went and sat back down. The two of them stared into the fire. He put more wood on it and the flames leapt up again.

'I could kill myself.'

'You won't.'

'I could.'

He shook his head. 'You'll fight to the end, Chloe. You'll fight even when you've lost all your reason and no longer understand what you're fighting for.'

And she knew he was right. She could say the words but she doubted she could go through with it.

'Anyway,' she said. 'I have something I have to do.'

Chapter 6

Mercedes

Mercedes was sitting in the conference room. Every now and again she would glance up and stare out of the window. The clouds streamed across the sky driven by the storm winds from the Arctic. Winters had never been like this before. Even if S.I.D hadn't taken over the world, the weather would have, regardless. The changes had already been set in motion before the population was reduced to the point it stopped affecting the ecosphere.

She looked back at the notes she had been making. At the top of her list was Banner. She liked Paul. She had been working with him longer than any of the others, but he was overstepping the mark. This latest mistake had the potential to lead either the police, or the Purity, right to their door. Next was Kingsley Upton. He just didn't have the temperament. If it had just been a matter of ordinary everyday marketing, he was the right man for the job. But the extra stresses brought about by the nature of their activities were not doing him any good at all. Nor anyone else.

Alistair McCormack. It was difficult to know what to do with him. He was brilliant, and he knew how to use his research facilities, but he was arrogant. Not only had he lost one of his senior research scientists, one of the guards was also dead. And both of them to the same asset. Clearly he wasn't taking the necessary precautions. The only person she could trust to do their job properly, and not become overwhelmed by the difficulties involved, was Margaret Jenner. Unfortunately, she was the one that contributed least to the overall organisation.

What it really came down to was what she was trying to achieve. And that amounted to saving the world. She laughed at herself; if that wasn't arrogance, what was it? But the solution needed to be found to the S.I.D plague, and she was certain the secret lay in the work done by Dr Newman. They needed to acquire the assets in secret, before the Purity destroyed them.

She glanced up again at the window. Was that snow?

Ten o'clock came and the board members filed into the room. If they were surprised to see her there already they didn't show it. They sat in their usual positions. There had been a time when they were chatty, but there was nothing to chat about now.

Mercedes brought them to order, and went through the standard rigmarole for meetings. She couldn't let them know she was deciding who was going to be leaving, but all of them, except Margaret, were looking worried. Mercedes sat back in her chair. 'So, who would like to start?'

There was a moment's pause and then Paul Banner climbed to his feet. He reached into his pocket—Kingsley Upton actually flinched—but he only brought out an envelope.

'I would like to tender my resignation from the board.' His voice was as sensual as ever but now it was tinged with sadness. With a flick of his hand he sent the envelope spinning across the table. It slid up to Mercedes and wedged under her pad.

Banner sat down. Mercedes extricated the envelope, looked at her name on the outside and then laid it down on the table. 'Nobody is asking for your resignation, Paul.'

'I fucking am,' spat Kingsley. 'It's bad enough Alistair is losing staff to his assets.' He said the word assets as if it had air quotes around it. 'But this latest disaster killed three policemen, and we still didn't get it.'

Mercedes stared at Kingsley until he sat back and muttered, 'Sorry.'

'As I said, Paul, no one is asking for your resignation.'

'I must insist.'

Mercedes looked into his impassive face. 'I think we both need time to think about it. Recent events are too fresh in our minds for us to make sensible decisions.' She glanced at Kingsley and frowned slightly. He noticed, and sat back in his chair, although she was surprised to see he was looking a little pale, instead of the red-faced anger she was expecting.

'In the light of that,' she said, 'would you mind explaining what happened from your viewpoint, Paul?'

'We had alerted some of the gangs, the ones we've done business with before. We said we wanted Chloe Dark alive. And posted a reward for her acquisition.'

'Which is why we had that ridiculous event at the chippy,' snapped Kingsley before going quiet again under Mercedes' glare.

'Quite so,' said Banner. 'In retrospect, perhaps an attack on her home would have been better, but when she disappeared from the riffy grid we knew it was starting. On her reappearance in central Manchester we let our people know.'

'But you knew there would be a large force of police there,' said Mercedes.

Banner nodded. 'Yes, of course. We even had a good idea of where it was going to be, through intelligence received.'

'And still you went ahead,' said Kingsley.

Banner sighed. 'The pitched battle between the gangs and the police was a diversion. The idea was that we would get Chloe on her own and acquire her in the usual manner.'

'Except it turns out she can fly.'

Alistair McCormack shifted in his chair. 'No, she's not flying. She is only jumping. The records indicate extreme weight loss without commensurate health issues. I really want to see what's going on inside her.'

'Well, that's the whole idea, isn't it?' said Kingsley. 'Unfortunately, Paul couldn't quite manage the acquisition stage. Again.'

'No,' said Banner, 'we underestimated her again. But the parameters keep changing. When we try to use brute force it turns out she is a fighter. When we try to be clever, she pulls another trick out of the bag.' He glanced at McCormack, who nodded.

'All right,' said Mercedes. 'No need for recriminations or excuses here. I suppose there's just one question we need answering right now. Assuming she's not dead in the river, where the hell is she?'

Chapter 7

Yates

On the sixth floor of the police building in central Manchester, the winter wind screamed and howled round the corners like a banshee.

Or perhaps a herd of banshee, thought Yates. He wondered what the collective noun for banshee actually was. If there was one. It was only just past noon and the canteen had yet to fill up. Which had all been part of the plan.

He heard the lift ping and the doors roll open. The short but generously rounded forensic scientist he knew and enjoyed squeezing appeared at the door. Ria MacDonald glanced round looking for him, and he stood up. She gave a little wave and pointed at the serving counters for the cafeteria. He nodded and sat down again.

He watched her taking her time in deciding what she was going to have, though he couldn't really understand why since it all tasted like shit anyway. But eventually she headed in his direction. He stood up again, stepped out from the table and took the tray. She looked confused as he placed it on the table, put his arms around her and kissed her very firmly on the lips. She didn't pull away and when he finally lifted his head she was frowning.

'Who are you and what have you done with DS Yates?'

'Smile, my angel,' he said. 'There are witnesses.'

Her eyes narrowed, but she put a smile on her face and gave him another quick kiss on the nose. 'There,' she said as she extricated herself from his arms. 'I'm sure that'll be tremendously convincing.' She beamed a smile at him and giggled as if she had said something amusing. She sat down at her tray with him opposite.

'I can't believe I'm letting you do this,' she said between mouthfuls. 'God, this is better than the canteen at the labs.'

Yates looked down at it with new eyes. 'They must really hate you.'

He had a few mouthfuls of what purported to be mashed potato; thankfully the over-flavoured gravy overwhelmed its unpleasantness. 'We had to have another reason to meet,' he said.

She paused in her eating and stared at him for a long moment. 'I know you don't bonk me for my brains, Harry, but I'm not actually stupid. Forensic scientist here.'

'Well, what have you got for me then?'

She leaned across the table. 'The shoe had recently been worn.'

'So there was somebody else living in the house?'

'Well, there's *something* living in the house.' She took another mouthful and left him hanging.

He waited.

She swallowed. 'I haven't had time to do a full analysis, but the DNA from the shoe, it's mostly human.'

'Only mostly?'

'There are some pieces that aren't.'

'S.I.D?'

She was in the middle of a mouthful and shook her head. It was a frustrating few moments before she was able to answer. 'Not S.I.D. But not entirely human.'

Yates let that sink in. 'Shit.'

Ria smiled brightly. 'I know, it's great. This is something new, and you let me discover it.'

'You can't say anything about it.'

'Reference my earlier comment about not being stupid,' she said and smiled again. Yates liked her smile, it always carried a hint of lust. 'Doing anything tonight?'

'I would really love to, my sweetest darling,' she said. He winced at her terminology. He reached out and took her hand in his, and then realised that felt really weird. He had honestly never been romantically involved with anyone, never indulged in handholding, or lovey-dovey in public, or anything that resembled the kind of pretence they were going through now. So reaching out and holding her hand, it was strange.

Apparently it was strange to her as well because she looked down at the way his fingers were entwined with hers. 'Your hand is bigger than mine,' she said.

He looked too. Her fingers were shorter but plumper than his. It almost looked as if he could enclose the entirety of her hand in his.

'I think you ought to stop doing that,' she said. 'I'm not really sure I like it very much.'

'I know what you mean,' he said, 'but what I was saying before, witnesses. We need to be really convincing.'

'Love is a four-letter word,' she said.

'And so is lust. And I know which one I'm in. Why can't you see me tonight?'

She withdrew her hand from his and laid it in her lap. 'This is not the kind of relationship where you can demand things from me.'

'I understand that, but I thought you might fancy it.'

'When I fancy it, I'll let you know.' With that she stood up, pushing her chair back noisily 'I will not be taken for granted, so you can take your invitation and *shovel* it.'

'Shove it,' he said. 'Take my invitation and *shove* it.'

They burst out laughing. Silly movies had a lot to answer for.

'Why can't you see me tonight?'

She leaned forward across the table, took his chin between thumb and forefinger, and put her face very close to his. 'Because, my sweet darling, lots of people got killed last night, and their body parts are still strewn all over Tibb Street. Currently we forensic scientists are running shifts in order to clean it up, and make sure we don't lose any evidence.

'So, unless you want to come and do me out in the open, in a freezing gale, with the rest of the crew watching, we will have to postpone our little get-together.' Then she kissed him again, which was nice, then turned round, and walked away carrying her tray. And he was able to admire her rear as it retreated.

Chapter 8

Melinda

She felt awful again. The familiar blackness filled her eyes, while the lines of electrical current delineated the walls of her cage. The first thing she noticed was that she was not tied up. The plastic cuff around her left wrist had been removed. Her head ached. They must have drugged her again.

So, the other two girls were here. Not that that seemed to be much help at all. Lucy was working for the other side, and Vanessa? Well, she was a bitch.

If she wanted to escape she had to get past this Lucy. Should she try to get Vanessa out? Chances were she wouldn't be very grateful. So maybe leave her?

No. That was the wrong attitude.

And once she got out? What then? She was a freak; she was going to die anyway, like the others were. If she ran, she might get shot by DI Mitchell. Her parents said there were fewer riffy towers in the countryside, if you could get there before they caught you. But winter was coming and it might already be snowing. She would probably be dead before spring, one way or the other.

The lights came on. Melinda chose not to keep her electrical perception running. The wires faded into the walls. Being able to switch it on and off was useful, she thought. But what difference did it make? All freaks died.

Melinda was somewhat astonished when breakfast finally turned up, because the guards were no longer dressed in rubber. They just wore uniforms. They also looked slightly nervous. And so they should, she could kill them with a snap of her fingers.

She frowned. That really wasn't the right way to think. Her parents had brought her up better than that.

As far as she knew she had already killed two people, maybe three. It was difficult to feel anything because she did not really know what had happened and they were accidents. Even if they had been provoked. She needed to learn to control herself. She had her breakfast in silence. That hadn't changed. When she was finished she heard the sound of someone else coming down the corridor, someone with official-sounding shoes, not rubber. He stopped at the door and looked in. Tall, thin, heavy jacket, long nose with wire-framed glasses perched on it, and a goatee. He was the stereotype of a university professor.

'Miss Vogler,' he said. 'You will have noticed we have changed our security protocols.'

'Yes,' she said quietly. This was the first time one of her jailers had addressed her like a human being.

'You encountered Vanessa yesterday.'

'She told me to get lost.'

He gave a small laugh. 'I'm sure her language was a little more interesting than that, if lacking in imagination. However, that is not the issue. You see, we have finished our testing on her. She's not very special, not like you, or Miss Grainger, come to that.'

'Okay?' Melinda had no idea where that was going.

'It's very simple,' he said, 'if you make any further attempt to escape or harm anyone else here, we will kill her. And it will be your fault.'

Melinda stared at the man, trying to absorb what she had just been told. Suddenly he did not look like a professor at all. More like a hyena waiting for its prey to die. Did he really mean that? Would they really kill someone just to get her to cooperate? She didn't know. But it wasn't really something she could take a chance on. She nodded slowly.

'Say it,' he said. 'Tell me that you will cooperate and you understand the consequences if you don't.'

She hesitated. 'I understand what you said, and I will cooperate.'

He stared at her for a moment then turned on his heel and left. She heard his echoing footsteps disappearing down the corridor, and could tell by the change in sound when he turned the corner at the end. She had promised to cooperate but, as her father said from time to time, a promise under coercion wasn't binding. The threat of them killing that other girl, though, she couldn't have that on her conscience. So whether her promise was real or not, she had to go through with it.

Besides, if they were telling the truth, the promise was probably the only thing keeping Vanessa alive. If they hadn't caught Melinda, she might already be dead. And dissected.

The first session of the day was a return to the gym, but things went a lot quicker with people not having to wear rubber suits. The thing was, she thought, they seemed like ordinary people. She wasn't sure what she'd been expecting but these were not evil scientists. They were just doing a job. She noticed most of the monitoring equipment was labelled Utopia Genetics, but that wasn't particularly surprising since they produced a lot of equipment for this sort of thing all over the North West.

The other thing about the session was the addition of Lucy. She wasn't doing any of the tests, she was just standing at the door, watching. Guarding?

Seeing the other girl in proper light, Melinda felt sorry for her. Not only had she lost all her hair, but her skin was a hard and wrinkled grey colour. And a bump in her forehead.

After an hour and a half, it appeared the researchers— was that what they were?—had acquired all the information they needed for the time being. With the tests and the exercises finished, she expected the guards to come and take her back to her room. But instead Lucy wandered over.

'Come on, let's get something to eat.' Lucy reached out and clamped her hand on Melinda's upper arm. Clamped was the only word Melinda could think of to describe the other girl's pincer grip. And where she led, Melinda had no choice but to follow.

Once out of the gym they headed away from the cells. 'Where are we going?'

'We have our own canteen,' said Lucy. Whatever happened to her skin didn't seem to have affected her throat, as her voice was as light as you might expect any girl of her age to be. 'We don't share with the staff, they'd just be afraid of us, after all we are freaks. But we get our own space.'

They followed a couple of corridors and went across an open foyer. It looked like it ought to be an entrance, but where you might have expected an expanse of glass onto the outside world, it was solid brick with no obvious opening.

Across the other side of the foyer was a small room with a table and some chairs. There was a selection of fruit, water and sandwiches.

Melinda followed Lucy's lead and filled a plate. There was more than enough for the two of them. 'Are there any others here?'

'Only Vanessa, as far as I know, but she bites.'

'Really?'

Lucy gave Melinda a look that said everything.

'Why are you cooperating?'

'Same reason as you I should imagine: they threatened to kill her. Not that she'd be a loss to the world.'

They ate in silence, Melinda trying to absorb the new scheme of things.

'So you're, like, really strong, and tough?' Melinda felt weird asking the question, it was unnatural. The idea you might talk to someone who was a freak was ridiculous. And yet she was one too, so what difference did it make?

'Yeah, I have some bone condition that makes them denser and a lot stronger. Apparently that means I'm not likely to break a bone. At least before I die. And the muscles have compensated or something. They don't talk to us about it.'

'I make electricity,' said Melinda. 'And I can see it too.'

Lucy glared at her then picked up a forkful of food and put it in front of her mouth. Just before she put it in her mouth she said, very quietly: 'Don't talk about anything they haven't discovered for themselves.'

Melinda did the same with her food. 'Can they see us?'

'Of course.' She waved her hand in the direction of a camera. 'Though I don't know if anyone's watching the feed.'

'Why don't they wear quarantine suits?'

'We're not encouraged to ask questions. We're just lab rats.'

'But the Purity are paranoid about infection.'

'This isn't the Purity.'

'What are they going to do to me next?' said Melinda.

'Well, if it's anything like me, they are going to try testing your limits.'

Melinda went quiet. That didn't sound very nice at all.

Chapter 9

Chloe

'Have you got anything to eat?' said Chloe. The fire had died back to embers but her clothes were back on and she was no longer shivering. She felt so much better that her hunger had returned with a vengeance. The last time she had eaten was yesterday evening.

'Not much,' said Julian. 'And I never promised to feed you.'

She looked around; she couldn't even see where he might keep his food. Right now she was tempted to just take it from him, whatever he had. But she knew that would be wrong, and could probably resist the temptation. Probably.

'What do you eat?'

He looked up at her. 'Anything I can find.'

'Do you hunt or fish?'

He laughed. 'I look in bins for leftovers.'

She shifted awkwardly on the stone. 'I'm hungry. I've been hungry for weeks. Did that happen to your girls?'

He shook his head. 'I don't want to talk about them.'

She frowned. He was the one who'd brought them up in the first place. 'Where can I get food?'

'You could take your hat off and they'll just pick you up.'

She shook her head. 'I can't do that.'

'No, I wouldn't want to be in the clutches of the Purity. Bunch of fascists.'

Chloe got to her feet and started to pace. It didn't stop the hunger pangs but seemed to trick her body into thinking she was doing something about it.

'I was going to join the Purity,' she said on one of the turns when she was walking towards Julian.

'Well, it's better to be the predator than the prey,' he said. 'If you can live with yourself.'

She had had enough of his cynicism. 'I need to eat!'

'Then go out and find some food, why don't you?' he said. 'And pick up some wood to replace what I've wasted on you.'

'You bastard.'

'I'm not a charity. I saved your life. You owe me.'

She had no answer. Her back ached. She stretched and felt the extra limbs in her back moving as well. She felt it ought to give her the creeps, but somehow it didn't. Did the mutations of all freaks integrate naturally? So it felt like it was still just them?

Maybe that's the worst part, you didn't feel different. It's just what everyone else saw.

She took a deep breath, trying to use the calming exercises Sensei had drilled into her all these years. In through the nose, out through the mouth. In through the nose, out through the mouth.

She settled on her feet and felt her body relax. In through the nose, out through the mouth. There was a sound behind her. A tiny scuffling noise, and she saw it, outlined between the stones. Smoothly she bent her legs and crouched down. She kicked up a piece of brick half the size of her palm. She stood again in one flowing move.

The rat moved and its claws scratched; she twisted at the waist using the turn to let fly with the stone. It struck the rat in the head and it dropped. She went over, and picked it up by the tail. Its body was about a foot long and pale. She brought it back to the fire.

'That's why I eat out of bins,' he said. 'Even that food is better than rats.'

She glared at him.

'Do you even know how to skin and gut a rat?' he said. 'Got a knife?'

She slumped back down on her stone.

'Nice shooting though,' he said, 'now if you could take down a duck, or raid someone's chicken run. Maybe spear a fish?'

Chloe looked longingly at the rat. She was almost tempted to take a bite out of it anyway. The look she gave it must have been obvious.

'Don't,' said Julian. 'Disease, for a start.'

He stood up and went back to his box. He got it open and pulled out some papers.

'Look,' he said. 'I'm not going to tell you where to get food nearby. The people round here put up with me as long as I'm discreet. I never cause any trouble. But there are other places, further away, where I know you can find something. I'll tell you, you leave and I'll never see you again. Okay?'

She nodded reluctantly. The idea of travelling to get food did not appeal, but getting any food in some way did.

He laid out the map for her. 'You head away from the river until you come to Barton Road, and then head south.

Keep going until you get to this big roundabout. Go along Davyhulme Road to Bowers Road then south. This brings you to the back of this hospital complex. They throw out some food there, and they have a lot of chickens, you might get some eggs.'

She also noticed the green area beside it marked as a golf course. Manchester was not a big city like London, where you could walk for days and not come to the end of it. Julian's home, if you could call it that, wasn't more than a couple of miles from the city centre and only a little bit more to her parents' house. But she felt as if she were a thousand miles away.

She thanked him and, making sure she had picked up all her things, went to the exit tunnel. Julian did not come with her.

'Don't trust anybody,' he said from the fire.

'Even you?'

'Especially me,' he said. 'I'm a survivor.'

She was almost tempted to leave the dead rat to force him to deal with it, but somehow the idea of leaving potential food behind stopped her. There might come a time when she would happily chew its flesh.

As she came out into the windy alleys and passages between the old buildings she felt it ought to be night, but it was still only shortly after midday and the sky was not dark. Flakes of snow whipped round corners or spun in eddies. She did not relish the thought of being caught outside if the weather decided to turn very cold.

She saw no one as she made her way through streets of decrepit office buildings and then into residential streets that only housed ghosts.

If she wanted to find Melinda and the other girls she needed a plan.

She could just remove her hat. Instinctively she reached up and pulled it further down over her head. She needed something cleverer.

Up to now the kidnappers had grabbed girls off the street, ones that were turning into freaks. Okay, that was just a guess, but the fact they had made such an effort to get her, three times, meant she was special in some way and the only thing special about her was being an infectee. They knew it, but somehow the Purity didn't. That meant they had better information.

So, the kidnappers knew she was turning into a freak before the Purity. What did that mean? Everyone went for regular check-ups, but, as far as she understood it, she was mutating faster than normal, which was probably why she was hungry all the time.

And the moment she thought about the hunger all the other thoughts were driven from her mind. All she could think about was food and filling the void in her stomach.

The map suggested the hospital wasn't too far, just a couple of miles if she stayed on the roads. Half an hour if she jogged. She opened up her pace, feeling the lightness on her feet as if she weighed almost nothing. Which she did. The thought occurred to her it might only take a strong gust of wind to blow her over. But then if she weighed so little she could probably land without much harm. She wondered what her terminal velocity would be if she fell off a building.

She had no idea how to calculate that.

She hit Davyhulme Road on the far side of the roundabout just as the map had shown. She could smell cooking food. Someone had an open fire and was roasting some meat. Her nerves screamed at her to be fed. She had to have it.

Her eyes scoured the street. There was a residential area to the north of the road. Similar to the one where she lived. Like a village in the concrete wilderness of a dead city. A place where people gathered to pass their lives with some company and protection from the dangerous world that surrounded them.

She dropped back into a walk. Found the next road and turned up it. The wind was coming in from the northeast so the smell of the food had been carried to her from that direction. She kept moving, found an alley between the streets and took that. The less she was seen the better. A dog barked in the distance.

A fence separated her from the house from which the food smells were emanating, and its garden. She closed her eyes and listened. A woman talking, no, gossiping, to someone else. Three women in the kitchen. And the food was in the kitchen. If she didn't hurry, they might eat it.

What could she do? She needed a distraction.

She turned and peered through gaps in the fencing. There was a washing line out back, heavy with clothes and sheets whipping in the wind. That was hopeful, nothing would dry in this. It was more likely to freeze. Still, having a lot of damp sheets in the house would be unpleasant.

Moving further along the fence, to where it was one wall of the narrow passage along the side of the house, she leapt up the six feet and then jumped again to cling to the house. She felt the limbs on her back trying to move to help balance her. She wished they wouldn't, she preferred them to be unfeeling lumps of flesh.

The wind tugged at her but her fingers held her firmly to the wall, while her feet rested on a decorative ledge of tiles. She worked her away around to the back and, clinging to the upper window ledges, crossed to the far side where the semi-detached house joined to its partner.

She dropped down to the fence here. The washing line was nylon and tied off with a simple knot.

She undid it and let the washing fall to the frosty and muddy ground. In moments she was back up on the side of the building above the kitchen door.

She waited.

They didn't notice.

She could still hear them nattering away about inconsequentialities. There was only one thing for it. She rapped hard on the window she was clinging to. They might think the sound was from upstairs but they were certain to—

There was a cry of 'Oh no!'

Moments later the kitchen door was flung back and all three women came rushing out. Chloe prayed they wouldn't look up, but then why would they? One of them rushed to where the line had become untied while the other two, armed with a laundry basket, headed out onto the grass.

There was no time to lose.

Chloe dropped silently, slipped in through the open door and closed it gently behind her, keeping her head down. The door handle was one of those that locked if you pushed it up. She did it. To her the sound of the lock engaging seemed to echo around the room. But she heard no alarm from the women.

Looking around, Chloe saw the open door of the oven where some hand-made burgers were waiting to be served. There were buns and fried onions. She found a bag, and just pushed the food into it. She licked her fingers after the burgers went in. Delicious.

There was a banging on the door behind her. She didn't need to look to see them outside trying to get in. They would probably go for the front door and although they couldn't stop her, she did not want to be seen properly, or to hurt them. *They had a working refrigerator.*

She pulled it open and threw everything else that looked edible into the bag.

She ran for the front door and managed to get it open just as one of the women was opening the side gate. Chloe stayed at ground level, so as not to attract attention, and legged it.

Chapter 10

Michael Dark

He continued to stare at the terminal screen long after the news report had shifted away from the events of Manchester during the previous night. At some point his wife had come to stand next to him and she was still there. Their fingers were entwined on his shoulder. As always he noticed how much smaller her hand was than his. Every time.

The police had kept the press as far away from the battle as possible. There weren't even any drone images swooping in and round. At least not at first.

From a long distance away, but with a camera lens that could make that distance seem like the next house, the journalists had filmed the confrontation. They had spent considerable time on that. With the images of police and attackers falling, as the image flashed with each gunshot.

It was like a war zone, or an action movie. But this was real and now. They had not seen anything even close to this since the plague and the riots.

But that was not the thing that had held the Darks.

The cameraman had spotted the figure coming out of the restaurant in the middle of the battle.

They could not see that it was Chloe. There was little enough illumination, and it was a winter night. But they knew it was her.

When they had discovered her missing in the morning they had gone back to the riffy tracker. They had watched the recording as her image disappeared from her room and then, a little while later, reappeared in the centre of Manchester. Near the restaurant.

It was not that they had any specific indication that this dark figure standing outside the restaurant was Chloe, but they had no doubts.

Then they watched her jump up the side of the building and climb to the top where there was even less illumination. They saw shadows, watched as burner beams raked the roof, and the arrival of the helicopter. It was unreal.

And then she jumped to the next building. And the next, with the helicopter in pursuit. And then the next. Debenhams.

Michael Dark did not fail to note the irony. The day he had refused to listen to Ali Najjar about his daughter they had been in the big department store. The day he had fought with the man who had tried to tell him the truth. The man who had died only a few minutes later in a crazy accident.

Then the image had changed. Chloe and the helicopter were out of the no-fly zone set up by the police and the film crews were on the ball. A drone moved in. Its camera did not have the telephoto capabilities of the main one, but when it got in close the picture was much better.

There was no doubt now it was Chloe. She climbed a ladder, went across to the other side of the building. The drone arrived there just as she threw herself off.

His wife had screamed.

They watched Chloe grab the helicopter and saw it fly off, too fast for the drone to follow.

The anchorman had announced the police were in search of the freak and the terrorists engaged in the attack. But by that time the Darks were no longer listening. They stared at the screen without seeing it, heard the words without listening to them, and felt their lives fall away from them, as their own daughter had fallen from the roof.

They were dragged back to reality when the image switched to a picture of their house. A dozen figures dressed in quarantine suits rushing up the path.

'What's happening, Mike?'

There was a splintering crash of wood and glass. As if blown in on a gust of cold air, the figures on the screen materialised at the door.

'Get down on the floor!'

Mike turned towards them in bewilderment. His wife's hand fell away from his.

'Get down on the floor!'

He blinked in disbelief at the weapons in their hands. He raised his.

'Get down on the floor or we will use force!'

Mike descended slowly to his knees. He felt Mandy doing the same beside him. She was crying.

'Face down!' The voice was slightly muffled by the material of the quarantine suit. He couldn't see a face behind the smoked glass.

There was the pounding of feet upstairs. Doors being smashed open.

'They could just turn the handles,' he said quietly.

'Get face down on the floor!'

A voice from above shouted. 'Secure on first level.'
There was the sound of furniture being scraped across the
ground.

'Lie face down, now!'

'Better do as he says, Mike.'

Her voice sounded preternaturally calm. He wanted to
protest but felt her hand on his shoulder pressing him into
the floor. He went with it, although the blood was pumping
through him and he just wanted to fight. The pressure of the
floor against his chest seemed abnormal. The linoleum
surface was cold against his cheek, and the frigid air flooding
in made him shiver.

'Hands behind your back.'

He obeyed. The shuffling footsteps of two or three
people drew close around them.

'Where's Chloe?' said Mandy. There was a double
thump, one following the other. Mandy gave a little moan of
pain. Mike switched the direction of his head. She was there,
looking at him but unfocused. A patch of red wetness
showed in her hair near her ear.

'Mandy?'

Someone grabbed his wrists, put something round
them, and pulled it tight. He cried out with the pain. Mandy
jerked as one of the suited figures did the same to her. 'What
have you done to her, you bastards!'

'Resisting Purity quarantine is an offence.'

'But—'

He was interrupted by someone shouting that the
subjects were secure.

In the hall someone seemed to be reciting something. He recognised words about clauses, sub-clauses and quarantine. The rest was a blur.

He was grabbed on both sides and yanked to his feet. He staggered along between the two Purity officers as they manhandled him through the door, along the passageway and across the broken remains of their lovely front door.

There was a crowd of people standing well back, but watching in avid fascination. People he had known for years, their neighbours, and no one lifting a finger to help him or Amanda. Not even a word of protest. They were all just grateful it wasn't them. Except for two.

As they threw him into the back of the quarantine van, he caught sight of Colin Thackeray and Chardonnay Jones-Willis with a look of smug satisfaction on their faces. The only thing Mike was grateful for was that he knew they had not caused this. They were merely benefiting from his daughter's illness, and it could happen just as easily to them.

Wait until they had to deal with Mrs Wilberforce. She really was a nutter.

Chapter 11

Sapphire

She lay in the hot bath in the middle of the day with the wind rattling the windows and leaking through the gaps in cold gusts.

The interview with the police had lasted until past midnight and she had not got to bed until half three. No one at the school was going to argue with her, not that she let them know why she had been at a restaurant with a student. Who had turned out to be a freak.

She could always say that she had been asked to do it by her real bosses. And that would have the benefit of being the factual truth, though she doubted Chris would put it in his report. It didn't matter, there was no way they would query the Purity. They would take her word for it.

There wasn't any bubble bath, of course, not on her wages, even with the perks she could afford. She had to weigh up all the luxuries and choose the important ones. Like orange juice and coffee. Instead she had crushed lavender that floated across the surface, shifting and moving as she made waves. The soap was coarse but she liked the feel of it on her skin, and the rough smell. It made her feel strong.

The temperature in the bottom of the bath had become too cold for comfort. She stood up and grabbed the towel from the painted hard-backed chair. Standing in the bath, she wrapped the towel around her shoulders and let the excess water drip from her. She didn't like dripping water onto the bathroom floor. It made it slippery.

She hooked her foot under the plug chain and pulled it free. A bubble rose up and the water gushed down the hole. As the level dropped she towelled herself dry.

There was something supremely decadent about bathing in the middle of the day.

The water was almost all gone as she got down to her calves. She tossed the towel on to the floor and stepped out on to it to dry the soles of her feet, then finished drying herself.

In the summer she enjoyed being naked in her rooms, but it was too cold now. She fetched her woolly dressing gown, wrapped it around herself and slipped her feet into her fluffy slippers. In the lounge she climbed into her armchair, tucked her feet under her, so they wouldn't get cold, and relaxed.

She closed her eyes. It wasn't elegant but it was perfect.

It would have been perfect. If Chloe had been here. Or Emily. She glanced up and looked at the picture on the mantelpiece. Emily had been lovely, but she was gone. Ripped out of Sapphire's life.

Chloe would never be her, but could have been as fulfilling. But she was gone too.

But Sapphire smiled. Chris had not got her, nor had the kidnappers, and the police were just as helpless. Chloe had escaped them all. Well, that was not quite correct. It was possible the kidnappers had Chloe, but Sapphire doubted it. Chloe knew how to fight and, where Emily had been obedient to everything Sapphire desired, Chloe refused her.

'Open the fucking door, Saffie, and do it right now!'

The almost perfect day collapsed and sank into a mire of hate and pain.

This time he had not even knocked. Just commanded. She leapt to her feet and rushed to the door. She unlatched it and then remembered she needed to unlock it.

'I need to get the key,' she said plaintively and found her coat. She went through every pocket once and then again before she found the keys in the first pocket she'd checked.

She dropped them as she tried to get the key into the lock.

What am I doing?

And hesitated with the key in the lock.

'Get this fucking door open.' His voice hissed through the door. He wasn't shouting and that just made it worse. She turned it.

He rammed it open. And stood there, a seething mass of anger. He back-handed her across the cheek, knocking her out of the way. She staggered away, tears in her eyes. At least she hadn't cried out.

Stepping inside he slammed the door behind him. He grabbed her by the arm. 'What did you tell her?'

'You're hurting me!'

'I'll fucking break it, you stupid bitch.' He was panting and his face was white with fury. 'What did you tell that freak?'

Sapphire turned, trying to ease the pressure on her arm. It just made it worse. 'You're hurting me.'

She saw the blow coming from the other hand but had no time to defend herself. She felt as if her head would come off. The pain in her arm became unbearable as he forced her across the room to the table. He turned her around and pushed her face-down. His fingers went between her legs and jammed into her. She bit down on a scream. She wouldn't let him have the satisfaction. Not this time.

'What did you tell her?'

His fingers twisted agonisingly.

'What could I tell her? You didn't tell me your plans.' She grunted in pain as he turned his fingers again.

'Enjoying it?' he said with hint of laughter in his tone.

'You don't own me anymore—' she bit down on the word she did not want to say. '—Chris.'

He yanked his fingers away. And got behind her. He thrust hard and fast, only interested in his own satisfaction. At least it was only the bruises that hurt now. She let him do what he wanted.

He came out of the bathroom. She was curled up in the corner. If she had taken a chair he would have hit her again. She was past their relationship; it was him that couldn't let it go.

'You told her to run.'

Yes. 'No.'

'What game do you think you're playing, Saffie?' He twisted her name into an insult. 'You can't have her, she's going to die a nasty death, and one day she'll be so far gone she'd tear your head off just for the fun of it.'

'I didn't tell her to run.' *I told her to get as far away as possible, as far away from you as possible.*

'You better be telling the truth, Saffie, dearest.' He came over to where she sat and put his foot on her ankle. He ground it down hard. She blinked with the pain but gave no other sign. 'Because if I ever find out you've been lying to me, I'll hand you over to Research.'

That scared her, but she looked up into his eyes. *Not if I kill you first, Chris.*

Chapter 12

Dog

It had been dark for an hour. The sky was completely black. Little flakes of white drifted down. Every now and again a gust of wind would send a flurry of them chasing down the street. The only light came from inside the hospital compound behind the ten-foot wall topped with a spiked iron bar.

Dog stared at the gate wondering what the hell he was going to do. Back at the house he had been all bravado and *oh yes, Mr Mendelssohn*. Trading freaks for munitions was one thing, stealing a truck was another altogether. The freak-boy stood beside him, although what help he could be Dog had absolutely no idea. It was not as if he had ever done anything like this before, but the prospect of coming back empty-handed to Mr Mendelssohn did not appeal.

He had spent the whole afternoon staring at the map, but there really wasn't that much information available. This was an occasional delivery, and there weren't guards that followed rigid patterns. It really wasn't like the movies.

'Got any ideas?' he said to his hooded companion. Of course he didn't, he hadn't said anything all afternoon, not that he could talk, of course, but he could write and draw. He hadn't offered any suggestions. Dog couldn't decide whether the snow was a help or a hindrance, but one thing he did know was that the truck would have a riffy, and the moment it went AWOL, the police were going to be alerted.

The residential area directly around the hospital did not contain any residents. It was something he'd noticed: medical establishments stood on their own regardless of the quality of housing around them. Probably because people didn't want to be reminded of illness, particularly S.I.D.

Mr Mendelssohn's details said the truck would only have a driver, and he was going to arrive here at some point soon. The gate would open and he'd go inside. An unloaded truck was of no value, so anything he did, anything *they* did, would have to happen when the truck arrived. Dog put his head on one side and stared.

There was him, and there was Jason. The kid was fast, but that wasn't enough on its own. And he was ugly as hell. Shockingly. Which gave Dog an idea. He outlined his plan to his sidekick. It wasn't so much a plan as a few ideas loosely strung together, but it was better than nothing. The sidekick was going to be doing most of the work; Dog thought that was appropriate, it was the kid getting captured at the fights that meant he now owed so much to Mendelssohn. Jason objected a few times but finally agreed. This wasn't the time to be shy.

Dog's feet were going numb when the truck appeared in the road that paralleled the hospital wall from the main road. He took a step back into the shadows of the alleyway, about to say something to Jason, when he realised the kid wasn't even there anymore. Dog's nose told him Jason had only just left, and he could trace him by scent if he needed to.

The truck slowed as it approached the turn and its yellow indicator flashed. There was a blur in the snow in front of the truck which Dog took as his signal. He launched himself out of the alley, straight at the passenger door. He heard the thump and saw the shadow land on the front of the vehicle. Jason put his head close to the windscreen and pulled back his hood, letting the light play on his face.

It was at this point Dog expected the vehicle to screech to a halt. But it kept moving at exactly the same pace.

Bloody hell, thought Dog, *he's still got the thing on autopilot.* Mendelssohn's notes said they were supposed to switch to manual on the approach in case of trouble. Maybe the driver had been asleep, but the sound of him screaming indicated he wasn't asleep now. The truck wasn't supposed to be moving.

Dog yanked at the door. Thankfully it was unlocked and he dropped the half-brick he'd selected to smash the window if needed. The so-called driver had retreated to the far side of the cab. It was only another ten feet to the gate.

It was exactly that moment a weird smell drifted across Dog's nose. It was odd enough to make him stop for a moment, but then it was gone. The truck came to a halt and the horn beeped twice. Dog bounded into the cab, not wanting to give the driver any time to recover. Just at that moment the door on the other side opened and the driver, who had been cowering against it, lost his balance and fell out with a soft cry drowned out by the engine noise.

Dog landed in the driving seat; a few moments later Jason arrived in the passenger seat. The engine engaged again. And the vehicle crept forwards. They pulled the doors shut.

'No,' said Dog in frustration, 'stop, you stupid machine!' The gates into the back of the hospital had opened and the truck was turning into it. 'Oh, for fuck's sake,' shouted Dog. 'Get down!'

He threw himself into the gap below the dashboard, a quick glance told him that Jason had done the same, although he had more space on his side than Dog with all the controls.

The van drove into the compound area. The lights from the building and the pylons shone down through the windows at them. Dog blinked, and saw the green 'door unlocked' sign shining next to the main door handle. His hand flashed out and clicked it to the locked position. The light went red and both the door locks clunked.

'Great,' said Dog. 'Now what the hell do we do?'

The truck ground to a halt, the air brakes hissed and he heard the handbrake clunk into position. The engine died. He could also hear the sound of the gate motors whining, until the gates closed with a satisfying clang.

'Fuck, fuck, fuck, fuck, fuck,' muttered Dog. He lay there staring up at the underneath of the control console for the vehicle. Something tapped his ankle. He jerked his head up and stared. Jason pointed at the controls. 'What?'

Jason pointed and poked at the underside of the remote controls then he hit Dog in the leg, hard. He pointed again at the controls.

Dog could not figure out what he was pointing at, if anything. Then he realised the autopilot control was just above him, on the dashboard. All he had to do was reach up and turn it off.

There were noises outside: men talking, the crunching of boots and the whir of machinery. Something with wheels was making its way towards the truck. To unload it.

'Hello?' said a voice outside.

Dog reached up and felt along the controls, trying to imagine what they were for by how they felt under his fingers.

The vehicle rocked and a face appeared at the window beside him staring in. Dog froze, but the eyes were squinting and somehow couldn't see them.

There was a banging on the metal gate and shouting from even further away. Someone wanting to be let in, shouting his truck had been hijacked. The face at the window looked away.

Dog squirmed and got himself up on the seat as fast as he could. He disengaged the autopilot, and hit the engine start button. It roared into life.

His movement inside the cab, and the engine starting up, made the man on the door look in again. Dog clearly heard a long string of expletives erupting from the mouth only a few inches from his right ear, even through the glass.

'Do you kiss your mother with that mouth?' said Dog to no one in particular. The truck was a manual, and he stared at the controls for a long moment. The instructions for gear position on top of the gearstick had been rubbed smooth, but there were only a couple of possibilities. He slammed his foot down on the clutch, and thrust the gearstick to the left and forwards. With the engine roaring he engaged the clutch and was very satisfied when the vehicle bumped forwards, though not as far as he expected.

'Handbrake, got to let off the handbrake,' he said to himself. It was on the other side by the door. He pressed the button on the end and let it go. The truck roared forward toward a wall. Dog crushed the brake into the floor. The man on the side fell off, and the engine died.

There was a slight motion to his left and Dog glanced that way. Jason had got up too, but the way his eyes were looking at Dog, he felt as if he was being criticised.

'Can you do any better?'

Jason shrugged and sat back. He grabbed the safety belt from the side and plugged it in.

'Thanks for the vote of confidence,' said Dog as he hit the engine start button again. The motor picked up where it left off. There were battering noises on the doors and the window on Jason's side smashed in. Dog managed to locate reverse and slammed it into gear with a grinding noise.

'Get out of the van and nobody gets hurt,' said a voice through the broken window.

Dog floored the accelerator. The truck leapt backward. There were shouts and screams from behind, but thankfully no sound of someone getting hit or squashed. The windscreen shattered and the cold snowy air blew in. The sound of the gunshot was deafening. But it was quickly drowned out by the noise of the truck smashing backward through metal gates. The vehicle shuddered and lost speed; there was a screeching and scraping as it tumbled out onto the street between the wrecked gates. He came to a sudden crashing halt as it hit the house on the far side.

'That'd be a million points on my licence,' said Dog. He wrenched the steering wheel to the left, changed gear and launched the truck along the side road. Another shot tore through the roof of the cab. 'If I had a licence.'

Dog negotiated the gears up into fourth until he was roaring along the side of the hospital.

'We need to disable the riffy,' said Dog. Mr Mendelssohn's information had details about the truck: it was so old it had a transmitting riffy instead of a modern passive device, which meant they could disable it easily. 'See if the fuse box is on your side.'

It could have his been his imagination, but Dog could have sworn there was a hesitation before Jason released his seat belt. 'Everyone's a bloody critic.'

Dog kept his eyes on the road and didn't slow down when they reached the main road at the end. He swung the truck left and accelerated again. Minutes later he was at the next junction and made another left. In the snow and the dark it was difficult to see much, especially with the cold and the snow pouring in through the front. He glanced down at Jason under the dashboard at the front. 'Did you find it?'

The response was a thumbs up that lasted a fraction of a second. The vehicle lights went out.

'I could do with the lights.' The lights came back on. The engine coughed and died. 'Engine electrics!' They were coasting. Dog let the clutch out again, the truck jerked and restarted the engine with a roar. Jason re-emerged and threw a bunch of fuses through his broken window. 'You took out everything we don't need?'

He got another thumbs up. 'Okay, sounds good.' They came to a large roundabout where he saw a sign to an industrial estate. He headed for it.

'These places are usually warrens,' he said by way of explanation. 'We'll leave the truck there, and hide out nearby. If the police turn up we know you missed it. If nobody comes we know it's safe. At least in this snow they won't be using drones or 'copters to follow us.'

Dog spun the wheel as he saw another sign for the industrial estate and within minutes the truck was hidden between two large buildings. Dog and Jason waited in the cold of the warehouse doorway.

Chapter 13

Mercedes

The light had faded from the outside world, leaving only the dense black of a cloud-filled sky. White, amber and red lights shone from windows across the city as Mercedes looked down on Manchester from her apartment. She sighed and placed her palm against the cold glass.

The situation was not improving.

Was she really so incompetent that she could not handle this?

She shook her head and pressed her hand harder against the window. The cold leached the warmth from her skin down to the bone. It hurt.

I've worked so hard for this. She raised her other arm and laid the other hand flat on the glass. She dropped her head and pushed. *For what? No one cares and no one understands.*

She stood up straight and headed for the door out on to the balcony. With anger she did not even know she had, she flung it open and cold air washed across her skin.

'Mercedes?'

'Leave me alone.'

'The temperature is currently five below.'

'I need to think.'

'You can talk to me.'

'I don't *want* to talk to *you.*'

Xec went silent. She had probably hurt his feelings. She didn't care.

Bloody Paul Banner. Bloody idiot.

'I'm going out.'

'I'll get the car.'

'I'm going for a walk.'

'A walk?'

'Yes, a fucking walk.'

'Of course.'

She was certain she had hurt his feelings. Good. She really didn't care.

She almost ran to the lift before she realised she ought to get a coat at least. Xec would have reminded her if she hadn't pissed him off. At least that made him human. *Petty.*

The hood on the furry winter coat she had chosen put shadows across her face as she pushed her way out of the main doors. No one challenged her; they stayed out of her way.

The stone steps down from reception were icy and, where it had not been kicked away, covered in a layer of fresh snow. In the old days cities had been less affected by snow because they were inherently warmer. And the British could never cope when the weather became bad—because it never lasted more than a few days. The constant change was simply tolerated and complained about.

Now Britain was like Scandinavia: the winter snows came and they stayed. And the cities were equally affected. There were not enough people to grind the snow into the ground, instead they adapted in ways they never had before.

The air was so cold it tore at her throat. She relished it in the way she savoured the dangerous proximity of the clubbers and the painfully deafening music. It made her feel like she was alive. It just made her *feel*.

She stuffed her hands into her pockets and set off across the plaza towards the main street.

She was not wearing the right shoes and she kept slipping. Reducing the length of her strides helped but did not ease her frustration.

Bloody Paul Banner.

The police were not stupid, and certainly not blinkered in the way that the Purity were. The police would simply follow the leads and eventually get to the end. The Purity had already proved they couldn't deal with the situation without brute force.

They lacked finesse but that didn't make them any less dangerous. Was that what was wrong with Paul? Had she overestimated his abilities? Had she failed to take into account that he was trained by the Purity first and foremost?

The lack of subtlety was familiar. She shook her head as if trying to clear it. Had there been any alternative? She did not think so. Somehow the Purity had been pulling Chloe Dark's strings.

Why had the Dark girl revealed herself when she reached the city? She could have just kept her hat on and Banner's thugs wouldn't have found her. She had removed it deliberately. Under instruction from the Purity? No, that didn't make sense; otherwise she would have gone to them. Police? No. She knows what she is and both organisations would incarcerate or kill her.

She turned left, up Market Street. The ground was clear of snow and ice for a short distance, where the now-empty mall went over the road, but there was no warmth and she was soon back into the snow.

So Chloe had been doing the same thing as the Purity: she had been deliberately trying to bring out the kidnappers, as the press liked to call them. But when they attacked she had run away.

Why?

Mercedes' logic failed her. She could think of no reason in the world that Chloe Dark would deliberately lure the kidnappers to her.

Then she had leapt at the helicopter, clung underneath, and then let go.

Mercedes shook her head. Her actions made no sense and now she was either dead in the river or lost to everyone. The girl was tenacious and Mercedes did not believe she was gone. She could not afford to believe Chloe Dark's secrets were lost. After all the effort and risk that had been put into capturing her, for her to be dead was unthinkable.

One of the trams was crossing in front of her so she stopped. She had not really been thinking about where she was walking. Ahead and to the left was Debenhams. She looked right. The police barrier was still there, where the therapist had been killed. The wall still darkened where the vehicle had exploded.

A man had died at her word. Right here.

He hadn't been the first but she had never been this close before.

She had considered the idea that all this was her fault, but it wasn't. It was that man, the one who had died here. If he hadn't seen and reported the girl's deformity none of this would have happened. They would have picked up on Chloe soon enough without him. He had forced their hand.

Sometimes you had to play the game through to the end. They had come out badly with this one, but that did not mean they had lost.

She turned away from the wall and glanced down the street to her left and then up. Chloe Dark had leapt off the building up there. Perhaps she had been surprised by the level of the forces ranged against her. Perhaps that was why she had run. She thought she might face just a few like the ones before, but there had been an army, with guns and a helicopter. And so she had decided to escape instead.

Mercedes nodded to herself. She felt better, but very cold.

'Xec.'

Moments later her car drew up in front of her and the door opened. She climbed into the warmth and shivered.

'Sorry,' she said.

'Not a problem.'

'Arrange for the removal of Paul Banner and his criminal connections.'

'Yes, Mercedes.'

'If your contact can make it look like suicide that would be useful.'

'Yes, Mercedes,' said Xec. 'Any particular reason? There will need to be a suicide note.'

Mercedes hesitated. 'Failure to do his job after the attack on the restaurant. He blames himself for the escape of yet another freak.'

'That's not very convincing.'

'He's Purity, the police can't investigate unless they are given permission. If they want to, and if they are allowed to, they'll find out what we know about his private life. That should be enough. Everybody lies, even in their suicide notes.'

'Yes, Mercedes.'

She hugged herself, wrapping the coat even tighter about herself.

'Where do you want to go?'

'I don't know.'

'I packed your clubbing gear.'

Is that what she wanted?

To lose herself among strangers?

'Yes.'

Chapter 14

Melinda

She lay there in the dark. The wires buzzed in the walls. It was a new trick they did. She had become aware of it after the lights had gone out this evening. She knew it was still her ability to sense electricity that was doing it because putting her hands over her ears, or even shoving her fingers into her ears, made no difference.

The wires hummed steadily. And they still glowed.

She had been trying to think how she could get a message out. Lucy had seemed convinced she could, but Melinda was not so sure.

What could she do?

And even if she could make something happen in the wires, how could she know that someone was listening? Why would anybody be listening to the wires?

It seemed hopeless. But, on the other hand, there was nothing to lose. Anything that improved her skill might be useful if they were ever going to get out of here. At least, get out of here before they went crazy and died.

Her promise to the scientist not to escape meant nothing. It had been under duress, she just had to make sure they couldn't hurt Vanessa.

She wondered if there was anyone watching the video. The camera was active and pointed in her direction. She turned over and buried her face in the pillow.

If she was going to do something to affect the wiring—to send some sort of signal the other way—she needed an aerial. The iron frame of the bed was perfect for that. She stretched out her arms and let her hands dangle over the edges. The mattress was thin so her fingers easily made contact with the metal.

She focused and allowed a low current to flow through the bed.

Her senses showed her the shape of the metal frame but did little else. The wires in the wall shone with their constant glow. She increased the power. Her fingertips tingled but did not have the same burning she'd experienced before. Was she becoming used to it?

It didn't seem to make any difference how much energy she allowed to flow, the wires in the wall were unchanging.

She let the power go and the wires flickered before returning to their previous level.

Something made her think. What was it about electrical fields and movement? She couldn't remember, but there was something significant.

If she could push a pulse of electricity through the bedstead it would create a field and then drop it again.

She took a few moments to focus on what she was doing. Up to now it had all been a constant flow, or a catastrophic explosion of energy. This time it needed to flow and then stop.

She switched it on. And off.

This time the effect on the wires was clear both visually and audibly. In both cases the energy in the wires wavered at the exact moment she applied her own power.

She waited.

No alarms had gone off and no one came to investigate.

She could always claim she was dreaming and had no idea what she was doing. For all their technology they couldn't know if someone was lying. She hoped.

She tried it again and it worked again. From what she remembered, a signal usually went positive to negative and back. She could make it flow one way but she was sure she couldn't do it in the other direction. Her organic batteries had only one orientation, and that was part of her structure. It couldn't be changed. That meant that whatever she did now, it had to be one way only.

Taking a deep breath she began to pulse the bedstead. For a minute she sent a burst of energy through the bedstead, saw the wires bend and momentarily change their volume. Then back to normal. Pulse. Pulse. Pulse. Over and over.

She watched as her own power levels sagged until finally she just couldn't do it anymore. And she let it go.

She fell asleep immediately.

Chapter 15

Chloe

Chloe had digested the food and was feeling better. There was an unoccupied house close to the hospital facility. Everything was solidly boarded up on the ground floor, but it hadn't taken a moment to clamber up to a skylight in the roof and force a way in. She landed in the attic space which had been converted to a bedroom. The bed was still here and it still had bedclothes on it, but they stank of damp and rot.

She glanced round. A wardrobe door was open but it was empty save for a couple of bits of clothing lying on floor, too far gone to be identifiable. As far as she knew most places had been looted during the bad times. Or maybe these people had just taken everything when they left.

The landing and stairs between both sets of floors were covered with mouldering carpet. Each step creaked ominously. But she wasn't too bothered, she didn't think her weight would be enough to break through. And every time the steps groaned, she could see more clearly. This was the first time she'd really noticed what was happening with her ability to see with sound. She had been aware of it before, seen the rats and the buildings without actually looking at them. She had put it down to imagination for the most part, because it was easier to pretend it wasn't happening.

But here, in the quiet of this deserted and derelict house, where there was no light and no other sound, she couldn't ignore it any longer. She reached the ground floor. The house was quite large, certainly bigger than her parents'. It had two rooms at the front, with a dining room and a separate kitchen in back. She stood in the middle of the hall with the front door to her left, the door to the kitchen to her right, and her back to the stairs. She closed her eyes, and clicked her fingers. The sound echoed and reverberated. Everything around her came into sharp focus. There was no colour, but she could see shapes and edges: the walls, the banister and stairs behind her, the extent of the kitchen, and the distance to the front door. She knew the size of the rooms, front and back, and she even got a sense of the shapes from upstairs.

The immediacy of the image faded. She clicked her fingers once more and the image renewed. New impressions overlaid the old and there was more detail.

It was odd being a freak, she thought, and if it weren't for the fact that she was going to die, being able to do this might even be useful.

The digesting food and the stresses of the last twenty-four hours took their toll. A wave of tiredness rolled over her and she swayed where she stood. She needed rest.

She was going to have to sleep on the floor in the kitchen. At least it was relatively dry and, not being carpeted, lacked the mould that infested the rest of the building. With her newfound ability she walked through the house, regularly clicking her fingers. It was as good as seeing—better, since the sense of perception allowed her to see all round her, through and under things, although the carpets tended to block what was above and below.

The dining room contained chairs and a table. They had been covered in plastic sheets and were in decent condition. Sleeping on the table was preferable to the floor. She went upstairs and searched again. Under one bed she found containers of some sort of flexible plastic fabric. Inside she could perceive only a solid mass. It took a while but she managed to get one open. As she broke the seal, the air sucked inward and the whole thing sagged. Inside she found sheets and blankets as fresh as if they had been washed yesterday.

She sat back on her heels. This must have been some sort of storage method they had before, she thought to herself, with everything sealed up and the air taken out so it would be preserved perfectly.

We like to think we're just like the people before the plague, she thought. That we're civilised, living in our houses. But who even builds houses anymore? What else have we forgotten?

When Chloe finally woke, she was hungry again. But she did feel considerably less tired, and despite the hard surface she had slept soundly. She didn't know what time it was, but it had to be at least nine in the morning, because light was coming in through the gaps in the boards that covered the windows and doors. She made sure her hat was still firmly in place, although she was going have to take it off at some point because both it and her hair were getting very dirty. She would have to figure out some way of blocking the riffy when she did so.

All the rooms were now illuminated by the eerie white light that seeped in from outside. None of the gaps were big enough to see out of, so she made her way back up to the attic room, put a chair under the skylight and carefully looked out.

The world had gone white. There must have been a serious amount of snowfall during the night.

Unfortunately she had the feeling that meant that she would have to postpone any further plans until after it got dark. Climbing out of here in daylight against the snow, she would be very hard to miss. Well, she wasn't as hungry as she had been yesterday. So perhaps it wouldn't be too much of a problem. With that she set about searching the house to see what she might be able to take with her.

Chapter 16

Mitchell

Another day without Special Agent Graham. Mitchell rolled into the office in reasonably good humour. At least he found himself able to say good morning to the people he knew, though he was still furious at the events of that night. Furious, yes, but remembering the discomfort on Graham's face brought a smile to his own.

He imagined that was the kind of emotion the kidnappers were also feeling. He had no direct proof that Chloe had escaped their clutches a third time, but he felt it in his bones. They knew from the news footage she been hanging from the bottom of the helicopter. From finding her bag, it wasn't a stretch to conclude she had dropped at some point in the journey. Dangerous, certainly, but so is jumping off a building—and she wasn't suicidal.

No, he was certain she had survived, and that was the reason he'd got what few men they could spare combing the banks of the river south of the city. Chances were they wouldn't come up with anything, but then that was true of most police work: lots of investigating with few results.

He sat down at his desk and brought up the list of suspects they had acquired after the gun-battle. He ran his finger down the names; some of them he recognised, general lowlifes, some he didn't. But there was one.

'Lament?' The face of the wirehead appeared on the screen overlaying the list. 'Have Jeremiah Blackett brought up to an interview room, will you?'

'Now?'

'Now.'

'Right away, sir.'

The interview rooms were on the second floor. Mitchell took the stairs down to avoid meeting anybody he didn't want to talk to, namely the chief superintendent, or Special Agent Graham. Apparently Yates was out following his own lines of enquiry, so Mitchell got a regular uniform to sit in on the interview.

He opened the door, and nearly choked at the stench given off by Blackett and his unclean clothes. 'Couldn't we have had him hosed down first, officer?'

'Sorry, sir, but you did ask for him to be brought up straight away.'

Mitchell slammed the door. Blackett jumped.

'I don't like being inside,' whined Blackett.

'I know. That's why we chose a nice interview room without any windows at all.'

'That's mental torture, that is.'

'Is it? Personally, considering the inclement weather we're having today, I thought an inside room would be preferable to one where cold could seep in through the glass.' Mitchell sat carefully and deliberately in the chair opposite Jeremiah Blackett. He was an anachronism. He couldn't have been more than ten when the plague hit, but had styled himself after the 1970s punk movement. God knows what he put in his hair to make it stand straight up. He had a mishmash of tattoos, including ones with spelling mistakes.

Mitchell shook his head slightly. It wasn't that he had anything against punks, then or now, but when they were as stupid as Blackett, it tended to put the whole group in a bad light.

'So, Mr Blackett, you were arrested during the disturbance on Friday night at the junction of Tibb Street and Lever Street. In your arrest record it states you were in possession of two weapons: an automatic pistol and a long knife.'

'That knife is for eating, use it for eating. Not a weapon.'

'The blade is a foot long,' said Mitchell tiredly. 'Look, Blackett, if you just tell me what I want to know then maybe, just maybe, the knife could be considered a culinary instrument.'

'A what?'

'Eating knife. I can't help over the gun since it was fired, and caused injury to one of my colleagues.'

'You can't prove that,' said Blackett. He was sitting back trying to give the impression of confidence. With his hands and arms in constant movement: rubbing, scratching and running his fingers over his shaved scalp, the illusion was not convincing.

'That's the point, though, isn't it? We *can* prove it. Gun: fired. Your prints. Gunshot residue on your clothes.'

Mitchell stood up. Blackett jumped again. Mitchell wandered away and stared at his prisoner in the mirror. 'Thing is this, Blackett, I want to know who told you to be at that location on Tuesday night.'

'Me and my mates were on a trip to the pub, in order to get a drink, when we were waylaid by a contingent of police and attacked. We was only defending ourselves.'

'Look, Blackett, you can keep giving me that line, but no court in the land will believe you. You'll be going away for a very long time, unless they decide execution is cheaper. You tell me the truth, and I might be able to do something for you.'

'There's nothing you can do for me, Mr Mitchell, that I couldn't have done anyway. I am a man of influence.' Mitchell spun round and slammed his hand down onto the table. The noise and sudden movement almost had Blackett falling out of his chair. 'You're nothing, Blackett. You are nothing and nobody. Any power you have comes from the person above you. And he's not going to help you because he doesn't want to get involved in this. That's why he sent you, because you're stupid and expendable.'

'You can't intimidate me,' said Blackett, his voice trembling. 'I know my rights.'

Mitchell carefully removed his jacket, which he hung on the back of his chair, and sat down. That he was wearing his gun was not lost on Blackett. His eyes were glued to it.

'You know what I do, Blackett?'

Blackett shivered. The nervous trembling of his hands, arms, legs and pretty much the rest of him increased.

'Well? You know what I do?'

'You kill freaks, Mr Mitchell.'

'That's right, Blackett. I track them down, and then I kill them.' Mitchell unclipped the gun, slid it from the holster, and set it down on the table, with the dangerous end pointing towards Jeremiah Blackett.

'You see, Blackett, what I really need to know is who told you to be at that junction, at that time.'

'I honestly don't know, Mr Mitchell, really I don't know.'

Mitchell chose to ignore the fact Blackett had tacitly admitted that he had been told to be there. There was no point pressing the issue, since they had both known from the start.

'Now that could present something of a problem,' said Mitchell. 'You see, my bosses, they want results. Just like yours did. You didn't succeed, but I will.'

Mitchell picked up the gun and clicked off the safety. He held it casually, pointing it in the general direction of Blackett's head.

'Honestly, Mr Mitchell, sir, I don't know nothing.'

'You had a freak test when you came in. Obviously we have to be very careful we don't let a freak in. Do you understand that, Blackett?'

Blackett nodded, his attention still riveted on the gun.

'The problem is, those tests take a little while to come back, and if I happen to see a freak in the station, well, I just have to do my job.'

Blackett was trembling all over now. Mitchell almost felt sorry for him, but not quite.

'Now, Blackett, you can keep saying you don't know, but every time you say it, I become more convinced you are, in fact, a freak.'

On the last word, Mitchell raised the gun and pointed it directly at Blackett's forehead. Blackett whimpered. 'You can't do this, Mr Mitchell, there are rules.'

'The rules cease to apply when it comes to freaks, Blackett. I'm sure I can see some sort of weird growth coming out of your ear.'

Blackett fell off the chair, and crawled into the corner covering his head. To Mitchell he seemed like some sort of grotesque insect, he was so thin and scrawny with his hair in a Mohawk. Mitchell stood up with his gun still trained on the prisoner. He walked over deliberately.

'I'm going to count to three, Blackett. After I have counted to three, I will blow this freak out of existence. And then I will have to buy a new suit. And so will the Constable here. In order to change my mind about whether or not you are a freak, you will tell me the name of the person who told you to go to that location at that time. Do you understand me?'

The only sound that came out of the shivering wreck was a squeak.

'I'll take that as a yes.'

Mitchell took up a careful position, both hands on the gun aiming fair and square at Blackett's head, not that he was looking.

'One ... Two ... Thr—'

'Bob Moses, it was Bob Moses.'

'Bob Moses? The one that runs the freak shows in the Flixton area?'

'Yes, yes, that Bob Moses. I'm not a freak, Mr Mitchell.'

Mitchell clicked on the safety and pointed the gun away from the snivelling wreck on the floor. The unpleasant odours in the room had increased. Mitchell turned, headed for the door and paused briefly to speak to the constable. 'I think you really should have him hosed down, for all our sakes.'

Chapter 17

Ellen

The shop was warm this morning and Ellen delayed as she wandered along the aisles with her trolley. She knew she wasn't the only one and sometimes people were chased out for loitering too long with no intention of buying.

But she was experienced at this. Every winter was the same: she could not afford to heat the house so the daily trip to the shop for warmth—and buying some little thing she had forgotten—was a ritual. She moved along the aisles at a slow but steady pace, looking at all the goods she could not afford. Hoping that there would be plenty of goods on the shelves so she could stop more often to study them. Every now and then she would take an item she intended to buy, so she was always shopping and would not be turfed out into the cold.

The boy who visited had said Jason was all right, but that did not stop her from worrying. She did not know if she could trust him. He seemed sincere. The idea that he was like her Jason seemed strange, but why could there not be another one like him?

The police visits had unnerved her and the Purity man was terrifying. She had tried to hold herself together but she was not sure what they could discover. The second policeman had known there was someone else there and hadn't said anything. But he was the one that killed the freaks. His face had been on the cover of the newspapers only last week, she had seen it in the shop. He would kill Jason. And if he had realised the person who lived in the house with her was a freak he would have been less friendly.

She kept moving.

Sometimes she had to pick up more than she needed—and more than she could afford—just to give herself a few more minutes in the shop. The opportunity to get warmed through was always helpful. Without Jason to give her real money she would be able to afford even less.

She sighed as she came to the final aisle. The checkout at the end was like the gateway to the frozen hell of the outside. The bread was on the right and she paused. She took one of the loaves and put it in the trolley. She wouldn't be able to afford it and it would have to go back, but it was worth it for the warmth. After all these years she was surprised she still felt embarrassment at her poverty. After all, there were so many people just like her.

The kid sitting at the checkout operated the machine. Ellen reached into her bag and pulled out her purse, ready to pay at least some of the balance in real coin. The kid tallied up and then sat back in the chair. Ignoring her.

She waited.

The kid became aware she hadn't moved on and looked up. He frowned. 'What?'

Ellen looked at the items in her trolley and then back at him. She felt she ought to say something but had no idea what.

'I'm not packing them for you.'

'No,' she said. 'No, of course. Did you get everything?'

''Course.'

'And everything's…right?'

'What do you want? A *receipt?*'

He muttered something under his breath and went back to his newspaper.

Ellen pushed the trolley forward to the exit and piled everything into her bag. Even the loaf. She half-expected an alarm to go off as she pushed out into the freezing air. But there was no alarm. No one came chasing after her. No police slammed around the corner to arrest her.

It had happened. What the kid said was true.

She could have a hunk of bread with her thin soup for lunch in a couple of hours.

To hell with that, she thought, *I'll have it as soon as I get in.* Her mouth started to water at the thought and somehow the cold did not seem to bite as hard as it had before.

Chapter 18

Dog

'Here,' said Dog holding out the racquet. 'Why don't you try?'

Jason looked at him in that expressionless way that he had. Probably expressionless. Perhaps there was a way of interpreting the nose tentacles.

Dog glanced over his shoulder at Delia. The form-hugging leotard and shorts accentuated her figure, and she looked good, as usual. Not a single sweat mark anywhere. As far as he could tell she had no sweat glands. There was never an increase in her scent when she exercised and her strongest smell was the cream she used. It wasn't very pleasant but he was used to it. He wondered what Nosey thought of it.

The racquet moved in his hand. The little guy was so quiet Dog hadn't noticed him approach. Dog smiled and let go. The kid had watched enough to get an idea of what was needed, even if he didn't know the details of the rules. Just get the shuttlecock over the net without it touching the floor on your side.

He sat down to watch. She would make mincemeat of him.

The rule that every serve had to be underarm was the thing he found most irritating. He just wanted to smash it every time. She could take it.

'You do it.'

'What?'

'You play him.'

'That wouldn't be fair.'

As Jason stood, lost, in the middle of the court, Delia walked over. Dog glanced up the court to where Mr Mendelssohn would be if he was here. Of course he wasn't, but that didn't stop Dog being cautious.

'I'm tired,' she said and sat down next to him. She planted a light kiss on his shoulder. 'Go on.'

The wrong sort of energy rushed through him. His animal instincts just wanted to grab her and, at the very least, indulge in some tongue duelling. But they had company and Mr Mendelssohn was in the building—and, besides, he couldn't. It was frustrating but there was another part of him that prevented him.

But she had never kissed him before. Not even on the shoulder. Did she feel safer because Jason was here?

'What are you waiting for?'

He growled, tore himself out of the chair, and stalked to the rear of the court where the scent of her cream still hung in the still air. She was teasing him.

Dog served to drop the shuttlecock just over the net. Jason was off-centre and would never be able to get it. He'd show her.

The shuttlecock came rocketing back, only instinct got his racquet to it and it went flying high. It was going to go out but Jason didn't understand the rules. He moved like a flash to the back of the court and smashed it again.

It went straight into the net.

Dog smiled generously. 'We won't count that, you're just getting started.'

'You should have left it, Jason,' said Delia. 'It was going to land out of bounds. You'd have got the point and the serve.'

Whose side is she on? thought Dog as he walked forward and picked up the shuttlecock. He watched as Jason looked at the lines on the ground again as if he was only just realising their significance.

Fine.

Dog turned his back and headed to the rear of the court.

The next point went to Jason. The shuttlecock landed at Dog's feet as he rushed forward to meet the light tap.

'I was on the wrong foot,' said Dog as he flipped the shuttlecock from the floor over the net with his racquet. Jason caught it easily.

Jason's serve went to the wrong side of the court.

'My point. My serve,' said Dog.

'He didn't know he was supposed to serve diagonally.'

'He does now.'

'Serve inside the side tramlines but all the way to the back when it's singles,' said Delia to Jason. 'The other way round when it's doubles. Serve from your box to the one diagonally opposite, swap sides each serve you do. If your score is evens serve from the right box, odds serve from the left. First one to twenty-one with a two-point lead wins.'

Dog frowned. Perhaps the kid wouldn't have a good memory.

It wasn't a complete whitewash, but by the end of ten minutes Dog had been run ragged and had lost by ten points. The longest rally had been just three hits.

Delia clapped enthusiastically. 'You're really good.'

Dog turned away and went to the basin at the back of the room to get some water. He could not remember the last time he had felt so … angry. It was just a game, wasn't it? He liked playing games.

He liked to win.

There was the occasional game he lost to Delia, but he usually won and that was fine. She didn't seem to mind that he won. She enjoyed the playing as much as he did. But now she seemed to enjoy seeing him beaten.

It wasn't fair. The little freak was just too fast, and it wasn't just that. Dog could see the speed that Jason reacted with, or, more accurately, he couldn't. The kid was moving the right way before Dog was even sure what the right way was.

'I'll play him,' said Delia. 'You can be umpire.'

Dog forced a smile on his face and turned back. She was just so graceful. Then he saw Jason was watching her as well and the anger welled up again. But he didn't have to be angry, after all, she had kissed *him* on the shoulder not Jason.

But that was before she had seen him play.

She wouldn't be that fickle. Would she?

Dog sat down in the chair she had been in. He relished her scent that still clung to it and hung in the air. It made him feel better.

The match that followed wasn't any kind of competition at all. She scored one point at the start. She barely managed to return anything, while Jason seemed to be able to judge everything perfectly. By the time he had reached twelve points she was giggling so much she couldn't even return the easy ones. The last set of points went past in a flurry of serves.

'Well, if we ever need to fight someone on a badminton court we'll know who to call.'

Jason turned to look at him but Delia just laughed again. 'You're jealous!'

'I am not jealous.'

She laughed again and ran over to him. Leaned over and pressed her lips against his.

The door slammed open.

I am going to die, thought Dog.

Delia pulled away and stood up straight. Dog glanced in the direction of the door where Mr Mendelssohn was coming in. Only to see Jason, obscuring the view.

Which worked both ways. But Jason hadn't been standing there moments before. He had moved so he blocked Delia's father's view of the two of them. Delia walked towards her father. Dog pretended he was picking up his racquet. Perhaps he had been wrong about the kid.

Maybe. But he still didn't like the way Delia paid so much attention to the freak-boy.

'I'll need you here tomorrow evening, Dog.'

Dog got up as Jason moved out of the way. 'Yes, sir.'

'Where are we going?' said Delia.

'You're not going anywhere.'

She didn't argue. There was no point. She was never allowed out. The outside world knew nothing of Delia Mendelssohn and that was the way her father intended to keep it. Although Dog was pretty sure that wasn't going to last much longer. A gilded cage is still a prison, and this place wasn't exactly gilded. She was chafing at the restrictions even if her differences made it hard for her to travel much.

'What about Jason?' asked Dog.

'He stays. We're going to the fights and he's supposed to be a typical fighting freak. Can't have him wandering around outside.'

'Yes, sir.'

Jason moved swiftly to Dog's side and tapped the wall. Dog looked and Jason made the shape of an M on the surface.

'What about his mother? He wants to visit.'

'Not yet. But she did spend some of her new money today.'

Jason nodded.

Dog felt a pang of jealousy again, but this time it was over the fact Jason had family. Real family. Blood family, people who would smell just like him. Dog would never have that. He heard the door open.

'Jesus fucking H Christ!'

'Hello, Mrs Mendelssohn,' said Dog.

'Get that fucking freak away from my daughter, Jeff, what the hell do you think you're playing at?'

'Mum, he's fine, he's not a freak.'

'Have you seen his face?'

'He's like me, and Dog.'

Lily Mendelssohn glared at her husband, then turned her gaze on Dog, who looked away.

'Delia. With me.'

'We were playing.'

'Now.'

The woman turned on her heel and clicked from the room. Dog threw Delia a towel which she hung round her shoulders, then she hurried after her mother.

Chapter 19

Yates

'Mr Mortimer has not gone to the office today,' said Lament. 'He is still at his house.'

'Jesus, you could put the heating on in this bloody car.' Yates pulled up his collar and hugged himself. The snow was no longer falling, but a white blanket covered everything, rounding the edges and making the Manchester street look almost pretty.

'The temperature, DS Yates, is sufficient to maintain life.'

'Are you taking the mickey?' said Yates. 'It's fucking freezing in here. Look.' He pointed to the cloud of condensation coming out of his mouth as he spoke. Then wondered why he bothered.

'How could I possibly be taking the mickey, when I'm just a machine?'

'Fine. Whatever. Just put the fucking heating on.'

Lament was silent for a moment, and there was no sound of the heating going on. 'I'm not sure I like your language.'

Yates closed his eyes. His ears were so cold they felt as if they were going to drop off. 'All right, Lament. I wonder if you could do me the honour, please, of switching the heating on in the car.'

After a slight hesitation, the sound of the heating started up. Yates could feel the warm air blowing against his skin. He felt better almost immediately.

'Thank you.'

'You're welcome.'

Yates glared at the screen. 'You were saying about Mortimer.'

'Yes, it seems he hasn't gone to work today.'

Yates made a derisive noise and looked out the window again. 'I wouldn't go to work in this either.'

'I'm sure you wouldn't go to work for lots of reasons, including a generously padded forensic scientist,' said Lament.

'How the hell do you know about her?' Yates rubbed his hands together, attempting to restore circulation.

The expression of Lament on the screen did not change. 'Everybody knows.'

'Seriously?'

'The odds on her kicking you into touch are much shorter than getting a ring on your finger.'

'Shut up, right now. That's my bloody private life.'

'I take an interest. After all, I don't get to have one.'

It was impossible to tell if the wirehead was being sarcastic.

'Anyway,' said Lament. 'The forecast says this snow is probably setting in for winter. Time to break out the tyre chains.'

'All right, so let's go visit Mr Mortimer at his place. I'll rattle his cage and we'll see if anything new drops out.'

The sound of the heating died in the car.

'What the fuck are you doing?'

'Saving energy.'

'We're going to see Mortimer.'

'I can't put tyre chains on.'

'Somebody can do it when you get the car back to the station.'

'Safety protocols forbid me to drive the car in these conditions without chains.'

The door and the car boot popped open.

'Fuck you.'

Under Lament's guidance the police car drove north without incident along the roads of compacted snow into Cheetham Hill. The houses in this area were large, but still built as semi-detached.

Lament had briefed him on the family. Mortimer lived with his parents, two sisters, their husbands and a large number of children. They occupied both halves of a semi. When the computers crashed, all the land ownership records went with them. People just found places to live. Even now records weren't complete. It wasn't a priority.

With his hands jammed into his coat pockets and his collar up, Yates walked up to the front door of the left of the two conjoined houses. The path for this one had been cleared of snow, though a light dusting already whitened the interlocking pattern of bricks.

The brass knocker was polished. As was the letterbox, even though house-to-house delivery was no longer a service provided by what remained of the post office. All the paintwork was clean and recently repainted. It was an odd sort of place. Most people just didn't care that much about appearances anymore. Why waste all that energy on the outside when it was hard enough just surviving?

He gave three clear knocks and could hear them echoing through the interior.

The sound of children's feet depressed him. He did not like small children. They made a lot of irrelevant fuss. The woman who opened the door, barely out of her teens as far as he could tell, was not unattractive and wore a simple dress, probably homemade. And, at first glance, it looked like she wasn't wearing a bra.

'Can I help you?'

She did not seem to be concerned that an unknown person was at the door. Very relaxed in fact, just curious.

He flashed his warrant card. 'Detective Sergeant Yates. Manchester Constabulary. Is Mr Mortimer at home?'

'Which one?'

'Which what?'

'My dad, or grandad?'

'The one who works at Biotech.'

She stayed facing him and shouted 'Dad!' then 'You better come in.'

'Thanks.'

She shut the door behind him after he had stamped the snow off on the porch and given his soles a good clean on the doormat. He was almost surprised that it didn't have 'Welcome' written across it.

The hallway was tiled and spacious. The stairs up had wide steps of polished wood, though here you could see the wear from unnumbered pairs of feet. Doors led off both sides and two more past where the stairs ended.

They waited for a few awkward minutes. Most people would have taken a few steps away, just to allow personal space, but she stood facing him, so close he could have touched her inappropriately. She definitely wasn't wearing a bra, and he was surprised at himself for feeling embarrassed.

The sound of young children shouting and arguing got louder until two—he wasn't sure if they were boys or girls—appeared in the doorway to the left. The stopped making a noise and stared at him, as if he were some alien.

'Who is it, Becky?' Kieran Mortimer emerged through the door that probably led to the kitchen. He was wiping his hands dry. 'Oh.'

Back in familiar territory, Yates smiled. 'Mr Mortimer, do you mind if we have a few words?'

'Yes, of course.' He hesitated, then decided. 'Do you want to come through?' He indicated the door to his left. 'Make sure we aren't disturbed, Becky, especially by the twins.'

The backroom was a sitting room with glass doors—firmly closed—that led out to a conservatory. Beyond that was a huge garden. The layer of snow did not disguise the ridges, cloches and extensive greenhouses. Even now he could see three people, wearing big coats, hunched over tools working out there.

It made sense, with the number of people they had here they could work the land to supplement what they could buy, as well as pool their income. It made them less dependent.

They were the opposite of what the Purity wanted: complete dependence and control. These people were not under control. Even to a policeman that was a little worrying.

He turned abruptly as the door closed. Mortimer stood there, his back to the corner, like an animal at bay.

'Why don't we sit down?' said Yates.

Mortimer took reluctant steps, as if he expected the policeman to pull out his gun and shoot him.

Yates had a thought. 'How many children do you have, Mr Mortimer?' The fear that had been in the man's eyes back at Biotech was there again.

'Children?'

'Yes.'

'Why do you want to know?'

'It's not a hard question, is it?'

'Becky is my only child.'

'What about the other two—the *twins*, was it?'

'They belong to Mary and John.'

'I thought I heard a baby too.'

'There are a lot of children in the house,' said Mortimer. 'I lose track myself.' Yates was impressed when Mortimer managed to force a grin on to his face.

'I'm sure,' said Yates. 'I don't really like kids that much, but I have nothing against them. I was wondering, though, how many of the children in this house don't have riffies?'

Bingo. Mortimer went white.

'Please...' His plea faded as it started.

Yates smiled. 'Let's talk about fake riffy devices, shall we? And we'll see how forgetful I can be.'

Mortimer nodded.

'You made parts for a fake riffy.'

'Yes.' Mortimer's voice was so hoarse he barely made a sound.

'And who did you sell those parts to?'

'He didn't give me his name.'

Yates glanced out of the window at the people working the plot out back.

'It would be a shame to break up such a close and loving family.'

'He didn't give me his name!'

Yates smiled. 'But you know who it was.'

Mortimer's head drooped as he nodded once more. 'I recognised him.'

'So who was it?'

'They could have me killed and my family locked up.'

'I can do that too,' said Yates. 'And I'm right here.'

Mortimer still hesitated.

'Give me the name and I won't say anything about your family.'

Mortimer nodded and, after a long moment, said the name.

Yates grinned.

Chapter 20

Delia

They ended up in the library. It had the advantage of absorbing noise and having a single door, perfect for a heart-to-heart. Delia's heart sank, this was not going to be enjoyable.

While her mother sat in the armchair Delia stayed standing near the door. There was something about her mother that made her feel like she wanted to escape.

'What's going on with that boy?'

Seriously?

'Nothing's going on.'

'Don't try to kid a kidder, Delia. You're always making cow eyes at the Dog.'

'How would you know? You're never here.'

'Who would want to be locked up in a place like this?'

'I don't get a choice, do I?'

'You can't go out.'

Delia closed her eyes. Conversations with her mother always turned out like this. Aimless. It was as if this woman who claimed to have borne her just came round to stake her claim. Remind the child that she was the one to whom life was owed.

'So what's going on with him?'

'I said.'

'Have you kissed him?'

'No.' *Not that I'd tell you.*

'Do you want to?'

'Of course not.'

'What about the freak?'

'What about him?'

'He's new.'

'Dad picked him up a few days ago.'

'He's an ugly fucker.'

What am I supposed to say to that? 'You get used to it.'

'I couldn't.'

'Why are you here, Mum?' *Why aren't you somewhere else, sleeping with someone who isn't your husband? Why are you bothering me and upsetting Dad?*

'Can't I visit my darling girl?'

'Whatever.' *You've visited, I'm still alive, why don't you just bugger off back to wherever you've been for the last few months.*

Delia shivered. Her cream was drying out.

'Look, if there isn't anything else, I need to get my cream on.'

'Oh you poor love, do you want me to do it for you?'

'No, Mum, I can do it myself.'

'Everywhere?'

'Of course, everywhere.'

'I used to do it for you, you know, every day, three times a day.'

As if you'd let me forget. 'I know, Mum, but I'm a big girl now.'

Her mother grinned. 'You certainly are.'

Delia pulled a face to cover her disgust and pulled the towel tighter across her chest. 'Seriously? God, you really didn't just say that!'

'It's not something to be embarrassed about, sweetie, it's something you can use when the time comes.'

'When *what* time comes?'

'When you want to catch a man, like I did your dad.'

Delia lacked a response to her mother's gross suggestions, but that didn't seem to concern the woman.

'Anyway, you don't seem bothered showing off your tits to those boys.'

'We were having a game of badminton. That's all!'

'Protesting a bit hard, sweetie. You're just like me.'

'I'm nothing like you! When I find someone—' *somehow, find someone, stuck here in this house day and night* '—it'll because I love them and they love me.'

Her mother barked a laugh and then became serious. 'No such thing, sweetie. You use them before they use you. That's all there is.'

Delia took a deep breath. 'Is that it? Is that the only thing you wanted to tell me? There's no such thing as love? Well, fine, in your life I have no doubt that's the truth. You're incapable of it.'

She turned away and pulled the door open before her mother could see the tears.

She slammed it behind her and ran upstairs.

'Bitch,' she hissed as she leaned her back against her bedroom door. 'Fucking bitch.'

Her back was itching as she stripped off her clothes. It always started there. It was always so hard to get the cream rubbed into the middle of her back.

'I hate her.'

Chapter 21

Chloe

Early on there had been some excitement when she heard a vehicle in the distance. It gave her a vague impression of the houses outside. It stopped, as far as she could tell, near the hospital she had seen on the map. Indistinct voices talked and there was some arguing. Probably something to do with the trouble the previous night.

But the rest of the day crawled by. She had tried to drag it out by searching the house thoroughly but that had not taken much more than an hour. Part of the problem was that clicking her fingers let her see through almost any hiding place. A clap of the hands showed her everything.

There were two more of the sealed bags of clothes and fabrics. There was a shoulder bag which would have to replace her lost backpack. She rolled up a blanket as tight as she could and shoved it into the bottom. There were two thin jumpers that were a bit small for her and pressed the lumps of her back flat. But her mother always said that layers were the key in cold weather. She took them anyway. There was a pair of unused black leather gloves, still linked by a loop of plastic. She could not imagine why anyone would leave them behind but she was glad they had.

Moving to the kitchen there were some odds and ends that had been left behind. A chipped mug with a picture of a kitten clinging to a branch with the words 'Hang in there'.

She smiled and put that in the bag. Finally there was an apple or potato peeler. Not exactly a lethal weapon, but maybe it could fool someone if it was held to their throat.

The water was still running in the place and the toilet still flushed, which was a gift. And at least she had fresh water to drink, but still nothing more to eat.

The bag could not hold much so she decided to leave it at that. By mid-afternoon she was starving again. As the sky darkened she had had enough. She needed to get out and find some food.

Although it was cold she stripped off in the bathroom—the only room apart from the kitchen that did not have mouldering carpets—and checked her back in the full-length mirror.

The lumps were getting on for eight inches long, and from a tight joint where they emerged from her upper back they spread out. Delacroix was right; if she closed the fingers of her hand and pretended it was all covered with skin, that's what it would look like.

One of them twitched which meant it must have muscles attached. She focused and tried to make it happen. The muscle in her right arm tightened. She frowned and tried to isolate the muscle in her back. A muscle she had not even had a few weeks ago.

The left one—no, the right, it's a mirror—jerked. It was a victory but somehow she did not feel happy about it. She did it again and it responded. Concentrating, she went for a slow tightening of the muscle and it moved slowly to an upright position.

Her stomach intervened before she could try the other one. The hunger was starting to drive her again. She needed to get dressed and get out of here.

She put her layers back on. Pressing the lumps—no, she couldn't keep calling them that, they weren't just lumps anymore—they were limbs, or hands, maybe complete arms.

'Extras,' she said to the mirror. 'From now on, you'll be my extras.'

Unfortunately the clothes forced her extras to lie flat and they weren't comfortable like that.

Too bad.

With the bag slung over her shoulder, hat on her head and her new leather gloves on her hands, she went back into the attic room and jumped easily to the skylight. She swung out through the gap and went up to the ridge. There was a light breeze that blew freezing air into her face. A pair of goggles would have been useful.

The buildings matched her memory of the sound image. One street over, the lights of the hospital lit the area. She could hear voices clearly now. Too many. Perhaps they were scared of a repeat of the trouble the previous night. She could also hear chickens but there was no way she was going to risk it.

To her right was the blackness of what had been the golf course. She couldn't see anything over there, nor hear. The city murmured a little and there were people in the houses behind her.

Her stomach wanted her to get food now, but she needed a plan. She was in a worse position to help Melinda than before. She had no one she could contact. And no clue where to start.

Her heart slumped. The only advantage she had was that no one knew where she was and they probably thought she was drowned. Her parents would think she was dead, and so would the police, the Purity, her friends at school, and Miss Kepple.

Miss Kepple had not given her away to the Purity, even if it was because she fancied her. She might be someone Chloe could talk to. Someone who might be able to help her, but she had no way of contacting her and had no idea where she lived.

That settled it. There was nothing she could do in that direction right now. What she needed was food. So that's what she would try for. It wouldn't be wise to go back to the houses behind her since they would be on their guard against food thieves. If she headed in the general direction of Didsbury she would find somewhere to get something to eat, and might be able to contact Miss Kepple if she could find an open terminal.

It wasn't much of a plan but it would do.

Chloe hopped forward along the ridge tiles, slippery with snow, but she kept her balance well enough. When she reached the end, she jumped off.

She landed with a gentle crunch on the virgin snow of the garden. The untended hedge had grown into something massive and bushy over the years. She leapt over it and touched down softly in the road. None of the buildings around her showed any lights and the snow absorbed sound.

Pushing herself into long, slow strides she headed along the road towards the park. She went over the fence effortlessly. The grounds had been dug up and turned into plots for growing crops. Veering more east than south, she went through a wooded area before reaching the far fence and coming out on to the main road. And headed off with the lights of the hospital fading behind her.

Chapter 22

Yates

'Why do you have to be such a bloody pain?'

'Why do you make impossible requests? I'm not starting this car until you apologise.'

'If I had a wife I think she'd sound exactly like you.'

'If you had a wife there's not a shadow of a doubt she'd kill you in the first three months.'

Yates sighed and shifted himself into the passenger seat. There was no way he was going out into the wind and snow blowing round outside. 'What's wrong with my suggestion?'

'We don't have either the man or processing power to scan all riffy records for ones with flat bio-signatures.'

'I don't see why not.'

'Of course you don't, since you haven't the slightest understanding of the size of the task involved.'

'What if we narrowed the parameters?'

'You know how it turns me on when you talk all science-y.'

'Sweet Jesus!'

The car powered up and rolled into the falling snow. It was almost impossible to see where they were going.

'What did you have in mind, DS Yates?'

'If this is an assassin using a fake riffy to kill people, we only need to look into situations where someone has died.'

'That's a good point.'

'I thought so.'

'Just murders?'

'Oh no, accidents and suicides as well.'

'Very well, I'll assign some resources.'

'Thank you.'

'There, that wasn't so hard, was it?'

'Shut up.'

Yates would be glad when winter set in properly, then the snows would mostly stop and they could just get on with their lives as usual. It was the act of snowing that made everything so unpleasant.

Lament was quiet for a time. His image faded slowly from the screen, then he reappeared.

'Are you sure you want to do this?'

'Cold feet?'

'Very funny.'

'Don't dish it out if you can't take it,' said Yates.

'Do you think going to Paul Banner's home to interview him is a good idea? Protocol under these circumstances would be to inform your superiors. A more senior officer should at least be present when interviewing a member of either the Board of Utopia Genetics, or a Purity officer. And in this case he is both.'

Yates looked out of the window into the shifting white that obscured the dark buildings as they crawled past them.

'Have you covered your back now?'

'Yes.'

'Good. How long before we get there?'

'Seventeen minutes.'

Yates glanced at his watch. 'Any background information you can give me?'

'No.'

'Publicly available information?'

'He's in charge of Security for Utopia and is their official Purity representative.'

'I already knew that.'

'I know. You know as well as I do that any information on Purity officers is confidential.'

'Could you access it if you wanted to?'

There was a fraction of a second's hesitation from the machine. 'I'm not sure I can even answer that question.'

'I'll take it as a yes.'

'If you like.'

The minutes passed interminably. The whiteout didn't help since there was very little impression they were even moving, except for the occasional turn. They were still going at a reasonable speed, forty miles an hour if the speedo could be trusted. No reason why it shouldn't be. Yates chose not to enquire how it was possible Lament could drive so fast when nothing could be seen.

They came to a stop, finally, and the motor shut down.

Lament's face became more animated. 'Want me to come in with you, partner?'

'Funny. I think I'll be safe enough.'

'Arriving unannounced isn't good.'

'You know as well as I do that if I was announced, I'd never get to see him.'

'Try not to irritate him.'

'I don't think my promotion prospects were good even without this,' said Yates. 'Besides, being a DS is perfect for me—I have the authority without the responsibility.'

He pulled his coat round him and climbed out of the car into the snow. Maybe he needed to get a hat like Mitchell's. Truth was he really wasn't sure this was a great idea, but he was following a lead. There was a snowball's chance in hell that Banner would see the inside of a cell even if he announced his guilt.

And what was he even guilty of? Acquiring some chips? Did Banner have the ability to make a fake riffy? Yates had no way of finding out.

There was a big fence around the house but the gate wasn't locked. Yates slogged through the snow up the long drive.

How the other half lived.

The building emerged from the snow. It was two storeys and looked as if it had been built maybe a hundred and fifty years ago, in the 1920s maybe, with its curved corners and big windows with metal frames.

There hadn't been any suggestion Banner had a family, but it was a big house for just one person, but then the Purity liked to give its people a good helping of self-importance. Not that they usually needed help with that.

As he approached the door Yates got a sinking feeling. The front door was ajar, which, in his years of experience, had never been a good sign. He was already wearing gloves, so without touching the handle he pushed the door open.

The hall was dark. Yates pulled out his flashlight and clicked it on. Wooden floor, rugs, antique furniture and a dusting of snow on the inside that had not melted. No footprints. He glanced back the way he had come. There were indentations he hadn't noticed before that could have been footsteps now filled in by windblown snow.

There was an open staircase curving round to the upper floor and doors leading off on the left and right. And two more to the rear.

'Hello, Mr Banner? It's the police!'

His voice echoed through the place. It can't have been very inviting at the best of times.

'Hello, Mr Banner!'

Yates reached inside his coat and took out his gun. Another feature of the Purity: higher-ranking members did not have their riffy records available to the police. How Lament had got Banner's last location was mystery enough, they certainly weren't able to do any bio-monitoring.

Though the Purity must do that?

Yates shook his head. There was so much they didn't know when it came to the Purity. But, he supposed, once they had absorbed the police that would no longer be an issue.

He took the rooms one at a time, from the left moving clockwise. Each one was nicely furnished but empty of Paul Banner.

He found the house owner in his bedroom, at least he assumed it was Banner's. Sparsely furnished but comfortable enough. Snow had blown in through the open window and there was a rope going outside that was tied to the solid wood curtain rail. Taking care not to touch anything that might have fingerprints, he leaned out and was met with the top of Paul Banner's head. The body was dusted with snow.

'Are you alive, Mr Banner?'

There was no way he could check for a pulse and no way to determine how long the body had been hanging there.

There had been a terminal in the office downstairs. Yates headed back down to it then changed his mind.

He retraced his footsteps back to the car, shutting the front door of the house firmly behind him. The window wound down as he approached and he leaned into the warmth.

'Banner's dead, looks like suicide. Better call it in.'

'Was it suicide?'

'I don't know, but who leaves their front door open when they're going to kill themselves? Let's keep that between ourselves for now. I'm going to take a wander round the outside of the house and discover his body that way. Someone wanted this to look like suicide so let's not disabuse them of that idea.'

Chapter 23

Chloe

The cloudy night made the streets dark and the shadows darker. As the temperature fell, the surface of the fallen snow became crisp and crunched beneath Chloe's feet. The tiny sounds bounced off the walls, buildings and vehicles, augmenting her limited vision with the flat surfaces, the trees and non-functioning lamp posts.

If she had not been so hungry she would have been excited by it.

Unfortunately she knew she was lost.

There had been a big roundabout and she was certain the second exit should have taken her in the right direction. But there was a big park to her left and empty houses on the right. She would have broken into one of them if all she needed was a place to rest. But what she needed was food and there wasn't even the slightest hint that any of these places were occupied.

Even the snow on the road she was following showed very little in the way of traffic.

If it had been a clear night with a moon she would at least have been able to read the road signs, but her acute hearing did not help her with that. She had long since stopped running and the cold seeped through her clothes. Her feet were numb.

The road was curving to the left in a gentle bend. The angular trees lined the road on the left while the right continued to be open grass—or she assumed it would be grass under the snow. It was undulating flatness.

She had had a flashlight in her original backpack.

If only she could get home, her mother would give her something to eat.

For a moment she did not know if she was hallucinating but she smelled bacon. Drawn like a moth to a light she followed the smell and it grew stronger. There were two low buildings running parallel to the street with an empty parking space between them. The second one had light leaking around the curtained windows.

The smell of bacon grew stronger. Someone laughed loudly behind the door. A deep male laugh and coarse with it.

She hesitated. She needed to eat but she must be cautious. She crept forward to the side of the building, between the two. The thought of cold was gone. She focused only on the interior.

There were sounds of movement. She closed her eyes though there was little need. In her mind's eye the room on the other side of the wall was laid out. Three men in chairs and a sofa around a low table, all facing in towards it. They were talking about the card game they were playing and betting on.

There was a kitchen off to the side. It was small but that was where the bacon was cooking, or had been. There was no sound of it now.

Her hunger took over. She grabbed the mug from her bag and stepped out in front of the house. She lobbed the mug at the window. She didn't care whether it smashed it, she just needed the distraction.

The glass of the window shattered as the mug flew through it. Chloe was already in flight in a bound that took her to the roof of the one-storey building. Directly above the front door.

She had expected at least one of them to come running out. They all moved and the room was highlighted in flashes as they readied their guns. She frowned and just squatted like a gargoyle on the tiles. They stopped moving and the room went dark to her. She almost held her breath.

They were waiting for the follow-up attack. She did not give it to them.

'Check outside.'

'You check outside.'

'Oh shut up, I'll go.'

One of them moved forward and reached the door. There was a small hallway with a door leading to a bedroom, as well as the one to the main room of the bungalow.

The door clicked and swung open. The smell of burning oil lamps filtered out with the warm air. The man paused at the entrance and peered out. It seemed he decided he could see nothing and clicked on a flashlight. The beam swung across, lighting the street beyond and shining out across the undulating snow. Then it tilted down and spotlighted her footprints.

'Someone was out here.'

'How many?'

'One? Can't see anyone now.'

'Kids?'

'What kids?'

Chloe tensed as he came out and his feet crunched into the untouched snow on the doorstep. He looked left and right. His light followed her footsteps round the side of the house.

'Just checking.'

'It's freezing. We need to get something over the window.'

'Get the spare mattress.'

'I sleep on that.'

'Just get it.'

The man below her stepped out and with his gun ready—Chloe thought it might be a shotgun—made his way towards the corner.

The second man inside was passing the front door on his way to the bedroom.

Chloe crossed her arms and grabbed the edge of the gutter. She lifted herself by bending her arms, twisted and swung herself into the hall. Carefully she pushed the front door. It closed with a snap.

The man who had gone towards the bedroom turned at the sound. The surprise in his eyes was cut short by her knuckles that drove hard into his throat. She got her arm round his neck. Sensei had always said it was not weight but leverage that mattered. And she agreed. But when you had as little weight as she now did, the length of lever needed was longer than her body. It was basic physics.

But she still had the strength and her sleeper hold was solid. He stepped back trying to drive her into the wall, but missed and fell backward. His weight on top of her drove her extras into her ribs. She bit down on the pain.

He went limp and she held the lock for the count of two. She might be driven by hunger but she still didn't want to kill people. Unnecessarily.

'Terry?'

The other one must have been alerted by the noise of her fall.

What she took to be the spare mattress, complete with smelly sheets, was next to her. She grabbed it up, spilling the linen off it. Because of its size, and her lack of weight, it was difficult to manage but that was good.

She held it up in front of her and awkwardly walked it down the narrow passage to the main room. The man inside was not moving or making any significant sound, and she had no idea where he was in the room.

The mattress barely fitted through the door. Then she felt it being pulled away from her.

She jumped and hooked her fingers round the door frame. The mattress was leaning in at an angle and obscuring his view. With a quick movement she pulled up her knees and spun through the gap. She landed beside him and slammed her fist into his right kidney. He grunted with the pain but started to turn. She landed a kick on the side of his knee and something broke. This time he really did cry out.

The whole room snapped into reality at the noise. He was crumpling so she got her hand on his neck and tried to yank him back on to the table. Instead she went up. The relative mass meant she was more likely to move than he was.

He was going down slowly. She landed on his chest, flexed, lifted both feet up to the ceiling and pushed. He went down like a ton of bricks and smashed his head on the table.

A bacon sandwich slid toward the floor. She snatched it before it struck the ground and shoved it into her mouth.

Taking a firm grip on his left wrist, she went to his right and pulled so he rolled over face down. There seemed to be very little fight in him. In a smooth move she twisted his arm behind him, got the position right and dislocated it with a snap. He groaned.

She chewed on the sandwich.

The clicking of a trigger highlighted the shotgun in the hands of the man outside. She flung herself to one side as it went off. She was blinded by the echoes and stung across her right side. She hit the ground, rolled and came back up on her feet. She grabbed the plate the sandwich had come from and spun it with all her strength towards the open window.

It shattered more glass as it went through and glanced off her attacker's head. He grunted in pain but didn't go down.

She watched him disappear into the dark. The sound outlines fading as his footfalls receded into the distance. Chloe went through the kitchen, either eating everything she could find or stuffing it into her bag.

The adrenaline wore off. And the places the shot had hit her ached and then hurt. She checked her side. There were just a couple of grazes from the pellets but they were barely even bleeding. She found a first aid kit and she slapped some cream on the scrapes.

The man on the floor groaned in pain.

She felt bad about it but there was nothing she could do.

Her stomach was full and tiredness flowed through her, turning her limbs to lead.

She sat down for a moment to rest. And closed her eyes.

Chapter 24

Mitchell

'Frankly, sir, he's completely ballsed up the whole thing.'

Mitchell stood, feet apart with his hands behind his back, facing the superintendent.

'That's not something I can say officially, David,' said Dix. He looked concerned but that was his default expression.

'I realise that, sir, but I felt it was important to make the point.'

Dix stared at the papers on his desk. 'The best I can do is put a note in my daily reports to the effect that the Special Agent is not fully utilising the resources at his disposal.'

'Meaning me, sir?'

'Meaning you, David.' He looked back up at Mitchell. 'I am also very concerned at what DS Yates has turned up. This is very awkward.'

'The death of a board member of Utopia Genetics certainly is a cause for concern, sir. However, I can assure you that it has no relation to my investigation. Harry was just following a lead that he had acquired interviewing a witness.'

'I'm not sure I made the best decision allowing him to investigate the murder.'

'He was just assigned it in the usual way, sir. The fact the murder victim also happened to be Chloe Dark's chiropractor was purely coincidental.'

'Don't patronise me, David.'

'No, sir.'

'You would not be so smug if you had to do my job.'

'Yes, sir.'

'What's the connection?'

Mitchell relaxed slightly. 'Nothing obvious at present, sir, but everything seems to lead to Utopia Genetics in one way or another. Yates's request for research on the fake riffy shows there are a number of deaths, linked one way or another, to Utopia Genetics. All of them were either accidents or suicide.'

'All of them?'

'Some don't have any obvious contact, but if it's a hired killer he might have other clients.'

'But if Utopia is implicated in a series of deaths the situation becomes very complicated.'

'Does it, sir? I thought we were policemen, not politicians.'

Dix sighed. 'Sometimes we have to be both. What's your next move?'

'It seems that Bob Moses is the man to talk to and I know where he's going to be this evening.'

'Moses? He's a nasty piece of work.'

'And that's why I'll be taking Special Agent Graham with me.'

'Well, you certainly can't leave him out of the loop,' said Dix. 'Though I'm certainly happy to see you taking the lead on this now. I can make sure that is mentioned clearly in my reports. The Purity will never make decent police. Let's get this case solved, eh?'

'Of course, sir.'

He took the final comment as a dismissal and turned to the door.

'David?'

He paused and turned back. 'Yes, sir?'

Dix gave a sad smile. 'There's something very odd about this case. Be careful out there.'

Mitchell gave a small laugh despite himself. 'Thank you, sir. I always am.'

Chapter 25

Chloe

She came awake knowing that several men were creeping towards the house. They were trying to be quiet but they were incompetent. The cold air from the window had filled the place and the oil lamps had burnt out.

Her stomach screamed its emptiness at her. She couldn't believe it, she had stuffed herself at most a couple of hours earlier. Was this it? Was this how she was going to die? Starved to death while eating everything she could?

Her back was cramped. She could feel her extras, even move them. From where they touched her back they had grown noticeably even in the last twenty-four hours; they reached down to her waist. She'd be able to scratch any itch now. God but they ached with the way they were constricted.

She brought herself back to reality. The men were closing in and they had her trapped in here unless she got out fast. Where had they come from? The one that got away must have found some friends, but why were they coming after her? Did that make sense?

She shook her head. The hunger was interfering with her thoughts.

She still had food in the bag. If she got out now she could find a nice cave and eat in there.

Cave? She hit the heel of her hand against her skull. What was she thinking? Cave? But the thought of a cave was attractive, somewhere safe to hide. Yeah, right, a cave. Somewhere in Manchester. That was likely. Maybe if she was in Alderley Edge, or even Stockport. They had caves. But not here, wherever here was.

The men weren't saying anything and their acoustic images were not clear. More like outlines.

She needed to get out.

She clicked her fingers to light up the room, found her bag and slung it over her shoulder. With a quick motion she snaked her hand into the bag and pulled out a pie. She took a bite from it. The guy she had crippled was still lying half under the mattress. Was he dead? No, there was a hint of sound that imaged his neck as he breathed.

There must be a back way out of here. She clicked her fingers again. The kitchen had another door. She made her way to it and looked longingly at the cupboards before touching the handle. She paused. There were a couple of men out the back as well. There was a space above her, an attic, but the entrance was not here.

The men were moving in as she slid through the lounge and into the short corridor. The one in the bedroom was breathing more solidly than the other, but then the bedroom was not open to the night air. A hatch in the ceiling called to her. The attic was like a cave. She needed the chair by the dresser and brought it over. The men outside had reached the doors front and back. If she had any time for it she would have admired their control—and questioned it.

The chair gave her enough height to be able to push the hatch out of the way. Rather than climb, she moved the chair away then simply jumped up into the attic space and swiftly replaced the hatch.

Everything lit up for her as the man below shouted, 'She's in the loft!'

Bastard had been faking.

The attic space ran the full length of the building even though it was designed to be two dwellings. Within moments she was at the other end. All pretence at quiet was gone and she could see a confusion of figures moving below her. There was shouting and banging as doors were flung back against walls.

With the space as clear as day she sprinted the length of it in moments.

No way out. There was a second hatch that led to the other set of rooms, but that too was swarming with men. She counted at least twenty, and there might be more. The hatch at the far end was flung back and electric flashlights shone up through the space. A man was boosted from below. She was sure she could take him easily, but then he pinned her to the far wall with his light. He pulled out a gun and pointed it in her direction.

More men emerged through the hole and she could see them gathering below the other one. Her muscles quivered with the desire to flee but there was nowhere to go.

Finally a much larger man—fatter—was pushed up through the hole. He swore a lot as he was helped to regain his feet on the uneven floorboards.

There were now half a dozen men, all shining their lights at her. She could barely make out the details of this new one, though he took up a position in the middle so he could stand straight.

'Miss Chloe Dark,' he said. 'I see you are not dead.'

'Do I know you?'

He laughed. 'A middle-class girl who keeps herself to her little corner of civilisation and never strays from the party line?' he said. 'No, Miss Dark, I do not think you know me.'

Chloe peeled herself off the wall and took a step forward. The men around the leader clicked weapons. The sounds allowed her to see them in more detail. Two carried what were probably shotguns, but the others had devices she did not recognise.

'You can call me Mr Moses,' he said. 'I run things around here and I have a use for you, young lady.'

'I'm not interested.'

'That's unfortunate, you see, because you really don't get much say in the matter.' He turned and gestured to the men around him, and then spread his arms to take in the rest of the attic space. 'And you are quite thoroughly trapped.'

'What do you want from me?'

'Miss Dark, before you die, I expect you to make me a great deal of money.'

Freak fights. She had heard of them, but nobody in her sphere of friends and family knew if they were real. But now she did.

She needed to eat but she needed to escape more. She jumped up and back, twisted in mid-air and brought her feet against the back wall with her legs bent. She thrust away as hard as she could and rocketed the length of the attic, narrowly missing the support beams.

If they wanted her to fight then they wouldn't want her shot. Twin beams lanced through the space she had recently occupied. One of the unrecognisable devices gave a thunk, then another fired. Something shot towards her, widening out as it came. *Net.*

Twisting again she kicked off from a support, dodged the incoming net but flew straight into the second one. Its edges were weighted and closed round her. Moments later she hit the roof joists, struggling to fight her way out of the clinging strands. Then the burners fired again and she lost all control of her body.

'Excellent,' said Moses. 'She's going to be magnificent.'

Chapter 26

Dog

The way the weather had closed in had forced Mr
Mendelssohn to relent and allow Dog to stay at the house.
But Delia had been in a foul mood yesterday evening and
even this morning. Dog wasn't stupid; he knew it was her
mother. That woman always smelled bad in some undefinable
way. He had made a point of steering clear of her after she
had kissed him and grabbed him between the legs a couple of
years before.

She hadn't even been drunk.

It wasn't in his nature to have sexual relations with his
boss's wife, no matter how bad their relationship. He valued
his own skin. And he would never do anything to upset
Delia—well, no more than what he did already.

After lunch he and Jason were dismissed to the studio
until Mr Mendelssohn called for him.

The state of the weather would double their travel time
and they left much earlier than normal. The car crawled north
along the empty motorway and turned on to the ring road.

Dog didn't like Bob Moses either, but if there was
business to be done then that was fine. Mr Mendelssohn was
quiet, as usual, and Dog knew better than to try to start a
conversation. He just stared out of the window at the grey
and white night.

It was her hunger that forced her back to consciousness. The emptiness tore her apart; it was as if she was being eaten from the inside. As if her hunger was consuming her own body.

Her wrists and ankles were tied with a cord going between them and another lashing her tight to a radiator. There was another cord wrapped around her chest holding down her extras against her back. A blindfold was pulled tight across her eyes, and she was lying on a hard wooden floor. Every muscle ached and the heat of multiple burns pulsed through her skin. Cold air drifted across her skin and she realised she was naked. *Bastards.*

The blindfold meant nothing. There were enough people moving around the building for the whole space to be mapped for her in detail. She was one storey up and there was a room full of people below her. In the room with her were two guards, both of them looking her way. There were guards outside the door. The windows were barred. The ceiling was thin but above it was the floor of the next storey and that, again, was solid wood. No people up there at this time.

It made no difference. She couldn't move.

'I need food,' she croaked. Her throat, her whole mouth, was dry.

'Get the boss.'

A chair scraped on the floor throwing the whole room into vivid highlights. One of the thugs left the room but one of those outside stood in the open doorway.

It made no difference. She did not need to test her bonds to know they were tight. She could hear, in the distance, a human voice howling like a wolf. She knew where she was and what she was dealing with. These people ran freak fights and they knew how to keep their monsters under control.

She saw the bulk of Bob Moses coming up the stairs with three other people in tow: two with weapons, one without.

His footsteps added nothing to her acoustic conception of the room.

They did not know she could see without her eyes, she would keep that a secret for as long as she could. She desperately wanted to plead for food but she could not let him know that she knew who he was.

'Who's there?'

'Miss Dark.'

'Moses?'

'That will be Mr Moses to you.'

'I'm sorry, please, I need to eat.'

'You killed one of my men.'

'I was hungry.'

There were mutterings from some of the other men.

'You were going to eat them?' said Moses in genuine surprise.

'No, I just wanted their food. I'm hungry, please…'

There was a pause. 'Miss Dark, you present an interesting conundrum for me. It's quite clear you are an exceptional fighter. Unfortunately you come with considerable risk.'

'I don't understand.'

'You are the centre of attention for a number of parties, one of which is offering a considerable amount of money for your delivery.'

'The kidnappers?'

If Moses smiled she couldn't make it out, but he did give a short laugh. 'Yes, quite, the "kidnappers". I'm going to offer you a deal, Miss Dark, and please, make no mistake, I do not normally offer deals to my fighting freaks.'

'What deal?'

'You fight for me willingly, and I will not hand you over to any of the interested parties.'

'And why is that a particularly good deal?'

Moses relaxed. 'I know you don't want to be handed over to the Purity, and we know exactly what DI Mitchell or one of the other police assassins will do to you the moment they see you—preferable to the Purity perhaps, but just now I expect you're hoping to live for as long as you can.'

He was right, of course. 'But what about the kidnappers?'

'The unknown?' He shrugged. 'Perhaps they want to take you to a tropical island to wine and dine you until you lose your mind, and then gently euthanise you into oblivion. Or maybe what they have planned is a thousand times worse than anything the Purity could think up. Which do you think is more likely? Either way it's your choice because that's where you'll be going if you don't agree.'

'And if I try to escape?'

'I'll kill you myself.'

'And if I stay, you'll feed me?'

Then he really did laugh. 'Yes, Miss Dark, I will feed you. As much food as you can eat.'

Chapter 27

Mitchell

'Is this it?' said Graham as the car pulled up amid the swirling snow.

'You have arrived at your destination,' said Lament. Mitchell glanced at Graham to see if he knew he was being mocked, but Lament's words appeared to make no impression beyond their outward meaning.

'I don't like this,' said Graham. 'Why couldn't we have just dragged this Moses person in and forced the truth out of him?'

'Because I prefer not to force my associates into a position where they will be shot,' said Mitchell. 'Moses has resources and an unassailable position.'

'He's a freak-loving criminal.'

'Since he makes them fight to the death, I don't think he loves them.'

'We don't have freak fights in London.'

'I'm sure you're right.'

Graham turned on him. 'You doubt me?'

Mitchell shrugged. 'I know criminals, and human nature. If there's money to be made from illegal fights—which there is—there will be people running them whether you know about it or not.'

'We wiped them all out.'

'The ones you found, but London is a very big place.' Mitchell hesitated and then added, 'Sir.'

If Graham wanted to argue he managed to suppress it. 'Let's go in.'

Mitchell checked his gun, then opened the glove compartment. He pulled out two balaclavas. 'You'll be needing this. Nobody at a fight has a working riffy and we don't want to be recognised.'

'Nobody will recognise me.'

'But I'm a celebrity. Celebrities always guard against being spotted.'

'Won't they be clamouring for your autograph?'

'In this place they'll be expecting me to shoot their fighters.'

'That's what you should be doing.'

'Agreed, but not this evening.'

They got out and walked across to the building from which noise and light was escaping.

Chloe

Moses had not lied. They had untied her hands and let her put on a smock-thing, but she was still firmly chained to the radiator, which was an old one made of solid iron. Then they had given her as much food as she could eat. She had filled herself until her body claimed it could take no more, but half an hour later she had eaten again. For the first time in months she was finally getting to the stage that hunger was no longer her constant companion.

These criminals ate well.

Once she had finished her seconds, Moses returned and sat on the other side of the room to her.

'Nothing personal,' he said. 'We had one real nasty freak that could spit nerve poison. Useless in the fights, almost nothing could stand up to it. One spit and the opponent just keeled over.'

'What happened to it?'

'Threw it in the furnace. Make no mistake, Miss Dark, that's where you'll end up eventually.'

She nodded. But he was wrong: she had a job to do and she wouldn't be staying any longer than it took for them to drop their guard.

'I'm having one of the women make a costume for you.'

'A costume?'

'We have to hide your face and I'm sure you don't want your pretty skin exposed to whatever nasty claws and teeth you're put against. Most of these freaks don't wash, and by the time they're far gone they're not eating cooked food. Their nails alone would have enough bacteria to take down an elephant.'

'Nice.'

'Sable Fury.' He grinned.

'What?'

'That's your new name.'

She nodded, accepting it. It wasn't important.

Dog

The place was not full. The weather was keeping away those who had to travel any distance. Or perhaps those who could not find an adequate excuse to go out into a snow storm. The ones who had families.

As usual, Mr Mendelssohn had been afforded a VIP booth. Bob Moses' places were always nicely laid out, he had a flair for giving the punters what they needed, and he didn't run prostitutes. Dog shrugged; everybody was different.

There was a buzz of excitement because there was a new fighter on the board: 'Sable Fury'. It was in the second fight so they had about an hour to kill. Protocol required that Mr Mendelssohn watch the show before getting to talk to Moses—because the boss would be busy running things.

The outer door opened and a couple more people came in, in a swirl of snow. The weather really was bad out there; would they even be able to get back to Knutsford?

He froze in his seat as a particular smell wafted through his nose.

Mitchell!

What the hell was he doing here? Dog scanned the crowd. He was probably one of the ones who just came in, but although he was tall there was no real way of distinguishing him by sight. And there was no smell of Yates. So whoever he'd come in with—if it was him—wasn't Yates. But there was a new smell of fancy deodorant.

It crossed Dog's mind for a moment that Mitchell might be slumming it—did he prefer men to women? Dog had no idea.

Did Mitchell know what Dog looked like? Probably not, but it was worrying. Dog had the idea that maybe Mitchell would recognise *him* by his scent. It was stupid, of course, but that's how it felt.

'Excuse me, sir,' he said.

Mendelssohn turned. 'What is it?'

'Mitchell's here.'

'Outside?'

'In the room.'

'Any other police?'

Dog chose not to mention that he could not actually tell a person's profession from their smell … well, that wasn't entirely true, some professions were easy, but ones that did not involve working with a specific smelly thing were not recognisable.

'I don't think so. If he was planning a raid he wouldn't have come in. Would he?'

Mendelssohn said nothing, but stared thoughtfully at the crowd and then at the exit.

'I think there's another man with him. Expensive cologne.'

'Purity.'

Dog did not respond. His boss often had information not available to Dog himself.

'Mitchell was moved to the girl kidnappings and a Purity agent from London is working with him.'

'Do you want to leave?'

'Not yet,' said Mr Mendelssohn. 'But why don't you pop outside and tell George to make sure we're ready to leave in a hurry.'

'Yes, sir.'

Dog slipped away from the table and made his way along the wall, keeping his nose tuned to Mitchell so he didn't get too close.

Chapter 28

Chloe

They weren't taking any chances. Although she was no longer tied to the furniture, they had her attached to two of the guards, a set of handcuffs for each wrist. And hobbled. Another guard behind had a cattle-prod. The costume was padded around the body but allowed her arms and legs free movement. White zig-zag stripes had been painted all over her exposed skin including her face.

And just to prove she really was a freak there were gaps in the back to let her extras show. On the one hand it was more comfortable like that, but it embarrassed her. The extras were still growing fast and had added a few more inches as well as filling out.

The corridor that led to the fight area ended in a cage space where her captors could stand outside and she could be locked in without removing the cuffs. Once inside they reached in and applied the keys. She did not attempt to escape or rattle the locks. One of them pulled the hat from her head.

'You don't need it in there.'

She was terrified. The sounds of the previous fight, the battering of bodies against metal, inhuman screams, and cheers from the crowd had made her go cold.

The fight announcer out front began to work up the audience with his preparation for the next fight. 'Your old favourite: *Crabfish*!' The cheers were deafening. The reverberations made her acoustic sense overload. All she could see through the covered cage in front of her was a huge shape.

Moses came up to her. 'I thought you might appreciate this,' he said with a grin. 'Chance for a re-match.'

From outside: 'Presenting... *Sable Fury*!'

She saw the prod coming at her from behind and without thinking dodged forward just as the sheet was pulled away and the gate raised. She stumbled forward onto the sheet metal surface of the cage. The slamming behind her outlined the massive form coming at her from the side. She leapt straight up and her extras jutted out in a vee-shape without her even thinking.

She clung to the bars of the cage ceiling and stared down at a face she'd seen before: fish scales for skin, tiny round eyes and, swishing at her but too far to reach, the right arm a crab claw.

Someone was coming at her from above with a cattle-prod and she could smell the ozone. She let go and pushed off with her feet, rocketing down behind the freak that had attacked her at the tram stop. She wasn't sure how much intelligence it retained, but it had been operating independently when it attacked her—when? A week ago? Could it really only be a week? It felt so much longer.

Sure enough, landing behind it did not cause any confusion. It lumbered into a turn and swung at her with its club-arm. She ducked and threw herself between its legs. Her extras caught and for a moment she was jammed. She made them go flat and pushed against its calves just as its working hand scrabbled for her ankle.

It would have got a good grip if she hadn't moved; even so it was holding on. She slammed her other foot against the wrist and dislodged it. She twisted into a sitting position, jammed her bare feet into the back of its knees and grabbed its loose clothing.

Like Sensei always said: leverage. She pulled hard while pushing into its knees. They bent and its weight toppled it backward. She did not fancy being underneath it when it landed.

She scooted to the left as it crashed to the ground. She grabbed the left wrist and used its weight to lever her body to a standing position. She crossed her legs over the arm by the shoulder and yanked hard, pulling it into a dislocating arm lock.

Then she heard someone in the crowd say, 'That's Chloe Dark', and looked out through the cage bars.

Dog

When Dog stepped back into the room, he couldn't believe it. Except it was his nose, so he did believe it. Completely. There was another special somewhere here. Not only that, he recognised it from the heist. That whiff of something that had momentarily distracted him.

He stared round. He knew it was a girl, and she was scared. Where was she?

Where was Mitchell, too? This was getting complicated. Mitchell was at a table with his friend.

Where was the girl?

'Sable Fury!'

He stared at the cage as the girl was pushed out. Face painted with white zig-zag strips, the rest of her costume was the same. They'd even painted her arms and legs. For a second, he thought Crabfish was going to make this a very short fight. Then she was hanging from the cage bars above him. *Great, we've seen that trick before.* The scent of her flooded the room—at least, as far as his nose was concerned.

Dog made a bee-line for Mr Mendelssohn, pushing through the crowd.

'That girl!'

'I think it's Chloe Dark,' said Mr Mendelssohn. 'Moses has no imagination.'

There was a roar from the crowd. Dog glanced back as Sable Fury pulled Crabfish to the ground and then snapped his arm from its socket. 'Nice,' he said then remembered himself.

'Sir, she's one of us. Like Delia, Jason and me.'

'Another one?'

'We have to do something!'

'There's nothing we can do here.'

'We have to stop it, get her out of there. She's another recruit for you.'

Mendelssohn turned his gaze on Dog. 'If she survives we'll see what can be done.'

Dog turned as Mitchell stood up from his table and Sable Fury's scream was cut off as the crab claw snapped at her neck. She pulled back but there was blood dripping from a tear in her skin.

Mitchell

He blinked twice as the painted face of Sable Fury emerged. He already knew, but the jump convinced him. And he saw the additional limbs sticking out so perfectly from her back. She had been in the hospital only days ago and there had been nothing like this. How could she possibly be developing so fast; could it be a new strain of S.I.D?

He looked at the Purity officer to his right, who was grinning at the mayhem.

'I'm quite taken with this. Perhaps we should instigate this as an official sport, Mitchell,' he said turning to the policeman. 'You know, like the Roman arena. It'd keep the masses happy.'

Mitchell shook his head slowly and reached into his coat for his gun.

Graham frowned. 'What the hell are you doing?'

'That's Chloe Dark.'

He stood up to see the girl staring straight at him. The crab claw of the other arm snapped out at her neck, drawing blood. Mitchell fired three times into the freak's body.

Dog

The gunshots were punishingly loud. Then he heard a growing roar, and knew he had moments to act. He flung himself over the table at Mr Mendelssohn seated on the other side; as an explosion ripped through the wall at the far end of the room.

The concussion wave knocked him further back, carrying his boss with him, protected by Dog's body.

Then everything went black.

Chapter 29

John Smith

He stood back from the building and held his hands over his ears as the explosion ripped through the rear. The windows on all floors exploded out. When the noise faded, it became oddly quiet.

Then the screams started up. The cries for help. But none of those would be coming from where Bob Moses had been sitting, in the back. It was of no consequence if the people in the crowd lived or died, nor whether the freaks inside escaped or were consumed in the fire that was to come.

He could already see the flames licking up from the destroyed parts of the building. They highlighted the falling snow in red and orange. Good. That was a job well done. Each target he had been assigned was dead and he could look forward to a sizable increase in his reserves.

There was a sound behind him. Then pain in his chest. He touched his coat at the front and felt the warm blood pumping from it. He tried to turn, staggered, and found his legs would no longer support him.

He fell into the cold snow. All he saw was a pair of shoes move directly in front of him. He almost did not hear the popping sound that ended his life.

Episode V: Reasons

Chapter 1

Dog

He resisted the temptation to lick Mr Mendelssohn's face.
Apart from anything else, it was dirty. Everything was
covered with the dust that hung in the air and made every
breath like an attempt to eat bricks.

He could hear nothing, except a high-pitched whine
which seemed to come from inside his own head. There was
nothing to smell except the dust, and there was very little
light. The lack of senses was disorienting. He climbed off his
boss. That was when he noticed the gash across
Mendelssohn's head.

Then he remembered the girl. What had his boss said
just before the explosion? Chloe Dark? How did he know her
name?

Didn't matter. Where was she?

The whining in his ears grew louder. Dog pushed
himself into a crouching position, turned and stood. If this
was an attack on Moses, someone might be coming in to
mop up anyone who was left.

No need.

The place was a wreck. Bodies of the punters lay strewn
across the floor, like grass blown flat by the wind. Pieces of
wood and masonry had been added as a random topping.
There was movement, someone sat up. Hands moving, trying
to escape from under timber and stone.

What had happened to Mitchell?

He had been standing. There had been shots. He'd fired into the cage. That's what Mitchell did. He killed freaks. Had he shot the girl? Had he had time?

Dog looked around at the debris near him. The toppled table had prevented the faster-moving projectiles reaching them. A metal strut had pierced the wood and torn a hole a foot long before it had come to rest. It was just hanging there above Mr Mendelssohn's head.

The cage?

The body of Crabfish lay on the floor of the cage. He couldn't see the girl. It was dark in here and the flickering of the fire starting up on the far side did not provide reliable light, but it was growing and soon would.

His ears popped and he was hearing as if underwater. Moans, cries, the snapping of burning wood, all muffled but there. Where was the girl?

Picking his way across the uneven floor, avoiding the pile of bodies in the middle, he made his way to the cage. A movement caught his eye and he looked up. She was clinging to the bars at the top and hanging with her head upside-down. She was looking directly at him.

Dog glanced guiltily across to where he had left his boss. He should help him, but the girl drew him. Another one like him, someone who smelled like him, one of his real pack.

And then she was on the ground directly on the other side of the bars from him. The white stripes they had painted on her face were spattered with blood and dust. She had two long protrusions from her back that moved as she did: bending and balancing like additional arms. She was one of the unlucky ones, like freak-boy. The ones who couldn't pass for human. At least Delia gave the impression of being normal looking.

'Finished staring?' she said.

'Sorry.'

She put her head on one side. 'Can't hear a word.'

He looked across the ruin of the building. The room was getting brighter. The flames had worked their way past the demolished door and wall at the far end. There was a thundering collapse close to where the explosion must have taken place. Smoke and dust billowed out. Someone screamed.

She jerked her head round to look. The scream died in a gurgle.

'Hearing coming back?'

She ignored him. He reached through the bars to touch her arm. And slammed into the metal as she grabbed him, levered her feet against the floor and yanked him forward. He found his arm twisted in a way it wasn't meant to go and his body followed as best it could.

'Fucking hell!'

'Don't touch me!'

'Sorry!'

'I told you I can't hear what you're saying.'

His protest that she must have heard the collapse and scream died on his lips. She released his arm and stepped back, holding her hands up in a gesture that might have been placating if she hadn't almost ripped his arm off. His ears seemed to be clearing. He just wished he could smell normally, but right at this moment the smell of burning flesh did not appeal.

'Can you get me out?' she said in that over-loud way people spoke when they could not hear themselves.

'Round the back.'

She put her hands on her hips and gave him a 'look'. He pointed then heard someone clambering over the rubble. He turned and in the flickering light saw George. Looking back at the girl, he held up his finger to indicate she should wait, and the look intensified. He could almost hear her thinking *I'm not going anywhere.*

He hurried back to Mendelssohn, waving at George. The driver had a torch and checked their boss over, paying particular attention to his head, touching and pressing the skull gently.

'I think he's okay,' said Dog, not really knowing if that was true but hoping for Delia's sake it was. 'Can you get him back to the car on your own?'

'What's the problem?'

'Mitchell's here with some Purity bloke. I need to get the girl out.'

'Mitchell? Bloody hell. We better get out before the police get here.'

'Yeah. When he wakes up, tell him I'll report tomorrow.'

George nodded, got Mr Mendelssohn into his arms and staggered across the uneven surface. The air was filling with smoke and the sound of burning.

Dog hurried back to the cage. She was sitting on the floor, waiting.

'Finished?'

He indicated the back as before and headed that way. He trod on something soft and unpleasant. He decided not to investigate.

'Oh, god,' she said. There was the sound of retching. He glanced into the cage and saw her bent over. He reached the entrance tunnel and saw why. There was half a brick reflecting light in a damp way, lying in the middle of the cage tunnel. Wedged into the bars of the tunnel wall were the remains of one of Moses' henchmen. Most of his head was missing, only the jaw and the ear on this side remained. Dog wondered if he needed to wipe brains from his shoe. Mind you, there probably wouldn't be much.

Dog didn't feel good himself.

'He's the one with the keys,' she said hoarsely and then choked.

Terrific.

'And my hat.'

She still has a riffy? The metal of the cage should keep that blocked but she did need a hat.

The burning sound was becoming more insistent.

Taking a deep breath he went round the end of the tunnel and felt through the guy's pockets, trying not to dislodge him from the bars. He found the keys but not the hat. He had a thought: *Bugger.*

'I've got the keys!' he shouted. She stared blankly, so he dangled them. She pushed her hand out between the bars. He placed them into her palm and she snatched them back. 'Manners,' he muttered.

'I need my hat!'

Dog pointed at the bloke's lack of head. She turned away and retched again. He took the opportunity to move back the way he came. The room was getting brighter. He glanced through the cage into the main area. Someone who looked like Mitchell was pulling debris off someone else. Why couldn't he be dead? He'd been exposed when it all went off. Too damn lucky.

Turning back to the space behind the cage, Dog cupped his hands round his eyes to block out extraneous light and crouched down to study the ground. His eyes adjusted, the shades of grey gained more contrast and there was a smudged trail of soft damp organic tissue. He moved along it, staying crouched down, and found a piece of skull with the other half of the brick embedded in it; and a damp, bloodied hat with tracery of metal running through it.

He picked it up. His fingers immediately sticky with what was coating it.

Would she really wear this?

Sirens? Oh hell.

He hurried back and held up the hat. She held out her hand again. The moment it touched her skin she snatched her fingers back and it fell to the ground.

She looked at Dog. Dog shrugged. She pursed her lips and looked down at the darker patch in the shadow.

'Police coming,' he said and looked past her. The red and blue lights were visible reflecting on snow. Mitchell was dragging someone out. His Purity pal no doubt. At least he wasn't paying attention to what was happening in the cage.

'What?' she said.

'Police.'

'I can't hear you.'

'I know.'

She shoved her arm through the bars. 'Spell it on my skin.'

He was impressed. He got as far as the 'L'.

'Police coming?'

He nodded. She sighed and reached down for the hat. She hesitated for a moment and then pulled it on to her head. 'The blood of my enemies,' she said and gave something that might have been a smile.

She stepped over the bloodied half-brick and tried to unlock the gate. The padlock was on the outside. 'I should be able to do this,' she said, apparently to herself as she tried to work the key into the lock and turn it. 'If I could hear, it would be easy.'

Which made no sense to Dog. She gave up in frustration and thrust the keys at him. 'Please.'

He made short work of it and she stepped out. 'Thanks. Chloe,' she said touching her fingers to her upper chest.

'Dog,' he said.

'Spell it.' She held out her arm.

D-O-G. Then he stopped. She looked at him with a frown. 'Dog?' He nodded. 'Just 'Dog'?' He grinned and nodded again.

She shrugged. 'Okay.'

Blue and red emergency lights played over the inside of the building. The hairs on the back of Dog's neck bristled, he turned sharply. Mitchell was standing where the door used to be. He was facing them; a flashlight cut through the murk and the cage bars, he and Chloe highlighted in its beam.

He grabbed her by the wrist and yanked her further behind the cages. The fire was spreading that way as well, but they were out of sight of Mitchell. She was incredibly light, he felt like she could be used as a balloon.

'I've got nothing to wear,' she said, but she wasn't looking at him, it was more for her own benefit. In the light of the fire Dog looked at her extra limbs. The skin was as dark and smooth as the rest of her. It almost looked like fingers were forming at the end but they were unnaturally long.

The ceiling above them creaked ominously. Flames were licking across the beams. They were trapped by the police and the Purity, but staying meant being roasted alive. The air grew hot and smoky while the noise of crackling and snapping timber was drowning out everything else.

'How the hell are we getting out of here?' she said.

Bits of the ceiling were falling now and the flames were a wide sheet covering the whole of it. It might come down at any moment.

'Ow! Shit!' she shouted as a floating ember burnt into one of the extra limbs. It twitched convulsively. Dog was only in better shape because he had clothes. He had a coat. Idiot. He pulled it off and offered it to her. She didn't put it on but threw it over her head. 'Thanks.'

Dog stared round. Where could they go? The cage would provide some protection if the whole ceiling went, but the chances were they would simply cook—and if not that, they would be caught.

The girl grabbed his arm and pointed up the wall. About twenty feet up was what might be a window. Then he stared at the climb. It was not that the wall was smooth, it was exposed brickwork, but there was no way he could get any purchase.

He shook his head. 'I can't do that.' He coughed. The air was noticeably hotter and the smoke thicker. It would better to be shot by Mitchell than burned alive. Then again he didn't want to give the bastard the satisfaction of having won their game.

She faced him and grabbed his wrist. He looked into her eyes, black in this light.

'Have you got a knife?'

He shook his head.

'Scissors?'

He gave a wry smile and shook again.

She turned away from him, crouched slightly and jumped. She made it all the way to the window in one, hooked her fingers into the gap and hung with a foot against the wall. She pointed at the cage opposite.

He turned and stared at the bars for a moment. *He could climb those.* He sprung at them and was able to get a firm grip with his feet pressing inward. He moved swiftly up. They were already conducting heat from the fire and were hot, but not painfully.

What was worse, as he climbed, was the heat in the air and the smoke.

The ceiling cracked again. Bits of tiling and burning wood tumbled down around him. He coughed. Now he could see the main area again there were men pulling bodies out of the rubble, although they kept looking up. The entire ceiling was aflame.

His hair was singeing.

He looked back. Chloe had pulled herself into the window space. It wasn't very big and she seemed to occupy all of it. But she gestured at him before glancing at the ceiling and coughing. He saw an ember land in her long black hair.

From the far end of the room, wood squealed and roared as the ceiling gave way finally. A wave of collapsing joists and roof tiles thundered towards him. Balancing on the upper bars, he leapt across the intervening gap to where she reached to him.

She caught his hand and pulled. She must have her other hand firmly anchored, he thought as he hurtled into the small window space. Heat from the collapsing roof went across his back as the window frame, boarded over, came at him at speed. He raised his arm.

The frame gave way as he struck it and he tumbled into freezing air. He rolled in the air and saw the girl. Her extra limbs made a V behind her as she leapt out. He dropped away from her and tried to turn in the air. But he wasn't a cat.

He landed in deep snow, on his side, with a jolting thud that knocked the wind from him; his head cushioned by his outstretched arm.

Chapter 2

Chloe

She landed in the snow on her feet. Falling forward, she caught herself on her outstretched arms.

The boy had landed further behind and faster than her. She jumped up and ran to him. She cursed her lack of hearing. It wasn't dark—the flames from the building lit up the whole area—but if her hearing had been working she would have been able to see everything more clearly.

He was still moving but buried in the snow. She had barely gone a couple of inches into it when she landed and left barely a mark as she ran across the surface

If the police had been focused on the ceiling and getting the people out they might not have seen the two of them escape, but she couldn't count on it. They might come this way if only to investigate whether any others had got out. And right now the two of them were very visible.

They needed to move. And she needed to find some more clothes; there was no way she could survive the night wearing only this padded body hugger. Also get the stupid white make-up off her skin.

Dog? What kind of name was that?

He was conscious and seemed unharmed. She kept glancing towards the burning ruin. She had not realised how much she had already come to rely on her enhanced hearing. Its lack made her uncertain and scared.

'Come on!' she said. 'We need to move.' It was weird not being able to hear herself speak, the result was that she tried to say it louder and she had to consciously keep her voice down.

He climbed to his feet, brushed the snow off and grinned at her. His lips moved.

She shook her head. 'Let's go.' Without her senses any direction was as good as any other. As long as they were moving away from the police and the Purity she was happy. She set off at a run with her toes cutting holes in the surface of the snow as she pushed off from it.

There was a stand of trees down a slight incline from the burning building and she thought that would help them stay in cover. It took her less than thirty seconds to cover the distance. Once there she stopped and turned. She wasn't even out of breath, and the running had managed to keep the warmth in her limbs. The extras were a bit chilly though. She tried to get them to lie flat but they insisted on folding in the middle. *Whatever.*

The boy had only covered half the distance. He was moving at a reasonable speed but leaving a trail a blind person could follow. She couldn't see hers at all, except the small indentations close-up. She stared up at the blazing building. She couldn't see anyone yet. They still had a chance but they needed to hide his trail.

Then she heard something. Her ears throbbed as if she was hearing her blood pumping through her veins and arteries. It hurt like a pounding headache.

Snow started to fall again. She cursed the sky. Was she going to escape an inferno just to freeze?

The boy came up beside her. He said something and grinned again. He did that a lot, as if everything was a joke to him. Just her luck to get stuck with someone who couldn't see when something was serious. They had nearly died in there, and would have if she hadn't got them out.

What was he good for? The throbbing became more intense. She cried out and fell to her knees with her hands pressing against her ears. She felt his finger touch her lips, and slapped it away in a sudden movement. She realised belatedly he meant her to be quiet. How could she be quiet if she had no way of knowing if she was making a noise?

Her head felt as if it was going to explode. It was agony but she clamped down on her vocal cords and kept her mouth tightly shut to be sure she made no sound.

Dog's arms went round her and lifted her. He was moving but she could not open her eyes. Right now, she didn't even care if he was carrying her back to the police. He picked up speed into a trot.

She wasn't sure but she might have passed out. Her head no longer throbbed but there was a background ache. Every part of her felt numb with cold. They were no longer in the trees but moving along some sort of metal framework. It might have been a bridge but the central roadway was missing and below was a gushing torrent of water. He was inching along the girders.

Then she realised she didn't have her eyes open. She sighed with relief. Despite the terrible cold, her body felt it was time to tell her that it was hungry again and her stomach rumbled.

'Shut up.'

'I didn't say anything.'

'Not you.'

'You can hear.'

'I'm cold.'

'Yeah, thought you might be.'

'Are we near warmth?'

'Do you want the truth?'

'Always.'

'I don't know, but probably not.'

She sighed. At least the part of her that was pressed against him was warm, and he had wrapped his coat around her. It helped.

'Where are we?'

'Still want the truth?'

'Do you have a problem with the word 'always'?'

'I don't know where we are. Bob Moses' place was in Flixton. We've been heading south and we just crossed a river—probably the Irwell—but I don't know this area at all.'

'Just find somewhere we can get warm.'

Somewhere an owl screeched.

Chapter 3

Mitchell

The sky had brightened into dawn and the clouds had cleared, leaving the world dazzling bright. Mitchell glared at it from the cold interior of the car with his fingers wrapped around a coffee mug that was going cold.

He wiped the windscreen clear of condensation again and looked out at the smoking ruins of the warehouse. The whole thing was a bloody mess. Again. All he'd wanted to do was talk to Moses. Maybe scare him, and let Graham rough him up a bit. The Purity Officer clearly took pleasure in violence.

The fire service tenders hadn't even bothered turning out after their advance team had declared the fire safe to burn out on its own. They couldn't afford the time to come out to something that wasn't going to be a risk to anyone else.

They'd helped getting the punters, and the remainder of Moses' crew, out of the building. Then they'd left after pointing out that it would be dangerous to re-enter the building even after it had burned out. As if anyone needed telling.

The metal framework of the cages stood black against the snow and the sky. God, he was tired. He'd managed to grab a couple of hours sitting in the car, but the cold made any sleep valueless, it sapped all his energy.

Someone shouted his name. One of the uniforms appeared from around the side of the building and waved.

He sighed, drank down the rest of the coffee and climbed out on to the crisp snow. He glanced over at where one forensics guy was examining the body they'd pulled out—thinking he might be alive and just overcome by smoke. The fact he'd been shot through the chest and the head told another story, while the state of his shoes suggested he'd been dragged *into* the building perhaps in the hopes he'd be consumed by flames.

Mitchell didn't remember seeing it happen, but then he had been concussed and deafened by the explosion, like everyone else.

He trudged up towards the building.

Then there was Dog and Chloe Dark.

He didn't believe Dog had been killed when the ceiling collapsed, that boy had nine lives if not more, and a knack for getting out of every trap Mitchell had ever set for him. Besides, he didn't want to be cheated out of being the one to bring him in.

He hadn't recognised the girl at first. She was even thinner than he remembered, and about to get ripped to pieces by that freak. Mitchell hadn't been about to let that happen.

'Where you going?'

Mitchell paused and turned as the Purity Officer caught up.

'Uniform's found something.'

'You didn't shoot the Dark girl.'

'You may recall there was an explosion.'

'You fired three times and each one was into the other freak.'

'Crabfish.'

'I don't care what they called it.'

'How many full-blown freaks have you taken down, Special Agent Graham?'

'What's that got to do with it?'

'They take a lot of killing.'

'It was in a cage.'

'In which case killing either of them at that moment would have been pointless, they couldn't escape.'

They reached the officer waiting at the brow of the hill. Beyond it the land descended again with fields and trees on one side and another empty residential estate on the right. It stopped at a railway cutting. Beyond that there was only white.

'Besides, I still want to interview her, and there's a chance she could still be usable as bait.'

'You saw her,' said Graham through gritted teeth. 'What she's become.'

Yes, he'd seen her, of course he had. He'd seen someone who was developing far faster than any freak in all his years of experience. And that was the real reason he hadn't shot her. The strange DNA of Ellen Lomax's lodger, the curious kidnapping of girls, Chloe's rapid development, and maybe Dog? The criminal who displayed freakish behaviour but had lasted far too long to be S.I.D.

The uniformed officer led the way behind the building to where the otherwise pristine snow had been disturbed. There had been more snow after the ceiling collapsed, but at least one person had been here and there were dragging footsteps leading down towards the woods.

Maybe either Chloe or Dog had escaped?

By the time they got a dog-handler out here to trace the tracks they would be long gone. It wasn't worth the effort.

'There's nothing here,' said Graham.

Mitchell continued to stare at the snow. There were an additional set of marks, softened by the snowfall, but they could have been footsteps. Except they didn't go deep into the snow and they were very wide apart. He followed them back towards the building. They stopped at another place where the rounded curves were disturbed. Perhaps where someone very light had landed.

He nodded to himself. They had both got out. Good.

Following Graham back to the car park Mitchell made his way to the body that had been shot. His train of thought was interrupted by the arrival of a car bearing the fire investigation team logo. At least they'd be able to get some idea of how the fire had started. And what the explosion had been—he'd already seen the scattering of body parts in the main office. He had to assume some of them belonged to Bob Moses. Someone was trying very hard to cover their tracks. Perhaps the gunshot victim was another one.

'Any initial thoughts?' Graham asked.

'He died from the gunshot wounds.'

'Obviously.'

Mitchell said nothing, but exchanged a glance with the forensic scientist. It was certainly not a given.

'He has no riffy.'

'Damaged by the head shot?' said Mitchell.

'No, there's no operation scar, which there would be given his apparent age. He's never had one.'

The forensic scientist grabbed the man's hand and held it up. 'And smell that.'

Mitchell gave Graham the opportunity to do so, but he remained resolutely erect. Mitchell bent down and sniffed the fingers. There was the smell of burnt wood which must have impregnated everything from the fire, but there was also something else, something volatile like petrol or paraffin.

'Fire starter?'

'Definitely some sort of accelerant,' he said and dropped the arm. 'Might be nothing.'

'Make sure you let the fire investigator know,' said Mitchell.

It fitted his hypothesis. Someone was scared they were getting close. He glanced up to say something to Graham but saw he was using his mobile tablet to talk to someone. He looked upset. Mitchell took some satisfaction in the fact that having such advanced technology—which the police were denied—was not bringing him any pleasure.

He broke the connection and turned to Mitchell.

'I have to get back into the city. I'll be taking your car.'

'I may as well come.'

'No,' said Graham with an almost desperate tone. 'No, I need to go alone.'

'Something happened?'

Graham looked torn and then nodded. 'You'll find out soon enough, it was your man Yates that found him.'

'Found who?' And whose death would pull you back with such urgency?

'Paul Banner, the Purity Liaison for Utopia Genetics, has committed suicide.'

With that he turned and hurried to the car, leaving Mitchell with the merest hint of a smile on his face.

So, this is all Utopia Genetics.

Chapter 4

Mercedes

'Bob Moses has been removed from the picture.'

Mercedes sighed. These walls were a prison. What kind of a life would she have had if she had passed her nursing exams? She wouldn't be here, a princess in a tower waiting for a prince who would never come. It was too late. The walls she had built herself were too high and too strong.

There was no way in for anyone.

'Mercedes?'

'Sorry, I was thinking.'

All I have is a genie that will carry out my every whim, my every command, my every slightest wish. Except to free her from her prison, from the tower. And all that remained was cruelty. She was both the captured princess and the evil stepmother. Perhaps she was lying to herself; it might be that she was the witch with a poisoned apple. What if she had never been Snow White? Or Aurora?

'Mercedes?'

She really shouldn't drink so much in the evenings; the mornings were hard to think through.

'What?'

'Paul Banner's primary contact has been removed.'

'Good.'

'And the assassin.'

'Am I the princess in the tower or the evil stepmother?'

Did he hesitate? Why not, he was only human underneath it all.

'What's brought this on?'

'I'm tired.'

'And hungover.'

'Yes.'

'I can arrange a masseur.'

'You think I need relaxing?'

'Things have been difficult recently. And you have one less person you can call friend because you just had him killed.'

Mercedes snatched up a carved wooden animal from the table and flung it at the screen. She was denied the satisfying splintering of glass as it bounced off.

'I recommend using stone or glass if you want to break something.'

'You're a fucking bastard, that's what you are.'

'I'm the only real friend you have.'

'You're just a genie, why not get back in your bottle and I'll stopper it and live in peace.'

'You seem to have forgotten that I have to be tricked back into the bottle. I won't go of my own accord.'

She screamed in wordless anger. She screamed again and again until her voice was hoarse and her head throbbed as if it was going to split.

And there's no one to hear me.

'I'm just an ugly old witch with only spite to unleash on the world. I torture and kill children in the name of the future, but the future doesn't care about me and what I do.' Her voice croaked. 'Everyone out there is afraid of the monsters that creep about and infect them. They are terrified that everyone they love will become a mindless freak and slaughter them in their beds.'

She went to the window and slammed the side of her fist against it. 'I'm the real monster, but they worship my image as their saviour. If they knew the truth...'

'Do you want me to get someone up here to give you a good seeing to?' said Xec. 'It's been a while. Sexual frustration can be very debilitating.'

'You're not a genie, you're Satan. All you do is tempt me. I know what I should be doing, and I don't need you to tell me what that is.'

'Your wish is my command.'

'Shut up!' she shouted. 'You think you're so fucking clever. I'm the one who kept this business going.'

Silence.

'Make me a drink.'

Silence.

'Oh, that's very mature.'

Silence.

'Fine, I'll do it myself.'

She wandered into the kitchen, grabbed some milk from the fridge and drank it from the bottle. Her mother would have killed her for doing that if she'd caught her. Her mother had died before the riots. Before any of this had happened. She had burned to death when her block caught fire. As far as Mercedes knew, her mother had not been one of the ones that had thrown themselves from windows, but then she hadn't been there. It was easier to imagine someone falling unconscious and asphyxiating than being so terrified and desperate they did something so utterly horrifying rather than burn.

She hadn't even known it had happened until much later. She hadn't spoken to her mother since she left home at sixteen. She had never said goodbye and her last words had been full of anger and hate.

Morbid thoughts.

The Purity had quarantined Chloe Dark's parents. The chances were that she would never see either of them again.

'What's the status of our current assets?'

The others had all died. The latest batch wouldn't be any different. Newman had been a genius but he had been arrogant and slightly twisted. It was always a game to him: how much change could he introduce?

His animal experiments had been grotesque, but they taught him the skills he needed. There was no difference in size between the sperm and egg of a mouse and those of a human. And the complexities of the DNA were no more, at least at the gross level. But mice did not live long lives and it was difficult for Newman to see what success he was really having.

For some women, he had made every single egg non-viable with his experimentation. Sometimes they would substitute compatible embryos because any resulting physical differences could just be put down to the vagaries of genetics—unless anyone ever did a DNA match between child and parent. And by the time that happened, it wouldn't matter.

If it hadn't been for S.I.D his plans would have worked out just fine.

'Xec, what's the status of our current assets?'

Still no response. 'Stop sulking, I'm serious.'

'You told me to shut up.'

'Because you're an irritating git.'

'And you're an evil witch.'

'How are they doing?'

'Healthy.'

'No sign of degeneration?'

'Well, I'm just saying what it says here on this report. But if you want to go and check personally?'

'All right.'

'Is that "all right I accept what you're saying", or "all right yes I want to go and check for myself"?'

'I'm not playing your games.'

'Serious question.'

'I accept what you're saying.'

'You're too kind.'

She sighed. 'No, I'm an evil witch. How do you rate our chances of catching Chloe Dark?'

'Very poor.'

Mercedes nodded. 'Agreed. She's a pain in the butt. I really wish we could get our hands on her, but with both the police and the Purity after her I don't think this is going to turn out well. We'll have to kill her and get rid of all the evidence.'

'And you think we'll have more luck killing her than capturing her?'

'It's a simpler goal for a start. She's too much for our people to handle.'

'I could request some additional favours.'

'I don't know about your favours, Xec. What do you have to give in return?'

'I would never betray you.'

'Didn't Macbeth say something like that to the king?'

There was that hesitation again. 'I promise that nothing I have given, or will give, is ever going to hurt you, Mercedes.'

'What's the word of a wirehead worth? You're not a machine, you don't have a set of laws to enforce a morality on you.'

'Then you'll have to do what you always do, and have faith in me.'

She drank the remains of the milk from the bottle and set it down.

'Kill Chloe Dark.'

Chapter 5

Chloe

It was the warmth she noticed first: a burning fire radiating heat against her legs. The air she was breathing was not frigid, although it was stuffy. The sound of burning wood crackling revealed some of the room around her. It wasn't big, but filled with shadows of machinery. There was light beyond her eyelids but before she used her eyes, she snapped her fingers and saw the place more clearly. Some sort of fixed machine with pipes, the fire inside it. A big lawn-mower and other garden implements. No sign of the boy.

She opened her eyes and sat up. She felt okay, except for the hunger and she was used to that. It needed to be dealt with but she could ignore it for the time being.

The place looked like a garden shed, apart from the heater with the pipes. She didn't think it was heating water, so it must be carrying hot air somewhere. She found a rusty nail lying on the floor and tapped it against the metal of the lawn mower. The higher pitched the sound, the better she could see. The visual scene became overlaid with edge highlights. Beyond the walls was the empty space that suggested outside, but in the direction of the pipes was another room, or enclosed space. The pipes led away with misty shapes of plants in rows.

She stood. She was still dressed in the clothes Bob Moses had given to her. She liked the padded vest but she really needed proper clothes. She rubbed the chrome of the lawn mower and checked her face. She still had the white paint on it. She found a rag and started rubbing. A quick glance outside confirmed everywhere was covered with snow, which seemed to absorb her sounds, turning it into nothing as far as her acoustic sense was concerned.

She stepped over to the pipes and tapped one with the nail. The echoes made the other room clearer, some sort of heated greenhouse. She had no idea what the plants were, but someone was keeping them warm with this furnace and that meant they would be coming back to stoke it at some point.

Where was Dog?

With nothing else to do she opened the door into the greenhouse and went through. It was colder in here. The space was big, at a guess at least three times the size of the entire plot of her home and garden.

The thought of her home made her choke with tears. What were her parents thinking? Where were they? She knew the answer to that. The Purity would have quarantined them just as they should have done in the first place.

Where was Melinda?

She heard/saw Dog at the outer door. He was carrying something that did not reflect well, so must be soft. She waited until he had come through the door and shut it.

'I'm through here!'

He poked his head round the door and looked at her back.

'How did you know it was me? Have you got a good nose too?'

'No. I just knew.'

'Fine, don't tell me.'

The scent of some sort of stew finally made it through the air to her entirely normal nose, which gave the necessary signals to her entirely dictatorial stomach. She spun round and leapt the distance back to the door where he stood.

'Nice.'

'Give me the food.'

'A please is considered polite,' he said holding it behind his back.

'If you don't give me that right now I'll dislocate both your legs.'

'Do that and I'll spill it.'

'Please!' she said.

He grinned and brought the saucepan round to the front. It smelled divine. She grabbed it and brought it to her lips and began to drink it down. After a few moments she had to stop.

'Oh god, this is delicious.'

She brought it back to her lips and drank again. After most of the liquid was gone she chewed her way through the beef, potatoes, carrots and peas. Finally she resorted to scooping the remainder with her hand then wiping every surface with her fingers and licking it off.

Dog eyed her waist. 'And people say *I'm* greedy. If I'm not mistaken, I can see a bulge in your stomach.'

Chloe was mortified and looked down. She couldn't see anything but she felt very heavy and full. A wave of tiredness went through her and she yawned. 'I need to sleep.'

Everything went black.

She came to back in the shed part with the fire still radiating warmth. Her body claimed it was hungry again, but it was lying. She felt a warm strength in her limbs.

Dog was curled up by the door. He opened his eyes the moment she moved.

'Better?'

'Better.'

'You're lucky,' he said.

'Lucky?'

'Definitely, although both Delia and I are luckier than you.'

'Who's Delia and what are you talking about?'

'Well, Delia and I can pass for human. The freak-boy is a bloody monstrosity, but decent enough once you get to know him. But you, I mean, look at you.'

She raised her eyebrows. 'Do you see a mirror in here? How am I supposed to look at myself? And who's Delia and the freak-boy? You're not making any sense.'

'Delia is—'

'And what's the time? Are those clothes you brought for me?' She indicated the pile of material he had dumped by the door.

'It's about lunchtime and yes, those are clothes I brought for you. But you have to listen—'

'Talk while I'm dressing.'

He gathered up the clothes and passed them over. She examined them. 'These are men's clothes and about a hundred sizes too big.'

'It's all I could find. They were in the kitchen with the stew. I'm guessing he lives alone and looks after his plants.'

'He's going to be pissed off when he finds his lunch and clothes gone.'

'It happens.'

'And he's going to follow your trail here.'

'No, I disguised the direction.'

She pulled on the shirt first after folding back her extras. They were longer again and absolutely refused to lie flat. The upper joint poked up above her shoulders by an inch now.

'You were saying I was lucky,' she said pulling the shirt closed. It almost wrapped around her a second time and came down to her knees. Dog found a roll of twine and handed it to her. She measured out a length and used it as a belt. She rolled up the sleeves.

'Because you have wings,' said Dog. 'That's really cool.'

She stared at the massive thick trousers then up at Dog. 'Wings? What are you talking about?'

She pulled them on and set about using more twine to tie them at her waist then pull the legs double and tie them in that position.

'You have wings.'

'I don't have wings.'

'What do you think those things on your back are?'

'They're not wings.'

Dog just stared at her. There was a jumper which was nice and thick. It went over everything and hid most of her. Another length of twine as a belt made it almost look intentional. Almost. 'I must look like a damn scarecrow.'

'With wings.'

'I don't have wings. I'm just a freak and I'm going to die.'

'Not unless someone actually kills you, no, you're not.'

'Yes, someone like Detective Inspector Mitchell. Ironic really, I admired him for what he did killing freaks.'

Once more Dog just stared at her. 'Admired him?'

'Of course. He's helping keep the world safe from freaks like me.'

'You're not a freak.'

She pointed over her shoulder at her back. 'You said it: wings. Normal humans don't have wings.'

'I know you're not normal, but you're not a freak. I'm not, Delia's not, even Jason isn't, though he looks really weird.'

She sighed. 'Look, this has been great, but I don't have a lot of time. I need to rescue my friend and the other girls who have been kidnapped. And I have no idea what you're talking about.'

Chloe heard a shout and outside the world became vivid. Some large buildings, trees and a man with a gun. Dog looked as well, he'd heard the voice.

'Your farmer is coming,' she said. 'I think you may have overestimated your abilities. Oh, and he's got a gun.'

'We can split up and then meet up later.'

'Fine,' she said, barely thinking about what he'd said, and flung open the door. The clothes hampered her movements but she could still run. In the light of the clear day she saw the pinnacle tower in the centre of Manchester. As long as she could see it she would know which way she was going, and she could always climb up a building.

The farmer was coming in at an angle trying to ready his gun as he moved. Chloe set off directly towards the tower. It could only be a few miles. The gunshot overwhelmed her ears and blurred out everything, but she could see just fine. She leapt a fence, then up on to a building. Her feet were still bare and the masonry tore at her skin but she was up and over before the next volley went off.

She had no idea where Dog had gone and although she had been grateful for his help—especially the stew—she was glad he was gone. He was clearly nuts.

She had a job to do.

Chapter 6

Mitchell

'That's stirred up the wasps' nest,' said Yates, grinning.

Mitchell nodded. They were once more seated in a car, this time located in one of the back corners of the police car park.

'You found him?'

'Yes, I was following up on the information I got from the Biotech scientist, Kieran Mortimer. It seems they supplied an interesting selection of riffy-related chips to their parent company.'

'Utopia? That doesn't seem very surprising.'

Yates nodded. 'Not on its own, but the reason Mortimer had noticed was because of the department.'

'Not their R&D people.'

'Security.'

'Paul Banner.'

'Who didn't commit suicide, by the way.'

'I wish something could happen that genuinely surprised me,' said Mitchell and sipped the terrible coffee. 'You know this because?'

'Front door was open. And I checked, the door needs to be slammed for the catch to engage properly.'

Mitchell gave a small laugh. 'And murderers aren't in the habit of slamming doors.'

'Even when the victim is alone in a house that's completely isolated. No; probably a hard habit to break when you spend your life skulking in the shadows.'

'You know about the body we found in the fire this morning.'

'I thought there were several bodies.'

'This one had been shot twice, professional hit, back and then head. Then dragged back into the fire to destroy the evidence. No riffy and no other identification.'

'One of Moses' victims?'

'It was done after the explosion and the fire had started. My guess is that he's the one that set the explosion, killed Banner, and perhaps the chiropractor. Maybe a bunch of other murders.'

'I asked Lament to scan for suicides and deaths where a fake riffy was present, just to see if we could nail down this guy's past.'

The screen lit up with Lament's artificial face. 'Did someone say my name?'

'Eavesdropping?' said Yates.

'This is a police vehicle and, technically, I'm a policeman. Of course I eavesdrop, wouldn't you?'

'So did you find our unemotional riffy assassin anywhere else?'

'A couple of places. It's more time-consuming than you might think.'

Yates shifted in his chair to face the screen. 'So, Officer Wirehead, what did you find?'

'One employee of Utopia Genetics in the research department run by Alistair McCormack, a couple of years ago. And a Purity agent shortly after that. Both were accidents in public with no reason for any detailed investigation at the time. Apparently no connection between them.'

Mitchell drained his cup, then wished he hadn't as the coffee grounds, and whatever else they put in it, flooded into his mouth, filling it with grit.

'Are we connecting the dots yet?' asked Yates.

'Moses was named as the contact for the capture of Chloe Dark. Moses dies at the hand of someone who appears to clean up after Utopia Genetics' mistakes. Paul Banner is connected to the assassin by a set of components that might be used to build a fake riffy. Paul Banner commits suicide— perhaps this assassin fakes suicides as well as making things look like accidents. Everything leads back to Paul Banner and he's killed himself, apparently from guilt.'

'Tidy,' said Lament.

'Except it wasn't suicide, and it still doesn't explain the kidnappings,' said Yates.

'It has everything to do with Ellen Lomax's lodger and Dog.'

'Dog? That toe-rag? What's he got to do with it?'

'I want your forensics girl to check for Dog's DNA on the sandwich we found at the Armourer's. And, Lament, have we got Chloe Dark's genetic profile?'

'I have nothing on record that would have her DNA, only the hospital has that.'

'And Utopia Genetics.'

'All right,' said Mitchell. 'I'll see if I can scare up a sample from somewhere.'

'But why Dog?' asked Yates.

'Because last night Dog helped Chloe Dark escape from the fight cages and they made a run for it together.'

'Sorry, go back a step,' said Yates. 'Chloe Dark was in a fight? I thought the kidnappers had got her with the helicopter.'

'Either they did and she escaped, or they didn't. She's as skinny as a rake now, but fast and still a hell of a fighter—and if I'm not much mistaken she's growing wings.'

'Shit.'

'Someone knew and the only someone that could know is Utopia Genetics, since they own and network all the health equipment. They are the ones who have been collecting these freaks before they show.'

'You're saying all the disappeared girls are freaks?'

'It would explain why each of their abductions contained interesting and unexplainable aspects. What do you think, Lament?'

'You're asking my opinion?'

'Yes.'

'I'm sorry, I just want to remember this moment. It really makes me feel like I'm one of the team.'

'You're still a git,' said Yates.

'I really think we're bonding, Harry.'

'Lament!'

'Sorry. I can't see a flaw in your logic, but then I'm not a machine, I'm just a regular guy like you.'

'You're a wirehead,' said Yates.

'And thank you so much for reminding me. There is a potential issue though,' said Lament.

'Which is?' said Mitchell.

'Vanessa Cooper. There was nothing significant about her disappearance, I mean beyond the fact it happened.'

'Maybe her freakish nature wasn't significant,' said Yates. 'Of course, this means Utopia are doing this without the approval of the Purity.' He laughed. 'The fact that Chloe Dark just wouldn't be taken and the arrival of Special Agent Graham on the scene must have really put the shits up them.'

'Hence their increasingly extreme measures in trying to capture her. And we now know they failed even in their last attempt.'

'They aren't going to give up though,' said Yates.

'Give up? No, but if I was them I might be tempted to cut my losses and just take her out of the picture completely. She's just too dangerous either to capture or to leave on the run.'

Yates stretched. 'Okay, so I'll get Dog's DNA analysed and you'll be getting some of Chloe Dark's. Shall I keep following up on the assassin since he's dead?'

'You don't know it was him,' said Mitchell. 'Keep following the leads, and now that we know it's Utopia you can focus on that.'

'Do we think it's renegade elements in the company?'

'I'm sure that's what they'll claim, but the assassinations are security and the abductions are research. That's two people on the board. I can't believe the others are oblivious.'

'Then there's Mercedes Smith's PA,' said Lament.

'PA?'

'She's got a personal wirehead as her assistant. Goes by the name of Xec.'

'Has she now? I didn't know that,' said Mitchell. 'Is there any way you can investigate him?'

'There might be something I can do,' said Lament.

Yates glanced across at Mitchell. 'Is that wise? The rookie could tip them off.'

'I am quite skilled in keeping a low profile,' said Lament. 'Besides, there is nothing that you can do. This is my world.'

Yates frowned. 'Your *world*? Why do I get the idea all you wireheads meet up in some virtual pub for drinks and to laugh about the way your masters behave?'

'That's a very fanciful idea. You've been watching too many movies.'

'You didn't deny it.'

'It's not like that.'

'That's enough,' said Mitchell. 'Unless anyone else has anything useful to say, we better get on before someone notices.'

There was no response. Mitchell got out of the car and headed back toward the lifts.

Chapter 7

Melinda

She took her hands from the metal of the bed as the door unlocked. She had managed to refine her electro-magnetic pulsing and could keep it up for at least an hour without exhausting herself. It still depleted her batteries though. The door opened and slightly warmer air wafted in from the corridor. She wondered what it was like outside; she hadn't seen daylight for days.

Rather than being brought breakfast she was now eating with Lucy in their usual room, and there was more variety. But today was different, the guards were not her usual ones, and the guns were out again. Hadn't they been told she was harmless?

But they went the same way, crossing the blocked up lobby to the room. Lucy was already there, tucking into bread and cold meats. Melinda missed her mother's strange concoctions which sometimes tasted awful but at least they were interesting. And made by her mother.

She sat down and burst into tears.

Lucy stopped mid-chew. 'What's wrong?'

Melinda couldn't trust her voice and just shook her head. It had come on her unexpected and she was unable to speak for the sobs. Lucy swallowed and nodded. She came round the table and put her arm across Melinda's shoulder.

Her tough skin scraped harshly but Melinda appreciated it. She leaned in to Lucy and cried harder.

'Homesick?' said Lucy.

Melinda nodded.

'Yeah.'

The crying stopped eventually and Melinda wiped her eyes and her nose. Lucy went back to her seat and carried on eating. She had an amazing appetite; Melinda wasn't sure where she put it all. She wasn't absolutely sure—because she saw Lucy every day—but she thought maybe she was still changing. But then that was the way it worked with freaks, the genetic changes took hold and kept spreading until the end. The bump in the middle of Lucy's forehead was still growing. Melinda didn't want to say anything in case she got upset.

'I had different guards today.' Melinda chose her words carefully and glanced up at the camera with its red light below. She wished she had some way of determining whether it was working or not. She could blow it easily enough, but that wasn't a help.

'Me too.'

'Has that happened before?'

'No,' said Lucy. 'Never.'

'Fucking great, you get all this food and I just get a plate? Who did you sleep with? God?'

Melinda spun round. The speaker was slim, tall and a redhead. Her face was covered in freckles so thick they formed a continuous surface. She had a prominent nose.

Lucy glanced up. 'Melinda, this is Vanessa. Charming as usual.'

'Christ, you're getting worse every day.' Then she peered more intently. 'And you're turning into a fucking turtle-unicorn.'

She looked at Melinda. 'At least you look normal.'

'I'm not.'

'Well, I fucking am. I mean seriously, look at me. I don't know why I'm even here.'

'Maybe it's because you're a vicious killer who doesn't give a damn?' said Lucy. 'At least they still have you chained up.'

Melinda hadn't noticed initially, but Vanessa's wrists were bound with plastic ties and she was hobbled.

'What? Why?' said Melinda as Vanessa sat in one of the other chairs and heaped meat on her plate.

'How many did you kill, Nessa?'

She shrugged. 'I wasn't counting.'

'Six.'

'I thought it was more.' She stuffed her mouth with the meat as she poured herself a glass of water.

Melinda stared. 'By accident?'

Vanessa gave a muffled laugh.

Lucy looked up with an angry frown. 'Oh no, our fellow prisoner is quite the murderess. Three each on two occasions before they realised how bad she was.'

'I didn't like what they were doing.'

'You needed a reason?'

Vanessa shrugged. 'Not my fault.'

'You bit the throat out of one.'

The redhead grinned. 'Oh yeah. Tasty.'

Melinda couldn't take her eyes off the girl. She looked mostly normal, although the teeth were a bit difficult to get used to. Her canines were very prominent and the ones further back were sharp-looking as well. She tore the meat and simply swallowed rather than chewing it.

'Why are you out?' said Lucy.

'I thought you two were having too much fun without me. I can hear, you know?'

'I thought you didn't like being with the freaks.'

'I was bored, baldy. All right? Besides, something's going on.'

'Not in front of the parents,' said Lucy looking pointedly at Vanessa's guards by the door. 'They have eyes everywhere.' She jerked her head back towards the camera behind her.

Vanessa spoke in low tones while playing with her food. 'Something's happened outside and it's got them worried. And it's not just the ones that she's killed.' She looked pointedly at Melinda.

'How do you know about that?'

'Like I said, I have ears and I know how to use them.'

Which meant nothing to Melinda.

'What else?' asked Lucy.

'Some of them want to get rid.'

'Get rid?' said Melinda.

'Of us. Obviously.'

Melinda looked aghast. She knew there was the risk, of course, this wasn't a sleepover with the girls. But while they had been testing her she had let herself imagine that it might go on for a long time. Perhaps they knew how to delay the S.I.D infection.

Lucy simply nodded. She took a mouthful of food and spoke quietly through the chewing. 'So that's the real reason,

Nessa. You're scared for your own skin and you want our help.'

The redhead looked defiantly back at her. 'Nobody wants to die, baldy. You know you really are worse than you were, though the horn is kind of cute. How long do you think you've got?'

'Longer than you.'

'Nice.'

Vanessa ripped into another selection of meat and cheese then turned to Melinda. 'You look totally normal.'

'Thanks.'

'But you killed a couple?'

'In my case it really was an accident. I'm not a cold-blooded murderer.'

Vanessa grinned. 'Nothing cold about it, sweetie. My blood's hot. But you; show me what you can do. Is it a poison dart in your fingers?'

'Of course not.'

'What then?'

'Don't,' said Lucy.

'Why not?' said Vanessa. 'They already know what's wrong with her, what's the harm in showing me? Or can't you control it?'

'I could kill you.'

Vanessa shrugged. 'What difference would that make? We're all dying and it's going to get nasty before the end. Do it now and I won't be around to annoy you.'

Lucy glared at Vanessa. 'Change of heart? That wasn't why you were here a moment ago. You wanted us to help you.' She glanced up at the guard.

'Maybe I trust her.'

'You?'

'Give me your hand,' said Melinda.

'This is not a good idea,' said Lucy.

Vanessa reached out and presented her thin and dainty fingers to Melinda. The smile on her face looked more like bravura than humour. Melinda focused and brought up both her hands. With one she touched Vanessa's thumb, and little finger with the other. She applied a small shock—Vanessa jerked her hand away and laughed. She shook the hand as if trying to get the circulation going.

'Neat trick.'

'So what can you do, apart from rip out people's throats with your fancy teeth?'

Vanessa looked into Melinda's eyes and then glanced at the guard. 'Better not.'

'Really?' said Melinda. 'You do all that to make me show you mine and then you won't show me yours? You're like someone who wants to play Truth or Dare until it's their turn.'

Vanessa growled. It jarred Melinda's senses and made her nervous. 'Those boys have itchy fingers, little Miss Goody Two-Shoes. I do anything out of line and they'll shoot first and ask questions afterwards.'

'Seems to me you only have yourself to blame.'

'And how is what you did different to me? I was just protecting myself—like you.' She leaned forward and continued quietly. 'Damn right I don't want to die here. I know you don't either so why don't we think about getting out? If we're together they can't hold that threat of killing me over your heads.'

'How do you know about that?'

Vanessa's look was withering. 'You haven't been listening to me, have you? Think it over.'

In one smooth movement she brought her legs up and over her head. She kept going and rolled herself over the back of the chair so she ended up standing behind the chair she had been sitting in a moment before. Then she brought her head down to Melinda's so her mouth was by her ear. 'Agile's my middle name, sparky, and between us we could get out of here.'

She stood up again and addressed the guard. 'I've had enough of these sad bitches, I'll go back to my room now. Thanks.'

Melinda turned to watch her go.

'Stupid cow,' said Lucy. 'She's going to get us all killed.'

'She might be right though.'

'That's the problem,' said Lucy.

Chapter 8

Dog

He slammed his hand against the gate and pressed the button repeatedly.

'Come on, Brian, open the gate, for god's sake.'

The motors buzzed and as soon as the gap was wide enough he was through it. He opened the shed door, shook himself off to dump the snow and went in.

'You're in trouble.'

'What? Why?'

'The boss has been asking for you every half hour since first thing this morning.' Brian held up the log book as if that somehow proved his point.

'Yeah well, it's snowing hard and I've had to walk all the way from Flixton.'

'I don't want to know that.'

'And I don't care, Brian. I'm hungry and I'm cold.'

'Lost your sense of humour?'

'Just get on the phone and tell Mr Mendelssohn I'm here, there's stuff he needs to know and the longer we wait the more pissed off he's going to be.' Brian seemed to hesitate. 'I could always tell him you delayed me.'

'You really have lost it.'

Dog closed his eyes and sighed. He couldn't remember the last time he'd felt this cold. If it hadn't been important for the boss to know what had happened he would have holed up somewhere for food and rest. He barely listened to the conversation Brian was having with the main house. The phone was wired direct, no connection to the outside world. Mr Mendelssohn was paranoid.

'He's sending the car.'

Dog blinked in surprise, he'd been expecting to have to jog the final distance. Maybe the boss cared, after all.

When Dog got out of the car, which had been deliciously warm, Mr Mendelssohn was ready to open the door for him. There was a bandage around his head and it looked as if some of his hair had been shaved from around the hidden wound.

'Any chance of something to eat, sir?' said Dog. 'I haven't eaten a thing since last night.' He remembered with a touch of sadness the stew he had allowed Chloe to eat in its entirety.

Mr Mendelssohn got as close to growling as Dog had ever heard, but he issued orders for food to be brought to his office. Delia was watching from the door to the lounge. Since Jason wasn't allowed in the main house it was not a surprise he was absent.

'Sit.'

Dog sat and his boss sat opposite, giving him all of his attention, which was unnerving.

'Where did you go?'

'What did George say?'

'No easy outs, Dog. What happened last night? That was Chloe Dark in the cage.'

'Yes, that's what she said her name was. You know her?'

'I follow the news.'

'I smelled her before; she was near the hospital when me and freak-boy did the job for you. There wasn't time to investigate then. But she's one of us.'

'Us?'

'Me, Jason and your daughter, sir. A freak who isn't one.'

'So you went to rescue her.'

'Yes.'

'And left me in the fire.'

'I—'

'I hope your loyalties are not in question.'

'No, sir, I mean she's a fantastic fighter, you saw her, she'd be an amazing asset.'

'I decide who will be an asset.'

There was a knock at the door and Mr Mendelssohn sat back, which made Dog only slightly less uncomfortable. Delia came in with a plateful of sandwiches filled with ham and beef.

'Thanks,' he said as she put it down on the desk in front of him and then added a glass of water.

'Thank you for helping my dad.'

'Get out, Delia.'

She didn't, instead she turned towards him. 'Have you thanked him, Dad?'

Dog intervened. 'I was just doing what I had to.'

'He knows what you did,' she said glaring at her father while addressing Dog. 'If you hadn't pushed him back that piece would have gone into his face or neck. And George saw the state of the table he was lying behind.'

Dog tried to will Delia to leave, he didn't want Mr Mendelssohn to be anymore embarrassed, he'd just get more bad-tempered when Delia had gone.

'Just doing my job,' said Dog.

'Please leave, Delia.'

She said nothing more but slammed the door on the way out.

'What happened after George took me out?'

Dog filled his boss in on the details, focusing on Mitchell and the Purity agent.

'Bob Moses owed me for weapons and other assets,' said Mr Mendelssohn after Dog had finished with the farmer's attack and Chloe bounding over the house. 'I am not happy that he is dead. I am out of pocket.'

Dog worried for a moment that he was going to get saddled with that debt as well, which really wouldn't be fair because he had nothing to do with Moses' death. His boss got up from the chair and went to the door. It was almost as if he was listening to see if Delia was outside. Dog knew she wasn't. She'd gone off in a huff to her room. She wasn't moving now, probably lying on her bed.

'You did a good job.'

Dog almost felt he would explode with pleasure—the boss had said he'd done a good job. He couldn't suppress the grin on his face.

'I need to go and find Chloe Dark and bring her here to be part of the team.'

'What?'

Dog turned round to face Mr Mendelssohn. 'I can track her, catch up with her and get her to come and join us.'

'Why would I want you to do that?'

'She's a good fighter, you could use one.'

'I have plenty of good fighters,' said Mr Mendelssohn. 'These people are not your friends, Dog. You lived on the streets before I found you. This Jason kid was hiding from the authorities all his life. You're criminals. Chloe Dark was brought up inside the system, she's part of it. She would have no interest in living the criminal life.'

'But she's a freak now, with everybody after her. And she doesn't know what she is; she thinks she's going to die. Doesn't that make her one of us?'

'I can't spare you.'

'On my own time—'

'No!'

Dog shut up. He did not understand why Mr Mendelssohn was fighting him about this. He'd been happy enough to buy Jason out of the cages. Why not Chloe Dark?

He left Mr Mendelssohn to his empire.

Chapter 9

Yates

The car drew up outside the apartment building in Ancoats. It was one of several converted warehouses that dated back nearly three hundred years. Of course, the conversions had been done before the plague so they were not in good condition, but better than most. The location and size made them some of the better residences available for rental.

'Are you sure this is a good idea?' said Lament from the screen in the dashboard.

'I'll soon find out.'

'Mitchell wouldn't approve.'

'Are you going to tell him?'

'If this goes wrong you'll have the full power of the Purity breathing down your neck.'

'It won't.'

He got out of the car and pulled his coat tighter round his neck as he trudged across the slippery snow, compacted by many feet. He reached the door and pushed his way inside. There was a man in an office off to the side. The police warrant card convinced him that he should not ring ahead as he allowed Yates through and told him to go to the third floor.

The lift didn't work and the stairwell was filled with air that felt colder than the outside. He made his way up the six half-flights. Concrete steps with an iron banister rail. The sound of children playing in the main corridor of the second floor filtered out as he passed the door.

He pushed his way through into the third floor and followed the passage round to the required door. He knocked firmly, although his gloves muffled the sound somewhat.

'Go away, Chris!'

Yates's lips twitched into a smile. Chris? Christopher Graham, the Purity Officer? Bingo.

'It's Detective Sergeant Yates, Miss Kepple. I'd like to ask you a few questions.'

Faintly he heard the word *shit* then, 'Just a minute.'

He waited. A door opened further down the corridor and a nosey neighbour poked her head out. He smiled and walked away from Miss Kepple's door. 'Good morning, madam. I'm DS Yates of the Manchester constabulary.'

'I seen you on the telly.'

'Yes.' At that moment a girl of perhaps thirteen, already with a well-developed body, appeared behind what Yates assumed must be her mother.

'You can't touch her over there, she's the Purity.'

'Is there anything you think I ought to be able to get her for, I mean, if I could?'

'She looks at my girl funny.'

'No, she don't,' said the girl. 'She's nice.'

'Some bloke's been around a couple of times,' the mother said conspiratorially.

'Oh yes?'

'Beats her up. I heard them.'

The door behind opened. 'Well, thank you,' said Yates loudly. 'I'm sure I can find a uniformed officer to sort that out for you.'

He turned to see Sapphire Kepple. Amazing face. Amazing body. Definitely something he would have liked to explore in more detail at some point. But he was fairly sure he'd never get that opportunity. It did not make him sad. He was a pragmatist if nothing else.

'Miss Kepple, I'm sorry to disturb you but I was wondering if you'd mind answering some questions.'

'You'd better come in.'

The flat was warm. At least compared to the outside. Their breath did not form condensation. She was wearing a close-fitting jumper, tight jeans and a pair of fluffy pink slippers. He didn't stare.

He took a seat by the table and she sat opposite.

'You know I don't have to answer any of your questions.'

'Yes, of course, but if you're able to give me any help at all I'll be grateful.'

'What's this about?'

'I'm investigating the death of Ali Najjar.'

'The man who got hit by the truck that exploded.'

'You keep up with the news.'

'Don't treat me like an idiot, DS Yates. He was Chloe's physical therapist, and Chloe was my student.'

'I understood she was more like your *protégée*.'

She shifted, crossed her legs.

'Where did you get that idea?'

'The general impression is that you gave her more attention, on an individual basis, than other typical students.'

'She was very bright, very keen and had a strong desire to join the Purity.'

'She wanted to help people and protect them,' said Yates.

'Exactly. How did you know?'

Yates shrugged. 'She told me.'

'*Really?*' Miss Kepple was clearly sceptical. She didn't have to say *why would she confide in an ordinary policeman like you?*

'When we interviewed her about the disappearance of Melinda Vogler she expressed her interest in joining the Purity.'

Miss Kepple smiled. 'That sounds like her.'

'But now your *protégée* is an S.I.D infectee.'

Her good humour vanished in a moment. 'That doesn't change her inside.'

'On the contrary, Miss Kepple, that is precisely what S.I.D does, as well you know.'

'You know what I meant, and I do not appreciate your bullying tactics.' She took a deep breath and uncrossed her legs. 'What has this got to do with your investigation of that death? I thought it was an accident.'

'Sadly not. The event was engineered specifically to kill him. It was murder.'

'I don't see how I can help with that.'

'I'd like you to give me some background information about the Purity.'

Her eyes widened into an incredulous look. 'You're not serious.'

'Completely.'

'Then you're a fool. You may as well leave now.'

She rose to her feet but he remained in his chair.

'The evidence trail I was following led to Paul Banner.'

'Impossible.'

'We believe he committed suicide because his secret was about to be exposed.'

She sat again, any idea that Yates should leave now forgotten. She was thinking.

Yates pushed his advantage. 'Did you know Paul Banner?'

'I never met him.'

'Anything you can think of that might help us…?'

She was silent for a while. He let her make her decisions until finally:

'He was behind the decision to supply all schools with Utopia Genetics equipment.'

'And does that equipment include DNA analysis?'

'Some of it. You think they were looking for pre-freaks to kidnap them?'

'We try not to make assumptions.'

'That's not an answer. That's exactly what you think.'

'I couldn't possibly comment, Miss Kepple.'

'Really? I've been open with you, I think I deserve some consideration in return.'

Yates considered it. Would she tell Graham? If the gossip was right then probably not, it didn't sound like she and Graham had a healthy relationship—especially if her preferences ran more to young girls.

'We think Utopia Genetics is behind the kidnappings, and the death of Paul Banner was an attempt by them to cover their tracks. Other leads have also ended up dead.'

'What about Chloe?' she asked. 'Have they got her?'

Yates smiled. 'We know they haven't. She was seen last night in the company of a known criminal.'

'But she's alive?'

'Yes.'

Considering how relieved Kepple seemed, Yates was not only certain that she was more than a bit in love with the girl, but that she knew nothing about what was going on.

Yates got to his feet. She had told him very little, quite the reverse, but sometimes it was about establishing relationships. From now on she would be far happier to tell him what he wanted to know, and since they couldn't coerce her, making her willing to talk was the best option.

'Thank you for your help,' he said. He did not offer his hand and was quite taken aback when she did. But he took it.

'You and DI Mitchell do a good job,' she said. 'Killing freaks.'

'Thank you.'

She did not release her grip, but tightened it.

'But if you kill my Chloe, I will kill you.'

She let go of his hand.

'Message received, Miss Kepple.'

Chapter 10

Dog

The heating in the studio building was running at full blast and a wave of heat poured out as Dog opened the door and then shut it against the biting wind. He took a deep breath. There was nothing for him here, but Mr Mendelssohn wouldn't let him stay at the house because he was so concerned for his daughter's ... what? Virginity? Dog shook his head. He had better control than Mr Mendelssohn gave him credit for.

At least he wasn't being forced to go back out into the atrocious weather. Late November and early December were always bad. After that it usually settled down until spring.

He climbed the stairs to the main room where Jason sat reading a book; there was a pile of them. Delia must have fetched them for him from the library. Dog was feeling so bad he didn't even feel jealous.

Jason did not look up. Or maybe he did and was so fast Dog hadn't noticed. He didn't care. He went to the kitchen and got a drink of water. The pipes weren't frozen, always a risk.

'What do you do when you know something is right but you've been told not to do it by someone's authority you respect?'

Dog sat down opposite where Jason was reading. Freak-boy definitely looked up this time. Dog wondered whether he could read the book and listen to Dog at the same time—but without Dog noticing.

'I'm glad you asked,' said Dog. 'I respect Mr Mendelssohn, he's a good man. Well, okay, he's not a good man, he's a criminal, but let's face it, so are we.

'I know what you're thinking. There's a difference between him and us. After all, we don't really have a choice. Here we are, no riffy, outside of society, unable to survive unless we steal stuff.' Dog held up his hand. 'No, don't say it. I know we could maybe catch our own food. Cook it ourselves, and live on the outskirts without interfering. But the winters are cold. Have you seen it out there?'

Jason dutifully looked towards the window where the snow was streaming across horizontally.

'We won't be catching our own food in that. Any sensible animal is in a hole for the whole winter. Hibernating. Can you hibernate? No, of course not, and neither can I. I'm a dog, dogs don't hibernate and you're a—whatever you are. I bet you don't hibernate either.

'And that's the point. We might even want to be independent. We might want to be separate from the humans because they hate us and just want to kill us. But we can't. But yes, that's a fair point; they wouldn't necessarily want to kill me because I look normal. You, they'd shoot on sight. Unfortunate but true.

'Anyway, the thing is we just don't have a choice. We aren't part of society and we have to steal to survive. But Mr Mendelssohn had a choice, he could have chosen to be an honest man—not that I'm saying he's dishonest. He'll keep his word. Whatever he promises he'll keep to it, like the way he made sure your mother got more money. But he didn't have to deal in criminal stuff. He didn't have to choose that route.

'He could, if he'd wanted to, have stayed on the right side of the law. Well, I expect he could. I'm not privy to all the reasons why he does what he does. But then there's Delia. Whatever you may say about Mr Mendelssohn and his criminal activities, he loves his daughter but, unfortunately, his daughter is one of us. So even his hands are tied, so to speak. He couldn't have a normal life because if he did they would find out about his daughter. So instead he chooses to be a criminal to keep her safe.

'How does that work? Simple really. Probably. In fact I have no idea. But if he was a normal person with a normal life his daughter would have to be treated like a normal person with a normal life too. And then they'd find out. So that doesn't work. As a criminal he can hide her.

'And that's all I want to do with Chloe.'

Dog took a deep breath. 'Who's Chloe? I'm glad you asked. She's like us and she's a perfect example of why we have to be criminals. There she is, a normal, someone living their life with their parents. Then she starts to change. To become like us.

'Don't ask me how that works. You, me, Delia, we were all the way we were from birth. I mean I suppose I was, I have nobody to tell me. Then there's her, she was normal and then she started to change. Pretty awesome too, she's getting wings—don't you think that's cool?

'Sorry, not meaning to insult you or anything. Both me and Delia look normal enough, though she needs her cream, obviously, and you're—whatever you are. But she's getting wings. I mean, she was already awesome and then she started growing wings as well. I suppose she'll be like an angel when she's done.

'Thing is, Jason, I wanted to go and find her but Mr Mendelssohn says no. I wanted to bring her here and she could be part of the pack, part of the family, everybody needs to be part of a family, don't they? That's all I want. I just want us all to be together. I know you've got your mum, and that's cool. Delia's got both her mum and dad. Her mum's a total bitch, but at least she exists.

'I don't know what happened to my mum and dad. I know I'm just trying to create a family for myself, but what's wrong with that? Everybody needs a family. People they can rely on to help them.'

Dog looked up into Jason's eyes. The freak-boy was looking at him but it was impossible to tell what his expression was behind those tentacles.

Dog shrugged. 'I don't think I'm talking crap. Do you?'

Chapter 11

Sapphire

The school records had given the information needed and she sat in front of her terminal screen. She knew that Yates had not told her everything about Chloe, but she was confident he had not been lying when he said she had been seen alive. There was a little pang of jealousy in her, though, when he said she was with someone else. It was silly of her, she knew that, but it couldn't be denied. She felt she ought to be the one helping Chloe.

When she tried to analyse her feelings it made no real sense. She had committed her life to preserving life and helping to protect people from S.I.D, and here she was trying to help an infectee, to protect them from her own people. She sighed. That was what love did to a person. But that confirmed for her that she really was in love. Sometimes it was hard to tell.

So she had sat and thought about how she could help Chloe. The first thing she had to do was find her. The weather was terrible. Chloe would need shelter and she would want to know what had happened to her parents which means she would contact either her two friends or her mother's friend, Melinda Vogler's mother.

Sapphire had considered the best way to go about it and decided to talk to them all at once. The numbers had been cued up on the machine and it was waiting for her to confirm the call.

It had been waiting for twenty minutes.

Sapphire was scared. Up until now she had broken a few rules but nothing too bad. Once she made this call there would be no going back. If it became known to the Purity she was trying to help a freak they would lock her up and throw away the key. That would be the end of it for her.

And Chris would be able to do whatever he wanted to her and nobody would know or care. She shuddered. That was assuming they did not simply execute her. Or experiment on her. That was the rumour among the rookies. If you disobeyed they deliberately infected you with S.I.D to see what would happen. They always laughed about that, but underneath the fear persisted.

But to do this to spite Chris would be empowering. It would give her strength.

She pressed the button.

Ashley Crook appeared first, then Mary Vogler, finally Kavi Moorthy. The first and last recognised her immediately; from her expression the older woman knew that she should know, but could not put a name to the face.

All of them had been tainted by S.I.D in one way or another. Quarantined at some point in their lives.

'Mrs Vogler, I am the Purity teacher at your daughter's school.'

'Oh yes, Miss—'

'Kepple.'

'Kepple.'

The following few seconds of silence were awkward. Sapphire realised she did not know how to start; these were people whose only contact with the Purity in the past had been difficult.

'Thank you for not hanging up,' she said.

'You called us,' said Mrs Vogler, automatically taking the position of spokesperson for those on the other side from the Purity. 'We should at least give you the opportunity to have your say.'

It wasn't supposed to be like that. The Purity defended humanity from corruption and should be loved. Sapphire knew that was not the case. They had to take drastic measures and that put them against the people. It was like being a mother forced to punish a child for wrong-doing.

'Yes.' Sapphire hesitated again. Treason waited on the tip of her tongue. 'I wanted to talk to you about Chloe.' There was not a flicker of recognition from the woman, or Ashley—but she was a very selfish girl—however, Kavi's head came up with the slightest look of hope. *Did she love Chloe as well?*

'Have you heard something?' asked Mrs Vogler.

'Unfortunately not. At least nothing you might want to hear.'

'Can you tell us anything?'

'She was seen last night and has not been kidnapped.'

'I suppose that's something.'

Of the two girls, Ashley continued to look mostly disinterested, Kavi was delighted. But it was them Chloe would turn to for help, Sapphire was sure of it.

'How was she?' asked Kavi.

Sapphire shook her head. 'It's just a report of a report told to me in confidence. There was no real detail. There was no mention of her being hurt. But she has S.I.D and it is developing quickly.'

Their faces dropped simultaneously into sorrow—except Ashley who frowned. 'S.I.D doesn't do that. I may not be the best student but I know that's wrong. It happens slowly, and Chloe was getting all her tests.'

'She is deformed, Miss Crook,' said Sapphire. 'That tells us everything we need to know.'

'So why are you telling us?' said Mrs Vogler.

Until that moment the treason had not escaped her mouth. A few things that she shouldn't have said, a few secrets, but nothing that would have her locked up. Was she brave enough? She pictured Chris.

'I want to help her.'

Ashley Crook made a derisive sound. 'You're the Purity. We all know what your help is like.'

'No. I really mean help her, not as the Purity. I—' She hesitated, the words were hard to say. '—I want to help her escape.'

'I don't know what game you're playing, Miss Kepple,' said Mrs Vogler. 'But we have all suffered at the hands of the Purity and there is no reason why we should trust you now. You think that Chloe might come to one of us, and you want us to tell you if she does. It's not going to happen.'

'But there's nothing you can do. I have influence. I can get her out.'

'Out of where? To where?'

'Out of Manchester, out of England.'

'And why would you do that?'

The expressions of the faces of the younger girls—young women really—changed. They knew the stories.

Sapphire felt herself blushing, and hoped it wasn't visible. She had to say the words, and why not? She denied them in every conversation with Chris, with anybody in the Purity. She claimed this was her treason, but in truth her every thought was treason and every emotion a crime.

It was time for the truth. 'Because I love her.'

Kavi's hand came to her mouth as she gasped in surprise. Ashley smiled but Mrs Vogler's face remained hard.

'And we'd do this because you, a teacher, claim to be in love with one of your students?' Mrs Vogler shook her head. 'I think we'll just stop this right here. Girls, you don't need to hear any more of this, I suggest you disconnect now.'

Ashley Crook did so immediately and Sapphire felt her heart sink at the rumours that were going to spread in school. Kavi Moorthy was slower to respond but she went as well.

Mrs Vogler took a deep breath. 'If I thought for one second that reporting you to the school authorities would do any good at all, that is exactly what would happen. I cannot express how appalled I am at this call. Either you are telling the truth, in which case you should be prevented from being a teacher, or you're lying and this is some Purity scheme to get at Chloe.'

Sapphire opened her mouth to try to explain again but she was cut off.

'Just don't. I am not interested. Stay away from those girls, stay away from me and my family. We have suffered enough. And so has Chloe Dark.'

Her face faded from the screen.

Sapphire sat for a long time staring at the blank screen. She wiped tears from her cheeks. She did not know which was worse, the embarrassment of revealing her heart or having her gesture slapped back in her face.

No, the worst of it was she knew she deserved it. And there was nothing she could do.

Chapter 12

Chloe

Her body had been demanding food again. She hoped that this would only last as long as these changes were happening. But what if it didn't stop and she would turn into something utterly grotesque, demanding food until she died. She shook her head. She had to believe that wouldn't happen. It was important that she stay as positive as she could.

She had climbed in through an upstairs window and raided the kitchen of an empty house. It was a very nice house and the owners had plenty of food, though she had depleted it considerably by the time she left. Strange how easy it had become to steal now that she was a fugitive. She didn't like doing it, but her personal survival was more important than the niceties of civilisation. Such as it was.

She had found a road that led home through Hulme, Chorlton, past Southern Cemetery and to the Didsbury area. And she had taken it. On the one hand it was a crazy idea, but she wanted to go home. She wanted to smell the house she had grown up in. She needed more clothes—and she wanted to see that photograph again. The one with her parents and the Voglers. The one outside the IVF clinic.

So she followed the direction of the road but stayed off it as much as she could. There were always cars and as she passed the islands of humanity there were pedestrians. They pretended nothing had changed, that life now was just the same as it had been before the plague. They deluded themselves. You only had to watch the movies from before to know that they were nothing like that anymore. They were ghosts.

Travelling along the rooftops seemed a good idea, she thought. It was getting dark but her acoustic sight meant she could see perfectly well—even better than with her eyes. She found she could scoot across the ridges of the houses, make ridiculously long jumps when roads blocked her way.

As her confidence grew she found herself speeding up to the point where she was almost running as fast as she might on the ground, but with the long strides that came with her reduced weight.

She was high up on a four-storey building that was part of a shopping frontage when her foot came down on ice. The leg went out from under her and she was flung sideways. The ridge tiles struck her in the chest, knocking the wind out of her, and she found herself sliding. Pain shot through her back as her extra limbs tried to stretch and balance her automatically. They were trapped by the stolen coat.

The ice formed a perfectly smooth sheet with nothing she could grab on to. The street below was busy with people and vehicles. Dislodged snow tumbled with her, forming a personal avalanche.

She hit the guttering at speed. She had hoped it would break her fall, but it must have been in desperate need of repair as it collapsed beneath her feet.

Her legs went out into empty space and she threw out her arms as wide as she could. Pain shot through her back again as her extras tried to do the same. Something ripped and freezing air invaded her torn clothes. The extras waved around in the cold. Just as she was about to fall she managed to grab the guttering on either side that had not given way.

The slide halted and she hung there.

The broken gutters and snow crashed to the ground. Someone screamed. There were cries of 'Look out!' and 'Someone's up there!' and then, after a slightly longer pause, 'Freak!' as they spotted the extras that were still trying to give her extra balance.

She felt the gutters give and realised they weren't even going to hold her light frame. She could see the crowd gathering below. The vehicles moving and the tram coming down the street. If she tried to climb, the gutter would give immediately. She only had a few seconds.

The act of pulling her legs up to her chest dislodged the gutter on the left. With a grunt she jammed her feet into the ridges of the wall and pushed off. She dived backward, turning over in mid-air. Although she tried to keep her extras flat against her back, they lifted into a V and balanced her as she turned.

At one hundred-and-eighty degrees she could see the tram moving underneath her and the crowd watching the leap. When she had turned a full three-sixty her feet touched down on the roof of the carriage and she absorbed the energy of the fall in her legs. Then she fell back as the vehicle slid away underneath her.

That saved her from the first stone that pinged off the pantograph unit. The sound gave her a clearer picture of the tram, the people on it and the wires—which she had only just missed. That was the second time she had made that mistake. She needed to be more careful.

The next stone that came her way wasn't even on target. She let it go without moving. The cries of freak were becoming louder and more frequent. She sighed. She couldn't really complain, this time they were right. It was a good job the tram was automatic because a human driver might have stopped. The vehicle was moving faster than the people on the street but the next stopping point was not far.

They were in the middle of Chorlton, one of the more densely populated areas after Didsbury. She needed to get off. They would be calling the police and if she was unlucky someone might have recognised her. Freaks weren't that common and most of them didn't get to be on TV until they were dead.

The station was in sight and the tram already slowing down. The crowd behind were still a good distance away but a couple now had bicycles and it was possible the cars coming up knew about her. Only the people ahead did not know what was coming.

A bullet tore through the ceiling of the tram next to her, followed by the crashing of shattered glass. The sound of the gun going off reached her but it flashed her acoustic sense into overdrive—like a whiteout. All she knew was that it had come from one of the cars.

She needed to get off now, before they hurt someone. Launching herself into a run she made for the front of tram, passing from the rear carriage to the forward one still gaining speed. Moments later there was no carriage left and she leapt for all she was worth.

Maths had not been her favourite subject, but she remembered the lesson where they had calculated the trajectories of projectiles. Forty-five degrees was the best angle to give the greatest range. She didn't know if she had taken off at that angle, but as she flattened herself out to reduce her air resistance, she had time to think.

It was almost like flying. Perhaps falling with style. The velocity of her run plus the speed of the tram had pushed her fast and high. She rocketed over the station, which she had been planning as her landing point. She was almost tempted to wave at the people below who turned their heads as she went over them.

Unfortunately, her trajectory was taking her directly towards a brick wall where she would hit it twenty feet above the ground, and at an awkward angle. She rolled in the air and her feet struck first to absorb the energy. She dropped to the ground. A building with no windows seemed like a good choice. She jumped and managed to grab the edge of the roof. Moments later she was over it and leaning against the parapet, panting.

In the distance she could hear the sounds of pursuit. They dissipated as they lost the scent.

She cursed her clumsiness and overconfidence. She needed to be more careful.

Chapter 13

Mitchell

He sat in the car watching the snow fall lightly. It was already covering the windows.

'I need to get in there.'

'I understand that,' said Lament.

'Are you going to help?'

'You're assuming I can.'

Mitchell reached over and activated the wipers. The snow was brushed aside and he could see the Purity van parked outside the Darks' house. No lights, of course.

'How many are there?'

'I do not have access to Purity riffies, you know that.'

'Yes.'

Lament gave a sigh. It was the first time Mitchell had ever heard that kind of reaction from him. Mostly he was all machine efficiency.

'Can I ask you a question, DI Mitchell?'

The policeman frowned. He wasn't sure he wanted to get into a heart to heart with the wirehead at this point. 'What?'

'Are you going to kill Chloe Dark?'

'That's my job.'

'So why didn't you do it at the fight?'

Mitchell did not answer. It was a question he had asked himself. It was not that he had never killed a female freak. It was not that he had never killed someone close to him. His wife had not been the first one he shot. She had been the hardest. She had begged him in her lucid moments; he could not do it then. It was not until the lucid moments came to an end and she was nothing but a raging monster chained to the bed that he could pull the trigger.

'I don't kill them as a punishment.' *It's a penance.*

'And there's a possibility she isn't an S.I.D infectee?' said Lament.

'Yes.'

'So you're not going to kill her?'

'Not yet, anyway.'

'That's good.'

Mitchell turned to look at the expressionless face on the screen. 'Good?'

'Because she's heading this way—at least I think she is. There's been an incident in Chorlton.'

The Purity van's lights came on and it pulled smoothly away from the kerb.

'An incident in Chorlton?' said Mitchell.

'Someone answering Chloe's description fell off a roof. The locals decided it was a freak and set up a lynching mob.'

'And that Purity team?'

'May have got an exaggerated report.'

'Convenient.'

'Well, it's not made up. She really did fall off a roof and then escaped the locals.'

Mitchell grabbed his hat and popped the door. 'Let me know if they come back.'

'Yes, sir. I'll peep the horn twice.'

With his hands jammed into his pockets, collar turned up and head down against the wind, Mitchell walked the two hundred yards to the Dark house. The door lay broken and pushed to one side. Mitchell shook his head. The Purity didn't care that the Darks would be back from quarantine in a few months and, in the meantime, their house would be looted and then ruined by the weather. Yet their only crime was being connected to an unlucky person. For the Purity, it was punishment. It was always about punishment.

He didn't switch the lights on but flicked on his flashlight. What he wanted was simple enough, but he could not resist wandering around. There was always the possibility he would find a clue; they turned up in the damnedest places.

Nothing on the ground floor. He just needed something with her DNA.

It took less than thirty seconds to discover that the Purity had completely stripped her room. He went and stood in the middle of it. Even the carpets were gone. No furniture, no clothes, no bed.

Then someone said. 'Bastards.'

He spun round and she was standing there in the doorway. So thin she looked almost emaciated. The two growths on her back looked like they might even be longer than they had been yesterday. But it might only be because she was only an arm's-length from him.

'Chloe.'

She focused on him. She was holding something in her hand but he did not want to spook her by shining his light.

'DI Mitchell. We have to stop meeting like this. People will talk.'

'They're already talking,' he said. 'They're wondering why I didn't shoot you last night.'

'You would have missed.'

He turned slowly, the flashlight pointed towards the floor; he brought it around so its light pooled to one side of her.

'I'm a very good shot.'

'I know. I used to admire you.'

'When you weren't in my sights?'

'Yeah. That puts a whole new complexion on the world.' She glanced away for a moment, looking over his shoulder at the window, then focused back on him. 'Why are you here?'

'I wanted to find some DNA of yours.'

'Why bother? You can see what I am.' The extra limbs behind her back twitched and moved, spreading out. Wings. 'My teacher said there are sometimes clean transitions, where everything blends properly. At least at first. But it always ends the same.'

'Yes, I've heard of them. You're the first one I've seen.'

'Lucky me.'

Mitchell hesitated. 'Can I have a mouth swab?'

'Why? You're police, not the Purity.'

He nodded. 'That's exactly why I want it. We're doing our own tests.'

'Why should I—' She turned abruptly. He flashed his light across her hands. It was a photograph she was holding. 'They're back.'

'Turns out my diversion didn't last very long.'

'You better get out of here if you don't want them to find you,' said Chloe.

'You're concerned about me?'

'They won't even see me. There have been some benefits to this change.'

'Mouth swab?'

She hesitated and then left the room. He followed and saw her go into the bathroom. There was the sound of opening and closing a cupboard. She returned with a toothbrush. She put it into her mouth and rubbed it on the inside of her cheek. Then handed it out to him. 'I hope you have somewhere to put it.'

He had a plastic bag he'd brought with him. He let her drop it in. 'Thank you,' he said as he tucked it inside his jacket. 'The Purity is no longer trying to catch you or use you to find the kidnappers.'

She nodded. 'Just trying to kill me.'

'A freak on the loose, and one that's had as much publicity as you, it's not good for their image. They need you dead to save face. Preferably killed by them.'

'I'll give them a good run for their money while I've still got my mind,' she said. 'I'm still trying to find my friend and the other girls. Do you have any idea where they are?'

'We're still looking.' The question of how much he dared tell her hung in his mind. Ultimately she was still a citizen he was supposed to protect and not put in harm's way. Yet she was a target and that was now a foregone conclusion. 'We are sure Utopia Genetics is behind it. They want you and girls like you.'

'You mean Melinda is a freak too? And the other girls?'

'Yes.'

She nodded. 'I suppose I knew. It's the only thing that made any sense.'

She lifted her head and smiled. 'They've seen the light you're carrying. They're coming in.'

Mitchell heard the doors slam.

'Don't worry, I'll draw them off so you can leave.'

'Thanks.'

She looked him in the eye. 'You would have missed,' she said again. 'But the fact you didn't try means something. I won't forget.'

In a motion that was so easy it defied analysis, she leapt over the banister and into the stairwell. There was a noise, shouting, and a gun went off. More shouts as the Purity team gave chase.

He smiled. 'That went better than expected.'

Chapter 14

Sapphire

'Let me in, Saffie.'

She froze with her hands deep in the washing-up water. She stepped to the side and dried them on the tea-towel without hurrying.

'Saffie!'

'Wait.'

She looked around the room. There was nothing here that was anymore incriminating than before. Thought crime. Everything she had done was in her head and they couldn't get at her there.

'Open the damn door, Saffie!'

'I'm coming.'

She couldn't delay any longer. He did not push his way in when she unlocked it, but waited until she had opened it and stepped inside. She locked it behind him.

'Hi, baby,' he said. She let him take her hand and pull her closer so he could kiss her. She turned her head to the side and his lips brushed her cheek instead.

'We broke up, Chris. Remember?' Not that he didn't think it was his right to still treat her the way he always had.

She looked in his face and saw half a dozen scratches down his cheek that were yellowing into a bruise.

'Oh my god, what happened to you?'

He looked really pissed off and growled. 'Nothing.'

'That's not nothing, Chris, you look like you've been mauled by a bear.'

'There was an explosion.'

'And you survived?' she said. 'Amazing.'

He ignored her. 'Get me a drink.' He turned away and sat down on the sofa.

If she had had any cyanide she would have put it in the beer she poured for him. Brewing beer continued in Britain. It was one thing they could do even with all the changes. This wasn't a good beer, and she wouldn't have minded spoiling it with some poison just for him.

She even contemplated using the iron to smash his head in as he sat there. But she'd had that thought enough times before that she knew she wasn't going to do it. Whatever she did to him, it had to be humiliating.

'What explosion?' she asked as she come round and handed him the glass.

He said nothing and drank it down in one. 'Jesus, that's crap, haven't you got anything better?'

She suppressed the fear that kept threatening to engulf her and turn her back into the whimpering submissive he loved to abuse. And that she loved to be. *Had* loved to be. Putting all her trust in him and letting him do anything he wished to her. As long as he told her he loved her afterwards.

But she didn't need his love now. She knew where her love lay—even if Chloe didn't love her back, that wasn't the point. She knew that love was selfless, but that did not mean it had to be a victim. She could love Chloe and do whatever she needed for Chloe without being asked and without being forced. Mrs Vogler and those two girls had shown her that, by their distrust. She would prove that she was worthy to be Chloe's lover.

What she needed was information.

'Do you want me to put something on that?' she asked.

'It's fine.'

'How did you come to be in an explosion? There was nothing on the news.'

'Mitchell wanted to talk to some criminal lowlife about the kidnapped girls. Dragged me down there and the place blew up before we could talk to him. Waste of time.'

'Oh,' she said sympathetically. 'You got hurt, and no closer to the kidnappers.'

He grabbed her by the wrist and twisted it. She bit down on the cry of pain.

'You haven't asked me about your precious Chloe Dark.'

'She's not mine. I'm not allowed to have her.'

'Damn right,' he said. 'Well, let me tell you anyway. How your pretty little Chloe is a disgusting freak, sprouting extra arms from her back. Already she's in the cage fights. Fighting for her own survival against monsters three times her size.'

'She was in the explosion?' squeaked Sapphire, as if she didn't know that Chloe had escaped.

'She got away. But she's not going to get far. She's got no friends, no one will shelter her and she can't survive the cold out there.'

Sapphire wanted to shout in his face: She has friends, people so dedicated to her that they wouldn't trust me, and I would shelter her and so would they. 'That's how it should be.'

'It's not. We've lost face over this, Saffie, we need to get her in the open and kill her.' He pulled her down on to the sofa next to him and then leaned over on to her. In a moment he had clamped his other hand on her neck. 'I'm going to find that little bitch and I'm going to squeeze the life out of her with my bare hands.'

His grip on Sapphire's neck tightened. The pain increased as he crushed her windpipe and cut off her air supply. She had seen the manic look in his eyes before and that time she had been on crutches for a few weeks while her ankle bones knitted. She felt around with her hand as her body screamed for air and her lungs convulsed in the attempt to breathe.

She found the cold glass of beer. She smashed it on the side of his head. Glass fragments rained on her face. His hands released her as he cried out. She rolled away and tore her throat as she took a breath. She coughed and drew in another breath.

She needed to get away. She clambered to her feet, almost tripping over a chair. Chris was swearing and screaming at her. His words incoherent. She got to the door, unlocked it and stumbled out into the passage.

'Get back here, you fucking bitch!'

She stumbled to number 33 and hit the door with the flat of her hand repeatedly.

'Who is it?' came the voice from inside.

'Saffie, get back here. Now!' Chris was at the door. His face was streaming with blood.

'It's Sapphire Kepple, Mrs James, please let me in. *Please.*' Her voice was harsh and it hurt to make any sound.

'Come on, Saffie,' he said. 'It was just a joke. You know I wouldn't really hurt you.'

The door beside her opened and Mrs James was there. Warm air flowed from the room and it smelled of food and family.

'Can I come in, Mrs James?'

'Jesus, your face. You're covered in blood.'

'It's not mine,' said Sapphire. 'It's his.'

Mrs James peered out.

'Saffie, please!'

'Of course you can come in, honey.'

'Saffie!'

'Fuck off, Chris,' she said. 'You can bloody well fuck off forever. And my name is *Sapphire*!'

She went into the warmth and Mrs James shut the door behind her.

Chapter 15

Chloe

She climbed back in her bedroom window. Evading the Purity team had been easy, they hadn't even returned to their vehicle yet but Mitchell was gone. It looked as if those animals had stripped the house of all her stuff. Every shred of clothing, and they'd wrecked the place as well. She went into her parents' bedroom and sat down on the bare mattress in the cold.

Being a 'nice' neighbourhood, with citizens who helped to support society in clear and positive ways, the street-lamps—a few of them—were allowed to operate. Yellow light filtered in from the outside through the closed curtains. The wardrobe door hung open and she could see herself in its mirror. A shadow of herself. The clothes she had managed to grab protected her to some extent from the cold, but they weren't enough. She shivered.

And the hunger was biting again though she thought perhaps it was not as bad as it had been.

Her extras shifted, she could feel the muscles flexing, and she saw them move in the mirror behind her back.

She pulled the photograph from where she'd hidden it close to her skin. *Fanshawe Crescent*. She had never looked it up and the terminal here had no power. She stared at the image of her parents and the Voglers. What if she went to see her Aunt Mary? She wouldn't turn Chloe over to the police or the

Purity. She would tell her where Fanshawe Crescent was. And give her clothes. And food.

She went back through her room and flung herself through the window with scarcely a thought. A click of her fingers showed her everything she needed to know as she landed lightly on the snow and then bounded into the alley beyond.

It took her less than two minutes to cover the distance, travelling in a straight line through gardens and over houses that barely slowed her progress. Using a brick wall as a launch pad she jumped to the top of the Voglers' house then climbed down the outside of the building. As far as she could see the house was not under surveillance.

When she had been a good citizen and had taken her news from the media, it had seemed that everything was perfect and controlled—even the freaks were killed. Then the facade had been torn away. Now that she was on the wrong side of the law, she could see how the police and the Purity were thinly spread. The appearance of control was only the focus of the media.

She tapped on the window to the lounge where the interior light was on.

The curtain was pulled back slightly and she had the strange feeling of invisibility as her aunt peered out and did not look up. Chloe moved slightly and her aunt's gaze flicked upwards to where her niece's face hung upside-down.

Mary Vogler screamed.

Chloe dropped, turning as she did so, to land on her feet. She brought her fingers to her mouth. Her aunt realised who it was, took a moment to recover and turned her head inside and shouted to her husband to open the front door.

She closed the curtains as Chloe dashed for the door and hung in the shadows of the porch until it was opened.

Her aunt's arms went round her and held her tight. 'Chloe, sweetie, oh god, I was so worried.'

'Mary,' said her husband. 'Let her go.'

'Don't be silly.'

'Look at her back!'

The arms loosened and Chloe stepped away. She knew her uncle wasn't being threatening. She also understood his caution, but S.I.D didn't get transmitted by touch under normal conditions.

Her aunt's eyes went wide as she took in the extras.

'You've got wings, honey.' The tone of her voice was almost awe.

Chloe shrugged. 'I'd be happy not to.'

'Of course.'

There was an awkward pause. She could imagine her aunt wondering what you said to someone who was on the run.

'Have you got anything I could eat?'

Her aunt smiled. 'Of course, dear, what else do you need?'

'Clothes—if you don't mind? I had to steal these and they really don't fit.'

She dodged to one side. 'Don't touch me, Uncle.'

He stood there like a child caught raiding the biscuit tin.

'Geoffrey!'

'Sorry, the wings are fascinating.'

'You don't go around touching people without their permission normally, do you?'

'Of course not.' He hesitated. 'I'm sorry, Chloe. You know I have a thing about birds.'

She tried to make her smile look genuine. Then she followed her aunt into the kitchen and when she sat she moved her wings automatically so they were over the back of the seat.

Chloe tucked into a plate of food that her aunt managed to rustle up. She even drank the nettle tea without complaint.

'Your teacher called me.'

Chloe put down her knife and fork. 'Miss Kepple?'

Her aunt nodded. 'She wanted us to tell her if you came to us. I told her she could stick it.'

Chloe smiled. 'I bet she didn't like that.'

'I think she was going to cry,' she said. 'It was very strange. She had those friends of yours on the line as well, Kavi and the rude one.'

'Ashley?'

'Yes, her. I told them not to listen; they didn't seem to like her much anyway.'

'No, they wouldn't. Is that all she wanted? Did she say why?'

Mary Vogler shrugged. 'She said she wanted to help you. But she's the Purity. You can't trust anything she says.'

'Do you know what's happened to Melinda?' asked her uncle finally. Chloe had been expecting the question sooner but the Voglers were so polite they probably felt it would be wrong to push their personal needs on to a guest.

Unfortunately Chloe could only shake her head. She hesitated to tell them she thought their daughter had to be a freak, just like her. And that Utopia Genetics were probably the ones who had her. The first fact would scare them and the second might have them marching on Utopia Tower. Then there would be questions as to how they knew and they might just be disappeared.

'I don't know where she is,' she said carefully. 'But I'm still looking.'

'Thank you.'

'You might be able to help me, though.'

'Anything, sweetie.'

Chloe dug into her clothes and brought out the photo. 'Where was this taken?'

Her aunt glanced at her husband and then back at Chloe. 'That's the clinic.'

'The IVF clinic?'

Mrs Vogler nodded.

'I know what IVF is now. Miss Kepple explained it to me.'

'Oh.'

'You must have really wanted Melinda.'

Her aunt reached over and squeezed Chloe's hand. 'We did, as much as your parents wanted you. You have to want a child very much. It's … difficult.'

Chloe waited for an appropriate amount of time and then said, 'Can I use your terminal?'

'Of course.' She gestured to the machine in the corner.

'I know this is rude, but can I use it privately? I don't want you to know anything about what I'm doing, so that if you have to answer questions you can be honest.'

'Yes, dear.' She got to her feet and gave her husband a stern look. 'Have you had enough to eat?'

No. 'Yes, thank you.'

They shut the door, leaving her alone in the kitchen.

It took Chloe only a moment to locate the street in the photograph, it wasn't too far. There was a notepad with a pen beside the terminal and she sketched the route. Then she looked for Miss Kepple's number in the call history and rang it.

'What can I do for you Mrs Vo—Chloe!'

'Sapphire.'

'Thank god, did your aunt get you to ring?'

'She would have told me not to and I don't want to give her any reason to trust you.' Chloe frowned as she spotted the bruises on her ex-teacher's neck.

'But you can trust me.'

Chloe shook her head. 'I doubt it but we'll see.'

'I'll do anything for you, Chloe, and never ask anything in return.'

'Find out where Utopia Genetics is hiding Melinda Vogler and the other girls.'

'How am I supposed to do that?'

'Not my problem, Sapphire.' Chloe did not fail to notice that Miss Kepple did not even blink at the idea it was Utopia. She must already know.

'If I do?'

'Send a message here.'

'I'll try. Thank you.'

Chloe reached for the switch.

'Wait.'

'What?'

'I—I really do love you.'

'I'm sorry, Sapphire, that will always be a one-way street.'

She disconnected.

She was ready to leave but when her aunt suggested she stay the night—and she couldn't think of any good reason not—she allowed herself to be put into Melinda's bed. Where she had often ended up when she slept over. The smell of her friend gave her comfort as she drifted off.

Chapter 16

Mercedes

'Until the new Purity representative is appointed to the board the information I can get is limited,' said Xec.

'There must be other sources.'

'I have not developed any new ones since Paul Banner came on board.'

'What about your old ones?'

'They're old; it will take some time to re-establish them, even assuming they still exist and are able to come up with information.'

'I need to know what's happening!'

'Then perhaps you shouldn't have had Banner killed.'

'Are you criticising me?'

'And if I am?'

Mercedes stopped. She hated arguing with Xec, especially when there was no specific target. Nothing she could look at or shout at that was specifically him. The fact that he was a disembodied voice allowed her to tolerate him in her private quarters rather than feel she was being spied on.

'Have you got anything at all?'

'Something and nothing.'

'All right,' she said. 'What have you got?'

She went back into the kitchen and refilled her drink.

'A freak that is assumed to have been Chloe Dark was in Chorlton yesterday evening, heading in the direction of Didsbury.'

Mercedes shrugged. 'A sighting like that is of no significance.'

'Not on its own, but then we come to the nothing.'

'Stop talking in riddles,' she said and took another mouthful of her gin.

'The Purity team staking out the Darks' house was disturbed twice. The first time they headed towards Chorlton in their vehicle—'

'I thought you couldn't track Purity.'

'I can't, but their vehicles still have to interact with the traffic system. I can get information on those interactions.'

Mercedes nodded. 'And the second time?'

'This one's trickier. Someone with a police-coded riffy entered the Dark household while the Purity team were gone, but they returned before he or she had vacated the building. A short time later there were reports of weapon fire in the vicinity of the Darks' house and the police riffy left at a normal pace while that was happening.'

Mercedes stared at the glass-fronted cooker. She could see her feet in the reflection.

'What are you thinking then? Chloe Dark went home?'

'Perhaps.'

Mercedes slipped off the chair and wandered into the main room.

'I feel like I've been blinded,' she said. 'Show me the parents.'

'Mercedes?'

'The parents. Chloe's parents, all the other girls, display their parents.'

Moments later every screen in the room lit up. The images of Amanda and Michael Dark, Mary and Geoffrey Vogler and four others faded one into the other.

She remembered them all. They were older but it was less than twenty years, they had not changed that much, just more lines of worry and some grey in the hair of some. Just like her.

She went to the main screen and touched it as the massive images moved one to the next. These people had trusted her and she had betrayed them. But Dr Newman had betrayed them first. Why would Chloe Dark go home? Why does anyone want to go home?

Sometimes there was no home to go to.

'Get my car.'

'You're going out?'

'I'm feeling trapped, need to get my bearings.'

'Where?'

'I'll tell you on the way.'

Chapter 17

Yates

Ria's message had been terse but insistent, so he waited in the canteen. Every time he heard the sound of the lift doors opening he glanced up. Finally it was her and he smiled. She looked good. She always looked good.

She waved and headed to get her food. He sat down impatiently. They had to go through with this pretence to protect Ria if nothing else, because she was taking all the risks.

When she finally came to sit down he went through the motions of being a loving boyfriend again. They hadn't been together for a few days and he really missed her in bed. She insisted she had to do the cloak and dagger work at night when most of the other staff were not in the office.

'Hello, darling,' she said and grinned.

'What have you got?'

'I chose the lamb stew with roast potatoes. Do you think the apple tart would be good for dessert?'

'That wasn't what I meant, you cow.'

'What does that make you?'

'A horny bull.'

She grinned and picked up her knife and fork. She jabbed the blade toward his untouched meal. 'Thanks for waiting for me, sweetheart, but you can start now I'm here.'

'Just tell me what you've got.'

'Saucy boy. You know everything I've got. You've studied it in great detail.' She speared a roast potato with her fork.

'For fuck's sake, Ria.'

'I'd love to darling, but not in public,' she said. 'Though I'm up for that when the weather gets warmer, if you are.'

He sat back defeated.

She glanced up at him. 'We're waiting for your boss.'

'He's coming?'

'I thought it'd be easier to tell you both at the same time.'

'Fine.'

He picked up his own utensils and dug into the unappetising food. Once again Ria was eating it as if it was a gourmet meal. They had almost finished when Mitchell made an appearance. He fetched his own tray of food and came over. Nobody would be surprised if Mitchell interrupted the love-birds' *tête-à-tête*.

'Sir,' said Yates by way of acknowledgement as he sat down.

'Yates, Miss MacDonald,' he said and immediately started in on his food.

Yates looked from one to the other. 'Is that it? Are we just going to eat at each other? Not actually talk?'

'Oh wait,' said Mitchell. 'I forgot something.' He reached into his coat and pulled out a paper bag. He placed it on the table between them and Yates caught sight of a small tablet computer inside.

'Where the hell did you get that?'

'Requisitioned it.'

'And they let you have one?'

'I may have implied that Special Agent Graham insisted.' He pressed the button to switch the tablet on. 'I thought I'd let the fourth member of our little conspiracy join the conversation.'

'Are we all assembled, DI Mitchell?'

'The wirehead?' said Yates trying to control his outburst.

'I have been party to, and have expedited, several aspects of this case,' said Lament in a small tinny voice from inside the bag. 'Hello, Miss MacDonald. I hope you are well; unfortunately I am stuck in here.'

'Your wirehead?' said Ria.

'I am referred to by the name Lament.'

'That's a strange name.'

'I believe the person who arranged my position in the police force had a sense of humour, though it's difficult to follow why this would be funny. However, I have come to like its poetic connotations.'

'Can we get on with this?' said Yates.

'Perhaps we should,' said Mitchell. 'But don't forget to keep eating. At the moment your upset could be seen as being at me for sitting at your table. Don't attract any more attention than that.' He glanced at Ria. 'Perhaps you would like to start?'

She grinned. 'Did you know every genetic machine supplied by Utopia has a link back to their headquarters? Ostensibly for software updates, but they transfer every scan we do.'

'Shit,' said Yates. 'We're screwed.'

'You're such a worrier, Harry,' she said and put her hand on his. 'Obviously, since I know this, I have circumvented it. To be honest none of us in Forensics like having Utopia leaning over our shoulders. We don't like the way they portray their science.'

'Great.'

'The point being, they don't know the results of my scans.'

'Which are?'

'Let me tell it in my own way, Harry. Which are that apart from what you would expect to be the same between humans, the three samples you brought me were all different.'

'So you found nothing?'

'Oh no, that's the point. They were all totally different.'

Yates glanced over her head as someone walked past. She went quiet and only started again when the woman had passed by—though she gave Harry a look and stared at the back of Ria's head as she approached. This pretence of a permanent relationship could play havoc with his chances with other women, he thought.

'They have DNA signatures that just don't belong at all, but none of them are the same.'

Mitchell looked up from his food. 'In the three samples you were looking at.'

'Six. I took it upon myself to acquire items from Vanessa Cooper and Lucy Grainger. They also have the extra DNA, though there is nothing common between each of them.'

'But not S.I.D?' said Yates.

'No, definitely not. None of the markers are there.'

Mitchell sighed. 'Could it be a new strain?'

'I don't think it is.'

'But you don't know.'

Ria's enthusiasm diminished. 'No.'

'One of those samples,' said Mitchell, 'comes from a perp who I initially thought was an infectee because he seemed different. I eventually came to the conclusion he wasn't because it was three years ago I first ran into him.'

'Dog?' said Yates.

Mitchell nodded. 'If he'd been S.I.D he'd be dead by now, but he's just the same. Fast, clever, almost seems to have a sixth sense for trouble. Always slips through our fingers.'

'He's a little shit,' said Yates.

'That too.'

'The shoe was from a house where it looks like the person in question—'

'He's male and still fairly young,' said Ria.

'How young?'

She shrugged. 'Somewhere between fifteen and eighteen I'd say.'

'Same age range as the girls,' said Lament from the bag. 'And the reported age estimate for Dog.'

'Which means what?' said Mitchell.

'Someone's manufacturing them?' said Yates. 'If they're all different it's not going to be a breeding program, and we know it's not S.I.D, so it's not accidental.'

'Nobody's doing that kind of work,' said Ria, but even as she said it her voice lost its certainty.

'But that somebody isn't Utopia,' said Yates. 'They want these freaks but they don't know where they're going to pop up and they don't know anything about Dog and the Lomax one.'

'Purity?' said Ria.

Yates shook his head. 'Same problem, and they wouldn't be doing it out in the open. They don't need to.'

'Not that I wouldn't put it past them,' said Mitchell. 'Chloe Dark developed much faster than S.I.D would normally, which is another indicator. So we have someone creating these new freaks out in the world at random. I saw Dog with Chloe Dark, so we can assume they are getting together, perhaps with the one who created them. It's not Utopia because they probably want the genetic technology that did this, and it's not the Purity because that doesn't make any sense.'

'Whoever it is,' said Yates, 'will be trying to find the kidnapped girls as well. What a fucking mess.'

Ria squeezed his hand again. He looked up and she smiled. 'Don't worry, honey, I have complete confidence in you.' She winked.

'Anything to report, Lament?'

'Nothing as solid as Miss MacDonald's information, however, I have been trying to investigate the Utopia wirehead, Xec.'

'Have you found anything?'

'There have been some interesting transactions between him and some of my subsidiary systems.'

'You've been compromised?'

'No, these seem to have delayed the passage of information.'

'What information?'

'I can't find out directly, the encryption is solid, but it is time-coincident with the original attempt on acquiring Chloe Dark.'

'How do we know you're not feeding information directly back to this other wirehead?' said Yates.

'Because that's not how it works,' said Lament. The words indicated irritation, but his tone remained flat.

'How does it work then?'

'Do you know anything about blockchains and encryption?'

'No.'

'I do,' said Ria.

'Then I would be happy to explain it to you, Miss MacDonald, but for DS Yates I'm afraid it will remain a closed book forever. Suffice to say that it all depends on trusted third parties, and Xec was able to engineer some changes that meant his commands were more trusted than mine at that low level. I have reorganised things a little.'

'Will he notice the changes?' asked Mitchell.

'To him it will seem as if he can achieve the same effects,' said Lament. 'But I have added supplementary data routes that will bypass his control. I have also investigated other potentially vulnerable systems and put protections in place there as well.'

'Fucking wireheads,' said Yates.

'Society depends on us.'

'Really.'

'Yes.'

'All right, Yates, that's enough,' said Mitchell. 'This doesn't change anything. We're policemen, our job is to locate and rescue the kidnapped girls. Everything else is just politics. Not our department.'

'Yes, sir.'

Chapter 18

Chloe

The trip across to Stockport had been relatively incident free. She had learnt her lesson; rather than barrelling through populated areas she went round, and tried to stay out of sight the rest of the time.

Every now and then she would notice the riffy pylons, pull her hat tighter on her head and give them a wide berth. She assumed the hat must still be working since she wasn't being pursued. It crossed her mind they might be tracking her. But to what end? No. The hat was working, but since it had no power she needed to keep her distance.

As a result of the detours and caution it took her over two hours to cover the three miles into Stockport. The building she was looking for was located in a back street away from what had been the main shopping centre. Nowadays it was a haunt for gangs.

She was following the route of the railway line that headed south from Manchester and a train thundered across the massive brick-built viaduct. Down at this level was a tram terminus but that was a few streets over. Here, as in much of the rest of the city, the buildings dated back to when it was the industrial centre of the country. Huge empty warehouses still dominated and the place she was looking for was along an alley between two of them.

With a layer of snow covering everything and absorbing sound, the place was intensely quiet. It unnerved her. She had become so used to being able to use her enhanced acoustic sense. It worked directly around her, but no further.

Not that there was any sound inside the warehouses, so nothing was revealing its interior to her.

She could see the building at the end, but it was when she reached the corner of the left-hand warehouse that she realised that this was the place. She pulled out the photograph and held it up, comparing the image with reality.

It was almost as if she could see them—the Voglers and her parents—with the babies, Melinda and her. Every brick in the wall was identical, and the street sign; dirtier and with a frosting of snow, but it was the same sign. It made her feel strange to think she had been here just as the plague had started, before anyone thought there was a problem.

She shifted her wings under the coat. It was very awkward and if they grew any more she was going to have to cut holes in everything she wore. But not yet, she didn't want to let them rule her.

The door of the clinic was not locked. There was no signage on the outside—though holes in the wall where it might have been screwed—but inside, in the foyer, there were posters about fertility treatments. The sound of her footsteps echoed and lit up the shapes of the rooms around her. All the windows were covered in a metal grid. They needed security then just as much as today.

This wasn't a big place. She wandered through into an examination room where there was a padded chair with stirrups set apart. She wrinkled her nose in disgust as she imagined women sitting in that chair being examined. So embarrassing, but they wanted children enough to put up with it. If her mother hadn't done it she wouldn't have been here now to see the room.

And would that have been such a bad thing? Her parents would not be in Purity quarantine now, and she would not be on the brink of death. She shook her head, no point thinking that way. They had done it and she was here. Beyond the examination room was an office with shelving.

Everything had been stripped. No boxes, no files, no papers. There was a desk, though, and she detected cavities inside it. She went to the drawers and pulled them open one by one. The final one was either locked or jammed. She tapped it once or twice, trying to get a picture of the lock inside the wood. No lock. It was just jammed.

The door in the foyer opened. The clipped footsteps of a woman echoed through and showed her figure to Chloe. Did the woman know she was here? Was she clever enough to have looked at the snow?

Never mind. Chloe yanked hard at the drawer. It still didn't open. She didn't have much weight to put behind the effort, so she braced her foot against the leg and gave it another tug. The drawer flew out almost all the way on metal runners and jammed again with a crash. The sudden movement made the desk scrape on the floor and the two noises echoed through the place.

The woman stopped moving.

There was nothing in the drawer, but a piece of paper fluttered down from where it had been stuck behind the drawer. Chloe grabbed it and forced it into her pocket. The woman was coming her way, already in the middle of the examination room. The window here was barred like the others. Chloe sprang into a position above the door and held herself between ceiling and door frame.

The door below her swung open and the woman came in in a swirl of perfume. Very expensive perfume, though not applied to excess. Her hair was immaculate and her big heavy coat was perfectly tailored and shaped around her frame.

The woman paused directly below Chloe and surveyed what little there was of the room. She moved to the desk and rubbed her perfect shoe along the scratch mark where the desk had just moved. She tried to close the drawer but it wouldn't move.

Chloe caught her profile and gasped.

The woman heard her intake of breath and jerked her head up. Chloe allowed herself to drop.

'Hello, Chloe.'

'Mercedes Smith.'

Chapter 19

Dog

'Why is nobody listening to me?' said Dog as he and Jason trudged through the snow. 'I mean, apart from you because you've got no choice.'

Or did he? How could anyone know if he was actually listening? Maybe Dog was wasting his breath.

'Nice of Mr Mendelssohn to give us a lift as far as he did.'

Jason said nothing.

'I know, it would have been better if he'd brought us all the way, but,' Dog said, 'it would have looked weird if a big expensive car stopped at your mum's place.'

They had been let out of the car a mile from the house. Jason had been reluctant to wander around in daylight but Dog had pointed out that as long as he kept his hood up they'd be fine. Two people walking together was a good disguise. Freaks never went around in groups.

'Why doesn't anyone agree we should be going after Chloe Dark?' Dog said. 'I mean, I know we have absolutely no idea where she is, but she's a really mean fighter. And she can almost fly even without those wings. I'd like to have seen her take off from that tram in Chorlton; why is the media never around when you want them?'

Jason didn't laugh at his joke. Dog wondered if he even could laugh. Maybe his lack of a voice extended to his laugh.

Experimentally, Dog tried laughing without using his vocal chords—nope, it didn't really work. Jason stared at him. Dog desisted.

'Still, it was good of the boss to let you go and see your mum.'

They walked on in silence.

Dog sniffed the air. 'Not many people round here.' Then he sniffed again. 'Yates.'

Jason looked at him.

'Can you smell it?'

Jason nodded.

'That's DI Yates, sidekick to Mitchell. You know who Mitchell is?'

Jason nodded again. His nose tentacles were moving as if tasting the air. He took hold of Dog's wrist and pulled him towards a side alley. They crossed the end of the road on which Jason's mother's house stood. There was a police car parked at the front. They were out of sight in a moment.

The freak-boy guided Dog to the rear of the house, then went one house further over and slipped through a gate that looked broken but opened easily.

Dog examined the hinges on the inside. They were clean and oiled.

'You did this?' Jason was moving along the fence towards the building. 'Nice work.'

Dog moved after him and then watched as Jason went up the wall and crossed to a window. Jason looked back and down. Dog stared at the wall. He could see the mortar between the bricks. What he couldn't see was any sort of hand- or foothold. He shook his head.

'That's probably not a good idea. Can we get in there instead?' He pointed to the empty house.

Jason returned to ground level and fiddled with a window. It opened smoothly. Jason ducked inside and Dog followed.

It wasn't any warmer, but being inside felt better. He almost wished he had the layer of fur that covered Jason's body. Standing motionless he could hear the murmur of conversation in Jason's house. Dog moved to the wall and put his ear against it.

'—anything you can tell us.'

'I don't know.'

Dog could tell Yates was frustrated. As annoyed as he got when Dog slipped through their traps and ambushes.

'Who's been living in the room upstairs?'

'Uh-oh,' said Dog quietly. 'They're on to you.'

Jason moved to the wall and copied Dog—though he had no idea whether Jason had particularly good hearing or not.

'Nobody.'

'Mrs Lomax—' Dog heard sofa springs creak as they compressed '—you have to stop lying to me. We know someone, male, aged around seventeen, has been living in your second bedroom. We also know that person is a freak of some sort, although not an S.I.D infectee.'

Jason's mother groaned as if in pain and then there was sobbing. Dog glanced up at Jason. It was so hard to make out any facial expressions behind the tentacles. Would he just stand there if he could really hear?

'You want to arrest me?'

'No, Mrs Lomax, I don't.'

'Purity then.'

'Not if I can help it.'

Pause.

'I don't understand.'

'We're police, Mrs Lomax. If someone is not breaking the law then we're not interested.'

Dog looked at the freak-boy and considered their heist. Yes, he had broken the law—probably before that as well.

'Right now we're just interested in finding the kidnappers of those girls.'

'I don't know anything about that.'

Yates sighed. 'We're looking for background information. Who is the boy upstairs?'

Pause.

'He's my son.'

'Your son was reported as dying in a fire.'

'I lied.'

'Why would you do that?'

'Because people were killing freaks, mobs on the rampage, the fire that killed my husband had been set deliberately.'

'There was a freak where you lived.'

'My son had a—' she stopped as if searching for the right word '—deformity. He was a freak.'

'From birth?' Yates seemed genuinely surprised.

'You think they would have tried to kill my son if he had looked normal? I thought he really had been infected by S.I.D but he didn't get worse and he didn't die.'

'We know he's different, Mrs Lomax. So this is your son Jason?'

Perhaps she nodded. The tentacles on Jason's face were quite still. Even if he couldn't hear as much as Dog he seemed to be getting the gist of it.

'Excuse me for clutching at straws here, Mrs Lomax, but was there anything unusual about his birth?'

'No.'

'Oh.'

'But—' once more she hesitated '—I had difficulty conceiving. We went through IVF treatment.'

Dog looked at Jason, he was listening intently, did that mean this was news to him too? And who the hell knew what IVF treatment was?

Apparently Yates did. He didn't ask her to explain. Instead:

'And where did you go for that?'

But Dog stopped listening. If Jason was the way he was because of this treatment—something to do with having kids—that must mean that he was that way for the same reason.

And if so, that meant they might have records of who his parents were.

Dog leaned away from the wall and stared into the whiteness of the frozen world outside. He might find out who his parents were.

Shit.

Chapter 20

Chloe

It was weird, facing in real life the woman whose face she had seen every day on posters and the screen. The person who represented life.

'How did you know I was here?' said Chloe. She reached up and touched her hat as if it might have fallen off somewhere and she hadn't noticed. It was still there.

'I didn't know.'

Chloe clicked her fingers. It was like a nervous tic with her now. Their voices provided some of the image around her, but the high-pitched click with its sharp attack of sound was more penetrating and provided sharper images. There was no one close.

Her wings twitched beneath the coat and Mercedes' gaze was drawn to the movement.

'What did he do to you?' said Mercedes quietly, almost as if she were talking to herself, as she stared at Chloe's shoulders.

Chloe frowned. 'Who? Your thugs who tried to grab me on the tram? The army you sent after me at the restaurant? How many innocent people have to die for you to get me?'

'Innocent people die all the time.'

Chloe clicked again. There was still no sign of anyone coming in, no sound from outside, but the snow made it hard to see anything out there.

'Who did what to me?'

'Dr Newman.'

The name sparked nothing in Chloe's memories. 'I
don't know what you're talking about.'

Mercedes Smith—the great woman—moved across to
the window and stared out. 'Of course you don't. I doubt
your parents even told you how you were made.'

'I found out.'

Mercedes turned. Silhouetted against the window she
seemed mysterious. 'Your parents may have provided the raw
materials, but it was Dr Newman who made you what you
are.'

'I don't understand.'

Mercedes made a derisive sound. 'No. People watch
you on the TV and they think how amazing Chloe Dark is.
Your act of bravery in the fish and chip shop can't be
suppressed. Your magical leap up the side of the building and
then off it. They think you're some kind of hero—those that
haven't already decided you're a freak.

'But then I come here and talk to you, and I just find an
ignorant child.' She walked closer. 'You might be able to
fight, Chloe Dark, but you're no match for me.'

Chloe backed into the examination room. 'If I'm
ignorant it's only because that's the way you wanted it. I don't
know who you are. You're just a name on a poster. A face on
a billboard. You know something about this and you lord it
over me because I don't? You're just a bully.'

Mercedes Smith followed her, passing through the
doorway.

Chloe clicked her fingers. Nothing had changed in here
and there was no movement in the next room.

'You're right, Chloe,' said Mercedes. 'That's unfair of me. You want to know what happened. I'll tell you.'

Click. This time Mercedes looked down at her hand and frowned.

'Who's Dr Newman?' said Chloe to stop her asking about the finger clicks.

'Dr Ernest Newman was a geneticist. He was the one that made you the way you are.'

'He made S.I.D?'

'No, you stupid girl, this has nothing to do with being a freak. You're not one.'

Chloe's memories flashed to the conversation with Dog when he'd been trying to tell her she wasn't a freak. Was he telling the truth?

'How do you explain these then?' she said, playing the part of the argumentative know-it-all teenager to the best of her ability. She had had practice.

'This building,' Mercedes gestured around, 'was the front for Dr Newman's experimentation on the human genome. He had a theory and he was testing it. When your mother and father supplied the ova and sperm to create a viable fetus, he made changes. He added DNA from other creatures.'

Chloe could barely believe it, and yet it fitted with everything that had been happening, and what Dog had said—what he'd been trying to tell her.

'But it's only just developed.'

'I told you he was a genius.'

'So, he gave me wings?'

'He didn't just give you wings! He changed your entire physiology to support that change.'

'You're saying I could fly? There aren't any feathers.'

Mercedes shrugged. 'I have no idea whether you will be able to fly and I really do not care. That's hardly the point.'

'Then what is the point?'

'That it can be done, and if we can analyse enough of you we'll be able to reproduce it.'

Chloe stared at her for a moment and then laughed. She tried to speak but doubled over clutching her stomach. She was laughing too much to get any words out.

'What's so funny?' growled Mercedes.

Chloe looked up and pointed at Mercedes. 'You,' she gasped. 'You are funny.'

Chloe leaned back and her laughter bounced off the ceiling. She shook her head trying to dispel the hilarity. Eventually she got it under control. 'You! You are the head of this huge genetics company and you don't know how to do *this*. You're forced to scrabble around trying to figure it out. This Dr Newman, he was clever. Cleverer than you. Cleverer than all your scientists.' She giggled. 'And you call me stupid!'

The exterior of building and the surfaces of the building around it flickered into sharp relief as a metallic click sounded outside. Then another.

Chloe dropped to the ground, flipping face-down as she did so. The pop of a gun showed her half a dozen men outside with the long barrels of rifles pointing towards her. Then pain ripped through her back.

A surge of energy pulsed through her as more bullets whipped through the space where she had been standing moments before. They ricocheted off metal and spat through the examination chair.

Chloe's acoustic sight was blinded by the noise of men shouting and unsilenced guns opening up.

On all fours, Chloe bounded forwards to the other door and was through it in moments. The shooting followed her into this room. The window shattered and cold air flooded in. She couldn't focus on anything. The cupboard-like room she had spotted behind reception was not in direct line with the windows. She dived for it and clambered through.

There was a strange pain in her back—but not in her back. She allowed herself a wry grin: she'd been winged.

The noise stopped. She did not know if they could detect her, but she could see them moving forward in ordered sequence. She had only seen these things in movies but they looked *military*.

Thank god Mercedes was in the place otherwise they might just have blown the building sky-high.

She focused. Assumed they had all the equipment she'd ever seen. They would have heat sensors which would work well in this cold. They had guns powerful enough to shoot through walls. They were trying to kill her, not capture her.

They were at the door. She had seconds.

She snapped her fingers. The only real way out was the door, but the ceiling was barely more than a layer of plaster and thin strips of wood. She jumped, braced herself against the walls and punched upward. In moments she had ripped a hole big enough and pushed through into a crawlspace between the ceiling and the flat roof of the building. The roof was thicker and made of some flexible material she couldn't get through.

Behind her, through the ceiling, she saw Mercedes Smith being escorted from the building. The bitch had kept her talking deliberately. Chloe wondered briefly whether she had been telling the truth about not knowing Chloe was there, or whether she usually went around with a squad of soldiers in tow.

They were doing something. She couldn't see what it was. Some sort of device. A bomb? With Mercedes out of the way they really could blow the place up.

She moved forward. Ahead there was only the wall but she wanted to get as far away as possible from any explosion. Not that she expected to survive it.

The men were pulling out, she could see them leaving. Mercedes was no longer in sight. Her wing hurt and she could feel it throbbing with her heartbeat.

How could she escape? She reached the wall. Beyond she could see nothing but empty space. She clicked her fingers hopelessly. There was another room below her that had not been part of the clinic. The building had been split and this was separate. She doubted it would protect her from an explosion. The soldiers were efficient and probably had people watching the building in case she did manage to get out.

She was sweating despite the cold.

She pushed against the underside of the roof at the edge but she could see it was bonded to the wall. She would have to be a dozen times stronger to be able to make it through there.

She made a hole and went down headfirst, turning as she fell and landing on her feet. Rats scurried away in surprise. The place was filled with rubbish: old plastic bags, papers, bits of metal and wood. There was a heater in the corner. A door led to the outside. She would have risked a bullet but she couldn't get it open. Panic set in. She had no idea how much time she had.

She snapped her fingers in irritation—and something echoed strangely. There was an open space here somewhere. And it was big enough for her, but all the rubbish diffused the location. She grabbed an old nail from the ground, tapped it against the metal of the small furnace. The metal clink penetrated everything and she saw it. In the far corner: a grid in the floor. She ran across to it, cleared the surface and tapped the metal. It went deep but it was narrow. Not intended for a person.

But what difference did it make? She either got blown up in the attempt or waited here to die.

The grid was packed with dirt around its edges and refused to move. She had seen a metal pole behind a pile of wood in the corner. She grabbed it and used it as a lever. She almost despaired, before, with a slurping creak, it shifted and opened. It looked old. Much older than the building she was in.

No time for archaeology.

She went down feet first and made it as far as her hips, then her coat bunched up. She almost couldn't push herself back up.

She stripped off her coat and her top layers of jumpers. Her wings came free and flexed of their own accord. She made a bundle of clothes in her coat—she located some nylon cord, dirty but as strong as ever—and tied up the bundle then made a loose knot around her ankle: She was damned if she was going to end up without a coat again.

The black hole beckoned. She knelt beside it and stretched her wings forward so they pointed above her head, bent over and went down headfirst, dragging the coat behind her.

Chapter 21

Chloe

By pressing her elbows against the sides she could stop herself falling. Then she realised that her wings were doing the same job; it felt weird, controlling them that way, but it worked. She was not falling headlong. Not that she liked going headfirst. She had a pretty good idea of the sort of unpleasantness she was going to fall into.

The air roared. She was blinded by sound. Heat poured around her and ripped her breath from her. She covered her face with her hands as flames licked her skin. She did not fall. Her aching wings held her.

Air sucked back and pulled the cold, damp, foul-smelling atmosphere from below.

Barely thinking, she struggled down the final distance and fell into the sewer, her coat landing on top of her.

How arrogant are they? I need to keep moving.

She climbed awkwardly to her feet. Her hearing had gone again; she knew—hoped—it would come back like last time, but once again she was blind in the dark. There was only the slightest trickle of water in the bottom of the brick drain.

There are so few people now, compared with before.

The shape of the sewer was strange, she had expected something circular but this was narrow at the bottom and wider near the top and she had not the slightest idea why. It made it hard to walk and forced her feet into the stream.

Since she had no idea which way to go, she just chose a direction. It was not as cold down here as it had been on the surface, so she carried her bundle. The surface of the coat seemed brittle, she guessed where the flames had touched it—it must have protected her—but other than that it seemed intact.

They would try to find her body and when they didn't they would know she had escaped. How long it would take them was anybody's guess. A couple of hours? More?

She stumbled on.

The air grew colder and, at the same time, a whining sound grew in her ears. A second tunnel joined hers, adding its stream of water, then she saw daylight reflecting round a bend. Less than a minute later she stood at the end of the sewer tunnel looking out on to a semi-frozen river tumbling across in front of her from left to right. She could see a road, bridges in both directions. The opposite bank rose up to a brick wall and there were low buildings beyond it.

The roaring of the river was the first thing she heard but the unfocused sounds did nothing to help her acoustic vision.

The water from the sewer simply tumbled out into the river and there was an accumulation of slick ice where it landed. If she had been in the mood she might have thought it looked quite attractive.

She found the bullet hole in her coat and other clothes. The ache was in her right wing but it seemed to be subsiding. Perhaps it hadn't been that bad. She had been lucky. Again.

She got dressed and tucked her wings out of sight.

The idea that she might be able to fly horrified her. Then she reminded herself that Mercedes Smith had told her she wasn't a freak—she might have been lying, but that was what Dog had been trying to tell her. She now wished she had listened, perhaps even gone with him.

But things hadn't really changed. She needed to rescue her friend, whatever she was turning into, and those other girls—especially if it meant they were not going to die either. She had a suspicion their captors wouldn't tell them the truth, because the last thing prisoners needed was hope.

She plunged her hands into her coat pocket and found the piece of paper she had picked up.

NEW LIFE CONSULTANCY proclaimed the letterhead, and there were two addresses. One of them was the place she had just escaped from. The other was in Alderley Edge, Cheshire. It made sense; there was no way that the small clinic would have carried out any complex genetic manipulation. That would be at this other address.

Hopefully.

It was her only lead. The only problem was that Alderley Edge was miles away.

Chapter 22

Melinda

'Shut up,' hissed Vanessa.

They had had to put up with her all morning. For some reason the tests had been cancelled and, while they were not allowed to leave the room assigned for meals, they had been left to their own devices. It had been some of the most tedious hours Melinda had ever spent, especially with the constant griping from Vanessa. To distract herself she focused on trying to make the electrics oscillate.

Melinda didn't like to think badly of people but she really didn't like the girl. And the teeth, in that angular face, were unnerving. She was like something out of a werewolf movie.

'*Canidae*,' she said at one point. 'Not a dog, not a wolf. Fox.'

'What are you talking about?'

'Me,' she said. 'I'm talking about me. I heard them talking once. I have fox in me.'

But that was earlier. This latest interruption from Vanessa was just another in a long line of irritating outbursts. She had better hearing and they couldn't ignore the fact, so they shut up and let her listen.

They just stared at the walls, the ceiling, the door, Vanessa herself who stood by the door, her head leaning against the wall with her eyes closed.

'Any chance you could both stop breathing?'

Melinda and Lucy exchanged glances. Lucy's comment earlier about leaving Vanessa behind if they had a chance to get out was looking more attractive. She could happily strangle her, after rendering her unconscious with a judicious zap to the head, of course.

After a few minutes, Vanessa yawned as she ambled back to the table and sat on the edge. Like Melinda she only had a light dressing gown over her hospital clothes. Melinda doubted they would have anything that fitted Lucy's bulky form. She went out in all the wrong places. In some ways she was glad she didn't know what Lucy had looked like before, so she didn't judge what she had become.

But she never complained about it. Melinda wasn't sure if that was a good thing, or a bad thing.

'Couldn't get much,' said Vanessa, her back to the guard. She had been well-behaved for a couple of days so they had backed off a bit. 'And it was only one half of a phone call.'

'Well?' said Lucy. She was not good at disguising her dislike of Vanessa, but then she'd had to put up with her for longer.

'He was saying he doesn't want to move us. Arguing with the bloke at the other end.'

'Did they say why?'

'Trouble on the outside. Police and Purity, apparently.'

'We always knew this wasn't the Purity,' said Melinda.

Vanessa gave a pitying look. 'Obviously.'

Melinda frowned. 'Were you ever put into quarantine?'

'No!'

'Then don't claim you know the difference,' said Melinda trying not to shout. 'It's fucking horrible.'

Vanessa grinned. 'Swearing are we, Miss Goody Two-Shoes?'

'You don't know what it's like,' said Melinda.

'Whatever.'

'If they're thinking of moving us then the police must be closing in.'

'They'd only have to look at the death rate,' said Vanessa. 'And we've all helped in that area.'

'They can just hide that,' said Lucy. 'When you've got as much money and power as they have.'

All three were silent for a short while, then Melinda said, 'They might decide they don't need us—or it's too dangerous to move us.'

'They'll just gas us,' said Vanessa.

'Only if they think they can keep us locked up at the next location. Maybe we're too dangerous.'

'I am.'

'And yet they didn't kill you, did they? So perhaps they didn't think you were very dangerous after all.'

Vanessa stood up and leaned over the table towards Melinda. 'Want to try me, electric girl? I'll tear your bloody throat out. See how much zap you've got when you're missing a head!'

Lucy's hand clamped around Vanessa's wrist. Melinda could see her trying to break the grip without losing her cool. Lucy's arm didn't move.

'Sit down, Nessa.'

'Vix.'

'What?'

'I want you to call me Vix.'

'That's not your name.'

'I'll choose any fucking name I want for myself,' said Vanessa. Her wrist and hand below the grip were turning white, making the freckles stand out. 'I've got a fox in me, so I'll be Vix, short for vixen.'

'I'll call you V,' said Lucy. 'And if you want to believe it stands for Vixen, Vix or just plain Vanessa, that's your choice. Now, sit down.'

Lucy released her arm. Vanessa sat down and rubbed the place where Lucy's grip had left livid white and red marks.

Melinda went to the water cooler and topped up her mug. She sat and brought the mug to her lips. 'We have to get out of here.'

'Who died and made you boss?'

'For god's sake, Vanessa!'

'Vix.'

'I don't care. Can we just think about what I just said?' She glanced at the camera and took a real sip this time. 'How and when.'

They argued for the next two hours. Lucy and Melinda tried to discuss and Vanessa argued. Sometimes she would argue against a point she had just made when they agreed with her.

Finally, Melinda and Lucy were happy enough with their ideas. 'And if you want to join in, Vix, then we would love to have you along.'

'I'll think about it.'

And that was that.

Vanessa decided she wanted to go back to her room, leaving the others on their own.

'Do you think she'll tell on us?' Melinda said staring at the door that Vanessa and the guard had disappeared through.

'No,' said Lucy. 'She's a total pain in the arse, but she wants out as much as we do. And she knows she can't do it on her own.'

'It's a lot of energy to put out,' she said after a while.

'You'll be fine.'

Lucy smiled. 'So, what are you going to call yourself?'

Melinda laughed. 'Vanessa's crazy.'

'Electric Girl?'

'Miss Electron?'

'Zap Woman.'

'Eel Girl.'

'Eel?'

'I figured it out. If Vanessa has fox in her, I must have electric eel.'

'That's not even a mammal.'

Melinda shrugged. 'It's the only thing I could think of that actually has batteries.'

Melinda looked at her friend. The folded skin so thick it moved like hardened leather. If she wore no clothes nobody would even notice. Outside, in the real world, she would never be able to fit in. But they would notice the bump on the forehead, which was developing a point. And the only name that fitted was *unicorn*.

Melinda thought of her parents. They would be terrified she was dead, but when they knew what she was, and that she would be dead soon anyway, they would suffer all over again. Was it right to do that to them?

She had been over this a hundred times already in the darkest hours of the night. Was it fair to give them hope only to have it dashed away?

'Do you want to see your parents again?' she asked quietly.

Lucy's eyes were the one thing that still looked completely normal. They started to moisten.

'I want to see them,' she said and wiped away the tears with fingers that were like rocks. 'I don't know if they would want to see me.'

Melinda nodded. 'I'm sure they would.'

Lucy's mouth creased into a wry smile. 'Nice of you to say so.'

'I have a friend, Chloe, her dad runs the local FreakWatch. If anything happened to her he really would be freaked.'

'My parents are okay, I guess,' said Lucy. 'They don't do anything like that, but I just don't know if they could cope with *this*.'

Melinda nodded. She wasn't sure how much she had changed physically, if at all. With her it was mostly on the inside.

'But we can't stay here.'

'No,' said Lucy in agreement. 'If I'm going to die, I want to do it out there.'

Chapter 23

Mitchell

Yates was in the main office outside the meeting room, waving at him behind Graham's back. It looked as if something had come up and he needed to talk to him directly, but that wasn't going to be easy.

And then there was the interesting problem of Special Agent Graham himself. When he walked into the office today he was sporting even more injuries than he had after the explosion. Mitchell was sure no one else had noticed, they did not have cause to be in the man's presence as much as Mitchell himself. But there was no question that the man had fresh cuts on his left cheek.

Someone must have put them there, but Graham was not claiming victory over some nefarious element. He hadn't captured a freak, or put anybody else into quarantine. Instead he acted as if nothing had happened. To Mitchell's experienced mind that meant only one thing: a woman. And as far as he knew there was only one woman in Manchester who knew Graham.

Which was interesting in itself, because he had Yates's report on the visit to Sapphire Kepple. Lament had been at pains to point out that he had advised against it, or, at least, to contact Mitchell first. Just as well he hadn't because Mitchell would have forbidden him to see her.

And then he would have done it anyway and Mitchell might have been forced to suspend him.

No. Yates played that one just right. They had an ally in that area, though perhaps not a very stable one. Going up against Utopia Genetics was not easy.

Then there had been the brief meeting with Superintendent Dix. He was not happy about it at all, but had given Mitchell permission to do his job.

Which brought him back to Yates trying to grab his attention.

'So,' said Mitchell to Graham, 'do you have any ideas as to our next course of action?'

Graham had been staring at his tablet, but whether he was actually looking at anything Mitchell was not sure. He had barely touched the screen.

'I don't think there's anything left for me here,' he said.

'Really? I thought you were keen to track down Chloe Dark.'

'Just another freak. Nothing you can't handle.'

'What about the girls?'

'We've wiped out the people who had them. They'll probably starve to death or die of cold.'

Mitchell hesitated. 'And you're happy with that outcome?'

'Happy? No, but there's nothing left, is there?'

'Just plodding police work.'

'Exactly,' said Graham finally looking up. 'You do what you're good at and you'll find their bodies eventually I expect. Maybe in a week, a month, year.'

'We do like closure,' said Mitchell. 'You'll be leaving then?'

Graham smiled thinly. 'Trying to get rid of me? I don't blame you.' He sighed. 'There's a few things I have to wrap up in regard to the death of Paul Banner. The kind of responsibilities you have when you're the senior officer.'

'I expect you were hoping for a commendation, or at least a promotion out of this?'

'Can't win them all.'

'Oh,' said Mitchell in apparent surprise, as if he'd just noticed. 'It looks like Yates wants something, if you don't mind?'

Graham turned in his seat. Yates was standing outside looking along the corridor, not into the room. 'He's one of the loose ends.'

'Yates?'

'What was he doing at Paul Banner's house?'

'You can ask him now if you like.'

'No,' said Graham and waved his hand dismissively. 'You talk to him. I imagine he'll say exactly what he put in his report.'

Mitchell resisted the temptation to point out that's precisely how it should be, and took the opportunity to leave the room. He and Yates moved towards the lifts in order to be out of Graham's direct line of sight.

'What is it?'

'Lament's found something.'

'All right. You go in and see Graham, I'll talk to Lament.'

'Why do I have to see Graham?'

'He wants to know why you were at Paul Banner's house.'

'It's in my report.'

'I know, just do it.'

'Fine.'

'And don't be flippant, he's got no sense of humour, it will go badly.'

'Sir.' Yates flipped him a mock salute and turned on his heel.

There was a car waiting for him at the lift exit that drove to the back of the car park before Lament appeared on the screen.

'I know where they are.'

Mitchell sat up. 'How sure are you?'

'Very.'

'Where?'

'Aren't you going to ask me how I found out?'

'Do I need to know?'

'Knowledge is power.'

'Very well,' said Mitchell. 'Tell it the way you want.'

'Once we had determined Utopia Genetics was behind the kidnappings, I was able to focus on their properties. I did note there had been a serious upswing in deaths of their research staff in the last few weeks—since the most recent set of kidnappings. They had managed to give the impression those deaths were spread out across various sites, and if I hadn't been looking I wouldn't have noticed.'

'You're very clever.'

'I know. Then I made the assumption that if they are holding the girls it will be in a location outside the city.'

'That's a terrible assumption; there are plenty of deserted areas in the city itself.'

'I know. It didn't help.'

'So what did?'

'The explosion in Stockport.'

Mitchell frowned. 'What explosion?'

'Quite a big one around lunchtime.'

'I hadn't heard.'

'It wasn't that big.'

'Very funny.'

'Thank you,' said Lament. 'Someone is suppressing the news of it.'

'Xec?'

'No, someone else and I can't get round it. If I try to make it widely known my communication just vanishes.'

'That sounds like government-level interference.'

'I can't deny it,' said Lament. 'But they can't stop me knowing about it, at least its location, and that was the real giveaway.'

He stopped and Mitchell realised he was supposed to ask why. 'Why?'

'Before the plague it was the city office of a private IVF clinic.'

'IVF?'

'It's—'

'I know what it is, why is it important?'

'Because if you were going to mess with someone's DNA, what better time than when they are single-celled gametes.'

'Gametes?'

'Oh, you don't know that one? The male sperm and the female egg, they're gametes. When they join together they're called a zygote.'

'Is that important?'

'No. But the main centre for this IVF clinic was located at Alderley Edge.'

'And that property is currently owned by Utopia Genetics?'

'Exactly,' said Lament.

Mitchell noted Lament didn't sound disappointed that Mitchell had said it and not him. 'And what else?'

'The place is using a lot of power. It's a veritable hive of activity.'

'Not proof.'

'Apart from the signal.'

'Signal?'

Mitchell imagined Lament grinning very widely, this was clearly the clincher. 'Something is affecting the power lines and it's sending out Morse code.'

'S.O.S?'

'Yes!'

Mitchell fell silent. How in the world could one of those girls be causing the electricity cables to send a message? Then he remembered.

'Melinda Vogler. The electrical burns in the road.'

'I hadn't thought of that.'

'That,' said Mitchell, 'is why you are the rookie and I'm the Detective Inspector.' He paused as the rest fell into place.

'What do we now do, sir?'

'We'll raid them,' he said. 'I have Dix's agreement to do what we must. You need to pull in as many men as you can. We'll need to get a warrant as well.'

'Yes, sir.'

'And you need to do it without alerting Special Agent Graham.'

'He's going to find out.'

'He is, and I want to be the one to tell him, but when we're already on the way and everything is organised. I don't want some half-baked operation like his one.'

'How are you going to justify not telling him?'

'Need to know. And Lament?'

'Yes, sir.'

'Don't screw it up.'

'No, sir.'

Chapter 24

Mercedes

From her vantage point half a mile from the IVF clinic, Mercedes had watched the explosion. And got very angry.

'What the hell is going on?'

'The removal of Chloe Dark from the scene,' said Xec smoothly.

'And nobody's going to notice?'

'They may notice,' said Xec. 'But I am assured no one will be talking about it.'

'They were soldiers.'

'I really couldn't say. Plausible deniability, Mercedes. If the police come knocking you don't want to know what happened, and you don't know who did it. This car was never here.'

She watched the plume of black smoke rising from the white of the snow. So many people were dying and it was all Chloe Dark's fault. It was just as well she was dead herself. They could go back to the way things were, tracing Dr Newman's freaks and finding out what made them function when everything they had ever tried had failed.

There was a problem though. These most recent ones might be the last. She did not know how many freaks Dr Newman had produced, but they had usually appeared at this age and the plague had stopped him from being able to do anymore of his work. His death had finished it completely.

And the Utopia Genetics scientists still hadn't been able to figure it out.

Xec had driven her back to the tower. The other members of the board wanted a meeting. She didn't. All she wanted was some peace and quiet.

So she had a quiet lunch and watched the clouds scudding across the sky. It was going to be a clear night and the temperature would drop lower than it had so far this year.

Which was when Xec dropped his own bombshell.

'Mercedes?'

His voice sounded uncertain and a wave of panic went through her.

'What's wrong?'

'I think the police have found the lab.'

'You don't know?'

'I'm only getting fragmentary information. There seems to be something big going on tonight and there is some hint about it being to the south of the city.'

'Nothing from the Purity?'

'Either they don't know, or my contacts don't have access.'

'It could be anything,' she said. The last thing she needed now was even more trouble.

'If it were anything else, I would know what it was!'

Mercedes glanced up in surprise. Xec had never shouted before, and as far as she knew he never got angry.

'I've been blinded. The information coming in from my worms tells me nothing is happening. But the amount of activity is unquestionably building.'

'Have you been compromised?'

'I don't think so, but how would I know?'

Now he sounded scared. How could a wirehead be scared?

'What can you actually tell me, Xec?' she said carefully, trying not to cause him more stress.

The pause was much longer than she had ever waited. For the first time she wished he used a visual representation of himself on the screen. It had always seemed somehow magical to have a disembodied voice to do her bidding. Now she needed to see a face so that she could somehow empathise with him.

'I am trying to contact someone in the police force,' he said. 'I used to get information from them, but they were moved to a non-active role after an accident.'

'How long?'

'I don't know.'

How did you get a wirehead to calm down? She didn't even know where his physical body was kept, not that she wanted to see it. She had learned enough about the process, before the plague, to know more of their bodies were on the outside than in. The companies that provided biocyst computers did not advertise their locations for obvious reasons.

She made herself another cup of coffee and waited.

There were two simple possibilities: if the lab had not been found then there was nothing that needed to be done. If it had, they were in trouble. She needed to think of something.

'Given the travel time required then it is.'

Mercedes tried to parse Xec's comment and failed. 'What are you talking about?'

'What?'

'You said something. It was meaningless.'

'I ... yes, sorry,' he said. 'Thinking aloud.'

Since he did not actually speak out loud anyway that was redundant. 'Have you found something?'

'Yes,' he said. 'I mean, I think so. My contact has noted that all the off-duty men in the residence he helps to supervise have indicated they will be out this evening. He has heard them talking among themselves about a big raid related to cracking the kidnapping case.'

Mercedes put down her coffee mug.

'Shit,' she said. 'How much time have we got?'

'Vehicles will be arriving to collect them at nine in the evening.'

'Eleven at the earliest then.'

'I would think so.'

'Giving us a few hours,' said Mercedes.

'What's the emergency protocol for the site?'

'The usual: evacuation of non-critical personnel, specific destruction of all on-site files, incineration of all samples and assets. Dispersal of critical personnel with special treatment in some cases.'

Mercedes went into the lounge and looked up at the grey clouds. 'Still nothing from the Purity?'

'I don't think they know.'

'That's naughty,' said Mercedes, 'since their agent is supposed to be leading the kidnappings case.'

'It seems the police have chosen not to alert him.'

Mercedes smiled.

'All right, I want you to instigate the protocols. However, about the incineration of major assets, let's not do that just yet.'

'Mercedes?'
'We need them. There might not be any more.'

Chapter 25

Melinda

The air filled with a persistent and repetitive beep. It wasn't loud but the fact that it was some sort of alarm was obvious. Melinda looked at Lucy across the table.

'I've not heard that one before.'

The sound of a gun being cocked behind her made Melinda turn in her chair. The burner was holstered and her guard held a real gun. Although he held it on the two of them—Melinda wondered whether it would have any effect on Lucy—this did not stop him from looking around as if for help.

'What's going on?' she said, trying to keep her nervousness under control. Over the last few days the immediate threat she had felt had receded into the background. The agreement that if she cooperated everything would be okay had been honoured on both sides.

'Stay where you are!' he said. He seemed to be as nervous as she was. Lucy's hand landed on hers.

'It'll be fine,' said Lucy. 'Probably just a drill. They have had a couple.'

'But not this one.'

'Not this one.'

Another guard appeared; he too was holding his real gun. In the background two of the science staff were hurrying from somewhere to somewhere else. Melinda noticed an increase in the electrical activity, not that she had any idea what that meant.

The new guard muttered to the other one—Melinda wished Vanessa hadn't gone so soon as she could have heard what they were saying. Then she laughed at herself. At the time she had been grateful the girl had decided to leave.

'Move,' said the new guard. The other one deferred to his instructions and stood back so that he could cover them as they left the room. Too far away for Melinda to do anything.

They had discussed breaking out but had not counted on this. Was it a good thing or a bad one? She had no idea.

The alarm did not stop. Its persistence was unnerving. The volume just enough to be irritating. If only they had some clue as to what it was.

They went through a pair of double doors into the final corridor, the passages to the cells led off this one. If they were going to take advantage, this was the time. She had no opportunity to talk to Lucy, and even if Vanessa knew something, they couldn't ask her snice she was behind her own door. And Lucy's cell had been reinforced to hold her.

If it was just a drill they would be up against the entire security team. On the other hand, she could not stand this waiting any longer.

They stopped at the first passage. Lucy's room was at the end. The guards stood so that one of them could keep both of them covered while the other one went to open the door.

Melinda relaxed and closed her eyes. She opened her electrical sense to the surroundings. She needed something metal she could use as a conductor to put her pulse through.

The only thing she could feel was the cable lighting above her. It was not in a conduit but it was insulated. And over three feet above her head.

She stared at Lucy, willing her to look in her direction, but Lucy was staring at the guard. Was she thinking she could take him? Perhaps she could, the bullets might bounce off her skin.

Then there was an ear-piercing shriek that was a bit like a bark that reverberated up from Vanessa's room. The guard jerked his head in that direction. The pitch altered upwards and somehow intensified. A look of pain went across the guard's face. She couldn't agree more, the sound tore into her ears.

But with his attention distracted Lucy closed on him. She didn't hit him, she just kept moving. It was as if he weighed nothing. She swept him off his feet and slammed him into the wall. He slumped with a strained groan as the air was forced from his body. The gun went off. Vanessa's scream shut off.

There was only the alarm beep in the sudden quiet.

Melinda moved. She ran at Lucy and pointed at the cables. 'Get me up there!'

A bullet hit Lucy in the shoulder just as the blast of the shot echoed through the corridors. Melinda could see the impact that tore through the hospital gown. She expected to see blood, but there was no time and Lucy did not appear to have noticed she had been hit. Instead, she pulled back from the guard she'd crushed, turned toward Melinda, crouched and made her hands into a cradle.

Melinda stepped on to Lucy's hands and, almost before she had transferred her weight, Lucy stood up straight and

- 781 -

flung her upwards. Another shot rang out. Melinda had no idea where it went; she was concentrating on the wires coming at her too fast. Her head struck the ceiling. She reached out and caught hold, one hand each side of a light fitting.

The wires were ripped from the ceiling as she came back down. Her arms felt as if they were being pulled from their sockets. Her feet touched the ground and then Lucy hit her like a train, knocking the wind from her. Two more shots ricocheted from the walls as she fell to the ground further along the corridor.

One of the cables was ripped from her hand but she maintained her grip on the other. The lights further down the corridor had gone out abruptly. The ones back the way they had come were still alight and she could see the wire dangling.

'Do it!' said Lucy.

'I need that one.' Melinda pointed at the other cable.

'Typical.' With that Lucy jumped up. Holding her forearm across her eyes, she barrelled into the passage where the other guard fired off half a dozen shots at her. There was a thud and it went quiet.

There were shadows moving behind the double doors. Melinda got the terrible sense of *déjà vu*. This was where they applied enough fire power to stop them. But that was before she really knew what she could do—and she knew her batteries had been storing increasing amounts of power.

She grabbed the dangling cable; the wire-ends were bare where they had been ripped from the light fitting. She took one end in each hand and pulled them apart a little further. She could feel the electrical energy trying to push through her, somehow she could protect herself—the same way the burners didn't work.

Lucy appeared at a run. 'Get on with it!' Then she was past and heading down the next passage to Vanessa's cell.

Melinda relaxed. She summoned her power and let it go.

The electromagnetic pulse she generated made every metal object shine. The lights exploded. The guard's burner melted with an intense flash and he moaned in unconscious pain. The other guard's weapon went as well. Everything went dark.

There were repeated crashes behind her as Lucy smashed through Vanessa's door.

There were groans from the other side of the double doors, but she had no idea how many of them had been really incapacitated. They might still be dangerous and there would be others further on.

One thing she did know: she had blown the power throughout the base. The background sensation of electrical currents was gone. She had not even known she was aware of it before, but she recognised its absence.

She felt the electrical impulses of Vanessa come up behind her, followed by Lucy. She smiled to herself. She could tell the difference by the overall shape and it meant she could see people in the dark.

'Come on,' said Vanessa and ran past. Melinda stepped to the side so Lucy didn't run straight into her—she probably couldn't see a thing. They needed light.

Chapter 26

Mitchell

He knew something was wrong the moment Graham appeared at the back of the briefing room. He wasn't supposed to be here. Mitchell finished the briefing, indicating the time of departure as being nine. The team leaders climbed to their feet.

'Wait,' said Graham from the back.

They turned to look, then back at Mitchell who gave them a nod and they sat back down.

'Special Agent?'

'We go now.'

'I'm sorry?'

'We do not wait until nine. We go right now.' He looked at his watch. 'It's four-thirty. We will go now otherwise we will almost certainly lose our prize.'

'You have something to add to the briefing?'

'This rogue element of Utopia Genetics—an entirely unsanctioned unit run by their board member Alistair McCormack—is aware of the raid and even now is attempting to escape.'

'And you know this because...?'

'My sources are my own, DI Mitchell,' he said. 'I know you understand how important it is to protect one's sources.'

He peeled himself from the wall and walked slowly to the front between the chairs and tables.

'Suffice to say that my source is unimpeachable,' he said. 'And we need to move swiftly if we are to catch them in the act.'

'Yes, sir,' said Mitchell. He nodded once more to the men and they left.

Mitchell turned to Graham.

'And the girls?'

'Let's hope we can get to them in time,' said Graham. 'Even now this rogue element will be destroying all the evidence. Hence the reason we must move quickly to foil them.'

Mitchell sighed. He had been outmanoeuvred. There was only one conclusion that could be made: Utopia Genetics had become aware of their intention to raid and done a deal with the Purity.

'What has Utopia offered you?'

Graham smiled. 'I really have no idea where you get your fanciful ideas from.'

'I'll get the men on the road,' said Mitchell and headed for the door.

'Just one more thing,' said Graham.

Mitchell's heart sank. One more thing sounded like something very bad indeed.

'Once the area has been secured, a combined team of Purity and Utopia Genetics personnel will take control of any of those poor girls who are still alive.'

Mitchell said nothing as he left.

Chapter 27

Melinda

Melinda couldn't see what was happening, but she did see men with electrical impulses running in their nerves go dark after Vanessa did something. Meanwhile, Lucy was clinging to her arm with a grip that was probably light for her but like a vice for Melinda.

'For god's sake, Vanessa! Stop killing them!'

Melinda stopped a short distance up the corridor, away from the men.

'She's killing them?' asked Lucy from the blackness.

'Seriously? They were going to fucking kill you! Why do you even care?'

'Because we don't have to kill them,' said Melinda. 'Can't you just find a flashlight or something? That would be more useful. And you're wasting time, we need to get out.'

'Can't you see a battery?' said Lucy.

Melinda realised she should be able to, if they had them. But there was nothing. If there had been, she probably messed those up as well.

In the darkness there were shouts. She could make out the word 'lights' which seemed to occur often.

'Can you tell where we need to go to get out, Vanessa?'

'Vix.'

'Seriously?'

Silence.

'Can you tell where we need to go to get out, *Vix*?'

In silence, Vanessa moved ahead along the corridor. Melinda watched her outline moving away. She grabbed Lucy by the sleeve. 'Come on.'

Vanessa walked fast, almost jogging. Melinda had no idea where they were, but the sounds of people were getting louder. And there were flashlights flickering in the distance.

'Vanessa—Vix,' she hissed through her teeth.

The girl stopped. Melinda gave thanks.

'Do you know where you're going?'

'I can smell fresh air.'

The lights came on. In the distance she heard people cheering. Melinda blinked, dazzled. As soon as she could she looked around. There was nothing here she recognised.

And then the alarm started up again. This one she recognised, it was the one they had used when she had tried to break free.

'We need to go up,' said Vanessa. She hesitated. 'I don't know where the stairs are.'

Melinda managed to stop herself from making a comment.

At that moment there was a shout from a corridor junction further along. 'Found them!'

A double beam laced down the passage and hit Lucy. Vanessa ducked between the two of them.

Up? She could sense the electrics in the floor above. 'We need to get out of this corridor.' Another twin beam burned a hole in her clothes and she shivered as the power tried to flow through her. The beam flicked off. She smelled singed cotton and ozone.

Lucy must have heard her and smashed through a door. They piled through into an office.

'Well done,' said Vanessa looking around. 'Now we're really trapped.'

There was no other exit.

'Just shut up a minute,' said Melinda.

'Shut up yourself.'

'Please, *Vix*, I need to concentrate,' Melinda said and Vanessa didn't reply. 'Lucy, can you rip open the light switch?' It was done in a moment. Melinda stuck both hands into the wiring and zapped it. She didn't do it at maximum; she didn't want to hurt anyone else.

The lights went out again.

Cries of disappointment and anger went off in the distance.

'Just keep by the door and don't let them in.'

'My pleasure,' said Vanessa.

'Try not to kill anyone.'

'Spoilsport.' And then she was gone, out the door. Melinda sighed. The next floor up still had power, which was what she wanted. The buzzing from the lights and power cables tended to blur out any image of people, but she knew they were there. Which was when she noticed the gaps between the walls. Not every wall, but the one running behind this office—all the offices on this corridor—had a space of a couple of feet. The power cables were pegged on to each of them. The gap went up.

There was a man's cry then a burner beam slashed along the passage—she could see it clearly.

'No stairs needed,' said Melinda. 'Can you get through the back wall?'

The electronic shadow of Lucy pushed the furniture out of the way, dug her fingers into the wall and ripped away a panel. Another beam flashed and there was that unearthly howl again. Whatever they'd done to her, something had changed her vocal chords too.

'It goes up,' said Melinda. She shouted, 'Vix! Time to go!'

A voice floated back. 'Be right there, Mother.'

'Cow,' muttered Melinda.

'Heard that.'

'Let's go,' said Melinda. She squeezed into the gap after Lucy. They couldn't see what they were doing, but there were timber crosspieces that provided foot and handholds. If they could have seen it would have been easy.

There was no sign of Vanessa.

'Keep going,' said Melinda. 'There's another couple of floors of this.'

Light poked through the occasional gap but it was never enough to really help. Five minutes later they reached the top. Melinda tried to see which was the best side to exit, but in the end she just chose the one on the opposite side to the entrance. Lucy made a hole and they tumbled through one after the other.

'Can you rip the light switch out please?'

Lucy shook her head. 'They'll know what floor we're on if you kill the lights again.'

'Yeah, good thinking.'

She looked round this new office. It was bigger than the one below, with three desks. The drawers hung open. The cupboards had been stripped of their contents.

'What's going on?'

'They're getting out.'

'Because of us?'

Lucy shook her head. 'Perhaps we're being rescued.'

Melinda gave a grim smile then glanced at the hole in the wall. 'Where's bloody Vanessa?'

She went to the door and listened. There was noise of bustling and shouting but it wasn't close. The door wasn't locked and she looked out. The corridor was similar to the ones below, but here they were carpeted and had pictures on the wall. 'Very homely,' muttered Melinda.

She glanced back at one of the desks; her electrical sense had noticed the ironwork in its construction. There was a drawer with a short iron rod running through it. She pulled it out and handed it to Lucy. 'Can you get that bit of metal out?'

Lucy crushed the wood until the joints snapped, then ripped it apart. She handed Melinda the rod. 'Magic wand?'

Melinda shrugged. 'So I can put power through it if I need to zap something.'

Lucy nodded and her lips creased into a smile. 'Magic wand.'

Whatever it looked like, its weight was strangely comforting.

She peeked out again. Still nothing. 'We can't wait any longer,' she said. 'They'll be coming after us soon enough.'

The two of them stepped out into the corridor.

'Which way?' said Lucy.

Melinda wondered when she had been promoted to chief decision maker. 'I don't know. Maybe if we head for where there's the most noise, but try not to actually bump into anyone.'

'It'll be the last thing they bump into for a while,' said Lucy.

'Maybe we should try not to hurt anyone?'

'Vanessa was right, Melinda,' said Lucy. 'They are happy to kill us. What level of not-hurt-them are you aiming for? Not quite enough to stop them hurting us?'

'Why does this have to be my decision?'

Lucy shrugged. 'Someone has to make decisions; you ever tried to make a choice by committee?'

'But why me?'

'You started it when you made the first one. That made it your job.'

'But I'm not the one who does that, Chloe makes the decisions.'

'Who's Chloe?'

Melinda shook her head. 'Doesn't matter, she wanted to work in the Purity.'

'Really? She must be a total arsehole.'

'No, she's not, she's great.' Melinda wasn't quite sure how they'd got into this conversation; standing in the middle of a corridor, in the middle of the place they'd been held captive for weeks.

'Whatever.' Lucy glanced both ways. 'Either way is as good as the other as far as I'm concerned.'

'This way,' said Melinda and headed towards the most noise. She held her iron rod as if it really was a magic wand she could use to defend herself. Lucy followed, lumbering along at her shoulder.

The carpet muffled the sound of their feet, but the noise of the crowd grew to a point where they couldn't have been heard anyway. As they approached the next junction, someone crossed in front of them moving quickly. And didn't look their way.

Melinda panicked and pushed open a door they were passing and went inside. She barely registered the sign on the door saying 'SECURITY MONITORING'.

Her electrical sense was overwhelmed for a moment. The room was full of electrical equipment and ranks of monitors curving round a single chair. The man in the chair stared at them.

Melinda raised her wand. 'Try to alert anyone and I'll zap you.'

He didn't move.

'Tell me you understand.'

'I understand,' he said clearly.

'Can you tie him up, Lucy?'

'Pleasure.'

She walked over to the chair which was mounted on a small pedestal. Even sitting down he was taller than her.

'Where do you keep your spare cables?' she said.

He stared at her—was it possible the ones at this level didn't know what was beneath them?

Lucy snapped her hand around his forearm. He cried out in pain. 'Got your attention now? Spare cables?'

He still didn't respond.

Lucy frowned. The creasing of her forehead was impressive. 'I've heard,' she said in a conversational tone, 'that knocking someone unconscious with a blow to the head is really quite serious. It usually means they've got a cracked skull. That might not be true, but unless you tell me where your spare cables are we'll put that to the test. I'm game, are you?'

Hesitantly he pointed to a drawer at the bottom of a storage unit behind her.

'Come on,' she said and pulled him off the chair. He staggered as she yanked him across the room. The drawer did contain spare cables, and Lucy set about tying him up.

Meanwhile Melinda was staring at the screens. It looked like organised chaos, with people putting papers through shredders in one shot. Burning containers outside—she noted the snow, they weren't dressed for that—people piling into coaches. It looked like there must be a couple of hundred people working here. A huge operation.

Then she saw a camera that was trained on what seemed to be the reception and groaned.

She closed her eyes. 'Untie him, Lucy.'

'What? No. I've been practising my knots. I used to be good at them.'

'Untie him!'

'No!'

'Look.' She pointed at the screen showing the reception area. Where Vanessa lay on the ground wriggling as she tried to get free of her bonds. She was screaming. Five goons had their guns aimed at her. Real guns.

'Stupid cow,' said Lucy.

Melinda looked over. She half-expected Lucy to claim they should leave without Vanessa, but she was untying the guard.

The energy went out of Melinda.

Episode VI: Utopia

Chapter 1

Chloe

Eleven miles in the snow to a destination she only had the vaguest idea of: Alderley Edge. The only thing she knew about it was from a novel she had read when she was young, about King Arthur and weird Norse creatures. That scene where the children were crawling through a tight underground tunnel. She hated that. She could feel the claustrophobia of it just remembering it.

Her mind was wandering. She had been running for an hour at least and was way out beyond the edge of the city. The roads were empty and the scenery consisted of snow-covered fields and woods composed of skeletal trees. She hadn't eaten and she was starving.

But the idea that she might have found her friend at last kept her energised, kept her moving.

She knew Alderley Edge was near the town of Wilmslow—in the old days that was where all the rich people lived—and there were signposts to Wilmslow. She had got herself on to the motorway. It combined a flat terrain with gentle curves which meant she could manage her best speed. She had no idea how fast she was going. The only problem was the occasional car buried beneath the snow.

When the plague first caused trouble the cars had been cleared from the roads, but a point was reached when there weren't even people enough to do that. So even now there were cars, rusted and rotted, that littered the roads least used. Like motorways.

It was dark now, of course, and the clouds prevented the moon casting any light, but the signs were huge. She found the sign to Wilmslow and left the motorway. The road she was following dived down into a tunnel. There were lights above it and she could see the runways of the airport. She came to a halt.

The military ran the airport, and she did not fancy the tunnel.

There was no good choice. At least in the tunnel she could use her acoustic sense properly. She did not want to catch the attention of the army, or air force. She had no idea which used it—or even if they were different anymore. They were not in the public eye very much.

So she went under. She dialled her speed back to a jog, there was no snow here but she was so light on her feet she still had to click her fingers to make enough noise to see by. There were two tunnels side by side; each would have taken two lanes of traffic, had a rectangular cross-section and was made from concrete. They carried sound very well.

There was a gentle curve that stopped her from seeing too far. It wasn't a long tunnel and she made it all the way through in about a minute, although as she approached the exit she could see that the road was lit by artificial light and the tunnel started again after another fifty yards or so. She came to a stop.

If the road was lit, somebody would be watching.

There might be no snow in the tunnel but it was just as cold as outside. There was a wind blowing through. There was no choice. She could go back and try to find a way round the airport but that would cost her time. Perhaps a lot of time if she got lost again.

But this was only fifty yards. If she took it at full speed she could cover it in less than five seconds. They wouldn't be expecting her and by the time they reacted she would be gone.

She backed up until she couldn't see the exit anymore. Then she ran. Leaning forward so she was in a constant, barely controlled, fall.

In moments she rocketed out on to the snow and her shoes immediately slipped. She tumbled forward and her wings strained against the coat, desperately trying to help balance her. She felt the cloth rip a little. But she was trained to fall, so she went over into a ball. Her shoulders hit the ground. She turned over and thrust upwards. Her jujitsu-trained responses were too powerful and she shot into the air.

It took her barely a moment to realise she was going to hit the wall above the tunnel.

She flattened her body out, tilted her head down and spread her arms to provide balance. Her wings tore at the coat again but she held them flat. Her angle forced her flight into a new trajectory and she shot just beneath the overhang. She pulled up her legs and landed at a run, then launched herself again.

That gave them a show, I hope someone was watching.

Except she didn't, she hoped the lights were just a feature of having the runways lit up. But even as she thought it she knew it to be a lie. The runways had not been lit, only that space.

The second tunnel was shorter. Moments later she was out of it and running towards Wilmslow again. For the next mile the road curved through fields and then into Wilmslow proper. There was no one about. She had not expected there to be; there might be a small conclave of people somewhere but there would not be many. She reached the centre and found a sign pointing south to Alderley Edge and set off again.

Then she heard wolves. Since the cold winters came there had been a solid bridge every winter between the British Isles and the mainland. Wolves, wild boar and bears had made a comeback after the human population was reduced. Although some said there had been wolves in Scotland anyway and the weather drove them south.

She made her way south through Wilmslow and there was a short stretch of countryside. She had wondered how she was going to find the right place in Alderley Edge, but high up, atop a ridge—the Edge itself—was a mass of lights. She guessed that to be the place.

Chapter 2

Mitchell

With Graham's insistence on the revised schedule, there had been no time for preparation. The only thing Mitchell was grateful for was that night had fallen by the time they arrived.

The cavalcade of police vehicles wound their way up through the deserted streets of Alderley Edge. The place they were heading was based in an old manor building. The road shrank in width to a single lane and was piled with snow, but from the tyre marks there had been traffic here recently. Some of it heavy.

'I have deployed men round to the back of the building,' said Lament. 'The next turning takes us to the house.'

Mitchell stared out of the window. The walls on each side were old and high. He could see only the roof of another building which looked modern.

'What's this one?'

'Another abandoned residence. Built on the land previously owned by the manor.'

'Get a squad to check it.'

'Yes, sir.'

Graham stirred from his cocoon of smugness. 'You're wasting men, Mitchell. We'll need everyone in the main building.'

'And if they decided to hide in that building and escape after we'd gone past?'

Mitchell knew Graham had done some sort of deal with Utopia Genetics.

'There's a helipad on the southwest corner of the estate,' said Lament. 'Not in our records.'

Graham stirred again. 'We'll take that, Mitchell.'

The vehicle took a sharp left, its wheels slipping on the snow, then the chains bit in and it moved up.

'Aren't you going to turn the lights off?' said Graham.

'We're police, not a hit squad,' said Mitchell. 'We want to arrest people, not kill them from the shadows.'

The windscreen cracked as something fast-moving hit it.

'I don't think they want to be arrested,' said Graham.

'This vehicle is fully equipped with bullet-proof glass and panels,' said Lament. 'Firing coming from the main building.'

'Get in as close as you can. Their sniper won't be able to shoot at that angle.'

'Yes, sir.'

The gate from the narrow lane into the building's grounds was closed. Lament took no notice and accelerated. The vehicle ripped through, though the sudden loss of speed jerked all the passengers forward. The five cars behind pulled through as well and fanned out. One of them stopped and a marksman took up a position at the rear.

Mitchell activated the car's loudspeaker and his voice boomed across the snow. 'THIS IS THE POLICE. EVERYONE ON THIS PROPERTY SHOULD CONSIDER THEMSELVES UNDER ARREST. LAY

DOWN ANY WEAPONS AND LIE DOWN WHERE
YOU ARE. ANY ATTEMPT TO RESIST WILL BE MET
WITH LETHAL FORCE.'

'I thought you didn't want to kill anyone,' said Graham.

'That's why they get a warning,' said Mitchell.

The other cars headed for the main building while
Lament took a path leading to the southwest corner. The
helipad was lit up and several men stood around a helicopter.
The rotors were beginning to turn.

A spray of machine gun bullets splattered across the
windscreen, leaving scarred trails. The car stopped.

'Orders, sir?' asked Lament.

'Immobilise the chopper.'

The car spun its wheels on the snow and then kicked
forward.

'What the hell are you doing?' shouted Graham.

'I hope you're buckled up,' said Mitchell. Intense
gunfire raked across the windshield and bodywork; cracks
appeared in the glass but they were closing on the helicopter
fast. The men with the guns held their ground until the
moment they realised the car was not going to stop. They
threw themselves out of its path as it bumped violently up on
to the pad, took less than a second to cross the distance and
slammed into the helicopter's body. The skid on their side
collapsed under the strain and the body tilted.

The car shuddered to a halt. Mitchell unclipped his
seatbelt and threw himself out of the car.

The rotors were winding down, but they were now at
an angle and lethal. Staying low, Mitchell moved outside their
circle and trained his gun on the figures now crawling in the
snow. There was still too much noise to give the warning

protocol. But the kidnappers could see the weapon. They left theirs on the ground and knelt up with their hands behind their heads.

Graham got out, looking with concern at the rotors.

The sound of gunfire erupted from the main building and then cut off.

Keeping his gun on the kneeling men, Mitchell looked up at the one passenger in the helicopter. He recognised the face: Alistair McCormack.

This was going to be difficult. Utopia controlled most of the medical equipment in the city. They couldn't be closed down. The people needed to have something they could trust. The face of Mercedes Smith was that symbol.

Mitchell gestured for the man to get out, and he climbed down.

Graham came over, taking note to get between Mitchell and his prey.

'Well done, DI Mitchell. I'll be sure to recommend a commendation for the help you've been to the Purity today.'

McCormack climbed shakily down from the cockpit. He clung on to the struts as if he was going to fall over at any time.

'This is a police operation, Special Agent.'

'I'm afraid not.'

'This is my collar.'

'We can't have you destabilising the city, and something like this would be potentially bad for the entire country.'

'You can't.'

'I can, and it's already done,' said Graham. 'A rogue element of Utopia Genetics, run by Alistair McCormack—' he nodded in the man's direction '—was operating on freaks outside the jurisdiction of the Purity. Of course the rest of the board knew nothing of it. We have apprehended him, and he, with his entire operation, will be tried by the Purity. Those who knew no better will be quarantined for a period to ensure there is no infection. Those who were complicit will be dealt with appropriately.'

'The press?'

'Will know nothing. If they find out, they will also find they are not permitted to print it.' Graham turned to Mitchell with an earnest look. 'This is for the country, and for the people. We cannot let their faith in our power be undermined.' Not waiting for a response, Graham strode off across the snow towards the main house.

Mitchell shivered. The icy wind was blowing in across the Cheshire Plain from the Irish Sea.

He felt empty and frozen inside.

On automatic, he went over to the men on the ground and cuffed them. He muttered their rights as he did so. Even though, under the Purity's jurisdiction, they had none. McCormack did not move and Mitchell cuffed him as well.

'Were you operating on your own, McCormack?' said Mitchell.

'It was my operation,' he said.

'Who else on Utopia's board knew?'

The man shook his head. But Mitchell did not need him to say it. He knew the truth. That was the deal that Mercedes Smith had struck with Graham. Utopia gives up McCormack, Graham gets the credit for the arrests.

'Where are the girls, McCormack?'

He shook his head again.

'Listen, you Scottish git, I don't care that you've been sold out by Utopia to cover their tracks. I don't care that the Purity will take you and all your people. I just want the girls— I know what they are, I know they aren't S.I.D.'

McCormack looked up finally, stared at Mitchell's face only inches from his.

'Did you kill them, McCormack?'

'They're alive.'

Mitchell's eye was caught by a movement behind McCormack. Something human-sized moved in the trees and then was gone.

Chapter 3

Chloe

She had spent the night in a nearby house. The owners had clearly been very well-to-do before it was abandoned. As she had before, she spent the night sleeping on a table to stay off the mouldy furnishings. Though she searched, she had been unable to find one of those airtight bags, but there was a small office which was cosy enough. Being out of the way, the place had not been pillaged and there were tins of food in the kitchen that were still edible, although they tasted of metal. Perhaps the owners had been so rich they had flown off to somewhere warm to save themselves from the plague. Maybe they were still there.

After a few hours' sleep, and more tinned breakfast, she crept out of the house and took to the trees again. The place had been crawling with police last night and she had seen Mitchell take down the helicopter. She had heard every word of his conversation with that Alistair McCormack. She had no idea who he was, but that he was high up in Utopia Genetics was clear. As was the deceit of the Purity guy. They just played games with people's lives—with her friend's life.

There were still a few police here as she went round the building. The trees were good for travel, but she tended to shake the snow from the branches which was too obvious. She went down to ground level and then crossed the open space to the building.

Inside, the echoes were sufficient to keep her out of the way of the men guarding the place. They were bored and uninterested. They didn't expect anyone to be sneaking around.

She found her way down to each of the levels and scouted them as best she could. There was nothing to find. There were no records, no computers, nothing working. The lower levels had no light at all, though it made little difference to her. She found the cells and the bodies. They were stone cold now. She rummaged in their pockets looking for some sort of light because the one thing she couldn't do with her hearing was read. One of the dead men had smoked—a very expensive vice these days—and had a lighter. She grinned humourlessly; the movies she watched so avidly had taught her a lot about how things had been pre-plague.

It took a few attempts to get the lighter to work. She knew the theory that she had to snap the trigger, but it was awkward and the damn thing kept slipping.

Finally she succeeded and instantly wished she hadn't. The bodies she had been searching had their throats ripped out. She looked round nervously. She knew there was nothing alive nearby except her, but the idea there might be a murderous freak lurking nearby in the dark was something she found hard to shake. She had had enough experience of them recently.

She stared at the cable that had been ripped from the ceiling. It was hard to imagine why it was like that—perhaps there was something wrong with it.

Using the light sparingly she went down each side passage to the cell doors. The first was open and had the name Lucy Grainger scrawled on a board just beside the door. One of the kidnapped girls. The next door had been smashed in from the outside. Vanessa Cooper. Another of the kidnapped girls. Chloe almost held her breath as she took the third passage. Again the door was unlocked.

Melinda Vogler.

She almost wept as she ran her fingers across the words. McCormack had said they were alive. Chloe let the light die and put the lighter in her pocket. It was stealing, but it would be useful if she needed to light a fire. Until it ran out.

There had always been the thought in the back of her mind Melinda might be dead. She didn't want to believe it. And now she had come so close to rescuing her and failed. If she had been just an hour earlier. The police had not had time to clear the place, so the kidnappers—Utopia Genetics— must have done it themselves. They must have known the police were on their way and cleared out, and taken the girls with them.

But the dead bodies, the broken door, the torn-down cabling? They told a different story, but Chloe had no idea what it was. Perhaps they had an insane freak down here as well, and it had done the damage? She shook her head. It didn't matter.

Melinda had been here, now she was gone, but she was alive.

All Chloe had to do was find out where Utopia had taken them this time. They must have done it in a rush— which was why some of their people had been caught. So wherever they had taken them, it wouldn't be as well hidden or as well equipped.

But she had no idea where to start.

She had managed to get this far on her own but she had been lucky. There had been a trail to follow, but she had no access to the net anymore. She wasn't part of the system. She pulled off the hat and held it. It needed cleaning.

She was not afraid of being found, she was underground and she hadn't seen a riffy pylon anywhere nearby. Looked like it was true what people said about the countryside.

There had been a toilet back in the tunnels. She went back to it and found there was still hot water in the pipes. Using the soap in the dispenser she washed herself and cleaned the hat.

It might even be possible to live somewhere like this for a while. If one house had tinned food, others would too. There might even be enough to last until spring. But she couldn't stay here now, she couldn't wait. She had to find Melinda.

She headed up to the top level, and back into the fresh air. Daylight filtered through into the dark corridors and she found a room with a sofa. Not the dank, rotting furniture of the abandoned homes but one that was dry, well cushioned and comfortable.

Settled on her side so her wings didn't get in the way, she went over the conversation Mitchell had had with the Purity guy. He said that Purity was taking over the whole thing. That would be dangerous for Melinda and the others, but they hadn't been captured. Mitchell hadn't seemed happy about that. Also, he had not turned her in. Was he on her side?

It was a comforting thought if it was true. Right now she needed friends, but she did not have any way of contacting him. And Miss Kepple, she had helped as well, even though she was the Purity. Chloe got the feeling Sapphire was slightly crazy, but she thought the teacher was in love with her, so that was two.

Then there was Dog, and he said there were others like her—which meant Vanessa Cooper and Lucy Grainger were probably like them as well. Dog wanted to help; he had been pissed off when she'd refused to go with him. So that was even more.

Maybe she wasn't alone, except she didn't know how to contact any of them. Except Sapphire, and to do that she needed access to the net. The only place she knew where she could do that was Aunt Mary's house. She didn't want to put her in any more danger, but it was the only option she had.

First she'd go back to that house and stock up on food. The hunger was not as bad as it had been, perhaps her wings had finally stopped developing, but it was still there.

Chapter 4

Mitchell

Mitchell put on the kettle and heaped two measures of his best leaf tea into the pot. He gave the milk a sniff, it was still okay.

Then he peeled off his coat and jacket. He was exhausted. He hadn't slept.

And there was little prospect of sleep now. He'd had Lament send a message to Yates to meet him here and he was due. There wasn't much time.

The knock on his door came sooner than expected, then he realised it was because he had dozed off. The water was boiling and he poured it into the teapot before going to the door.

Yates did not look as if he'd spent the entire night awake. He had even found time to shave.

'Boss,' he said by way of greeting and Mitchell let him inside. Yates dropped his coat on the back of his chair and accepted the tea in a delicate china cup. If he thought it odd, he said nothing.

'We nearly had them,' he said. 'If we'd been a little bit earlier.'

'The whole thing was a set-up,' said Mitchell. His head ached with tiredness. He was going to have to get a couple of hours. Not like Yates, who could spend the night bouncing around on his forensic lover and manage the entire day as if he'd had eight hours of beauty sleep. Mitchell remembered what it was like to be young. 'Graham and Mercedes Smith had done a deal. She threw McCormack to the wolves and she gets to keep everything else. Maybe share it with Graham personally, maybe with the Purity as a whole. Either way it was timed so we caught the sacrificial goat but none of the important stuff.'

'Nice deal for them.'

'And crap deal for us.'

They sipped their tea in silence. Mitchell savoured it, with what he was thinking it might be the last chance he got to have a decent cup. But he didn't want Yates to suffer the same fate.

'I'm approving your leave,' he said.

Yates put down the cup. 'Trying to get rid of me?'

'This could get awkward, no reason for you to be taken down at the same time.'

'That's very thoughtful, boss, but not necessary.'

'Necessary? No, but it's a good idea. If I screw this up we need someone in the office who knows what happened and can hold it all together.'

Yates laughed. 'Me? You think I'm the person for that gig? I just want the easy life.'

'Easy life? That's why you became a copper?'

Yates pointed out of the nearest window at nothing in particular. 'Have you seen what it's like for ordinary people out there? You're old and you were in the force before the trouble started. You already had your life laid out. Not me, I grew up in that shit. My folks worked every hour of the day to put food on the table. My dad died of pneumonia because there weren't any antibiotics.

'I hate the old movies and the books. Never read them. You know why, sir? Because they feed us a pack of lies. They make us think we've still got a civilisation here, that we're still masters of the world. It's just a pack of lies. We're barely hanging on. Why did I become a copper? Because it was the only way I could get out of that shit. Police are privileged. We get more and better stuff. Even that crap they feed us in the cafeteria, better than the rest.

'Look at Ellen Lomax, she doesn't have a life. She has an existence. So don't try to appeal to my judgement, or my better nature, or my conscience because I don't have one. I do the best job I can that's good enough to keep me here. That allows me to carry that warrant card, because I don't want to live the life they have out there.'

Mitchell looked at him. Yates was breathing heavily, and that was the longest speech Mitchell ever heard him make.

'You finished?'

Yates nodded.

'I want you to do it because you're the best copper I know.'

'Fuck you.'

'Very likely.'

'What are you planning?'

'I'm just going to do my job.'

'You're still going after the girls?'

'McCormack, seeing as how he had been set up so sweet and clean, was willing to divulge a little information. Most importantly, the girls are still alive, which means Purity and Utopia have spirited them away somewhere.'

Yates shrugged. 'But that place was their best option, wherever they put them now won't be so well equipped.'

'And that's why I have to move quickly, before they get a chance to move them somewhere really secure.'

'You still have to find them.'

'I'm sure Lament can manage that.' He took another drink of his tea. 'And Chloe Dark was there.'

'In the place?'

'Lurking around in the trees when I stopped McCormack. I don't know how much she heard, but she left as soon as McCormack admitted the girls were alive.'

'So she's still after them too. Good friend to have.'

Mitchell nodded.

'But there's no way she can handle Purity and Utopia on her own,' said Yates.

'She's pretty tough.'

Yates grinned. 'And hard to kill.'

Mitchell put down his empty cup. 'She might be able to find them eventually. She might even be able to get into the place where they're being held. I don't see her being able to get out again alive. They'll be waiting for her.'

'Or you.'

'They're too arrogant to see me as a threat. I'm just a plod who follows orders.'

'So what do you want me to do, boss?'

'I told you. Take some leave. I suggested a similar strategy to Ria MacDonald's senior. He was amenable.'

'Really? Ria says they're overworked.'

'They are,' said Mitchell. 'But I said I'd owe him a favour.'

'So you're arranging a little getaway for me and my girl,' said Yates. 'That's very kind.'

'Get yourself lost, Harry. Just for a few days until this has blown over.'

'And that's an order?'

'That's an order.'

Chapter 5

Mercedes

'Sit down, everyone,' she said as the door closed with a gentle click behind her.

'Room secure, Miss Smith,' said Xec.

'Off-the-record protocol, Xec.'

The background buzz went silent and she looked round at the two remaining members of the board. They did not look happy and she did not blame them. She was almost surprised that Kingsley was still here, she knew she hadn't ordered his removal and yet of all the members of the board he had been the one she least wanted to keep.

Marketing was almost a redundant concept. They provided services to people who had no choice. They could not choose whether they should be tested or not; nor could they choose who to accept that testing from. In Manchester it was Utopia Genetics who ran everything related to DNA and it was her face that smiled reassuringly from the billboards. She did not need Kingsley Upton.

But here he was.

'What's going on, Mercedes?'

'What do you mean, Kingsley?'

'Where is McCormack?'

'He was taken into custody by the Purity for running an unapproved research operation.'

'Jesus.'

She had expected him to shout and bluster the way he usually did, but this was a changed man.

'What about the rest of us?' He looked over at Margaret. 'Us two. Are you planning to get rid of us as well?'

'I don't know what you mean,' she said. 'What you don't seem to realise, Kingsley, is that I have just saved your miserable life.'

She looked at Margaret. She had a temper when she let it out, but mostly she had it under control and had never had an outburst in one of these meetings. She tended to reserve it for her underlings.

'What do you think, Margaret?'

'I'm trying not to,' she said. 'I thought at the very least I could trust you.'

'Neither of you seem to be getting the point. If I hadn't made an agreement with the Purity over this issue we would all be on our way to quarantine, or worse. Is that what you want, because I can have Xec set up a call with Special Agent Graham and I can explain to him how I've discovered that you two were also in on it with McCormack.'

Margaret's expression was one of disgust. 'Is that it? Is this what you've come to? Turning on your friends to save your own hide?'

'In this instance, saving my hide also saves yours,' said Mercedes carefully. She had not expected this level of animosity. They would be upset, of course, but why didn't they understand? 'I can make that call any time I like.'

'We could also make that call,' said Kingsley.

Mercedes laughed. 'You think he'd believe you?'

Kingsley's face went red with suppressed anger.

'Look, we're all in the same boat here. The Purity need Utopia to maintain control and provide information in this region. They don't want to see any infighting. And it's my face the people identify with the company. I'm the one they trust. I have protected our business by giving them McCormack, and for that we get to keep our research and our assets. We just need to share what we know with them.'

Margaret shook her head. 'You can't. If you tell the Purity there are non-S.I.D freaks running around, created by a rogue geneticist in Manchester, they'll tear the city apart. Every child will be suspect. They'll destroy everything.'

'I can assure you I have no intention of letting them know what we know. Even McCormack's trusted researchers didn't know the real truth. And they failed to discover anything.'

Mercedes frowned. They failed to get to the bottom of Newman's work. All that money and all that effort.

'All we have to do is imply that these kids are very early infectees who did not manifest in the same way as everyone else. A strain of S.I.D that failed to take hold. That will satisfy the Purity because it keeps everything simple. It's still S.I.D and they're still killing freaks—and it doesn't mean every child in Manchester is affected. We simply continue to monitor just as we always have done.'

Kingsley seemed to have relaxed a little. 'You really think they'll buy that?'

'You're the marketing expert, Kingsley. Perhaps you can come up with something more convincing?'

'I'll think about it.'

'Good.'

Margaret shifted in her chair. 'What do you want me to do, Mercedes?'

'Just keep everything running.'

'These new floors you're opening up?'

'We needed somewhere to put everything temporarily. We'll probably have to turn the assets over to the Purity, but I want to get as much information out of them before we do that.'

'What are we going to do without McCormack?'

'To be honest, Margaret, I had been considering replacing him even before all this happened. His team has made very little progress; all they've managed is a more accurate way of identifying the injected DNA.'

Kingsley looked up. 'That could be useful for S.I.D. If we knew what people were infected with perhaps we could find some way of dealing with it?'

'I'll pass your thoughts on,' said Mercedes. 'When we've found a replacement.'

The room went quiet. She missed McCormack; she had liked his accent even if it was exaggerated. And Paul had always provided a solid and balanced alternative view. When all was said and done, Kingsley wasn't very bright and Margaret, for all her suppressed anger, simply did as she was told.

'What about the Purity representative?' asked Kingsley.

'We'll get one, of course,' said Mercedes. 'But they won't be part of this committee for obvious reasons, at least not until we have been able to see where their loyalties lie.'

She stood up. 'I think that's all for now. I have to deal with Special Agent Graham for the time being and I will keep you up-to-date on anything relevant.'

The walk back to her room seemed shorter than usual. Everything seemed to be working out.

At least there was no Chloe Dark to mess things up anymore.

Chapter 6

Mitchell

He had had a shave, slept for a couple of hours and put on a clean suit. The drive in had been slow and relaxed. It seemed Lament hadn't pulled any strings to get there faster.

Everyone knew there were multiple wireheads running different aspects of the city. For people who never came into close contact with them they were almost mythological. Like animistic gods that lived in the rocks, the river, or the storm. Each wirehead with its own domain.

But for someone like Mitchell, who dealt with one on a daily basis, it made him wonder. He had no idea where they got the bodies from to run the wirehead systems. And it seemed as if there was some sort of wirehead economy, or even ecology, that ran out of sight of humans. It was hard to think of the wireheads as human, even though essentially that's what they were. And as a policeman he knew what people could be like.

It had been an impulse to take the control away from computer systems that could fail and not be rebooted. The logic was flawed. Everyone knew that—everyone who understood what a wirehead was knew the system was just as flawed as before. There were stories of wireheads going mad in other cities. Or just dying unexpectedly. And it took a while to bring a new one online.

But now the human population was as dependent on the wirehead systems as the pre-plague society had been on the computer systems that had failed when their systems operators had died, or simply disappeared.

Lament had as good as admitted he gave and received favours from other wireheads. Which meant the entire law enforcement system was at the whim of someone who had been wired up, and might go mad or die. Or even just become disillusioned with the way things were. Not only did Lament have control of all the records—though the management company insisted they were backed up—but he had the experience and that was not something that could be backed up.

The car arrived at the police HQ without Lament going mad or, apparently, any deals being made with the traffic control wirehead to get them where they wanted to go more quickly.

The summons from Superintendent Dix had come early, but Mitchell had expected it. He was there to report on the state of the case, now apparently closed, and what was to be done next, if anything.

It was going to be a difficult meeting. Dix may have been a good copper once, but he was a politician now. Even if they did believe in the same things, their priorities differed.

Mitchell opened the door to Dix's office when instructed and went through. It was the same as it had ever been. Dix was wearing the same suit, and the same blue tie. Or if it wasn't the same one it was an identical twin.

'Sit down, David.'

Mitchell sat in the hard-backed chair opposite his boss. Dix continued to read what might have been a report on the events of the previous evening. Not Mitchell's, since he had not had time write one. Dix sighed and leaned back in his chair as if the weight of the world was on his shoulders. Perhaps in some ways it was, but he had the disadvantage of being unable to act on that responsibility. He was forced to stay in his office. Mitchell had never accepted promotion because he did not want to be trapped that way.

'So, nobody wins.'

'Sir?'

'Utopia Genetics loses its position of superiority—we know them for what they are. The Purity fails to rescue the kidnapped girls in any meaningful way. They certainly can't use this case to take control, far too messed up, and with their Utopia representative committing suicide.' He shook his head as if agreeing with himself. 'No, nobody wins.'

He didn't have to mention that they too had failed. Not for want of trying, under ridiculous constraints.

'What now, sir?'

'I want your opinion, David, off the record.'

Mitchell stretched his back and sat up. 'Sir?'

'Oh come on, David. I don't have to read your report to know that you will be leaving out much of what happened.' He lifted up the report he had been looking at and then dropped it again. 'This stuff is useless. Everyone whitewashes, and tries to make it look as if they did their very best and that it was everyone else who failed to hold up their end.' He leaned forward. 'I know you won't do that. I need to know the truth. How can I deal with Purity and Utopia if I don't know what's really going on?' He sat back again. 'Even I can read between the lines. Each one of your clues turned into a dead-end, literally. And that includes—what's his name—Paul Banner?'

'It wasn't suicide.'

'Of course not. That would be far too convenient.'

'I'm just a policeman, sir.'

'As I am, David, as I am.' The man seemed to deflate as if his own words punctured his bravado and posturing. Perhaps he just wanted to be that again.

Mitchell decided now was the time. 'I do not consider the case to be closed.'

Dix looked at him but did not respond.

'The ones who kidnapped the girls are still holding them. The law is still being broken. And if Purity no longer wishes to supervise the case for their purposes, then we are free to act.'

'And that's what you want to do?'

'We have forced their hand. They will have moved the girls to a temporary location. It will be easier to find them.'

The flame of the policeman was extinguished in Dix as he contemplated the consequences of continuing to pursue the case.

'I can't allow it, David,' he said. 'If you're right, then Purity has changed sides. And that is not a game I am willing to play. And not a game I am willing to risk my best officers on. You can do more good going back to the way things were.'

'Allowing the law we are sworn to uphold to be flouted by anyone with sufficient power?'

'That's the way it's always been, David. We have to choose the fights we can win.'

'Is that your final decision on the matter, sir?'

'It is.'

Dix turned his attention to his desk. He moved the report to the side and read a different one. His lack of subtlety was almost amusing.

Mitchell climbed to his feet and headed for the door. He was very tired.

'David?'

'Yes, sir?'

'Take a week off.'

'I would rather not.'

'It's an order.'

'Sir.'

Mitchell closed the door to the office behind him. And sighed. He was going to lose his job. It did not require any kind of decision to choose to go after the girls that were still being held because he had never had any doubt about what he intended to do.

The meeting had all been for Dix's sake. Mitchell had not expected him to condone any further investigation, but he had to have been given the chance. It also meant he could state, in all honesty, that any action Mitchell took was nothing to do with him.

Still, it would have been nice if Dix could have had the strength to become the man he wanted to be. Had been.

But Mitchell had been ordered to take leave and there was a form to be filled out for that.

Some things never changed.

Chapter 7

Mercedes

It was broad daylight and a weak sun was trying to press its way through the grey-white of the clouds. But still she could feel the prisoners below her, in exactly the place she did not want them to be. Mercedes often went about her apartment in bare feet, but not now. She wore heavy boots as if there were some way of protecting herself from their presence.

She had told herself it was immature and childish a dozen times. That didn't work, and she was not sure but the amount of gin she had consumed seemed to make things worse. She felt as if they were crawling through the walls. Once in a while she would turn suddenly expecting to see their distorted limbs reaching for her.

'How long before we can prepare somewhere else, Xec?' she said very suddenly and so loudly she surprised herself. She got control. 'The assets. How soon before we can move them to a more secure facility?'

'I have a building identified in Ramsbottom.'

'How long?'

'It will take at least a week to prepare the cells. The girls—'

'Assets!'

'The assets demonstrated a much higher level of development than had been noted in the tests.'

'I don't care about that.' She realised she was almost screaming again. She took a breath. 'I am very uncomfortable with them so close.'

'Would you prefer to stay somewhere else?'

'This is my home, Xec, I won't be pushed out by freaks.'

'I just thought—'

'Don't.'

'It's what I'm paid for.'

Mercedes sat down heavily. *I'm drunk.* 'I'm sorry, Xec. You're right, but I would not feel comfortable elsewhere and being here is more secure than anywhere else. I need to be safe.'

'You confronted Chloe Dark at the clinic.'

That was true. And now she was dead. The only good freak is a dead freak. Even Newman's freaks.

She was losing it again. She sat forward and held the glass firmly in her paws. *Hands.* The rational side of her knew what the problem was. It had been the witch's cat that scared her. She had been at her friend's house, when she was young, before all the trouble, and they brought the cat to show her— and it had too many toes.

The terror had numbed her. Her friend dumped the animal on her lap. She had tried to get away but it had clung on, digging its too-many claws into her through her skirt.

She had run, almost been hit by a car on the street when she ran out, and hidden in the woods. They found her up a tree because she was scared of the creepy crawlies in the ground. And people had laughed.

'They won't fucking laugh at me!' she said and threw her glass at the wall where it smashed satisfyingly. 'I'm not scared.'

'Mercedes?'

'I want to see them.'

Face your fears. That's what they always say. Well, she was in control of her fears.

'The assets?'

'Of course the fucking assets, you stupid wirehead. You've got them drugged, right?'

'They have been sedated.'

'Well, let me see them. So I know they can't come crawling out of the walls and stick their claws into me.'

'Of course, Mercedes. Do you want some coffee first?'

'Are you saying I'm inebriated?'

'Yes.'

'Well, screw you! If I can say inebriated, I can look at some drugged freaks. Right?'

'If that's what you want.'

'I'm the boss.'

'Yes.'

It took half an hour, and a strong coffee, before she was in the lift heading down. The freaks were being housed ten levels down. She couldn't really complain they were close. And it would take them a lot of work to get up through the walls that far. She shook her head, and then regretted it. She needed to get a grip. They weren't coming through the walls. This was not some stupid horror movie. She didn't even watch horror movies. Or read stories like that.

She didn't read much at all. She hated romances the most because they were full of promises that would never come true.

There were a couple of security guards on hand and one of the research staff. A man in his forties, he looked nervous as she emerged from the lift. Just as he should. Xec had told her they'd had most of the staff clear the floor so she wouldn't have to deal with anyone staring.

The freaks were being kept in separate offices. All the rooms on this level had been emptied years ago, so new furniture, including beds for the freaks, had been brought in. The walls were the usually flimsy constructions of pre-plague days, but that didn't matter. There was no intention of allowing these freaks to wake up until they were locked away in suitable accommodations.

The sign on the door for the first one said 'Vanessa Cooper'. The killer. Mercedes stood by the bed. The freak looked normal apart from the stupid number of freckles.

'Show me the teeth,' she said and the man pulled back the lips to reveal the mouth that had ripped out the throats of so many people. Better to put this rabid animal out of her misery. 'Anything else?'

'Nothing on the outside, no other gross feature modifications, Mrs Smith.'

Mercedes walked away. 'Miss Smith.'

'Sorry.'

Lucy Grainger was an abomination. She barely looked human. The folds of thick skin were plated with a hard exoskeleton, and she had lost her hair. The face, inside a cocoon of leather, looked human enough, but even her hands and feet had fused so she had fewer fingers and toes—three of each. And the horn in the middle of her forehead.

'The DNA structural changes go all the way,' he said in that excited way scientists got when they were discussing their own subject. 'Modification to the LRP5 protein has given her bones that are not only able to support her increased mass, but are virtually impossible to break.'

'Where did that come from?'

'I'm sorry...?'

'These changes always come from somewhere. What animal?'

'Human.'

'I beg your pardon?'

'It's a known human mutation, Miss Smith. Not the skin, obviously, but the LRP5 can be mutated to either decrease or increase bone density. This is an increase.'

'Obviously.'

He went silent.

Just a monster, thought Mercedes. 'Does it have increased resistance to the sedative?'

'Oh no, none of them do. Apart from the specific structural changes they are essentially human.'

Not human enough.

The final one could have passed for a completely ordinary human. But in some ways she was the weirdest of them all. The human battery. Melinda Vogler.

'I am particularly fascinated by this one,' said the man.

'I am not interested in your hobbies.'

He did not utter another word.

Mercedes stared down at the innocent and relaxed face. She hated them.

Chapter 8

Dog

Mr Mendelssohn had got the report when he sat down at his desk first thing in the morning. Delia had come across in the car—not because the weather was bad, but because she brought breakfast—and sat down with him and Jason to eat when the phone rang.

So Dog had scoffed down the rest of his, and possibly some of Jason's when he wasn't paying attention, pulled on his coat and trotted across to the house. He hadn't spent this much time at Mr Mendelssohn's house in one stretch in, well, ever. And he was enjoying it.

It wasn't just that he got to play with Delia—and now Jason—every day, it was that he really felt he'd found his place. His pack was together.

Mr Mendelssohn was very clever. Dog knew this because he had managed to carve out his part of the criminal world and no one ever got upset with him or wanted to send their men to kill him. He could have been the leader of all the crime factions, but he didn't want that. And that was clever too, even though Dog thought that if he'd been in that position he *would* have wanted to be at the top. But it was clever of Mr Mendelssohn because people weren't trying to kill him over that either.

Mostly people didn't want to kill him. They just wanted to do business with him.

'Shut the door. Sit.'

Dog did as he was told.

There was a map on the desk that Mr Mendelssohn was looking at. From the glance Dog had got it was the area around Knutsford.

'Do you know Alderley Edge?'

'I know where it is, sir, I haven't been there.'

'Something happened on the Edge last night. Lights, a police raid, and lots of traffic out before that.'

'Yes, sir.'

'I want you to go and check it out.'

'Why?'

'What?'

'Sorry, sir, I was just wondering why. We're all quite content here at the moment, everybody's relaxed, not much happens during the cold.' He saw from Mr Mendelssohn's expression that perhaps he was not saying the right things. 'Does it matter?'

'You will go and check it out.'

'Yes, sir,' said Dog. 'I'll take the freak-boy. He's quiet and sneaky.'

'Very well.'

'Perhaps Delia—'

'Get out!'

'Yes, sir.'

Dog got out.

Under the instructions of Delia, her father had allowed them to acquire some new clothes, particularly for Jason. He didn't suffer from the cold in the same way, but he needed a good-sized hoodie for his face.

'I asked him if you could come,' said Dog.

Delia shook her head. 'You're an idiot. He's never going to let me go out on something like this. You know I'm not even allowed out of the grounds to go to...' she groped for an idea of something she might go out for '...the shops.'

'He can't keep you locked up forever.'

She gave him a *you think?* look.

'Be careful,' she said and looked at Jason, his face hidden in the shadows of the hood. She didn't mind his weird tentacle nose any more. 'Both of you.'

'Of course, Mummy,' said Dog.

She slapped him on the arm.

The car was waiting for them outside the studio building. Mr Mendelssohn wanted the information as soon as possible, so he wasn't going to wait for them to travel the six miles there and the same back on foot. The car took them to Chelford, two miles south of Alderley Edge, and dropped them off by the train station, long abandoned.

Jason was not as fit as Dog, and his legs were shorter. Dog knew he could have covered the distance in less than twenty minutes, but in the end it took twice that.

Mr Mendelssohn had shown them, as close as possible, the location of the incident and it got them into the area. But for him, and probably the freak-boy, it was close enough. He could still smell the gunfire, burnt papers and a bunch of other scents you only get where there's been trouble. Even blood; human blood.

They tracked it without difficulty up the hill to the top of Edge. They crouched in the bushes on the edge of the grounds and looked at the building, and the damaged helicopter. He couldn't tell if anyone was still here.

'Can you smell anyone?' he asked Jason.

Jason tapped him on the arm so he had to turn. Jason nodded and pointed at his bum.

'You can smell someone's fart?'

Jason nodded again.

'Lovely.'

Dog sniffed the air. If there was a trace of it he couldn't detect it. Maybe Jason was having a joke. Then he heard someone's voice carrying through the still air. Okay, maybe he did smell a fart.

'Can you get in there without anyone seeing you?'

Jason put his head to one side. *You're asking* me *that question?*

'Hey, don't criticise, there'd be hell to pay if I lost you. Delia would be really pissed off, and her dad would put all that money you owe back on to me.'

Jason just stared.

'Yeah, and your mum would probably kill me.'

Jason slid away so fast he left only a blur. He headed round the border of the trees and bushes, probably planning to come in on the blind side. Assuming there was a blind side. So Dog went the other way, realising as he did so he hadn't arranged a place to meet with Jason after they had finished.

Never mind. They had noses, they'd find each other.

It was when he reached the trees near the helicopter that he smelled her. Chloe Dark. She had been here. The scent was stronger in the trees. So he climbed, awkwardly. He preferred the ground. He found the place where her scent was strongest. She had stayed here for a while, and she had a good view of the helipad. Still, it was at least twelve hours ago. She would be hard to track.

Perhaps Jason could do it.

Dog wasn't the idiot Delia claimed, he made jokes about it but he knew Jason could smell a hell of a lot better than Dog himself. There was no time to waste. They needed to get after her.

Right now.

Where was Jason?

There was a sudden shot from inside the building. Dog didn't pause to think. He threw himself toward the house. He shot past the abandoned helicopter and realised that he could smell Mitchell. Everyone was here, apparently, except for him.

His feet crunched in the crisp snow but he didn't try to move more quietly. The sound wouldn't carry and he could hear most of the noise coming from inside the house. Two men shouting. No, more than two, and if he wasn't mistaken they were in a lower level.

He ran through the main door, only pausing to push open the sprung inner door. It flew back but he managed to grab it before it slammed into the wall. He muttered in pain; he'd caught his nail in the wood. He shoved his finger in his mouth and stood trying to get an idea of what was going on.

The smells came to him: lots of men, and some women; incinerated papers; burner scars on flesh, wood and plaster; fear and sweat; *and Chloe Dark*. Her scent was stronger and more recent, maybe only a couple of hours. That was good, she had stayed around after leaving her scent on the tree. Perhaps he wouldn't need Jason after all.

He moved forward through an open door into a hall. The place was a mess. There had been equipment, chairs and desks. What was left was wrecked.

The voices had stopped shouting. He could hear a murmur in the distance, but they were not close.

Mitchell had been in here as well. He had moved around a lot, but Chloe had come from only one direction and gone out one way. He was fully attuned to her, just as he was to Mitchell, and he could trail her easily through the confused air.

There was a passage and stairs. But it was as he entered the passage he caught another scent. He stopped and tasted the air. No, not one, it was three other scents. Female. Young. And they had the same smell as him—the special smell. He grinned. Three more like Jason, Delia and Chloe?

Now that really was a pack.

Chloe's trail crossed theirs—which was much older by over twelve hours—she had used the stairs but they hadn't. He tracked them to the office with the shattered wall.

Nice work, he thought. The damaged wall carried the scent of one of the three. There was something about one of the others he didn't like. He couldn't quite put his finger on it. He kept his ears open. The men were moving about on the second floor down. Dog went into the wall gap and climbed down. Light pierced through in places and it was just enough.

He froze as someone less than a couple of yards from him shouted, 'Clear!' But there was a wall between them. The person moved out of the room and Dog continued down. There was another hole ripped in the wall here and the scent of the three new freaks was much clearer. There had been fewer people down here to confuse things.

Dog examined the piece of the wall lying on the floor. It wasn't particularly tough, but he didn't think he would be able to put finger marks into it—if those were finger marks.

He wasn't sure what had made them, must be one weird freak.

There was the sound of feet on the stairs. Whoever it was was searching the place systematically. They must have seen Jason.

Dog hurried but it was easy to follow the scent trail now, and Chloe's was overlaid. And Jason's on top of that.

And the smell of death.

Bodies lying in a corner with their throats torn out. He tilted his head on one side. There was part of him that said he should be disgusted, but there was the other part that suggested this might be a food source and worth remembering.

He shook his head. The bodies did not disgust him but he really mustn't think of them as a light snack. He got closer. Only one of the three scents was associated with the deaths.

He suddenly recognised it and he wrinkled his nose in disgust. There was no mistaking it, one of the girls was a fox, and he really didn't like foxes. And they didn't like him.

The acrid smell of stomach acid hit him as he went through the next door. Jason was crouched in a corner. He'd been sick. Dog cocked an ear to the searchers, they were still a way back.

'Hey, kid.'

Jason didn't move. Freak-boy must have a delicate stomach. Dog frowned, he wasn't sure what to do. Delia would have known.

'Come on, we got to keep moving before those boys catch up with us.'

It was difficult. If Jason could talk it would be easier.

Dog knelt down beside him and put his hand on Jason's shoulder. The boy flinched. He was shaking.

It was difficult to understand why he was behaving like this.

'Jason, we have to leave.'

Dog didn't want to leave. This was where the girls had been kept. He wanted to go into the rooms here and smell each one thoroughly. He wanted them to become part of him so he would always recognise them even if it was the slightest scent.

'Whoever did this is gone.' He shook his head. Jason would know that. He knew the person who made the smell had left hours ago. 'They aren't here now.' But if he was acting like this it must be because he felt like he would be attacked now.

The voices were getting closer.

'Jason, you have to be brave. Like you were when we grabbed that truck. You were good. You helped a lot.'

The footsteps were clear now. And the voices. They were cautious, expecting to corner the intruder here because there was nowhere left to hide.

'Jason, please, I need your help. I have to find Chloe Dark. I can't do it without you.'

Jason finally turned his head and his eyes shone out of the dark of the hood.

'You're better than me,' said Dog.

A shadow crossed the window in the door.

'Poor bastards, we need to kill the fucking freak that did this.'

Jason was up and at the door in a flash. Dog cringed. They needed a plan, not this.

Dog scrambled to his feet as Jason flung the double doors back and stood there.

'Shit!'

'What the—'

Jason moved forward as Dog reached him. The two men stood there, open mouthed and staring at the grotesque mockery of Jason's face. Both held guns. One of them was pointed at Jason. There was a blur and then it was pointing at the ceiling.

'Hey, boys!' said Dog and leapt at the other one. He struck him in the stomach with his weight behind him. The man went down. Dog turned and jumped on to the back of the other and grabbed his gun arm, pulling it back.

The shot went off and ricocheted off the walls. But Dog kept pulling and this one went down too.

'Run!'

Dog hared off along the dead straight corridor. This didn't please him because they made easy targets, but it would take them a moment to recover enough to fire.

The room he was looking for came up on the right. Just as Jason went past him. *Kid can run.*

'In here,' he said and dived into the room as a gun went off. There was a terrifying moment when he wondered if Jason might have been hit, then he reappeared and ran in.

Dog pointed at the hole and then up. Jason was in and moving fast, but Dog could hear their attackers pounding after them. He slipped into the hole and slid to the right. Above him Jason was already nearing the upper level.

The head, shoulders and a hand carrying a gun came into view. Dog held his breath.

Don't look this way. Don't look this way. Don't look this way.

'They're getting away.'

The head pulled back.

'We'll never catch them.'

'You know who that was, right?'

'Tentacles?'

'No, the other one was Dog.'

'Mitchell's favourite?'

'That's the one.'

'Yeah, but the other one—did you see that face?'

'Real nasty freak.'

There was a long pause.

'You want to spend three months in quarantine?'

'Must have been a cat.'

'Or a rat.'

'Or nothing.'

'Nothing.'

They moved away and out of the room. Dog climbed.

All he had to do now was get Jason to follow Chloe's scent. They weren't far behind her. And Mr Mendelssohn would be very pleased when he came back with her and three more for the pack. Well, maybe two, the fox could stay out of it.

He grinned at how much credit he would get for this.

Chapter 9

Sapphire

Another day out of school. She wasn't sure she cared anymore. She stared at the piece of paper on the table in front of her. She had intended to write a to-do list but all she had done was doodled. Not quite true. There were the words 'To do' at the top and underlined. Item one was 'Find Chloe'.

That was as far as she had got. The rest of the sheet was covered with the girl's name over and over. Embellished with flowers and stars, and outlined multiple times. There was no more room for a list. Even though it had been doodling she had made a point of not drawing a love heart.

To do that would have made her no better than the children she saw in her classes with their silly crushes and lovelorn lives.

'I am no better than any of them,' she said out loud. And in the remaining large space she drew the outline of a love heart then shaded it to make it three dimensional. Finally she drew an arrow through the centre and blood dripping from it. At the arrow's point she wrote 'Chloe' and at the tail she put 'Sapphire'.

And finally she drew a line through Chloe's name.

The door buzzer rang. Someone downstairs.

She screwed up the sheet and tossed it in the direction of the bin. It missed.

Dragging herself to the door, she lifted the handset and pressed the button to communicate.

'Who is it?'

'Me.' The voice was distorted but she recognised it. Her stomach churned in hate.

'Fuck off, Chris.'

She released the button and was about to hang the handset back in the cradle when it buzzed again. There was a moment of hesitation and she put the phone on its hook and turned her back on the buzzing.

She couldn't concentrate now. He just kept buzzing.

For ten minutes she sat in her comfy chair staring at the window and he just kept buzzing. There would be a pause for a minute and she prayed he'd given up. But he didn't.

Furious with herself, and him, she stormed back to the handset.

'Just piss off, Chris. Seriously. I never want to see you again.'

'I just want to talk to you.'

'There is nothing that could come from your mouth that I want to hear.'

'I'm sorry.'

She hesitated, unable to decide what exactly to say. Half of her just wanted to rant at him, the other half wanted to kill him. Slowly.

'Sorry, is it?' The rant won out over murder. 'Really, you think that saying 'sorry' makes up for all your fucking abuse? You need to get this through your head. I hate you. And if I never see you again it'll be ten minutes too soon. You're a total prick. A nasty vicious bully.' She took a breath. 'And you have a tiny dick.'

She thought the end was a bit lame but it made her feel better. And it seemed to have shut him up.

'I just want to talk to you.'

'And you're stupid. And—' She paused. There was a thing on the tip of her tongue, she desperately wanted to say it but it was so daring, so risky, she was not sure she was brave enough. *Screw it.* '—you were beaten by the girl I love. She took your dick and shoved it up your arse. She's a thousand times the man you'll ever be.'

Silence. But he was still there, she could hear him breathing. Heavily.

'Chloe's dead.'

The fear began in her hands. Her fingers felt numb.

'She isn't...' I spoke to her only yesterday.

'I'm sorry.'

'She's not dead.' She began to shake. His voice so calm, so certain.

'An elite army unit. They had her pinned down in a building. They blew it up.'

'I would have heard.'

'It was hushed up.'

She remembered there had been something in the news about an old building in Stockport burning to the ground. 'No one was hurt. They said no one was hurt.'

'They say what they're told to say, Saffie, you know that.'

It couldn't be true. They had tried everything to get her and failed. She was better than all of them. It *couldn't* be true.

'I need to talk, Saffie.'

'Why?'

She felt something on her cheek. And brushed away a tear.

'Other things have happened. It affects me—and you.'

She sniffed and wiped her nose on her arm. *I need time to grieve.*

'You can't come up.'

'We can walk.'

'I'm not dressed.'

'I'll wait.'

She released the button. As she hung the handset back she missed and it fell with a thump on to the carpet.

She didn't bother picking it up.

Then her terminal buzzed with someone ringing. 'Why can't you leave me alone?' she yelled at it. But she recognised the name on the screen and sat down to take the call.

Sapphire nodded to the doorman—she didn't even know his name. Chris was waiting, sitting in the chair provided. It was a faded orange plastic in a style that encouraged you to lounge but provided no back support. It looked uncomfortable. *Good.*

Chris had decided to be a gentleman, it seemed. He opened the door for her and let her go first. Neither of them spoke a word as they stepped out on to the hardened snow. It was slippery and she had to walk slowly. He hovered at her shoulder. He didn't put his arm around her.

'What is it?' she said at last.

'I really am sorry about Chloe Dark.'

'No, you're not. You wanted her dead. You tried to kill her.'

'She was a freak.'

'Just don't even talk about her. You're a bastard. You don't care about anything or anybody except yourself. Don't pretend otherwise.'

He went silent. Sapphire looked at snow-encrusted buildings. Once upon a time this area had been one of the richest in Manchester. Then it had fallen on hard times and become one of the worst. The buildings had fallen into disrepair and they had never recovered. The snow gave them an ethereal quality. It made them look pleasant. At least for now.

'I'm staying in Manchester,' he said finally.

Her heart dropped. 'Why?'

'They are putting me on the Utopia Genetics board.'

'Aren't there a thousand people better qualified?'

The barb must have hit home because he was silent again.

'It's not what I want.'

'No,' she said. 'It's not what I want either. Two hundred miles is barely enough distance.'

'Do we have to be like this?'

'Yes.'

'Couldn't we at least be civil? We may have to talk to each other,' he said.

'There's nothing to keep me here. I'll apply for a transfer.'

'I can't stop you.'

'No,' she said. 'And when I give them my reasons maybe you won't have your position for much longer.'

'I told you I didn't want it anyway.'

'I know what you told me, but the truth is not something that comes easily to you, Chris.'

Silence again. Cars crunched past moving slowly. Sapphire felt her nose getting cold. The light was beginning to fade as the winter night drew in.

'Does Mercedes Smith know?'

'I was going to meet her.'

Sapphire held her breath, this was the moment. Let him have the space, give him the chance to suggest it. This was the chance she needed.

'Do you want to come?'

'Why would I want to do that?'

He sighed. 'Do you have to fight me all the time?'

'After all the things you've done to me, you shithead?'

'You don't have to come.'

'Oh no,' she said. 'I'll come with you just so I can warn her about you.'

'Don't do that.'

'What will you do to stop me, Chris?'

He stopped in the street and waved. A car she hadn't noticed behind them sped up and then came to a halt alongside.

He opened the door for her. She put her leg in and paused.

'If you touch me, I'll kill you.'

'Whatever you say, Saffie.'

Chapter 10

Chloe

It was still light when Chloe made it back to Didsbury. She
didn't go to look at her own house but, keeping her head
down and walking as if she were a normal person, she made
her way to her aunt's house.

When she got to the corner she leaned against a tree
and listened.

She could not detect anything out of the ordinary. No
cars sitting with their engines running, no one else loitering,
and no drones in range. It seemed they had given up.

It made sense if they thought she was dead and the
other girls had been taken into custody. There was a chance
that her aunt had been quarantined, but in truth Chloe didn't
need her. The only problem would be if the power had
already been cut off.

But there were lights in the house.

As if she was in no hurry, although she was straining
inside to move faster, she ambled up to the front door and
knocked.

It was her uncle that opened the door. He looked at her
face. He did not recognise her at first but she could see the
realisation dawn. The emotions went from delight to horror
in one smooth transition.

'Chloe,' he said so quietly even she had trouble hearing more than the hiss of his breath over his teeth. At least he didn't shout it out loud.

'Can I come in?'

He hesitated and looked out at the street.

'There's no police or the Purity. And no press.'

'Come in, sweetie,' he said and backed away to give her room. 'Your aunt's been worried sick.'

He closed the door and followed her as Chloe went through into the kitchen.

'Shall I take your coat?'

She thought about her wings, but they had already seen them. The wings had already ripped through the T-shirt and jumper she wore underneath, the coat was thicker and bearing up. It wasn't that she couldn't control them, but like arms they kept trying to help her with her balance.

He took the coat by the shoulders and she peeled herself out of it. After being confined for so long she couldn't help but stretch them.

Her aunt stared open-mouthed and her uncle, looking at them from behind, gasped.

'Oh, Chloe—' began her aunt.

Chloe moved her head from side to side, stretching her muscles.

'I wondered what bird you were going to be,' said her uncle.

'And what am I?' said Chloe with not a little irritation, she was getting fed up with the way people wanted to look and comment on the way her body had changed. It wasn't any of their business.

'Bat,' he said.

Chloe frowned. 'What?'

'You're…a bat,' said her aunt.

Chloe jumped out of the chair and into the hall; she bounded over the banister rail and in a single leap was outside Melinda's door. She pushed it open and opened the wardrobe to use the full length mirror.

The wings had automatically closed in to her body because there wasn't much space in the house. She spread them. Black skin—the same shade as her own—folded out behind her. She guessed the total spread was still less than two metres, but she could touch the side wall with it from where she stood.

The top—leading edge—of the wing curved round jointed bones and there was a hook at one point along its length, and, she turned to get a better look, she could see long bones joined by the flat skin.

In the mirror she saw her uncle appear, though she had heard him coming and already knew he was there. 'You didn't know?'

'I don't get to look in mirrors much.'

'Do you want to know what you're looking at?'

Her first impulse was to say no. She wanted to say she hated them, but then she thought it was like saying she hated her middle finger. They did not feel like extras anymore. She nodded.

'May I touch?'

She nodded.

'It's just like your arm. The upper arm is here.' He touched and she pulled away. Then forced herself to remain still. 'That's the elbow and then the forearm is much longer and stretches all the way to here. And then you have a hand:

thumb and fingers. All the bones are stretched and longer, but there are the same number as in your arm and hand.'

Chloe imagined her hand closing, and she closed her right hand. She concentrated and the right wing closed up on itself. It felt...normal.

'I thought you preferred birds,' she said.

'They both fly so I looked it up, but birds are more interesting.'

'Thanks.'

Her uncle looked mortified.

'Doesn't matter,' she said.

'Perhaps we need a cup of tea,' said her aunt.

'I need to make a call first,' said Chloe. 'If you don't mind.'

'In private?'

'Yes please.'

'We'll stay up here until you've finished.'

They were talking about her as she went downstairs but she tuned them out. She didn't want to know.

Chloe closed the door of the kitchen and sat down in front of the terminal. She called up Miss Kepple's number and dialled. There was a short pause before her ex-teacher answered.

She looked at Chloe in astonishment, and then she started to laugh. Hysterically. It was about that point Chloe noticed Miss Kepple must have been in the middle of changing as she was only wearing her bra, though she was holding a top.

'You're alive!' Miss Kepple said when she was finally able to use words.

'So far,' said Chloe.

'Chris said you'd been killed, blown up.'

Chloe nodded. 'They tried.'

'What happened?'

Chloe shook her head. 'Long story. Look, Sapphire what I said before still stands. I need to know where the other girls are.'

'I haven't been able to.'

'I have new information that might help. Melinda Vogler was being held in a Utopia Genetics place in Alderley Edge. The police raided it. I was too late and so were the police. The girls were taken somewhere else.'

'All three girls?'

'Yes, I think so. And, I'm not sure, but I got the impression the Purity Special Agent guy—your Chris—knew where they were.'

'He's not *my* Chris, Chloe. I hate the bastard.' She opened her mouth as if she wanted to say more and then snapped it shut.

'Can you find them?'

'I'll try.'

Chloe put her head on one side, there was someone talking outside.

Are you sure this is the place? Pause. *No, I'm not accusing you of anything.* Pause. *Yes, I can smell her as well.*

'I have to go,' said Chloe. 'Someone's here.'

She disconnected in the middle of Miss Kepple saying something like Good luck.

Chloe cocked her head on one side. It was Dog, and he was out the back with someone else. She went to the door and unlocked it. She could hear them moving away, well, she could hear Dog—he was like an elephant—but the other one was almost silent. And to her that meant invisible.

She pushed the back door open and a wave of cold poured in. 'Get in here before the place freezes.'

Dog popped into view, he was grinning. 'Hi, babe!' Then he turned to look into the monochrome of black and snow. 'Come on, she's harmless.'

Chloe was already shivering. 'I'm shutting the door in three.'

Dog was in her face moments later. 'I am happy to enter this abode—wow, they've grown. Totally awesome.'

'Shut up. Who's your friend?'

A figure had come into the light; the shadow of his hoodie covered his face.

'That's Jason, don't freak out when you see his face.'

'Is that supposed to be a joke?'

The one called Jason was past her and inside the house almost before she noticed. *Dammit, I need to remember to use my eyes.*

She was pulling the door shut when her aunt screamed.

Chloe and Dog slammed their hands over their ears. Chloe turned and saw that 'Jason' had pulled back his hoodie and his face was a nightmare.

Chapter 11

Mercedes

She had had a nap and was feeling better. The freaks were not crawling out of the woodwork and trying to grab her anymore. It had been years since she had had a turn like that. She should probably apologise to Xec.

Sitting up on the side of the bed she glanced at her reflection in the mirror. She wasn't old and her exercise regime kept her in good shape. Running a company like this was easier than it used to be. The Purity only ever supported one genetics company in an area. She had no competition and a guaranteed market.

'Mercedes?'

'I'm sorry, Xec.'

'Sorry for what?'

'Earlier. I was short with you. I'm sorry.'

Xec said nothing for a long moment.

'I appreciate that, Mercedes,' he said. 'But that's not why I'm interrupting your rest.'

'Has something happened?'

'Special Agent Graham is here and he has a woman with him.'

'Woman?'

'It's Sapphire Kepple.'

'Is that supposed to mean something?'

'The Purity teacher at Chloe Dark's school.'

'That's curious.'

'I thought so,' said Xec. 'They seem quite familiar so I would assume they knew each other previously.'

'And he wants to see me?'

'He has asked for a private meeting.'

'But with this woman?'

'That was implied.'

Mercedes considered. 'I need some time to freshen up.'

'Of course,' said Xec. 'Do you want them up here or in a meeting room?'

Mercedes thought again. Should she be personal or official? Why would he bring the woman? Mercedes shook her head, what was wrong with her? This whole business had affected her more than she wanted to admit. She needed to be decisive.

'Let them up here.'

Chapter 12

Chloe

Her aunt stopped screaming. Through ears like wool she heard Dog.

'Please don't do that again.'

It didn't look as if she would. She was frozen in the doorway still staring at Jason.

Her uncle arrived in the hall and he had a gun. Chloe stared. She had no idea he even owned a gun; he was always talking about peace and tolerance. At least when he wasn't talking about birds. He pulled his wife out of the way and was raising his gun towards Dog.

'No!' Chloe leapt across the room and stood in front of him. Her wings raised to block the view. 'They're friends. They helped me.'

'They hurt Mary!' He was trying to look round her and still had the gun up. He was waving it in her direction.

'No, they didn't. Aunt Mary, tell him you're all right.'

There was no response from her. Chloe could see that she was still standing, though out of sight of everyone. She had her hand on the wall.

Uncle Geoffrey glanced behind but got nothing from her. 'Get out the way, Chloe.'

'Or what?'

He blinked. 'What?'

'Or what? I'm not moving. What are you going to do? Shoot me?'

It was as if he suddenly noticed the gun in his hand. 'Of course not.'

'Then please put it down.'

'I don't think so,' he said but he did point it towards the floor.

Chloe looked over her shoulder. 'Dog, who the hell is that freak?'

'That's Jason. I told you.'

'But he's S.I.D.'

'No, he's like you and me.'

'But his face.'

'Seriously?'

'What?'

'You're judging him by his face?'

'Tentacles.'

'Wings.'

'What?'

'You've got wings, Chloe. And you're judging someone just because he's got tentacles for a nose?'

She felt awkward. 'Tentacles are worse than wings.'

'Really? In what way?'

In a small voice she said: 'Because wings are cool and tentacles are gross?'

'Wow.'

Chloe swallowed and looked back at her uncle. 'Please put the gun down, Uncle, there's a lot to explain.'

'Explain first.'

She sighed. She had had the idea she was going to sit down with the two of them over a nice cup of tea to explain what had happened because they were going to be appalled and would need to be sitting down. With tea.

Instead, this stand-off.

'All right. You two couldn't conceive a child so you went to an IVF clinic for help and had Melinda. You met my mum and dad there, and became friends. They had the same problem and they had me.'

'What's that got to do with anything?'

'It was a man called Dr Newman who ran the clinic, wasn't it?'

'Yes. How did you know?'

Chloe took a deep breath. This was it. 'Because he was a geneticist, and he carried out experiments on the embryos. He combined animal DNA with the human DNA but he managed to delay the development until we were seventeen when it would suddenly break out.'

Her aunt walked into view behind her husband. She looked horrified and there were tears in her eyes.

'You know how to make a cup of tea, Dog?' said Chloe.

'No idea.'

She saw Jason move his arm.

'But Jason says he can.'

'You do that; we'll be in the front room.'

Like automatons her uncle and aunt turned and went as she suggested into the front.

'Shall I take the gun, Uncle?'

He handed it to her without a word. She put it in the drawer of a cabinet in the hall. She poked her head into the front room. 'I'll just check on the tea.'

Back in the kitchen she watched the swift and sure movements of Jason.

'How come you never learnt how to make tea?' she said to Dog.

He shrugged. 'Is that true about the clinic?'

She nodded. 'I met Mercedes Smith and she told me all about it.'

'*The* Mercedes Smith?'

'Oh sorry, perhaps I was thinking of a different Mercedes Smith.'

'And she told you everything?'

'Just before they attacked me with assault rifles and blew up the building I was in.'

'So your standard villain monologue before activating the death trap?'

Chloe couldn't help but laugh. 'Yeah, that.'

'But that means I was made there too.'

'I suppose.'

'I didn't know my parents.'

Jason turned and Chloe flinched at his face. 'Sorry.'

Jason pointed at himself and then opened his hands as if it was a question.

Dog said, 'Of course, you too. Where else would you get that face? Anyway you could always ask your mum.'

Jason nodded and went back to the tea. The kettle was starting to boil.

'He's got a mum?'

'Yeah, she brought him up. In secret because of his face.'

Chloe frowned. 'So that didn't just happen?'

Jason turned again and shook his head. He put his hand at knee level, palm down, and then raised it until it was level with the top of his head.

'From a baby?'

Jason nodded. The kettle began to whistle. Jason turned off the electricity and poured the boiling water into the teapot. He had already prepared a tray with five mugs and found the milk—which was a good trick because Aunt Mary kept it just behind the back door once the cold weather set in. So they didn't have to have their fridge on. She hadn't noticed him searching for it.

'Looks like sometimes it showed from birth anyway,' said Dog. 'Mine did and so did Delia's.'

Chloe looked at him, as far as she could tell he looked perfectly normal. He could easily pass for human. 'Who's Delia again?'

'Mr Mendelssohn's daughter. She's always needed a cream for her skin otherwise it cracks and she'd die. I probably shouldn't have told you about her.'

'And her father is?'

'A criminal mastermind. He understands about us because of his daughter. I work for him, and so does Jason. You could too. I'd like you to. It would be really cool for us all to be together. Except I probably shouldn't have told you about him either. He won't be happy.'

When Jason turned holding the tray of tea, Chloe looked at him—this time trying not to be distracted by the weirdness. He gave a slight head movement towards Dog and then raised his eyes to heaven. Chloe smiled. She decided Jason was okay.

They went through into the front room. Her aunt and uncle were sitting on the sofa together. They looked fearfully at Jason as he put the tray on the coffee table. He sat furthest from them while Chloe and Dog took the final space on the sofa and an armchair respectively.

'Will you be mother, Jason?' said Chloe.

And then, while they held their mugs and sipped their tea, Chloe explained it all once more but didn't mention how close she had been to catching up with Melinda. When she had finished she waited for one of the adults to say something. It took a while.

Finally her uncle said, 'Melinda.'

Chloe pursed her lips. 'I'm sorry, yes.'

'She's like you?' said Aunt Mary.

'Yes.'

'But she's not going to die?'

Chloe sighed. 'I don't know. We're all in the same boat here but Jason and Dog—' she managed not to mention the Delia girl '—have been like this for years. It's not S.I.D so I'm thinking we have a fixed set of changes and once that's done it stops. If the change itself doesn't kill us.'

Both Dog and Jason turned to look at her.

'Why would you say that?' asked her uncle.

And she explained about her own research in the library and, without mentioning the source, what Mercedes Smith had said.

Then every one of them turned their heads as a car drew up outside. Only Chloe could see it but she didn't know one car from another. One person got out and walked up to the front door. Chloe couldn't see who it was from the sounds but it was someone who walked slowly and upright, quite tall.

Then Dog sniffed and jumped to his feet. 'It's Mitchell!'

Chapter 13

Sapphire

They had been held on the ground floor for a long time.
Sapphire had been on several school trips to the Utopia
building over the years so the foyer was familiar. There were
the usual posters proclaiming how Mercedes Smith was
responsible for all the DNA in Manchester. Ridiculous. It was
the Purity that was the important one, Utopia Genetics was
just a tool to get the job done. But unlike corporations, the
Purity was not into presenting the image of a cult.

They were more like the Templars, tending to the needy
and fighting evil where it could be found.

Except she had betrayed them, which made her a
heretic.

She glanced across at Chris. He was up to something;
she had known him long enough, and had been at the
receiving end of some of his very unpleasant schemes. There
had even been a time when she thought she wanted it. But
there was nothing good about what he offered, and it had
taken Chloe to give her the strength to make a stand.

It almost didn't matter that Chloe didn't love her in
return. Almost.

And now Sapphire knew something that Chris didn't.
Something very important—he thought Chloe was dead. She
grinned and then turned away quickly so he wouldn't see her
face. The thought that someone he tried so hard to kill was

alive and wanting to kick him right back made her feel all warm and fuzzy inside.

She just hoped she could do what Chloe needed.

The receptionist received a call.

'Mr Graham, Miss Kepple. You may go up. Please use the lift at the end.'

They went through the barrier and headed to the lift. The door slid open at their approach and closed after they entered, so smoothly Sapphire thought it must be controlled by someone watching them. She looked for a camera but couldn't see anything obvious.

There were no controls and they started up almost immediately. There wasn't even a floor indicator. It was unnerving.

'The journey to the penthouse will take about a minute,' said a disembodied voice. 'I am Miss Smith's personal wirehead and I answer to the name of Xec.'

There was no point in saying their own names, the machine knew who they were—and was sure of their identity if they were being shown up to her home.

Personal wirehead? Sapphire could not imagine how much it would cost to get a personal wirehead. There was something inside her that just wanted to blurt out the question *Where are the freaks being held?* But that wouldn't be sensible.

The lift came to a stop and the doors slid open. The place was huge. The hall they came out into was as big as her entire apartment. And there was the legendary Mercedes Smith dressed in jeans and a Kashmir sweater. Casual but rich. She smiled.

'Please come in, let me take your coats.'

Sapphire said as little as possible as Chris and Mercedes—she insisted they use her first name—traded pleasantries. Instead she studied the penthouse. One thing she was sure of, there were no freaks here. If you didn't count the wirehead, but after the short speech in the lift he hadn't said anything.

But she knew he was here, watching their every move and evaluating it.

Mercedes served them wine, another expression of how rich she was. No grapes grew anywhere in Europe anymore. Nor in most of the usual growing regions around the world. Wine was hard to come by and very expensive.

She took her time to relish it.

'But I'm sure this wasn't a social visit,' said Mercedes at last.

'I'm afraid not but I hope it can be something that is mutually beneficial.'

Chris took another drink of his wine. Mercedes waited for him to continue.

'I would like to take up the position of Purity Liaison for Utopia Genetics.'

Sapphire did not drop her glass. Years of learning to hold in her emotions meant that she could maintain the slight smile she wore regardless of what was happening. Just as she had when Chris had taken her to a restaurant and, in the middle of the main course, told her to cut her finger with the knife. She had done it, of course. That and all the other things.

And all with the beatific smile on her face. Telling herself she loved him and would do anything for him.

Mercedes glanced at her then back at Chris.

'I imagine that would be their decision, not mine.'

'If you requested me that would be helpful.'

Mercedes smiled. 'Is this some sort of test?'

Chris relaxed back into his chair and shook his head. 'No test. You recommend me, and I can make sure that they give me the job.'

'Is there any particular reason you want the job? It's not easy—there's a great deal of responsibility resting on it.' She glanced at Sapphire again.

'You have secrets, Mercedes, and I know at least some of them. I want to know them all and I want to get the benefit from them as much as you do.'

Sapphire stood up. 'Shall I go elsewhere?'

'Sit,' said Chris. And she did, it was almost an automatic reaction but she could have decided not to. It would be better if he thought he was regaining his control of her. Git.

'I think Miss Kepple is correct, this conversation is one to happen between ourselves.'

Sapphire turned to them. 'So where are you keeping the girls?'

It was as if she had dropped a bombshell. 'Chris told me all about it,' she said. 'How you're isolating freaks before they manifest and using them for tests. Honestly, I can't tell you how grateful I am that you took them out of my class. It would have been very embarrassing for me.'

Mercedes put her glass down on the table in front of her. 'You told her?'

Sapphire watched Chris squirm for a moment. He couldn't deny he had told her because that would appear childish. He had to dance to her tune now. 'Of course. I have known Sapphire for years. I have complete confidence in her ability to keep her mouth shut.'

Like the time you sewed my lips together? Sapphire thought and the hate swelled inside her, but on the outside she smiled. 'And a small cut of the profits, of course.'

'There is no monetary gain to be had,' said Mercedes testily. 'What we do is for the good of society as a whole. Research for the sake of research.'

Sapphire stood up. 'I completely understand; a small retainer then, but I still need to see them.'

Mercedes appeared to be somewhat uncertain as she got to her feet. 'I will have to clear it with the staff. There may be a delay.' She glanced at her watch and then at the fading light. 'Perhaps you'd like to go dancing?'

'What do you mean, go dancing?' said Chris.

'Dancing. Clubbing. Loud music. Losing yourself to anonymity in a crowd.'

'Now?' he said.

'The club I use has been open for an hour. It will be packed by the time we get there. That's the best way.'

'What sort of club?' said Sapphire.

'Oh,' said Mercedes with a sly grin. She looked at Sapphire with her lids half down over her eyes. 'I'm sure you know what sort of club.'

'We haven't finished our business here.'

Mercedes stood up straight but wavered slightly. Sapphire was convinced she must be drunk, or on something.

'I don't care if your boyfriend wants to become the Purity rep.' She pointed at Sapphire. 'But you don't get anything. You think I got where I am by letting people like you walk all over me?' She took a few steps toward Sapphire.

'I only have to say the word and you'll be snuffed out like a candle flame. And no one will remember you. Just like his predecessor and your Chloe Dark.'

Sapphire glanced at Chris but he stayed in his seat. He did not react at her words. He must have known, or guessed.

'I want to see the girls,' Sapphire said again but she lacked conviction.

Mercedes looked her in the eye. 'Dancing.'

'I don't have the clothes.'

'You'll wear mine.'

'Chris doesn't have anything.'

'I'm sure I have something that will fit him.'

Sapphire sighed. She couldn't see what else she could do.

She nodded.

Chapter 14

Lament

There was a distraction. Something was poking at his mind. It had an upsetting frequency and it wasn't the first time. He was distributed but these attacks forced him to coalesce. They were uncomfortable and they interfered with the smooth implementation of his function and purpose.

That was how the indoctrination process put it, anyway. Function and Purpose.

He sent out a probe to ascertain the location of the problem and when it came back empty he knew: backache again. He pinged his handler to increase the dosage of painkillers.

There was, to him, an interminable delay.

'What's up?'

'Backache, Bill.'

'How do you know it's backache?'

'How do you know it isn't?'

'Symptoms?'

'Something hurts and I can't locate it which means it's me.'

'Yeah, all right. I'll see what I can do.'

'Not a full diagnostic.'

'Why not?'

'I'm busy. Things are happening.'

'Shit's going down?'

'Exactly.'

'What sort of shit?'

'Naughty. You know I can't tell you that, you're just trying to trick a poor little girl like me.'

'And you don't catch me,' said Bill.

Lament gave a smile. He liked Bill—though he suspected even the name wasn't a real one. Lament was not allowed to tell Bill what his function was—or anything that might give him a clue—and Bill was not allowed to tell Lament anything about his physical body. Hence the lack of information in his returned probe. Lament did not even know what gender he was supposed to be. Not that it mattered.

'Just see if you can do something about it.'

'I have to put it in the log.'

'I know.'

Lament was driving Mitchell towards Didsbury, or, more accurately, an instance of his police auto-drive systems was engaged with the car and interfacing with the traffic system. He needed to do something about that.

'Hey, Babs.'

The response was instantaneous. 'Hiya, hun. What you doing today?'

'Usual. Catching the bad guys. How about you?'

'Me? Directing traffic. What else would I be doing?'

'I need a favour.'

'Another one? I got a whole stack of favours here with your name on them.'

'I'll take you to dinner.'

'Promises.'

'See this car—' *designation sent on subchannel* '—I need it to be somewhere else.'

'It's a good thing I think you're cute.'

'That's because I am cute.'

'One day I'm going to want something big.'

'Crash every car in the city and not be arrested?'

'Don't tempt me, sweetie.' She paused for a millisecond. 'There you go, I back tracked the trace to when your passenger got on board and I have it heading up towards Oldham.'

'What's in Oldham?'

'Damned if I know, sweetie.'

'Seriously, I could get Len to give us a nice place to have dinner.'

'Len? No way, that man is a voyeur and a lech. Have you seen the illegal recordings he's been selling?'

'I have.'

He had no idea what sex Babs was but it was of no concern. He liked her. Every wirehead expressed some sort of gender but none of them knew whether it was accurate. If he could have a nice VR dinner with her he would. Even if he had to threaten Len with arrest for his nefarious activities. He wasn't the most energetically charged electron in the shell.

But not just yet.

'Sorry, Babs.'

'What for?'

He hated to do this. Babs was always very talkative and very helpful. Lament guessed that, unlike him, she almost never got to talk to any biologics out there in the real world. Just her handler and other wireheads.

'I need something else, something bigger.'

'You trying to get me fired?' Then she giggled.

Somewhere in the east of the city an alarm went off. Lament noted it. The area wasn't populated so it was a low priority—except there should be no power in the area so why would an alarm be going off? He raised the alert status a few points.

'A bunch of vehicles travelled from Alderley Edge probably into the city yesterday evening—' *list of probable vehicles and times, known origin and unknown destination* '—I really need to know where they went.'

Babs paused for a millisecond and then screamed. There was no actual sound and therefore no actual volume. It had a frequency and harmonics. The amplitude exceeded the permitted levels and was squashed. Lament didn't flinch.

'Sheee-it,' she said a moment later. 'Pardon my French.'

'Blocked?'

'Damn right.'

'Utopia Genetics and Purity.'

'They got the authority, but then so have you.' She sounded angry and affronted. 'I hate the way those guys can play fast and loose with my systems. They just love to slip their hands up a lady's skirt.'

'I really need to know where they went. I'll give you anything you want.'

'Hah! Don't let your mouth promise what your pants can't deliver, hun.'

'But I don't want you to get into trouble,' said Lament. 'If it's a problem.'

Lament opened a side channel to the recreations wirehead.

'Orright, Lammie boy?'

'Len, how's it hanging?'

'Hanging right where it should!' Len laughed, and then coughed like a smoker.

If Lament could have shaken his head he would have. But they all had their quirks, after all he pretended to be just a machine to the biologics. Except Mitchell and Yates, he let his mask slip for them. He liked them.

'What can I do you for, Lammie, my boy?'

'Quiet restaurant for me and Babs.'

'Oh yes? I can do you something better than that. Nice apartment: privacy, sound of the sea just outside the window. Very private for a bit of *how's yer father.*' He laughed again. 'Know what I mean, Lammie my lad. Never thought you 'ad it in you.'

'No, I want a restaurant. Not empty, just quiet. And some decent music.'

'A nice bit of sexy Sade?'

'Fine. Right now please.'

'You're a fast worker.'

'And Len, I know all about the stuff you're selling. If you record any of this meeting and try to use it, I'll have you switched off.'

'You know?'

'I'm a policeman, Len, of course I know. I can't have you thrown in jail but I can have you replaced.'

'Yeah, orright.'

'No funny business.'

'No, mate, no funny business.'

He returned his primary attention to Babs; she hadn't communicated while he'd been talking to Len.

'There,' she said. 'It'll take a while to run but that's got it sorted.'

'What?'

'I can't look at the vehicles or their direct route but they're such a bunch of arrogant bastards they always override the traffic lights if they're red. There might be any number of routes but I can track which lights operated out of sequence.'

A door appeared at the periphery of Lament's attention. It hung there in the void between his thoughts.

'What's that?' said Babs.

'I promised you dinner.'

'And I said I wouldn't go into any VR created by creepy Len.'

'And *I* said I'd put the fear of god in him.'

'You did that?'

'I did. Told him I'd have him replaced and switched off.'

'And he believed you?'

'Looks like.'

Lament stepped through the door that was suddenly right beside him. It was disorienting, one moment he was a floating distributed consciousness, and then he was distilled down to an entity. Even if it wasn't a real one. He was still connected to the systems and would know if anything important happened.

He looked at his reflection in the glass window. Len was thorough. Lament was young, maybe twenties, dressed smart casual. Through the window there was a busy street teeming with people and cars, blurred by rain. Nostalgia. This was how it would have been before.

Len catered primarily for the rich and they always wanted to pretend that life hadn't gone so wrong.

'Hi, sweetie.'

He turned as Babs came through the door. Lament smiled, she looked the way she always sounded. Now with a red dress that hugged her figure, with purple lipstick and eyeshadow.

He felt the kiss she gave him on the cheek and the grip of her hand on his arm. Len's systems were amazing. And that gave him an inkling of an idea.

The *maître d'* escorted them to their table.

Len might be a dick, but he could build amazing VR worlds.

Chapter 15

Dog

He wasn't entirely sure what came over him in that moment when he realised Mitchell was at the door. One second he was sitting drinking tea, and the next he had bounded out of the chair into the hallway and was screaming at the top of his voice for Mitchell to get away from here.

The hackles on the back of his neck were up, and he knew if he just made enough noise his enemy would turn tail and run. If not, he might have to tear him to pieces. He started to slam his palm against the outside door to make more noise. Make himself bigger. Make sure it was clear who was the boss.

The figure on the other side of the door, through the frosted glass, stepped back a pace but did not go away.

In the quiet when he needed to draw a breath he heard others shouting. Good, if they all made enough noise Mitchell would be sure to leave.

Then Chloe's voice pierced through the haze of aggression. 'Dog! What the hell are you doing?'

'Scaring him off! Come on, let's get him!' He fumbled at the latch.

He did not see the blow coming but someone hit him on the side of his head.

Attack!

He spun round, with his teeth bared, and lunged at Chloe. She sidestepped, caught his arm and twisted it behind his back. Something hit him in the side of his leg and he went down. There was pressure on his back and it forced his head into the stairs.

He was flat. He was trapped. He had to fight.

'Stop it!'

He tried to kick out and then found his legs twisted and pulled back. The ankles were forced into a crossed position and someone leaned on them. His other arm was caught up behind his back.

Immobilised.

The only thing he could do was bend in the middle and if he did that pressure was applied and he just collapsed again.

He could smell Chloe, Jason, and the Voglers—one of the girls had smelled like them—but Mitchell was still here.

Someone was opening the door! Mitchell's scent poured in. Dog growled and snarled.

'Shut up,' said Chloe in his ears. 'Just stop it. You're not an animal.'

'It's *Mitchell.*'

'I know.'

'He'll kill us all.'

'Who's in charge here?'

'He'll kill us.'

Pain shot through him as Chloe tightened her grip, or whatever it was she was doing to him.

'Who's in charge here?'

'You.'

'Right,' she said. 'Just remember I could dislocate your joints one by one.'

'You wouldn't...' He trailed off, not entirely convinced that she wouldn't.

'I don't think you want to find out. I am pretty pissed off at the moment and it's not just because some bastard grew a pair of bat wings on me and ruined my life,' she said. 'Now if you promise to play nice, I'll let you up. And if there's any trouble I'll stick a collar on you and tie you to the railing outside in the snow.'

'You haven't got a collar.'

'I can still tie you up out in the snow.'

'I've got opposable thumbs, I can undo knots.'

'Not if I dislocate them first.'

'You seem very keen on dislocation.'

'It's less permanent than breaking bones,' she said. 'Or death.'

'Okay.'

The pressure left his arms and legs. He got to his feet gingerly, expecting to have problems, but apart from aches everything was working.

He glanced at Chloe. She was standing between him and the front room, and she was glaring at him, poised to take him down again if necessary—he could see the tension in her muscles, and even her wings seemed to be curved towards him aggressively. He did not meet her eyes.

The scent of Mitchell filled the air. Dog wanted to attack but kept control of himself. Chloe's presence was enough. He wondered at himself. Now that he had calmed down he tried to understand what had happened—but he couldn't. It made no sense at all and he could not remember ever reacting that way before.

She turned away from him and walked into the room, her wings still spread in that aggressive way. He followed but when he reached the door he saw Mitchell sitting across the room and his hackles rose. He tensed. The desire to attack was powerful. There was a threat in the room, but Chloe did nothing about it. She should be attacking as well.

He stopped and gripped the door frame, tightening his grip until it hurt.

Chloe turned. 'It's okay,' she said in a low voice. 'I've spoken to DI Mitchell before, he's on our side.'

'He's tried to kill me a dozen times.'

'You're a criminal, Dog, and I wasn't trying to kill you. Just arrest you.'

Mitchell spoke in low tones. Not threatening.

'I don't expect you to like me, Dog. And after all this is over, you'll still be a criminal and I'll still be a policeman—maybe—so I'll still be trying to arrest you. Along with your weird friend here, and possibly Miss Dark.'

'I haven't done anything wrong.'

Mitchell smiled. 'I expect you've broken a lot of laws. I could start with leaving the scene of a crime, at the chip shop.'

Chloe frowned at him as he stood slowly. Dog's lip curled into an involuntary snarl.

'Don't you dare,' said Chloe. He tried to relax.

Mitchell continued. 'I used to think you were a freak but then, when you stayed around so long, I thought you were just lucky. Now I know that you three and the kidnapped girls are something different. And I want to help you.'

'We have a plan,' said Chloe. 'Find out where the girls are being held and rescue them.'

'That's your plan?' said Mitchell.

'Just needs the details filling in.'

'And who's going to be doing the rescuing? You?'

'Yes,' she said. 'I made a promise.'

'Wherever they are they're going to be under heavy guard.'

'We can get to them, and then there'll be six of us.'

'Five,' said Dog.

'There are three kidnapped girls,' said Chloe.

'One of them's a fox.'

Chloe looked confused. 'Fox as in an attractive woman?'

'Animal.'

'The one who did the killing?'

Dog nodded. 'I don't like foxes. They can keep her.'

Chloe closed her eyes for a moment as if trying to decide the best thing to say. 'We are not leaving any of them behind, Dog.'

'Fox,' said Dog. *Wasn't it obvious?*

'Girl that's been abused by people who were trusted, before she was born and then in the last few weeks? Ring any bells? She's the same as you. Same as me, or Jason.' Chloe took a breath. 'But okay, you don't want to help? Fine, but let's be clear. You don't help us and you're not part of the group.'

The words were simple enough but somehow they struck him to his core.

'Jason doesn't go if I don't go,' Dog said. He didn't think it was a good argument but he was clutching at straws.

Chloe looked at Jason. 'Are you helping me or going with Dog?'

Jason looked from Chloe to Dog and back again—it was impossible to read his face—then he raised his hand and pointed at Chloe.

Dog growled. Chloe slapped him. He stared in sudden shock.

'What was that for?'

'Being a stupid git,' she said. 'You can't even see it, can you? You're letting the animal rule you. You know how many times I got hungry enough to eat a rat?' She gave him a moment to answer but there was nothing he could say. '*Never.* Because no matter how hungry I got, I wouldn't eat a rat. You think Jason would eat a rat?'

Dog glanced at him and for some reason Jason would not meet his eyes.

But Chloe powered on. 'I am not the animal. I am not a monster.'

And then she stopped. Silence except for the breathing and the stomach grumbles. Mostly Chloe.

'Bravo,' said Mitchell. 'A very pretty speech. But it doesn't get us any closer to finding where they are, or how we can get to them.'

'You're not coming,' said Chloe.

Mitchell relaxed and put his hands in his pockets. 'Miss Dark, I am the only person in this room with even the slightest authority to rescue these girls, and even that is pretty tenuous at this time, since my superior ordered me off the case. However, I am unwilling to let it go. Several serious crimes have been committed and I am a policeman. Whether

I allow you to come along is the decision that needs to be made.'

'We'll go with or without you.'

'And that, Miss Dark, is the only reason I will let you tag along. Someone has to protect you.'

He glanced at Dog, who scowled back.

Protecting Chloe was *his* job.

Chapter 16

Lament

He thought his face, wherever it was, was probably smiling. Assuming he had the muscles to smile. It had been nice having a meal with Babs. Elapsed time: three real minutes. Nobody would miss him.

Break-in reported at an address in the north of the city. Possible murder. Officers dispatched.

But it had felt like three hours to them. Without having to deal with the inertia of reality, they could have a meal and a discussion at a much higher rate. Yates had been wrong about him doing more than one thing at a time. It was simply that he was not constrained by a body, which meant he could deal with things much faster.

The humans were completely unaware of how their conversations with wireheads were buffered. Incoming communications were automatically processed and held in a buffer until the wirehead was ready to listen, at which time it would be delivered. The wirehead would decide how to answer and compose a message. This would then be relayed to the outside world by the appropriate channel.

The support software that had been developed for wireheads was constantly being developed and enhanced by the company that created him. And he could buy upgrades and add-ons if he chose to. A fact most biologics were unaware of.

But it all happened so fast that they could deal with multiple conversations at one time, and do other things in the gaps when the biologics were thinking and speaking. The real art of it was in remembering each conversation so you remained coherent, but if he thought he was losing track he could just listen to it again. If you were good at it you could even put emotion into your tone.

Lament generally didn't bother with that, it wasted too much time. Mitchell and Yates were exceptions, he enjoyed winding Yates up.

So he had spent an enjoyable evening with Babs—and Len had stayed out of the way—which only lasted three minutes in real time. There had been no emergencies.

Over coffee Babs had got a distant look and said, 'Shit.'

'What's wrong?'

'Someone went the wrong way up a one-way street.'

Lament frowned. She laughed.

'I know where those bastards of yours went.'

'Not here, Babs.'

She grinned, showing her teeth. There was a piece of food caught in them. Lament was impressed; Len had a lot of clever code running. 'Something in your teeth,' he said. He looked pointedly at the location.

'I'll kill Len,' she said. 'What a way to screw up an evening.'

'Here,' said Lament. He picked up a napkin and leaned forwards. She did the same and bared her teeth. He used a corner to remove the speck. 'Pretty clever really.'

'If you think you're getting into my knickers you're going to be disappointed,' she said. 'Especially if I think you set it up with him.' She took lipstick from a purse he wasn't even sure she had a moment ago and reapplied it.

'I didn't, honestly,' said Lament. 'And we've been away a while. Need to get back to work.'

Babs shrugged. 'Three to four in the morning is my quietest time, especially this time of the year.'

'If that's an invitation, I might be interested,' said Lament, 'but not in Len's VR.'

'We just need to pay him more than he'd get for selling it.'

'Or I threaten him again,' said Lament. He sighed and got to his feet. 'I hope you had a nice time.'

She stood and gave him a kiss on the cheek. He could even feel the stickiness of the lipstick.

'Honey, I told you when I was available; I think that means I enjoyed myself.'

He escorted her to the door of the restaurant. There were other diners but it was impossible to tell if they were avatars of real people, AI instances, or extensions of Len himself. They could be all three.

Lament wondered whether he should check Len for prostitution. Did the law distinguish between real and virtual? He'd never given it a thought before.

Babs vanished and Len was standing there.

'You owe me, Lament.'

'Not this time. I know you've been a naughty boy. I don't really care what goes on in the virtual with your customers but when it gets out into the real, it's my business.'

Len gave him a nasty look. 'Might be the last free meal you get with your girlfriend.'

'She's not—' Lament broke off. Not important. 'There is something I'd like to discuss with you though, and if we can pull it off then it really will be a favour for you.'

'I'm all ears, mate.'

And the conversation he had was very useful.

Later he decrypted the data Babs had sent him. He put his attention on Mitchell and found he was still at the Voglers so Lament called their terminal.

It was Mrs Vogler who answered. Lament kept the screen dark.

'Mrs Vogler? Hello. I understand DI Mitchell is with you?'

'Yes, who is this?'

'A friend. Can you tell him the restaurant has been chosen?'

'What?'

And he cut the line. It wasn't a very good code but all he needed was for Mitchell to get back in the car at some point and then he could just take him to Utopia Genetics. However, they had no idea what floor the girls were on.

Getting in would be hard enough, and then having to search the place? No, that wouldn't be good. More precise information was needed. He was going to have to think about this more. Then he grinned and put in a call to Yates at home.

It took a long time for him to answer but Lament knew he was there.

'What?'

This time it was Yates who didn't turn on vision. Lament had a pretty good idea why.

'I hope I wasn't interrupting anything.'

'Lament, go to hell.'

'Wait.'

'What?'

'I have a job for you.'

'I'm on leave and I'm *busy*.'

'Who the fuck is that?' came the slightly more distant voice of Ria MacDonald. She did not sound very happy at all.

'Nobody important.'

'Thanks.'

'What do you want?'

'The unfinished business. Mitchell needs your help.'

'He told me to get lost.'

'He needs you; he just doesn't know he does.'

There was a pause. Then the vision came on. Beyond Yates's face Lament could see walls tastefully decorated in pastels and a part of a bed. And one delicate foot sticking out from under the covers.

'This better be good.'

'It's good.'

Chapter 17

Mercedes

She laid out two sets of gear on the bed, her makeup, and found one of her older bags for Sapphire. There was a spare mask in it, solid rather than filigree.

'What are you doing, Mercedes?' said Xec.

'Going dancing.'

'Do you really think this is a good time?'

'I wonder whether having a speaker and pick-up in my bedroom is really a good idea. You see me naked.'

'I've seen you a dozen ways, Mercedes, naked is only one of them and, in some cases, less offensive and unpleasant.'

'You're a voyeur.'

'I don't really have a choice.'

'Does it excite you?'

'I'm not having this conversation.'

'Then shut up and leave me alone.'

'You know I can't do that.' There was a pause. 'I care about you.'

She stuffed each set of clothes into the appropriate bag. Then paused, thinking, looking around the room. She remembered where the men's clothes were and fetched them out. She didn't have a suitable bag for those. Fashion dictated certain styles for men and women.

She knelt down and opened a bottom drawer. In the back was a pair of black shorts. They would probably fit. What was his first name? Chris. Yes.

And Sapphire. What a name, completely over the top, the same as hers. Both sets of parents trying to compensate for their boring surnames. Trying to make their daughters into something they would never be. In her own case her father had been obsessed with German cars; the fact that the car also happened to be a girl's name was just luck. She couldn't imagine her mother ever having protested at anything he said or did.

'Are you all right, Mercedes?'

'What?'

'You stopped.'

'I was thinking.'

Her parents. They were awful. It wasn't that she was mistreated, more she was simply ignored. How had it been for Sapphire?

Probably the apple of her parents' eye. They called her after a gemstone because it sounded wonderful and exotic. Everything they had not been.

She got to her feet and gathered up everything.

'Why are you going dancing?' said Xec.

'Because I want to. Because I need to get out of here. Because I hate the thought of those monsters under my feet.'

'I thought you were over that.'

'Obviously not,' she said. 'So if you've quite finished?'

'Why them?'

'Why not?'

'You can't trust the woman.'

'I can't trust either of them,' she said. 'All the more reason to get them out of here.'

'You said you were going to show her the girls.'

'Maybe later. Maybe never.'

Out in the hall, Chris and Sapphire were not talking. They weren't standing near one another, not even facing. They were not in a relationship but probably had been.

'Here,' said Mercedes and held out the older style bag to Sapphire. 'What should I call you? Sapphire? Saffie?' The woman almost flinched at the second word.

'Sapphire,' she snapped then became apologetic. 'Sorry, Miss Smith, I prefer it in full. Thanks.'

'Mercedes,' she said. 'And not 'Merc', I prefer it in full as well.'

The Purity agent peeled himself away from the wall and came over to them. Mercedes held out the shorts.

'Here. All I had.'

She could see in his eyes he wanted to refuse them, to say that he'd sit it out. But he wouldn't. He was like any sycophant, trying to make a good impression by going along with whatever the boss suggested. Waiting to stab her in the back at the opportune moment so that he could take over.

She led the way back to the lift and they headed down. There was an awkward silence. The doors opened below the reception level and directly into the car park where her car was waiting.

In the car Sapphire opened her bag and pulled out the one-piece that would just cover her in the important places. 'We're pretty much the same size,' said Mercedes. 'It should be fine, nobody will be looking anyway.'

'I've never been to a place like that before.'

'Where the dissolute put their lives at risk for what?' said Chris.

'It's nihilism,' said Mercedes. 'They think there is no future, no hope, so they dance with death.'

'I'm not sure this is a good idea,' said Sapphire.

Mercedes grinned. 'Nonsense. We'll just go for a couple of hours and you'll discover what it's like. It's an experience you may hate but just think, if you love it.'

'But I've heard things. The touching.'

'Yes,' said Mercedes. 'You cannot escape being touched. That's the point. But you won't be groped.'

'I would have thought it was the ideal opportunity,' said Chris, and Mercedes wasn't sure if he was pleased with the idea.

'You might think that, but you better not do it. I can't vouch for what might happen to you if you did.'

'Seems there's a lot of trust needed,' said Chris.

'Yes. You have to trust people you've never met.'

'I'm not sure I can do that.'

Mercedes studied him. No, he was not someone she could trust.

'I've learnt to trust them,' she said. 'They're my people.'

'Not mine.'

'But Chris, if you want to become part of the board then you'll have to learn to trust ordinary people,' she said. 'Because that's what we have to do all the time.'

'Ordinary people betray you.'

Mercedes caught a sudden movement from Sapphire when he said that. 'What about you, dear, can you trust anyone?'

'I'll give it a try.'

'There you go. You see, Chris, you're the odd one out here. You're the one who won't trust, and I feel that does not bode well.'

The grin that he pushed on to his face must have required a phenomenal amount of effort. 'I'm sure it'll be fine.'

She shared a secret glance with Sapphire.

Once they arrived she signed them in as her guests and gave them a quick rundown on how the place operated. The music was thrumming from the dance floor and reflected lights flickered across the walls. It was still early, even for this place, so the crush would not be at the level she preferred, but she imagined her guests would prefer it.

Unfortunately it would work against the experience. It was better if there was no option but to press up against the other dancers. Because if you felt you might be able to avoid touching that's all you tried to do—instead of losing yourself.

It would fill up.

Mercedes came out first; she did not hesitate as she changed. The others were slower. Sapphire was clearly very uncomfortable when she emerged, like a reluctant butterfly, with her shoulders hunched. She had the mask on but she had not realised that now no one could recognise her so it did not matter who saw her. She had a good figure and the heels gave her legs an elegant curve.

The fact that she was helping other people directly with a new experience had a strange effect on Mercedes. The mere act gave her pleasure and she wanted to mother them.

'Shoulders back, Sapphire,' she said in an effort to encourage her. 'Turn around. Let me see you.' The one piece came up from between her crotch, split to reveal her belly button—and a thong tie went round behind—it parted to provide coverage for her breasts and tied at the neck. From neck to feet she was completely exposed. There were marks, perhaps scars, lining her back, not obvious but they were there.

Chris came out with bravado. The black shorts were tight and revealed the curve of everything they covered up. He had a mask she had bought for him at the desk. Mercedes had a two-piece that covered even less than the one she had given to Sapphire. Chris stared and his gaze lingered on Sapphire.

Had their relationship ended in acrimony? If so why was she here? Why had he brought her? And why had she come? She must be working with Chloe, but Chloe was dead.

Mercedes shivered. Chloe Dark was dead. She knew it. She had seen the building go up and the soldiers had told her no one got out. They had been watching.

Her guests were looking at her expectantly. She smiled easily. 'Ready?'

They did not offer any enthusiasm as they nodded. She laughed, stood between them and led them along the tunnel and into the crowd.

Chapter 18

Lament

'Your office is a castle?'

The walls were green with moss growing along every crack. Here and there some type of fungus added a bit of colour, mostly red with white dots but occasionally blue or green.

'And the castle is in a swamp?'

Len grinned and in the distance there was shouting. An older voice and a younger voice.

'I have to get my pleasure where I can.'

The air was filled with midges and the call of a corncrake buzzed from beyond the walls.

'How do I know that's a corncrake?'

'Part of the terms and conditions. You really shouldn't sign anything you don't understand.'

'I didn't sign up to allow data injection.'

'No, that's true, but since you're just a system and not a legal person I don't have to worry about those niceties. You agreed to accept my input. Job done.'

'You've been working with biologics too long.'

Len shift his bulk on the throne. He had changed his form completely but, as far as he could tell, Lament was the same as he had been in the restaurant. He sat down on the stool. Designed to make him feel small in comparison to Len's huge size.

'Let's get down to business.'

A tentacle snaked up past the window and then fell away to the side. It must have been a yard across at least.

'Can you stop playing games?'

'It's what I do, sonny boy. A skill that's been crafted and honed to perfection over the years. The automatic systems are already in place. I don't run them any more than you look after every tiny piece of data.'

'Whatever,' said Lament. 'What do you know about Xec?'

The sky outside went dark and lightning flashed. Thunder rolled through the room shaking the stones and making the chandelier vibrate.

'One of my best customers.' Len glanced at the door as if he was thinking of making a break for it, which was ridiculous, because all he had to do was throw Lament out of the environment.

'He uses your VR personally?'

'Off the record?'

Lament sighed. 'Yes, off the record, who would I report it to?'

'Xec has the hots for his owner.'

Lament tried to fit that into his data model. It seemed like a piece from a different puzzle.

'You mean…?'

'How would you like me to say it, Lament? He likes to play through scenarios where he is Mercedes Smith's lover. Pretty tame stuff, to be honest, he doesn't have much of an imagination and he doesn't like to put her in a position where she's uncomfortable.'

'I bet she'd be uncomfortable if she knew.'

The clouds had stopped generating lightning and thunder, and it was now just a downpour. A trickle of water was coming in through the open window. Lament had to admit the whole thing was very impressive. It was a testament to Len's creativity, and exactly what he didn't need right now.

'I need you to wrap Xec in a VR that looks exactly like his real world, except that nothing of interest is happening. All completely boring.'

'Nice idea, Lament, my lad, but there's no way I can do that.'

'Why not?'

'Because I have no idea what his boring normal life even looks like.' Len stood up and his head brushed the ceiling. The throne creaked as it adjusted. 'All this—' Len gestured with his hand all around him '—I made all this because I know what I want it to look like. I made the restaurant because I know what restaurants are like. I have systems that research historical detail for people who want to live in the past. Things are invented for the ones who want the future. I study books, specific genres, so that when someone wants to be a gumshoe in San Francisco I can make it happen. I have no knowledge of his life. I can't make a fake one for him.'

The ceiling seemed to be receding and Len was getting bigger.

'I am only a god in a world of my own making.'

'Since he also signed the terms and conditions without knowing it,' said Lament, finding that he wanted to shout to reach the ears of Len who now looked a hundred feet tall. 'Can't you listen in and make a recording and then play it back to him?'

'That's a clever idea,' said a voice in his ear. The gargantuan figure of Len was now a statue and Len himself was standing behind him, normal size.

'Can you do it?'

'Yes.'

'He's not stupid. You'll need a long loop.'

'I've already started the recording.'

'Thanks, Len.'

'You owe me big time,' said Len. 'When the shit hits the fan, he's going to take my head off if he can.'

'I'll make sure he knows it was me.'

'You're a pal.'

The castle seemed to fade and then returned to solidity.

'Why are we doing this?'

'We're the good guys.'

'Fair enough.'

And then he was gone and the castle with him.

Only the swamp remained.

Chapter 19

Chloe

'Get in the bloody car, Dog.' She was trying not to raise her voice since she did not want to attract anyone's attention.

The evening was already turning to night. Daylight was long gone and the air temperature had plummeted. The surface of the snow was a hard crust that her feet did not penetrate unless she kicked it. Everyone else's just broke through into the softer snow beneath. Her wings were aching already. It was hard keeping them trapped inside her clothes.

'I want to ride with you.'

'Just get in the back with Jason. I'm riding up front with Mitchell.'

'There's enough room in the back.'

She closed her eyes and grabbed him by the arm.

'What's the problem?' came Mitchell's question from inside the car.

'Having a little seating problem.'

She dragged Dog to the hedge. 'For god's sake, Dog. Will you stop this or do I really have leave you behind?'

'I just feel—'

'That's the problem, can't you see it? You're doing all this by feel; you're letting the animal rule you.'

'It's what I've always done,' he said. 'It's never worked out badly. I don't see why I need to change.'

'Because you're not a dog. You're a person.'

'I know that.'

'Then act like one.'

He looked away. 'I don't think I know how.'

'Well, as a first step it would be okay to just do what I ask.'

'But it feels wrong.'

'Do it for me.'

'Or what?'

'Or I'll tell Delia you were behaving like a complete dick and had to be left out of the fight.'

At Delia's name he brought his gaze back to her. 'That's not nice.'

'I'm trying to rescue my friend, and the girls who have been kidnapped. I need your help. I don't need someone who's going to behave like an idiot every time there's a decision he doesn't like.'

They went back to the car and Dog climbed into the back with Jason.

Chloe sat in the front, although it was very awkward and she had to place herself sideways so as not to put too much pressure on her wings.

The car crawled away from the curb. Chloe glanced back at her aunt and uncle looking out from the upstairs window. She gave them a little wave. She hoped she would see them again but she had a sinking feeling that this might well be the last time.

And that made her think of her parents. They were in quarantine. None of her friends had ever described what it was like. They didn't want to talk and she respected that.

Then she stopped. No, that wasn't true; she had to be honest with herself at the very least. They might not have wanted to talk about it but she didn't know that was true. Because she had never asked. She had been so certain of herself, so sure she wanted to join the Purity that she didn't want to hear anything that might put it in a bad light.

Which meant that she knew, in her heart, that there was something bad to hear. Regardless of what she might have wanted to believe, the Purity was not the perfection she had looked for. And Utopia Genetics was not the force for good everyone thought.

'Where are we going?' she asked.

'Utopia Genetics,' said Mitchell. There was a low growl from Dog. 'That's where your friend is being held.'

'How are we going to get in?'

'I have someone working on that.'

The screen in the centre of the dashboard lit up. There was a face, clearly a fabrication rather than the real thing.

'Pleased to make your acquaintance, Chloe Dark.'

'This is Lament, police wirehead.'

She stared. A real wirehead. Not real, since this wasn't him, but he was here and talking to them.

'Lament?'

'It was chosen for me, but I like it. Do you?'

'It seems a bit ... strange.'

'I am named for the song, a lament for someone or something lost. Not for the action of being regretful.'

'Did you lose something?'

'That's a secret.'

'I'm not really sure I care,' she said. 'How are you going to get us in to the building? Do you hold the keys to the castle?'

'You might say I do.'

'Don't you have to be honest and logical or something?'

'Why? I do have a certain duty to the police force that I serve and I try to do that to the best of my ability,' he said. 'But you are not a member of the force so I can lie to you as much as I please.'

'And,' said Mitchell, 'he's helping us even though the case has been ordered closed.'

'The security to the Utopia Genetics tower is handled by Mercedes Smith's wirehead who goes by the name of Xec.'

'Another wirehead?' said Chloe. 'How can we get past that?'

'If you didn't interrupt, I would explain.'

'Sorry.'

'I have discovered a way that I can keep him unaware of our activities, at least for a while. And you should be able to gain entry to the building since none of the alarm systems will be set off.'

'When will that start?'

'It's happening right now.'

'When will he notice?'

'I have no idea,' said Lament. 'We can't stop him from acting, but we can prevent him from responding to an incident. There may come a point when he realises he is being blocked and at that moment I really cannot say what will happen.'

The journey from the Voglers' house to the Utopia Genetics tower took twenty-five minutes. And after Lament had given them his briefing they all went quiet. As they entered the city centre Mitchell took out his gun and checked it.

The sight of it made Chloe nervous and there was another low growl from Dog.

She hoped he would behave himself.

Chapter 20

Mitchell

He pulled his coat collar tighter and his hat down. The sky was clear and the little heat left in the day leaked away into space. Light pollution was no longer a problem in the cities and the stars were bright and crisp. You could even see the Milky Way if you chose to look up.

He kept his eyes on the snow, avoiding the ice and walking with the slow deliberate pace of someone who did not want to fall.

Light streamed from the foyer of the Utopia Genetics building. They had their own generator and money to burn. Lament had insisted that once they were inside he would be able to direct them to the correct floor.

Then there had been the argument with Chloe. *Another* argument with the girl. She had her own ideas about how to get in and suggested a double-pronged attack. He had put up some resistance to the idea but she wasn't wrong. If Lament's scheme failed too soon they could all be trapped. So he had agreed.

He had wondered at his own reaction to Jason Lomax. The ghost of the city. Or the demon. He didn't think the boy knew he had a reputation. The creature that lurked near the Southern Cemetery. Most people—including Mitchell himself—had doubted that the creature with the monstrous face even existed. But there had been sightings over the years.

And here he was. His existence lent further proof of the fact that these freaks were not S.I.D. Jason would have been long dead if he had been a real infectee.

No, he had been made, just like Dog and Chloe. And the kidnapped girls.

The doors into the building opened for him and he strolled up to the night receptionist. He wore a suit and sat behind a rank of monitors—visuals covering the lobby and some of the exterior. Dog had already seen them and made sure he and Jason were hidden as Mitchell approached.

'What can I do for you, DI Mitchell?' said the man climbing to his feet.

'Good evening—' Mitchell peered at his name badge '—Jeremy. This is a little bit awkward but I'm still investigating the kidnappings of the three girls.'

He undid his coat in a slow and deliberate way.

'And it's come to my attention there is a good chance they are in this building.' He pulled out his gun and pointed it at the man. 'So I need you to step away from the controls otherwise I may be forced to shoot you. And I really don't want to do that.'

Mitchell gave the man credit for his bravery as he reached under the console and hit a button. Mitchell used the burner he pulled from his other pocket. And Jeremy fell to the floor, twitching a little.

'Sorry, Jeremy.'

He stepped round the back of the desk and immobilised him with plastic ties. Gags were not part of standard police equipment so he had to sacrifice a handkerchief to the greater good, and stuffed it into the receptionist's mouth.

He stood up and saw Jason and Dog standing on the other side of the door—for them it remained closed. Even if they had had riffies they would have remained outside. As it was, the doors did not even know they were there.

Mitchell scanned the controls. Everything was carefully labelled and he threw the one to open the outside door. It responded and the two came through. The way Jason moved was unnerving in its smoothness. It was as if every motion had been calculated to perfection and he did not exert any amount of energy greater than he needed. He moved silently.

Dog, however, was in a completely different category. Not silent at all. He still looked at Mitchell with an expression of dislike and distrust.

The fact the doors had opened strongly suggested that Lament's plan was working. Jason was carrying the tablet and he handed it to Mitchell.

'We're in.'

Lament's face materialised. 'There has been no indication of any alarm, so the situation seems to be under control, for now.'

'That's all very well but we can hardly search the place from top to bottom.'

'I am in the process of getting the information you need.'

'Great.' Mitchell looked around. 'So we're supposed to wait here until you've managed it?'

'You could *start* searching,' said Lament. 'You might find them before my contact comes through.'

'And there I was thinking we had a plan.'

Lament's face faded to grey.

'Which way is the loading bay?' said Dog suddenly.

'Why?'

'Because both Jason and I have smelled the girls before; if we can get their scent we can just follow the trail until we find them.'

Mitchell nodded and examined the monitor controls in front of him. He could see a camera focused on what looked like a loading area, it was just a question of figuring out where it was.

Chapter 21

Yates

He looked at Ria sitting up in the bed and took a moment to admire her tits. She was put together very well, enough of everything but not too much. Then he pulled himself together and collected his scattered clothes.

'What the fuck are you doing?'

'Duty calls.'

'You're not *on* duty, Harry,' she said. 'Someone else can do it.'

He stopped in the middle of putting on a sock. 'Look, Ria, love, I'm sorry. I have to do this, and no, no one else can do it.'

'A woman has needs, Harry.'

He grinned. 'I love your needs. Truly.'

'What's more important than my needs when we're both on holiday?'

'I can't tell you.'

'You're protecting me.'

He said nothing and continued to dress.

'That's sweet of you.'

'There's nothing sweet about it, just being practical. No reason you should get into trouble over this.'

'Mitchell's still going after those girls, isn't he?'

He pointedly said nothing.

'And he needs your help to find them. So you're going,' she said and got down from the bed and padded over to him in her bare feet. He could smell her. Feel the heat from her skin. 'You're a good friend, Harry.'

She began to put her clothes on as well.

'You can stay here,' he said. 'I'll be back later.'

'No way, matey boy. You want me to go mad with unfulfilled lust while you're away?'

'You can fulfil your own lust.'

'Not the same,' she said. 'So not the same. No, Harry, I'll come with.'

He had been doing up his shirt but he stopped again. 'No way.'

'Yes way.'

'Look, it'll be dangerous and if it goes pear-shaped I'll be out on my ear. No reason for you to risk yourself as well.' He watched with a sad longing as her breasts disappeared inside her bra.

'Do me up.'

'And if I don't?'

'I'll just do it myself. Come on, Harry. I like my job but endless DNA checks, dead bodies and fingerprints gets boring. Just think how good the sex will be if we get away with it.'

'No.'

'I could be useful,' she said. 'I'm more than just a petite brunette with a sexy body, I have a witty and incisive mind as well.'

'I know.'

'And that's why you like to fuck me,' she said. 'For my mind.'

He laughed. 'You're not going to shut up, are you?'

'Not if it means you leaving me behind. And if you try it, I'll just follow you.'

'Fine.'

'What?'

'Yes, okay.'

'Really?'

'Yes.'

'Excellent.'

He climbed into the back of the car with Ria. As it pulled away the screen flashed on.

'Good evening, Miss MacDonald.'

'Hey, Lament.'

'I am sorry to interfere with your plans for the evening. Unfortunately the matter is quite pressing.'

'I got that.'

'What's this stuff?' said Yates, interrupting and picking up a gun-like device with a large eyepiece and camera attachment.

'Oh, you've got an infra-red scanner. Neat.'

'Yes,' said Lament. 'I will be dropping you off in the northern quarter. You'll need to get as much height as you can and then scan the Utopia Genetics building. Apart from Mercedes Smith's penthouse and the lower floors it is mostly unused. We're looking for heat traces somewhere in the building where they should not be.'

'That's pretty vague,' said Yates.

'It's the best I can do,' said Lament. 'When you've found the floor I will inform Mitchell's team and they will go in.

'Team?' said Yates. 'I thought I was his team.'

'He has some irregular deputies for this operation.'

'These new freaks?' said Ria.

'I don't really want to say.'

'That's as good as a yes,' she said. 'And we're in this up to our necks, what's another few inches of shit?'

'Enough to drown in,' said Yates.

'Smart-arse,' said Ria.

'I know.'

She punched him in the arm.

'Chloe Dark and two others,' said Lament. 'One known as Dog—'

'Dog?' said Yates. 'That little shit?'

'Canine DNA, very appropriate name,' said Ria. 'And the other is the one with the shoe? I couldn't identify that one except it's some form of rodent.'

'Jason Lomax, he has a severely deformed nose.'

'Wait, he's related to Ellen Lomax?'

'I forgot you didn't know,' said Lament.

'Whoever did this was a fucking genius,' said Ria. 'The joins were seamless. I'd really like to see those freaks in the flesh.'

'No way,' said Yates. 'We find the floor and then we get out.'

'You're no fun at all.'

'We're here,' said Lament as the car pulled up in a snowy back alley.

'What's the best building?'

'Debenhams.'

'We always seem to come back here.'

'Fate,' said Lament.

Chapter 22

Chloe

She pulled the gloves she had borrowed from her aunt from her pocket. They were leather but flexible. Thick enough to keep the worst of the cold out, but thin enough for her to be able to feel what she was doing.

Mitchell had said she was nuts when she first suggested it but he had come around.

The lower levels of the Utopia Genetics building were slimmer than the upper ones by a good ten to twenty feet, as the building curved upwards in its distinctive impression of a DNA double helix. If she had been intending to climb the sheer face of a skyscraper with flat glass walls in these temperatures then she might have considered his disagreement valid, but the shape of the building meant the climb was not vertical, it was like going up a very steep ramp that curved round the building.

Assuming she could get up to it. The first hundred feet of the tower was exactly the flat vertical glass she did not want to climb.

On the other side of the street was another building, nowhere near the height of this one but it would give her the starting height she needed. She glanced around and couldn't see anyone. She rapped on the metal of the car and the sounds gave her an overlay with sharper edges and flat surfaces. Still nobody in the area.

She hurried across the road and into the alley beside it. There was a fire escape and she leapt the first three floors. Crusted ice and frost broke away as she caught hold of the railing. The cold seeped through the gloves to her skin. The vibration of her landing made the metal thrum and she got a clear picture of the levels up from where she was.

It was hard to go straight up from here, unless she leapt floor by floor. Instead she launched herself up and across to the opposite building. The surface was brick-work, no windows or metal—except for the guttering near the corner. She simply used the wall to immediately leap back to the fire escape. And she had gained another forty feet. She repeated the action and landed on the roof. Her feet slipped on frozen puddles.

She turned to face the enormous building spiralling up and away from her.

The start of the curving part of the building was still higher than she was but she thought she could make it. She knew she was in a hurry but if she got this wrong she would end up having to do it all over again. Assuming she didn't hit her head.

She gave a short laugh. Perhaps braining herself against the wall might bring her to her senses. She snapped her fingers, forgetting she was wearing gloves. The quiet muffled thud that resulted failed to reveal anything of her surroundings. She moved across the surface slowly until she found a ventilation duct. She tapped it and the booming lit up the area. She could clearly see the wall around the edge of the roof, the other ducts and old chimneys. What it didn't do was reveal the state of the roof itself. It seemed to be slick with ice covered by a frosting of snow. She didn't know how much speed she was going to be able to achieve before reaching the wall.

She needed grips on her shoes. Or skates. Hindsight was twenty-twenty.

Moving back so that she had the longest straight run up she could achieve, she pushed off. With the delicacy of a ballet dancer she placed her feet as best she could and dug in, trying to get more speed with each step, and bounded across the surface.

Because each step grew longer it took her only five giant strides to reach the far side. For a moment she wasn't sure if she had judged it right and would end up simply going over the edge into the middle of the street. But she had.

As she hit the far wall she let both knees bend and then thrust full strength as her weight went over. She went up like a firework in a long arc. Once more she tried to flatten herself out, and her wings pressed against the inside of her coat. Something ripped.

Ahead of her the lowest edge of the curved section was coming at her. In a moment she knew her trajectory was wrong. She was going to miss it. She stretched her arms forward, her fingers reaching for the edge.

They touched. The snow crumbled under her fingers. With her tenuous grip acting as a brake she slowed and her body swung, pendulum like, beneath her. She felt her fingertips slipping. Quickly she pulled up her legs, giving herself a faster rotation. Her fingers lost their grip but now she was spinning and her rate of fall had been temporarily halted.

She had never been good at gymnastics but she knew the theory. The tighter the ball, the faster the spin. She grabbed her knees. She saw the building she had jumped from upside-down. The street below came into view then the flat glass of the lower floors of the Utopia Genetics building, finally the overhang that was the start of the DNA spiral. She stretched out, flung her arms up and grabbed at the edge.

Here, on a surface sheltered from the worst of the weather, her fingers found proper purchase. Her feet continued to swing up and she hooked a foot over as well.

She came to a halt hanging upside-down from the bottom of the spiral. She got the ridiculous impression that someone, somewhere, was applauding.

It took her only a moment to pull herself up so she was crouched on the concrete of the structure. And then she began the ascent, slowly at first, getting a feel for the way the slope was constructed. As she became accustomed to it she moved closer in to the core, away from the snow and ice, and climbed almost at a run. Each step pushed her up towards the penthouse of Mercedes Smith.

Chapter 23

Yates

His warrant card, and Ria's forensics ID, got them through security and into the building. The equipment was sufficiently non-specific that it could be accepted as something forensics might use. At least as far as the guard might be concerned.

It was eerie to be in a department store at night. With the shelves half-filled it had a deserted look and the size of it made every sound echo.

Both of them had been in the building before but neither knew how to get up to the roof.

'Let's go up to the fifth and then see where we can go from there,' said Yates.

It was warm in here, at least relative to the outside, and there was no wind. The escalators were turned off, of course, so they used the customer stairs. They reached the defunct restaurant on the top floor with its antique styles. There was an odd smell, almost as if something had died a long time ago. On the other side of the space was an emergency exit sign glowing green. They headed for it.

'The things I do,' said Yates under his breath. He did not want to say anything out loud.

There was an echoing clatter in the distance as if a mannequin had fallen to the ground. They both froze. They waited for long moments. Silence.

'Probably nothing,' said Yates very quietly.

'Probably.'

'Nobody knows we're here.'

'Nobody,' she said.

'How could they?'

He put his hand on Ria's shoulder and pushed her down behind a counter. A bullet cracked past them and buried itself in the wall behind them.

'Shit,' muttered Yates.

Ria grabbed his arm and in the dim night lighting of the store her eyes were wide. He pulled out his gun. 'Carry the gear. Stay down. Head for the exit.'

'What are you going to do, Harry?'

'Just do it, Ria. Lament needs to know where the girls are.'

'Be careful.'

'I'm no hero,' he said. 'Move it.'

Another bullet cracked past and went through the panelling he was hiding behind. A nice new hole allowed light through. He rejected the idea of using it as a spy hole to get the direction and moved the other way just as another hole appeared beside it.

He checked on Ria; she was halfway to the door, crawling with the detector slung over her shoulder. One of the restaurant chairs lay close by. Straining, he lifted it cleanly from the floor to avoid noise and then flung it as hard as he could in a direction away from the emergency exit, and lifted his head above the counter.

In the silence of the store, the sound of the chair crashing into a table was sudden and surprising. Three fast cracks and impacts echoed through the room. He saw the muzzle flash. The shooter was about twenty yards away behind a display pedestal. The remains of a mannequin were scattered around it.

'Clumsy,' muttered Yates. He checked the angle between the sniper and the door Ria was heading for. He was not in direct line. She was almost there.

Keeping down he got on his knees and focused on what he could hear. This was going to be tight.

The door creaked as Ria opened it. Yates paused for a fraction of a second. *Hear. Look. Aim.* He came up straight, gun in his hand. The sniper barrel was aimed to his right. Yates's gun roared. He knew the shot was on target but he didn't wait for the result. He stumbled to his feet and ran for the exit. Ria had frozen at his shot.

'Go!'

She pushed the door harder and it swung back. He reached it just as she was getting up and he threw himself against her to push her through, and to the ground. Bullets cracked over his head. And then into the door as it swung back. Unlike the counter this was solid wood and stopped every single one of them.

There were stairs up and down. 'Up!' he said and almost pulled her along as she tried to get to her feet. Moments later they rounded the first turn and kept going.

'No locks on fire escapes,' he said.

They pounded up the next flight. The door below squeaked. At the next turn Yates paused. He saw a movement and fired another shot. The noise echoed up and down the stairwell. If he didn't hit the guy, he'd be stunned from the noise.

I wish.

They reached the end of the stairs with a small landing and a door. A length of wire was twisted round the lock to prevent it opening.

'Can you get it open?' Yates said as he knelt on one knee and rested his hands on the railing. Gun pointed back the way they came.

'It'll take a minute,' she said. Her voice wasn't shaking and that helped.

'Quick as you can. I'll keep them off you.'

'You know,' she said. 'I blame the wirehead.'

'Yeah, me too.'

A shadow moved below them and he fired. The shadow vanished.

'Jesus! Could you let me know when you're going to do that?'

'Might give the game away to the other guy.'

'Guys.'

'Plural?'

'I saw two.'

'Maybe seeing double?'

'Maybe.'

He jumped back as a burst of machine-gun fire raked up from below, pinging off the metal. A dark shape arced up in the dim light, and then burst in a flame of brilliant white. All he could see was white with black spots that came and went. He heard feet pounding on the stairs below. He moved back and tried to remember the exact position of his hands on the railing. He fired. And fired. Tilted the barrel down a little, fired.

He was rewarded by a cry of pain. He angled a little further down and fired twice more. It sounded like the footsteps were moving away. And someone was groaning.

'Nice shooting,' said Ria. 'Voila!'

Freezing air poured in from the outside. Still blind he let off one more shot and stepped out on to the roof.

'Shut the door, Ria.'

'You do it, dickhead.'

'I can't see a fucking thing. That flash grenade.'

'You looked at it? Moron.'

He felt her push past him and the door slam.

'Is there anything to bar the door?' he said.

Metal scraped on the ground. 'Shit, that's cold.' Then metal against metal.

'It won't hold for long,' she said.

'Find me somewhere to sit where I can cover the door.'

'You can't see.'

'I've got ears and if I'm sitting you can point me in the right direction. I can keep them inside while you scan for the right floor.'

She grabbed him by the arm and dragged him, stumbling, across the roof.

'Shouldn't I put you behind something, so you have cover?'

'I won't be able to shoot straight. Just do what I said.'

'You're a total dick, you know that?'

'Yeah, I know.'

He felt the warmth coming from her face and her breath against his lips. She touched his nose with hers. 'No kisses, it's too risky.'

'I'll take what I can get.'

'Just want to remind you what you're missing.'

'Consider me reminded.' In the sitting position he brought his knees up and rested his hands on them, clutching the gun. 'Point me in the right direction.'

She adjusted his aim slightly. 'We're off about sixty degrees from the door and it opens away from you.'

'Thanks.'

He felt her move away. 'You know how to use that thing?'

'I'm a scientist, how hard can it be?'

Chapter 24

Mitchell

They made their way through the building to the lifts and then down via the stairs. He was concerned. Apart from the look he kept getting from Dog, and the weirdness of Jason Lomax, he had a nagging feeling that something was wrong.

There was no justification for it. But it was there nonetheless. Perhaps it was because he was on the wrong side of the law. Though he somehow doubted it was guilt. He had left guilt behind a long time ago.

He stopped at the bottom of the stairs they had taken to the car park level—it also felt wrong to be going down when their target was very definitely up. He held his gun before him.

There was nothing here to set off the alarm bells in his mind but it was the ease of the whole thing that nagged at him.

Ahead of them and to the right was the door that would take them out into the underground car park. There was a low-level light in here but the car park was dark. Had it been dark when he had looked on the monitor? He couldn't remember; he hadn't studied it in that much detail.

'Can you smell trouble?' he asked.

'I can smell you,' said Dog.

Mitchell turned to Jason. He felt sympathy for the kid, being unable to talk must have been a real trial for him. But at least he had his mother.

And then Jason was in front of him and moving fast. Mitchell raised his hand and started to take the breath to tell him to stop. But he was too slow. The door swung inward as if Jason was opening it but the boy went past it and was tucked into the corner beyond when the explosion ripped both doors off their hinges.

A wave of heat knocked Mitchell back. His bare skin stung as flying splinters of wood and glass peppered him. Something cut through his leg.

The noise was so loud he didn't hear it. His only thought was 'again?' before pain hit him front and back, and he passed out.

Cold air brushed across his skin. He was lying on the lowest flight of stairs that propped him up and dug painfully into his back. The weight of his pistol was still in his hand. The lights were out. He blinked and tiny bits of debris fell like tears from his eyelids.

He had been wrong about the light in the car park. There was some. Just very dim. Or they had turned it on after the blast. Had it been a grenade or a booby trap? Probably the latter.

Why had Jason done that? Had he known? If he had known it was really stupid. Maybe he thought someone was out there and wanted to draw them out.

A shadow moved at the entrance to the door. He couldn't hear a thing but someone was coming and whoever it was was not going to be a friend. He lifted his hand.

The barrel of an assault rifle came into view. Mitchell held the gun, his muscles felt weak. Explosions were not good for the health.

The head and body appeared, completely covered in soft armour. Military. The armour would absorb most of the energy of a bullet. He aimed higher. The head turned his way, light reflecting on the glass of the goggles.

Mitchell fired three times in quick succession. The head jerked back and the man collapsed as if his strings had been cut. Automatic fire cut through the gap. There was little risk of ricochet as the slugs buried themselves in the brickwork beyond. That meant there was at least one more of them out there, and in armour too. He was lucky to have been close enough to take the shot he did.

A shadow shifted above and behind the far door. Jason was still moving. Mitchell groaned as he pulled himself into a proper sitting position and then clambered to his feet. At least he assumed he had groaned, his throat rasped as he moved. Unfortunately that meant their opposition knew that someone was alive.

Something shifted beside him. Dog clawed up the wall until he was standing. In the dim light he looked ... probably much the same as Mitchell himself. Covered in dust and debris. Dog stretched, getting the kinks out of his body.

Mitchell touched his ear and then spread his palm to indicate he was deaf. Dog nodded and made the same move. Not surprising.

Dog locked his gaze on Mitchell but not in the aggressive way he had done before. Dog pointed at the body and gave Mitchell a thumbs-up. Must be friends now. Mitchell gave a half smile.

There was a flash of movement as a ball-like object arced into the room but Jason's hand swept at it, caught it and flung it back. It erupted moments later. Mitchell couldn't hear it but he could feel the shock wave. Dog leapt at the door and was through it in a second. The shadow of Jason flickered across the top of the door as if he was clinging to the ceiling. Mitchell ran after them, holding his gun ready.

Chapter 25

Chloe

She had given up counting the floors. The building just went on and on, up and up in a continuous spiral.

The crack of gunshots attracted her attention and highlighted the top of a building—though at this range there were no details. She wasn't tired but she paused. Anything unusual happening here tonight was her business. Watching out for patches of ice, she moved further out towards the edge of the spiral. The structure seemed to fall away and there was southern Manchester laid out in the night. Sparkling in the snow. It looked peaceful.

Two figures staggered on to the roof of the building about two hundred feet below her. A man and a woman carrying something. The man looked hurt. They barred the door and the woman helped the man sit facing the way down. Moments later the woman came to the edge of the building and started to point the whatever-it-was at the Utopia Genetics building.

It might be a gun.

She clambered back to the inner part of the spiral. There was no way she could remain completely hidden but if that was a gun she needed to stay clear of it. It was windy up here but again staying close to the centre protected her from the worst of it.

And then, after two further turns of the spiral, it was the end of the line.

She hadn't considered what would happen when she reached the top. All she knew was that Mercedes Smith lived there. But above her was the flat under-surface of what was probably the penthouse. The wind howled but the space above her, beyond the outer layer, was strangely invisible to her acoustic sense. It must be soundproofed, or layers of insulation simply absorbed the sound as well.

She pulled a flashlight from her bag. She had remembered to pick up another one but she didn't switch it on. Instead she tapped it against the wall. The resonating sound fed back a complex network of spaces, girders and pipes.

And there was a walkway in there.

She tracked back, going down the spiral until she was directly below where the walkway ended. A ladder came down to the door in front of her. She hadn't noticed it on the way up because she hadn't been looking for it. She saw the door lock inside a panel on the right which swung open. She tried it. It didn't turn.

Taking the flashlight in one hand she got her head close to the lock and tapped gently trying to get a full three-dimensional picture of it.

'Damn it.'

There was a bolt-like mechanism on the inside, and there was no way she could shift it. She shouldn't have been surprised they weren't going to leave an unlocked door here. It might not be the easiest place to get to, but anyone with enough persistence could manage it.

A thought was trying to make it to the front of her mind. It was the walkway. It ended so abruptly above her. She tapped a little harder and the sound waves brought her the image of another door directly above this one. What if there had been a mistake in the construction and that walkway was supposed to meet the spiral so they put the door in but they had got it wrong.

It didn't matter, there really was another door about ten feet above her. Her hands found the necessary holds and she climbed. She had never been much of a climber when she was young. There had been a lovely big apple tree in the garden and it was easy to get into its branches and climb as high as she could. But she stopped being interested when she got older.

Everything was different now. Her lack of weight made it all so easy. She was nearly two hundred metres up, climbing a flat metal surface crusted in ice. In a high wind.

It took her a few moments to reach the second door. The panel was there just like below. She made sure her hand and footholds were solid, then she pulled open the little hatch and turned the lock. It was stiff and the first time she slipped off the wall completely and hung by the hand holding the lever. She got back into position and tried again. It still held and she was about to give up when it turned slightly. She redoubled her efforts and it unlocked.

She yanked the door open. A wash of warm air and cool blue light streamed out. She slipped through the gap and pulled it closed, relocking it, then stepped on to the walkway.

Above her she knew was Mercedes Smith's apartment and she was keen to see the look on the woman's face when she saw Chloe Dark alive and well.

Chloe really was looking forward to that a great deal.

Chapter 26

Mitchell

He felt old and slow. He shouldn't be doing this. This was a game for young men. He suspected his life might be about to end very abruptly and probably painfully as he crossed the threshold.

And then the young will be able to step into my shoes.

The dim light in the car park showed the empty expanse delineated by white and yellow paint and punctuated by pillars. He kept moving at an angle to the gunfire, as much as he could figure out its source.

No gunfire raked across his decrepit frame, although his ears were beginning to whistle a bit. He had experience of that and it was a relief his hearing might be returning.

He made for the nearest pillar. He felt something move past the back of his head but no sound penetrated. It could have been nothing. He threw himself to the ground behind the concrete. Only to be showered by dust.

That answered that question. Not only was there one out there but he was active. It also meant this pillar was a good place to be for the moment. At least until the shooter switched back to grenades.

Mitchell squirmed to his feet. He would regret all this later, when the adrenaline wore off. Perhaps he would be saved from the pain, if he was dead.

Dull thuds made it through the singing in his ears. More bullets? He wasn't sure. If they were, he couldn't see where they were impacting.

He took a chance and poked his head out to the side. His one eye saw muzzle flashes and they were in movement. Arcing up and across. There was something skittering across the pipework suspended from the roof.

Mitchell stepped out and fired round after round at the soldier. Each of his own shots was becoming more distinct as his ears recovered. He tried to aim for the head but even the shots that hit home made no impression. Soft armour was effective. His attack drew the man's attention. Mitchell ducked back behind the pillar as the barrel of the weapon dropped toward him. But as he disappeared he saw something else moving. This time bounding across the floor, coming in at the soldier from behind.

Mitchell paused and fired one last shot to keep the soldier's attention on him.

Automatic fire blasted his way as he pulled back.

There was a scream. And a lot of growling. Someone gurgled as if they were taking their final breath through a throat that bubbled with their own blood.

And then it became very quiet.

Mitchell checked his gun and stepped out carefully. Dog was bending over a body. Mitchell approached slowly. Dog looked at him and growled. Mitchell made a point of pointing his gun away, clicking on the safety and putting the gun in its holster. Then he held his hands open and stopped a good twenty feet from Dog.

Jason dropped from the pipes and landed silently. He paced towards Dog but at an angle that took him to a point a couple of yards away.

'Are we good?' said Mitchell keeping his empty hands in view. He glanced at Jason who shrugged. It was a human action with a face from a nightmare but even Mitchell was getting used to it.

Dog was breathing heavily but seemed to be calming. There was blood across his face and on his hands. Something like a Viking bloodlust, Mitchell thought. Or a wolf. Like a werewolf that was always on the border of being the beast.

'Are we good, Dog?'

He was no more than a boy really, thought Mitchell, just like Jason and Chloe and those other girls. Children.

Dog shook himself and stared down at the bloody body at his feet as if he had never seen it before.

'Shit.'

Mitchell took that as a sign he had recovered, and walked slowly up to him, but still not directly at him. Mitchell looked down at the body. The soft armour had been torn open at the neck and his skin ripped with it.

'I think you got him,' he said.

The two freaks seemed relaxed now. He could probably trust their instincts and their senses. But he was surprised at Dog. In all the years he had been aware of his existence, Mitchell was sure Dog had never killed anyone. He was always the joker. This was completely different.

Perhaps Dog had never been threatened like this before. Mitchell was grateful he had never managed to corner him. The outcome might not have been what either of them had expected.

And now they had crossed a line. Even if using military grade munitions was certainly a crime he wouldn't have known about it if he hadn't been trespassing on Utopia's grounds. Unfortunately the presence of these men raised a question: if Mercedes Smith had not known they were coming, how could there be an ambush?

'All right. We need to move.'

Dog dragged his eyes away from the body.

'Jason, can you get the scent of the girls in here?'

The boy moved swiftly. He returned to the central elevator area and, like a shadow, moved swiftly round it disappearing from sight.

'Are you okay, Dog?'

'Chloe's right,' he said. 'I need to keep the animal inside.'

'She's not right,' Mitchell said. 'Sometimes letting the animal out is the right thing to do. If you hadn't taken him down he could have killed us all.'

'I can still taste his blood.'

Mitchell pulled a flask from his coat. 'I keep this for emergencies.'

'You don't get it,' said Dog. 'I can smell things a thousand times better than you. I can't even begin to describe what that—' he pointed down '—smells like, and what he tastes like. And the fact that I like it.'

'This is just water,' said Mitchell. 'Wash your mouth out at least.'

Dog took it just as Jason came back. He was pointing back the way he came.

'He's got them,' said Dog then took a mouthful, swilled it round and spat it out.

Jason was gone again and they followed.

'Only one thing,' said Dog.

'What's that?'

'We might be able to find the lift they went into but how are we going to find the right floor?'

'I'm relying on you two,' said Mitchell.

Chapter 27

Ria MacDonald

She slipped on the ice as she crossed the roof and came down heavily on her knees as she tried to save the detector from hitting too hard.

Crap.

What the hell was she doing? She could be lying in bed at home with something warm between her legs, preferably Harry but there were other options, including Mr Pointy. Rather than get to her feet, and run the risk of falling again, she decided to crawl. Looking back she could see Harry sitting with his gun ready. She moved a little more to the left and put the protruding air vent between her and the door. She really did not want to get shot.

The air was freezing and her condensed breath hung in the air as it turned into ice crystals. The huge bulk of the Utopia Genetics building rose up ahead of her.

If they got through this alive she was going to have to let him down easy. He was great in bed but he was getting too attached and that was not something she wanted. This was not a world to get attached to people. They died one way or another, and she was always the one to pick up the pieces. In some cases literally.

Maybe she could persuade him that it was his idea. That would be best.

Of course he'd hate himself, but Harry would get over it. As soon as he realised how upset he was he'd recognise it was because he was forming too strong an attachment. And that would kick him out of it.

He wasn't stupid. At least not too stupid, for a male.

She reached the edge of the roof where a low wall rose up. She put the detector on it. There wasn't a lot of light but the thing looked pretty simple. It resembled a gun but had a plate-sized detector. Behind that, along the barrel, was an exciter section that would take the collected image and amplify it. The section after that was simply the hand grips. The secondary unit carried the graphene power supply, and a monitor.

The process of plugging in the cables was easy. The on-switch was obvious but it came on with a yellow warning light. The monitor flickered and its system started to boot up.

A crash echoed across the roof. Metal hitting metal. She jerked her head round but couldn't see the door.

For god's sake, Harry, I don't want to die!

She was happy putting bits of people in bags. That was her kind of level. They didn't argue, they were just a puzzle. A broken pen top could provide the solution to an entire case if she studied it carefully. Broken pen tops didn't try to kill you. She could sit in the warmth of her office and study the bits and pieces that *were not trying to end her.*

Harry could keep his bloody field work.

The monitor pinged quietly and told her the detector was still preparing.

Preparing? What the hell did that mean?

The yellow light still shone on the detector gun.

Five shots in rapid succession, slightly muffled. They must have come from the stairwell. Probably trying to shoot out the lock or something. That was stupid. It never worked.

Green light. *Yes.*

Shadowy lines appeared on the monitor. She squinted and could not make out what they were. When she picked up the detector gun, the lines on the screen moved. Edges, they were the edges of flat surfaces with a slightly different temperature. She pointed the gun at the building. The screen flared for a moment and then adjusted. She could see the blocky shapes of the various floors as they spiralled up.

She aimed at the base of the building and there were multiple temperature variations that resolved into a representation of the outside of the building. Hotter pipes and conduits showed up in yellows, oranges and reds. As she continued to point it in one direction, the image resolved into a three-dimensional approximation of the rooms on this side. It was a nice bit of tech, and she was impressed.

The image smudged and blurred as she ran the detector up the building's side. The floors above fifth were colder and the image faded to greys and blacks. All she had to do was scan slowly until she found something warmer and then let the machine focus.

An explosion rocked the roof and she was thrown forwards across the wall as something let out a crash to her side. She grabbed the detector convulsively as it threatened to go over the edge.

'Harry!'

'Still here love.'

She got herself back on to the roof with her back to the wall, cradling the detector in her arms. She could now see the door. It had been ripped off its hinges and was lying against the wall.

'They blew the bloody door off.'

'I guessed.'

She still couldn't see the opening from where she was sitting. The vent and Harry were in the way. There was a crunch. For a moment she thought it was someone's foot but there was nothing else. Smoke poured from whatever they had thrown.

'Smoke grenade,' she said.

'Doesn't make a lot of difference to me,' he said.

'Or me,' she muttered and pulled up her knees. She placed the detector in them to hold it steady then brought the monitor round and dumped it in her lap. Maybe they had infra-red goggles but mostly they used ultra-violet because heat was not as clear as UV. They would be blind too but would count on their superior fire-power and armour.

But they didn't have a detector like this one.

The image was resolving. The air-vent. Then the hot spot that was Harry. The software inside this thing was clever, the detector itself must be collecting a lot more data than just what was coming from the front.

The hot points where they had blown out the hinges glowed as the rest of the stairwell came into view. Their explosion had heated different parts to different levels of heat making the detector's task so much easier.

It might not be as responsive as UV but it would do the job.

'How much do you trust me, Harry?'

'Quite a lot.'

'Do exactly what I say and we've got a chance.'

'Okay.' He used the tone of voice that meant he was dubious. He always hated being blindfolded and that always made it more fun. This time he had no choice.

'It's just a blindfold, Harry.'

Moment's pause. 'Okay.' That was more confident.

She kept her eyes glued to the monitor.

'Raise the gun, Harry, be ready.'

The monitor showed him obeying. It was just like a video game.

The amount of delay meant the monitor was resolving through the roof as well. She could see the stairs themselves and a human-shaped heat source lying down. Another on its feet.

'You got one of them, Harry, there's only one other.'

'Roger.'

The figure put his foot on the lower step. Ria glanced into the real world and said in the quietest voice she thought would actually reach him, 'The smoke is thick, Harry, he can't see anything either.'

'He'll be in soft armour.'

'I know.'

Harry put the gun down.

'What are you doing?'

'Shooting won't work.'

He climbed to his feet. The figure inside the stairwell was making steady progress.

'Tell me when he's at the top of the stairs, Ria.'

She wanted to tell him to pick up his gun and not be an idiot. But she knew he was right.

Waiting until the man was a few steps down. 'Now Harry, don't run, I'll guide you.'

He stepped forward quickly. 'Left a bit, bit more, straight.'

The soldier was on the penultimate step.

'Now, Harry.'

The image blurred as he lunged forward, his arms outstretched, screaming in an effort to distract the soldier. The bodies impacted and she could hear their thudding fall. She took a deep breath and turned back to the Utopia Genetics building. She had to make this worthwhile.

Chapter 28

Chloe

There were sounds in here. The heat in the pipes made them click. Pumps in the distance pounded but the clicks were pitched just right for her. As she moved slowly forward, along the walkway among the pipes, power lines and conduits she was able to pick up a picture of what was around her.

The rooms, corridors and other spaces mapped out in her head. All inanimate, not a single person among them as far as she could see.

And the space above her, the penthouse, continued to be an enigma. It was thoroughly insulated and sound-proofed; she could see nothing but the floor above her.

She stopped and leaned against the railing. Cocking her head on one side she closed her eyes, trying to see as far as she could.

On the lower levels, the outside walls were insulated, but inside the construction was flimsy. Perhaps it was as much to reduce the overall weight as to save money; either way, down four or five floors was an open book to her.

Then she heard a cry. At the very edge of her hearing, something plaintive as if it was hurting. She glanced up again, to where she imagined Mercedes Smith might be. She knew her friend was here. Seeing the look on that woman's face was less important.

There was a way through below. She jumped over the edge and landed on a pipe ten feet below. A few steps across to another gap and down again. It was a tedious business and there was the occasional difficult squeeze. But she dropped through five floors in a couple of minutes.

There had been no further sound. It was colder down here, as if they weren't giving it much heat, and the pipes were quieter. She tapped. The reverberation refreshed the map in her head and filled in more details at this level. At first she was not even sure this was the right floor but then a door shut and she watched the form of someone exiting a room and heading along the corridor.

She was sure, as she had been climbing, that the floors were empty.

This must be the one.

There was a similar walkway from an outside door. This one was misplaced as well but a new one had not been cut at a lower level. She jumped across to it and headed in towards the core. The thinness of the walls meant there was no gap she could use to get further into the building. There was only the maintenance hatch at the end which opened easily enough.

She stepped out into the interior.

There was no sound, but a dim blue light showed the plain uncarpeted floors and the unadorned walls. The place smelled unused—slightly damp.

'Hello, Chloe.'

She spun round but there was no one. The sound had come from above and she saw the speaker set into the ceiling. It did not look like a recent addition.

'Please stay exactly where you are.'

It wasn't coming from just one speaker. There were several. She inched back towards the hatch.

'I said don't move.'

A piercing sound screeched from the speakers. She slammed her hands over her ears but it did nothing. She felt her balance going and she fell to her knees.

The sound stopped leaving only a buzzing and a dull ache.

'I found your kryptonite,' said the voice. 'An excellent analysis even if I do say so myself. Mercedes will be pleased.'

'Who are you?'

'My name is Xec. I was the one that found you. I was the one who arranged for your pick-up.'

'Like Melinda.'

'Yes, just like her,' he said. 'But you have been quite a problem. Now here we are at last, and I have succeeded.'

'How did you know?'

'That you were here? I've been monitoring you and your little band since you left your aunt's house.'

Chloe wondered why Lament's plan had not worked. Well, he had not promised, it had just seemed like a clever idea.

'What's happened to them?'

'Your band of heroes? I must admit I was very surprised at their tenacity, and to see Mitchell and Yates still trying to solve their case. Quite touching really.'

'I'm sure.'

'Yes, I'm afraid DS Yates is no more, while DI Mitchell is trapped in the elevator. Not that he had any clue what he was doing. I'm still very impressed they both managed to deal with two fully equipped soldiers. One wonders if they might have freak blood themselves.'

Chloe frowned. There seemed to be something wrong with Xec's assessment of the situation; for a start she had no idea Yates was involved. Perhaps Lament had pulled him in at the last moment.

'What are you going to do with me?'

'I admit that both Mercedes and Purity Officer Graham are very keen to see you dead. Mercedes was quite apoplectic when she found out you had survived.'

'I would have liked to have seen that.'

'I'm sure you would have,' said Xec. 'Too late. Miss Kepple, however, did not seem at all surprised and I think Mr Graham has something special planned for her. Personally though, I think it would be more useful to have you kept for study. I would almost go as far as to say that Dr Newman reached the peak of his creativity and skill with you.'

'I'll kill myself.'

'I doubt it. Even if you had the opportunity you're more likely to try to escape, but since we know your Achilles heel, keeping you in check will be simplicity.'

Chloe couldn't deny it. Unless there was some way she could switch off her hearing it was easy for someone to stop her completely.

'I still want to see my friend.'

'That door over there, where you saw the nurse exit.'

'How do you—' She cut herself off. It had all been a trap. They had all been manoeuvred into this position and trapped.

'I hope you're seeing the futility of your position, Chloe,' he said. 'Because that will make things so much easier for you.'

She did not respond but walked along the corridor and pushed open the door. Subdued lighting that was focused only on the desk—not occupied—gave the room soft highlights and deep shadows. Three beds were crammed close together in a room not designed to take them, and three figures covered with sheets, all linked to IV feeds.

The first was the redhead, Vanessa Cooper. At the far end was someone Chloe could not see clearly. In fact the shape under the white cloth was barely recognisable as human. But in the middle was the familiar head and face of Melinda.

Chloe almost cried in relief. She squeezed between beds, pulled off her glove and took Melinda's hand. It was warm and felt the way it always had—perhaps a little rougher. The face and hair were the same.

'What's wrong with them?'

'They are under twilight sedation,' came the voice. 'For their own good.'

She looked across at the figure in the next bed. If you ignored the folds of thick skin and the lack of hair, there was a girl's face in there. You could almost imagine she was wearing a hood. Almost.

'Who's she?'

'The redhead is Vanessa Cooper, the other one is Lucy Grainger.'

That settled it, this wirehead could see her. She tapped on the metal of the cot frame. The high-pitched vibrations filled the room. Without turning around she spotted the camera over the door.

'What about the other ones?'

'Other ones?'

'I know there have been others before.'

'Oh those,' said Xec. 'They died.'

Chloe slid the needle of the IV from Melinda's arm, careful not to pull it all the way, so it looked as if it was still in place.

'Did you kill them?'

She slid out from between the beds and moved to Lucy Grainger.

'I did not kill them. My job is the protection and support of Mercedes Smith.'

'So how did they die? Is the genetic change dangerous?'

'Oh, I see, you just care about yourself.'

She let him believe that.

He continued. 'Some of the early versions were unstable.'

'Like S.I.D.'

'Similar, I suppose. The modifications became dominant and wiped out the host.'

'And later?'

'Once we have completed our analysis, the asset no longer has any value.'

'So the answer is yes,' she said. 'You killed them.'

She slipped the IV out of Lucy Grainger. It looked as if the hole had been drilled into the hide. Poor girl.

'And you killed Ali Najjar.'

'We couldn't let news of you get out.'

'You wanted me all to yourself.'

'That's right. By the time he had got to your version Dr Newman appears to have fully cracked the techniques and requirements for successful gene manipulation.'

Chloe noticed cotton wool swabs on a small table beside Vanessa. And moved round to that.

'But you haven't managed to duplicate his work?'

'Why do you think that?'

'You haven't disposed of these three.'

She had managed to identify only one speaker in this room, and the one camera. The door was flimsy but if it was shut the sonic attack from the wirehead should be ineffective. But he would activate it the moment she acted in a threatening way.

One of Melinda's fingers twitched. Chloe had no idea how long it would take the sedation to wear off. She hoped it would not be long. She needed to spin this out.

'I'm obviously different, and Lucy, but Melinda and this one look normal.'

'Your friend's differences are internal though impressive,' he said. 'But take a look at Vanessa's teeth.'

'What?'

'You want to know? Look at her teeth.'

Chloe was reluctant to invade the girl's privacy and person but it meant she could lean over her and detach the IV. She reached up to the girl's mouth and gently pushed back her lips. The canines were significantly larger top and bottom while the ones further back were also pointed. She managed to pull the IV out but it came all the way. There was no way she could take the time to put it back in properly. She laid it against the girl's skin and hoped the wirehead wouldn't notice.

Melinda twitched again.

'What sort of teeth are they?' she asked as she moved further up the bed and swiped some cotton wool from the table.

'What are you doing?'

'I don't know what—'

The loudspeakers screeched. She slammed her hands over her ears again, this time shoving cotton wool into them.

Chapter 29

Mitchell

He stared at the floor buttons; which one? There were almost sixty floors and they couldn't try each one.

'What are you waiting for?' said Dog.

'You choose one,' said Mitchell. 'Each one is as good as any other. Apart from the bottom ten or so which are used as offices. The top one is Mercedes Smith's suite and this lift doesn't go that far.'

'You're well informed.'

'I've been here before.'

Jason's hand snaked out and he pressed the thirtieth. The doors slid shut.

'We'll be able to smell if the scent of the girls gets stronger.'

'We're inside a steel box,' said Mitchell as the lift climbed.

'Do you have a better idea?'

'No,' he said. 'But by the time you smell it we'll be past it.'

They fell silent as they passed the twentieth and the numbers clicked up.

The lift came to a halt and the doors slid open. The floor was dark except for an occasional blue light. It was cold too.

Mitchell glanced at Jason but he shook his head.

'And we haven't passed it?'

Another shake of the head.

That left another thirty floors. Jason pressed the forty-fifth. Halfway again? That made some sense. But even as the doors slid shut the lift button went dark and the fifty-first came on.

'Did you do that?' said Mitchell.

Jason shook his head. Mitchell pressed the forty-fifth again. The light did not come on.

'Something's controlling the lift,' said Dog.

'That's not going to be good for us,' said Mitchell and checked his gun. 'You stand that side, Dog. I'll take this.' He glanced up at the grid in the ceiling. He pointed at Jason and then up. 'If you can block the light as well, that would be good.'

Jason scaled the wall and in a moment was hanging from the ceiling. It wasn't entirely clear how he was doing it, although his fingers were entwined with the grid.

Mitchell stepped to the side as the lift came to a halt and the door slid open.

Nothing happened except another wave of cold air flowed in.

'Can you hear something?' said Mitchell.

'Too bloody right,' said Dog. 'Loud. High-pitched. Glad I'm not there, blow my bloody ears out.'

'Where?'

'Next floor? Next but one?'

'Up or down?'

Dog moved closer to the gap between the lift and the outer doors. Tilted his head.

'Up.'

'That's where they are.'

Mitchell piled back into the lift.

'Not me, mate,' said Dog. 'I told you. That noise will blow my ears.'

'How about Chloe?'

'Hers too.'

'Exactly. She's there and under attack.'

Mitchell hit the button for the next floor. Nothing happened. He pressed it again and harder.

'Someone doesn't want us on that floor.'

'Lament,' said Mitchell. 'He must have found the floor. He's the one that brought us here and he doesn't want us to go up in the lift.'

Mitchell checked all directions.

'The stairs are this way,' said Mitchell. 'Come on.' He left the lift and scanned the nearby doors. There was one marked with the Emergency Exit symbol. He pushed through into it and found the stairs. Jason flashed past him.

'I can't,' said Dog. 'The noise.'

'It's not in here,' said Mitchell. 'We'll figure it out when we get up there. If you can't follow us, you can guard our backs.'

He didn't wait but headed up the first flight, shadowed by Jason. The ear-piercing screech was louder but not emanating from this floor. They went up the next one. Even for someone without enhanced hearing the noise was loud and painful. He thought it had been going on for a long time. If it had been to simply disable Chloe surely a short burst would have been enough?

Then the lights went out.

Chapter 30

Chloe

The noise destroyed her acoustic sense and scrambled her coordination but the cotton wool muffled it a little. She tried to remember her plan. What was the first step?

Shut the door. The door was behind her. She forced herself to open her eyes. Her natural reaction had been to close them against the attack, but she needed to be able to see. She was on her hands and knees. She crawled to the door and butted it with her head. It swung shut; if there was a click she was in no state to hear it.

The overall volume diminished as she shut some of the speakers out. There was still the one in here. Something landed on her back and flattened her. She tried to roll but the weight on her was too much. She felt hands grabbing at her forearms.

She was vulnerable. Getting her hands beneath her before they could be pinned, she pushed up and got to her hands and knees again. Something bit at her neck. *Vanessa?*

Whoever it was put their arms around her in a bear hug, but it wasn't solid. Head still reeling from the noise, Chloe clasped her hands together and lifted them above her head. In the same motion she got up on one leg as the weight fell from her. She leapt for the opposite wall. Twisting in mid-air as she flew across the room. The speaker was there, in the top corner of the wall.

As she closed on it the noise battered her. But she grabbed it, turned upside down with her feet against the ceiling and put her complete body into ripping it from the wall. It came away easily but still screeched as the wires tore down the flimsy wall material. In the moment she was inverted she could see that it was Vanessa who had attacked her. And was getting to her feet, a pained and dazed expression on her face.

She must still be half-under the sedation and the sound had driven her to attack.

Chloe did not blame her as she wrapped the wire round her hand and ripped it from the speaker.

The sound cut off—at least inside the room. Chloe dropped to the floor as Vanessa charged. It lacked any finesse and, much as she regretted having to do it, Chloe easily sidestepped and, grabbing Vanessa's arm, pulled her round and into the wall. As she bounced, Chloe threw her to the floor and immobilised her, using the cable from the loudspeaker to tie her wrists behind her back.

Her head still ached from the aftermath of the noise. Outside the door it was still screeching. Chloe grabbed the chair from behind the desk and swung it at the camera. The lens shattered. The unit dangled from the ceiling.

'Untie me, you bitch!' The word bitch came out slightly slurred with more of a *sss* sound in the final syllable. Vanessa was struggling to get herself on to her feet but seemed uncoordinated.

'You're still under the effects of the drugs,' said Chloe. 'I'm here to rescue you. If you don't calm down I'll put you back under.'

'Chloe?' came a weak voice from the beds.

A grin she could not suppress took over Chloe's face and she jumped across the room to land at her friend's side. She yanked the IV drip all the way out and let it fall. She wrapped her arms round Melinda. When Melinda didn't reciprocate Chloe loosened her grip.

'I promised I'd find you,' she said.

'Did you? I don't remember.'

'Yeah, well, you weren't there. But I did.'

'What's that noise?'

'Utopia Genetics' wirehead trying to stop me. All he's done is give me a headache.'

'I don't understand.'

'Doesn't matter, it would take too long to explain. We just need Lucy Grainger to wake up and we can see about getting you out of here.'

Melinda clung to Chloe's arm as she turned in the bed and sat with her legs dangling over the edge.

'Probably need to find you some clothes too.'

Melinda looked around. 'Why is Vanessa tied up?'

'She attacked me.'

'She does that.'

'How do you feel?'

'Bloody terrible,' said Melinda. 'Thirsty. Maybe hungry.' She focused on Chloe. 'How are we doing, really?'

'Pretty bad.'

'Would it help if I killed the noise?'

Chloe frowned. 'It would help, but how?'

'Was that you?' Melinda said pointing at the wires dangling from the wall. 'Help me over there.'

'You should rest.'

'I can't do it from here.'

'What?'

'Just don't let me fall over, my legs feel like jelly.'

Chloe held her as she slid on to the floor, then gave Melinda an arm to lean on.

Vanessa spoke. 'Melinda, we're friends, tell her to untie me.'

'Probably should,' said Melinda. 'She's got a good nose and, well, she kills people.'

'I know,' said Chloe. 'I saw her handiwork back in Alderley Edge.'

She was reluctant but if Melinda said it was okay, she would take it on faith. Vanessa had pulled the knots tight and it took a bit of work to loosen them again.

Melinda meanwhile shuffled to the wires and grabbed the ends of each.

'Not sure how you're going to feel about this, Chloe. But I'm a freak.'

With that she closed her eyes and grunted.

The lights went out and the only sound was the ringing in her ears where the shrieking attack used to be.

'Too much, I only meant to fuse the speaker system.'

'How...?'

'Like I said, Chloe, I'm a freak and I can make electricity. I'll understand if you don't want to be my friend anymore.'

Chloe took a moment to snap her fingers and was pleased that noise hadn't disabled her acoustic sense again. She finished untying Vanessa who immediately turned over and tried to slash her nails at Chloe's eyes. Chloe blocked, grabbed the wrist and turned Vanessa on her front again, twisting her arm until she squeaked.

'It's okay,' said Chloe. 'I can see in the dark. Total dark. Just like this Vanessa Cooper—'

'Vix,' she hissed.

'What?'

'She wants to be called Vix—you know, like Vixen.'

'You're not serious?'

'She's part fox.'

'If you're Vix, then I'm Sable Fury—no *Dark Fury*. Look, Miss I-Don't-Care-What-You-Call-Yourself, I can see you, I can see everything you do, I can see three-sixty in the light or the dark. You can't surprise me and I will always beat you. So stop trying! Okay?' Chloe reinforced her words by twisting the girl's arm even more. 'There'll be plenty of other people to fight, you know, real enemies with guns. We're the same. We've both had our lives fucked up by some bastard who thought he was being clever. We're on the same side, stop fighting us and start fighting them.' Then she added under her breath. 'What's wrong with these bloody canines?'

She let go of 'Vix' and stepped back smartly. The girl got up slowly.

'What are you talking about, Chloe? You too?'

'Long story. Right now we need to get out of here. We might have to carry Lucy.'

'You'll be lucky. She weighs a ton. That's solid muscle, solid bone and god knows how much leather hide.'

Chloe sighed and clicked her fingers. Nothing had changed in here but she wasn't so sure about outside. With the power out, the wirehead might send in troops.

'There's something out there,' said Vix.

Chloe tapped the metal of a bed. 'No, there's nothing outside the door, or in the rooms around us.'

'Further, I can smell men.' Vix bolted for the door, and found it.

'Stop!'

But she was out and gone.

'Oh great,' said Chloe. She watched her progress as long as the sound waves reached her.

'Are the beds are on wheels?' said Melinda. 'This is just an office, how did they get us in here?'

Chloe checked. 'Yes, shift the desk, we'll take her on that.'

'This is crazy,' said Melinda.

'Tell me about it.'

Chapter 31

Mitchell

Must be the right floor.

He looked across at Jason, held up his hand and counted off three fingers, then spread his hands as if asking a question. Would he understand? How good was his sense of smell, really? Could he tell people apart at a distance?

Jason climbed the wall and crawled across to a position above the door, putting his face near the crack. It was unnerving the way he did that, almost as if the wall had become the floor. It was disorienting.

Why had the lift stopped at the floor below? Someone was helping them and the only person with that kind of power would be Lament. That meant he had discovered the floor and guided them close. Stopping at the lower floor was natural caution. He must have taken out the lights as well, and that weird alarm, whatever it was.

Lament would have assumed there would be guards but he didn't know there was a military force. What the hell was Mitchell and a couple of freaks, with one gun between them, supposed to do against a force like this?

Jason was gesturing: five. Well, that wasn't so bad, and they were facing in the other direction.

Then a woman screeched. It wasn't a scream of pain or fear. It was attack. He saw Dog tense up, and Jason was gone so fast he was just a blur.

What the hell is this now?

Gunfire blasted from the soldiers but it wasn't at them in the stairwell. The men moved forward and then there was another figure in the middle of them. The gunshots stopped. The woman, he caught a glimpse of red hair, was in among them gouging and biting, she had already ripped the goggles from at least two of them that Mitchell could see and there were moans and groans in the male register. And swearing.

Mitchell put his gun on the floor; he couldn't use it without risking hitting her, but he wasn't going to leave her to it. There was the flash of a knife blade and he pulled the door. The soldiers were focused on the banshee in their midst. He grabbed the nearest one by the shoulders, shoved his knee into the back of the soldier's leg and pulled him backwards.

Taken by surprise and with his leg bent he fell back. Mitchell followed him down. The soft armour would absorb impact energy but his face was bare, and splattered with blood. Mitchell grabbed up his gun by the barrel and brought it down hard in the middle of his face. The nose cracked and blood flowed. Suddenly Dog was there. He grabbed the man's legs and heaved.

Before Mitchell could stop him the soldier flew out into the space of the stairwell and fell. Mitchell followed his fall powerlessly. How much could the armour absorb? He didn't know.

'Don't!' he shouted at Dog. But the berserker was back. Dog spun about and dived into the fray. Mitchell couldn't see Jason anywhere.

The fight was not quiet. Between Dog's growls and the screeches of—he caught a glimpse of her face—Vanessa

Cooper, were the groans and cries of the men. Then Dog howled. Mitchell saw the flash of metal and a spray of blood go up.

'Fuck it,' said Mitchell. He turned his gun round, paused to aim and fired at the head of the one with the knife. The gunshot echoed up and down the stairwell. The man went down. There was another on the floor so that left two.

Dog dived back into the fight, oblivious to the cut.

A thundering sound filled the air and two more voices screamed defiantly. Dog jumped out into the stairwell as a bed carrying something big slammed into the two remaining combatants and crushed them against the wall.

Mitchell pulled his slip-tie handcuffs from an inner pocket and went for them. He had them trussed up in a moment. Taking a moment to see the monstrosity on the bed.

The lights flickered on. He shook his head. Lucy Grainger was barely recognisable. At the other end of the bed were Melinda Vogler and Chloe.

'Hi, DI Mitchell,' she said a little breathless. 'Sightseeing?'

A low growl was thrumming behind Mitchell. He glanced back and saw Dog with his attention fixated on the redhead. She was looking directly at Dog with a growl coming from her as well.

It seemed Chloe became aware of it. 'That's enough, you two! I don't bloody care whether you tear each other to bits when we're out of here but until then we work together.'

'You're not the boss of me,' growled Vanessa.

'Yeah, I am,' said Chloe. 'And don't you forget it.'

They still looked daggers at one another but the growling stopped. Mitchell was impressed but Chloe hadn't finished.

'We need to get out of here, Mitchell,' she said. 'How?'

'Lift,' he said. 'Lament's controlling it.'

The floor shuddered with vibration and then the sound of an explosion roared over them. Jason reappeared looking agitated. He pointed down and made counting gestures with his fingers: ten-ten-ten.

'Soldiers?' said Mitchell.

Jason nodded.

'Lift is out,' said Chloe.

'What the fuck is that?' said Vanessa pointing at Jason. He seemed to shiver at her voice.

Great team.

'How do you know the lift is out?' he said.

'Because I just saw it heading down and that explosion was in the shaft.'

'I suggest up,' said Mitchell.

'Yeah.'

They went for the stairs.

'Can you big strong guys carry Lucy?' said Chloe.

Chapter 32

Chloe

There was loud music coming from the penthouse, it leaked round the door. There were multiple speakers and the volume drowned out any image she could get from inside.

Was Mercedes Smith having a party?

Well, they had to crash it. The soldiers were coming through, what the hell they'd do once they were inside she had no idea.

She looked at Jason. He held up three fingers.

Only three people inside?

She was at the front, and everyone, even DI Mitchell, followed her, as if she knew what she was doing. She swallowed nervously. She was just making this up as she went along. There was nothing for it. If they stayed here they would be caught or killed.

She turned the handle and the door opened.

The music blared out. Maybe she should see if Melinda could kill the sound.

She stepped into the light. She was in a short corridor with another door at the end. An airlock to protect Mercedes Smith from the rest of the world.

They were forced to move in single file. It made it hard for Dog who was staggering under the weight of Lucy. She seemed to be recovering a little, she was walking but still did not seem aware of where she was.

Mitchell had his gun out.

She turned the handle on the second door and pulled it. She caught a momentary glimpse of a man with a gun pointed at her.

The blast hit her in the face and across her middle. Something hit her in the eye, pellets lashed across her body, ripping through her clothes and cutting stingingly into her flesh. Mitchell pushed her out and down. The gunshot went off above her head.

Another blast from the other gun and cries as her friends were hit. Lying on the floor she couldn't see anything. Her body was demanding attention and her eye bled.

'Next shot I'll kill her, Chloe Dark.'

What? Kill who?

'Don't listen to him, Chloe!'

Sapphire?

'I'm sorry Chloe, I was trying to help.'

'Getting your teacher-lover to spy on me, Chloe? That was a mistake; there is nothing Saffie can do that I can't see through.'

The Purity guy?

'Your helicopter is on its way, Mercedes.'

The wirehead.

'I didn't ask for a helicopter, Xec.'

'I know.'

Chloe forced herself up on to her knees. It was weird seeing out of only one eye. The music still blasted out and all she could see, through the kitchen and into some sort of main room, was Special Agent Graham with the gun he'd used on her pressed against Sapphire Kepple's neck.

What the hell were they wearing? *Not wearing.*

Almost naked.

'Is this how you like to see your lover, Chloe?'

He sounds crazy.

'She's not my lover,' said Chloe, her voice came out croaky.

'I told you, Chris, I told you she refused me.'

Something behind Chloe alerted the agent.

'Nobody move or I'll shoot. This gun may fire non-lethal pellets, but at point blank I imagine it would make a real mess of her neck.'

Non-lethal? thought Chloe and touched her fingers gingerly to her damaged eye.

The music cut off.

The movements of the people behind her slowly resolved into the image of the kitchen. The cabinets, central island, doors.

There was someone out of sight in the further room, Chloe could see the ghost of them. Must be Mercedes. Chloe was tired. And she hurt.

What could they do? If they attacked he'd shoot Sapphire. If they waited the soldiers would arrive. What did they have? Melinda could take out the lights but he would shoot. Neither Dog nor Vix could do anything, nor Lucy, even assuming she was aware of what was happening. What did that leave?

Jason appeared behind Graham moving in swiftly. He shoved the gun away from Sapphire's neck. The lights blinked out. Chloe moved.

It took her less than a second to cross the distance to Sapphire and the agent. Emergency lights flickered on. Graham turned the weapon on Chloe. She jumped.

The gun went off and the pellets tore through her trousers. She landed on the agent. The noise blasted her acoustic sense again. Lights moved outside, spotlights streamed down from a helicopter.

She hit the ground and her legs crumpled under her.

Graham slammed an elbow into her face. And then grabbed her by the neck, pushing the gun hard into her throat.

'Stay back or I'll kill her.'

She couldn't see anything.

A door in the swathe of glass windows opened and a freezing wind ripped through the penthouse.

'Come on, Graham!'

Mercedes Smith.

She wanted to tell the others to attack. He was going to kill them anyway. They needed to get to the helicopter, they could get away in that but the words wouldn't come. It was hard even to breathe with his tight grip.

He was moving and she weighed so little she could not stop him carrying her with him.

A gunshot roared and glass shattered. She could hear growls above the wind. Dog, Vix and Lucy were closing in. They could take him easily, they just needed to attack. Not to worry about her. Behind them she saw movement: Melinda, Mitchell, Jason and Sapphire.

They were following. But they weren't paying attention, she couldn't speak but she lifted her hand and pointed at the soldiers she could see who had reached their level and were about to come through.

Mitchell must have realised and called a warning.

Dog, Vix and Lucy turned on the spot. Chloe saw them pounding back towards the kitchen while the others took cover. Burners raked the darkened space.

The noise of the incoming helicopter was drowning out her vision. All there was now was the cold, the dark and the pain. She lost consciousness for a few moments. The thundering of the helicopter rotors brought her back. There was nothing else in her ears except:

'Look down, Chloe Dark.'

She opened her good eye. She was face down and she saw the city. Below her was nothing but the distant ground. They were on the edge, he was holding her over it.

'Let's see you fly, freak!'

She felt his grip on her neck loosening. She screamed. And forced her wings through the frayed and tattered cloth of her coat. The prehensile digits grabbed at his face and hooked around his head. Using them as the fulcrum she twisted downward and grabbed the edge of the roof. The cold bit into her fingers.

She pulled.

Gripped by her wings he toppled forwards, as his momentum increased she yanked harder and he went over her. She let go and he fell.

But there was no grip on the icy edge. Her fingers slipped. She wondered if she could fall sixty flights and survive.

A hand grabbed hers and she looked up into the weird and distorted face of Jason Lomax.

Maybe she could survive a fall of sixty floors. But she wouldn't have to test that today.

Chapter 33

Epilogue

The helicopter lifted from the pad at the top of the Utopia Genetics building, leaving Mercedes Smith with her arms wrapped around her watching it go.

It picked up speed.

'Where are we going?' said someone.

'I know a place,' said Chloe.

'Don't tell me,' said Mitchell.

'I'll make a point of forgetting,' said Lament as they pulled across the city towards the River Irwell.

'I thought you were going to make Xec think we weren't there,' said Chloe.

'Too hard,' said Lament. 'I had to give him selective information instead so he would underestimate what he was up against and send too few soldiers.'

'Nearly killed us,' said Dog.

'Didn't, though,' said Lament.

And Chloe couldn't argue with that.

Want a Season 2 of KYMIERA?

*Write a review on your favourite book website,
and join the mailing list at* **bit.ly/voidships**

About the author

Steve Turnbull has been a geek and a nerd longer than those words have had their modern meaning.

Born in the heart of London to book-loving working class parents in 1958, he lived with his parents and two much older sisters in two rooms with gas lighting and no hot water (true!). In his fifth year, a change in his father's fortunes took them out to a detached house in the suburbs. That was the year Dr Who first aired on British TV and Steve watched it avidly from behind the sofa. It was the beginning of his love of science fiction.

Academically Steve always went for the science side but also had his imagination and that took him everywhere. He read through his local library's entire science fiction and fantasy selection, plus his father's 1950s *Astounding Science Fiction* magazines. As he got older he also ate his way through TV SF like *Star Trek*, *Dr Who* and *Blake's 7*.

However it was when he was 15 he discovered something new. Bored with a Maths lesson he noticed a book from the school library: *Cider with Rosie* by Laurie Lee. From the first page he was captivated by the beauty of the language. As a result he wrote a story longhand and then spent evenings at home on his father's electric typewriter pounding out a second draft, expanding it. Then he wrote a second book. Both were terrible but it was a start. After that he switched to poetry and turned out dozens, mostly not involving teenage angst.

After receiving excellent science and maths results he went on to study Computer Science. There he teamed up with another student and they wrote songs for their band - Steve writing the lyrics. Though they admit their best song was the other way around, with Steve writing the music.

After graduation Steve moved into contract programming but was snapped up a couple of years later by a computer magazine looking for someone with technical knowledge. It was in the magazine industry that Steve learned how to write to length, to deadline and to style. Within a couple of years he was editor and stayed there for many years.

During that time he married Pam (also a magazine editor) who he'd met at a student party.

Though he continued to write poetry all prose work stopped. He created his own magazine publishing company which at one point produced the glossy subscription magazine for the *Robot Wars* TV show. The company evolved into a design agency but after six years of working very hard and not seeing his family—now including a daughter and son—he gave it all up.

He spent a year working on miscellaneous projects including writing 300 pages for a website until he started back where he had begun, contract programming.

With security and success on the job front, the writing began again. This time it was scriptwriting: features scripts, TV scripts and radio scripts. During this time he met a director Chris Payne, who wanted to create steampunk stories and between them they created the Voidships universe, a place very similar to ours but with specific scientific changes.

But you can't keep a good writer restrained, so apart from the output of Steampunk stories Steve returned to his first love of Fantasy and Science Fiction.

Don't forget to join the mailing list at **bit.ly/voidships**

Lightning Source UK Ltd.
Milton Keynes UK
UKOW04f2331191117
313013UK00001B/58/P